ALSO BY HA JIN

Between Silences

Facing Shadows

Ocean of Words

Under the Red Flag

In the Pond

Waiting

The Bridegroom

Wreckage

The Crazed

War Trash

A Free Life

The Writer as Migrant

A Good Fall

Nanjing Requiem

A Map of Betrayal

The Boat Rocker

A Distant Center

The Banished Immortal

A Song Everlasting

· THE ·

Woman
Back from
Moscow

· *In Pursuit of Beauty* ·

Ha Jin

OTHER PRESS
NEW YORK

Production editor: Yvonne E. Cárdenas
Text designer: Jennifer Daddio / Bookmark Design & Media Inc.
This book was set in Mrs. Eaves OT and Poiret One
by Alpha Design & Composition of Pittsfield, NH

1 3 5 7 9 10 8 6 4 2

Library of Congress Cataloging-in-Publication Data
Names: Jin, Ha, 1956- author.
Title: The woman back from Moscow : in pursuit of beauty / Ha Jin.
Description: New York : Other Press, 2023.
Identifiers: LCCN 2023006309 (print) | LCCN 2023006310 (ebook) |
ISBN 9781635423778 (paperback) | ISBN 9781635423785 (ebook)
Subjects: LCSH: Sun, Weishi—Fiction. | Theatrical producers and directors—
China—Biography—Fiction. | China—History—20th century—Fiction. |
Zhongguo gong chan dang—Fiction. | LCGFT: Biographical fiction. |
Historical fiction. | Novels.
Classification: LCC PS3560.I6 W66 2023 (print) | LCC PS3560.I6 (ebook) |
DDC 813/.54—dc23/eng/20230424
LC record available at https://lccn.loc.gov/2023006309
LC ebook record available at https://lccn.loc.gov/2023006310

For Lisha

· *Characters* ·

Ah Jin, Deng Xiaoping's ex-wife, who perished in the
   Battle of Moscow
Alya, Russian woman employed by the Comintern
Bo Gu, top Party leader, educated in the Soviet Union and
   in charge of the Chinese Red Army's political work
Bogdanov, head of the International Red Aid in Moscow
Otto Braun, German officer, sent by the Comintern to
   China as a military adviser to the Red Army, summoned
   back to Moscow in 1939
Budyonny, Soviet marshal who commanded the Red
   Square parade in November 1941
Burhan, Sun Yomei's schoolmate at the Russian Institute of
   Theater Arts, who helped her and Lily flee Moscow
Chen Boda, Mao Zedong's political secretary, who actively
   collaborated with the Gang of Four during the Cultural
   Revolution
Chen Changhao, one of the Twenty-Eight and a Half
   Bolsheviks in Yan'an. He went to the Soviet Union
   on the same planes with Yomei and later became a
   translator in the Chinese Communist Party (CCP).
Chen Xiaoda (Little Tiger), Chen Boda's son, who went to
   the Soviet Union at age six in 1939
Cheng Yuan-gong, Premier Zhou Enlai's chief of guards

Valko Chervenkov, Bulgarian Communist, the principal of the Party school outside Ufa

Chiang Kai-shek, the head of the Nationalist government

Deng Xiaoping, top leader in the CCP

Deng Yingchao, Zhou Enlai's wife and Yomei's adoptive mother

Nikolai Fedorenko, Soviet orientalist who often served as a Chinese translator for Soviet leaders

Nikolai Gorchakov, Yomei's professor at the Russian Institute of Theater Arts

Grania, illiterate Soviet woman who was Chen Changhao's wife

Guo Moruo, pro-Communist poet and man of letters

Ho Zi-zhen, Mao Zedong's third wife (1930–37), who gave him three children. She went to the Soviet Union for medical treatment in 1938 and returned to China in 1947. From then on she lived in Shanghai for recuperation until 1984.

Hou Min, head of Yomei's interrogators

Hsiao Chih, an actress who played Cassy in Yomei's production of *Black Slaves' Hate*

Hsiao Yuehua, Otto Braun's first Chinese wife

Hsiaolin (Lin), Lin Biao's daughter

Huang Zongying, movie star and Zhao Dan's wife

Jiang Ching, actress who used to be associated with Yomei. She later became Madame Mao and started the Cultural Revolution.

Jin Minju, spoken drama actress in Harbin

Jin Shan, Yomei's husband, a movie star and stage actor and director

Kang Sheng, ideologue in the CCP, active in persecuting others. He died in 1975 and was stripped of all his titles and influences posthumously.

Lisa Kishkin, Li Lisan's wife and Yomei's friend

Kiushin, Soviet official at the Comintern, in charge of Chinese affairs

Ivan Kovalev, Soviet official in charge of Mao's accommodations in Moscow

Katina Lestov, lecturer at the Russian Institute of Theater Arts, Yomei's teacher

Li Lilian, movie star and Otto Braun's second Chinese wife

Li Lisan, a founder and a top leader of the CCP, Yomei's friend

Li Tianyou, a three-star general, Yomei's schoolmate in Moscow

Liao Chengzhi, active in propaganda work in the CCP. Later he headed the Youth Union of the People's Republic of China (PRC). He hired Yomei as the stage director in chief at the National Youth Art Theater.

Lin Biao, marshal and minister of defense in PRC. During his stay in Moscow, he fell in love with Yomei and was later still obsessed with her.

Lin Bochü, Lily's father, who was in charge of the Red Army's finances in the 1930s, known for his honesty and integrity. He was one of the Five Grandpops in Yan'an.

Lin Lily (Lin Li), Yomei's close friend in the Soviet Union and in the PRC. She served as a translator, from Chinese into Russian.

Lin Mohan, propaganda official in the CCP who helped Jiang Ching produce her revolutionary model plays

Linlin (Lin Lin), Lily's younger sister, who grew up and was educated in the Soviet Union

Liu Aichin, Liu Shaoqi's daughter, educated in the Soviet Union

Liu Ch'un-hsian, Bo Gu's wife. Perished in the Battle of
Moscow.

Liu Shaoqi, top leader of the CCP and president of the
PRC

Liu Yalou, a schoolmate of Yomei in Moscow, he pursued
her passionately. Later he became the founder of the
PRC's air force, which he also commanded.

Liu Yunbin, Liu Shaoqi's son, who went to the Soviet
Union as a student and married a Russian woman

Lu Ju, cowgirl at the oil field in Daqing

Luo Rui-ching, minister of public security in the PRC, a
four-star general

Mao Anqing, Mao's second son, who became mentally
unstable due to stress and anxiety

Mao Anying, Mao's oldest son, who was killed in Korea in
November 1950

Mao Zedong, the head of the CCP, Chairman Mao

Anastas Mikoyan, Soviet statesman and top leader of the
Communist Party of the Soviet Union (CPSU)

Reslie Mironov, Yomei's classmate at the Russian Institute
of Theater Arts. He shared the stage with her in *Three
Sisters*.

Vyacheslav Molotov, Soviet foreign minister (1939–49)

Niu Lang, high-school history teacher in Harbin, an
amateur stage director

Ryo Nosaka, Sanzo's wife, stranded in Moscow

Sanzo Nosaka, founding figure of the Japanese
Communist Party

Oyang Fei, Yomei's friend, nicknamed Feifei. She grew up
in the Soviet Union and served as a Russian translator in
the CCP.

Oyang Yuchien, dramaturge who was Yomei's neighbor
and theater colleague

Peng Dehuai, marshal, the commander of the Chinese army in Korea

Ren Bishi, active leader of the CCP, staying at the Comintern as the representative of the CCP

Ren Fukun, Yomei's aunt, who adopted her little sister, Yolan

Ren Jun, Yomei's sixth aunt, who grew up together with her

Ren Rui, Yomei's mother

Nikolai Roshchin, Soviet diplomat, ambassador to China (1949–52)

Eva Sanber, Jewish German woman working at the Comintern. She married poet Hsiao San and moved to Yan'an in the mid-1940s.

Shao Yan-hsiang, poet who, with Yomei, adapted Vsevolod Kochetov's novel *The Brothers Yershov* into the play of the same name

Sheng Shicai, warlord in Xinjiang in the 1930s and early 1940s

Shih Chee, Sun Yang's wife, Yomei's sister-in-law

Shi Zhe, Mao's Russian secretary

Joseph Stalin, the head of the Soviet Union

Sun Bing, Yomei's niece, daughter of Sun Yang and Shih Chee

Sun Bingwen, Yomei's father, who joined the CCP in 1925, after being recommended by Zhou Enlai, and who was murdered by the Nationalists in 1927

Sun Jishi, Yomei's second brother, who remained in Sichuan

Sun Ming, Yomei's nephew, son of Sun Yang and Shih Chee

Sun Mingshi, Yomei's younger brother

Sun Ning, Yomei's nephew, son of Sun Yang and Shih Chee

Sun Yang, Yomei's elder brother, who served as Zhu Deh's assistant and later wrote his biography

Sun Yolan (Sun Weixin), Yomei's younger sister

Sun Yomei (Sun Weishi), adopted by Zhou Enlai. She went to Moscow to study theater arts for seven years, and later became an eminent stage director in China.

Sun Zaoli, amateur actor for Yomei in Daqing Oil Field

Tian Cheng-ren, actor who played Uncle Tom in *Black Slaves' Hate*

Vilkov, head of the International Red Aid

Vitaley, midlevel official at the International Red Aid

Wang Dongxing, head of general affairs in Zhongnanhai compound, Mao's butler of sorts

Wang Jia-hsiang, top official of the PRC, the first ambassador to the Soviet Union

Wang Jin-hsi, model worker (driller) and friend of Yomei's, nicknamed Iron Man Wang

Wang Yida, Ren Jun's husband

Wang Ying, movie star, Jin Shan's first wife

Xu Yi-xin, Yomei's first lover, and also her teacher in Yan'an. He was the "half" of the Twenty-Eight and a Half Bolsheviks, the runt. In the new China, he served as ambassador to Albania, Syria, Norway, and Pakistan, and eventually became a vice foreign minister of the PRC.

Yang Shangkun, in charge of political work in the CCP. In the late 1980s he became president of the PRC.

Yang Zhicheng, friend and schoolmate of Yomei's in Moscow, nicknamed Grandpa

Yeh Jian-ying, a major leader of the CCP, and later a marshal in the People's Army

Yeh Qun, Lin Biao's wife and Yomei's persecutor

You Benchang, comic actor for Yomei

Zeng Yongfu, petty Chinese official who remained in the Soviet Union and who ran after Lily for a while

Zhang Mei, Lin Biao's wife before 1941, also Yomei's friend

Zhang Wentian, top leader in the CCP. He lived in both America and Russia and served as the first foreign minister of the PRC.

Zhao Dan, movie star and Jin Shan's longtime friend

Zhang Guonan, Jiang Ching's personal Russian translator

Zhang Ruifang, actress and movie star, and Jin Shan's second wife

Zhen-yao Zheng, actress directed by Yomei in *The Little White Rabbit* and *The Storm*

Zhong Chibing, Yomei's schoolmate in Moscow. Although disabled, he managed to graduate from the Frunze Military Academy. A two-star general in the PRC, in charge of China's civil aviation.

Zhou Enlai, a major leader of the CCP. He was the premier of the PRC, and Yomei's adoptive father.

Zhou Yang, cultural official and translator of *Anna Karenina*, in charge of propaganda and literary theories in the CCP

Zhu Deh, marshal and founder of the Red Army

Zhu Ming, Lin Boqu's fourth wife, Lily's stepmother

Zongchang (Li), Sun Yolan's husband, chemist educated in the Soviet Union

Zutao (Chen), Changhao's son, who went to study in the Soviet Union in 1939

· One ·

Yomei was wondering why Jiang Ching wanted to meet after the evening class. They were both at Lu Hsun Academy of Literature and Arts in Yan'an, the legendary Communist base in the remote Shaanxi Province. Ching was an instructor, Yomei a student. Both had come to this place the previous year, 1937.

Yomei was seventeen and Ching twenty-four. But their seven-year age gap set them as apart as if they belonged to different generations, especially when they were onstage and in the arena of love. They had known each other since four summers before in Shanghai, when they were in the Oriental Troupe of Modern Drama—Yomei had been an apprentice there and even taken an acting class taught by Ching. At that time the girl was still too green to perform in plays, while Ching, called Lan Ping then, was a burgeoning actress seeking her place in the metropolitan's theater circle. In *The Government Inspector*, the Gogol comedy, Ching played only a minor role, a locksmith's wife, despite her moderate success as a starlet in several movies. That same year, however, she had managed to snatch a leading part—Nora, in Ibsen's *A Doll's House*—and then another major role—Katherina in Ostrovsky's *The Storm*. But here in Yan'an, Yomei, younger and more talented, could easily outshine

Ching onstage. A few months before, they had acted together in *The Blood Sacrifice in Shanghai*, which commemorates that city's fight against the Japanese invasion six years earlier. Yomei performed the leading female role—the daughter of a rich capitalist—whereas Ching had to settle for a secondary part—the rich man's concubine. The play had been so successful that it was performed twenty times in the town of Yan'an alone, watched by more than ten thousand people. Some even perched on the trees around the platform to get a better view. Numerous Communist leaders saw it and praised the performance. It was said that Ching had met Mao Zedong personally at one of her performances. Mao was so impressed by the troupe's recent productions that he suggested establishing Lu Hsun Academy of Literature and Arts, and his colleagues unanimously supported the idea. After the performance season, both Yomei and Ching became well known—even children in the streets would call Yomei "the Miss" and Ching "the Concubine." To a degree, Ching was annoyed by such notoriety, and she knew that as far as acting went, Yomei may have been getting ahead of her—in recent years, after her apprenticeship and before coming to Yan'an, the girl, Yomei, had acted in several movies and plays in Shanghai and earned a name for herself. She was already like a professional.

Now the two of them were going to meet beside the grand Catholic church that boasted a pair of belfries and stood next to their academy. Yomei had never liked Ching, who, to her mind, was a second-rate actress who engaged in one affair after another in Shanghai. Some men had abandoned their families or attempted suicide thanks to her casual entanglements with them. Ever since coming to Yan'an, Yomei had tried to avoid Ching, following instructions from her mother Ren Rui, who had arrived in Yan'an soon after Yomei and had also been a student here, at the College of Marxism and Leninism. Ren Rui believed Jiang Ching was bad news, so Yomei had better not mix with her.

There Ching was, walking toward Yomei with feet slightly splayed in suede boots. Tall and willowy, she wore a gray-blue woolen coat and an army cap. She was a kind of sartorial expert, good at giving advice to other women on what clothes to put on and how to alter a tunic or jacket. In this red base, most women just wore baggy gray uniforms like their male comrades, but Ching seemed determined to stand out by dressing differently.

"Yomei, my little sister," Ching said with a faint smile, "I'd like to talk about Yi-xin." In the silvery moonlight her mouth stiffened, her left cheek's muscles twitched a little while her large eyes glowed.

"All right, what about him?" Yomei asked, having in a way expected this. Yi-xin headed the Education and Training Section of their college and was also a teacher in socialist thought. A lean, intelligent man, he could speak Russian, having studied in the Soviet Union seven or eight years before.

"Yomei, I'd like to advise you as an older sister who has gone through more in life," Ching went on, her voice a little husky and uncertain. "You know, by rule, you're not allowed to carry on with a man like Yi-xin. An affair between a teacher and a student is strictly forbidden here. You might get him and yourself into trouble if you don't stop soon enough."

"He's been kind to me and I can't just brush him aside," Yomei replied honestly, even though she was unsure of her own feelings for that somewhat attractive man. "I know you like him, Ching, but you mustn't blame me if he doesn't leave me alone. I'm only seventeen, too young to date, so I'm not that eager to go with any man."

"Don't you hope he'll stop chasing you?" Ching looked her in the face, her eyes shimmering in the moonlight.

"Well, he's a leader of our college. I can't be rude to him."

"Can I tell him to leave you alone?"

"Please let me handle this by myself. Right now I can only say this: if you two are in love, I'll step aside without interfering with your relationship."

"I'm glad to hear that. Keep in mind, Yomei, you're still a young girl, and there'll be infinite opportunities for you. Everybody views you as Zhou Enlai's daughter, the Red Princess of Yan'an, but I am new here, with no one to rely on."

"So you need a man like Yi-xin?" Yomei asked, knowing Ching was often blunt and brash. A practical woman indeed.

"Yes, I need a man here. Truth to tell, Yi-xin is handsome and smart, but he may not be powerful enough to protect his woman yet. He's probably running after you because he intends to be associated with your dad, Vice Chairman Zhou."

"I don't think Yi-xin is that calculating," Yomei said, her anger rising. "If I'm fond of someone, I'll never bad-mouth him behind his back."

"You're still young and innocent and believe in the purity of romantic love."

"You don't then?"

"Honestly, I don't, perhaps because I've been betrayed by too many men. Trust me, Yomei, most men just use women to advance their careers or satisfy their lust and vanity.

You must take more precautions to protect yourself against them."

"Thank you for telling me." Yomei felt annoyed and hoped to end their conversation.

"Actually, you're such a smart girl that I don't need to dwell on this. You've already transformed yourself into a Red Princess—to be sure, you know how to promote yourself."

"You think too highly of me," said Yomei.

"You know I've always appreciated you. Do give thought to what I've told you."

"Of course I will."

Ching turned and strode away as if peeved. Her slanted shadow was wavering ahead of her in the pale moonlight. The night smelled of charcoal fire and was peaceful. A dog barked sleepily in the distance as Ching moved away with a swinging gait. It was whispered that one of her feet had six toes, but nobody had ever seen them. Legend had it that a person with six toes on one foot could be either a saint or a demon. Ching never revealed her naked feet, always donning socks. Even when wearing straw sandals, she would decorate the fronts of the shoes with red strings, which made them pretty and unique. People all agreed that Ching had refined taste and knew how to make herself up and dress smart. At a big locust tree, she veered to the left and faded into the night.

Yomei turned around, heading back to her lodgings. A cockerel, confused about time, crowed as if dawn were breaking, even though it wasn't yet midnight. Here and there, bean-oil lamps were glowing behind paper window screens, some flickering on hillsides. Yomei could tell that Ching must be irritated by her—by her having to take such a drastic step, personally admonishing her rival to stay away from the man they both liked. That woman could indeed act aggressively. Even without provocation, she could be outrageous and menacing.

Without further delay Yomei headed for the cave room she shared with four other female students. A sentry demanded loudly: "Password?"

"Flying red flag!" she cried back.

The man shone a flashlight on her. "Oh, the Miss," he snickered, then bowed a little and let her pass.

· Two ·

But Xu Yi-xin continued to pursue Yomei. The next
morning, after teaching his class, Introduction to Social
Sciences, he caught up with her and asked her to meet
after dinner. Such a request flustered her, but it also pleased
her. For the whole day she was under the spell of a peculiar
sensation, as if she were blushing constantly even when she
was alone.

To some extent Yomei adored Yi-xin, who had a lean face
and was in his late twenties. He was also a noted figure in
Yan'an. Within the CCP there was a group of senior cadres
nicknamed the Twenty-Eight and a Half Bolsheviks, who
had all come back from the USSR, where they had attended
Sun Yat-sen University, a school in Moscow established
by the Soviets for training and educating Chinese
revolutionaries. The group was headed by Wang Ming, a
short, dapper man who, sent back by Stalin, was almost
equal to Mao Zedong and Zhou Enlai in power. Wang
represented the Comintern (the Communist International),
which had been founded by Lenin two decades before as the
international headquarters of Communism, so even though
Wang was not experienced in Chinese revolutionary work,
he carried a lot of clout, was backed up by the USSR, and
had been in charge of the United Front that tried to bring

together all the forces in China to support the CCP. Yi-xin
was the runt among those Chinese Bolsheviks, the "half"
after the other twenty-eight, because he'd been so young, so
inexperienced, that he hadn't always been able to function
like the full Bolsheviks, and he was also less contentious
than the others. Nevertheless, he was intelligent, with a
strong memory, easygoing, and amiable. Every once in a
while, he even served as Mao's Russian secretary. By the
time he arrived at Lu Hsun Academy of Literature and
Arts, he was already a full-fledged revolutionary, a capable
and outstanding leader in cultural affairs. In class he
would drop a Russian word or phrase, which impressed the
students all the more. He was such a kind and articulate
man that many young women were fond of him. His
attentions to Yomei flattered her, though she was nearly ten
years his junior. Now she was wondering if she should bring
up the topic of Jiang Ching to him.

When Yomei reached the side of the Yan River, a little
creek actually, he was already there waiting. He was wearing
a flapped cotton hat and leggings, which made him look like
a soldier on the front. His small eyes flashed as he smiled.
"I'm so happy you came, Yomei."

"Well, I'm here. What's new?" she said, her heart
expanding with delight.

"I just want to talk to you." He held her hand as if to
claim a unique intimate relationship with her.

Instinctively she wanted to pull her hand out of his
grip, but didn't. Together they turned, strolling along the
gurgling stream, its surface shimmering while the water
wound away into the distance. A crosswind tossed up some
dried leaves, which skidded along the riverbank with a
tiny crackling sound. Yomei noticed that his legs were
slightly bandy, and that in spite of his wiry physique, he was

healthy, sturdy like a Mongolian pony. He must have had women before, considering he had once lived in Russia, where he had undoubtedly rubbed shoulders with female revolutionaries, but Yomei knew that may have been part of his work.

She asked him, "You know, as a student, I'm not allowed to have a relationship with a man, especially a leader."

He smiled and said, "But I'm already twenty-seven, entitled to look for a wife."

At that word, her heart leaped. She felt herself going red. Luckily, the darkness covered her hot face. She ventured, "During your career, have you ever played the role of husband to a woman comrade?"

"Not really, but I have often carried out tasks together with female colleagues."

She'd heard that revolutionaries often lived together as couples, especially in the area of the White Terror, which was occupied by the Nationalists and warlords, and Communists had to operate in disguise. Some of the ad hoc couples had become lovers eventually, even though many also lost their marriages because their spouses couldn't stomach such infidelity.

"Do you know Jiang Ching well?" she asked him.

"Not really, but she often comes to my office. She's eager to learn and has a lot of questions."

"She's interested in you for sure."

"Probably, but I want to be with you. She seems too smooth to be trustworthy."

Yomei stopped to face him. "Ching and I talked last night. She warned me not to mix with you."

"Why did she do that?" He sounded surprised and a little irritated.

"Because I'm just a student of yours."

"Even if you weren't here, I wouldn't feel comfortable spending personal time with Ching. Of course, I can respect her as a comrade. She's a decent actress."

What he said put her somewhat at ease. If push came to shove, she might tell Ching candidly that she wouldn't have a chance with Yi-xin anyway, so it would be unnecessary for her, Yomei, to back down. Before they turned around toward their quarters, Yi-xin kissed her on the cheek, and she kissed him back, but on the mouth. She liked his male scent, pungent like fresh grass, and his palm on her chest, for the first time, gave her such a thrill that she shook a little.

Two weeks later Yomei was amazed by a new development—Jiang Ching left the academy and began to work at Chairman Mao's office as his personal secretary. The rumor was that an affair had just started between her and the top leader. That must be true. The two of them had appeared together at theatrical shows the week before—they were seated in the very front row, as if to flaunt that they were a couple. Ching also rode in the minivan (known as a breadbox car) designated for Mao's personal use. The vehicle had been donated to the Red Army by the immigrant community of New York's Chinatown for fighting against the Japanese aggression. Many young women here were astounded by such a breakthrough in Ching's life. How could she, without extraordinary looks or talent, manage to hold the great man in thrall? This was simply beyond everyone.

Yet some people in the know believed that such a quick development—Mao's having another woman—might be inevitable. He was known as a kind of skirt chaser and often went to dance parties, which had been introduced to Yan'an by the radical American writer Agnes Smedley and also by Sophie Su, the wife of Shafick Hatem, an American medical doctor. The Hatems had a phonograph in their cave house, which was a common dwelling in the Yan'an region, a cave dug on a hillslope serving as a home of two or three rooms. The couple often held dance parties, at which coffee and soda were served in place of alcohol. As a result, social dancing was quite popular among the Communist leaders, as relaxation after the day's work. Some young women frequented those parties, but Yomei's mother wouldn't let her go, saying she was still too young to mix with men publicly. Her adoptive father, Zhou Enlai, was one of the best dancers among the leaders, able to move nimbly and gracefully; besides, he was good at chitchatting with his dance partners, showing a lot of personal interest and concern. Naturally, many women went up and invited him to dance. In comparison, Zhu Deh, the commander in chief of the Red Army, would dance as if he were marching formally, always moving forward without retreating. It was so hard for his partner to accommodate him. Still, the Office of General Affairs would make arrangements with some young women beforehand so that Zhu Deh wouldn't feel left out. Mao was notorious for his casual way with his dance partners, touching them here and there while moving with stiff steps. At times he embarrassed them; yet they never said a peep. One of the women had once told Yomei in private that if another man had touched her behind in a dance, she would have given him a loud slap on the face. But with Chairman Mao, she had to bite her tongue and lower her eyes.

Ching was an elegant dancer and had a sizable following, some of whom were young women eager to learn from her

Mao with his third wife, Ho Zi-zhen

how to dance well. Naturally she caught Mao's attention, and they began to exchange letters. After paying Mao a visit and staying a night with him, she was transferred to his office and put in charge of handling his correspondence. Ching was shrewd enough to seize the opportunity of his wife Ho Zi-zhen's absence, and pretty soon they lived together like a couple.

It was known that Mrs. Mao, Zi-zhen, had gone to Xi'an together with their daughter Min after a fight with her husband. Zi-zhen had caught him flirting with Wu Lili, who was Agnes Smedley's English interpreter. Zi-zhen even attacked the young lady, calling her "a rotten slut." She cursed Smedley as well, accusing her of shamelessly seducing Chinese men. Zi-zhen was a markswoman with a fiery temper who used to command a detachment of guerrillas. She saw her husband in the cave house shared by Smedley and Wu Lili and began cursing the young woman. Even though Mao yelled at her to stop, she got louder and louder instead, so he ordered his bodyguards to drag her out of the cave room. Wu Lili was a beauty of a sort who spoke English fluently and could quote Byron and Shelley and Keats off the top of her head. She and Mao had started carrying on clandestinely; though encouraged by Smedley, Wu Lili was still frightened of Zi-zhen. Smedley had bragged to others that she intended to wreck Mao's marriage because she despised Zi-zhen, while taking it upon herself to westernize Mao. On some level, to her, he may have seemed like a bumpkin who had never set foot outside China and had no clue what other countries were like, even though he was well read and could toss out an English word or phrase from time to time. He had been learning the foreign tongue since his youth.

Owing to this scandal, Agnes and Wu Lili sneaked away from Yan'an. Their departure, plus Mao's wife's absence, left a vacancy in his personal life. By now, Zi-zhen was in Moscow for medical treatment and refused to come back to Yan'an. Mao's comrades grew concerned, believing that he needed a female companion, since he worked day and night, being totally absorbed in military operations and the underground activities in the region occupied by Chiang Kai-shek's regime. If a woman, ideally a wife, could take good care of him, that would make him emotionally stable and curb his nasty temper.

Ching's new role in Mao's office surprised not only many young women but also some men. Among them was Yi-xin, who for several days didn't know how to cope with such a turn of events. Yet his gut told him not to rush in developing his relationship with Yomei. He mustn't rile Ching. Instinctively he felt that a vengeful woman could be implacable and destructive, so he refrained from seeing Yomei from then on. Obviously Ching had become a power he'd have to reckon with. One thing was clear now: he could not afford to antagonize Mao's woman, who might sway the Chairman with her pillow chats, so Yi-xin stopped seeing Yomei, not even speaking with her in front of others. She noticed him avoiding her. She got the message and felt hurt, but she began to shun him too, knowing that at heart he must be a timid man. Despite her effort to distance herself from him, she felt he had stolen her heart, and she was tormented by the loss. Yet she knew that however painful it was, she'd have to take her heart back from him if she could.

· *Three* ·

Yomei heard that her adoptive father, Zhou Enlai, had just returned from Wuhan, so she went to see him and his wife, Deng Yingchao. The Zhous resided in a cave house on the hillside near Mao's quarters, about half a mile from where Yomei lived. Even though they were her parents in name only, she had been calling them Dad and Mom ever since she came to Yan'an. Her birth father, Sun Bingwen, had once been Zhou Enlai's close friend and had joined the Communist Party in Berlin in 1922 together with Zhu Deh, the current commander in chief of the Red Army. Zhou Enlai recommended both men, Zhu and Sun, to the CCP, though he was younger than they. Three years later, Sun Bingwen went to Russia and then came back to China to become an active revolutionary. In April 1927, he was arrested by the Nationalists and they swiftly executed him. He left behind five children. His wife gave away their youngest daughter to her elder sister, unable to raise all of the kids on her own. Then she took her sons and Yomei to cities like Suzhou and Beijing and Shanghai, where with the help of the underground Communists, Yomei began to learn acting.

Then, in the fall of 1937, Yomei and her elder brother Yang went to Wuhan, where they found the office of the

Communist army. They entered the three-story building
and begged the staffers to send them to Yan'an, saying they
wanted to join the resistance force to fight the Japanese
invasion. The men in the office laughed at the girl and
asked how old she was. "Sixteen," she said.

They laughed again and told her, "You look fourteen,
too young for us. Please go back to Shanghai." They kept
Yang, however, who was well educated and already a lanky
twenty-one-year-old. He could speak Japanese, having just
returned from Japan after the war broke out full-scale.

Upon exiting the stucco office building, Yomei burst
into tears. At this point, a handsome middle-aged man in
a fedora got out of a limo, sauntering toward the entrance
of the building. He asked why the girl was crying. She said,
"I want to follow in my dad's footsteps, but they won't let me
join the Red Army."

"Who's your father?" he asked, amused.

"Sun Bingwen."

"What, let me look at you again!" The gentleman was
astonished. "Are you little Yomei?"

"Yes, who are you?"

"I'm your uncle Zhou Enlai."

Indeed, he had first seen her when she was still a baby.
Later, when she was five, Sun would bring her along to meet
with Zhou so that she could keep watch for them over her
dad's shoulder while they talked business. In other words,
the girl had participated in revolutionary work when she
was still a little kiddie in pinafores.

At Zhou Enlai's mention of his own name, Yomei
stepped closer and looked him in the face. She then hugged
him and said, "Uncle Zhou, they already took my brother
Yang, please tell them to have me too. I want to go to
Yan'an."

That was how both she and her brother came to the remote Communist base, where Sun Yang began to work for Commander Zhu Deh as his secretary, while Yomei entered the Party's Political College to study revolutionary theories. Soon their mother Ren Rui also came and joined them. Mother and daughter enrolled in the same school and often attended the same classes. They became a topic of town gossip, a kind of legend. After graduation, Yomei continued her studies at the arts academy, while her mother went to work at a kindergarten for the time being.

Yomei felt attached to Zhou Enlai. He was warm and gracious, an attentive listener and ready to give a helping hand to whoever needed it. His bright eyes, bushy brows, and elegant figure tended to produce a cheerful and charming effect on people. Yomei often heard young women talk about him, saying they'd do anything for him. Just the other day a slender foreign reporter, whose mother was Swedish and father Cantonese, had openly declared she was willing to lay down her life for Zhou Enlai if he ordered her to die.

Unlike those women who were bewitched by him, Yomei had mixed feelings. No doubt she was attracted to him as a man in his prime, but on the other hand, she also felt attached to him like a daughter. She had few memories of her birth father, who had been so dedicated to the revolutionary cause led by Sun Yat-sen that he had seldom spent time with his family. At heart she had always tried to confine her feelings for Zhou Enlai within father-daughter parameters. Yet, she could tell that whenever she was with him, he would become excited, his eyes radiating with happiness and his lean face glazed with a warm sheen. She was sure that his wife, Deng Yingchao, was aware of this too. That must be one of the reasons Mrs. Zhou had

suggested they adopt Yomei as their daughter, since they had
no children of their own. That plain, plump woman with
smiling eyes and a pug nose was smart enough to establish
a boundary between her husband and this beautiful girl—as
long as they remained father and daughter, no extramarital
affair would develop between them. Such terms were
entirely acceptable and comfortable to Yomei. When she
told her birth mother the Zhous' intention to adopt her,
Ren Rui was delighted and encouraged her to stay as close
to the couple as possible. In her heart of hearts, Ren Rui
intuited that to survive in Yan'an, within the Communist
rank and file, Yomei would need some protection. There
wouldn't be more suitable adoptive parents than the Zhous,
with whom the Suns had been longtime friends. Yomei's
mother could trust the couple. Above all, Zhou Enlai was
one of the most powerful men in the CCP, second only to
Mao.

   The Zhous looked delighted to see Yomei when she
stepped in. Their room smelled good, redolent of tasty
cooking. "Have you eaten?" asked Mother Deng.

   "Yes," Yomei said, "but I wouldn't mind sharing a bite.
You know what a glutton I am, Mother."

   At that, Zhou Enlai laughed. "Sit down and let us eat
together."

   "Thanks, Dad. I'm so happy to see you back."

   Dinner consisted of four courses: steamed dace, sautéed
cabbage with cured pork, scrambled eggs with scallions,
and a tofu seaweed soup. Thanks to Zhou Enlai's high rank,
such fare was standard. All the top leaders here could have
four-course lunches and dinners, whereas regular soldiers
ate corn buns, boiled millet, black beans, and vegetables.
At the Communist base, such dining distinctions were
strictly kept. For instance, even Yi-xin, a midlevel cadre,

would eat two dishes at dinner or lunch. Top leaders like Mao Zedong, Zhu Deh, Zhou Enlai, and Zhang Wentian could also have one pound of fresh milk per diem. One reason Yomei loved to visit her adoptive parents was that she usually could have a hearty meal with them.

Zhou Enlai was fond of fish and foreign wines. He picked up a big chunk of dace with his chopsticks and put it into Yomei's bowl of millet. "Try to eat more," he said kindly.

They were seated in wicker chairs at a square table. While eating, they chatted about life in Yan'an. Father Zhou was curious about the lectures Yomei had been attending. Indeed, she often went to talks and shows. The Zhous had no time to attend, but wanted to know about them, particularly who spoke about what and how well the talks were received. Recently, Yomei reported, she had gone to a lecture given by Chen Yun, the head of the CCP's Organization Department. The topic was how to become an excellent Communist. The skinny man was lucid and eloquent, his talk quite engaging. Toward the end of the lecture, he asked the room whether there were any questions. A slip of paper was passed

Yomei and her adoptive parents, Zhou Enlai and Deng Yingchao

to him. He looked at the question, then, with his eyebrows lifting, read it out: "The basic principle of Communism is equality, but in Yan'an, why do we eat different meals? It's said that Chairman Mao eats a chicken a day, whereas common soldiers like us haven't tasted meat for months. Why is that?"

"Well," Chen Yun said with a straight face, "Chairman Mao indeed eats a chicken a day, but that's not his choice. Our revolution needs a strong, healthy leader, so he has to keep himself in good health. In other words, he eats chicken on our behalf, as a task." Such a clever answer cracked up the whole room.

Zhou Enlai chuckled and said Chen Yun was smart and hadn't wasted the time he'd spent abroad—that small, bony man had just returned from the USSR, where he had served as a representative of the CCP at the Comintern. Yomei was amused by Father Zhou's remark about Chen Yun. The dapper man was indeed quick-witted and had the gift of gab. It seemed that those who were trained and educated abroad were much smarter than those spawned in China's villages and wilderness, and that they tended to have a broader perspective and a deeper understanding of the revolution. They all seemed more knowledgeable and more articulate.

After dinner, over aster tea, they chatted about matters at Lu Hsun Academy of Literature and Arts. The Zhous had met Jiang Ching at Mao's office the previous day and were eager to learn more about her. Yomei said she had known Ching for more than four years, that they used to be in the same drama troupe in Shanghai. She was cautious not to reveal too much about Ching and just said the woman had been married before, maybe more than once.

"She broke many hearts," Yomei added without emphasis.

"You mean she was promiscuous?" Mother Deng asked as if surprised.

"I can't say that for sure, but she had some complicated relationships with men."

The Zhous exchanged glances and seemed alarmed.

"Actually," Yomei added, "I would say she always keeps her eyes on useful men. For example, she spoke to me just a month ago, warning me to stay away from Xu Yi-xin."

"You mean she was after Yi-xin?" asked Zhou Enlai, who occasionally used the young man as a Russian interpreter.

"Yes. She warned me that I'd break the rules if I had a relationship with Yi-xin."

"Are you interested in him?" asked Mother Deng.

"He's fine, but I'm not going with him. He brushed Jiang Ching aside and often came to me. Ching was unhappy about that, of course. But now she's at Chairman Mao's office and might not bother about Yi-xin anymore."

"It's hard to tell," Father Zhou said broodingly. "But, Yomei, she's right about your breaking the rules, which forbid a young student like you to mix with a school leader like Yi-xin."

"You mean I should stay away from him?"

"Yes, you mustn't start a relationship so early," he went on.

His wife added, "Besides, don't cross Jiang Ching. An acrimonious woman can be dangerous."

Father Zhou continued, "I'll speak to Yi-xin. Both of you must be careful from now on."

"Of course, I'll focus on my studies," agreed Yomei. "Yi-xin seems to avoid me these days anyway."

Later she shared the content of that conversation with her birth mother, who had known Ching personally for six or seven years. She also demanded that her daughter stop going with Yi-xin in case Ching were to take offense. Yomei assured her mother, saying with blazing eyes, "No need to worry, Mom, I have torn him out of my heart."

· *Four* ·

Zhou Enlai's talk with Yi-xin seemed to have shaken the young man. From then on, he avoided Yomei. When they ran into each other, he would just nod at her and at most say a few words in greeting. She could tell that he was breaking up with her, perhaps because Father Zhou had pressured him to do so, though she wasn't sure whether Zhou had done that out of worry about Ching's new role as Chairman Mao's mistress or out of paternal feeling for her, Yomei, since few fathers were willing to see their young daughters get intimate with another man. She wasn't really worried, because Yi-xin was ten years older than she was. And she felt she was too young to look for a man. True, she was drawn to him, but she wouldn't say she loved him. Probably it was merely a crush.

She had a young aunt, Ren Jun, who was only one year older than her. Jun was small-boned and had smiling eyes. The two had grown up together like sisters, wandering through different cities and provinces. Together they learned acting in Shanghai, where the actors treated the two of them as a pair of young apprentices. As a result, Jun also knew Jiang Ching personally. In some ways, Yomei was closer to Jun than to her mother—the two had so much to share, and were able to confide in each other. Jun was also

Yomei (left) and Ren Jun

in the arts academy. She'd take a minor role in a play now and then, since she was less talented than Yomei and without her niece's kind of popularity. This was also largely due to the fact that she didn't have Yomei's looks and vivaciousness. Still, Jiang Ching tried to befriend both of them. These days, whenever they ran into Ching, she would invite Yomei and Jun to visit her at Mao's residence. They knew the woman was vain but didn't know that Ching was doing her best to befriend them for another reason, namely that she didn't want them to prattle about her past, particularly her many affairs and scandals back in Shanghai—any revelation of her former ill repute could undermine her chances with Chairman Mao, because an amorous relationship between her and Mao would have to be approved by the principal leaders of the Party's Central Committee, in which Zhou Enlai was a key figure with a decisive voice.

Nowadays, whenever Ching saw Yomei and Jun, she'd say, "Please come see me at my new place. We'll have tea and candies together."

They would reply that they'd pay her a visit soon, but they never made good on their word. As a well-known beauty in Yan'an and also as the daughter of a late revered revolutionary, Yomei was familiar with many senior leaders' families. She knew Mao's wife, Ho Zi-zhen, and also their small daughter, Min. Yomei had been to Mao's office twice, and the Great Leader had seemed happy to see her there, speaking with her like an amiable uncle. But now her feelings about that place had changed. Neither she nor Jun liked Jiang Ching, believing she was an opportunist, something of a social butterfly. Yet, no matter how displeased Ching was with them, she had to be polite to them because she badly needed Zhou Enlai's support.

In fact, Ching also tried to ingratiate herself directly with Zhou Enlai, whose graciousness and affable manner she admired. Every once in a while the two of them went out strolling or even riding together. Zhou Enlai was eager to ensure that everything was well with Mao's life and staff. Zhou used to be the CCP's number one leader, well above Mao, in full charge of both the Party's political and military affairs. But he had no military talent or strategies. Worse, the German military adviser sent over by the Comintern, Otto Braun (aka Li Deh), was a capable strategist only on paper—neither he nor Zhou, who both had a European background and training, had any concrete sense of the topography of China's countryside or the rural people involved

Jiang Ching as movie actress

in the revolutionary struggle. Consequently, in the early
1930s, they lost one battle after another to the Nationalist
forces, which drove the Red Army out of its bases to embark
on the so-called Long March, which in reality was a
protracted flight. Not until January 1935, in the small town
of Zunyi in Guizhou Province, did Zhou turn around,
and, overruling the majority of the CCP leaders, let Mao
command the Red Army. Since then, with the military fully
in his hands, Mao's supremacy in the Party could no longer
be challenged. Zhou was convinced that Mao was much
more capable and farsighted than he was. Indeed, ever since
coming to power, Mao had led the Red Army to outsmart
Chiang Kai-shek's forces at every turn and defeat their
attacks. Zhou believed that only Mao could navigate the Party
through all the perils down the road. That was why he was
willing to serve Mao, playing second fiddle. For him this
was a matter of survival, not just his own but that of the whole Party's.

One afternoon in the early fall of 1939, after giving a talk at the Party school, Zhou Enlai left for his cave home at Yang Jia Hill, riding his Mongolian pony and followed by his bodyguard Jiuzhou, a short, eighteen-year-old marksman. Somehow Jiang Ching appeared on the road, also riding a horse. So she and Zhou were heading back together. But

Jiang Ching and Mao in Yan'an

upon reaching the Yan River, Ching struck her horse to urge it to speed up. That startled the animal, and it collided into Zhou's horse, which sprang up and threw him off. To protect his head, he put up his right arm, which landed first. The fall smashed his arm. Lying on the riverbank, he couldn't get up. His bodyguard dismounted and rushed over to help him to his feet. Zhou groaned, unable to move his arm anymore.

Back in his cave home, his wife tied a band of cloth around his neck as a sling. They both thought he'd feel better after a good night's sleep, but he hurt all the more the next morning, perspiration soaking the back of his shirt, so they sent for a doctor. The doctor found that Zhou's arm was fractured—he'd have to be treated without delay. But the medical services in Yan'an were so primitive that he'd have to go elsewhere for surgery.

At the news of Father Zhou's injury, Yomei hurried to Yang Jia Hill to see him. She was angry at Jiuzhou and blamed him for not being careful enough while keeping her father company. But Mother Deng stopped her, saying it was not the boy's fault. Father Zhou also demanded, "You must apologize to your younger brother Jiuzhou." She did. She was just a few months older than the young bodyguard, but he was shorter and looked like he was in his early teens, so she often called him younger brother. He was fond of her, and not really offended by her outburst.

Mao, after consulting with some leaders on the Central Committee, decided to send Zhou to the USSR for treatment. In no time, the Soviets agreed to arrange a plane to fetch Zhou. In its reply, the Comintern also summoned Otto Braun back to Russia on the same flight. The telegram didn't explain why; it just said there was a new task for him in Moscow. But Braun was already married to a Chinese woman, Li Lilian, a famous movie star who had come to Yan'an from Shanghai two years before. Initially, after he'd graduated from the Frunze Military Academy in the spring of 1932, Braun was sent to Manchuria to gather intelligence on the Japanese Kwantung Army that garrisoned on the southern edge of Siberia, poised to invade the USSR. He soon moved to Shanghai, where he could communicate directly with the Soviet Union and the Chinese red bases in the remote provinces. In the summer of 1933, orders came from Moscow that he go to Ruijin, the capital of the Chinese Soviet State in Jiangxi Province, to join Wang Ming, the Russian-educated and -appointed head of the CCP, assisting him in military operations. In the beginning, Braun gave disastrous suggestions right and left, which his Chinese comrades took for orders because he represented the Comintern, to whom the CCP was willing to defer. But Braun was sensible and discerning enough to see his own faults and limitations. Even after he lost his leadership, he openly acknowledged Mao's strategic superiority, and was willing to learn from his Chinese comrades. However, Braun had another weakness—he was unable to control his lust or tear himself away from pretty women. From the moment of his arrival at the red base Ruijin, he asked the CCP to find a woman for him. Worse, whenever he chanced upon a pretty woman, he would accost her, offering gifts and inviting her out. Some of the women were already married, so his untoward attention often outraged their husbands, who kept complaining to the CCP's Central Committee about him.

To contain him, they found him a woman. Her name was Hsiao Yuehua. She was in her twenties and from a peasant family. Yuehua wasn't pretty, but she was strong

and capable, good at singing and playing basketball. Yet
when the topic of marriage was broached with her, she
was reluctant, because Braun was ten years her senior and
also fat and bespectacled, with protruding teeth, an odd
smell, and a totally different lifestyle. All the same, some
women cadres in the Party worked on her and managed
to convince her that this was an invaluable revolutionary
task entrusted to her. So she and Braun soon married,
and that made him happy and steady, though Yuehua
wasn't pleased at all. She still had to eat differently, not
being qualified for the kind of dining privileges Braun
was entitled to. Worse yet, he often blamed her for stealing
his food and powdered milk—his cookie tin always had
some of its contents missing. They later had a child, a son,
though soon after the Long March, in 1935, she filed for
divorce, and Braun agreed to let her go and to pay alimony
of six hundred yuan a month, which was a huge sum,
considering that a schoolteacher in the local county could
make around one hundred yuan a year at the time.

Then Li Lilian came onto the scene. She was attractive
and charming, already a famous movie star. The moment
she greeted Braun in English at a party, he was smitten
and began chasing her. Since she was already divorced,
she agreed to give him her hand. In most ways, Braun's
lust and vanity were satisfied, and their married life was
uneventful. Yet now, the summons from Moscow threw
the couple into panic. He had to go back, he told her, and
she wanted to leave with him, saying she mustn't live like
a widow with a husband still alive and far away. But the
Central Committee denied her request on the grounds
that she had no passport, so they couldn't possibly get
a visa for her on such short notice. Having heard that,
Lilian cried so hard that she passed out.

Now Otto Braun was leaving on the same plane with the
Zhous. Lilian didn't show up, although several leaders were
at the airport outside of the town gate to see Braun off. The
night before, at Yang Jia Hill, there had been a farewell
party for him, which she hadn't attended either. Braun got
drunk and told Mao and Zhu Deh that he hoped to come
back soon to fetch his wife if he had to work in Europe for
a long time. His Chinese comrades still liked him in spite
of his shortcomings. They all wished him good luck and
promised to take care of his wife.

The plane on the single runway turned out to be a large
American DC-3 with twenty-four seats. This was the biggest
aircraft that had ever landed here, and it surprised the
Communist leaders. Most passenger planes that came a few
times a month were small Russian Kharkiv KhAIs, with
only six or seven seats. Together with the Zhous and Otto
Braun there were some other passengers, including Chen
Haochang, a tall, bulky-faced man who was a professor
at the Party's Political College, one of the twenty-eight
Bolsheviks in Yan'an. Professor Chen had lived in the
USSR for three years and was fluent in Russian. He was
suffering from a severe stomach ulcer and going to Moscow
for treatment. Yomei recognized his eleven-year-old son,
Zutao. She wondered why the boy was with his father. Zutao
explained to her that he was leaving for Russia too and that
his dad hadn't expected such a large plane. The previous
day, the professor had even told the boy that they might
head for the Soviet Union by buses and trains if tomorrow's
plane was small, with limited seats. Now father and son
were elated to see such a spacious DC-3 that could carry
everyone here. It was said that this U.S. aircraft was Chiang
Kai-shek's personal plane, and that he had dispatched it to
fly Zhou Enlai to the Soviet Union for medical treatment.

Since the Nationalist government had lately agreed to join hands with the Communists in fighting the Japanese Imperial Army, this was an occasion for Generalissimo Chiang to show his magnanimity.

To her surprise, Yomei saw that together with Zutao was "Tiger"—Gao Yi, the ten-year-old son of Gao Gang, the CCP's regional chief of Shaanxi Province. Both boys had powerful fathers and were going to study in the USSR. A twinge of envy jabbed Yomei. She knew that many children of the top CCP leaders were already attending school in the Soviet Union, such as Mao's two sons and Lin Bochü's daughters. Suddenly a small boy broke out wailing, stamping his feet and refusing to get off the plane. He was Chen Boda's son, merely six years old. His dad was running Mao's office of military affairs and was here to see the Zhous off. The six-year-old, nicknamed Little Tiger, wanted to leave together with his older pals, and no matter how hard his nanny cajoled him, he wouldn't leave the plane. All the adults were astonished, not knowing what to do about him. Some laughed. His dad was embarrassed, but since he was always indulging the boy, Chen Boda said to Professor Chen, "Can you take him along?" All the men on board laughed again, but the boy wailed, "I wanna go to Russia like Yi and Zutao."

Zhou Enlai said to his father, "If you feel comfortable letting him go abroad at such a tender age, maybe he can go with his pals too. It will do him good in the long run."

Mr. Chen lowered his eyes, then raised his round chin. He said to his son, "All right, you can go with your buddies, but you must listen to the uncles and aunties after you get there."

The boy nodded with a smile and went over to sit next to his friend Zutao.

Yomei worked up her courage and pulled the front end of Jiuzhou's jacket, saying, "Younger Brother, I want to go to Russia too; can you speak to my parents for me? I can help take care of my dad."

The bodyguard went up to the Zhous and said, "Yomei wants to go study in Russia too. Can't you take her along? She'll be a good student there."

Zhou Enlai, his thick brows pitched together, answered, "No, we might not be able to take her with us. I'm going to Moscow for medical treatment and also for work, and I was instructed by the Central Committee to go there only with my wife. It's like a job or a task I'm supposed to carry out. If Yomei tags along, what can I say to Chairman Mao?"

Overhearing those words, Deng Fa, a dimple-cheeked man with sparkling eyes, the president of the Party school, half-joked, "Yomei, the plane won't leave for an hour. You still have time to get Chairman Mao's approval."

To their astonishment, she said, "All right, I'm going to his office to ask for his permission."

She borrowed a bay horse from Deng Fa's bodyguard and mounted the saddle and dashed away.

On arrival at Mao's courtyard, Yomei ran into Ching, who stopped her. "I want to see Chairman Mao," Yomei told her.

"What for?" Ching asked, batting her large eyes.

"To get his approval. Please, Sister Ching, let me in. The plane is waiting and I need Chairman Mao's permission immediately."

"You should have scheduled an appointment—you can't just barge in. Chairman Mao is extremely busy and mustn't be disturbed at this moment."

"Who's there?" came Mao's metallic voice.

"Chairman Mao, I want to see you and need your permission," shouted Yomei.

He stepped out, smiling with his eyes tilting toward his temples. "How can I help you, Yomei?"

"My parents are at the airport. I want to go to the USSR with them, but my father won't take me along unless you approve."

"All right, I will let you go with them. You need a note from me?"

"Yes, please tell them you allow me to go?"

She followed him into his office. He took out a piece of paper and wrote with a squat pen: "I agree to let Comrade Sun Yomei go to the Soviet Union." He paused to ask her, "For what?"

"To study."

He added those two words. "Off you go," he said and handed the note to her. "Study hard in Russia."

"You haven't signed this yet," she reminded him.

"There's no need—they can tell it's my handwriting."

She thanked him with a bow and went out. At the sight of Ching, she cried, "Thank you so much, Sister Ching. I'm leaving with my parents for Russia. Take care." She waved the piece of paper, which crackled as if the words on it suddenly came alive.

Ching's lips twitched and stiffened. She smiled and said, "Lucky girl. Safe travels and come back soon." She waved as Yomei strode toward the horse tethered to the willow outside the courtyard.

"I will." Yomei mounted the horse, galloping away.

When she got back to the airport, the plane's propellers were already spinning, tossing up dirt from the new runway that went through the middle of a threshing floor. She showed Mao's approval to her parents. They nodded, both pleased to take her abroad with them.

As the plane was taking off, shaking like a boat, Father Zhou chuckled and said to her, "You're still wearing sandals like a country girl."

She looked at her straw shoes, which were almost tattered, held together with hempen strings. Mother Deng said, "Don't worry. We'll get you a new pair in Lanzhou."

Braun, who looked gloomy, was seated at a tiny, square window. He didn't say anything to the Chinese passengers, though he knew the Zhous and Professor Chen well. He still seemed unhappy about the summons from Moscow.

· *Five* ·

I n spite of the turbulent din, Otto Braun, still heartsick
about having left his wife in Yan'an, managed to talk with
Zhou Enlai through Professor Chen's translation. Braun
was upset, his eyes flickering with red rims. His lips curled
and stopped just short of a grimace.

"How come it's so easy for these kids to go to the Soviet
Union? They all have a visa?" he asked.

Zhou smiled and said, "We made an agreement with our
Soviet comrades long ago to send some children there to
study, so we had their papers prepared beforehand."

"Then I still don't understand why Lilian can't come
with me. She's my legal wife. This makes me feel like a fraud
just using a Chinese woman."

"We double-checked with the Comintern. They
instructed us that you go back alone. I'm sorry about this,
Otto."

"That will make Lilian believe I've taken advantage of
her all these years."

"I totally understand," Zhou said amiably. "We're all
revolutionaries and often have to sacrifice our personal
interests and happiness."

"I know that, but I don't see the necessity in my case."

"We're in a similar situation, having to obey orders from the Comintern even though we might not understand their reasons."

"You think they're all rational?"

"I don't see why I should doubt them."

Yomei had been following their conversation attentively, though she didn't appear to be listening. She liked and even worshipped Li Lilian for her vivacious personality and mellifluous singing voice and for her gorgeous figure. Few actors at the time could act in both movies and musicals like Lilian. Now, that woman, only in her midtwenties, may have been abandoned. How heart-wrenching this situation must be for her! Yomei also felt that Lilian had been used or misused. Intuitively, she reminded herself that she must take care to avoid that kind of situation in the future. So many revolutionaries seemed to have no second thoughts about leaving their spouses behind when they were ordered to pull up stakes. If this was the way they would act, why get married in the first place? It was irresponsible.

At the Lanzhou airport, Yomei saw squadrons of fighter planes and asked Father Zhou why those Russian aircraft were here. He explained that those Soviet pilots were helping China fight Japan, which was also Russia's perpetual enemy. Lanzhou was a transitional point where the materials and weapons sold to China by the Soviet Union were gathered. The fighter planes were shipped here straight from the USSR and then flew inland to deliver themselves to the Chinese military or to participate directly in air battles. Yomei had witnessed Japanese planes bombing and strafing civilians, but never had she thought that China had its own air force, even if it belonged to Chiang Kai-shek's army.

The Zhous stayed in Lanzhou for three days and then
flew to Tihwa, present-day Urumuqi, where Father Zhou
bought Yomei a pair of brown leather loafers with tassels,
which made her beside herself with joy, never having worn
such nice shoes. Seeing the girl's new footwear, Mrs. Zhou
frowned a bit, then told her husband with a smile, "You've
never been so openhanded for me, Enlai."

"Yomei is a young girl and we mustn't let her appear
shabby in front of foreign comrades."

"Mother, I'll buy you beautiful shoes when I make
money," the girl enthused.

Mrs. Zhou nodded and said, "Just enjoy yourself. I was
joking with your dad. You don't need to worry about the
future."

They stayed in a spacious suite in a two-story building
for the night. The hotel was quite elegant, surrounded
by weeping willows. It used to be warlord Sheng Shicai's
personal residence, but now served as a guesthouse, mainly
to accommodate the Communist cadres and officers
passing through, because Sheng Shicai needed the capable
military personnel of the Red Army to help him build his
mechanized battalions equipped with Russian vehicles and
automatic weapons. Two more children joined the Zhous at
the guesthouse—Liu Yunbin and his sister Aichin—whose
father was Liu Shaoqi, a key leader of the CCP, running
its Central Plains Bureau. The boy was fifteen and the girl
eleven. Together with them were also those boys who had
arrived on the same plane with the Zhous. Yomei was the
oldest among these youngsters. In total, there were six of
them, all regarding her as an elder sister.

After dinner the kids gathered in the room shared by
Yunbin and Aichin. Over hot cocoa made by Yunbin,

they chatted about their future plans. Little Tiger was too
young to know what he would like to study in the Soviet
Union. He just wanted to go there and have a good time
with his buddies. The other older boys all wanted to study
sciences and specialize in industrial fields. Their parents,
all experienced revolutionaries, had urged them to avoid
military academies, because the officers sent to China from
the USSR had turned out to be incapable and often made
terrible blunders and because the CCP had adept officers
galore but lacked experts in almost every civil field. So the
parents all wanted their children to specialize in a subject
that could be more useful for the new China they'd been
fighting to establish. Unlike Yomei, none of them was
interested in the arts or the humanities. She realized she
might be a black sheep among them, because she was eager
to study theater, which was her passion. She had talked
about this with her adoptive parents, who both supported
her choice, saying she could specialize in whatever she
preferred and that the revolutionary cause could use all
kinds of experts.

That night she wrote a letter to her aunt Jun, to whom
she hadn't been able to say goodbye when she left Yan'an in
a hurry. She didn't reveal her destination to Jun and just
said she'd write her again once she settled down. She also
gave Jun her mother's new address in Chongqing, where
Ren Rui had just transferred to the office of the Eighth
Route Army, where she was to direct its library. Yomei
enclosed a five-yuan bill for Jun, saying she had no need for
such money anymore. Indeed, she'd soon be using rubles
instead.

The Zhous stayed in Tihwa for about a week. Zhou Enlai
had many matters to attend to, talking with Sheng Shicai
and meeting the Communist cadres working in the region

Sun Weishi's letter to her sixth aunt, Ren Jun,
signed "Yomei"

to ensure that this place, so close to the Soviet Union,
would serve as a secure base for the CCP in the future.

There were other children and wives of the Communist
leaders on their way to Russia for medical treatment and
recuperation, and also for education, but some of them
were yet to arrive at Tihwa. So the Zhous and Professor
Chen, unable to wait for their arrival, were going to leave
for the Soviet Union before them. The two men and Mrs.

Zhou and Yomei bid the kids goodbye, hoping to see them in Moscow soon. Meanwhile, the children needed to learn as much Russian as possible from Uncle Peng, a senior officer who knew some Russian. The next morning, the Zhous and the Chens boarded a smaller plane to Almaty in Kazakhstan. Yomei was thrilled to see down below the Great Wall, battered and broken in places, like a giant sleeping python stretching along mountain ridges to the edge of the sky. Then the forest disappeared, replaced by an immense desert swelling with endless sand dunes.

"Now China is behind us," said Professor Chen. Zutao, his son, and Yomei nodded solemnly, as if too awestruck for words.

n Almaty, they boarded the train to Moscow. The trip
took them four days. When they arrived at the capital, at
Kazansky Railway Station, Ren Bishi, a chubby man in his
midthirties, was there to meet the Zhous and the Chens.
Yomei recognized him—Uncle Ren, who was the CCP's
envoy to the Kremlin and had come here two years earlier
to brief Stalin on the progress that the CCP had made
in recent years and on China's resistance war against the
Japanese. Yomei had known Ren for years; he was a sweet
man who treated her like his own child. When he smiled,
his thick mustache would tilt up at both ends like a pair of
little bird wings. They got into a flat-topped passenger van,
which took them downtown, directly to 10 Gorky Street, to
the Hotel Lux, which was also the Comintern's dormitory.
This was where the Zhous would stay, since many Chinese
Cominternians were also living in the midrise building.
Professor Chen and his son would lodge elsewhere—the
professor had lived in Moscow for some years and still had
friends here who would accommodate him and his son.

Zhou Enlai would be treated at the Kremlin Hospital by
the best doctors there, though he wouldn't be hospitalized.
An interpreter, Shi Zhe, would accompany him. Mr. Shi
was Ren Bishi's secretary and represented the CCP at

the Monino international children's home, which had
received the majority of the CCP leaders' children in the
USSR, some of them orphans. Shi Zhe had once studied
engineering at a military academy in Kiev and was the
most fluent Russian speaker in the CCP. The Zhous were
pleased to have him as their companion at the Kremlin
Hospital, which was known to the Chinese as the Russian
Royal hospital, so Mrs. Zhou thanked Ren Bishi for all the
arrangements he had made. Meanwhile, Zhou Enlai was
also to work on behalf of the CCP and the Comintern. He
knew many people and had a lot of business to handle here.

After lunch in the Hotel Lux's cafeteria—tomato soup
and smoked sausages and artisan rolls—Professor Chen
and his son left for his friend's place. Still unsure of what
she was going to do, Yomei was pleased to stay with her
parents for now. Their suite had three rooms and was
rather shabby, with two north-facing windows that didn't let
in a lot of sunlight, but the Zhous had become accustomed
to a bohemian lifestyle when they had been young
revolutionaries, so they were satisfied with the lodgings.

From the next day on, Yomei would go out to see the
surroundings. She was greatly impressed by the architecture
and artwork in public places. There were even sculptures
in some parks—bronze and stone figures of workers,
soldiers, national leaders, proverbial heroines, mounted
warriors, even some gigantic birds—eagles, doves, swans.
The Russians must be art lovers, better educated than the
Chinese overall. Their excitement over the public display
of artwork made Yomei more determined to study here. She
hoped she could get into a theater school, but that seemed
out of the question before she learned enough Russian.

Two days later, when Uncle Ren came again, they talked
about Yomei's plans to stay here. He hadn't expected to hear

that she would specialize in theater arts. Indeed, she was a
rarity among the youngsters from China, who all wanted
to study a useful subject like one of the hard sciences. To
Yomei's delight, Ren produced two books that could help
her learn Russian: one was a concise Russian-Japanese
dictionary made of thin, glazed paper and clothbound
(at the time there was no Russian-Chinese dictionary
yet); the other was a book of Russian grammar by Liu
Zerong, a well-known professor who had taught Russian
at Peking University before the Japanese invasion. Yomei
loved the books so much that she could hardly put them
down. Even though she didn't know Japanese, thanks to
the Chinese characters Japanese shared, she could figure
out the meanings of most of the Russian vocabulary. She
remembered that Yi-xin, the man who had courted her
briefly in Yan'an, had owned a copy of such a Russian-
Japanese dictionary, which was even harder to come by in
China. The wordbook had been published by Whitewater
Press in Tokyo, in a small printing, mainly for the
Kwantung Army stationed in Manchuria as part of the
preparations for Japanese soldiers to invade the Soviet
Union.

    Since Yomei couldn't be of much help to the Zhous,
Mother Deng urged her to start her studies as soon as
possible. The girl could see that her presence in the suite
was a hindrance to Father Zhou, who constantly had to
meet people in private. Uncle Ren suggested getting her
enrolled for now at the KUTV, the Communist University
of the Toilers of the East, so that she could settle down
and start her student life without delay. At the mention of
that school, her heart leaped and her eyes lit up. She knew
it was a mecca of sorts for international revolutionaries
and that numerous renowned figures had been educated

at the KUTV, including the heads of some nations and
Communist parties in Asia and Africa. Yomei knew there
were many KUTV alumni among Chinese dignitaries—
Deng Xiaoping, Liu Shaoqi, Chü Chiubai, General Yeh
Jian-ying, Tsao Jing-hua (professor of Russian), and even
Chiang Kai-shek's young son Ching-kuo. But Uncle Ren
Bishi made clear that she was only going to be a temporary
student there, mainly to study Russian so that she could get
into a theater school in the near future. The Zhous believed
this was a sensible arrangement, saying they entrusted their
daughter entirely to Uncle Ren.

Yomei left with Ren in the minivan. They were going
east to a suburban town called Kuchino. It was already late
fall, the streets strewn with leaves, and pedestrians wearing
windbreakers and hats and headscarves. On the way, Ren
Bishi explained to her that they were going to Section Seven
of the KUTV, where two dozen or so Chinese comrades
were already enrolled. He said that the KUTV was also
his alma mater, and that he was still well connected with
it, so Yomei mustn't hesitate to ask him if she needed help.
Twenty minutes later, they entered Kuchino district and
then pulled up in front of a long, two-story building that
housed the school's administration and some classrooms.
Pointing at the building shaded by acacia trees, Uncle Ren
said that Yomei should come here to register and fill out her
paperwork after she settled in.

Having walked across a playfield and then a poplar
grove, they stopped at a white wood cottage with tall
windows. This was obviously a dorm, cozy and gable-
roofed—the surroundings were peaceful and bucolic. Yomei
liked the solidity of the house. She had noticed that Russian
architecture was much sturdier than that in China, as if
everything here was built to last—a lot of stone and brick

and timber were used. They went up to the second floor and entered a room with wide planks on its floor. At the sight of its occupant, a round-faced Chinese girl, Ren said, "Hey, Lily, I brought you the friend I mentioned." He turned to Yomei and introduced them: "This is Lin Lily."

The two girls shook hands, grinning at each other as if they'd met before. Indeed, Yomei had already known quite a bit about this girl—Uncle Ren had told her about Lily in some detail. The girl had come to Moscow the previous year with a group of children and sick wives of CCP leaders, including Deng Xiaoping's ex-wife, Ah Jin. Lily was the third daughter of Lin Bochü, one of "the Five Grandpops" in Yan'an who had joined the CCP in 1921, the very year it was founded, and who used to be in charge of the Red Army's finances and logistics. The old man was revered for his integrity and frugality in managing public funds. Lily had been at the KUTV for fifteen months and was already attuned to the environment and could speak Russian decently. Uncle Ren said that from now on, the two of them would stay together and that Lily should help Yomei get accustomed to life here. The girls seemed to like each other instantly and promised him that they'd get along.

He gave Yomei a sheaf of crisp banknotes—seven hundred rubles—saying she should get some suitable clothes and things for everyday use. Lily told him, "Rest assured, we'll go out shopping this afternoon."

"Also help her get registered for a Russian class and a political course."

"By all means, she's my charge now," Lily said with a smile, which dimpled her left cheek.

When Uncle Ren had left, Lily took Yomei out to show her the college grounds. Lily had heard that the premises were a gift recently given to the CCP by the Soviet Union.

Yomei was pleased to stay at such a tranquil place like a village back in China, but this was definitely inside the city, like an oasis. Her new friend went on to explain that she, Lily, hadn't joined the other Chinese youngsters at the international children's home that was about to move away from Moscow because she was older, and the CCP officials here thought she might start dating soon. Lily giggled and said, "I guess you'll be the same—how old are you?"

Yomei swatted her on the shoulder. "I'm eighteen. How about you?"

"Me too. I was born in October 1921. I'm also a Rooster. We're the same—two domestic creatures, and should get along fine."

"I was born in June, four months older than you, so you should call me Older Sister."

"All right," Lily agreed. "I'd love to have an older sister here."

Together they walked farther into the campus. Behind the classroom building, on the other side of the playground, stood several white clapboard houses that served as dorms and a kitchen and a canteen, and there was also a kindergarten that cared for about twenty kids, a few of whom were Chinese and whose mothers were students at the KUTV. Beyond those houses spread a wood of pines and oaks, through which a trail curved away. As the two of them followed the path, Yomei saw squirrels chasing one another in treetops, their fluffy tails flashing. A few were running on the ground, now and again foraging through the year's decaying leaves. At the end of the woods flowed a babbling creek, its water clear and cool. On the waterside, a flock of wild ducks were waddling with heavy behinds, flapping their wings and letting out lusty quacks. Yomei was amazed to see the waterfowl unafraid of people.

Lily said that besides studying Russian, she had been taking three courses this semester: the Soviet Constitution, Political Economy, and the History of World Communism. Every class was taught by a Russian teacher and then translated by a Chinese interpreter in the classroom. But some concepts were nebulous and even alien to the Chinese students, such as productivity, superstructure, surplus labor, worth and value, and the stages of capitalism, and the interpreter didn't know how to render them into concrete, comprehensible terms. In such cases, the students just wrote down the words. They were told to remember them in Russian for now—by and by, the words would make sense to them.

After lunch in the school's canteen—cabbage soup and rye bread with butter—the two girls went out shopping. At a large clothing store, Yomei spent almost three hundred rubles for two shirts, a pair of pajamas, some underclothes, and two brassieres. Lily said Yomei must develop a different sense of money from now on—here everything was expensive, but they each received a decent stipend— four hundred and sixty rubles a month from the Chinese program at the Comintern, so they mustn't appear shabby and should even splurge every once in a while, going to the movies or the theater. Yomei said she'd like to see every play staged in town.

Yomei joined Lily in the Russian class. They were taught by Vera, a housewife who conducted conversation with them with the help of her son Sasha, a meatball of a little boy who had milky skin and orange hair. Can we learn genuine Russian this way? Yomei wondered. But she was glad Lily was also in the class with six others. She told her

Chinese classmates that she was here to study theater arts, so she must give all her time and energy to mastering the foreign tongue first. Her explanation prevented others from making her join their political curriculum. They all believed that specializing in theater studies was a task assigned to her by Chairman Mao. It was known that the Great Leader had personally allowed her to come and study in Moscow.

Though she had enrolled at the KUTV, she did her best to avoid taking courses of abstruse and slippery revolutionary theories, which might be beyond her. She would even try to use as little Chinese as possible so as to learn Russian faster.

Lily could speak the foreign tongue, though she still hesitated when using it, and had an accent. Yomei had learned a bit of Russian back in Yan'an, so she could tell that Lily conjugated her sentences quite well without making obvious mistakes in gender and cases and tenses, although she still tripped over a word or phrase once in a while. Lily was amazed to see the grammar book Uncle Ren had given Yomei, saying she had been looking for this very book for some time without success. Yomei was more than willing to share it with her. In return, Lily showed her the textbooks she had been using. Whenever Yomei had questions, her friend was ready to explain to her patiently. Yomei was behind everyone in the language class and had to work harder to catch up. Every morning she would stroll around, reading out passages and memorizing words and sentences. It was already winter, and sometimes the cold air, plus her overused voice, gave her a sore throat, but she forced herself to practice oral Russian for at least two hours every morning. Lily was impressed by the progress her friend was making. Indeed, Yomei soon could say some basic phrases in Russian with ease, such as "Thank you very much," "This is great," "Let us go," "What a beautiful child!" and "How are you?"

On Sundays she'd go to downtown Moscow to see the Zhous. Father Zhou had just gone through surgery, which, he was told, was successful but wouldn't be effective enough to restore the full use of his arm. Yomei was delighted to see that Father Zhou could move his right arm a little in spite of his tourniquet. He said he had gone through three rounds of diagnosis by expert orthopedists at the Kremlin Hospital and that the chief surgeon had suggested opening the elbow fully and reconnecting the bone, but Father Zhou had preferred the less invasive procedure—have only the protruding piece of bone cut off, which could restore the arm to its original form, in appearance at least. He was told that after the procedure, his arm should recover enough to become functional in the near future but wouldn't regain its full use. That was good enough for Father Zhou, who had so many things to deal with here and was unable to be an invalid for long.

Thanks to the successful treatment, the Zhous decided to return to China in the spring. Uncle Ren Bishi was also going back to Yan'an with them, but Father Zhou assured Yomei that he'd make arrangements with the Comintern to ensure that she could continue to stay and study here, provided that she was accepted by a drama school. That was something she'd have to achieve by herself.

Uncle Ren also talked with Lily and told her that most of the adult students at the KUTV would return to China soon, while she and Yomei should stay in Moscow on their own for seven or eight years. The Party would need all types of experts, and the two of them, still so young, should study for several years here to become more capable and more useful to the CCP. Lily said of course she'd be happy to remain in the USSR.

With Uncle Ren's help and through an office of the Comintern, Yomei was put in touch with the Russian Institute of Theater Arts. She was excited but also nervous, unsure if she could get into that school, which was regarded as the heart of theater studies in the Soviet Union. She shared the good news with Lily, who was thrilled for her too.

Then, in mid-February, Yomei and Lily moved to the Hotel Lux, which would become their dorm once the Zhous left. Yomei wanted to stay with her adoptive parents as much as possible, even though she and Lily shared a room below the Zhous and had to ride the tram to the KUTV for classes. The two also went to plays downtown, especially those at the Moscow Imperial Theater, where they saw *Carmen*, Tolstoy's *The Power of Darkness*, and Gorky's *The Lower Depths*. Though they loved the performances, the tickets were expensive, usually more than ten rubles a seat. On occasion, they got free tickets from the Comintern's office in charge of the affairs of the Chinese students and visiting cadres. Whenever that happened, it was like a holiday for the two girls, who would spruce themselves up a bit for the evening. By disposition, Lily was more somber and wanted to study philosophy or revolutionary theories, but she was fond of Yomei for her vivacious personality and her hearty laughter. She was eager to help Yomei figure out how to get admitted to the Russian Institute of Theater Arts.

"You must think I'm nuts to study theater here, don't you?" Yomei once asked.

"No, it's a great career choice," Lily said. "Who's to say that a drama artist won't be more useful than an architect or a bridge engineer to our country in the future?"

Yomei seized her friend's warm hand and gave it a shake. She knew Lily had in mind the Chinese boys, who were all eager to study weaponry and technology. They even looked down on those who wanted to specialize in the arts and the humanities, viewing them as having inferior minds.

Then, Yomei heard from the theater institute officially— its letter stated that she'd have to pass an audition to get admitted. That thrilled her, though she knew this wouldn't be easy. Fortunately, she was never afraid of performing in front of strangers.

On Monday morning, February 12, 1940, Yomei and Lily went to the theater institute for her audition. A stalwart professor in his midforties named Nikolai Gorchakov and a woman in her midthirties, Katina Lestov, led them into a rehearsal hall. Through Lily's translation, they told Yomei to perform something, anything—a song or a dance or a scene of a play—to demonstrate her ability. They understood that Yomei couldn't speak Russian well yet, but she could use any language as long as she could show her talent. Together with the teachers were several men and women who must have been actors, and they all took seats in the front of the rehearsal area. Behind them stood some set pieces: a black upright piano, a brown organ, a floral screen, and a grandfather clock whose brass pendulum was motionless.

With supple footsteps, Yomei got to the center of the room, which had floor-to-ceiling windows. She said she was going to sing a love song called "The Blue Flower" that was quite popular in northern China, particularly in the red Soviet region in Shaanxi Province. The professor nodded his approval. She asked for a stool or chair, and a young man came over with a leather footstool and placed it next to her. Yomei sat down on it and began acting as if at a spinning wheel. Then she started the song, her voice crisp and so energetic that it sounded rather piercing, while her hands were busy weaving at a piece of phantom fabric:

Green thread and blue thread,
All the bright colors
Are forming a blue flower,
So lovely it delights me.
Among all the crops
Sorghum stands the highest.
Among the girls in the thirteen provinces
Blue Flower is the most beautiful.

In January comes the marriage broker
And the engagement takes place in February.
The bridal money is handed to my father
So my groom will come to bring me home in April . . .

When she was done, she stood up and bowed to the spectators. They clapped their hands, all looking uncertain, as if a little puzzled. Katina accompanied the two Chinese girls out of the rehearsal hall and said they would inform Yomei of the results in a month or so.

On their walk back, Lily confessed that she wasn't sure how well the folk song had worked on the auditors, but Yomei's performance was lively by Chinese standards. Lily also felt it might have been a little too rustic, though she was impressed by the bell-like clarity of Yomei's voice. But who could tell what those theater professionals really liked? They might take the love song as something original, full of joie de vivre. She assured Yomei not to worry. The die was already cast, and all they could do was wait patiently.

When Yomei told her parents about her audition, Father Zhou was pleased to know she had performed "The Blue Flower," one of his favorite songs. He said that Chinese artists ought to stick to their own tradition in order to find their place in the world. Without question, Yomei had made the right choice with that song.

As a top leader of the CCP, Zhou Enlai wanted to meet with some Chinese students at the KUTV and see how well they were doing. The announcement of his visit excited the students, some of whom were his comrades sent over to study and get trained for more consequential jobs in the future. Yomei accompanied Father Zhou to the KUTV on a windy afternoon, and Lily went also with them. The classroom turned livelier the moment Zhou Enlai entered. He waved at the smiling faces and said, "Hello everyone, I'm so happy to see you here."

Right in the front row was a wavy-haired man in his late twenties. Father Zhou recognized him and went up to shake hands with him. The man was Liu Yalou, who used to be in charge of educating the cadres and officers at the CCP's Counter Japanese Military and Political University back in Yan'an. Like Yomei, he had just arrived and had been learning Russian so as to get into the Frunze, the military academy nicknamed the Brain of the Red Army, to study the combat operations of large corps.

Yomei went to the front, turned around to face her schoolmates, and asked them, "Can we sing a song together to welcome Vice Chairman Zhou?"

They all supported such a suggestion, so she started a song while beating time like a conductor without a baton, her chestnut-shaped eyes smiling. Together they belted out the folk song "The Vagrants' Ballad of Fighting the Japanese Invaders":

The curved moon is dragging a long shadow
Over the hills and on the roads.
We're wandering around and miss home.

Tell me, where is your home?

My home's beyond the Great Wall,
Beside a broad road.
Our village faces the Songhua River.

Is it Wang Village?

Yes, that is my home village,
But I haven't seen it for nine years . . .

It was a long ballad that told the story of how the vagrants' homes were robbed and burned down and how ferocious the Japanese soldiers were to the civilians. Most of the students in the room were not good at singing at all, and many sang out of tune. Yalou, his sparkling eyes trained on Yomei the whole time, followed her hands while crying out the lyrics. He couldn't sing at all, but he was so excited that he just recited the words loudly. The whole room could hear him reciting the lyrics. Lily loved Yomei for her ability to organize a chorus so spontaneously—though new here, Yomei often went to the front of a classroom and taught others how to sing a song that was popular back in Yan'an, beating time with her narrow hands while smiling merrily. In the beginning, Lily had butterflies in her stomach for her friend, but Yomei seemed to have no sense of stage fright. She was such fun, full of spontaneous grace. No wonder so many men enjoyed her presence among them.

Zhou Enlai was amused, and the instant they finished singing the ballad, he told Yomei, "Let us sing another song that everybody knows. This is really delightful." So she started another one, "The Big Sword March." It was a popular song among the soldiers of the Twenty-Ninth Army, who had fought the Japanese Imperial Army in Hebei Province. Now the whole room chorused in one voice: "Big swords fall on the devils' heads. / All our armed brothers, / Now's the time to battle against the Japanese invaders . . ."

Unlike most leaders, Zhou Enlai did not enjoy giving formal talks, so after the singing, he started conversing with the students. They asked him about the prospects of the war against the Japanese aggression back home. He explained that the CCP had been doing its best to collaborate with the Nationalist government so that China could maintain a united front, but there had been problems, even skirmishes, with Chiang Kai-shek's regime, which seemed more determined to undermine the CCP's efforts to keep the autonomy of the red bases. Therefore, the Party and the Red Army must remain vigilant against the reactionary forces in China and must continue to build the popular trust and confidence in the roles that the CCP had been playing in the war.

In answer to Liu Yalou's question about the importance of the Soviet Union to China, Zhou Enlai spoke more like a top Communist leader, saying that in his opinion the revolution led by the CCP was a continuation of the October Revolution started by Lenin, though the Chinese Communists were facing their own domestic tasks and challenges. For instance, China was a poor country with a huge population and lacking in natural resources. As he spoke he was clearly aware of a Comintern cadre, a skeletal man wearing a tawny soul patch, among the audience, and Zhou was certain that whatever he was telling the Chinese students here would be reported to the Russians. But with diplomatic savvy, he praised the USSR, saying that the Soviet Communists had been big brothers to the CCP, helpful and generous with their resources and experiences. He emphasized, "The Soviet Union is our rear base, on which we have to rely in order to survive the White Terror. See, some of you were sick and wounded back in China and came here to get treated and to recuperate. Without the support of the Soviet Union, we wouldn't be able to survive all the upheavals that plunged our Party into danger time and again." He stressed that this was also Chairman Mao's view. So the CCP had to follow in the CPSU's footsteps to build a strong socialist China ruled by the proletariat, but they had to drive the Japanese invaders out of their homeland first.

Zhou Enlai also discussed the European situation with the students. He said he worried about Germany, where Hitler seemed to be going to extremes in his so-called national socialism. In Zhou's view, Hitler was dangerous and could become detrimental to the European Communist movement; for example, the Nazis had already started persecuting Jews in Germany and had invaded Poland. But he believed that the Soviet Union was the invincible bastion against all the international reactionary forces. So every one of them here should be hopeful and confident. The world had no use for pessimists, and true revolutionaries must be optimists and always believe that the human race is capable of self-improvement and making social progress, that a better life awaits us ahead. In short, they all should feel fortunate to be at the KUTV, able to concentrate on their studies while their comrades back home were fighting bloody battles.

It was a warm, inspiring conversation. Afterward, many students told Yomei that they admired Vice Chairman Zhou very much. Some also tried to get close to her, even saying she was undoubtedly actress material and wishing her luck with her application for the Russian Institute of Theater Arts. Yalou was also one of those who had been following Yomei. He often turned up at the table where Yomei and Lily were having lunch or dinner in the mess hall. He would just shoot the breeze with them. From the Zhous, Yomei learned that Yalou had been married and had a son. Yomei, having noticed Yalou's interest in her, was very careful when mixing with him, because he was a family man. At the same time, she wouldn't want to offend him, knowing he was one of the most brilliant young officers in the CCP—he had been a division commander even in his early twenties. Because he was better educated than other officers, Chairman Mao didn't send him to the front to fight for almost a decade—the Great Leader wanted to preserve the best officers for the Red Army. That was why he had been dispatched to Moscow to study—once he learned enough Russian, he would attend the Frunze Military Academy to learn to become a military strategist.

Lily, however, didn't like Yalou that much, mainly because she felt he was pursuing Yomei too aggressively. He even warned other men to back off because only he himself was entitled to make friends with the beautiful new arrival. To Lily, Yomei, youthful and charming, deserved a better suitor than him. So whenever Yalou sat down with them, Lily would snort, "Why are you here again? We're all students and have tons of homework to do." She also tried to persuade Yomei to avoid him. In fact, Yomei wasn't eager to be associated with him, knowing that, though divorced, he had been quite thick with another woman, Su Liwa, who had been helping him with his Russian and was living in Moscow with her mother and younger brother. Above anything else, Yomei pictured herself differently and dreamed of becoming an artist who would act in plays and even direct a few. She felt vaguely that theater arts should be the center of her universe, though she couldn't articulate this thought yet, knowing that as an artist she must serve the revolutionary cause as well.

· *Seven* ·

Those youngsters who had come to the Soviet Union
after Yomei were now at a children's home called
the Interdorm, which was about to move to Ivanovo,
a city known for its large state-run textile mills, about
two hundred miles northeast of Moscow. Before the
youngsters left for Ivanovo, the Zhous went to see them at
the Interdorm's current location, in an idyllic compound
in Monino, an eastern suburb of Moscow. They brought
the children some toffees and peanut brittle as a gift from
the CCP. Yomei helped her parents distribute the presents
to the youngsters. She gave Lily's younger sister Linlin an
extra pack of candies; the girl, in her midteens, was lovely,
with a sunny face, and stood out among the Chinese kids.
Yomei was delighted to see the boys and girls who had finally
gathered here. Little Tiger was almost half a head taller than
last fall and already spoke Russian without hesitation, having
played with local kids every day. Even when Yomei asked
him questions in Chinese, he would answer in Russian. His
face was still pale, though it had lost some of its baby fat and
developed some delicate features. He said he disliked the
food here and missed his mom and dad.

Before heading back to China, the Zhous again went to
Yomei's campus, Section Seven of the KUTV, to see some

wives of the CCP leaders, such as Mao's third wife, Zi-zhen, and Deng Xiaoping's ex. Yomei accompanied the Zhous on these visits, knowing the women personally and calling each of them Auntie, though they were only in their thirties. Chairman Mao had married Jiang Ching the previous winter, although he hadn't officially divorced Zi-zhen yet, so people here still regarded her as Mao's wife. Zi-zhen was staying in a dorm on campus, together with her four-year-old daughter Min, who had just come from China to join her. Mother and daughter lived in a suite with a bathroom, two beds, and a square dining table that could seat six and that also served as a desk. Zi-zhen's eyes were fierce, radiating a hard light, in which Yomei could see anger, probably exacerbated by a touch of madness. Recently Zi-zhen's friends here had read a TASS journalist's interview with Mao in Yan'an, which in passing mentioned that the Chairman was accompanied by his "gracious young wife, Jiang Ching," so Zi-zhen concluded that Mao may have married another woman. But to her mind, the marriage was illegitimate, because they were not divorced yet. She often said that Mao always used women relentlessly and had to have sex every day. Wearing a glossy bob with crimped bangs, Zi-zhen told Mr. Zhou, "Enlai, our Party ought to give a right name to my status now that Mao Zedong is living with another woman. The Russians must already know he dumped me. That's why the personnel here have begun treating me and my daughter like a nuisance. The other day, the head of this program even threatened to put me in a mental asylum. I can't remain in limbo like this. I want to know who I am."

Yomei could see that physically Auntie Zi-zhen was already a wreck. The woman was often short of breath and perspired copiously whenever she got excited. She had been injured many times in battle and still had more than ten pieces of shrapnel in her body, which even the best Soviet doctors couldn't take out and which still gave her dull pain on rainy days. The agony had made her more irritable. Mr. Zhou tried to console her, saying he would certainly pass her request on to the Central Committee back home, that everything would work out properly. For now she must take it easy and focus on her recuperation. She didn't seem to listen to his advice, nor could Mother Deng's consoling words calm her anger. On the other hand, Zi-zhen seemed happy to see them, partly because she and Mother Deng were longtime friends. She thanked the couple for bringing her the box of Chinese books that the Zhous had obtained through Ren Bishi's help, some of which, the illustrated ones, were for Min. Yomei noticed that emotionally Zi-zhen was no longer stable—whenever her small timid-eyed daughter wanted to go out, Zi-zhen would yell at her and even pinch her cheeks, which were already chafed. The woman seemed to take her rage out on the child randomly.

As the Zhous were leaving, Zi-zhen said to Zhou Enlai in a rasping voice, "Please tell Mao Zedong that he still has his family in Moscow, even though we just lost our youngest son Leowa to pneumonia. I buried the boy in the flower garden on campus and I go visit him every morning."

The Zhous had heard about the loss of the eight-month-old and agreed to relay the sad news to Mao. They knew that Mao's two sons from his previous marriage were both studying here and living away from the other Chinese students in their own lodgings on Gorky Street downtown. But the two boys got on well with their stepmother Zi-zhen and often came to see her. That was why she claimed that Mao's family was still here in Moscow. She seemed

determined to keep her hold on her husband and his
children, still acting like the matriarch of the family.

The visit to Auntie Zi-zhen threw a shadow on Yomei's
mind. The woman used to be full of vigor and guts,
but now at age thirty she was already a madwoman of
sorts. Evidently she had been damaged, perhaps by her
entanglement with the captivating ideal that had inspired
so many young people to join the revolution, or simply by
the powerful man, Mao, who had chosen and possessed her,
and finally ruined her.

The Zhous also went to a hospital downtown to see Ah
Jin, who had been Deng Xiaoping's second wife (his first
wife had died in childbirth). Yomei knew quite a bit about
Ah Jin, a legendary woman with bold eyes and heavy brows.
She had loved Deng Xiaoping enough to marry him, but
their marriage had not survived the relentless persecution
within the CCP, which had once gotten Deng stripped of
all his positions and also incarcerated. Later, when he was
released and rehabilitated, their marriage crumbled—Ah
Jin had by then fallen for Li Weihan, who was in charge of
investigating Deng's case and had been Deng's perennial
rival in the arena of love. Li and Ah Jin had been attracted
to each other long ago, and now they began to resume
their relationship. Deng Xiaoping was crushed by the
disintegration of his marriage, but he never blamed Ah Jin.
Here in Moscow, it was reported that she had lost her mind
and was being treated as a mental patient in the hospital.

Inside the ward—a large room for five patients—Ah Jin
looked normal, wearing brown sneakers and a gray woolen
jacket that brought to mind the uniform of the Red Army's
senior officers. Yomei was surprised to see her hair shorn
at the nape. Ah Jin used to have long, abundant hair,
which was envied by other women, but she looked so odd

and crazed now that Yomei tried hard to avoid her gaze.
Yet Ah Jin appeared calm and at ease, and was evidently
delighted to meet with the Zhous. She thanked them for
coming to see her. She said she liked it here, and was able
to read a lot, but she missed her child back in Yan'an. She
regretted having left China without her two-year-old boy,
and she begged the Zhous to keep an eye on her son when
they got back.

"Of course, Ah Jin," said Mrs. Zhou, "your child is also
ours."

"Tell Weihan, I'm all right here and will speak Russian
better than him."

Her current husband, Li Weihan, as well as her ex, Deng
Xiaoping, had both lived and studied in the Soviet Union
long ago, so for her, to come to Moscow for treatment
and recuperation was more or less like a return to a home
base. At the moment Deng Xiaoping was the commissar of
the 129th Division of the Red Army and had just married
another woman. Ah Jin even urged Mrs. Zhou to come
join her here in a year or two so that they could go pick
mushrooms together in a nearby forest. Yomei was startled
by such a bizarre suggestion and wondered if the woman
had a screw loose, but Mother Deng, though healthy and
hardy, said she would consider coming here for a restful
vacation after their revolution succeeded. That meant once
Red China was founded, which might take decades, given
all the formidable odds the CCP had to fight against.

In fact, Ah Jin wasn't an ornery woman at all, but
at times she looked flighty, her broad eyes shifting and
flashing. She kept smiling at Lily, who was serving as their
Russian interpreter on this occasion. The girl used to be
under Ah Jin's leadership at the KUTV before the woman
entered the hospital. Ah Jin had once served as the secretary

of the CCP branch among the students here; even though
Lily wasn't a Party member yet, she'd still had to report her
thoughts to Ah Jin regularly. Now it was awful to see this
respected auntie in such a wretched state. To Yomei, Ah Jin
might be another damaged woman if her mind was really
as cracked as people believed. It was indeed difficult for
women to survive the revolution, especially those brimming
with vitality and idealism and elevated sentiment. The
brightest and the most capable of them tended to break
down first.

At the same hospital, they tried to see another woman
from Yan'an, Liu Ch'un-hsian, who was Bo Gu's wife,
not yet thirty years old, and who had also come to Moscow
for medical treatment. In Yan'an she'd been notorious
for having come up with this wisecrack: "On the Long
March, every donkey or mule was superior to a husband."
She'd said that because so many men had gotten their
wives pregnant regardless of the women's suffering and
desperate struggle on that arduous, dangerous trek. It was
whispered that her husband Bo Gu resented her flippancy,
which set their marriage on a decline, since the popular
remark embarrassed many leaders of the CCP. Here she was
diagnosed with dementia and placed in the mental ward
on the top floor. Through Lily's translation, a head nurse
told the visitors that Ch'un-hsian was dangerous and that
was why she was confined to a single room. They stopped
at the door, but were allowed to see her only through a tiny
opening on it. Indeed, the woman's eyes were dull and
stiff, her strong face harder and manlier than it used to
be. The sight of the madwoman upset Yomei, though she
said nothing. To her knowledge, Ch'un-hsian's husband
Bo Gu, a Soviet-educated leader in charge of all the CCP's
cadres, hadn't remarried yet, but he was cohabiting with

another woman in Yan'an. What was unusual was that
Bo Gu and Ch'un-hsian had married in Moscow twelve
years before, when they'd both been enrolled at the Sun
Yat-sen University here, so they had viewed this city
like a hometown—the cradle of their idealism, love, and
revolutionary careers. Now she had landed here again,
alone. Oddly, the wife's return to Moscow reminded Yomei
of the conventional custom: a bride would go back to her
parents' home when her marriage ran into trouble.

She knew that Father Zhou had been seeing some Soviet
officials to make arrangements for the Chinese children
and expats who were in the USSR. He had also been trying
to persuade the Russians to release a former top leader of
the CCP, Li Lisan, imprisoned since the previous year on
charges of being a Trotskyist and a foreign spy. Zhou Enlai
assured the Soviets that he had known Li Lisan, one of
the twelve founders of the CCP, for many years and could
vouch for his loyalty to Stalin. In reality, it was the CCP's
Central Committee that had ordered Li to stay in the
Soviet Union as its liaison. In other words, his gathering
inside information on the Kremlin was largely due to his
official mission here. In addition to that role, Li Lisan
had been editing a newspaper, *The Times of National Salvation*,
in support of China's fighting the Japanese invasion. Zhou
Enlai pledged to the Soviets that in every way Li Lisan was
a dedicated revolutionary, a trustworthy comrade. In terms
of seniority, Li was similar to Zhou and had been the Party's
de facto head in the late 1920s. He was a man of integrity
and charisma, though he could be a little too radical and
hotheaded and lacked real experience and flexibility.

What's more, among the top CCP leaders, Li Lisan
was one of those deeply connected to the Soviet Union.
Besides having lived in this country for more than a

decade, he had married a young Russian woman, though he'd already had two broken marriages. Yomei had met his wife, Lisa Kishkin, a foreign language student at a teachers college who had lucent, prominent eyes, her dark hair twined into a long braid. Lovely and sturdy, Lisa was at least fifteen years Li's junior. From time to time Lisa came to see the Zhous, imploring them to intercede on behalf of her husband, who she insisted was a good man and a genuine Communist. Yomei admired Lisa, who seemed to love her husband unconditionally. Lisa said that the Department of Internal Affairs (the predecessor of the KGB) had demanded that she divorce Li Lisan and expose him publicly as an enemy of the Soviet Union, but she had refused. Instead, she went to one prison after another in search of him. She feared they might have banished him to Siberia or the island of Sakhalin. Sometimes, after a whole day's looking for him in vain, she wandered alone in the city at night for hours on end. Finally, one afternoon she located him in the notorious Taganka Prison, known as Moscow's central detention house, where an old warden told her that she could bring her husband some money. But she was just a graduate student, with a monthly scholarship of two hundred fifty rubles for living expenses. Still she managed to give her husband sixty rubles every month, plus the food she took to him—bread, cheese, butter, peanuts, tomatoes, carrots, onions, cucumbers, pickled mushrooms, and eggplants. Also tobacco leaves.

Thanks to Zhou Enlai's intercession, Li Lisan was released toward the end of 1939. Lisa was rapturous to have him home again and told Yomei, "I always believed Lisan would come back, liberated and reinstated. He's a pure man I can trust. He and I are both beholden to your dad now."

Lisa's effusive words touched Yomei and set her mind spinning with thoughts. To her, this was an example of what true love should be like—constant and unaffected by circumstances, serving as an inner compass for one's life.

But the Lis had lost their lodgings at the Hotel Lux when Li Lisan was arrested, so the couple had to go and stay with Lisa's mother now. To make matters worse, Li Lisan had no job, and for months had been looking for work to no avail. Yomei had heard so much about this man and would love to meet him, though their paths would cross only years later. For now, even Lisa seemed to have disappeared.

· *Eight* ·

n early March 1940, Yomei heard from the theater institute that it had accepted her, offering her a full scholarship that was renewable annually, provided that her grades were decent, above B on average. Finally she could study theater arts in Moscow. The acceptance letter stated that she was the first Chinese student they had ever admitted and that they hoped this would herald a significant beginning. She wasn't sure whether they had accepted her because of talent they had perceived or thanks to some assistance from the Comintern. Probably both. She believed that Father Zhou must have spoken to some officials in charge of international affairs there. The Soviets might intend to educate her in dramaturgy as a kind of cultural aide to the CCP. To some extent this was verified when she broke the news to her adoptive parents: Zhou Enlai smiled, obviously delighted, and said to her, "Our Party needs all kinds of experts. You must study hard and make the best use of this opportunity and turn yourself into an accomplished artist."

"I will, Dad," she promised.

"Now I can tell Chairman Mao that the Soviets want to train you to become an expert in theater."

"Please thank him for me too."

Before heading back to China, Zhou Enlai spoke with some Soviet officials about the children of the CCP leaders studying in Russia. He asked them to treat the Chinese kids generously and also to avoid putting them in danger, because many of them had already lost their parents. The Soviets agreed to do their best to preserve the bloodlines of the Chinese Communists embodied by these children. Yomei was almost nineteen now, so she was on her own and was treated like a regular international student. Zhou Enlai entrusted Yomei and Lily to a Comintern cadre named Margelov. The man promised to watch after the two young women, but he also suggested that they get naturalized, because that would facilitate their full participation in Soviet life and society. The suggestion took Zhou Enlai by surprise, though he knew that some young Chinese had married Russians and other foreign nationals and decided to live abroad for good. He told Margelov, "That should be up to the girls to decide for themselves."

Yet when Margelov spoke with Yomei and Lily about this, they both shook their heads and refused to apply for Soviet citizenship. Among the Chinese students there was a moniker for those who had married foreigners and settled down in the USSR permanently—"Musty Bread," which referred to the type of food that had lost its freshness and nutrients after being kept somewhere for too long. Neither Yomei nor Lily wanted to become Musty Bread, and they were convinced that they'd go back to China in the future, so the Comintern no longer insisted on their naturalization.

Yomei's theater institute was downtown, far away from the campus of the KUTV, but fortunately she and Lily could continue to live at 10 Gorky Street after the Zhous left for Yan'an. Uncle Ren found a new room for them in

the Hotel Lux, one with two beds and some basic furniture.
Both Yomei and Lily were elated about this arrangement,
which would improve their lives considerably, even though
Lily had to take the tram to school twice a week. But she
would graduate in a month or two, so they were happy to
have their new lodgings downtown now.

After the Zhous and Uncle Ren had left, on the first day
after they had moved into their new room, Yomei lit their
small butane burner and made dough-drop soup with oats,
eggs, crushed tomato, and sauerkraut. She cooked a whole
pot of it for dinner, which Lily loved and ate with a lusty
appetite, saying she hadn't tasted Chinese food in ages.
Yomei had two big bowls too, but she said cooking took too
much time, so they should avoid making meals. Lily agreed,
also believing they ought to devote more time and energy
to their studies. So from the next day on, they subsisted
mainly on bread. Yomei liked sweet stuff and lathered her
toast with jam or jelly, while Lily ate hers with butter or
cream cheese. Occasionally they also had pickled vegetables,
like mushrooms and gherkins and onions.

In the mornings the two of them often went out
together, trudging through the snow-covered streets and
crossing the Moskva, on which children skated or rode
on sleds drawn by husky dogs. On the way to the libraries
or Yomei's theater school, the two of them often bought
breakfast at bakeries, each having a Danish or a puff,
munching on the pastry while walking. Along the streets
sometimes the fresh snow was so heavy that the electricity
lines dipped into long, diving curves. Near the bridge they
found a small patisserie that sold fried turnovers stuffed
with apple or eggs mixed with rice, somewhat like the
vegetable buns they used to eat back in China, so whenever
there was no line at the store, they'd each get a large

turnover for one ruble and twenty kopecks. The owner, pink faced and with crisp white hair, would beam at them while wrapping their purchase in wax paper and then tell them to come again. They both looked younger than they were, so the man took them to be in their midteens and called them girls. When they left the bakery, their fingers would be interlaced as they strolled away chewing on the turnovers.

Every once in a while some international figures would appear at the Hotel Lux to speak to the Cominternians from various countries. One afternoon in the spring of 1940, Lily came back and said excitedly to Yomei, "Do you know Li Deh, the German officer who used to command the Red Army in China, is going to speak here tomorrow evening?"

"You mean Otto Braun?" asked Yomei.

"Yes, that's the man. He's going to talk about the Chinese Red Army to some international comrades."

"He flew back to Moscow on the same plane with me, so I should go listen to him and say hello."

The next evening they went to the conference room on the ground floor to hear him talk. Otto Braun looked exhausted, a little haggard, and apparently he hadn't been doing well. In the introduction, Kiushin, the man in charge of Chinese affairs at the Comintern, mentioned that Otto was working at the Foreign Language Press now as a translator and an editor and was going to update them about the CCP's military affairs. At the lectern, Otto grew more animated as he spoke about the structure of the leadership in the Chinese Red Army, which was basically a force composed of rebellious peasants and troops who had surrendered from the Nationalist army. Obviously, the audience here, especially those from European

countries, were unfamiliar with his topic, so he was patient
in explaining the details and some terminology he used.
According to him, the CCP still had some thirty divisions
scattered in different provinces—each, on average, consisted
of about seven thousand troops. But the army was poorly
equipped, each division having only four or five light
mortars and less than fifty machine guns and two or three
hundred horses. In contrast, Chiang Kai-shek's Nationalist
army had a great deal of aid from international capitalist
powers and was equipped with German and American
weapons, including tanks and heavy artillery pieces,
armored vehicles, and bombers.

But the CCP's military leadership was strong and
capable. Otto admitted that he had been less adequate
compared to his former Chinese comrades because he hadn't
known the countryfolk and the geography well enough to
give effective directives. During his tenure there, he based
his assessments and analyses mainly on telegrams and
statistics gathered by his aides. With a touch of bitterness,
he praised Mao as a strategist, saying the man was brilliant
and thoroughly seasoned with battle experiences, though he
was sure Mao couldn't even fire a gun or pitch a grenade.
Otto had attended several talks given by Mao, who he could
tell was humorous, earthy, and charismatic, a natural
leader, although at times Mao could be diabolical like a
bandit. Knowing Otto couldn't eat red chili, Mao had once
announced to a crowd, "Fried red chili is a revolutionary
foodstuff. Whoever cannot eat fried red chili is not a
revolutionary." Otto's account cracked up the audience.

He also mentioned Bo Gu and Luo Fu, top leaders
of the CCP who had both studied in the USSR for years,
and were fluent in Russian. He liked Luo Fu (Zhang
Wentian) a lot, saying the man also spoke good English,

having lived in the United States for years too. In every way the two foreign-educated men were international revolutionaries. Sometimes they were both uncomfortable about Mao's nationalistic vision and narrow-mindedness, but they did their best to accommodate Mao for the sake of the Party's solidarity. Unlike them, Mao was natively bred, never having stepped foot outside China, yet he was full of vitality and peasant cunning, and particularly good at guerrilla warfare. He was a far superior leader to the others in the CCP. In comparison, Zhou Enlai was a great administrator, unflagging, astute, and always adaptable, but he was not a capable military strategist. For some years Zhou had been the actual commander of the Red Army, but about six years back he had switched to Mao's side and supported Mao unconditionally. Indeed, Mao stood out among the top leaders, who all seemed willing to follow him even when they didn't fully understand his intentions. Otto was confident that with Mao as its top commander, the Red Army would continue to flourish and might take over the whole of China in the future, despite its shabby current state.

Yomei was impressed by Otto's candor and bigheartedness. The man had been defeated by his China mission and disliked by his Chinese colleagues, but he showed little bitterness. Yomei had overheard the Zhous talking about Otto as an inexperienced military adviser, a bookish cadet from the Frunze Academy. To many CCP military leaders, he had been the cause of numerous setbacks and disasters, a jinx of sorts cast by the Comintern on the Chinese Red Army. They may have felt relieved to see him removed finally.

After Otto's talk, Yomei went up to him. He recognized her and held out his hand, saying he was impressed that she could speak Russian now. "Just a little," she said with a smile after shaking his meaty hand.

She asked him about Lilian, whom she still remembered fondly. His eyes dimmed, then began shifting. He grinned, laugh lines bracketing his stout nose. He said, "I haven't heard from her since I left Yan'an."

"Is she still there?" she asked.

"She might still be teaching music at the Yan'an Arts Academy, but I'm not sure." He shook his head of curly hair, more grizzled than the year before.

"Don't you miss her?"

"What can I do?" He grimaced. "We have to take losses as part of our lives."

Yomei thought to ask him about his son in the care of Yuehua. She was curious to know if he was still paying the six-hundred-yuan monthly child support to that woman, his first Chinese wife; perhaps it was the CCP that shelled out some cash on his behalf now, but Yomei refrained from asking and just told him that she had enrolled in the Russian Institute of Theater Arts, to study acting. He was impressed and said he was glad to see her making such progress here. Yet the brief exchange with him disturbed Yomei a little, especially when she saw him leaving the conference room with a young blonde wearing knee-high boots and a brown peacoat, who was holding his arm with both hands as they walked away to the street. She must be his current woman. Yomei knew that the Bolsheviks had introduced the notion and practice of casual sex to the Chinese Communists, so marriages among the CCP members were not stable at all. In Yan'an there was the popular euphemism for sex—"a glass of water." Such an attitude embodied sexual liberation, a theory and practice advocated by Alexandra Kollontai, the famous Bolshevik

feminist, who viewed sexual liberation as an integral part
of proletarian revolution. Even here among the Chinese
expats at the KUTV there was the witticism that went,
"In the Yangtze one wave pushes away another, while in
life new lovers replace the old ones." This was only some
men's justification for chasing tail. Yomei knew there'd
been a secret slogan among male Communists back in
Yan'an, which, it was said, had been started by Ho Long,
Ho Zi-zhen's brother: "All girls are ours." Intuitively she
felt this sexual liberation was upsetting, having seen so
many women left behind by their men like detritus of the
revolutionary cause.

Back in their room on the fourth floor, she talked to
Lily about Li Lilian, whose movies Lily had seen. Lily was
appalled to hear that Braun had left his glamorous wife
behind in China. Such a separation signified another kind
of marital trouble, which had been prevalent among the
revolutionaries. The two of them chatted about the broken
marriages in Yan'an, a place Lily had never been to but
was eager to learn about. They sat at the small round table
under the only window in their room, which had frosted
over and was covered in white floral patterns. They couldn't
see the outside through the ice. Between the double panes
was sawdust, about one and a half feet high, to keep out
cold air. All the cracks in the frame had been sealed with
putty prior to the wintertime, and for ventilation there was
only a little transom at the top, which they kept open for a
few minutes in the mornings. Both of them believed that
Otto Braun was a kind of scoundrel, having abandoned his
wife, who deserved a much better man than him. Evidently
power and love could hardly be harmonized, and it must be
dangerous for women to get entwined with powerful men.
They both believed that such entanglement was something

they must avoid. That was why Yomei wanted to study theater arts, preferring to pursue artistic beauty, and she urged Lily to find her passion unrelated to political power as well.

They had heard that the Comintern had recently investigated Otto Braun's activities in China and concluded that he had made serious mistakes, but he was pardoned without any disciplinary action against him, because his role in the CCP had been as an adviser with no power to make decisions. Both Yomei and Lily felt that the conclusion was unfair, too protective of their own man, since everybody knew how much weight and influence Otto Braun's opinions had carried with the CCP leaders, who had all revered him as the representative of the Comintern. His opinions may have been construed as orders from Moscow and sometimes even followed to the letter. In other words, even though without commanding power, he was obeyed like a commander.

Yomei and Lily both loved art and music, though Lily, always modest, believed she herself had no artistic talent. Concerts were too expensive for them, but most galleries and museums were free to the public. There were also cheap seatless tickets at various theaters, in which they often watched plays while sitting on stairs or on the steps along the side walls. Yomei happened to know a middle-aged actor who taught part-time at her theater institute and who could get free tickets for some productions. Whenever he gave her a pair of tickets, she and Lily would go to the play together and often celebrated such an outing with a night snack afterward. The Russians were passionate about art, and even the metro stations were constructed like miniature museums, decked with sculptures and murals and gorgeous colored chandeliers. Sometimes Yomei would linger in the marble halls underground, standing before the artwork, observing their intricacy and beauty.

Somewhat out of duty, she and Lily went to see the museum of Lenin so that they could learn more about the history of the Soviet revolution. To their amazement, they were actually moved by the story of Lenin's dedication to the Communist cause (even though the narrative was officially made for propaganda's sake), and the exhibition was unexpectedly stimulating and even inspiring to both of them. Another place they enjoyed visiting was the Gorky Central Park of Culture and Leisure downtown. It was immense, full of local people who went there for relaxation, exercising on the flagged terraces or promenading by the waterside. When spring came, more courting couples appeared in the park, spending private time among the trees and blossoms. Yomei and Lily also paid a visit to the museum of Nikolai Ostrovsky nearby. They both had read and loved his novel *How the Steel Was Tempered*, which was renowned throughout the socialist bloc as a masterpiece of Communist literature. They were amazed to see that the director of the museum was Ostrovsky's wife, who was still in her midthirties, with a youthful, energetic face, bright round eyes, and a broad forehead. In a chesty, warm voice, the woman explained to them how her late husband had managed to study and write even though he was paralyzed and blind. Indeed, the man had possessed a willpower like steel. His wife's face, as if animated by the memories, shone with a pinkish sheen as she was speaking about him to the two Chinese women.

By far, Yomei's favorite place was the Tretyakov Gallery, which was also close by in Lavrushinsky Lane. It was a museum with a huge collection of Russian art, more than two thousand paintings and drawings, mainly from the

nineteenth century. Yomei and Lily often went to the brick
building that looked small, even shabby, from the outside
but was immense inside, consisting of two floors and dozens
of high-ceilinged halls. Sometimes they would spend
hours in there, observing the paintings or just absorbing
the ambience they felt the artwork capable of creating. For
Yomei, this was part of her education too. She felt that in
spite of their vibrant colors and youthful freshness and
occasional romantic spirit, these paintings embodied the
essence of Russian arts: serious, somber, and noble, with a
tragic feeling close to pathos, a deep, innate resonance of
life. Usually, however bright a scene was, there were always
shadows on a grassland, clouds in the blue sky, and a haze
over a cityscape. Whenever Yomei was in this gallery, she
was moved and even felt a little purified by the beauty of the
artwork. Therefore she would visit that place whenever she
had free time. If Lily wasn't available, she'd go alone.

Nine

Yomei and Lily didn't live at 10 Gorky Street for long because they were soon employed by the International Red Aid. They were told that from now on they were no longer the Comintern's responsibility, even though the IRA was an organization under the Comintern. So the two of them moved to the administration building of the IRA, which was also in downtown Moscow, close to the Hotel Lux. They were given a room on the top floor. Their life hadn't changed much—Yomei, in spite of her part-time employment, could continue with her theater studies while Lily had already graduated from the KUTV and was now on her own, working full-time at the IRA, keeping records of material donations, which came from various countries and the satellite states.

Despite living away from other Chinese, the two still kept some contact with the expat community in Moscow. These days some expats were excited, having learned that General Lin Biao was now living in town. They were eager to meet him and hear him talk about China's military effort against the Japanese invasion.

Lin Biao was respected as a national hero, because two years earlier his troops, the 115th Division of the Red Army, had fought the first successful major battle in the

war against the Japanese. After a forced march, his men
had reached Pingxing Pass in Shanxi Province, where
they ambushed the Eleventh Independent Mixed Brigade
of the Japanese Imperial Army. They defeated the enemy,
having inflicted more than a thousand casualties and seized
over one hundred truckloads of supplies. All at once, Lin
Biao was celebrated as a hero throughout China. Several
captured Japanese officers had presented to him a general's
uniform set and a katana sword, both of which he would
later don whenever he went out to inspect his troops and
their positions.

Then one day a sharpshooter in the warlord Yan
Xishan's army, which had also participated in fighting the
Japanese, spotted Lin Biao from afar and mistook him
for a Japanese officer riding a big sorrel tarpan horse. So
the man fired, and the bullet grazed Lin's head and threw
him off the horse. The fall injured his back and paralyzed
him briefly. Though he was treated straightaway at the Red
Army's Central Hospital, its doctors were unskilled, and its
facilities too primitive and inadequate. Consequently his
wound began suppurating. That was why, in the winter of
1938, he came to the Soviet Union for medical treatment.
Originally he and his wife stayed at a sanatorium, and then
they moved to Section Seven of the KUTV in Kuchino,
though seldom had he come out of his house or mixed
with others. As his health improved, he began to resume
some light work at the Comintern on behalf of the CCP.
In the spring of 1940, when Ren Bishi, his wife, and his
secretary, Shi Zhe, left Moscow together with the Zhous,
Lin Biao took over that man's role and served as the top
representative of the CCP at the Comintern. He also
inherited Ren Bishi's flat at 10 Gorky Street. That made

some Chinese expats in the Moscow area eager to have him
speak to them.

Yomei knew Lin Biao personally, and back in Yan'an
they had met a number of times. He headed the Chinese
People's Anti-Japanese Military and Political University,
where her mother Ren Rui used to study. When the Zhous
were in Moscow, Yomei had once accompanied them to
Kuchino to visit the Lins. She enjoyed spending time with
Lin Biao's wife, Zhang Mei, and the two young women
became friends. When Yomei later stayed with Lily at the
KUTV briefly, she often went to see Lin Biao's wife. The
two of them would sing folk songs together, which helped to
mitigate their homesickness. On the Zhous' next visit to the
Lins, Yomei's adoptive parents noticed the change in Lin
Biao, who had become more cheerful and talkative. Father
Zhou told Yomei afterward, "You really made Lin Biao
happy. He used to be so taciturn that he rarely expressed
his feelings. See, when you and his bride were singing, he
enjoyed listening to the songs so much that he even beat
time with his knuckles on the desk." Mother Deng grinned
and added that she had never seen Lin Biao so lively either.
He was known as a reserved man and wouldn't even speak to
his troops more than necessary.

Having heard that Yomei was living near the Lins, some
Chinese expats asked her to represent them to invite Lin
Biao to give a talk. They knew that Yomei's elder brother
Sun Yang was an aide to General Zhu Deh, who was one of
the few military leaders above Lin Biao in the Red Army,
so Lin might be willing to accept Yomei's invitation. She
was glad to represent her follow expats, and together with
Lily, they went over to the Hotel Lux to invite the general.
Lin Biao was delighted to see the two young women again

and, without thinking twice, agreed to come and speak to
the expats in the building of the International Red Aid. He
even said this was part of his work in Moscow anyway.

Three days later, about forty men and women gathered
in a large room in the basement of the IRA building,
waiting for Lin Biao, who was regarded as the most capable
CCP general, completely trusted by Chairman Mao. Some
of the expats had known Lin Biao personally and were
amazed to see him so warm and friendly now. He sat next
to Yomei and spoke animatedly about the situation back
in China, specifically about Chiang Kai-shek's intrigues
and conspiracy against the revolutionary forces there.
He believed that with the generous support of the Soviet
Union, the CCP would thrive and develop rapidly in spite
of the Japanese aggression and the pressure put on the
Communist Party by domestic reactionaries. Answering the
question whether the red bases in various provinces could
survive the blockade imposed by both the Japanese and
the Nationalist regime, he assured them that the CCP had
lately started a movement called "the Great Production,"
which aimed to make the central Communist base of
Yan'an economically self-sufficient. He also mentioned
that there were even several ordnance factories in the Red
Army now, and that they could produce light artillery pieces
like mortars and small flat-fire guns in addition to rifles,
grenades, landmines, and shells, though the quantity of the
production was limited. In short, the Communists would
prevail, not just in China but throughout the world.

The expats were inspired by his talk and wanted him
to speak to them more often. They regarded him as their
direct connection with Yan'an, and also, his style was more
casual and more engaging than regular political speeches.
Indeed, he was the number one leader of the CCP in

Moscow now. He promised to keep himself available, saying he was supposed to report to the Central Committee back in Yan'an on their life and work here anyway. Yomei was glad to serve as a liaison between the expats and Lin Biao. Besides inviting him, she also meant to visit her friend Zhang Mei, who was already in the second trimester of pregnancy. Zhang Mei was eager to have Yomei over and chat with her so that she could learn more about the world outside their building. She was pretty and used to be nicknamed the County Belle back in Yan'an. In truth, Zhang Mei was a beauty, with a round face and large glossy eyes and a shapely figure, and in spite of her pregnancy she still looked lovely. She was fond of theater too, and whenever possible would go to Yomei's institute to watch the rehearsals. Yomei also gave her free tickets for plays staged at local theaters, especially those performed by students, which were open to the public. Zhang Mei loved to attend the plays, saying they were much better designed and produced than those back in China. By comparison, she said that the folk drama back home was a little too primitive, and that she admired Yomei for studying foreign theater arts, which would definitely help China develop culturally. She regarded Yomei as a pioneer of a sort; for that, she respected Yomei more. Although Yomei usually gave Zhang Mei a pair of tickets to ensure the couple could enjoy a play together, Lin Biao never went with his wife. He disliked crowds.

One afternoon, on arrival at their three-room flat on the third floor of the Hotel Lux, Yomei overheard the couple exchanging sharp words. She paused at their door.

"Why do you go out every day?" Lin Biao demanded.

"I want to see what Russia is like," his wife said.

"You came here as my companion. That's your job, so you should stay home in case I need you."

"I'm a free woman. You mustn't treat me like you own me, like I'm a servant of yours."

"But you're carrying our baby and mustn't go out too often."

"That's why I should move around as much as I can before my belly gets too big."

Yomei walked away. After overhearing their exchange, she wouldn't give her friend play tickets as often as before. She sensed that there might be some problem in the Lins' marriage, so she mustn't be more involved in their life. Still, Lin Bao continued coming to the IRA building to see Yomei and Lily. He even invited them out, taking them to the nearby parks and waterfronts.

And even more than before, he was always ready to join the expats, some of whom were no longer students at the KUTV and had begun working for the Soviets in the city. Whenever he turned up at their gatherings, he'd sit next to Yomei and speak excitedly, showing he was truly happy to be among them. Once, Yomei couldn't attend his talk, and as a result, he looked lost, his mind scattered, and all his amination vanished. When answering questions, he couldn't speak coherently, meandering instead. Some women in the room realized it was Yomei's absence that dispirited the general. After the meeting, Liu Yalou, who had been after Yomei all along, said to Lin Biao, "Wake up, man, Sun Yomei has her own life here. She's busy with her drama studies and can't always come to support you. I love that girl too. She's like a fresh breeze that always brings you life and joy, isn't she?"

Wordlessly Lin Biao stared at him.

Yalou went on, "Let's face it, my general. She's a beautiful girl, but unavailable for either of us. We're both family men and had better leave her alone. That will make everyone's life easier and more comfortable."

Lin Biao spun around and strode away, his hands clasped behind his thin back. Yalou shook his head and sighed, murmuring, "Every old ox wants to chew tender grass, myself included." Indeed, he had recently married his Russian teacher, Su Liwa.

Soon it was whispered that Lin Biao was head over heels in love with Yomei and that he often fought with his wife. Lily told Yomei, "Some young women at the Comintern are green with envy, seeing you can turn General Lin's brain into a bucket of paste."

Surprised, Yomei stammered, "I respect him like an uncle. He's thirteen or fourteen years older than me and already has a family. I can't take him as a boyfriend, you know."

"Still he's a top commander in the Red Army, second only to Zhu Deh. To many women and girls, he's like a demigod of warfare. Also, he's rather handsome, isn't he?"

Indeed, Li Biao had a youthful, oval face with bright eyes and mothy brows, though he had a slight build. By conventional Chinese standards, he was quite good-looking, the scholarly type with sensitive features, but Yomei didn't feel attracted to him. She told Lily, "I like Lin Biao, but only as an older comrade, so please don't join others in gabbing about this. Besides, Zhang Mei is my good friend, how could I wreck her marriage?"

Nevertheless, the gossip unnerved Yomei. From then on, she took care to avoid Lin Biao as much as possible. But every once in a while, Zhang Mei would turn up at Yomei's dorm and beg her to come to her flat because Lin Biao had gotten moody again, downcast and unable to hold back his temper. "He's having another nasty fit," in his wife's words. True, whenever Yomei appeared in their home, he'd become a different man, mild and even warm to others. So Yomei felt obligated to help her friend and would still visit the Lins when Lin Biao was so down in the dumps that Zhang Mei couldn't but beg her to help. Lily often joked about this, saying it was ludicrous that her nineteen-year-old friend was becoming a babysitter of that man, who in name still commanded tens of thousands of red troops far away.

· *Ten* ·

At the theater institute, Yomei mainly studied with Professor Gorchakov, a tall man with a whiskered, square face and a belly-deep voice. He was full of enthusiasm about the plays he directed and would yell at his students if they didn't follow his instructions exactly. If a student did something wrong or clunky in a rehearsal, he would bang a desk and let out a torrent of complaints, some of which Yomei couldn't understand yet. She also took courses taught by other faculty members. She enjoyed Katina's performing class and always practiced the small parts the teacher assigned her, even though she still stumbled when trying to speak lines in Russian. Katina was kind and praised her whenever she did something right. She said Yomei was smart, a natural. Even though at times Yomei felt frustrated, unable to grasp the full meaning of the teachers' instructions, she cherished the time she spent in the studios and the rehearsal halls and could see the progress she had been making. In such a nourishing environment, she would definitely grow into a capable artist of spoken drama.

Although not yet fifty, Professor Gorchakov was already revered in Moscow's theater circles. He had been a student of the late Stanislavski's for many years and

had even directed plays with him. He often talked about
that monumental figure, saying that his teacher had
revolutionized Russian theater and that their institute was
meant to follow in Stanislavski's footsteps—their practice
and style were based on the method invented by him.
Gorchakov emphasized to his students that this staging
method was a *process*, not a theory, so they must not expect
a system of theoretical constructs from him. What they
could learn from him about Stanislavski's system was the
actual practice of how to stage plays. Gorchakov often got
excited when talking about Stanislavski—his eyes would
turn dreamy and at times even teary. Yomei respected him
for his ardent passion and total dedication to dramatic arts.
He often repeated, "The theater is the school of the people.
What we're doing here is a spiritual pursuit that provides
Russians with artistic nourishment and ethical guidance.
Therefore, theater is a noble profession." He couldn't
tolerate any trace of laziness or vulgarity.

Yomei regretted not having come to Moscow earlier,
since Stanislavski had passed away just the year before. Back
in China, like most theater students and professionals,
she had read Stanislavski's *An Actor's Work*, a book regarded
as a must-read about the skills of stage performance. Now
she felt fortunate to be studying Stanislavski systematically
at the very place where the giant practiced his art and
developed his method. Someday she'd bring this dramatic
practice back to China and make it blossom on the stage
there. In a way, she viewed herself as "a granddaughter of
Stanislavski's" because Professor Gorchakov saw himself as
an authentic disciple of that founding figure, a son of sorts.

He was pleased to hear that Yomei often went to art
museums and galleries. Indeed, her familiarity with

Russian painting helped her theater studies. Deep within, she could feel the undercurrent of Russian arts—serious, spiritual, passionate, soul-stirring. Since the beginning of the academic year, Professor Gorchakov had been directing some one-act plays as an initial step for the acting and directing students. At the moment he was doing Chekhov's *The Anniversary*, a short comic play set in a bank that is celebrating its fifteenth anniversary. It is a small piece, so there were not many students involved. All the same, Yomei felt she'd been learning a lot from the staging of the play. Because she wasn't good at speaking Russian yet, she was given a tiny role, which pleased her nonetheless.

A small number of students were picked for the cast, and every participant was excited and went about their assignment conscientiously. A few of them had many lines to learn and engrossed themselves in the rehearsals. Yomei's role was merely as a servant who helps lay a table of snacks and beverages toward the end of the play. Such a scene was minimal in the original script, but it was expanded by Gorchakov to get more students involved. Even for her small part, Yomei had to participate in the rehearsals fully like the others, studying the text carefully, writing out her understanding of it, and even the biographies of the main characters. This was to make every acting student familiar with all the aspects of the production. Gorchakov emphasized that one must enter the character and act out the role from within, as though the actor manifested his or her own personality onstage—their performance had to be their personal creative contribution to the play. Likewise, they mustn't imitate any performance. He often said, "Imitation means the death of art."

Yomei took a lot of notes about the rules and the process and tried to grasp the director's intentions, which by and large reflected Stanislavski's method. Since *The Anniversary* was a comedic piece, some of the actors strove to be funny. This often made Gorchakov lose his temper. One afternoon, he flung up his thin hand and cried out at Yuri, who played the grouchy clerk, Khirin. When his superior Shipuchin, the bank's chairman, let him deal with the silly, pathetic old woman who has come to the bank for help even though her sick husband should turn to the military health service for aid, Yuri, playing Khirin, began to jeer at the woman. With a smirk on his long face, he told her, "To put it plainly, you don't have a brain in your head. What's in your head is sawdust!" Suddenly Professor Gorchakov cried out, "Don't try to be funny. Don't show your effort to make the audience laugh."

"We're doing comedy, aren't we?" Yuri asked timidly, smiling as if still amused by his own attempt to be ostentatiously funny.

Gorchakov's high forehead was shiny, coated with beads of perspiration. He stepped closer to Yuri. "When you're trying to make the audience laugh, you ruin the comedy. You must be absolutely earnest—the more serious you are onstage, the stronger the comic effect you'll produce. Don't ever lapse into a caricature."

Yomei made a note of that exchange and could see that Yuri's later earnest performance got sharper and funnier in manifesting the clerk's irritability and the absurdity of the situation, which at moments could even become disturbing in spite of the laughter from the spectators. Professor Gorchakov always emphasized that acting must be based on the actor's own creative impulse and personal interpretation, which must reflect the actor's inner life and dramatic urges.

Yomei hardly did anything in the play. She stepped onstage, then stood beside a tall samovar, holding a platter of refreshments.

Still, at the first dress rehearsal, she just followed the others onto the stage without doing anything. She stole a glance at the teachers and students below the stage, all of whom were observing them as attentively as if this were a real performance. She tried to follow the characters, moving her body with the people around her and nodding her head and letting out an "Ah" or "Oh" now and again with the other servants. She tried to appear jubilant.

Afterward Katina grabbed hold of Yomei and took her to the side of the auditorium. She said under her breath, "You didn't act well enough in the rehearsal. You must keep your attention on the stage action."

Taken aback, Yomei mumbled, "I joined the others in the play the whole time."

"But you looked away from the stage action," Katina persisted, her voice rising a little.

"How? I don't know what happened."

"You looked at the audience instead of acting from within the drama. I saw you glancing at me. Didn't our eyes meet once?"

"They did."

The teacher blinked her deep-set eyes. "You see, that's why in the scene you appeared like an outsider. You must concentrate on the drama unfolding onstage. If your mind is not in it, your performance will get out of character and detached from the play. The truth is that the more you focus on the stage action, the more likely the audience will participate in the drama—both the actor and the audience must be actively involved in the dramatic development. That is a fundamental principle of our acting method."

"I will remember this and won't let my mind wander away from the stage action again," Yomei said in a subdued voice.

That evening she wrote in her journal: "Remember no matter how small a role is, it must be an integral part of the whole play, as essential as any of the major components. Your mind and body must stay in the drama constantly— you're supposed to create the stage action, not just imitate someone. Everything must come from within."

· Eleven ·

Though a good number of men were eager to get to know Yomei better, she treated them equally and at times even lightheartedly, without slighting anybody. If someone invited her out, she would feign ignorance, saying, "How about Lily? Can she come too? She's like a younger sister of mine."

In reality, she meant to give all her energy to her studies and to the work at the Red Aid. At this stage of her life, she wasn't interested in any romantic relationship, since she was unsure where she would settle down in the future.

In a way, she was a jester, good at ribbing others without hurting their feelings. For instance, at the KUTV she had an older classmate, Yang Zhicheng, who was thin like a picket and had a wrinkled face. Yomei called him Grandpa, though Zhicheng was only in his midthirties, but he was so good-natured that he never took offense. Whenever Yomei called him Grandpa, he would nod as his way of responding to her. He knew she treated him as a genuine friend. Even after Yomei had left the KUTV, Zhicheng would still chat with her warmly whenever they ran into each other. He would introduce her to others as his friend and former classmate. Several of those military men in their class, including Zhicheng, would become two- or three-star generals in the People's Liberation Army a decade later. They all treated Yomei as a younger sister of sorts and never got offended by her jokes and antics.

Through her friendship with Yomei, Lily felt enlivened and rejuvenated. She confessed to Yomei that before they met, never had she experienced the joy of youth, and that was why she felt so attached to Yomei, as if they had been born friends. Indeed, even some older women expats had noticed the change in Lily, saying she was no longer the broody, studious girl she used to be. Like Yomei, she now laughed a lot too, even out loud in front of others. Yomei mulled over Lily's confession, which brought back to her the memory of her little sister, Yolan, whom their mother, unable to raise all her children by herself, had given away to their oldest aunt's family. How was Yolan doing in Sichuan? Yomei hoped her little sister was doing well at school. Yolan's absence from her life might have helped build the strong sisterly friendship between her and Lily.

At the beginning of 1941, Lin Biao came to call on Yomei again. Lily was not in but might return any minute, so Yomei went out with him, reluctant to let Lily find him and her together in their room privately. As they were strolling in a birch grove where the mottled boles were turning silver and glimmering in the setting sun, he told her that he was leaving for Yan'an together with a few other expats, mostly those young officers educated here. The CCP had recently called them back, so they had to head for home. He planned to take them to Mongolia first, and from there they would cross the border back into northern China.

Yomei was caught unawares and asked, "What about Zhang Mei and Hsiaolin? Are they leaving with you too?"

Hsiaolin was their newborn baby girl. He said, "Mei won't go back with me. She loves it here and will stay."

"Can she take care of your child by herself here?"

"She says she can. I want you to know that Mei and I are going to split up. Our marriage has hit rock bottom, and there's no way to salvage it anymore."

"How does Mei feel about this?" Yomei was alarmed, wondering why he was telling her this. To her mind, Zhang Mei was an excellent wife for him.

"She has agreed we'll part ways. I'm wondering if you might be willing to go back with me to Yan'an."

Flustered and with her face burning hot, she managed to ask, "What for? If we went back together, people would ask who I am to you."

"I promise I'll marry you as soon as Mei and I are divorced. She and I have already agreed on this. You know my feelings for you, Yomei. You're the best young woman I've ever met. Please go back with me to make me a happy man."

Under his intense gaze, she felt her face reddening, her mind groping for an appropriate answer.

"Please," he almost begged her, "I'll be good and considerate to you."

"I know you're an extraordinary man," she at last found her words, "but it was Chairman Mao who sent me here to study theater arts, and I still have four years to go. If I quit now, what can I say to Chairman Mao? I would become a failure in people's eyes. Before leaving Moscow, Uncle Ren Bishi talked to me and Lin Lily and wanted us to study here as long as possible. Now I can't just head back alone and abandon Lily here."

His brow furrowed. "In that case, I can take Lily back to Yan'an too. I can explain to the Central Committee and Chairman Mao. I'll tell him that I need you so I can work better for the Party and the Red Army. You will become my fiancée for the time being so people can't wag their tongues about your return with me."

"Truth to tell, this makes me very uncomfortable. Zhang Mei is my friend, and I can't destroy her marriage."

"Believe me, with or without you, she and I will get divorced. You can go ask her."

"Please understand, I'm just a student. I love the theater studies here, which are so hard that I can barely survive, but I have to persevere. I don't want to start dating so early. You know our Party wants me to become an expert in spoken drama. The institute I'm in is a great place for my studies, and I must cherish such a privilege."

"Well, I'll be patient. You don't have to give me a final answer now."

"Please don't count on me. My future is still uncertain, and I'll be here for several years. Anything might happen in the meantime."

"I'm very certain about my feelings for you, Yomei. I can assure you that Zhang Mei and I will get divorced pretty soon, then I will wait for you in China. I won't be with another woman until I hear from you."

She was touched but managed to reply, "You're a good man. Any woman would feel delighted and honored by such an offer, but please don't place all your hopes on me. My life is still unpredictable."

"Rest assured, I will wait patiently."

He held out his hand, and they shook goodbye. She said that the local Chinese expats would love to give him a farewell party before he left. He didn't respond to that and just gave a faint smile, shaking his angular chin slightly. He spun around and walked away, the soles of his leather boots making tiny screeches. She noticed that in spite of his thin frame, he had a straight back and sturdy legs, which must have resulted from his many years of military life. In the back of her mind lingered another shade of unease. Why was he so sure that she was attracted to him? He was a very confident man indeed.

That evening she mentioned his proposal to Lily, who had become her confidante of late. They were having coffee with cubes of brown sugar. Lily was annoyed that Lin Biao had even suggested bringing her back to Yan'an without consulting her first. But she was also amazed and excited by his offer to Yomei. She was certain that many young women would kill to be with that legendary young general. At the same time, Lily wouldn't say Lin Biao was a completely decent man. The previous summer he had often come to take both of them out while leaving his pregnant wife alone at home. Now he wanted to divorce her so that he could marry Yomei. What kind of man was he? At least irresponsible.

Lily also confessed that usually she was afraid of men and might not see anyone in the near future. This fear dated back to her early childhood. When she was five years old, her mother had taken their family from Shanghai to Guangzhou by boat. One afternoon, she was playing near the prow of the steamer and saw a drunk man grab a young woman passing by, forcing her to sit on his lap. As the woman was struggling to get away, the man exploded and lifted her and dumped her into the rolling sea. The ship stopped to retrieve her, but she was already drowned when they pulled her up to the deck. "Ever since that terrible episode," Lily confessed, "I've been scared of men."

"It's so hard for a woman to live a good, fulfilled life in this world," said Yomei.

The two of them also talked about the kind of men who might be suitable for them. Yomei revealed that she actually felt uneasy about going with a dedicated revolutionary, because a powerful and extraordinary man might be hard for a young woman to keep up with. "Look at Auntie Zi-zhen and Auntie Liu Ch'un-hsian, and also Auntie Ah Jin," she said to Lily. "They used to be the brightest and the strongest women in the Party, but Auntie Ch'un-hsian lost her mind while Auntie Zi-zhen is a total wreck, abandoned by the powerful men they were married to. Do you know Chairman Mao has a young woman living with him now, even though he and Auntie Zi-zhen are not divorced?" Just two weeks before, they'd heard that Zi-zhen suffered a breakdown and was sent to a mental hospital, where the doctors feared that she might attempt suicide.

"I've heard of Chairman Mao's new wife," said Lily. "It's rumored that she used to be an actress in Shanghai."

Yomei nodded. "She was a second-rate actress, and I've known her for many years. She's good at using men."

"You mean Jiang Ching was promiscuous?"

"I wouldn't say that, but she had trouble with some men in Shanghai. Her ex-husband Tang Na attempted to kill himself because of an affair she had with another man." Yomei felt she might have disclosed too much about Ching, so she returned to the original topic. "Think about Auntie Zi-zhen and Auntie Liu Ch'un-hsian. What if they hadn't married Mao Zedong or Bo Gu to begin with? Also, remember Li Lilian, left behind in Yan'an by Otto Braun? What kind of women might they be now if they hadn't married men with great power?"

"Good mothers and loving wives, to say the least," Lily said thoughtfully. "I would also say they might be better company, and better friends. They'd be normal people. You're a smart girl, Yomei. I see your point—powerful men can be destructive to women. The ancient adage 'A hero and a beauty ought to be together' is a fallacy, totally wrong."

Yomei smiled, nodding her assent. "Powerful men are less capable of human feelings, I believe."

"How about your adoptive parents?"

The question threw Yomei, but she scrambled to answer, "Well, Mother Deng is a plain woman—in terms of looks, she can't match Father Zhou at all."

"You mean their marriage is stable because she's browbeaten by him?"

"Probably." For now Yomei couldn't tell Lily everything. She had once overheard her adoptive parents fighting—Mrs. Zhou was yelling at her husband, accusing him of flirting with a pretty young woman. He hung his head a little and kept mum about the accusation, which might have been true. Nonetheless, Mother Deng must understand that in the public eye, she wasn't a good match for her husband, so she often caved in to him.

Lily continued, "My dad is a major CCP leader, and my mom has never had a peaceful time with him. Such a marriage can be heavy going for any woman. Look at the Rens—when Uncle Ren Bishi and his wife, Auntie Zongying, were going back to Yan'an last year, they left their one-year-old daughter behind in the international children's home. It's awful to keep a family broken like that."

"I wonder if the child might grow up troubled," Yomei echoed. "Kids in a parentless environment might develop emotional problems down the road. At least they'll have a lonesome childhood. Oh, Auntie Ch'un-hsien's daughter, Little Jima, is also in Ivanovo now. That's another shattered family among the top revolutionaries."

"And her husband Bo Gu doesn't seem to care how mother and daughter are doing here."

"For the sake of the revolutionary cause, those powerful men are always ready to sacrifice everything, including their families."

Lily agreed, "Some of them view such sacrifice as necessary and even noble."

Sensing that they were straying from their original topic, Yomei returned to the current situation, saying, "I don't feel I have many things to say with Lin Biao. What can we talk about—battles, cannons and howitzers, bombers and fighter planes, tanks and armored combat cars? You know I don't like military or political stuff. I love art and want to be an artist. As a woman, I want to live a life in pursuit of beauty. If I marry, I want to do that only for love."

"Not for happiness?"

"Without love, how can a marriage make you happy? One thing I'm certain about—I can accept neither a statesman nor a general as a lover."

"Then you'd better fall for a scholar or an artist." Lily batted her eyes, smiling as pinkish patches were creeping up her smooth cheeks.

Yomei sighed and went on, "Now, I'm afraid that Zhang Mei might become another wrecked woman left behind by her husband."

"It must be hard for her to raise Hsiaolin alone," added Lily.

For some reason, Yomei couldn't keep Zhang Mei out of her mind the next morning. Then, speak of the devil—she ran into Mei on Gogol Boulevard that very afternoon. To her amazement, Zhang Mei appeared more vigorous in spite of her sad face; she was striding with brisk steps while carrying a bag of groceries and a bottle of milk. She stopped to greet Yomei. Her round eyes suddenly smiled. The two friends swept away the dusty snow from the slats of a bench on the sidewalk and sat down. They chatted warmly, their shoulders touching from time to time. It was turning dusky, snow blanketing the wide street, on which people wrapped in furs and long coats and children in dark-blue duffel coats passed by. The kids brought to mind giant, stumbling penguins. Yomei asked her friend about Hsiaolin, and also about how the two of them would get on once Lin Biao went back. Zhang Mei was in placid spirits, shaking her thick bob calmly. She said, "We'll be OK. Actually, without him around, life might be more peaceful for us. I'm just tired of staying indoors all the time as a housewife, listening to him gripe without a break."

"Do you plan to go back soon?" asked Yomei.

"No, I'll stay here for some years. Our marriage is over, and we'll get a divorce." Zhang Mei's lovely eyes blazed as if she suddenly remembered something hurtful. "Oh, I see. Did you meet Lin Biao recently? How come you know he's leaving?"

"He did come to see me."

"What else did he say? Did he bad-mouth me?"

"Not at all, he only said you two were splitting up—your marriage was not salvageable anymore."

"Why did he bring this up to you?"

"He invited me to go back with him," Yomei admitted. "But I refused to leave. I'm still a student here and can't stop in the middle of my studies. Also, you're my friend, and I can't do you such a mean turn. I told him that I couldn't let people think I wrecked your marriage."

"Actually I won't care if he marries someone like you, who can make him happy," Mei said crossly. "He does like you, a lot. He once said you were enchanting. I can see that a beautiful woman like you can bewitch many men easily. Lin Biao is yours, Yomei. I don't want him anymore. He has

Zhang Mei and Yomei

made me feel ten years older since our baby was born."

"In all honesty, sister, I'm not interested in Lin Biao. He might be brilliant and powerful, but not the type of man I like. Please don't tell him I said that."

"Sure, I won't let on we've met."

"Still, it's hard for me to see how you and your baby will get by."

"He has made some financial arrangements for us. I guess I'll be in a situation similar to a Chinese expat here."

"Do you want to study or do something you like in Russia?"

"I'll have to wait and see how things work out."

"I'm sure there'll be some opportunities."

"Perhaps I might go to college here. But unlike you, I didn't attend school back in China and I'll have to start from scratch."

"Still, you should make good use of your time in the Soviet Union."

"That's what I've been thinking too."

The meeting with Zhang Mei comforted Yomei some. But soon she heard that Lin Biao had left Moscow quietly without saying goodbye to others. That was typical of him: he avoided meeting people as long as he could.

· *Twelve* ·

Try as he might, Lin Biao couldn't take those expatriate officers back to China by way of Mongolia, because the Japanese military, as well as Chiang Kai-shek's army, sealed the Sino-Mongolian border. Even he himself couldn't get out of the Soviet Union until three months later. Yet thanks to his reputation as a national hero, Lin Biao was allowed to return through Kazakhstan. He had once been Chiang Kai-shek's student at the Whampoa Military Academy, and the CCP had joined forces with the Nationalists to fight the Japanese invaders, so the Generalissimo meant to display his magnanimity, even dispatching a plane to Almaty to fetch Lin Biao to Tihwa. Still, he couldn't bring the whole group of expat officers with him; he could have only his personal doctor accompanying him back. Once he landed in Tihwa, he managed to bring a few capable military officers stranded there back to Yan'an with him. Yet even without his help, those expats in Moscow set out for Mongolia anyway in hopes of crossing the border on the sly, but only two or three of them got across to the Chinese side, while the rest, including Grandpa (Yang Zhichéng), were all scattered in Central Asia. It took them several years to set foot in their homeland again.

One morning in late June, as Yomei was reading aloud
a Russian lesson behind the IRA building, a loudspeaker
announced that the German army had crossed the border
in the west, attacking Soviet positions. In the past few years,
she'd heard the ominous news: Czechoslovakia had fallen to
the Nazi forces, then Poland, then France, but no one had
expected such a blitzkrieg on the USSR. She was stunned,
and everyone on the streets looked dazed too.

She ran back toward her room, bounding up the stairs
two at a time, and found Lily also in a state of agitation,
with blazing eyes and pale cheeks. Lily had been listening
to the radio, which was reporting the event in more detail.
As they ate a breakfast of buttered toast and milk, they
talked about what they should do. It looked as if the Soviet
forces, unprepared for such an avalanche of attacks, had
been overwhelmed. It was said that the front resistance was
collapsing. Like the Soviets, Yomei and Lily both viewed
Nazi Germany as the archenemy of world peace and wanted
to fight the invaders. Unlike Lily, Yomei knew how to use a
rifle and throw a grenade, having already trained in Yan'an.

For days, the two tried to find out whether they could
join the Soviet army or the guerrilla forces or any armed
resistance. The city was chaotic, a lot of people fleeing while
many institutions were talking about evacuating. The two
of them met some Chinese expats still in Moscow to see
what their options were. Liu Yalou said he would try to
join the Soviet army—he was already an officer, enrolled at
the Frunze Military Academy. This seemed to be the only
sensible option for him. Yet most young Chinese expats had
no idea what to do, though they were all eager to fight the
Nazi forces and defend the USSR.

One day, after lunch, Yomei and Lily saw a line of
people outside a kiosk on a sidewalk. They went over to take

a look—at the front of the line was a desk, at which sat two
officers wearing peaked caps. About fifty men and women
were queueing up to join the army. Yomei and Lily stood
at the end of the line, in the middle of which Yomei saw
an acting teacher from her theater institute. She knew the
man with salt-and-pepper hair, so she went up to him and
bowed. Lily followed suit. They both said they too wanted
to join the Soviet citizens and fight in the Red Army. Then
they returned to the end the line, waiting for their turn to
register. Fortunately, they both had their IRA ID on them,
which could prove they were adults in spite of their youthful
looks. They talked about where to put their belongings after
they joined up. Yomei suggested selling them to get as much
cash as possible. They were unsure where they might land
in the future.

When an applicant finished registering at the front of
the line, he or she would step aside to another desk, where a
doctor-like man asked them a few questions and sized them
up and at times looked into their mouths with a flashlight.
Some of them were asked to do a couple of squats or push-
ups. Once they passed this cursory physical, they were given
a certificate—formally conscripted. Next, the new recruits
would go to a warehouse nearby to receive uniforms and
weapons, each getting a rifle plus a bandolier and a pair of
grenades. Then some of them went home to say goodbye to
their families.

Finally Yomei reached the desk, and the middle-aged
officer fixed his pale-blue eyes on her and asked, "What
country are you from?"

"China," she replied. "My friend here is also from
China." She pointed with her thumb at Lily behind her.
"We both want to join the Red Army to fight the Nazis."

"No, no." He shook his whiskered face.

"Why? I'm already twenty." She produced her ID to show him her birthday.

"Me too," Lily joined in, though she was still four months short of twenty.

"Miss, I'm sorry," the officer said. "We're not allowed to recruit foreign nationals."

"The German invaders are also our enemy. Why can't we take part in fighting them?"

The man jotted down their names and contact information. He told them that he would double-check with his superiors to ascertain that he was abiding by the rules. He would let them know the exact policy of the Soviet government, but today he just couldn't register any foreigners. Yomei and Lily had no choice but to leave.

They were upset and spoke with their superior Michail at the IRA about this. The man made a couple of phone calls on their behalf. The Comintern office in charge of Chinese affairs told him that there was an agreement between the CCP and the USSR about the matter: none of the youngsters from the Chinese revolutionary families would be allowed to fight on the front.

This explanation brought to mind what Lin Biao had once told Yomei. She was amazed by the memory and shared it with Lily. They were drinking black tea in their room. Yomei said, "Before leaving Moscow, Lin Biao predicted there might be a war like this. He said that was why he was eager to bring those expat officers back to Yan'an. Lin Biao believed that the Germans might attack the Soviet Union. If this happened, the Nazi army would come to take Moscow as soon as possible. Once the capital fell, he said, the whole Soviet Union would collapse." At the time Yomei didn't know how to take his opinion and just kept silent. She didn't believe that Nazi Germany could conquer the Soviet Union.

"We have to give Lin Biao credit—he was clairvoyant, to say the least," said Lily.

"He also told me that some Soviet officers laughed at him, saying his prediction was absurd and groundless. Now that it has come true, he might feel vindicated far away in Yan'an."

Later Yomei and Lily learned that Zhang Mei, together with her baby Hsiaolin, had left for the children's home in Ivanovo to join the other Chinese youngsters and staffers there. Among all the forty-odd Chinese students in the Soviet Union, in spite of their eagerness to go into the Soviet army, only Anying, Mao's eldest son, was allowed to join up. Before leaving, Anying had left his seventeen-year-old brother Anching, who was troubled as a result of constant anxiety in his childhood, in the care of some other Chinese students. Then Anying went to the Polish front, where he served as an artillery officer, shelling Nazi positions and vehicles.

Soon antiaircraft guns appeared in the capital, mostly deployed at makeshift batteries, which were large pits dug on street sides and on open ground. Hundreds of light artillery pieces and heavy machine guns were also placed on rooftops in downtown. Some were accompanied by giant searchlights. Every evening huge balloons were flown up to interrupt the Luftwaffe bombers that came during the night. When it was dark, hundreds of shafts of light would scrape and illuminate the sky, making it look as if a holiday celebration were underway.

As expected, soon German planes came, dropping bombs randomly on residential areas. Though the Nazi

army was still far away from the city, the bombers were
intended to dissolve the Russians' resolve to resist. But
the Soviet artillery and air force were fierce in fighting
back—most of the bombers were brought down before they
could enter Moscow's sky, which was lighted as if on fire.
Still, once in a while a few planes managed to penetrate
the network of gunfire and dropped bombs on the city.
That brought about more chaos. Every day Yomei ran into
Muscovites scrambling to flee the city. There were also
new arrivals from the western and southern provinces,
which were already ravaged by German forces. Some of
these refugee families, made up mostly of old men and
housewives and young kids, were carried into Moscow
by trucks spattered with mud and drilled with bullet and
shrapnel holes. Children looked famished, while adults
were all bedraggled and dazed, many with dusty faces
stained with sweat and tears.

One afternoon, as Yomei was passing the hospital that
she and the Zhous had visited a year earlier to see Ah Jin
and Liu Ch'un-hsian, both of whom had been treated there
as psychiatric patients, she wondered if the two women were
still in there. They must be. Yomei made a mental note that
she and Lily should come and pay a visit to Auntie Ah Jin
and Auntie Ch'un-hsian. That was something she and Lily
were obligated to do. Ahead of her, Yomei saw a short line
of people—old men and middle-aged women—all with a
sleeve rolled up. She stepped closer and realized they were
donating blood. There was a window at the head of the line
where the donors registered, then moved to a room in the
building to have their blood drawn. After the donation,
they were each given a slip of paper with which they could
get some foodstuffs in an office down the hallway, usually
a small bag of potatoes, four or five pounds. Yomei could

see that the donors didn't intend to give blood just for food.
They meant to help the people fighting at the frontline.
Now and again, an old man would shout to demand that the
nurse draw more blood from him. But an accented female
voice cried back, "No more than two hundred milliliters
per person."

Yomei stood in the line, waiting to donate some blood.
Half an hour later, she reached the window, behind which
was a thirtysomething woman who looked Egyptian, with
an angular face and slim hands. Yomei put down her name
and age and said that her blood type was O—she was a
universal donor.

She then went into the lab, where she was led to a chair
that had a board attached to the armrest. Three nurses were
busy drawing blood. A stocky woman stepped over with a
needle and a small bottle. A tapering finger pressed a vein
at the top of Yomei's elbow. Then the masked woman said
in Chinese, "I know you. You came to see me with Zhou
Enlai and his wife last winter." She took off her face mask.

"Auntie Ah Jin!" Yomei cried. "Why are you here?"

"I can't join the army to go to the front, so I started to
help at the hospital. They'll train me to become a nurse.
Eventually I'll tend the wounded soldiers."

"Why are you here alone? I mean, why are no other
Chinese comrades working with you? Is Auntie Ch'un-
hsian still here?"

"She's the same, still in the solitary ward." Ah Jin tied
a rubber belt around Yomei's upper arm to make the
vein swell, then went on about Ch'un-hsian. "She hasn't
improved much. I've been working to show the medical
personnel that I'm all right and able to do things on my
own, and don't need their attention. They'd better let me
out soon. Now, don't be scared. I'm good at this, so it'll only

be a pinch." Ah Jin jabbed the needle into Yomei's vein, and instantly a crimson line of blood began flowing into the plastic bottle.

"Auntie Ah Jin, do you think they can take me on here? I want to help too. They won't let me go into the army either. Please ask your superiors whether I can join you here."

"Can you do the overnight shift if they take you on?"

"No problem. My school is closed, so my schedule is flexible now."

"In that case, I'll ask them for you. Now you're all set. Press the cotton ball like this for a minute or two."

"My blood type is O and can be transfused into anyone. Can you draw more? Three or four hundred milliliters will be fine with me."

"No, I can only get two hundred at a time. That's the rule. Besides, if they allow you to start here, you'll have to save energy for work. So go collect your food now."

Yomei was impressed by Auntie Ah Jin's poise, her speech lucid and her work skilled—there was no trace of madness at all. Even though sick and somewhat unbalanced, Ah Jin was clearly still a dedicated revolutionary at heart, eager to work for the war against the fascists. She was truly a remarkable woman.

Yomei went out to collect her share of potatoes in a paper bag. Before leaving the hospital, she reentered the lab and told Ah Jin that she would come again to check with her whether she could work here. They agreed to see each other in two or three days. Yomei didn't mention Lily to Ah Jin, believing that once she started here, she could help her friend get a spot too, so for now she mustn't rush things. Ah Jin's heavy-boned face kept smiling. She said it would be great if she could have someone speaking Chinese with her at work, so she hoped they could accept Yomei. As Ah

Jin was speaking, she narrowed her eyes dreamily. Yomei
felt drawn to this vivacious woman, who seemed warm to
everyone. On the other hand, Ah Jin's reason for working
at the hospital on her own made Yomei uneasy, because
much like Mao's wife Zi-zhen, Ah Jin had been viewed as
unhinged, a madwoman of sorts. Yomei felt that in a way
both Ah Jin and Zi-zhen were like flotsam jettisoned by the
red revolutionary fleet of China. She'd heard that Zi-zhen,
angry with Mao, often took it out on others from Yan'an
who visited her. Indeed, it was hard for a woman, no matter
how energetic and intelligent and resourceful, to remain
sound and sane in a strenuous struggle together with her
man. Such a condition ought to be taken into account as an
additional sacrifice for women to join the revolution. They
should also conceive of the possibility of hysteria incited by
their political zeal, by their shattered ideals, and by their
men's betrayals. On Yomei's walk back, those thoughts were
on her mind like pebbles rubbing each other continuously.
On the stairs inside the IRA building, suddenly she felt
drained and woozy, having to sit down for a few moments to
gather a second wind to climb the steps back to her room on
the fifth floor.

Yomei mentioned to Lily her encounter with Auntie
Ah Jin. Her friend was impressed and amazed and wanted
to work at the blood donation center too. Yomei promised
that once she started there, she'd do her best to persuade the
clinic to take on Lily as well.

The next night German bombers appeared in the sky
again. There were five or six of them droning around,
initially as if unsure what to do while sailing through the
net of artillery fire. Then one dropped two bombs in the
downtown area, and the others followed, doing the same,
each releasing a pair of bombs at a time. Some buildings

collapsed with loud, dull thumps, raising dusty waves of air.
The antiaircraft guns were firing at the planes like crazy,
drawing blazing lines and curves across the sky. Whenever
a bomber got hit, it began nose-diving and howling like a
dying animal. Then a giant fireball jumped up from the
spot where it crashed. Yomei and Lily couldn't go to bed
until the small hours. They stayed in the basement of their
building until the bombers disappeared. Many Muscovites
had descended into the metro stations, using them as bomb
shelters.

Yomei and Lily went out after daybreak to see the
damage. To their horror, the hospital where Auntie Ah Jin
and Auntie Ch'un-hsian stayed had collapsed. The rubble
of the building was still smoking in places, shattered floors
and loose bricks and concrete covering the spot and showing
no human trace. Only embers and ashes were everywhere.
Yomei and Lily got nervous, wondering where Auntie Ah Jin
might be. They went to speak with the official, Kiushin, at
the Comintern in charge of the Chinese expatriate affairs.
The man made some phone calls, but nobody had seen Ah
Jin or Liu Ch'un-hsian at all.

Then word spread among the Chinese expats that Ah
Jin and Liu Ch'un-hsian had been killed in the hospital
when it was flattened. Some of them, including Yomei
and Lily, went to the site to see the casualties in hopes of
finding the two women, but the place remained the same.
People were too busy with war preparations to remove the
rubble, in which obviously some lives were still buried.
Yomei even got hold of the head of the hospital, but the old
man looked crumbled by the loss of his staff and merely
shook his white head, saying he wished to heaven he could
have some excavators on hand, but all the equipment had
been commandeered for digging moats and building

defense works outside the city. Even all the fire brigades were dispatched to construct bunkers and set up Czech hedgehogs against German panzers in front of the defense fortifications.

Now clearly Ah Jin and Ch'un-hsian were gone, and all Yomei could do was write to her adoptive parents and report their disappearance so that the CCP might name the two women as revolutionary martyrs. Maybe the Party would even hold a memorial service for them back in Yan'an. In her letter to the Zhous, Yomei said, "Please share the sad news with others about this heroic woman, Auntie Ah Jin, who was an example of dedication and self-sacrifice. Please also let Uncle Li and Uncle Deng know that Auntie Ah Jin lost her life defending the Soviet Union. She was a brave woman, a model for all of us." By "Uncle Li," she was referring to Ah Jin's current husband Li Weihan, whereas "Uncle Deng" was Deng Xiaoping. It was said that Deng had loved Ah Jin so much that he had shut himself in a room for several days after he came to know of her death. He was more upset than when she'd left him for her perennial lover Uncle Li.

Yomei also reported to the Zhous that Little Jima, Auntie Ch'un-hsian's daughter, had been sent to the international children's home in Ivanovo to join the other Chinese kids there, so Uncle Bo Gu shouldn't worry about his child's safety in the Soviet Union.

· *Thirteen* ·

As a result of the indiscriminate bombing and the advancement of the Nazi forces, some departments of the Soviet government began to evacuate, moving to the countryside and remote towns and cities. By October 1941, most of the officers among the Chinese expats had left Moscow, either for Thiwa through Kazakhstan or for northern China by way of Mongolia. The latter route was impossible, but still a number of the expat officers went to the Far East anyway. In the Soviet Union, there were still some sick wives of CCP leaders, most of whom had gone to Ivanovo, where their children enrolled at the Interdorm, the international children's home. Yomei heard from Zhang Mei that she had become a music teacher at the Interdorm and liked the job there very much. Zhang Mei wrote that her daughter was doing fine and that she wanted to stay with little Hsiaolin so that the child wouldn't have her mother absent from her childhood. Evidently Zhang Mei could speak some Russian now, or the Interdorm wouldn't have employed her. Her letter amazed and touched Yomei. She showed it to Lily, who said Lin Biao's ex-wife must be a good mother.

Now only a few Chinese expats remained in Moscow, working for the Comintern or the Soviet government, but

Yomei and Lily had little contact with them. They both
felt as though they were now the only Chinese left in town.
What should they do?

Yomei believed they must act. If unable to join a force
fighting the Nazi troops, they mustn't sit tight waiting for
them. On October 14, a Tuesday, the two of them went to
the Cadre Department of the Comintern and inquired
what to do. An official with a bald head named Vilkov
received them, and right away he phoned Bogdanov, the
chairman of the IRA, and asked him what arrangement
they had made for Lily and Yomei. The chairman couldn't
give a definite answer but assured Vilkov that he was
responsible for the two young women. Having no idea
what else they could do, Yomei and Lily returned to their
lodgings in the IRA building.

That night a commotion woke them up. They went
downstairs to take a look. All the lights in the building were
on, the doors of most offices were open, and many IRA
employees were passing to and fro in the hallways. Yomei
and Lily stepped into Bogdanov's office and found the
chairman, his florid face a bit gray now. He'd been pacing
up and down. Yomei asked him what was happening,
but he responded absentmindedly, irrelevantly, saying
he'd leave Moscow only when the Red Army retreated. As
for the two Chinese women, they'd better flee with the
other IRA employees on a heavy-duty truck early in the
morning. He then called over Vitaley, a middle-aged man
in charge of general affairs, and told him to issue the two
women some food. The man led Yomei and Lily into a
large room, where there were stacks of food. He gave them
each a pack of crackers and a length of sausage, more than
a foot long. Yomei wondered if they should ask for more,
but said nothing and just thanked him. Then the two of

them wandered through different floors of the building and saw many rooms piled with foodstuffs and clothes, including hats, shoes, duffel parkas, rain capes with hoods, trench coats. Lily told Yomei, "I keep records of all sorts of donations, but I've handled them only on paper and never thought there was so much stuff right in this building." Indeed, the IRA had been parsimonious to the foreigners they sponsored. Yomei said, "They should have issued us at least an army coat or a down parka. That would make the winter here more bearable."

They entered a room and came upon a stack of fine boots in boxes. They each took a pair of white knee-high boots back to their room. Yomei touched the leather of her boots that had zippers on the side, and said, "I've never worn such a nice thing." Then, as if hit by a fit of contrition, she sighed, "We can't keep these, I guess. It's not right to take them without permission."

Lily agreed, "Besides, these are so eye-catching that people can see we have new boots."

So they sent the boots back to the original stack downstairs. As a matter of fact, all the IRA staff were in the grip of disbelief and fear, and nobody cared about the things under their charge anymore. Even some people from the streets came into the building and grabbed things they needed. A man was carrying two boxes of canned food, hurrying away down the corridor while calling to his little boy to follow him. A middle-aged woman in a floor-length army coat was scouring the rooms for something else she'd take, a few new bedsheets and blankets draped over her shoulders. This kind of looting made the atmosphere more panicky. Yomei whispered to Lily, "We can't stay here anymore. We'd better bolt."

Lily nodded in agreement. Early in the morning, they each packed a small suitcase, plus a canvas satchel, and went out to look for the departing truck. At the front of the building, they saw two trucks with double tires and a sky-blue sedan. One of the trucks was loaded with food and money, and the other was for the people in flight, so Yomei and Lily spoke with Vitaley, who allowed them to climb onto the back of a truck. As for the blue car, only the chairman of the IRA and his wife could use it. By now a lot of expats, foreigners who were in Moscow due to political persecutions back home, gathered at the front entrance of the building, some crying and begging to be taken along, a few asking what they should do. Some staffers, who were to stay behind, were sobbing too, believing the fascist troops would wipe them out once they broke into town. But the IRA officials ignored them all and ordered the vehicles to drive off. As the trucks clattered away, loud curses were hurled behind them, while Yomei lowered her eyes and clutched Lily's hand.

After a series of streets, they pulled up in front of a train station. Vitaley suddenly turned desperate and ordered the two Chinese women to get off, saying the truck was overloaded and unable to go fast. This would make their journey more perilous, more likely to be attacked by German planes, so they had to lighten some. He had dark pouches under his eyes that reminded Yomei of a panda, and he was wearing an Ushanka raccoon hat like a colossal mushroom. He told Yomei and Lily that there were Cominternians inside the train station, so they should go and join that crowd. Regardless of their protests, they were both pushed off the truck and then their suitcases landed beside them. Two other people were also dropped—a Polish expat and a salesman who worked at a convenience store. The four of them looked at each other, totally at sea. Yomei and Lily were furious, their hearts seething.

They decided to go in search of the Cominternians, but the station was so crowded that they couldn't find where they were. They came across a phone on a desk and dialed the number of the Comintern, but no one picked up. Obviously the staff of that organization had all taken flight. The two of them went to the platform instead and got on a train. Then Yomei remembered they had no tickets. So they asked the passengers where the train was bound and how they could get tickets. A man said it was going to Kuybyshev. As for the tickets, he just smirked without a word. Apparently some of them hadn't bought tickets at all. In such chaos, who cared! Still, they got off the train.

Yomei knew Kuybyshev was far away, five or six hundred miles to the east, so she wasn't sure how serious that answer was. She and Lily weighed their situation. Evidently the entire Comintern had fled, and the whole city was at sixes and sevens. Now, they had lost contact with any official association; without any resources and with the little Russian they could speak, how could they survive? If the German army broke into town, what would happen to them? Wouldn't they be killed or taken prisoner and then shipped away as slaves? After considering all the dire possibilities, they decided to get back on the train, which was going east at least, in the same direction most refugees were fleeing. But the train was too packed now, and couldn't let in a single person more. Some of the train cars were reserved for the editorial staff of major newspapers like *Pravda* and *Izvestia*. They forbade any stranger admittance.

Having nowhere to go, Yomei and Lily returned to their room at the IRA. Exhausted and hungry, they each

ate a hunk of bread with hot tea. Then Yomei said that
since her school was nearby, she should go there and see
where her fellow students were heading. Maybe she and
Lily both could join them for protection. So Yomei went
to the theater institute, where she stumbled across a class
of minority students, who said they were going homeward,
back to Central Asia. Some Russian students were going
to leave with them for the east too. Yomei hurried back to
tell Lily about this: the minority students were willing to
take them along, but there might be no trucks or trains on
the trek—they might have to walk. Yomei and Lily decided
to leave with them, feeling that they might find some
international organization on the way. Considering they
might sleep in the open air at night, they brought along a
blanket. Since they were going to walk, they'd have to wear
flat-soled shoes. Lily had a pair of old felt sneakers, but
Yomei's low-heeled shoes were already tattered. She packed
a pair of leather high heels used for the stage. On the way to
the theater institute, she bartered them for a pair of boots
from a young man, who said he was happy to surrender his
own footgear for these heels for his aunt. Yomei was pleased
about the exchange and put on the boots on the spot, even
though they were a little too big.

It was noisy and chaotic inside the theater institute. The
man in charge of the fleeing group was thirtysomething, an
acting student. He had been talking in all directions, and
told Yomei and Lily to rest on a long bench for now. When
it was time to leave, he would come fetch them.

Not until the next morning, when it was full light, did
they start out. They walked along the streets and reached
a suburb, where they got on a tram. To Yomei and Lily's
amazement, they were heading toward Kuchino, a familiar
area where the campus of Section Seven of the KUTV was

located. On arrival at the terminal, the man in charge
led them to a freight train made up of more than a dozen
flatcars, all loaded with cannons. Apparently the guns,
mostly disabled, were being sent back to a rear base for
repairs. Yomei and Lily, like some others, sat under a
cannon on a flatcar. Burhan, an Uzbek in his late twenties
wearing a short coat, sat down with them under a gun
that had a long barrel. The trio each hugged their own
shoulders. With his back against the ruptured tire of the
gun, husky Burhan grinned and said it might snow, his
wide-set eyes gazing up at the gray clouds. In spite of his
young age, when he smiled a pair of fishtails appeared at
the ends of his eyes. He asked them what food they had on
them; they showed him their crackers and sausages. He said
that obviously they had no idea what the trek ahead was like,
so they must take it easy and eat while they still had grub.
He showed them what he had brought along: a small sack of
bread and an iron kettle. "So, let's eat," he said cheerfully
and handed them each a bun glazed with egg and speckled
with tiny raisins on the top. Yomei took a bite. "It's so fresh
and delicious, thank you," she said. Lily added, "You're so
nice." They shared their sausages with him.

The train was trundling eastward. Most stations along
the way had hot water in supply, so the kettle came in handy.
Whenever they stopped, Burhan would get off to fetch
boiled water for the three of them. He was so kind that he
fed Yomei and Lily until all his bread was gone. As he had
predicted, it dropped some dusty snow that night—Yomei
and Lily couldn't stop shaking in the freezing wind, though
they were snuggling together to keep warm under their
blanket. They both put sheepskin hats over their faces while
asleep. In spite of the thin layer of powdery snow that had

accumulated on the blanket, Yomei was amazed that they'd both slept soundly for many hours on end.

It took them more than two days to reach the train's destination, Gorky city (present-day Nizhny Novgorod), two hundred and sixty miles east of Moscow.

Their team's head led them into the city. They entered a theater house, in which they were all put up on the second floor—the balcony inside the auditorium. Then Yomei and Burhan went out with the kettle to get hot water. Just outside the entrance of the theater, she caught sight of Vitaley in his sheepskin overcoat and big raccoon hat.

She ran up to him. He was astonished to see her in this city, his jaw hanging open. He said that the IRA group in his charge hadn't been able to travel during the day, that the roads were muddy, so they had moved slowly east. That was why they were also here. Yomei got angry and said, "You shouldn't have dumped us at the train station like that. Now we're stranded in that playhouse. You must help us or else we won't know where to go. We feel like garbage discarded by the IRA."

"But we can't take you along. You should go with the Comintern group. Some of them are in town too."

"How can we find them?" she asked hotly.

"I'll come to the theater to get you and take you to them."

"Thank you, Vitaley. We'll wait for you."

Despite saying that, she didn't trust the man, considering he'd gotten rid of them heartlessly. She hurried back, without going with Burhan for hot water, to tell Lily about her encounter with Vitaley on the street.

"I can't hang my hopes on that man either," Lily said. "He's like a gangster. He just abandoned us like trash and might make himself scarce again."

Burhan came back, so they began eating bread and pickles, which their team leader had just handed to them. Meanwhile, a play was still being enacted on the stage below. Yomei recognized it as Gogol's *Marriage*. The first floor of the auditorium was only one-third full. In times like these, just staging such a play was already phenomenal. Regardless of the noise and chaos outside the theater, the audience laughed and cheered, at times even applauded.

Unlike the others, Yomei was eating halfheartedly while lounging on a front seat on the balcony and watching the performance below, her heels rested casually atop the rail of the balcony. Now and again she laughed out loud, having to take a sip of water to calm herself down.

"I love that woman playing Agafya. She's so funny and vibrant, a little hysterical," Yomei said to Burhan.

He had been watching too, not as attentively. Munching on his artisan roll, he said, "I guess any girl who receives so many suitors all at once can get overwhelmed and lose self-possession easily. All this slapstick can sure keep the audience feeling high. Actually, the small guy playing Ivan is quite good too. His getup is outrageous."

"He's so dynamic, so earnest," agreed Yomei. "The old matchmaker is well acted too—she's like a crazy witch. It must take a lot out of her to perform that wildly." Indeed, the flighty crone kept stumbling around onstage like a gigantic crab. The bell attached to her waist made a loud tinkle.

Ivan, the younger suitor, wearing a bright-green coat and a tall hat and a checkered vest, appeared confused and intimidated by those rich and powerful suitors who all showed up simultaneously. Yomei could see that the actor was playing Ivan with more subtlety and more of an inner struggle than those enacting the other suitors. Before

she and Lily could finish lunch, Vitaley turned up. His
appearance surprised them both, and they couldn't help but
give a whoop of delight.

He said with a forced smile, "All right, girls, I talked
with the Comintern people. They can take you along. Now
let's go."

Yomei brushed the breadcrumbs off her jacket and
trousers and thanked Burhan for taking care of them on
the way. Then she fished some tattered rubles out of her
pockets and handed the money to him. Lily also gave him
all the banknotes she had. In toto, there were more than
one hundred thirty rubles. They knew that once they joined
the Comintern group, they'd be provided for adequately, so
the money could do more for Burhan. They picked up their
suitcases and left the theater with Vitaley.

Fourteen

Vitaley took them into the half-deserted sanatorium where the Cadre Department of the Comintern was located. Kiushin, a gaunt fortysomething man who was in charge of Chinese affairs, received them. He was so sympathetic to the two young women that he accepted them on the spot, led them to a temporary shelter, and found them each a thick blanket and a sheaf of banknotes, three hundred rubles. From then on, they stayed with the Comintern's administrative staff and followed them on the way eastward.

They boarded a train that even had sleeper compartments, which were all occupied by the families of the Comintern cadres. Shouts and rumpus went up inside those enclosures, wives berating husbands and men yelling at others and spanking kids. People were ill-tempered and desperate— everybody seemed on a short fuse, after being suddenly overtaken by such a tumultuous flight and such ominous prospects. Yomei and Lily couldn't get a sleeping bunk like the real Cominternians, but they were allowed to sit on the jump seats in the narrow hallway. This was comfortable enough for them. It was warm in the car, and the seats were at windows, which showed valleys and small villages streaking past. Yomei was excited by the view of the landscape scattered with lakes and rivers, and at times with a backdrop of the undulating taiga of firs and oaks. There were also spruces and pines, queueing up like a swarm of giant warriors. Once she saw a herd of deer running on a grassland below a birch wood, their drifting movement as light as if they had been weightless. She called Lily to look at those gliding creatures. Lily exclaimed, "Wow, they're so lovely!"

"They look so at ease, the war must have nothing to do with them," said Yomei.

Once they caught sight of a moose far away, whose coat was shiny and whose large antlers resembled a small cluster of coral. Neither of them knew what kind of animal it was. Yomei asked the gray-haired Kiushin, who happened to be padding by, what that behemoth was. "Must be a *laos*," he told them.

Following his pronunciation, Yomei found the word in their dictionary, in which the Japanese explanation said it was "a camel deer." They had no idea what it was called in Chinese, so they settled with *laos*.

The next afternoon they stopped at Cheboksary, a small, charming city on the Volga. Mr. Guliyev, the stalwart official of the Comintern's Cadre Department, told them that this was their train's destination. That meant they'd go to the port and take a boat down the river. A few trucks, all caked with mud, pulled up by the train, from which sacks and boxes were carried out, piled on the ground. In a booming voice Guliyev asked the male passengers to come off and help the truck drivers load the sacks of documents onto the vehicles, but no man on the train paid him any mind. Yomei and Lily rose and asked him, "Can we help?"

"No, no, we don't need you girls," Guliyev grunted. "What a shameless bunch those fellows are." He was referring to the men in the berth compartments.

He went ahead and lifted the sacks and boxes by
himself. Among the Cominternians, he was the only man
who helped the truck drivers. The incident gave Yomei
a bad taste in her mouth. She and Lily talked about the
male passengers and couldn't help but feel contemptuous.
Compared to regular Soviet citizens, who were eager to
fight the Nazis, those cadres seemed only proficient at
escaping danger with their families. Many of them looked
well preserved, disdaining menial work.

After the loading was done, they climbed into the backs
of the trucks, which shipped them to the riverside. There
they got on a white steamer that could carry hundreds of
people. When the boat cast off, sailing down the river, the
sun had nearly set behind them, showering its last rays on
the colorful roofs sprawling away from the shore—blue,
red, green, yellow, orange. Among the houses stood a
stone cathedral, squarish and imposing, boasting a cluster
of gleaming onion domes. Behind the steamer, the broad
water turned grayish and calm. There was a swarm of
rowboats moored in a bay, as if all forsaken by their owners.
Some big birds were sailing above the river, diving into the
shifting wavelets time and again to catch a fish or frog. On
the green bank, hundreds of goats were trotting away in the
gloaming, herded by a few young boys and dogs. Yomei was
fascinated by the peaceful sight and kept saying, "Life is so
idyllic here. The war seems to be raging on another planet."

"But everything will be destroyed when the Germans
arrive here," said Lily.

"In some ways, I appreciate this opportunity to move out
of Moscow and see the Russian land and feel its immensity."

"Me too," agreed Lily.

The steamer sailed for a whole night, during which
Yomei and Lily slumbered head against head on a long

leather bench in the lower cabin while the engine moaned
monotonously. The next morning they entered a bay
that they were told was the confluence of the Volga and
the Kama. Lily said the area of the joining waters was so
vast that it was like the harbor outside Guangzhou. Some
white birds with broad, black-tipped wings were gliding
around. Yomei had never seen such a wide river before and
murmured, "Amazing. Now I understand why everything in
Russia is so grand."

After breakfast—bread and beef kielbasa—they pulled
in to the shore at Ulyanovsk, the waterside lined with reeds
and bulrushes, whose seeds bent the heads of the long
stalks. The air was touched with an herbaceous smell. They
debarked from the steamer and unloaded the parcels and
boxes, which were put onto some trucks. Together with
their baggage, the people in flight were driven into the
town and then to the train station, which was a squat, white
building with a tall spire, its tip sporting a large red star.
The square in front of the station was muddy, covered with
puddles of rainwater. Against the wall of the station house
were some food and fruit vendors, now and again hawking
their wares. Yomei was under the impression that, generally
speaking, when viewed from a distance, Russian cities and
towns appeared prettier and better ordered than those in
China. But up close they were similar to some Chinese
towns and cities, with littered grounds, potholed streets,
fetid wafts of sewage, battered curbs, and railroad tracks
overgrown with weeds. Also, mud was everywhere.

They boarded a train to Ufa, the capital of
Bashkortostan. It took them fifteen hours to reach the
city, but by now the trip made Yomei feel that the war was
already far behind them. The Comintern's administration
was put up in a schoolhouse, a two-story brick building. In

front of it, a pair of flags were flying, the red one decked
with a hammer and a sickle below a golden star, and the
white one flaunting a green band at its bottom and a
bounding squirrel with a waving tail. Yomei and Lily were
curious about the animal flag and were told that it was
the city's flag. Inside the building, the rooms were large,
without any furniture but with thick layers of straw spread
against the walls, contained by timber beams nailed to the
floors. The Comintern staffers slept in the straw. Some
complained about the crude sleeping arrangement, but
Yomei and Lily felt comfortable lying in the straw bed.

They went out after breakfast the next morning to
look for a bathhouse. For three weeks, they hadn't taken
a bath, so they often joked about it, saying to each other
"you stink." Now as they walked along a street, they saw in
front of a cottage with green walls and a gray roof a line of
women and girls, each holding a washbasin and a reticule
containing a clean change of clothes and towels. Apparently
it was a bathhouse for the masses, without a sauna or
individual tubs, though when observed from the exterior,
the old-fashioned cottage hadn't lost all the glamour of a
former *banya* (steam bath). At the southern end of the house
was a hair salon that was also a barbershop for men. Yomei
and Lily joined the people in the queue. Without a basin
with them, they each borrowed one from the babushka
manning the ticket counter in the foyer.

In the bathing hall, dozens of women and girls, all
naked like giant turnips, were steeping themselves in the
two steaming pools, while many others stood under the
cones of warm water sprayed by the showerheads attached to
the tiled walls, rubbing themselves with hand towels. Lily
slid into the smaller pool, sat down, and reclined on a step,
stretching her limbs. She looked so happy and comfortable,

but Yomei pulled her on the arm and said, "We shouldn't get into this water. I'm not sure it's clean."

"All these women and girls look healthy, with smooth skin," Lily said. "Don't worry about the water. Didn't we join others in a bathing pool back in Moscow?"

Yomei shook her head and remained outside the pool. Unlike Lily, she washed herself only with warm water from a showerhead. Yet they gave each other a rubdown. Yomei lay prone on the concrete side of the pool and let her friend scrub her back with a towel. She then did the same for Lily, who moaned with pleasure from time to time, "Oh, I want to stay in here for a whole day!"

The bath was so enjoyable that, stepping out of the house, they felt a little lighter than an hour before. Yomei said maybe they should come once a week if they stayed here for long. Lily agreed.

But that night Lily's back got itchy and burning. She tried to scratch the irritated areas but couldn't reach them all. So Yomei helped her. Lily took off her shirt and lay facedown on her blanket in a corner while Yomei kept scratching her back. "How about this? Feeling better?" she asked Lily.

"Oh yes! You're always smarter than me. I shouldn't have waded into the bathing pool."

Yomei worked on her back for three hours that night, until Lily fell asleep.

For several days, the two of them talked about what to do and concluded that the most sensible way was to stick close to the Comintern administrative staff, who at least had enough provisions. Then one morning, as they were reading the news on a large blackboard in the lobby of the schoolhouse, a tall man in his midforties approached quietly and stood nearby. Feeling a presence behind them,

they turned around. He said, "Girls, it's time to go." Seeing
them at a loss, he smiled, with his narrow nose going
up a bit while nodding his lumpy face. He went on, "I'm
Vladimirov and will go with you. The Comintern has
decided to send both of you to the Party school, where you
can study together with other international comrades. We
can go there together."

"Where's the Party school? Far away?" asked Yomei.

"No, just outside Ufa."

It was early November, but the Belaya hadn't frozen
yet, so they could travel by water. They said goodbye to
Kiushin and took a boat up the river. Soon they figured
out that Vladimirov was the principal of the Party school,
and like many of its foreign students, he was also stranded
in the Soviet Union by the war. He was Bulgarian, an
international Communist, and his real name was Valko
Chervenkov (in the early 1950s, he became Bulgaria's prime
minister). They sailed north, against the current, for more
than an hour and stopped at a small town, from which
the three of them climbed a long hillslope toward their
destination on the top of a mountain.

· Fifteen ·

The Party school was located in a deserted technical academy, which consisted of a dozen or so wood cottages. The dorms, dining rooms, and schoolhouses were scattered at different spots on the mountain. There were already more than sixty students in the Party school, who were from different European countries. Vladimirov was to head this new school, thrown together mainly for the young internationals stranded in the Soviet Union and assembled in the Urals to avoid the flames of war.

Soon after arrival, Yomei and Lily went to the clinic in a log cabin. They told the nurse, a blonde in her early thirties who had her coppery hair pinned tightly in a bun on top of her head, that Lily had a skin problem. Indeed, some tiny blisters had appeared on her back, probably also thanks to the scratching, and even her armpits and crotch were itching like crazy now. Seeing the bloody spots on Lily's skin, the nurse was appalled and said this was a kind of tinea, a fungal infection, which was contagious. She wouldn't touch Lily's skin and instructed that she move out of the dormitory room and be quarantined. Yomei was alarmed and protested that it would be inappropriate for Lily to live alone in isolation.

"In that case, you can keep her company, can't you?" asked the nurse.

Yomei nodded and then told Lily not to be scared. She said, "I'll be with you no matter what."

Lily suddenly grasped Yomei's forearm as if in need of her support to remain on her feet. The nurse gave her a jar of salve whose main ingredient was sulfur, saying she must apply it all over to her skin. As for the affected spots, she should rub the ointment on them at least three times a day. From now on, she mustn't step out of her room and must avoid meeting others before she was healed.

Yomei was surprised by the medical instructions but told Lily not to worry, and that they'd figure out what to do. Together they moved into an empty room in a house that must once have been a kitchen, on whose eaves outside was hanging a deserted dovecote. Every day, Yomei went out to fetch water and meals for Lily. Inside the dining room crowded with people, she would finish eating in a hurry and then bring a bowl of cabbage or onion soup and a hunk of bread back to their cottage. Without fail, Lily would be standing at the door, watching her coming back. There were flickers of fear in her eyes, as if she was afraid Yomei might not return. Once Lily took over the food, she would wolf down everything in great haste. Amazingly, her appetite was exceptionally hearty these days. "Slow down," Yomei often bantered. "Nobody's fighting with you for food."

Lily replied, "It must be waiting for you in here that worked up my appetite."

Yomei gave a ringing laugh and said, "Come on, silly girl, you thought I might clear out of here? Where could I go in the sticks of the Urals? Moscow is more than thirteen hundred kilometers away. I need you too."

It was getting colder day by day. In their room there
was a cooking range, a large stove with flat iron rings that
formed its top. Maybe they could start a fire and keep the
room warm at night. So Yomei went out and gathered some
pieces of wood, but they were unfamiliar with the stove, not
knowing how to control the fire and smoke. They didn't
make sure that the pipe and chimney would draw fully.
Soon after they fell asleep that night, smoke leaked out and
filled the room, choking them. In spite of their coughing
and tearful eyes, they managed to stop the fire in the
cooking range. From then on, they didn't dare to light the
stove at night again.

Fortunately, Lily's skin disease was subsiding. Many of
the spots on her back began to dry up and heal. In spite of
staying together with Lily and applying the salve for her,
especially to the spots Lily couldn't reach by herself, Yomei
wasn't infected at all. Even the nurse was amazed, saying
she'd been doing a great job, like a medical professional.
The nurse suggested Lily discard her current underclothes
and then take a hot bath. Right away, Yomei went out
and found a wooden washtub. She also lugged back three
buckets of hot water from the room next to the kitchen.
Lily bathed slowly and leisurely, then put on the clean
underclothes and pajamas that Yomei had gotten for her
from a Czech student who was the same size as Lily. Yomei
had paid her thirty rubles for the used clothes.

The next day Lily's quarantine was lifted. Now they were
allowed to join the other students, but it was crowded in
those dorm houses. So they moved into a large room in a
two-story cottage, inhabited by not only students but also a
married couple and an old woman with a little girl. Yomei
and Lily got along well with those who slept in the same

room, where everyone tried to adapt to this odd lodging arrangement.

As the winter deepened, it grew colder at night, so at times they lit the stove, the only one in the room. In the beginning, they went out to gather firewood, but soon they discovered a big pile of abandoned furniture in another room: broken chairs and desks, some with their legs missing. They dismantled the furniture and burned the pieces of wood in the stove. It was manufactured furniture, so nobody felt bad about using it to heat the room.

A week later, Yomei and Lily were ordered to move into one of the students' dorm houses. Their new room had people from various countries: four Poles, three Germans, a Bulgarian, and two Albanians. In it, there was a colossal stove, tall enough to reach Yomei's chest. Every morning, an old woman wearing a balaclava came to kindle it, despite her hacking cough and slight limp, so the room was quite warm in the daytime. This room was at the end of the hallway of the house, and on both sides of the corridor were several smaller rooms, which accommodated married couples. By far, the largest foreign student group was from Spain, but the Spaniards lived in another house, which was shared by a number of Romanians. The Slavic students were grouped into one class, which was also sizable, more than a score of students, and they were taught in Russian. Yomei and Lily were put into this class. There was only one student from France—Lucas, a young Communist, had lived in the area near Belgium and been drafted by the German military and dispatched to the eastern front. Once he got into Russia, he crossed the fighting line and surrendered to the Red Army. The Soviets handed him over to the Comintern, and after an investigation into his background, he was sent to the Party school.

Their curriculum was quite simple—the history of international Communism, current affairs and policies, and a course of military knowledge and drill. For the current affairs and policies, they mainly read the materials published by TASS. The study was mostly in the form of discussion, which was so lively that Yomei and Lily felt stimulated and occasionally enlightened. At times the classes were conducted by Vladimirov, who was considerate toward the two young Chinese women. They couldn't speak Russian well enough to participate in discussions, but he designated them as speakers. Once forced to speak up, they managed to express themselves hesitantly, groping for words and phrases. Sometimes they used an odd expression, which brought out peals of good-natured laughter. In the class on the history of international Communism, even though both Yomei and Lily had studied most of its contents before, they still had to read Lenin's works, such as *The State and Revolution* and *Imperialism, the Highest Stage of Capitalism*, in the original. It was hard going for them, but with the aid of the Russian-Japanese dictionary and with dogged perseverance, they struggled through both books. As a result, their Russian improved greatly. When they spoke to their classmates, they felt more at ease now. Yomei could tell that some of the Eastern Europeans were not fluent in Russian either, although most of them were better at expressing themselves orally.

The military course was taught by Filip, a middle-aged Croatian who was called Professor by the students and who was said to have once been an officer in the Red Army and to have seen action in the war. The swarthy officer taught them how to give orders in Russian, like "Put down your arms!" "Don't move or I'll shoot!" "Stop serving the Nazis!" "We treat POWs humanely." But those short sentences were

hard for the foreign students to cry out. When they shouted
the orders at the drill, the recipients were often thrown into
a fog. Seeing the mistakes they made—some turned in the
wrong direction or did something in the opposite manner—
the class would break into laughter. Yomei and Lily, young
and energetic, enjoyed moving around outdoors, running
in the snow while soft, white billows of breath were swirling
around their faces. They took the drill as good exercise, but
some older students grumbled about the training, saying
it was too much for them. What a waste of time! Students
from the Mediterranean region often complained that
they had never lived in such a cold climate. Indeed, if the
temperature reached ten below zero Celsius, it was already
a warm day here. At night it could easily plummet to minus
forty. During the day, long icicles formed under the eaves,
gleaming in the sunlight; now and then, a few pieces of the
ice were blown off by a gust of wind, hitting the ground
with sharp cracks.

The Polish students in class were kind and warm to Yomei
and Lily. They knew Russian better and would help the two
Chinese read articles and books in Russian. Outside class,
they also chatted with them. From them Yomei learned that
the Polish Communist Party had collapsed, so they, the Poles
at the Party school, were being prepared to be air-dropped to
the enemy's rear so that they could start underground work
in Poland. Later some of them did go back and got killed by
the Germans, though a few rose to eminence in the Polish
government after the war.

Lucas, the Frenchman, was younger than most of the
other male students. He was in his early twenties and
obviously attracted to Yomei. He once heard her humming
a sprightly tune, so he offered to teach her some French
songs. He had a baritone voice that sounded mellow, like

an older man's. It was too cold for them to go out, so they
stayed in a corner in the big dorm room, and he sang the
first verse of the old folk song "Au clair de la lune." Yomei
liked the simple melody that sounded like a nursery rhyme,
though she didn't understand the French lyrics. They
managed to speak simple Russian between them. He said it
was a pity that he didn't have a fiddle with him; otherwise he
could have performed with the instrument for her as well.
She liked Lucas, especially his large ginger-brown eyes that
would turn moist when he was singing, as if he remembered
something sad. He was always friendly and must have been
eager to get close to her, though they were always indoors,
confined to the high-back chairs they were sitting in. Still, at
times she felt stirred by his closeness, which kind of thrilled
her. If they had been in Moscow and could have spent
more time alone, she wouldn't have minded taking him as
a boyfriend. He was handsome and sensitive, also sweet.
Nevertheless, she was clearheaded about this, knowing she
mustn't rush into an intimate personal relationship at a time
like this. The war was raging, and she might go anywhere
on short notice. Deep down, she intuited that she and Lucas
might have to part ways soon, so for now she'd better keep
some distance from him. To Lily, the Frenchman didn't
seem reliable. His background was still murky.

One afternoon, the moment Lucas had left after singing
with Yomei, Lily, chewing her fleshy lower lip, said, "You
shouldn't rub elbows with the French fellow like that."

"Why? He's like a friend and has always been nice to us,"
Yomei asked in surprise.

"He's flirting with you, haven't you noticed? Everybody
can see that plainly."

"But he's no harm. It won't hurt if I have some fun every
once in a while."

"You're such a careless girl. Haven't you noticed that others look down on Lucas?"

"I don't care what others think of him. He treats me as a friend, so I can't be mean to him."

Lily sighed, chewing her lip again, and shook her round face. Yomei knew that some of her classmates didn't respect Lucas because he had once served in the Nazi army and later become a POW. She'd heard them snort or seen them laugh behind their hands when he started to sing a song. They wouldn't consider the fact that he had fled the German position and returned to the Communist rank and file of his own volition, that he hated the Nazis with a passion. She believed that since the Party school had accepted him, she should treat him as a comrade as well.

She noticed that some Spanish women here were quite open about having boyfriends. Those female Spaniards were young, barely out of their teens, and most of them were pretty, with strong teeth and large, vivid eyes. They had come to the Soviet Union after the civil war in Spain. Every morning they'd make themselves up and arrange their hair into their personal styles. Some even penciled their eyebrows and put on pearl earrings and rouged their lips. It was believed that they must have gotten up before five o'clock to make themselves up like that; otherwise they couldn't have had the time to join the setting-up exercises at six. No matter how cold it was in the mornings, they wouldn't put on fur hats for fear that the headgear might mess up their hairdos; they wore headscarves instead. They also wore skirts and woolen leggings instead of pants. Most of the Spanish girls were beautiful, radiating youth and health, and some even had new Spanish boyfriends at the Party school. Yomei befriended Amaya, a tall, oval-faced girl who was quiet and looked rather humble. Through their conversations, Yomei discovered that Amaya's mother was Dolores Ibarruri, the general secretary of the Communist Party of Spain. Yomei shared her discovery with Lily, who was impressed, saying, "No wonder Amaya doesn't put on all her pretties like the other Spanish girls." (Later those Spaniards were dispatched to Yugoslavia so that they could open a route to Western Europe and then back to Spain, but most of them got killed fighting the fascist forces on the way.)

Lily didn't have warm, suitable shoes for the winter. Amaya suggested bartering with the locals, who might come up with some decent footwear. Yomei and Lily thought it was a good idea and each began to save one piece of bread a day. A week later they had a small bag of dried bread, which they took to the marketplace in a village down the mountain. An old man with a gummy smile offered Lily a pair of used boots, which were good enough for her. So she was pleased about the exchange and put on the shoes at once. She wore them all the way back, saying they were pretty comfortable, though a bit too wide for her feet.

Approaching the naked top of the mountain, Yomei and Lily paused to scan the landscape down below. The Belaya was winding through the land in snow; the river had frozen, yet was steaming in places, glittering in the setting sun and curving away southward, until it vanished into the forest. A line of electric pylons stretched through the woods and beyond the shoulder of a hill. The western sky was burning red, a couple of clouds rolling across the setting sun. Yomei and Lily tied their earflaps tight and continued toward the Party school. The wind grew gusty while they trudged along, as if they were wrestling with some frisky shadows.

Life on the mountain was hard, since they had to do everything by themselves. After the broken furniture was

used up, the male students took turns going into the woods
to fell trees for firewood, some of them wearing balaclavas
for the job. The work could be dangerous. Once, a falling
tree crashed into a Spaniard's shoulder and twisted his
back, so he had to lie in bed for half a month. The female
students did kitchen duties by turns, helping the staff cook
and dole out meals. Naturally, the food wasn't as good as
before the war, but they all had enough to eat: a plate of
vegetable soup, a few potatoes, and a hunk of black bread.
Most times, the bread wasn't fully baked yet, still damp,
so the students often brought it back to their dorms and
baked it on the stoves again. Yomei would place her bread
on the top of the stove while sitting by to read or memorize
Russian words and phrases. She wanted to learn some short
sentences by heart so that she could use them as samples
of collocations. Once she left the door of the stove open,
unaware that her face was too close to the fire. As a result,
her upper lip was singed a little. In no time, small blisters
appeared on her lip. Her roommates razzed her, saying she
must have kissed someone too hard. "Is Lucas the culprit?"
asked Hilda, a German girl who often entertained her
boyfriend Max with coffee and sugar, which were so rare
here that the other students would fan with their fingers the
coffee fume into their noses while sniffing at the pot. But
like the other German women, Hilda wouldn't share the
beverage with others, except for Max. Both Yomei and Lily
felt that was quite bizarre. Back in China, such behavior
would surely alienate one's comrades.

They all had to relieve themselves outdoors, in the
privies behind their dorms. The outhouses were primitive,
not much different from the latrines back in the Chinese
countryside. As soon as they emptied their bladders and
bowels, the urine and feces would freeze solid. In the

early mornings, some villagers would come to gather
the excrement as fertilizer. They used a stick to dislodge
the frozen feces that piled up like tiny pagodas, some of
which even stuck out of the pits. If not knocked down and
removed, they would make it impossible for anyone to
squat over a pit. The women students often joked about
the accumulations in the outhouses, saying that those little
stalagmites were their miniature Christmas trees. Yet in
spite of the cold weather and the harsh conditions, very few
got sick up on the mountain. No one even caught a cold.
Only once was there a serious illness: a Polish professor
contracted typhus and was sent away to the hospital in Ufa,
where he stayed until the Party school was disbanded.

In late January, they watched a documentary film about
the Red Square parade on November 7 the previous year.
The movie was a part of their political studies and it moved
and inspired them. It showed that unlike many fleeing
officials and Muscovites, Stalin had made a point of staying
in the capital. He spoke from his Kremlin office regularly
to the whole USSR and swore he would fight their common
foe to the death.

Still, the situation looked precarious—the Soviet defense
lines were collapsing. It was reported that more than
eighty German mechanized divisions were approaching
Moscow from the west and the southwest, and that Hitler
had ordered his army to seize the Soviet capital within two
months, before it snowed. Soon a good part of Belarus fell
to the Nazi army, and then Smolensk was captured, and
that was a key strategic point on the route to Moscow. As
the Germans approached, a lot of people started fleeing the
city. All this time, numerous soldiers with Asianic features
appeared on the streets, having come from the Far East to
reinforce the defense of the capital.

The documentary film also showed that many civilian men, middle-aged, with stern and grave faces, were lining up to join the militia. Some were still in suspenders and overalls and hard hats, apparently having come directly from work. After registering their names, they were each given a quilted jacket, a rifle, and a cartridge belt. Wearing those, they marched away to join the militia units in the defense lines outside the city. Some of them were assigned to help load bullets for machine guns. If they could drive, they would be sent to field hospitals as ambulance drivers. Occasionally there were also young women marching away with the men. Those women all wore a white armband marked with a red cross, some carrying folded stretchers.

Inside Moscow there were groups of housewives and old men building street barricades at bridgeheads and intersections. They shoveled sand into straw sacks, then stacked the sandbags on the streets so that the defenders could lean on them while firing at the incoming enemy. In spite of such a dire scenario, people still believed the Soviet army could block the Nazis' advancement, but they had to prepare for the worst—if the enemy entered the city, the Muscovites would fight them street by street and house by house.

It was getting cold in the city, and the first snow fell, light and dry, the streets strewn with leaves that scudded and swirled around in the wind. The fighting in the south and southwest was getting more ferocious now. Yet the Germans couldn't make progress as they had planned, lacking logistic support and having lost so much equipment. Even their tanks no longer had enough fuel, not to mention the fact that their troops were without warm clothes for the brutal Russian winter. In comparison, the Soviet army was better provided for the severe weather and also better supplied. So the Battle of Moscow had reached a stalemate.

Rumors flew that the military parade on November 7 was canceled this year. Indeed, among the Soviet leaders, there was a debate over whether such a celebration of the national holiday should be held as in other years, but Stalin overruled them and decreed that it be held notwithstanding.

The city was no longer crowded by November, so common citizens were allowed to join the official spectators along the side of Red Square to watch the military parade. In the south, the spires of Saint Basil's Cathedral gleamed a little, though the grand church was partially obscured by a grayish mist, having lost most of its bright colors. Then Marshal Budyonny, a short man wearing a walrus mustache and a fur toque and a long sword, rode a raven Percheron horse to the front of the terrace on top of Lenin's mausoleum, on which many Soviet leaders were standing. In a stentorian voice, he reported to Stalin that the troops were ready for inspection. Then the Supreme Commander, in a woolen overcoat, saluted back and began to address the celebrators in a calm, nasal voice. Stalin said that the Nazis' panzers were just tens of miles away from Moscow. Now the victory of this war depended solely on the people of this city. He declared, "The whole world is looking to you as the force capable of destroying the plundering hordes of German invaders. The enslaved peoples of Europe who have fallen under the yoke of the German invaders look to you as their liberators. A great liberating mission has fallen to your lot. Be worthy of this mission! The war you are waging is a war of liberation, a just war."

It began snowing again, thin flurries swirling in the air while the wind was whistling. Stalin ended his speech by shouting: "Death to the German Invaders! Under the banner of Lenin, forward to victory!"

Following that, the troops hoorayed, wisps of breath dangling from young faces. Most of their hats were whitish with snowflakes now. The civilian spectators also shouted to show their support and enthusiasm. Then Marshal Budyonny declared that all the troops here were marching directly out of the city to take part in the Battle of Moscow. Katyusha rocket launchers mounted on trucks, artillery pieces—some drawn by teams of draft horses and some self-propelled, columns of T-34 tanks, cavalry raising banners and swords, infantrymen holding rifles with fixed bayonets, even young women—nurses and medical personnel—wearing medicine cases slung across their chests, all passed the saluting leaders and the clapping throngs, marching south to the defense line outside the city. Yomei was amazed to see on the screen a battalion of men all wearing white camouflage uniforms stride past, shouldering long skis and with submachine guns hanging at their chests. Evidently they were special troops that could move fast and stealthily in snow.

Watching those brave men and women heading to the battle outside Moscow, some of the students couldn't stop their tears. They were all convinced that the Soviet Union would surely win the war. How they wished they could have joined those fighters.

· Sixteen ·

In late February, the Party school dissolved, and all the students were going to different places. The Spaniards were heading for Slovenia to join some guerrilla force there and eventually fight their way back to Spain, while the Eastern Europeans and the two Chinese would go to Ufa city, where they were to work for the Comintern, which needed new hands. Lucas was assigned to leave with the Spaniards. He was willing to set out with them, believing this could be his way of getting back to France.

Before departing, Lucas invited Yomei out, but they had nowhere to go and just stayed behind in the classroom cottage. It was cold, the wind piercing them to the bone. The ground was icy and slippery, so they couldn't stroll around. It was dangerous to do that at night, besides; there were marauding wolves in the woods. "I will miss you," Lucas said in an undertone. "Hope we'll meet again."

"Of course, we will run into each other in the future. Maybe in France or another country," Yomei said. Even though she had been fond of him from the day he had begun to teach her French folk songs, she had purposely kept herself from getting too close to him, certain that they'd go separate ways because of the precarious circumstances. After living among the Communist

revolutionaries for so many years, she had by now become
used to saying goodbye to people close to her. She felt that if
she and Lucas had spent more time together singing songs,
their mutual affection might have developed into something
more intense and serious. But they were in the midst of
a war and mustn't make any long-term plans. Yet in her
heart of hearts, she'd like him to remember her, so she had
prepared a souvenir for him.

"Here's the keepsake you asked for." She handed him
half a photo, then giggled. The grainy picture used to have
both her and Zhang Mei in it, but she cut off her friend's
half, since she had several photos taken with Zhang Mei.
Two days before, Lucas had asked her for a photo, which
she'd promised to give him.

He was delighted to have her picture and put it into his
jacket's inner pocket. He said, "Thank you so much, Yomei.
I'll keep it here all the time and let it warm my heart." He
placed his palm on his chest as if to protect her photo. "I
wish we could have taken a picture together. Sorry, I don't
have one on me—the damned Germans stripped me of
everything."

"I will remember you even without your photo," she said.

At this point, the bedtime bugle started blaring, so they
had to go back to their rooms. They hugged and also kissed
au revoir. For the rest of the night, she felt her face burning
and her chest sizzling, even though she knew she mustn't
take Lucas too seriously. He might just be a passerby in her
continuous wanderings.

The group heading for Ufa set out before the others
the next morning. Yomei and Lily got on the large sleigh
with one Lithuanian and five Polish students who were
also going to work at the Comintern. Wrapped in their
thick blankets, Yomei and Lily were lounging together

on the sleigh, which had no guardrail on either side and was drawn by a piebald Clydesdale. The horse trotted with ease, now and then snorting through flared nostrils. It was wearing a bell, so the sleigh was moving rhythmically, dragging a cloud of snow dust behind it. Above them, three vultures were flying in a triangular formation, squawking intermittently. A flock of crows was gyrating in the distance, as if caught in a tiny whirlwind. Despite the stinging cold, in the high sun, the snow-covered mountain sparkled silver here and there. Because she hadn't slept well the previous night, Yomei soon nodded off. As the sleigh was making a sharp turn down the slope, she fell off into the snow. Yanek, a tall, olive-skinned man, jumped off and pulled her out and helped her aboard again while the others were laughing. This happened to Lily once too.

After they had arrived at the Comintern's administration in Ufa city, Yomei and Lily were assigned to its Chinese bureau. They were supervised by Zeng Yongfu, who was in his late twenties, the youngest among the group of Chinese employees there before Yomei and Lily's arrival, so people called him Young Zeng. Though he was older than Yomei and Lily and was their supervisor, they would still call him Young Zeng between themselves, while in front of him, "Teacher Zeng," or "Cross-eye Zeng" behind his back, because he had slight esotropia. Their job was to sort and classify the archives in a warehouse. The work was sheer drudgery, mechanical and mind-numbing, and they soon grew sick of it, but they had to continue. They felt staggered whenever they looked at the immense amount of archives, mostly in Chinese, which recorded the personal activities and histories of their compatriots who had joined the international Communist movement over the decades. Sacks of personal files were stacked together in numerous

piles, most of which were lined in rows in the vast room.
Yomei and Lily couldn't help but wonder how long it would
take to sort out all the stacks.

One morning, while going through the dossiers of the
Chinese students at the KUTV, Lily chanced upon her own
file in a bag. To her astonishment, she found a nasty report
on her character that had been written because she had once
complained about the poor quality of the interpreters' work
in the classes that she took at the university. It stated that she
was tainted by "the petty bourgeois outlook." Lily showed
those negative notes to Yomei, who was outraged. Without
a second thought she took those pages and tore them to
pieces, stuffing the scraps into her pants pockets. "You're so
bold, girl," Lily said with flashing eyes. "But thanks."

"I don't see any point keeping this kind of trash against
you," Yomei said matter-of-factly. "We all know how much
energy the Communist Party has misused in hurting their
own comrades. What a waste!"

"I guess there must be a lot of this sort of garbage in
these stacks," Lily said.

They both grinned.

When they took a break, Yomei burned the scraps from
Lily's file in the bathroom and flushed the ashes down a
toilet. Before leaving the ladies' room, Yomei cranked open
the transom window to let out the smoky air.

Besides Zeng, there were four Chinese men in the
archival bureau. Alya, a Russian woman, was also in the
group. She was the wife of Xu Jiefan, who was on staff
too. All those older employees felt apprehensive about the
presence of Yomei and Lily among them, having heard that
Kiushin had told Young Zeng the bureau needed "fresh
blood." Alya was particularly agitated, because she and the
men all guessed that the two young women were meant to

replace some of them. It looked like one or two of them would get fired soon. But neither Yomei nor Lily were cognizant of the animosity toward them, and they even took Alya as a friend and often complimented her on the silk attire that her Chinese husband bought for her.

During their work there, an investigation was underway into the International Red Aid's pell-mell flight from Moscow. Knowing Yomei and Lily used to be with the IRA, the Comintern asked them to write a report on their ordeal in the evacuation. Both Yomei and Lily remembered the experience with the IRA's chairman, Bogdanov, and the chief of general affairs, Vitaley, so they wrote out everything—but without pointing the finger at anyone—and submitted the report. Evidently their writings contributed to the investigation. Bogdanov was soon dismissed from his office, and in late March Vitaley came to see them, saying he was sorry that they had gone through so many difficulties. They found his voice hoarser than before, which might be due to the scathing investigation he had gone through. Yomei and Lily felt somewhat contrite about reporting Bogdanov and Vitaley. They wouldn't do that again.

They both had many cards from the Comintern administration: a work pass, meal tickets, residential papers, personal IDs. They were both absentminded and careless about their cards. Once, they left their work passes on the large desk in their office and then went to the cafeteria for lunch. When they returned, their passes were gone and couldn't be found anywhere. The loss of such official papers was a serious breach that might lead to criticism. Fortunately, at this time—April 1942—the entire Comintern was planning to move back to Moscow, which was safe now that the Germans had been pushed back, so nobody paid attention to the loss of a couple of small official documents anymore, because all the passes would be obsolete soon, replaced by new ones. Yomei and Lily were both ordered to return to the capital, together with their colleagues.

The Chinese bureau all boarded the same train to Moscow. Because Yomei and Lily were the youngest among them, they were more active in serving their older colleagues—whenever they stopped at a station, they'd get off to fetch hot water and buy snacks for their comrades. At most stops, there were peasant women carrying wicker baskets up and down the platforms, hawking honey biscuits, Rossiysky cheese, raisin buns, pirozhki, boiled potatoes, apple pears. The vendors would take only kopecks, but no paper money. Yomei and Lily were especially considerate to Alya. Although the woman was Russian, she was obsessed with mahjong and had even brought along a set for this trip. Now, on the train, she wanted Yomei and Lily to play with her. They had no choice but to oblige. So they traveled and played for several days, making lively conversation whenever they could. As a result, Alya began to grow affable. On the last day, as they were approaching Moscow, she opened her purple handbag and produced a pair of work passes. She kept a poker face and asked them, "How come your papers got into my purse?"

Yomei and Lily were thrilled to see their passes, then wondered aloud how this had happened—why had their papers landed in Alya's hands?

"Goodness knows," said Alya.

Though astonished, neither Yomei nor Lily pressed her for the truth, given that they liked her husband Mr. Xu, who was a gentleman, always kind to them. (Many years later Xu became Zhang Mei's husband. To Yomei, beyond question Xu Jiefan was a better man than Lin Biao, suiting her friend better.) Yomei and Lily were pleased about the recovery of the work passes and wouldn't mention them again, since the passes would be obsolete soon.

Back in Moscow, the two of them resumed staying in the Hotel Lux. The faculty and students of Yomei's theater institute hadn't returned yet, so she and Lily continued working for the Comintern. In fact, the Comintern had built an administration center a few years before the war. The new office building was spacious and bright, but far away from 10 Gorky Street. To get there, Yomei and Lily had to walk a long way, past several streets and the extensive structure of the Agriculture Exhibition Hall. It was still cold in April, and the freezing wind penetrated their clothes, which were just quilted jackets and thin woolen sweaters. They often said that they each should have snatched a warm overcoat when they were fleeing the IRA building half a year before. At the Comintern's administration center, they shared an office with Alya and Li Kuo-dong. Li had come to the Soviet Union many years before and was fluent in Russian, so he was supervising Yomei and Lily—their job as a trio was to read Chinese periodicals published by the Nationalist media and glean news on women and young people, translate the useful information into Russian, then send the translations to Kiushin. Some of the information would be shared with other offices, particularly those handling foreign affairs. Yomei and Lily could speak the foreign tongue with some ease now, but they couldn't write it well. Whenever they got stuck on a word or phrase, they would ask Li Kuo-dong how to render it into Russian, but Li often got impatient, becoming reluctant to answer them and even ribbing them, saying their college studies here hadn't really educated them. Meanwhile, Alya became hostile again, seeking opportunities to pester the two young women. Once, Lily cracked a joke and Yomei broke out laughing. Somehow her carefree laughter bothered Alya, who phoned Kiushin, who came up right away, his reddish goatee bristling. Alya complained in a grating tone of voice that the two young women always distracted her. Their boss spoke with Yomei and Lily and was convinced it wasn't that serious. He shook his head and left without another word. Yomei could tell that Kiushin didn't believe Alya at all and might take her as a mere fussbudget. Yet thereafter both she and Lily began to keep quiet at work, knowing the woman might be bent on alienating them from their colleagues and superiors so as to drive them away from the Comintern.

Lily often said in private, "It's so hard to please a Russian Big Sister."

Yomei quipped, "Generally speaking, it's easier to make a Russian Big Brother happy." She laughed out loud, amused by her own jest.

Lily cracked up too.

But they no longer rubbed shoulders with Alya these days. They began to work at night, individually. Since June, the trio—Li Kuo-dong, Yomei, and Lily—had worked in the radio room, following the broadcast of Chongqing, China's wartime capital. They had to listen to the radio constantly, day and night, so they rotated, each doing an eight-hour shift, jotting down useful news. Consequently, Yomei and Lily couldn't spend much time together; even if they didn't work during the day, they had to sleep some to prepare for the night shift. Due to the long distance, Chongqing's broadcast signal tended to be feeble, but most of the time they could find it. Oddly, once in a while there was a Doppler effect, as if both the transmitting and the receiving sides had been on the move. When alone, Yomei and Lily would try to search for the broadcast from Yan'an but never could locate it. Yomei knew there was a radio station in the red base of the CCP, because Father Zhou had asked the Soviets for a transmitter so that Yan'an could build its own broadcasting station. The Russians promptly gave them such a machine. When the Zhous had been heading back to Yan'an two years before, they had it taken apart and packed the pieces into their baggage. Uncle Ren Bishi managed to have the equipment smuggled through the customs controlled by the Nationalist government without a glitch. Yomei was sure that Yan'an already had its broadcasting station now.

"So obviously their radio isn't powerful enough," said Lily.

"True, it must be below par," agreed Yomei.

Though Yomei knew Yan'an's radio didn't have enough wattage to send the broadcast to Moscow, she couldn't help but attempt to search for its voice every once in a while. But as always, she tried in vain.

Their work with the radio wasn't hard, but it was boring. Still, it was peaceful. In comparison, it was more frustrating to mix with their other colleagues, because it was hard to maintain a congenial relationship with them. Besides the nagging Alya in the Chinese bureau, Young Zeng, who was working in another office now but continued to act like their superior, was also a pain in the ass. Sometimes Zeng even attempted to intimidate Yomei and Lily. He once accused them of often visiting Lisa's family and meeting with her husband Li Lisan. That was a total fabrication—they hadn't seen Lisa in the past two years. Nor did they know what had happened to the couple, though they both believed that Li Lisan was a decent man, or Lisa wouldn't have been that loyal and devoted to him.

But they didn't defend Li Lisan in front of Young Zeng, knowing Lisan was still a target of the investigation by the USSR's Department of Internal Affairs. Yomei and Lily just denied any connection with Li Lisan. Yet Zeng wouldn't stop there, and instead told them that some people from the Department of Internal Affairs would come and talk with both of them. This scared them, but on the spur of the moment, Yomei told Young Zeng, "We're employees of the Comintern, so by rule we're not allowed to talk directly to people from outside. If the investigators want to speak with us, please let them go through the Comintern so that we can get authorized to meet with them. We have to follow the rules here." That stopped Young Zeng. From his withdrawal, Yomei surmised that the whole maneuver must have been part of Zeng's own machinations and that his threat was idle. The man seemed to enjoy tattling on others and lording it over people, but to Yomei, he was merely a hanger-on in the Department of Internal Affairs, like a lackey, and yet he seemed very nice to Lily, so Yomei managed to be polite to him.

The work at the Comintern had advantages—it guaranteed them their livelihood. They were each given a windbreaker, which kept them from shaking on the chilly days. Better still, there was always enough to eat. The cafeteria provided three meals a day at a discount. In addition, they each received a city resident's rations— they could buy their daily bread like a Muscovite. The Comintern paid them each a salary—six hundred rubles a month, which might have been at the lowest end of scale at the time. They each could keep three hundred rubles for themselves after the warfare tax and the childless tax (as foreigners, they didn't have to pay the latter, but Yomei and Lily didn't mind contributing their shares like regular

Soviet citizens). Such an amount was enough for their keep.
Other than work, they didn't have anything else to do. Most
places were still closed, and even the theater arts institute
hadn't reopened yet. Yomei couldn't wait to resume her
dramatic studies.

There was little nightlife in Moscow these days. Seldom
did they go out in the evenings, when the streets were unlit
but still bustling with pedestrians. Some areas were teeming
with pickpockets and robbers, some of whom roamed the
city in packs. Many people got their hats snatched away
in the dark. It was reported that one night in early June,
Muscovites had lost more than one hundred hats to robbers,
whose faces couldn't be seen under cover of darkness.
Then, one afternoon, Yomei and Lily returned from work
together. As usual, Lily was carrying under her arm the
leather purse that contained both their hotel passes, ID
cards, ration books, banknotes, keys, and lip balm, because
Yomei could be absentminded and might misplace such
things. They got on the A-line tram, heading for Pushkin
Square, where they would alight. On arrival, as Lily was
trying to get off, she felt somebody pull her from behind.
With a forward lunge, she landed on the ground next to
Yomei. To their horror, the purse was gone. Immediately
they clambered aboard again and looked around for the
leather pouch, but there was no trace of it anywhere. They
got off at the next stop and tramped all the way back with
their hearts in their boots.

Luckily the old concierge at the Hotel Lux knew them
and let them through without asking for their passes.
But having no key anymore, they had to contact Igor, the
superintendent, who came up with the spare copy. Once
in their room, they made a list of their lost items: besides
the keys and a lip balm, there were their work permits,

the Moscow residential certificates, meal tickets for the Comintern's cafeteria, the bread booklet for the city's rations, and upward of one hundred twenty rubles. What a disaster! Lily turned tearful, but Yomei said, "Don't worry. We will sort this out one way or another."

Nevertheless, it was very inconvenient for them. Even to work in the Comintern building became a problem—they each had to obtain a temporary pass for that. Then two days later, before they left for the office in the morning, the concierge sent for them, saying a woman wanted to see them at the front desk. They hurried down and saw a thin, red-haired woman in her early thirties with a small boy standing next to the bearded concierge. The woman said her five-year-old son had chanced upon the purse while playing on the street and had brought it home. She opened it and found many official papers and also two young women's photos on some certificates, so she realized that the loss to the foreign ladies must have been like a calamity. Then she saw an envelope with the recipient's address on it (the letter was from Lily's younger sister Linlin in Ivanovo), so following the address, she came to the Hotel Lux to return the purse. Yomei and Lily found their papers all in there, and became ecstatic, thanking the woman again and again. Yomei happened to have two hard candies on her, which she gave to the boy. Without a word, he unwrapped one and popped it into this mouth, sucking it with relish. They would love to give the woman something as well, but all the cash, bread coupons, and meal tickets were gone, so they could thank her only with words.

At work that day, they mentioned the recovery of their stuff to Li Kuo-dong, saying there were still good-hearted people around nowadays, but the man was more skeptical. He deduced that most petty thieves in Moscow

wouldn't implicate themselves in politics, and they knew
that appropriating official documents could be treated as
a political crime. If they happened to steal official papers,
they would send the documents to a lost-and-found center
or have them delivered back to the owners.

Without the meal tickets anymore, Yomei and Lily
couldn't eat in the cafeteria for the time being. Fortunately
it was already close to the end of June. In just a few days they
each got a new booklet of meal tickets for the month.

Since Yomei's theater school hadn't resumed yet, she
and Lily often went out to do volunteer work, visiting
the wounded soldiers at a school nearby that had been
repurposed as a makeshift hospital. In there, many patients
were staying on gurneys, and even the corridors smelled
of bleach and antiseptic. Yomei and Lily served as nurse
aides—getting hot water for the patients, wiping their faces
with warm hand towels, and carrying sanitary trays. On top
of that, the two often went to the clinic to donate blood. As
before, Yomei told the nurse that she was type O, that she
could give more blood, but every time they would draw no
more than two hundred milliliters, because she had passed
out once after they had drawn three hundred from her.
Nowadays Yomei would always get her blood drawn first, so
that Lily could take care of her if she blacked out again. But
such an incident didn't recur.

· Seventeen ·

n the summer of 1942, a movement started among
Muscovites to help with agricultural work in the
countryside. Lily joined a group of Cominternians and
went to a suburban town in the south called Serpukhov,
where they were to labor on a collective farm. Most men
in the countryside had left for the army, so there were
mainly women and children working in the kolkhoz now,
led by a one-armed, middle-aged veteran. Yomei didn't go
with Lily because her theater institute had just restarted.
Every week, Lily wrote to her, reporting on her life in the
countryside. She enjoyed herself despite having to get up
the moment roosters crowed, usually before five thirty, and
having to toil for a whole day, until it was dark. There was
an hour lunch break at noon, during which she could nap
a little on a ridge in a field. As for food, every meal was the
same, a chunk of black bread and a gourd ladle of porridge
or soup. But the fare was filling, and breathing the fresh
air constantly, Lily felt she was getting healthier by the
week. She also mentioned that the helpers from the city
could eat as much as they wanted of vegetables in the fields:
lettuce, carrots, cabbages, zucchinis, cauliflowers, even
turnips, though they mustn't have tomatoes or cucumbers
or radishes. Yomei was amused to read her friend's letters,

wondering why some of the vegetables were not allowed to be consumed freely and whether there was an orchard in the kolkhoz. How she wished she could be with Lily.

Now Yomei worked only part-time at the Comintern, two shifts a week in the radio room, for which she could have four meal tickets. Her drama school again offered her a stipend of two hundred eighty rubles a month, but food was rationed, and one could get bread only with the coupons issued by the city. In contrast, whenever she ate at the Comintern's cafeteria, she could eat her fill, so the meal tickets were essential for her nourishment.

On the other hand, she was obsessed with theater arts again, for which she was willing to go hungry if need be. She tried to work at the Comintern as little as possible so as to have more time for her studies. At the theater institute, people were amazed by Yomei's Russian, which she could speak more fluently now, almost with ease. Many male students and faculty members had left the previous year to join the army or the militia. It was said that Professor Gorchakov, though already middle-aged, had become a political instructor in a guerrilla force that was fighting the Nazi army in the south. It was also reported that some of the male theater students had fallen on the front. By now the German forces had bogged down, unable to push forward as they had planned. The tide of war seemed to have turned—the Red Army was fighting back vigorously and gaining the upper hand.

Due to the loss of some students and faculty, the theater institute was smaller in size now, but the instruction and dramatic practice resumed, and people were as busy as before. Yomei was happy to rejoin them and actively participated in the school's activities. All of a sudden she felt her life had a concrete purpose again.

These days, the acting department of the institute had been talking about staging a play, even though they knew it would be out of the question for them to attract a big audience in a time like this. They wanted to produce a play mainly for pedagogical purposes and wouldn't worry about audience or profit at all. A few students complained that they should suspend theatrical performances altogether, since shows might make them appear to be fiddling while the whole country was burning with the fire of war. But most faculty viewed this matter differently, arguing that however dire the times were, they had to continue practicing their art. This was their artistic duty, their way of preserving the essence of Russia onstage.

Because most of the best male actors among the faculty and students were absent now, the acting department believed they ought to stage a play that leaned heavily on female actors. They decided on Chekhov's *Three Sisters*. All agreed this was an excellent choice, though they would still need a few men for the play, but this wasn't difficult, because most of the male characters in *Three Sisters* are unremarkable, and some are old. With a little adjustment and makeup, even a middle-aged actor could play a man of a different age, younger or older. So they should be able to form an appropriate cast. Yet their ambition in staging this masterpiece was modest. They were to do it mainly for the students to learn how to act, specifically in the convention of the Stanislavski method. Not aiming for a hit in town, they would stage it in their own venue. If one performance could bring an audience of two hundred, that would be a success.

Most of the young main characters were to be played by students. Because Yomei spoke Russian well now, she was assigned to play Masha Prozorov, the middle sister, a role

she desired in spite of the tremendous challenge it posed.
Her classmates were to play the other sisters—Zina would be
the elder sister Olga, while Yelena would become Irina, the
youngest. Lecturer Katina Lestov, serving as the director,
wanted them all to study the play script carefully on their
own—everyone must write out their understanding and
analysis of the character they were going to play. Sometimes
the trio of the sister actresses worked together, comparing
notes and sharing their personal interpretations of the
characters' longing to leave their backwater for Moscow.
Yelena, blinking her blue eyes, said that even though she
was in the capital now, she already missed the former
city life terribly, so there was no lacking of emotional
connection with the three Prozorov sisters. Yet Director
Lestov emphasized that they mustn't imagine imitating a
character but instead they must look into themselves to find
their own emotional response to the dramatic situation
and follow that impulse to create their personal experience
when they were onstage. In other words, they were not just
to present the character but also embody the character from
both within and without. Katina Lestov revealed to Yomei
that she had chosen her for Masha because she, Katina,
could see something passionate and impulsive in Yomei
despite her Chinese background, and because those inner
qualities would help create the character of the middle
sister, who had a love affair with a married man, Colonel
Vershinin. The director's revelation made Yomei blush, the
tips of her ears even became hot for a few minutes, but she
liked to be considered that way: passionate and impulsive,
also attractive. Vershinin was played by Leonid, a middle-
aged acting teacher, who had a short ginger beard and fit
the role well. In the play, the colonel was a fortysomething,
already a father of two little girls.

Masha is the only married one among the three sisters. Her husband Kulygin, a local high-school teacher, was played by a student named Reslie Mironov, who was in his midtwenties and pale-faced, with a bump at the bridge of his nose. His appearance seemed to suit Kulygin's dull but kindhearted disposition. Reslie had attempted to join the army but gotten rejected due to asthma, which had grown more severe during the wintertime. He was talented in his own way, able to play the flute and speak both French and German, but he had been told he couldn't be useful as soldier. Now he was happy about this role in *Three Sisters* and worked hard on the preparations, together with the other participants. In the play, Kulygin loves his wife unconditionally, whereas Masha is at times sarcastic and doesn't always reciprocate his love. Indeed, in her eyes he used to be the cleverest man in town, but as time goes by, she finds him dull and visionless. Unlike him, all three sisters dream of leaving for Moscow, where they imagine living a life full of meaning, purpose, and also happiness. Still, the mundane existence in the small river town takes a toll on them and wears them down. Olga has become an old maid, a headmistress of a local school, while Irina consents to marry a man she doesn't love. In Masha's case, she starts an affair with the middle-aged colonel whose uniform and whose habit of philosophizing fascinate her and inflame her reveries and feelings.

The complexity of Masha's character posed a challenge to Yomei, who had never really fallen in love before. In her comments on the scene in which Colonel Vershinin expresses his infatuation with Masha ("I love your eyes, your gestures; I dream about how you move"), Yomei put triple question marks behind Masha's response to his sugary words, then pondered Masha's mixed reply ("When you talk to me like that, I want to laugh, even though it frightens me. Stop, please! . . . [*Sotto voce*] No, say it anyway. It doesn't matter. [*Covering her face with both hands*] I don't mind"). Yomei was nagged by the realization that Masha might know the man was just toying with her, but why would she encourage him? What would she, Yomei, do in such a situation? She thought hard about this and wrote out her true feelings: "I wouldn't mind having a fling with a man if he is really good and attractive to me. I want to expand my life, including my life with men." She was disturbed by her confession, even though it was only on paper and only to herself. She was glad to play the role of Masha, which seemed to offer a clear glimpse into her own soul. Yes, if she ran into a gorgeous man, whether he was single or married, she'd go with him, even give herself to him. She concluded in her notes on this episode: "Love and passion—the essence of life." She thought about Lucas and wondered if he was such a man. No, he's not, she concluded.

On the other hand, she shared Masha's conviction about the sine qua non of life's meaning. Masha claims to Vershinin: "It seems to me one must have some faith, or must look for a faith, otherwise one's life is empty . . . To live without knowing why the cranes fly, why babies are born, why stars shine in heaven . . . Either one knows what one lives for, or everything is futile and worthless." Yomei put an exclamation point at the end of those sentences and added, "Totally agree. That's why I am studying theater arts, so as to make my little contribution to China's cultural development, adding a beautiful nuance to the Communist revolution. A good life should result from a combination of passion and purpose, also dedication."

In the play, the Prozorov sisters' brother Andrei is an inveterate gambler and has lost tens of thousands of rubles

at cards. Without his sisters' knowledge, he sells the house
that belongs to the four of them. Masha's response to this
treachery is more visceral than her sisters'. She confesses
to them, "I cannot get it out of my mind . . . It's simply
disgusting. It torments me, like a nail driven into my head.
I can't remain silent. I mean about Andrei . . ." Never having
owned anything valuable and then having lost it as Masha
does in the play, Yomei couldn't feel the misery of loss that
excruciatingly, but she took such a liking to the expression
that she adopted the analogy as part of her language.
Whenever she was pained, agonizing over something, she'd
say, even in Chinese, "like a nail in my head that I can't
have pulled out."

Still, the biggest challenge to her in the performance
was language. She had to articulate like a native Russian
speaker, and for that, she spent at least five hours a day
improving her speech, which had to be delivered naturally,
without any hesitation. Her stage partner Reslie, who played
her husband, helped her practice whenever he could. By and
by, she sounded more natural, and was even able to manage
naturally the retroflex R sound, which needed her to turn
and curve her tongue backward. She had an extraordinary
memory and could learn everything by heart with ease.
So Katina Lestov was pleased to see the progress she was
making.

After the phase of character preparations was over,
they began rehearsing. For this, they divided the play into
different segments so that they could be more focused in
the rehearsals. Some of the passages in Chekhov's original
script were too long, so Leonid (Colonel Vershinin
onstage), being an amateur playwright, condensed them.
The shortened passages, tighter and more energetic now,

suited Yomei better in her playing Masha and also made the drama more dynamic and move faster.

The rehearsals went well by and large, but at the last act Yomei appeared slightly out of character. The soldiers are leaving, and so is Colonel Vershinin. When he says farewell to Masha, who can't get some poetic words out of her mind, repeating, "A green oak by a curved seashore, / upon that oak a golden chain," she is agitated and might now realize that the affair between them might become nothing but a fling. Having seen that all the officers are gone, she speaks to her sisters, neither of whom is dreaming of going to Moscow anymore, saying, "They are leaving us. There's one who has gone for good, forever. We are alone now and have to start our life over again. We must go on . . . We must go on living . . ."

Yomei delivered those lines quite rationally. Throughout the final scene, she tried to act like a reasonable woman, but Director Lestov said to her afterward, "You were rather detached onstage just now. Even your sobs at Vershinin's departure didn't seem right. Think about the good times you spent with the colonel. Were you not in the garden or in a room with him before his departure? What did you do to each other? Try to re-create that experience of joy and pain for yourself."

"This is really hard for me, like a nail in my head," Yomei confessed. "Different from Masha, I have no such experience with a man." She meant to say she hadn't slept with any man yet, but she was too bashful to let that out.

"But you're not supposed to imitate Masha. Use your imagination," Katina said with a straight face while her index finger was cranking at her temple. "As an artist, you must participate in the drama that is also part of your own

creation. Imagine the kind of mixed emotions you might
have at such a moment."

What Director Lestov was trying to convey was the actor's
total participation in the drama—even when absent from
the scene, her new presence must manifest that she has been
in the drama the whole time. Their institute's principle
of acting was that whether the actors were onstage or not,
psychologically they must be in the drama from start to
finish. Likewise, Yomei was supposed to manifest Masha's
continuous affair with Colonel Vershinin throughout the
second half of the play, and every one of her appearances
must reflect this continuity. Therefore, Vershinin's
departure must upset her deeply, both physically and
psychologically, which must be shown in Masha's convulsive
sobs while she wraps her arms around him, unwilling to let
him go.

Following the director's guidance, before entering the
final scene in the dress rehearsal, Yomei sat alone in a
corner and, eyes closed, began making out with the tall
and handsome Colonel Vershinin mentally so that she
could appear turned on. She imagined kissing him hard
on the mouth and enjoying his touch on her body here and
there. Indeed, when she took the stage, she radiated with
a flushing face and flashing eyes, even her chest swelling
a little. Everyone was struck by her new appearance.
Afterward both Zina and Yelena complimented her on
her tormented beauty. Leonid even said to others, "My
goodness, she'd so bewitching and so passionate. How could
I leave such a woman behind? What a dolt I am!"

Hearing him, people all laughed. Yomei tittered too,
saying she had just been acting. Reslie also complimented
her, saying, "You did marvelously. You made me envy
Colonel Vershinin." In the play, even though he knows

there has been an affair going on between his wife and the officer, the good-hearted Kulygin, without showing any trace of irritation, promises Masha he will love her all the same and will never "make any allusion" to it.

Katina Lestov was so pleased that she told Yomei, "You're downright striking, a born actress. You know how to make yourself act like an experienced woman in love—her mixed feelings, both her hunger for fulfillment and her heartbreak."

"Did I overdo it?" Yomei asked hesitantly.

"Not at all. Please continue to perform like that," Katina said.

Yet as expected, some people began to complain about Yomei's playing the role of Masha. They argued that *Three Sisters* was quintessentially a Russian play, a crowning jewel of the nation's dramatic achievement. How did they dare to let a foreign lady play such a major part? In spite of her charm and beauty and her excellent acting skill, and in spite of the sandy wig, the shell necklace, and the heeled pumps she wore, everybody could tell she was not a Russian. She spoke their mother tongue with traces of an accent and with slight hesitation, so her playing Masha was a bad choice, inappropriate to say the least. But such grumbles dissipated after the theater institute officially explained that the performance was only students' coursework and that Yomei, as an international student, was supposed to learn how to perform in the Russian way. It was part of her education assigned by the Soviet government.

· Eighteen ·

Lily had been away for seven weeks. On the evening of the last Sunday of September she phoned, and Yomei went down to the front desk to speak with her. Lily was coming back in two days and asked Yomei to receive her at the train station, because she had things to carry. Yomei was thrilled and agreed to meet her there.

She was delighted to see Lily getting off the train, smiling with a face that was slightly weathered but glowing with health. Lily was carrying a sack of vegetables, more than fifty pounds of them. Yomei took the bag and threw it on her shoulder, then they were moving toward the exit of the platform. "How much did you pay for this?" she asked about the vegetables.

"Nothing," said Lily, a proud smile on her lips. "They let me take as much as I could carry."

Back in their room at the Hotel Lux, Yomei emptied the sack. There were three big heads of cabbage, half a dozen squashes, some twenty potatoes, four long cucumbers, a couple of stout eggplants, two stalks of celery, even a small pumpkin. She told Lily, "What a windfall—I haven't eaten fresh vegetables in weeks."

"I took with me only the uncrushable produce. They were nice to me."

That evening Yomei cooked a vegetable stew spiced
with chili flakes and soy paste, which she'd bought at a
small Korean grocery store. They each ate two large bowls
of the dish. Lily said this was the first time she had tasted
homemade food since she'd left for Serpukhov. She also
told Yomei that she'd go to the public bathhouse first thing
the next morning, because she might still have a couple of
lice and must get rid of them. Yomei reminded her not to
wade into a bathing pool again. "Of course I'll be more
careful," said Lily.

Lily was excited to learn that Yomei was to act in
Three Sisters. She enthused that no Chinese actor had ever
performed such a major role in a Russian play, but Yomei
reminded her that it was only a students' effort, purely
pedagogical.

The premiere of *Three Sisters* was scheduled for the
following week, after the play had gone through more
than forty rehearsals. This was much less than a play
produced for the general public, which usually had at
least one hundred rehearsals. On the opening night, the
small theater at the institute was crowded with some three
hundred people, mostly from local communities and the
theater circle. There were also a few Chinese expats who
had heard that Yomei was going to perform in the play.
Most of the audience were seated on oak bleachers, which
formed a sloping semicircle. Some were sitting on the floor
at the front. The back windows were all open to show a
view of the riverside. On the stage, a couple of thick birch
boles stood to give a country ambience. Inside the Prozorov
house, there was a long table with a vase of mixed flowers
at its center for Irina's name-day party. The stage props
were basic and minimal, but rustically authentic, with
some pollarded willows whose drowsy branches wavered in

the backdrop, outside the open windows that overlooked
the abruptly dropping banks of the Moskva. A large carpet
covered the center of the floor, on which stood some chairs
and a pair of brown sofas.

Most of the male characters had on a military uniform,
and Colonel Vershinin even bore a sword. As for the
women, they had donned long dresses. Masha was wearing
black, while her younger sister Irina was in white and her
elder sister Olga was in a long, pea-green sleeveless dress
and a beige shirt. All the female servants wore black with
large white aprons around the waists, their hair wrapped
in red bandannas. In spite of their nervousness at the
beginning, the cast gradually grew at ease, proceeding
smoothly. They managed to put the audience under a spell,
and they didn't move, even though some had to remain on
their feet the whole time. Deep inside, Yomei was antsy
largely due to her struggle with the lines she had to say in
Russian, yet since she was playing Masha, having an affair
with the colonel, her state of nerves did give a touch of
neurotic intensity to her acting.

When the last episode was over, applause exploded, and
some in the audience whistled. Katina was so pleased that
afterward she told the cast with her eyes smiling, "I wish
we could pop champagne to celebrate." She thanked them
with a small bow and with her hand on her chest, as if this
were a high-quality professional production. Then the
teacher pulled Yomei aside and told her, "To be honest,
I was nervous about you, but you were excellent. The
audience couldn't tell you're a foreigner. They might have
assumed that you were a Soviet minority from Central
Asia."

"Thank you so much, Katina, for your encouragement
and for all the help."

Reslie Mironov, still wearing the brown vest and the felt hat for the part of Kulygin, came up to Yomei and said shyly, "Can I take you home?"

Yomei laughed and said, "You act like you're still onstage." Indeed, at the end of the play Masha's husband is supposed to offer to take her home. Seeing him a bit embarrassed, Yomei added, "Maybe we can walk back together another day. My friend is here waiting for me, and I ought to go with her." She threw her arm around Lily, who had been standing next to her waiting the whole time. There'd be another performance in two days, but she wasn't sure she'd like to walk home with Reslie, still unable to shake off his stage image—Masha's boring, ridiculous husband, Kulygin.

"Good night then, see you soon," the good-natured Reslie said, and with his slim fingers, adjusted the steel-framed, powerless glasses he wore for the stage.

The moment Yomei and her friend left the theater institute, heading south to their dorm, Lily said, "That Reslie fellow must be interested in you. He might be after you."

"I can't date seriously here," Yomei said thoughtfully. "Reslie Mironov plays my husband in the play, so I ought to be nice to him. We have to be together onstage."

"How about offstage then?" Lily giggled.

Yomei smacked her on the shoulder. "You're such an imaginative girl that you're trying to catch shadows— nothing will happen between Reslie and me. Remember how we all refused to become Soviet citizens, saying we didn't want to be Musty Bread?"

"Sure, but that's not my point. I mean it's natural for a young woman to have feelings for a young man, even a foreign man. Actually, even my little sister Linlin has been dating seriously."

"Going with a foreigner?"

"A Russian boy in the same international children's home."

"How are your parents taking it?"

"They're too far away to interfere with her life or mine. Things change constantly. We all have to adapt to circumstances, don't we?"

"OK, I can see that you've become a true internationalist at heart," Yomei said, swatting away the mosquitoes buzzing around her head.

"Just now, you were gorgeous onstage. Seeing you in the last scene, for the first time in my life I understood the word 'sexy.' My goodness, you were sexy like a filly in heat. What happened to you?"

"I was just acting. You shouldn't mix drama with life."

"But you were blooming like a real woman frustrated with her dull marriage—everything came out of you so naturally. Did you have to prepare yourself for that kind of presentation?"

"In our field we call it 'expression' instead of 'presentation.' One has to express the emotional experience onstage. Everything must come from within. I have to prepare myself psychologically for every one of my appearances in the play."

"Then I can see why so many men are drawn to you. You could easily turn some of their heads."

"Come on, you're taking me to be a fox spirit that keeps men bewitched."

"I guess deep down most girls want to become a coquette, even though we don't say we do."

"You know, Stanislavski used to play the part of Colonel Vershinin. If he were doing that tonight, I might have been so unnerved, sharing the stage with him, that I would have peed my panties."

Lily laughed. "You know, Yomei, at heart you're a wanton woman."

"Ha ha ha, maybe only at heart."

A tram passed by with a jangling bell, and they continued south and entered the Hotel Lux. They didn't go to sleep until after midnight, lying in the dark with the heads of their beds against each other, chatting about their dreams of going back to China to build a new country. Both felt their hearts swelling with the lofty feeling of dedication and self-sacrifice. They wanted to work ardently for the revolution back home.

At one point, Lily mentioned Lucas, the French man at the Party school outside Ufa who had run after Yomei, but there hadn't been a word from him. All Yomei had heard was that the group of Spanish students, Lucas among them, had gone to join a partisan force in Yugoslavia to fight their way back to Spain, and that some of them got killed on the way.

Director Lestov was pleased about their performance as a pedagogical success. For those students who had actually acted in the play, this opportunity helped them understand the dramatic art more intimately. Whether or not they continued to major in acting or directing, the experience of performing in *Three Sisters* was invaluable to them. Among the Chinese expats, word spread that Yomei was truly phenomenal. It was said that she acted brilliantly, and what was even more amazing, that she spoke Russian like a native speaker onstage. But those who knew her in person acknowledged that she must have worked extremely hard on her lines, considering that in everyday life she still hesitated

a bit and even paused to find the right word or phrase when
she spoke the foreign tongue.

The performance continued twice a week for the entire
month of October. From the second night on, Reslie
accompanied Yomei on her way back to the Hotel Lux. He
was excited while walking beside her: his voice dropped
whenever a car passed by, and then he would resume talking.
He said he had attempted in vain to join the army again, but
that they had kept a file on him and rejected him for his flat
feet and asthma. In fact, when it was warm, he could breathe
normally. He believed that the recruiting officers may have
been biased against an educated, urbane young man their
age, since they even accepted Professor Gorchakov, who was
already forty-seven, though Gorchakov was stalwart, like a
draft horse. Still, he, Reslie, could have been more useful for
the military by far. At least, he believed he could have carried
artillery shells and loaded cartridges for a machine gun. "But
I'm happy now," he said, eyeing Yomei sideways mysteriously.
"Because I was left behind, I got to act together with you and
to know you better. I have my reward. Life is truly amazing,
unpredictable."

Actually, Professor Gorchakov hadn't been taken by the
army. He just marched away with the militia, serving as a
commissar in a resistance force, but Yomei didn't correct
Reslie. His shoulders hunched some as he was walking
beside her. She could feel his pain from being rejected by
the military—she too had been denied an opportunity to
fight the Nazi invaders on the front.

Before they said good night, he hugged her and even
gave her a peck on the cheek, which she believed was
harmless, though it did make her face hot for a moment.

After the next performance, on their way downtown,
they didn't go back to her dorm directly. Before crossing

the bridge over the Moskva, they strolled a little along its southern bank. Some nimbus clouds were gathering in the city's shimmering sky, while faint lightning zigzagged, cracking a wall of dark clouds. The air was damp, and no mosquitoes and gnats were flying. In the dark a boat was blowing its horn, which sounded mysterious to Yomei. She was sure there was no passenger service on the water at this late hour. Neither could it be a fishing boat—the loud noise could scare fish away. She asked Reslie, "Why are they tootling like that while sailing on the water?"

"I'm not sure, perhaps they are signaling to someone they are going to meet."

At this point, a male voice shouted and then a harmonica began shrilling from the boat. In response, a flourish of polka music on the accordion and the balalaika started in the distance. Reslie said, "There must be a party somewhere in the woods down the river."

Yomei gave a loud whistle, like Masha does in *Three Sisters*, but the boat didn't respond to her. Instead, a young female voice started singing:

> *My dear nightingale,*
> *Please stop warbling before dawn.*
> *Let my beloved sleep a little more.*
> *He's going to ride to the front in a few hours*
> *To fight the horde from the south . . .*

"I like that song," Yomei said. "What's it called?"

"I don't know. It must be a folk song. This is the first time I've heard it too."

In a flash, the boat disappeared downstream. A few waterfowl let out sleepy cries, and the river turned quiet again.

The moon came out suddenly, and its silver light rendered their faces clear to each other. Yomei said, "Moscow is such a spacious city. There's still a lot of nature around here."

"Would you mind living here for good?" he asked with a smile.

"I'm not sure. Probably, if I meet someone I really love—I will be happy to be a good wife and a loving mother."

"Would you mind someday resuming our roles like in *Three Sisters?*"

In spite of his even tone of voice, his question, eager and heartfelt, threw her. For a moment, she didn't know how to reply. Finally she found her words, saying, "But I don't want to have Kulygin for a husband."

He laughed, a bit nervously. "You know in real life, I'm not like Masha's husband at all."

"OK, I like you, Reslie, and will be happy to be a good friend of yours, but as for the other kind of relationship you mentioned, it can get complicated."

"In what way?"

"Right before I enrolled in our theater institute, some official here asked me to get naturalized and said that with Soviet citizenship in hand, it would be easier for me to study and live here. Now I can see he was right, but I refused the offer."

"What does this mean?"

"It means that without Soviet citizenship, it might be hard for me to settle down here. Eventually I'll have to go back to my country, where I'll be more useful."

"You can always apply for Soviet citizenship, can't you? Besides, I wouldn't mind going to China and living there as long as I can be with you."

Although he said those words readily, as if without thinking, she was still astounded. She had no doubt about his sincerity. He may have given a lot of thought to that scenario. On the other hand, she knew many Russian men were extroverted and more likely to change their hearts in the matter of love. All the same, she was touched, even though she didn't feel very attracted to him.

From the next performance on, she had Lily accompany her back from the theater institute, so that she could prevent Reslie from sticking to her and pressing her for a definite answer to his question. She needed time to think through this matter, and by instinct she knew she must concentrate on her schoolwork for now. Lily was happy to serve as chaperone, since she also believed they must keep their life as simple as possible. Without any emotional complications here, they'd be able to go home for a clean start.

· *Nineteen* ·

For months, Reslie joined Yomei whenever he could. He
seemed to want to show others that they were dating
seriously, but she was ambivalent about this relationship,
unsure of her future. What's more, she couldn't dispel
from her mind Kulygin, the wimpy and nondescript
character that Reslie had played. For a long time she had
been mystified by this unpleasant impression left by Reslie
in her mind; then she realized that actually he must be
an excellent actor if he could overcome his fear to show
the audience a somewhat negative character who was quite
different from him. Only an accomplished actor could be
that dedicated and brave. With such a realization, Yomei
felt closer to Reslie. She tried to be kind and warm to him
and often reminded herself that he had helped her so much
when she practiced for the role of Masha.

Early in the summer, Reslie was finally recruited by the
Red Army. Thanks to his skills in German, he was assigned
to become a radio monitor, following the communications
among the enemy forces to gather information. He joined a
radio company of the Eighth Guards Motor Rifle Division,
which had come west from the Kyrgyz Republic. He was
happy about his conscription, even though he had to go to

the Demyansk front in the northwest. One afternoon, he came to break the news to Yomei. She brewed jasmine tea for him and then placed a saucer holding a few cubes of sugar next to his cup. His gray eyes blazed at the sight of the sugar, which was a rarity nowadays. She was able to pay a high price for it, which she could afford because she drew a small salary from the Comintern besides her scholarship from the theater institute.

It was midafternoon, and Lily wasn't back yet. Yomei and Reslie were sitting at their dining table. She said she was happy for him, while he was so excited that his plain face shone with reddish patches. He said, "I'm sorry, Yomei, but duty is calling, and I have to go to the front." Reslie managed a smile as a frosty sparkle flashed from his eyes. He was acting as though they had already gone steady, so even his departure mustn't break off their relationship, although it might break his heart.

She exhaled a feeble sigh, then added, "I understand. I would do the same if I could join up."

"I'll write to you."

"Please do. But what if our letters go astray? You know letters get lost easily in times like these."

Her earnest voice seemed to faze him a bit. He lowered his mop of auburn curls and said, "I have an idea." He took out a pen and wrote on his tiny spiral notebook. "I am leaving with you my parents' address in Kansk. You can write them directly if we lose touch. I'll let them know who you are." He ripped off the page and handed it to her.

She carefully folded the sheet into fourths and slipped it into her shirt pocket. Despite her uneasy feeling about his passionate interest in her, she ventured to ask, "If I go back to China in the future, will you really go there too?"

"I'll follow you wherever you are."

He said those words solemnly, as if making a promise, which touched her. She realized that at a minimum she must treat him as a good friend.

At this point, Lily came back, so Reslie rose to leave—he had intuitively felt that Lily wasn't supportive of their relationship. Yomei went out with him. It was hot outside, the sun intense, while cicadas droned from the tops of young maples that lined the wide street, every one of the tree trunks lime-painted three feet up from the root to prevent the attack of insects. When Reslie and Yomei got close to a plaza, a flock of white-breasted swallows appeared, darting back and forth, catching gnats and midges. Their wings were fluttering and whistling faintly. The moment the two of them neared a man-made fountain, a tram arrived noiselessly. Reslie turned and hugged her, saying, "I'll miss you, Yomei. Remember, I'll always love you."

"I'll miss you too, Reslie. Don't forget to write."

"Of course I won't," he said.

Then he turned and leaped onto the tram, which went rolling away with its bell ringing. He waved and blew her a kiss.

She returned him one. As she watched his cream-colored shirt fade into the bustling thoroughfare, her throat tightened and her eyes misted over. It was always hard to see someone close to her leaving, and she was unsure if she would ever see him again.

Soon after Reslie Mironov left for Demyansk, Professor Gorchakov came back to the theater institute. In less than two years, he had aged considerably, his hair half-grizzled and his face marked with deeper lines. But he was still in buoyant spirits, his eyes sparkling when he laughed. One afternoon he called Yomei into his office for a conference.

Seated behind his hardwood desk, he asked about her life and experiences over the past year. She said she had an unforgettable time at the Party school outside Ufa and felt enriched by the sojourn into the regions of the Ural Mountains. She was greatly impressed by the openness and vastness of the Russian land. Above all, her participation in *Three Sisters* seemed to mark a new phase of her professional development.

"Actually, that's what I'd like to talk with you about," Gorchakov said in his deep voice. "All the teachers and students have praised your performance. Beyond question, you are a quite brilliant burgeoning actress. Tell me, what's your plan after graduation?"

The question took her by surprise, though once in a while she had wrestled with the same issue. Even if she was certain she'd go back to China afterward, she wasn't sure where she could have an acting career; at most, that might be feasible if she settled down in one of the major cities. Another question kept nagging her in secret as well. What if she fell in love with a foreign man before her return? To date, she had tried to prevent emotional entanglements, but she wasn't certain she could always keep hold of herself. She said to Professor Gorchakov, "Anything might happen in one's life. I still have three years to go before graduation. At this point, I believe I will return to my motherland."

His green eyes lit up. "I too hope you will go back to China and become an influential figure in the spoken drama circle there. At this point in your career as an aspiring theater artist, you should think about your concentration, which should be part of your lifelong plan too. To be frank, if you live in Russia, you might be able to keep acting and ultimately become a fine actress, but bear in mind that even though you're brilliant and beautiful, you might not grow into a preeminent actress in Russia, given that you are not a native speaker and there might be unexpected obstacles to you. But if you go back to China, you might have a different career altogether."

What Gorchakov said made her wonder if he was representing some official power in speaking with her like this. This was nothing untoward, as she was already accustomed to arrangements by the Party and by her superiors. She smiled and said almost naughtily, "I guess I can still act after I go back to China. I can be a decent actress after my education here."

"No doubt about that, but we, I mean our institute, would want you to be more useful in China."

"Can you expand on that please?"

"Let me put it this way: a successful actor is at most a flame that can illuminate a stage, but a director can become a torch that brings new light to the field. You should concentrate on directing instead of acting in our school. We hope that someday you can bring the Stanislavski method back to China. That will be a great contribution you can make to your country."

His words made her heart swell with a surge of emotion. She said, "I will think about what you said. But do you think I can become a good director?"

"Why not? We've all witnessed the progress you've made. You're observant and sensitive and have a distinct sensibility, which is usually innate, not something that can be taught. To be frank, if you specialize in directing, I can see a bright future ahead of you in the field of spoken drama in China—your work might become more significant in Chinese theater."

"Thank you for having such confidence in me."

"My teacher, the late Stanislavski, used to say that the director was a midwife who becomes more experienced and even like a sorceress as she grows older. Later he revised this analogy and said the director was also like a thoughtful teacher, having to make the audience ponder the issues of their time. What I'm trying to convey is that a director can have a lifelong career—the older you are, the better you'll become."

"I want a directorial career then," she said. "I appreciate what you just told me."

He waved his slim, almost feminine, hand, indicating this was part of his job. "Do let me know what you think, so that we can design your curriculum."

"I will soon."

Yomei talked with Lily about Gorchakov's suggestion, which her friend urged her to follow. Lily even added her own spin, saying that actors, however talented, usually had a short stage life, after which only a small number of them could manage to transform themselves into directors. "Unless you hanker for stardom, you'd better focus on directing from the outset," Lily concluded.

"I know myself," said Yomei. "I cannot become a great actress. Also, a woman loses her looks in a matter of a few years, but artistic beauty in a play can be renewed if not everlasting."

The exchange with Lily helped Yomei cement her resolve, and she informed Mr. Gorchakov that she would concentrate on directing. The professor was delighted to hear that. She enrolled in his directing class, and from that point whenever he worked on a play, she became an assistant on his directorial team.

· *Twenty* ·

Lily resumed working full-time at the Comintern, where everything remained the same. Both she and Yomei were pleased that they didn't have to deal with office politics there, since they stayed only in the radio room following the voices from Chongqing. With her friend back now, Yomei felt her life stabilized some. She was always halfhearted about her job at the Comintern; Lily disliked her work there in spite of the stable meals they were able to have. Similar to Yomei, though less passionate, she wanted to continue with her studies too, believing that with more college education, she would be more useful when she returned to China.

Toward the end of 1942, they were informed that the Comintern was about to disband. The news unsettled them. They asked to be released from the radio program so that they could continue with their education. Their request was granted, so both of them left the Comintern and felt liberated at last.

But soon the issue of livelihood grew more pressing. Without employment, they couldn't have regular meals as they used to have. They had to manage like the unemployed Muscovites who depended on the city's rations. Yomei and Lily each had a provision booklet, which allowed one to buy

550 grams of bread a day—300 grams of black bread and 250 grams of white bread. Since the beginning of 1943, the monthly rations also included some other items: 100 grams of fat, 100 grams of sugar, and two kilos of meat. But most times the shops had only empty shelves and often sold substitutes for the real thing, such as pastry in place of sugar, egg powder in lieu of meat, and man-made butter for fat. Even the substitutes were not always available. Yomei and Lily were so hungry that sometimes they ate up their daily bread right in the shops where they bought it. Then, for the rest of the day, they had to drink hot water to mitigate hunger pangs. Never had they felt so weak. At times, when climbing the stairs, all of a sudden their legs would go all cottony and they had to sit on the steps to rest for a spell before continuing up.

One day Chen Daonan, a man in his late thirties also living at the Hotel Lux, came to see Yomei and Lily. He was a translator at an international Soviet radio station, and had come to the USSR many years before, and had been assigned by the CCP to stay on and work here. Then he had married a Russian woman and become a Soviet citizen. Seeing Yomei and Lily's predicament, he suggested they work for his radio station as quality checkers, which was an easy job for educated native Chinese speakers. The two of them could share the work. All they did was listen to the Mandarin broadcast of the Soviet station—if they came across any error in the pronunciation of a broadcaster, they made a note and let the person know so that it could be corrected in the future. For this job they were paid nine hundred rubles a month, plus one meal ticket a day. This was enough to support both of them, so they accepted the job readily. From the first week on, they alternated, so that each day one of them could eat her fill at lunch. Then

Yomei persuaded the supervisor of the dining hall to allow them to use their meal tickets on different days, so that she and Lily could have lunch together every other day. The food was filling, and they could eat as much bread and butter and milk as they wanted. Once in a while there were also sourdough and fish soup. They both loved the garlic bread, which was warm, soft, and tasty. So their hunger pangs were staved off.

To be able to eat one's fill three times a week was a kind of luxury that most Muscovites couldn't have. People tried various ways to nourish themselves. The Russians loved potatoes and used to discard the peels, but now they saved the skins and dried them—they then ground them into powder and mixed it with a bit of cornmeal or wheat flour and baked the "dough" into small puffed cakes. Such a "pastry" could be quite tasty, and Yomei and Lily were often treated to such potato cakes by their Russian friends. Usually there were potatoes for sale at marketplaces, but the sellers were farmers from the suburban villages. They also sold cheese, butter, jerky, honey, apples, dried prunes, carrots, beets, mushrooms, all at an exorbitant price. Yomei once chanced on a vendor selling red-skinned potatoes for ninety rubles a kilo.

Actually the climate here made it easy to grow produce, and there was plenty of farmland in Russia. When spring came, many urbanites began to grow their own spuds. In most cases, their departments or companies allocated them each a little piece of cropland in the suburbs where they could plant their own vegetables. But Yomei and Lily were not officially on staff anywhere, so they were not entitled to have their own land. Again, it was Chen Daonan who helped them. He cut a small piece from the land allotted to him and gave it to them, so that they could also grow their own produce. Yomei and Lily didn't want to spend too much time farming, so they just planted some potato peels with eyes on them in their land and let the crop grow by itself. They neither weeded nor fertilized their "garden." The black soil was rich anyway, so they didn't bother to do anything about their spuds. Not even once did they go there to take a look at their tiny patch.

In spite of the food shortage, the capital was still rich with cultural life during wartime. Their occasional financial straits were never severe enough to prevent Yomei and Lily from enjoying public entertainment. They went to the theater quite often. Together they saw many performances, some of which were Russian masterpieces by Chekhov, Tolstoy, Ostrovsky, Gorky, and other playwrights. They saw some foreign plays as well—Ibsen's *An Enemy of the People*, Goldoni's *The Servant of Two Masters*, Shakespeare's *Othello* and *Much Ado About Nothing*. There were also plays that reflected the contemporary spirit and realities, like Ivanov's *Armored Train 14–69* and Bulgakov's *The Days of the Turbins*. The former was a massive production with at least fifty characters and many large group scenes. The latter, a play about the collapse of the German-Ukrainian regime under the attack of the Bolsheviks, had impressed Stalin so much so that he claimed he had watched it fifteen times and granted his approval for its performance to the public. All those plays, old or new, domestic or foreign, had been in the repertoire of the Moscow Art Theatre, which had several studios in the city—each of those houses could give the plays a full run. Both Yomei and Lily noticed that Soviet citizens didn't spend a lot of time on political studies and meetings (unlike back in China) and instead, derived their revolutionary enthusiasm and inspiration mainly from the arts, particularly theater and cinema, which functioned to educate the populace, raising their morale and ethical spirits and instilling in them the love for the country and fellow citizens. It stood to reason that Stanislavski had once declared, "The theater is the school of the people."

Unlike Lily, who didn't mind working, Yomei became reluctant to work at the radio station. Even for a part-time job that guaranteed her a full meal whenever she went to the office, she wouldn't sacrifice her time. She said she wanted to concentrate on her studies at the theater institute. There was so much to learn that she wished she hadn't needed to sleep at all. Lily said Yomei was like a willful young girl. Indeed, Lily had become the guardian of their livelihood. After Yomei quit her job, Lily began working full-time at the radio station. She also did extra work for them, checking the Chinese scripts before they went on the air. With the limited income Lily was pulling in, the two of them managed to continue to live in Moscow.

· *Twenty-One* ·

Yomei was excited about Gorchakov's directorial seminar and felt it was more invigorating than an acting course. The directing class was quite small, with only seven students, and they were like an elite group within the institute. Gorchakov was going to direct two plays each year: one traditional and the other contemporary. His plan was to make his students learn through actual participation in the directing projects so that they could experience how the plays were produced. His choices of the traditional plays all used to belong to the Moscow Art Theatre's repertoire, but now the institute needed to reproduce them to educate the younger generation of actors and directors and to familiarize them with the Stanislavski method, which their institute was proud of and determined to advocate for and disseminate domestically and abroad. Besides directing, the students also attended business meetings, during which various aspects of the production were discussed, such as budgeting, promotion, scheduling, and hiring temps, because most of the students would go to different places after graduation and take charge of a theater and build their own directing careers. Yomei was fascinated by the elaborate planning a production required and eager to learn how the theater operated.

The first traditional play Professor Gorchakov directed with his class was Charles Dickens's *The Battle of Life*, a romantic play performed in Moscow nearly two decades before. When Gorchakov expressed his desire to reproduce this play, there was a debate among the faculty about its suitability. Those who had reservations thought the play already too dated to suit the age of the proletarian revolution. Moreover, in a time of war, a sentimental play like this one might be going against the zeitgeist. But Gorchakov insisted on the production, saying that self-sacrifice, the central idea of the play, should serve the modern age well. More important, his teacher Stanislavski had participated in directing this play and Gorchakov had seen how the late master worked on the production, so he would like to pass his firsthand knowledge on to his young students. The argument over the suitability of this play couldn't be settled at this level, and the issue was sent up to the Ministry of Culture and the Kremlin.

To Gorchakov's delight, the official approval came within two weeks. The cultural officials gave two justifications: First, Britain was an ally of the Soviet Union in fighting Nazi Germany, and putting on Dickens's play might help build rapport between the USSR and the UK. Second, the spirit of self-sacrifice must be promoted now among Soviet citizens in resisting the German invasion, so a play like this one could inspire people.

Without delay Gorchakov began to pick the cast of actors and also the stage designers. His directing students all served as his assistants. He was candid about why he chose *The Battle of Life*, confessing that it had been his graduation work at the Moscow Art Theatre two decades prior, so he knew the play and its staging process thoroughly. More essential, after Stanislavski had seen the run-through of the

play directed by Gorchakov, he had offered to help make
it into a permanent piece in the theater's repertoire. He
worked with young Gorchakov and the actors for more than
two weeks and rendered the production splendid and more
artistically expressive and intricate. Now Gorchakov wanted
to walk his students through the same process so that they
could learn the Stanislavski method more intimately. His
confession made the students, both the aspiring directors
and actors, more excited.

He urged Yomei to devote more time and energy to the
stagings of the traditional plays, because these were the
ones that Stanislavski had left his mark on, so she could
learn more of his method. As for Gorchakov's directing
of the current plays, she should be involved, but they
should not be essential to her studies, because the new
plays might be less accomplished artistically (this was just
between him and her, the professor emphasized). She had
been keeping a directing journal meticulously. She would
also review her notes in order to fully grasp the meanings
of Gorchakov's instructions and impromptu decisions at
rehearsals. He told the directors-to-be that ultimately the
most important part of the theater business was to build
a significant, lasting repertoire. In his words, "Try your
best to keep the plays youthful." By that he meant a fine
play in the repertoire should have a kind of permanent
relevance to human life, which could keep the work "new
and youthful." He used *The Battle of Life* as an example. The
younger sister Marion makes a tremendous sacrifice for
her sister Grace because she finds out that Grace loves
Alfred, Marion's fiancé, more than she does. The whole
plays centers around this timeless idea of self-sacrifice,
which always strikes a chord in the human heart. Such a
magnanimous feeling can also assume different forms,

such as parents' sacrifice for their child, citizens' sacrifice
for their country, a lover's sacrifice for the beloved,
and an ordinary person's sacrifice for a noble idea. In
Gorchakov's opinion, as well as Stanislavski's, it was
this permanent and universal idea that had kept the play
youthful, so its production must focus on this perennial
theme, making it as vibrant as possible. In the structure
of a play, the central idea should be its mainstay, its
throbbing heartbeat, whose manifestation should reflect
the clarity of the dramatic purpose.

Every time at the rehearsal, Yomei got excited, though
she wasn't playing any role now. She was eager to see how the
director in chief conducted his business, specifically how
Gorchakov helped the actors improve their performances.
She believed that her teacher, after a fashion, embodied
the spirit of his mentor Konstantin Stanislavski, so she
must observe carefully and grasp the meanings and logic of
Gorchakov's criticism and decisions.

Her friend Zina, lovely and expressive, with large and
lucent eyes, was an excellent actress now, able to act like a
professional. In *The Battle of Life*, she was playing the role of
Marion, the heroine. One afternoon, the cast rehearsed
the garden scene in which the two sisters talk about
their love for Alfred, and Marion makes up her mind to
sacrifice herself for Grace. The younger sister, moved by
her own plan to run away while reading a ballad to Grace,
is supposed to turn tearful, but Zina couldn't summon up
her tears. At most she could sound teary with her voice.
Zina justified her dry eyes by saying she couldn't fake tears,
though she was obviously frustrated.

Gorchakov retorted that every worthy actor must be
able to simulate emotions, which was the prerequisite for
her admission into their theater institute, so Zina mustn't

evade her task in the performance and must produce tears. Gorchakov's tone of voice was sharp and even harsh. As a result, Zina started crying.

Seizing the moment, he shouted, "Let's do the scene again. Begin!"

This time Marion couldn't stop her tears while reading the ballad to her sister. All the spectators observed with approval. Yomei was so impressed that she was about to congratulate Zina the moment the scene was over.

But Gorchakov shook his head of wavy hair and said, "Something is off here. Tell us, Zina, what did you think when you were crying onstage?"

"I was thinking of my poor grandmother, who wanted to eat herring on a piece of baguette and a bowl of sauerkraut soup when she was dying, but we couldn't get any of those for her." Again her eyes began welling up.

"Stop it!" Gorchakov said. "The nature of your emotion was wrong here. Marion couldn't be struck by sorrow when she was reading the ballad to her sister. The right emotion should be self-pity. On the one hand, she was touched by the noble spirit of self-sacrifice, and on the other, she hoped Grace could perceive her true motivation, but Grace was wrapped in her own bliss of love for Alfred and was blind to her younger sister's true feelings. That must be Marion's right emotions, mixed ones."

Zina's heart-shaped face contorted a little, as if she had eaten something sour. She said, "Self-pity is base, close to selfishness, isn't it? I'm supposed to show the nobility of Marion's self-sacrifice."

"What you're talking about is emotional purity," the teacher replied, "but there's no purity in human motivations. In Marion's case, some mixed emotions can make her more authentic, more human. Let's try this episode again. Let your inner struggle manifest on your face when you speak to Grace." He turned and cried, "Begin!"

This time Marion became a completely different girl, dynamic and complicated, obviously struggling to get something out but unable to. Her face showed both joy and bitterness. Clearly she was also in anguish. The spectators were watching with rapt attention, as if in thrall.

"Bravo!" shouted Gorchakov the second the episode was over. "That was spectacular, Zina. Let's take a breather. We can pick it up here tomorrow."

Yomei was so impressed by the great improvement that she went up to Zina and said, "It was a tremendous rehearsal. I hope you still have tears in your eyes."

Zina smiled and said, "Sure, I always have some. Professor Gorchakov has made me see that acting is also an artistic creation, and an actor must look deep into herself for inspiration."

That night Yomei jotted down in her journal: "Absolutely no emotional purity! Also look into your own soul for emotional authenticity."

At every rehearsal she picked up something new. She was so excited about the directing class that she often went to the studio long before the rehearsal started. She found out that Gorchakov would arrive fifteen minutes early, and that he'd go around to check on things and talk with other faculty members and administrative staff. He once told her that Stanislavski had always come to his rehearsals before his students. "It's a good habit, so I do the same."

Yomei scribbled in her directing journal: "Must arrive before your actors." She put an asterisk at the end of the sentence as if to remind herself of this as a rule.

In addition to writing every character's biography, the directing students were also instructed to read Dickens's

novel carefully so that they could have the original story
as a reference for creating the right mise-en-scènes and
stage actions. Yomei did all the homework carefully. She
enjoyed reading the novel, in the Russian translation, and
could see that it was richer and more nuanced and with
more shades in its characters' feelings and psychology,
even though the play was adapted by Albert Smith, a
contemporary of Dickens's, who had been quite faithful
to the novel. Gorchakov was frank with his students about
his own missteps in his original production and about how
Stanislavski had helped him correct them. There is a law
firm scene in the middle of the play. Michael Warden, the
villain, believes he has succeeded in seducing Marion, who
has agreed to elope with him so that her sister Grace can
marry Alfred. It follows that Warden has to make financial
arrangements with his lawyers, Mr. Craggs and Mr.
Snitchery. In the beginning, Gorchakov decided to let the
two lawyers dominate the law office so that Warden would
appear at their mercy.

   He asked the directing class what kind of props they
should put in the scene. More like a law office, with fine
furniture, or just a regular business room? Most of the
students believed the setting should be a professional office,
with shiny furniture. Gorchakov smiled and told them, "I
made the same decision, putting in a fancy desk and high
stools. So in the scene the two lawyers perched on the stools
like a pair of ravens and looked down at Warden when they
spoke with him. But in Stanislavski's rehearsal, he suggested
getting rid of the fancy furniture and using a regular
square table and armchairs instead. I was mortified and
tried to defend my position. It happened that he had just
read the novel again and figured out the right psychological
undercurrent of the scene, in which Warden must be the

center because he still owned most of his estates, although a part of them had been misused and wasted by the two lawyers. So Stanislavski placed Warden at the center, let him sit at the square table facing the audience while the two lawyers were seated at his sides. When Warden expressed his intention to elope with Dr. Jeddler's second daughter Marion, the two lawyers turned aghast, showing a peculiar kind of emotional intensity and complexity. The doctor had been their reputable client, so they had to be decent to Dr. Jeddler and attempt to stop Warden so as to protect Marion. On the other hand, Warden had been a major source of their income for years, too profitable for them to give him up. Warden was intelligent and cognizant of their greed. He defended his scheme, saying he had once lived with the Jeddlers for six weeks and knew how to read them. As a result, Warden wrested an agreement from the law office, which would send him six hundred pounds a month while he was abroad with Marion."

Having heard Gorchakov's explanation, the directing class all supported the use of a regular square table and armchairs for the law office.

As the drama unfolds, Marion doesn't run away with Warden. Instead, she goes to her aunt's and stays there for six years. In the final scene, Warden and Marion both return to the small town. Everyone is shocked except for Dr. Jeddler, who has been in correspondence with Marion all these years. In fact, with a broken heart Warden has never stopped looking for his love, Marion, and his misery and suffering have made him a better man now. In the end, he and Marion get married, so the play ends in a reunion.

Such a perfect ending bothered Yomei, however. She felt this was too neat, somewhat like a grand reunion in

traditional Chinese drama, which could feel too facile.
She shared her misgivings with Professor Gorchakov and
asked him whether the director could change the ending
if necessary. He looked surprised, lowering his eyes for a
moment, as if lost in thought. He then said to the whole
class, "The director can change any part of a play. As a
matter of fact, Stanislavski never hesitated to make changes.
For instance, in the play *The Two Orphans*, directed by both
him and me, we added a beginning, a scene at a bakery
to highlight the food shortage, that wasn't in the original
script at all. The French playwrights' version started with a
scene of revolt—such a historical happening was so powerful
that it could have overwhelmed the audience. Yomei's
question touches on a serious issue, namely how much
creative freedom the director can have. There shouldn't be
any restriction on small changes. As for a drastic change
like altering the perfect reunion at the end of the play, we
have to be very careful. If we make a major change like that,
we must give convincing justification." He then raised his
face to the class and asked about their understanding of the
final scene. None of them agreed with Yomei.

Gorchakov continued, "Behind Yomei's question lies the
uncertainty of whether we believe that a rake can reform
himself into a decent man. In Warden's case, I believe he
can—he has suffered for love, and it's love that has made him
a better man with a soul now, so I have no problem with his
final union with Marion."

"That's true," Yomei agreed, feeling the sincerity of her
teacher's remarks and glad that the issue was clarified for
her. Now she was clearer about the possibilities and the
limits of a director's creative freedom.

Besides *The Battle of Life*, Gorchakov was directing another
play, *Tanya*, by Alexei Arbuzov. It was a contemporary

work, which Yomei had seen two years back, staged at the
Revolution Theater in Moscow. But the war had scattered
the actors of the play, so now Gorchakov was responsible
for reassembling an acting crew and bringing the play
back to the stage. Yomei loved this play and felt it was
closer to the current zeitgeist. She was amazed to see the
heroine Tanya's emotional growth parallel her separation
from her husband. Tanya overhears her husband Herman
expressing his love for another woman in their own home
in a Siberian town; then, without letting him know, she
leaves home to give birth to their son alone, determined
to bring him up on her own in a suburb of Moscow. But
the boy dies of illness, and then she is sent to practice
medicine in a mining area in Siberia. One afternoon she
risks her life, trudging twenty miles in a blizzard to save
the life of a sick child, who turns out to be Herman's son
with the other woman. What impressed Yomei was that
Tanya used to think she might become helpless with love
at the sight of her husband again, but it turns out that she
finds herself changed when they actually meet toward the
end. In her own words, now her "girlhood is over." Indeed,
she has become a woman, a strong, remarkable one. Yomei
especially loved some small details in the play. For instance,
the miners, to express their gratitude for her pulling the
baby out of danger, present Tanya with a gift—a large,
fresh cucumber, grown by the scientific method in the
wintertime. At the very end, Tanya and her new lover plan
to enjoy the cucumber together that evening, presumably
to make a salad with it. Such a small touch made the drama
concrete and memorable. Another marvelous detail that
stuck in Yomei's mind was a thermos flask of coffee the
mine's manager gives Tanya before she sets out into the
blizzard to save the sick child. Such a considerate gesture

foreshadows the genuine friendship and love between them in the end.

Because of her fondness of this play, Yomei would always hang around when Gorchakov was working with the cast of student actors, even though she was supposed to focus her directing coursework more on *The Battle of Life*.

· *Twenty-Two* ·

The first weekend of September, Yomei and Lily went
to their little piece of land to gather the potatoes they
had planted. For months they'd done nothing about
the crop, but they were now amazed to see the abundant
yield. They dug around the plants with a small spade and
let the spuds dry in the sun before they put them into
cloth sacks. They were excited to see such a bumper crop,
which felt like a godsend. The Russian soil was so rich that
you could practically plant any crop into it and let it grow
by itself. It was so different from back in China, where
you at least had to water the seedlings to keep them from
withering. That afternoon, they carried back two bags of
potatoes, each about sixty pounds, which kept them fed for
three months.

With Lily working more hours at the broadcasting
station, there was enough food for both of them. They were
like two birds in one nest, sharing everything. With the
heads of their beds adjoining, they chatted at length every
night before going to sleep. Lily confessed that Young Zeng,
the man with shifty round eyes who was formerly in charge
of the section of Chinese archives at the Comintern and was
now working for the Department of Internal Affairs of the
USSR, often turned up at the broadcasting station to see

her. Apparently he was eager to get close to her, probably wanting to start a relationship. "What do you think of Zeng?" she asked Yomei in the darkness one night.

"Well, it depends on whether you like him. Do you?"

"I don't know. He's a little slippery. Every time we meet, he'll say something bad about others, as if he has inside information on everyone. I can't trust him."

"Did he bad-mouth me?"

"Not really. He just said you looked down on him."

"I'll try to be good to him if you go with him. But doesn't he look handsome to you? He has a strong build."

"He looks fine, but he's full of airs and always tries to show how consequential he is. I often wonder what can justify his kind of insolence. Honestly, lots of men give me the creeps. I still can't forget the woman dumped into the sea by the drunk from the steamer I was taking with my mom."

"That was long ago. You were just a toddler then."

"But I can't get it out of my head. How about you? Have you heard from Lucas?"

"No," Yomei said matter-of-factly. "I don't take him as a boyfriend, so I don't expect to hear from him. I'm wondering what has happened to Reslie, though. He promised to write to me, but I haven't heard from him."

"So he's your boyfriend?"

"I wouldn't say that, but we share the same passion for theater. He was a fine actor and should have a bright future if he stays in the field."

"You know anything can happen on the front. Also, letters go astray easily nowadays."

"I hope he's all right," Yomei said in a half whisper.

That weekend she wrote to Reslie's parents in Kansk and asked about their son. She just said she was a fellow student

of his, using the common term "comrade" and not wanting
to give the impression that she was his girlfriend. She
wrote: "All his friends at the theater school are concerned,
because none of us has heard from him after he left. Please
share the news about him if you have any."

Soon they wrote back, saying they hadn't heard from
Reslie directly either, but three months earlier they'd been
informed that their son was injured in an air attack by
the Germans. He was sent to some field hospital, then no
word about him came anymore. They had made inquiries
with the military and were told that Reslie was classified as
missing in action.

This news upset Yomei and others who knew Reslie,
including Gorchakov. The professor kept saying Reslie was
quick on the uptake and could have become an excellent
director if he had continued to study at the theater institute.
"This damned war has destroyed so many young talents!"
said Gorchakov.

To Yomei's surprise, toward the end of 1943 she heard
from Lin Biao from Yan'an. He wrote that he'd gotten
married in the summer and that his bride was Yeh Qun,
whom Yomei might know since they both had attended the
Counter-Japanese Military and Political University at the
same time years back. Honestly, Lin Biao wrote, he hadn't
planned to marry at all, but his friends and colleagues in
Yan'an had all urged him to form a family without further
delay so that he could concentrate on work and military
operations. That was how this marriage had taken place.
He didn't say whether he loved his new wife, and was just
writing to inform Yomei of his current marital status. He
also mentioned that he still remembered her fondly and
thanked her for the wonderful time he had spent with her
in Moscow.

His letter puzzled Yomei in some way. She showed it to Lily, who chuckled after reading it. Lily said, "Do you know Lin Biao's bride?"

"Not really. I don't remember her at all. But her name sounds familiar."

"He seems unable to forget you. This means you can still bewitch him."

"Come now, he's more like an uncle, fourteen years older than me."

"Any young woman can fall for him easily. He's a top commander in the Red Army, also the youngest."

"Why did he tell me he was married?" Yomei mused out loud.

"Didn't he promise to wait for you? Now he broke his word, so he asked for your forgiveness."

"He doesn't sound apologetic at all."

"He doesn't need to. He means to tell you not to wait for him anymore. He's decent in this regard."

"Truth to tell, I've never waited for him. I didn't take him as a boyfriend or fiancé."

"But from his perspective, you might have been waiting for him."

"I can't see why he was so self-assured."

"He's remarkable. One of the most capable generals in the Red Army. How many women can resist that?"

"You sound like you might be interested in him." Yomei smiled, narrowing her eyes.

"You know I like capable men. For me, a man's looks don't mean much. It's the inner strength that matters."

"But shouldn't a man be attractive to you first? There're distinguished men I know personally, but I can think of them at most as friends. As a woman, I can't be attracted to them."

"To be honest, I prefer to become single if I can't find an outstanding man." Lily let out a sigh.

"But isn't a man like Lin Biao outstanding? Would you marry him if he proposed?"

"Well, honestly, Yomei, I'm not sure if I could refuse. Any girl would feel greatly honored to be with a legendary man like him. You're luckier than others, you know?"

"I wish I were attracted to him, but we don't live in legends. I just can't love him like a woman ought to love a man. You know what I mean."

"Of course I know. You mean you can't go to bed with him, but look at our mothers and all the aunties. How many of them got married for love? A lot of them were assigned by the Party to form a union with a man chosen for them."

"I wish I could be like them, but I just can't do that. I have to be faithful to my own heart."

"You're the only Chinese woman I know who thinks this way."

"So I'm an odd one?"

"In a manner of speaking, you are. Perhaps to our compatriots, we're all oddities. When we're back in our country, I'm sure many Chinese might peg us as foreign girls, also as social cripples."

"Probably you're right."

Yomei wrote back to Lin Biao to congratulate him on his new marriage and briefly described her situation in Moscow, saying that she and Lily were like sisters now and helped each other manage their life and work and studies here, and that she was going to go back to China in two or three years.

· Twenty-Three ·

Besides her busy studies at the theater institute, Yomei still did volunteer work with her schoolmates. In the spring of 1944, she was assigned to help in Red Aurora Confectionery factory, which was now mainly manufacturing military rations: canned food, hardtack, soft drink powder, even cigarettes. She went there two days a week. The volunteers were not paid but were allowed to eat their fill in the factory. One of the workshops was still making sweets: taffy, orange drops, hard bonbons, assorted chocolates. The volunteers were allowed to eat as many candies as they wanted, especially the malformed ones, but they mustn't take any home. On the first day, Yomei was excited to have free candies, but soon she was sated, in spite of her sweet tooth. From the third day on, she didn't touch the candies anymore. Yet she liked the work there, which enabled her to help the soldiers on the front. The women workers were cheerful and often sang patriotic songs together, and Yomei would join them in their songfests and jot down any lyrics that were new to her.

Lily was fascinated by Yomei's volunteer work at the confectionery factory and said she wished she could go there once a week so that she could eat so many candies that she wouldn't have needed the sugar ration anymore. Yomei

promised to swipe some sweets for her, though it might be
hard, because the candies were also a military ration, and
the factory's rule prohibited anyone from taking them out
of its premises. The next time Yomei worked there, she put
on a denim jumper skirt with a belt at the waist. When her
shift was over, she slipped two pieces of chocolate into the
front of her dress in hopes of smuggling them through the
front gate. If the guard frisked the leaving workers, she'd
loosen her belt beforehand so that the candies could drop to
the ground before she reached the gate. Lucky for her, the
middle-aged guard recognized her as a volunteer, so with a
gappy smile he just waved her through.

Back in the Hotel Lux, Lily was so thrilled to have the
chocolates that she ate only half a piece at a time. Yomei said
this was the first time she had ever pilfered something, but
she was happy to see her friend so beside herself with joy
and satisfying her sweet tooth.

She planned to take back candies for Lily more often,
regardless of the rule and her unease. Fortunately her
volunteer work at the confectionery factory ended a
week later, and the students were sent to help dismantle
barricades and antitank hedgehogs to facilitate traffic
and restore the former cityscape. The Nazi army was in
retreat now, and unlikely to come again. Evidently the
Soviet and Allied forces would be able to defeat Hitler's
army. From time to time columns of German POWs in
tattered uniforms and collapsed boots marched through
the streets of Moscow. Some wobbled along on crutches.
In silence people watched them pass by, some limping and
a few hobbling, all hanging their heads. In spite of their
anger, the spectators never turned violent. At most, a few
babushkas spat at them. Now, even the few Chinese expats
in the capital grew restless, and some started talking about

going back to China to fight the Japanese invaders and also
to found a new country.

As the war continued, with one victory after another,
food supplies improved considerably in Moscow in 1944.
Late that year, there were even U.S. cans for sale in some
stores—Spam, tuna, corned beef, luncheon loaf, beans
and peas, beef stew, sardines. Both Yomei and Lily could
see that the final defeat of fascism was on the horizon.
Though their life had become somewhat normal now, they
were busier than before. As the war seemed to be winding
down, more Chinese youngsters from the children's home
in Ivanovo were coming to Moscow for college. To facilitate
school admissions, they were supposed to get naturalized,
and some of them became Soviet citizens. Yomei and Lily
often went to the railway station to receive the girls. A
number of boys got into Bauman Moscow State Technical
University, but they had friends in the city and didn't need
Yomei and Lily to help them. Among the girls they received
were Lily's younger sister Linlin, Oyang Fei, Zhang Maya,
and others. Maya's mother was Zhang Ch'in-ch'iu, the
highest-ranking female officer in the Chinese Red Army,
who used to be the only woman commander of a division.
Unlike the others, Oyang Fei, nicknamed Feifei, was an
orphan and had no idea who her parents had been. It was
only known that she had been saved and brought over to be
raised in the Soviet Union after her parents had been killed
in the mid-1920s by the Nationalists. Yomei and Lily did
their best to accommodate the girls and also showed them
around a little.

But when it got cold, they couldn't receive others as
before, because they no longer had their own room in the
Hotel Lux. To save fuel, half of the houses and buildings
in Moscow were shut down—people had to share heated

rooms with others in the winter. Yomei and Lily's room was closed, so they'd have to stay with others. Unexpectedly, Ryo Nosaka, a short, plump woman who was the wife of Sanzo

Linlin, Yomei, and Lily in Moscow, July 1945

Nosaka, the president of the Japanese Communist Party, noticed the two young Chinese women's predicament. Ryo and her adopted daughter were living in a heated suite on the third floor of the Hotel Lux, so she invited Yomei and Lily to stay with her family, telling Yomei that her father Zhou Enlai was a good friend of her husband's. "Your father is so handsome, like a movie star," Ryo once told Yomei. Yomei replied, "Yes, that was why I have him as my dad." Both Mrs. Nosaka and Lily laughed. Ryo said it should be the other way around because a child couldn't choose its parents.

Yomei happened to know something about Nosaka, who was in Yan'an now and who had been close to the top CCP leaders. Under the Comintern's order four years before, he had gone there to help the Chinese people fight the Japanese invasion, supervising a small institute of Japan studies

in Yan'an. His staff combed newspapers and magazines
published in both Japan and China, followed the radio
broadcasts, and analyzed the information they gathered.
Thanks to Nosaka's dedication, Yan'an's intelligence work
on Japan and its military was brought up to date. In the red
base he began to publish in Chinese as well, using the pen
name Lin Zhe. As Otto Braun had, he asked for a female
companion, and the CCP assigned a pretty young woman
named Zhuang Tao to be his partner. Yomei shared what
she'd heard about Sanzo Nosaka with Lily, saying that Ryo
might have been abandoned by her husband, though the
woman often bragged that she and Sanzo had been married
for two decades. On the other hand, Yomei felt that Ryo
may have known the true situation of her marriage and
accepted her husband's cohabitation with a young Chinese
woman as a fait accompli—like most Communists would
under such circumstances. Every Party member had to
sacrifice their personal interests for the revolutionary cause,
so even Ryo's marital trouble might be due to the kind of
arrangement made by the former Comintern. In spite of
their unease, Yomei and Lily were pleased to have a warm
room in the Japanese woman's suite.

Soon after they had moved in with Ryo, she asked them
to fetch lunch for her because she couldn't leave her small
girl alone in the flat and the cafeteria was too far away, in
the basement. Yomei and Lily agreed to get lunch for her,
since Ryo would let them keep the soup served for her at the
meal. The two would alternate running the errand, but as
it wasn't easy to climb with a plate and a bowl full of soup
up all the way from the dining hall to Ryo's suite, they just
ate the soup in the cafeteria before bringing back lunch.
Often they complained between themselves that Ryo was
too stingy to let them have any solid food. For her work at

the broadcasting station, Lily got one meal ticket a day, but
Ryo, even though not working, received two meal tickets
every day. More unfair was that she ate much better food.
Living in the same suite with her, Yomei and Lily saw what
mother and daughter would eat at breakfast: white bread,
hard butter, sour cream, raspberry jam, cheese, fried
peanuts, bologna, ham, preserved fruit; some of those items
had been hard for common people to come by even before
the war. More amazing, Ryo would drink coffee and tea
with honey and creamer every morning. Small wonder the
woman didn't need the soup served at lunch—she already
got enough nutrition from other foods.

   More outrageous was that they soon discovered that Ryo
had foodstuffs stashed away deep in a closet, which Yomei
called "the little granary." In there were stacked bags of
rice, millet, cornmeal, wheat flour, peas, and soybeans,
some already moldy and wormy. In private, Yomei and Lily
often sighed, saying that was "a lifetime's supply of food,"
and they complained that while most people were starving,
here so much stuff was uneaten in the closet and might be
consumed only by worms and mice! Even though they knew
this was a rare case, they couldn't stop griping between
themselves. Yet despite their unease about Ryo Nosaka,
they both admitted that the woman was composed and
good-natured, always treating the child like her own. Even
though she must know her husband was living with a pretty
young woman in Yan'an, she looked untroubled and even
serene. She was an experienced Communist, and together
with her husband had been to different parts of the world,
including the United States, about which she often talked
to Yomei and Lily. She said America was a wild country,
with little civilization except for New York City and San
Francisco, but its environment was pristine, the air so

clean that you didn't need to shine your shoes for months. She often sucked her teeth when speaking, as if having a toothache. Her chubby face and bespectacled eyes plus her shiny, severe bun made her appear like a professional woman, an office lady. Ryo had met Zhou Enlai several times and told Yomei that she admired her father. "Such a nice man," she'd say, her eyes turning dreamy.

When it was getting warm, Yomei and Lily returned to their former room on the fourth floor and didn't use Ryo's lunch soup anymore. At long last, in early May the news of German surrender came, and many people, especially foreigners in Moscow, took to the streets to celebrate, singing and dancing with abandon, though most Russians remained quiet and looked sober and grim, perhaps because the weight of victory lay heavy on their minds. So many families had lost their loved ones in the war that they couldn't take the great news with the jubilation of triumph now.

Soon, many Chinese expats stranded in Central Asia returned to Moscow. They had failed to cross the Mongolian border to get back to northern China, and now they hoped they could find another way to return, either through Kazakhstan and Xinjiang or through the Trans-Siberian Railway network. But first they had to come back to Moscow to get official approval and papers. For months, Yomei and Lily were busy receiving expats who resurfaced in the capital. Among the returnees were those officers who had studied at the KUTV and who were known to Yomei and Lily. First came Li Tianyou, a handsome young officer with a ramrod bearing who used to command a division under Lin Biao. Li had begun to attend the Frunze Military Academy in the fall of 1938. When Lin Biao was returning to Yan'an from Moscow at the beginning of 1941, Li left too, but he couldn't take the same route through Almaty and Tihwa that

his superior was taking. Instead, he left with some expats
for Central Asia in hopes of crossing the Sino-Mongolian
border. But like the others, he got stuck in Siberia and
couldn't move around. His return to China was smoother
than that of the others, partly because he came back to
Moscow earlier than they did—at the end of 1944. He set out
for Kazakhstan right away. Before he left, Yomei and Lily
treated him to lunch at the broadcasting station's cafeteria.
Known as the Tiger General, he was expected to return to
Yan'an as soon as possible. Now that the war in Russia was
finally over, he had to depart without delay. He said he'd tell
Lin Biao that he had met Yomei in Moscow again and that
she was prettier than before. She was about to say that Lin
Biao had a new wife now, that Li Tianyou shouldn't bring
her, Yomei, up in conversation, but she thought better of it.

A few months later their friend Grandpa, Yang Zhicheng,
came back to Moscow too, wearing a squashed felt hat as if
it were still winter. In spite of the sobriquet given him by
naughty Yomei, Yang was still not that old, only forty-one,
but he was so famished that he was scraggy and a little bent,
hardly able to walk steadily. He arrived at the Hotel Lux and
told the front desk that he wanted to see Sun Yomei and Lin
Lily. At first, the two women didn't recognize him due to his
emaciated, misshapen face. Then Yomei cried out, "Yang
Zhicheng, Grandpa, why are you here?"

"Didn't you go back to China?" added Lily.

He explained that he'd gotten stranded in Siberia and
couldn't get across to Inner Mongolia. Yomei realized he
must be hungry and had to eat at once, so she and Lily
told him to wait for them in the lobby and they'd be back
in a moment. They rushed up to their room to get their
meal tickets. But when they came down again, Grandpa
was gone. So they went out in search of him. Yomei was

worried, knowing he had no place to stay. Her plan was to
let him eat something first, then find a bed for him, but
why wouldn't he just wait for them? He must have assumed
that the two women were unable to help him, or maybe he
thought that he didn't want to be a burden to them. They
shouldn't have both gone back for the meal tickets, leaving
him alone at the front desk. Now they had to find him.

Lily found Grandpa at a tram stop and brought him
back. Yomei blamed him for running away like that. They
took him to the hotel's cafeteria, where Yomei bought a
plate of fish soup for him. He began to wolf down a hunk
of kringle, together with soup made of burbot and crushed
tomatoes. He was eating so fast that he bit his tongue, which
bled a little. "Gosh," Yomei said, "don't rush, don't eat your
own tongue!"

He grinned and nodded his shock of tousled hair. Lily
went away with a mug to get some hot tea for him.

While munching on another piece of bread, he kept
saying he must find a way back to join Commander Lin
Biao's army in Manchuria. Once he had some food in
his stomach, he grew more alive. He said the two women
friends looked prettier than before, more like foreign ladies
now. He even asked Yomei whether she was still carrying on
with General Lin Biao. To that, Yomei just answered, "He
wrote me a year and a half ago and told me that he married
a young woman in Yan'an. They might have a baby now."

"Oh, that's too bad," Grandpa said with a shrewd
twinkle in his eyes. "That wasn't like him. He should've had
more patience with a beautiful girl like you."

Yomei clapped him on the shoulder and said, "Shut up!
We'll have to find a bed for you somewhere."

They went to see Igor, the superintendent in the Hotel
Lux who was employed by the IRA, and asked him to help.

Igor was a squat man in his midthirties, with a large head and a toothbrush mustache. He was fond of the two young women and often asked if he could do something for them. To Yomei's amazement, Grandpa could speak Russian with ease now. He and Igor chatted about the Lake Baikal region, which Igor was familiar with, having grown up in Siberia. How he missed ice fishing on the lake, he told them. He assigned Grandpa a room just for himself. Yomei and Lily were delighted and told Zhicheng that they could find more food for him.

When Yomei had free time, she'd go see Grandpa and chat with him over tea. Sometimes Zhicheng would get carried away while talking to Yomei, whom he took as a close friend. Once he mentioned something that disturbed her. He said one and a half years back, in December 1943, there'd been a conference among the top CCP leaders in Yan'an. Chairman Mao presided over the meeting and demanded that every attendee do self-criticism so as to reform themselves properly. Somehow Mao singled out Zhou Enlai and asked him to confess his misdeeds in front of everyone. Zhou was so flabbergasted that he sank to his knees and apologized to Mao while blaming himself for not always having taken Mao's side in the past struggles within the Party. Grandpa described the incident to Yomei vividly. At the beginning of the conference, Chairman Mao had announced to the audience what he was doing by using the analogy of taking a bath: "This rectification effort is to make some Party members undress and drop their trousers to show their bodies. Then with the help of your comrades, you can wash yourself clean, and some will help you scrub your backs. Once you get cleaned, you will feel comfortable again, like a sick person who has recuperated." Mao concluded by declaring, "Now is Zhou Enlai's turn. Please undress yourself and drop your trousers." To everyone's astonishment, Zhou dropped to his knees instead and said, "I admit my crimes, I admit my crimes, Chairman." Mao was startled and cried sharply, "Why are you doing this? This is like calling me names, as if I were an emperor." Zhou replied, "Chairman, you're the emperor of China's revolution. Both Comrade Liu Shaoqi and I agree about this—you're our emperor. Without you at the helm, our ship would capsize."

"That might be just hearsay!" Yomei said crossly.

"Anyhow," Grandpa went on, "you shouldn't take this to be merely a rumor. We all know that on the Long March Zhou Enlai at times washed Chairman Mao's sore feet. That was his way of showing his love and reverence for our great leader."

Yomei knew that Father Zhou had opposed Mao several times in the past decades, but she didn't believe what Grandpa had told her. That must be a malicious rumor or slander. She demanded to know the source of this hearsay. Hard as she tried, Grandpa wouldn't reveal anything more and just said he'd heard about the incident from someone who was at the conference. He shook his head and kept giggling.

In spite of Yomei's disbelief, the rumor did throw a shadow on her mind, and for weeks she couldn't shake off the image of Father Zhou kneeling in front of Chairman Mao at a meeting, calling him "Emperor" and begging for mercy.

Early that summer came Zhong Chibing, who had been a comrade in arms of Grandpa's, so Igor allowed them to share the same room in the Hotel Lux. The superintendent was so generous that he gave them each a meal ticket for dinner in the cafeteria. They could eat there six times a week. That solved the problem of their board. Like Li Tianyou and Yang Zhicheng, Zhong was also a remarkable officer, but he looked more like a scholar—he wore horn-rimmed glasses and had lost his right leg and left thumb after being wounded in battles back in China. With a single leg, he had managed to complete the nine-thousand-mile trek (the Long March) and become a legendary figure in the Red Army. Then, in the summer of 1938, he was sent to the Soviet Union to get medical treatment and to study. The Russian doctors operated on the stump of his right leg and stopped it from getting infected again. (He had undergone three operations back in Yan'an, treated intermittently by the Canadian surgeon Dr. Norman Bethune, but the infection couldn't be checked. As a consequence, he'd lost the entire leg.) Then he attended the Frunze Military Academy together with Grandpa and Li Tianyou, and they all graduated at the same time in the summer of 1941 when the Germans started the blitzkrieg on the Soviet Union. But Zhong Chibing was particularly close to Liu Yalou, Yomei's other passionate suitor among the expat officers. Together with Yalou, Chibing went to Central Asia, but Yalou was recruited by the Soviet Eighty-Eighth Infantry Brigade in Khabarovsk and was still serving there as a colonel. Chibing revealed to Yomei that his friend Liu Yalou had often mentioned her, saying that the only woman who could possess his heart was Sun Yomei. Evidently he hadn't given up on her, so she'd better be prepared for that man to pop up in her life again, given that the war was over and he might leave the Soviet army. Yomei

Liu Yalou, Yomei's
passionate suitor,
in the Frunze Military
Academy, 1940

begged him, "Please, don't deputize your buddy like this! Liu Yalou is already a family man."

Liu and Zhong would remain close friends indeed. In the following decade Liu Yalou and Zhong Chibing would still work as a pair, Liu in charge of China's air force and Zhong running the country's civil aviation.

Those officers who resurfaced in Moscow would play significant roles in the CCP's military. Soon after the establishment of the PRC in 1949, Li Tianyou and Yang Zhicheng became three-star generals, though Zhong Chibing was given two stars, probably because his work focused more on the civil services by then.

Left to right: Yang Zhicheng ("Grandpa"), Yomei,
Li Tianyou, Lily, and Lu Dongsheng, who was also a general
educated and trained in the Soviet Union

· Twenty-Four ·

Following the returned officers, some cultural workers also resurfaced in Moscow. Five years earlier, the CCP had dispatched a filming crew to the Soviet Union to complete the last portion of a documentary titled *Yan'an and the Eighth Route Army*, which was intended to boost the image of the CCP and the Red Army internationally. But the war kept the crew from going back, and they had become expats stranded in the interior of the USSR. Among them were actors, cameramen, directors, and playwrights. There was also the composer Sinn Sing Hoi, who also resurfaced in Moscow now. Sinn had attended the Paris Conservatory, studying composition with Paul Dukas and Vincent d'Indy. Legend had it that when he had passed his audition and been admitted by the French conservatory, the school had intended to grant him an award and asked him what he'd like to have. Already delirious with hunger, he had managed to say, "Meal tickets." So they gave him a thick booklet of them. Later, Sinn composed music in all the major forms and became the author of China's national anthem. He came to the Soviet Union with the filming crew and was marooned here with them by the war. He had gone to Kazakhstan but not been able to cross the border, because Sheng Shicai, the warlord in Xinjiang, had turned

against the CCP and begun suppressing red elements in his
territory. Thus travel between the USSR and Tihwa stopped.

During this hard period, Sinn Sing Hoi composed
continuously. Even in the Soviet Union his music found
admirers, thanks to a distinct style that often combined
Chinese folk music and classic European music, and he
became a popular figure in Almaty, where he had been
biding his time before returning to China. It happened that
a young woman, Leora, the head of a local music school,
fell in love with him and offered to take care of him. Soon
they began living together. He was uncomfortable about
her devotion and affection and told her that he was already
married and loved his wife, to whom he'd go back sooner or
later. But Leora had no problem with that, saying she just
loved his talent and wanted to care for him while he was
in the Soviet Union. In fact, he did need her help, because
he had TB and the only foreign language he knew was
French. With Leora's assistance, he could get around and
mix with the locals. And with some Kazakhstan composers'
endorsements, he often performed in the cities and towns
in that region and gained some popularity.

Now that the war was over, he thought he might get
back to China by way of Moscow, so he came to the capital,
accompanied by Leora. He had no idea where to get help
and went to the Foreign Language Press, which had once
published his music. The Chinese Communist Li Lisan
happened to be a translator at the press, and, seeing Sinn's
plight, he offered to take him and Leora home and to find
them the help they needed. But first they had to eat, so Li
Lisan took them to the press's dining room and got lunch
for them. While they were eating, Lily came to deliver a
piece of translation—a rush job that she had just completed
for the press, where she had heard about the arrival of Sinn

Sing Hoi. It was big news to her, since Sinn was regarded
as the number one composer in China. She thought Yomei
must have known Sinn personally, so she hurried back
to the Hotel Lux to tell her friend about his appearance
in town. Indeed, Yomei had attended the arts college in
Yan'an, where Sinn used to head the music department.
Above all, she loved his music, especially his *Yellow River
Cantata*. Right away she and Lily set off for the Foreign
Language Press to see the composer.

Yomei was shocked to see how sickly Sinn looked. He
used to be strong and handsome in Yan'an, but now he
was so pallid that he looked like an old man, with half of
his hair gray, though he was barely forty. Worse, his jacket
draped on a chair in Lisan's office was like rags, its lining
tattered with holes. Yomei hugged him, trying hard to
force down her tears. Following them, she and Lily went
to Li Lisan's home, which they were told was nearby. She
hadn't seen Li's wife Lisa for more than three years and
was eager to reconnect with her. Lily had told Yomei that
Leora must be Sinn's mistress, so Yomei couldn't warm up
to the Russian woman. She had met the composer's wife,
Chian Yunling, an excellent music teacher and a loving
wife to Sinn. Mrs. Sinn had once treated some students
at the Yan'an arts college to a kind of makeshift coffee she
prepared herself—baked soy powder mixed with brown
sugar. That was the first time Yomei had tasted "coffee,"
which, despite its fakeness, had nonetheless left with her the
fond memory of that mild, kindhearted woman. Yomei also
knew that the couple had a lovely baby girl, but now why on
earth would Mr. Sinn cohabit with this Russian brunette,
who was skinny like a whippet and had glassy eyes? All the
way, Yomei kept some distance from Leora, though Lily said
a word or two to her from time to time.

To their astonishment, Li Lisan's home was merely a single room, less than two hundred square feet, which belonged to Lisa's mother and was shared by six people. It was partitioned along the middle by a row of bookshelves. Li Lisan and Lisa and their two-year-old girl used half of the room, and the other half was for Lisa's mother and sister-in-law and her little nephew. Li Lisan's "home" had only one bed, which he let Sinn and Leora use, while he and Lisa and their baby were going to sleep on the floor. Yomei and Lisa hugged warmly like friends. Lisa said, "It's miracle we can meet again. So many people disappeared in the war."

Yomei turned to the baby girl: "Inna, what do you call me in Chinese?"

The two-year-old stared at her with amazement and confusion. Her mother stepped in: "She hasn't learned Chinese yet. How could she call you Auntie in Mandarin?"

Lily held up Inna, who giggled, eager to play with both young women. She looked similar to her father, with the same color of eyes, skin, and hair. Yomei showed her a book, and pointing at the characters on the cover, she asked the girl, "Do you know this word? It means 'one.'"

The girl didn't know any Chinese characters either, yet when Yomei gave her another book, whose title was upside-down, the girl looked at it, then turned it right. That made both Yomei and Lily laugh and wonder aloud how she could tell the correct order of the characters. Lisa assured them that it was in the girl's blood. If they had handed the book in the wrong order to her nephew, the five-year-old wouldn't have noticed anything unusual at all.

Yomei then told Lisa that Mr. Sinn used to be a teacher of hers, and she thanked her for being so generous to him. Evidently, Lisa was devoted to her husband in spite of his trouble with the Soviet government. Yomei had heard

that for a long time Li Lisan couldn't find employment
and that only the Foreign Language Press had hired him
lately because he was fluent in Russian and could translate
Chinese books. They paid him on a piecework basis. On
their way back, Lily and Yomei talked about the Lis. They
were both touched by the Lis' accommodating Sinn and
his mistress. Lily again mentioned how Young Zeng at the
Comintern used to bad-mouth Li Lisan, referring to him
as though Li were contagious with a disease. Indeed, for a
long time Lily had viewed Li Lisan as a problematic figure
tainted with historical mistakes he had made, but today she
couldn't help but think differently. Yomei told her that she
had met Li Lisan and Lisa three years go and would never
believe they were potential enemies. Instead, she took them
as friends.

Yomei's view cast a shadow on Lily's mind and forced
her to reevaluate the character of Young Zeng, who seemed
to enjoy belittling others and seeing them suffer. She
told Yomei, "Young Zeng is a liar—he said Li Lisan was a
Trotskyist, an enemy of the Soviet government, so we must
shun him. But just now we saw how solicitous and generous
he was to Sinn Sing Hoi. I believe Li Lisan is a genuine
comrade, a good man."

Yomei said, "I can't tell what political faction Li Lisan
belongs to in the Party, but the way he treats his family and
his comrades has shown he's a decent man, kindhearted and
trustworthy. I just cannot take Young Zeng's admonishment
seriously. He is a mean and small-minded asshole. You
should stay away from him."

They talked about Sinn's plight as well, believing
they must do something to help. They went to see
Superintendent Igor and described Sinn as an artist with
international renown and asked him to help the composer

in extremis. He should give Sinn the room vacated by Grandpa and his one-legged buddy Zhong Chibing, who both had just left for Harbin by the railroad. Igor jotted down the information about Sinn and said he would report to his superior and figure out how to help.

Back in their room, Yomei realized they had left behind their galoshes at the Lis, thanks to their excitement just now. But they'd be going there anyway, to give whatever help they could to Mr. Sinn, and could retrieve the overshoes then.

To their delight, Igor informed them the next afternoon that his superior at the IRA had instructed him to provide room and board for Sinn. Without delay, Yomei and Lily hurried to the Lis and told them the good news. Lisa was relieved and kept thanking them. She said to Yomei under her breath, "Mr. Sinn coughs a lot and must have TB. I was worried last night. We have a baby, who is vulnerable to infectious disease."

Yomei said, "That was why we felt it imperative to find private lodgings for him and Leora."

Li Lisan went into ecstasies too and told Yomei that this solution helped relieve his feeling of guilt toward his in-laws. He thought that everyone in Lisa's family had been suffering for his sake.

"I'll write to Father Zhou and Mother Deng to report your generous help for Mr. Sinn," Yomei told him.

He smiled appreciatively.

The Soviet government intervened on Sinn's behalf as well. Stalin liked his music and gave orders to the IRA administration that they arrange medical help for Sinn. He was soon shipped to the Kremlin Hospital, but by then his condition had deteriorated. Yomei and Lily often went

to see him, and he told them about his relationship with
Leora, saying it was just a temporary arrangement and he
couldn't wait to return to his wife and daughter back in
Yan'an.

  Though he was hospitalized, Leora was now using his
room at the Hotel Lux. She presented herself as Sinn's
woman, and felt the IRA ought to make arrangements for her
as well, finding her a job, getting her a residential certificate,
a ration book, and assorted coupons. In the Hotel Lux,
there were a good number of Jews from other countries.
Because Leora was partly Jewish, she got to know some of the
international Jews living at the hotel. Yomei and Lily found
them as close to each other as if they had been from the same
town. Some were ready to give Leora a hand when she needed
help. Somehow they also viewed her as Sinn's woman, so
they believed she should be the responsibility of the Chinese
comrades too. When bumping into Yomei and Lily, some of
the Jewish women blamed them for not taking care of those
connected to the Chinese community, like Leora. But what
she needed were rubles. At most the two of them could get
five hundred a month after taxes, just enough for themselves.
At this time, their room was under repair, so they stayed
in a big suite together with seven foreign women—three
Spaniards, one Romanian, two Italians, and one Hungarian.
Out of obligation, Yomei and Lily felt they had to help Leora,
so they borrowed money from their roommates and handed
two hundred rubles to her.

  By and by, Leora's situation improved. She got a teaching
position in town and wore a tartan skirt and knee-high
boots with brass buttons when going to work. She would
also have on a black cape with a lavender silk lining. If it
was chilly, she would put on an embroidered purple shawl
with tiny tassels. Even more unexpectedly, she managed to

hold on to all the rights to Sinn's unpublished music. She didn't go to the hospital to attend him anymore. In contrast, Yomei and Lily often went to see Sinn, who was still in high spirits and had wild hopes, telling them that once the revolution succeeded, the CCP would build a grand musical hall in the capital, constructed of white stone. He hoped he would perform in it someday. He was particularly delighted to know that Yomei was studying theater arts and urged her to master the Stanislavski method and bring "the artistic fire" back to China. "Our country will need genuine artists more than generals and engineers," he told her.

In late October, his illness took a turn for the worse, and he slipped into a coma. The doctors couldn't do a thing for him anymore, and he died at the end of the month.

Yomei and Lily did as much as they could to help Li Lisan and Lisa in arranging for Mr. Sinn's funeral and memorial service. He was interred in a suburban public cemetery. At the funeral service, the Soviet Georgian composer Vano Muradeli delivered a moving speech, a part of which he later used as the lyrics of the popular song "Russian Man and Chinese Man Are Brothers Forever," which he himself composed:

Russian man and Chinese man are brothers forever.
The unity of peoples and races grows stronger,
A simple man has straightened his shoulders,
A simple man strides forward with a song
While Stalin and Mao are listening to us . . .

Some people in Soviet music circles were eager to put on a concert in Sinn's memory to have his most recent compositions performed, but they couldn't get permission from Leora, who held all the rights now. Later a Moscow publisher was interested in bringing out the collected sheet music by Sinn, but they could not secure the rights from Leora and had to give up the plan.

Two weeks after Sinn's funeral in Moscow, there was a huge memorial service in Yan'an attended by the top CCP leaders and people from various walks of life. Despite Sinn's radical political stance his death was considered a great loss to the Chinese music world. Many major newspapers printed his obituary.

· Twenty-Five ·

As more and more expats returned to China, Lily wanted to go back too. She had finished her education in the Soviet Union and was eager to participate in revolutionary work back home, now that Japan had surrendered and there was so much to do in China. In the late fall of 1945, she submitted her request for permission to the CCP's External Liaison Department, which was in charge of the expats. She would be allowed to go back toward the end of that year or at the beginning of 1946. She was excited about the prospect of seeing her father in Yan'an. Also, she missed her homeland.

But Yomei couldn't return together with her now, since she still had a semester to go at the theater institute. She insisted that they go back together, so Lily should wait for her until she graduated. Lily could see that Yomei might not be able to survive on her own in Moscow, since she was careless about her life, even willing to starve so as to have more time for her studies at the theater school. She had become an assistant director to Professor Gorchakov and was busy directing two plays as her graduation projects. Once the plays were staged, she would graduate as a full-fledged director and could go home. Her ambition now was to become a pioneer figure in Chinese spoken drama, bringing back and

disseminating the Stanislavski method. Some senior faculty
at the theater institute had mentioned to Yomei the goals of
the Soviet Ministry of Culture, which viewed her as an expert
in theater arts—a kind of cultural export to China. But she
wasn't bothered by the official goals at all. She took herself
as an artist, entirely dedicated to theater arts, who should be
able to exist outside the arena of politics.

Lily agreed to wait half a year for Yomei. In the
meantime, she'd keep working at the broadcasting station,
where some other expats were employed too, so her job was
more pleasant now. Insofar as one of them worked, Yomei
would be fed. For her friend, Lily was willing to endure
another harsh Moscow winter.

Young Zeng somehow came to know of Lily's request
for return, so he began to visit her more often, most times
wearing a checked cap and a plaid button-down. He went so
far as to ask her to live in Moscow for good, implying they
might wind up a couple, but she made it clear that she was
staying on only for Yomei, not for him. Yomei once ribbed
her, saying, "To many women, Young Zeng seems a suitable
man. He's smart and savvy about life in Russia. In some
ways he's remarkable. Don't you think?"

"True, a remarkable snob," Lily said. "I can't trust him.
I find him odious. He always puts on a mysterious air,
wearing a woolen army greatcoat in the winter. He enjoys
looking powerful. He's vain and likes showing off his
connections, as if he were superior to the other expats and
has lots of friends in high places. He makes me disgusted."

"I'm floored. I thought you and he were seeing each
other in earnest of late."

"Come on, you and I have been together all the time.
How could I start seeing someone seriously without letting
you know?"

"That's true, but keep in mind, no one is perfect. Maybe you should be more tolerant of a man if you really want to date someone."

"At this point in my life, I don't want to date anyone at all. I'm not a tolerant person. I can tolerate you but not somebody like Young Zeng," Lily said with a straight face.

"Am I that awful, having to be tolerated?" said Yomei with a twinkle in her eyes.

"You're my friend I can trust totally, but Young Zeng is different. If I can't find a trustworthy man, I will remain single. I don't mind becoming a spinster."

"Neither do I. We can stay together as a pair of old maids."

"Please, Yomei, everybody can see you're beautiful. There're always outstanding men smitten with you. Your problem is how to stay away from them."

"But I still want us to be together, always. Can you promise me that?"

"OK, that's what I want too. That's why I'll be waiting for you to graduate."

Yomei hugged her tightly, saying they were true sisters.

· Twenty-Six ·

I n the summer of 1945, a Chinese cultural delegation came to visit the Soviet Union. Among the delegates was the pro-Communist poet and scholar Guo Moruo, who had been a longtime time friend of Yomei's father's. So she was eager to see the old man, who was also from Sichuan and who used to visit Yomei's parents back home. But then Young Zeng appeared at the broadcasting station one afternoon. Flapping his red-rimmed eyes, he told Lily that none of them should go see Mr. Guo because the man was affiliated with the Nationalist government in Chongqing and was a reactionary. Though it was already hot these days, Zeng was wearing a black trilby hat that covered his balding head and that made him appear foppish. Lily was baffled by his eagerness to prevent others from meeting Guo Moruo. In fact, Guo was known as a progressive intellectual and a Communist sympathizer. On top of that, he had been a friend of Zhou Enlai's for decades. Mao Zedong also liked him.

Young Zeng's meddling infuriated Yomei, who believed that his admonishment was merely his own little maneuver. Regardless, she went to see Guo Moruo and even took Lily along with her, saying it would do her friend good to get to know the dignitary, who was also an accomplished

playwright and archeologist, a man of letters par excellence.
Together they went to the Moskva Hotel, where the cultural
delegation was staying. Mr. Guo, wearing a herringbone
suit and a silk necktie, was delighted to see Yomei. He
noticed Lily's nervous state but didn't ask why. He praised
Yomei for studying theater arts, saying she would become
a force that the older generation in China's theater circle
would have to reckon with, and that it would be wonderful
if she could direct one of his plays someday. He gave them
each a business card whose embossed words said that
he was the head of the Third Bureau of the Nationalist
government's Political Department, that he was the author
of the long poem *Goddess*, and the translator of *War and Peace*.

They also talked about Father Zhou and Chairman
Mao, who had both been in Chongqing lately and met Mr.
Guo. He assured her that they were well, that there should
be a peaceful time ahead now that Japan had surrendered.
Seizing a moment when Lily was away to get some beverages
for them, Yomei asked him, "Uncle Guo, I have a personal
question that I hope you won't mind me asking."

"Of course not. What do you want to know?"

"It's said that two years ago my dad, Zhou Enlai, knelt in
front of Chairman Mao at a meeting. Was that true?"

"Well," said Mr. Guo. He looked astonished, his silver-
bound glasses flashing. "I was not in Yan'an, so I was not
at the scene. I heard of the rumor, though I can't tell if
it was true. Please don't take it seriously, and don't let it
affect you. You're going to be an expert in spoken drama.
Try to live a life somewhat detached from politics, which
can be capricious and perilous. Only the arts are constant
and can last."

At this point, Lily returned with a few bottles of kvass.
She said to Mr. Guo, "Try this Russian soda and see if you

like it." She uncapped a bottle and poured the foaming drink into handleless cups.

"This is rich and tastes like beer, but fruitier and yeasty," he said after a large sip. "Is it alcoholic?"

"No," Lily told him. "Everyone drinks it here, even small kids."

"This is good. I can't get tipsy as I will have to go to a public gathering."

There was a literary event that evening, a poetry reading by both Russian and Chinese poets. Mr. Guo invited Yomei and Lily to attend it with him, but they couldn't, saying they had to work and study. They knew Young Zeng would be there to keep an eye on the attendees and then report to the USSR's Department of Internal Affairs, so they'd better avoid the gathering.

Uncle Guo's indirect confirmation of the hearsay about Zhou Enlai's going to his knees made Yomei mindful. She loved Father Zhou and was glad she regarded him as no more than a paternal figure. Deep down, she knew she was attracted to him, loving his handsome looks, charismatic personality, sophisticated demeanor, discerning intelligence. If there had not been a father-daughter relationship, something more intimate might have developed between them, but now she could say for certain that he was just her father, and she ought to accept him as just that, with both his virtues and flaws.

Twenty-Seven

This academic year, Professor Gorchakov was directing two plays, a traditional one that Stanislavski had supervised originally and a contemporary one that reflected the spirit of the age. The old play was old indeed: *The Two Orphans*, by the nineteenth-century French writers Adolphe d'Ennery and Eugène Cormon. The story takes place in Paris on the eve of the French Revolution in 1789. It's about two sisters, Henrietta and Louisa, who go to Paris to live with their uncle, but then are forced to separate—Henrietta is kidnapped, while Louisa, the younger girl, who is blind, falls into the hands of thieves. Gorchakov had directed *The Two Orphans* with Stanislavski twenty years before and even given it a different title, *The Sisters Gérard*, so he knew the play like the back of his hand. Everybody viewed it as a melodrama, a genre drastically different from the drama in vogue.

Gorchakov made clear that he wanted to stage the play again mainly for the directing students to learn more about the practical aspects of theater arts. According to him, as a form, melodrama is more demanding on both the actors and the director. It is a more physical genre, packed with events and actions, totally different from the lyrical and poetic drama represented by the Chekhovian plays. It looks

simple but is actually more complicated, because it involves
so many intricate components of the theater business. The
director has to know how to build the acting cast and how
to make the best use of the actors, exploring the inner
creativity in each of them. As a form, melodrama can train
young actors and develop their potential and teach them to
act lively and passionately while still remaining expressive
and subtle. Conventionally, the actors capable of playing
melodrama occupied the highest positions in theater
companies. Therefore, Gorchakov emphasized, every one
of the directing students must participate in the rehearsal
intently and keep meticulous notes, which might come in
handy in the future when they directed on their own.

Since it was a historical play, they worked on certain
aspects carefully, such as the wardrobe, makeup, lighting,
and stage sets. They also discussed the music, which in
melodrama is often employed to generate a mood for a
situation or to get the actors ready for a bigger moment.
Every detail had to seem authentic, and there mustn't be
anything out of place or time. Because Louisa is blind, at
moments the lighting had to go darker to match her fear
and confusion in a new, unknown environment. Even the
rags worn by the beggars had to be appropriate in material
and colors. It was said that Stanislavski had always respected
the audience's attention, saying they could tell whether the
polish on an actress's fingernails was right for the period of
the play.

Yomei found it quite illuminating to work on *The Sisters
Gérard*. She was constantly learning new rules or "secrets"
about the directing business. Gorchakov often reiterated
what Stanislavski had taught him. For instance, he told
his students, "The first movements after the curtain
goes up must hold the audience's attention. That means

the beginning of a play must be simple and clear, able to establish the dramatic situation right off so as to draw the audience into the story." Yomei wrote that down and added triple asterisks next to it.

Gorchakov's way of working on the actors' dialogue was quite enlightening to her too. He did what Stanislavski had done in building the psychological intensity in a scene. He instructed the three main actors in an episode to talk only with their eyes. In other words, none of them was allowed to say a word and must "speak" just with their eyes and facial expressions. The actors and the spectators were confused at first, but as they were performing voicelessly, the drama and the message they were trying to communicate grew clear and largely comprehensible. At some point Yelena (Henrietta) couldn't hold back her words anymore and began to speak. The others followed her going verbal as well. Everyone in the rehearsal hall was struck by how colorful and intense the dialogue at once became—it was charged with inner feelings. That approach, often employed by Stanislavski, was called "the art of inner dialogue." It followed that the actor must give full attention to other actors in a scene and keep communicating with them psychologically, so that even the gaps in dialogue can become expressive. In short, actors onstage must earn the right to open their mouths.

Gorchakov summed up the principle of ideal dialogue: "Let your heart burst through your lips."

Yomei noticed a stack of large plywood boards, all coated with lacquer, leaning again the back wall of the rehearsal hall and wondered what they were for. In one scene, people in desperate search of the blind girl keep shouting, "Louisa! Louisa, where are you?" Even after they stopped calling, their voices still lingered in echoes.

Gorchakov smiled and told the students, "It took us a long time to find the way to reproduce the echoes on the stage, with a special arrangement of those boards." He went on to explain that at a rehearsal two decades before, after the shouts some echoes lingered, which pleased Stanislavski greatly. The master director asked, "How did you make that happen?" No one could answer. Then they figured out it was the ceiling design that reflected the voices. Later Gorchakov tried numerous ways to reproduce the echoes and finally settled on a special arrangement of large boards.

"The lesson is," he told the directors to be, "never neglect the minutiae, no matter how infinitesimal. You must do everything to make your play more colorful. Try to be a stickler for minor details. The accumulation of small, original touches can transform the quality of the work eventually."

That was another lesson Yomei wrote down and cherished.

For the contemporary play, Gorchakov had been directing Leonid Leonov's Invasion, whose plot used the Battle of Moscow as a backdrop, though the play was set in a small, central Russian town. Three years back, it had been staged at the Maly Theater, one of the oldest playhouses in the capital, and performed by some famous actors. For this play, Leonov received the Stalin Prize (1943), and its appearance was regarded as a significant event in contemporary Russian letters. After the war, the original actors were either too feeble to act or simply unavailable, so Gorchakov intended to bring it back to the stage again, even though he wouldn't have an experienced crew. He believed it would be better to train the younger generation, so he decided on *Invasion* as one of the last projects for the directing seniors.

Gorchakov had six assistant directors this academic year, and Yomei was one of them. She studied the play script thoroughly and wrote out the biography of every main character. She found the power of this grand, historical play rested not only in the vast canvas of the war against the fascist invasion but also in the central idea of redemption or atonement. The principal figure is Fyodor, Doctor Talanov's son, who was imprisoned for three years for killing a young woman out of frustrated passion. His release and return to his hometown coincide with the arrival of the German troops. Fyodor is embittered, cynical, and rough-edged. Naturally, his family receives him with reservations and trepidation. He asks his father's patient Kolesnikov, chairman of the District Soviet's Executive Committee, to let him join the partisan detachment so that he can fight the invaders like them. But out of caution, Kolesnikov turns him down. Later, Fyodor becomes a lone fighter, killing the Nazi soldiers on his own, but always in the same secretive manner as the partisans, leaving a "Welcome" note on the dead bodies that is signed with a pseudonym, "Andrei." On the eve of the Nazi army's attack on Moscow, Fayunin, a rogue believed already dead by the town and now handpicked by the Germans as their puppet mayor, gives a celebratory party. The German officers and the Talanovs, as dignitaries in town, are supposed to attend. But the German commandant Wibbel and his four bodyguards are shot dead on the street by a single attacker right before their arrival at the party. The attacker, a Russian man, is brought over for interrogation. The Talanovs are shocked to find that their son Fyodor turns out to be the hero, but he insists he is Andrei, the head of the partisans. The Germans can't believe him, but Fyodor counters, saying, "Do you think I want to acquire the honor of swinging from the gallows on someone else's behalf?" So his parents finally accept him as Andrei in front of the enemies and also as their son at heart.

Yomei carefully studied the scene of Fyodor's return, in which the son coughs wheezingly and asks his father to prescribe some medicine for him. Dr. Talanov does, but the prescription turns out to be the words "Justice to human beings!" Fyodor suddenly gets emotional and cries out, "Justice?" But the father offers his explanation, saying, "I had someone brought to me in the hospital recently—a young gentleman of draft age, who was also his mother's pride and joy. He shot a young lady no older than he was and then he shot himself. Unrequited love."

Those words are supposed to be the foundation of the drama, namely the idea that Fyodor killed a young woman and did a three-year prison term for it. That prompts his father to give him the "justice" prescription. Yomei believed that such a detail was so crucial for the emotional basis of the play that it should be emphasized to make a firmer dramatic underpinning. Perhaps Dr. Talanov should add a phrase to his explanation, saying to Fyodor, "Unlike you, he shot himself as well." That would emphasize the drama more. Gorchakov was delighted to hear this and agreed to add those words. He told his students that a capable director mustn't hesitate to make this kind of small adjustment to improve the dramatic effect.

He also said this play was a great challenge to both the director and the actors, because every sentence and every phrase must be said naturally and be psychologically right. While still striving for subtlety, there is the historical magnitude that must manifest the zeitgeist. Every small detail must echo the rest of the play. Indeed, Yomei could see the sophisticated directorial skills employed in developing the drama. Initially Fayunin, the puppet mayor, is like a mummy, a dead man who has returned to life, withered and subdued, but once the Germans appear, he becomes more alive. Every exploded bomb dropped by the Nazi planes pumps him up some, both mentally and physically. But in the end, when the occupiers learn that they have lost the Battle of Moscow, Fayunin begins to shrink. Eventually the Soviet army arrives and liberates the town, and he returns to his mummy state. Such an evolution of the character along with the development of the historical drama gave Yomei an indelible lesson in directing.

Unlike the plays they had produced before, *Invasion* needed original music to create a suitable mood and aura. Two theater composers were used for that job. They also made a piano piece, to be played by Mrs. Talanov. In every way, this play demonstrated the complexity and intricacy of being a director.

Yomei was working devotedly to make the best use of her last few months before graduation.

· Twenty-Eight ·

For fifteen years Li Lisan had been confined to the Soviet Union, sometimes suspected as a Trotskyist, and imprisoned for years under the false charge of espionage. But at heart, he was a revolutionary and always acted like one, so even the Soviets weren't sure what to do about him. The true reason for his prolonged sojourn in Russia was that his return to China might have interfered with the other leading Communist figures there, who had also been trained in the USSR and already had its backup, such as Wang Ming and Kang Sheng. Li Lisan intuited the true reason for his displacement and had nearly given up hope of ever setting foot on his native land again. Seven years ago, when he was arrested, he had been informed that he'd been expelled from the CCP. Although he was no longer a Party member, his wife Lisa believed he was a real revolutionary, a fine man, so she loved him as before. Yet whenever he asked the Kremlin to let him go back to China where he could become "more useful to the revolution," they turned him down.

However, in spite of his fall within the Party, he and Mao had always gotten along. He'd never done anything against Mao, unlike the Soviet-supported Wang Ming in the CCP, who'd been a strong opponent of Mao's. So Mao

hadn't forgotten Li Lisan. Li had another great virtue:
he had always admitted his mistakes openly if he found
himself wrong. That deeply impressed some of his comrades
and earned him a reputation for uprightness. Therefore,
he hadn't been totally discarded by the CCP. On January
1, 1946, the USSR's Department of Foreign Liaisons
summoned him. This plunged Lisa and him into agitation.
The couple assumed that he might be sent to the Far East
to work as a translator at the Zhong-Chang Railroad, the
eastern section of the Trans-Siberian Railroad, which
stretched from Chita city in Russia to Mudanjiang, the
eastern border region of Manchuria, and beyond, to other
Chinese cities in the northeast. But to Li Lisan's surprise,
the Soviet officials informed him that he had been elected
to join the Central Committee of the CCP, even though he
assumed that he was no longer a Party member. Even his
Soviet comrades were amazed that he had been elected to
such a consequential post in absentia.

Stunned though he was, he recovered his wits on the
spot and asked for permission to go back to China right
away. His request was granted. Lisa was happy for him and
supported his return. She was determined to follow him to
his homeland.

After Li Lisan left Moscow, Yomei and Lily knew that
soon they'd be on their way homeward too. Together
they submitted their request to the CCP's Department
of International Relations, which approved it and even
urged them to head back as soon as possible. Yomei started
winding up at the theater institute. The two plays, *The Sisters
Gérard* and *Invasion*, had already started dress rehearsals and
would be staged publicly within two weeks, first the old
play and then the contemporary one. Once the directing
work was over, she could graduate. She'd be the first

Chinese person to earn such a diploma in theater arts from Russia. These days, she could feel the pull of her homeland building up in her, to the point of being almost irresistible. Homesickness often came over her like a bout of nausea.

As she and Lily were busy preparing to head back, Young Zeng turned up again, wearing spit-polished oxfords and a camel-hair blazer with leather elbow patches. He said he wanted to see them before they left. Yomei excused herself to give Lily and Zeng some time for themselves, assuming that Lily might need some private moments with him, though Lily had often insisted that she wouldn't live in Russia any longer. She also revealed to Yomei that Young Zeng wouldn't be going back to China anymore because he believed his career could advance more quickly in the Soviet Union. His position here allowed him to stay above his Chinese comrades, some of whom depended on him to keep in close contact with the USSR. Indeed, over the years, he had been serving as a small facilitator between his Soviet Department of Internal Affairs and the CCP's External Liaison Department, and he thought he could continue playing such a role. Lily looked down on him for that, feeling there was something sneaky and pitiful about him.

Yomei bought some puff pastries and a pack of bratwurst and six eggs. She wanted to keep Young Zeng for dinner. She'd do that for her friend's sake, even though she had never liked him. She thought Lily might still want to keep some kind of relationship with Young Zeng, who, over two years, had often come to see her and even bragged to others that Lin Lily was his girlfriend. When Yomei came back to the Hotel Lux, he was gone, and Lily looked upset, her face flushed and her eyes blazing with annoyance. Yomei put her purchases on the dining table and said, "I thought we could treat him to dinner. He left without giving me some instructions?"

"Don't ever try to fix me up with him again. I hated spending time with him alone! I cannot abide his studied gravitas. He's a minion, a pipsqueak with superior airs, and he's always obsequious to the Russians while throwing his weight around when he's among the Chinese. He's a cat that acts like a lion, nothing more."

"I thought you and he might need to say goodbye in your own fashion, so I went out to pick up a couple of things. Well, we can enjoy these ourselves."

"I don't like him and won't see him again."

"What happened?"

"He said Li Lisan was in Harbin now, working under Lin Biao and in charge of international affairs. But Young Zeng gave me orders as if he were representing Stalin, saying I must let Lin Biao know that Li Lisan couldn't be trusted, so that the CCP mustn't put him in charge of serious work. Zeng even emphasized that this conclusion was made by the Kremlin. Somehow he knew that Harbin was our first stop in China. I could see he was just playing the big boss with me, so I told him that if the Soviet comrades had such a negative opinion about Li Lisan, they could communicate it to Lin Biao directly, since they had their official channels. I wouldn't carry such a secretive message for him. Actually, I gave him a piece of my mind and refused to serve as his messenger. He was upset, saying I was too myopic and he would like to see me in China someday. I didn't respond to that. I don't want to have anything to do with him. He just annoys me, and his drivel makes my ears wilt."

"Why is he so determined to ruin Li Lisan?" Yomei said, amused by the Russian idiom Lily had adopted. It made her language more colorful.

"Li Lisan must know some secrets of his, so Young Zeng wants to make him appear untrustworthy to the CCP leaders."

"Then I don't understand why he treated you like that. He can't act like a snot if he meant to please you and win you over. He doesn't seem to know how to get along with a woman."

"He knows how to manipulate others by mendacious moves. Clearly he just believes in power, as if he thinks that so long as he has a consequential position, any woman will fall for him. He's just a philistine, a snitch plus a lackey. If my dad weren't a senior leader in the Party, Young Zeng might not even give me a glance."

"This is insane. Then you should wash your hands of him. Down the road, it might be dangerous to have such a man in your life. At least we know we can't trust him."

"I can't stand him. So don't ever try to put him and me together again. He used to be a nail in my head, which I have finally pulled out."

Yomei was amazed that Lily also seemed fond of that Russian expression, which sounded so fresh in Chinese coming from someone else's mouth and which Yomei herself had also often used after she had learned it from acting in *Three Sisters*.

Josip, a middle-aged official at the Department of International Relations, told Yomei and Lily that Lisa Kishkin and her child were going together with them back to China to join Li Lisan, who had been very active in Harbin. Josip, slight but barrel-chested, in a flannel rolled up at the sleeves, helped them with their papers.

He said he wasn't sure whether the CCP could resist the
Nationalist army supported by the United States. It looked
like Chiang Kai-shek would take back the northeast of
China soon after the Soviet army withdrew from there.
Such an opinion agitated Yomei and Lily. Still, they were
happy to bring Lisa and Inna with them. They decided to
depart in mid-September, and Lisa agreed.

Both Yomei and Lily were traveling light, each carrying
only a small suitcase, as when they had come to Moscow
seven or eight years before. There was no direct train to
Harbin, and they'd have to switch trains at Chita to reach
the border town of Otpor (now Zabaykalsk). Through the
customs there, they would cross into Inner Mongolia, where
they'd have to change trains again to Harbin. It was said
that the journey could be precarious and that there might
be disruptions due to the remnants of the White Army
and Chinese bandits. But Yomei and Lily were excited and
couldn't wait to embark on the homeward trip.

On arrival at Yaroslavsky railway station, they were
amazed to see how much baggage Lisa had—three large
suitcases and five bags, some of which were as heavy as
stones, since they were packed with books. Yomei and Lily
helped her drag the baggage onto the train, which pulled
out of Moscow the moment they sat down.

Lisa was antsy, never having stepped foot out of her
native country, but Yomei assured her that Li Lisan must
have made proper arrangements in Harbin, and that
everything should be in order. Actually Yomei wasn't as
certain of the prospects as she claimed to Lisa, but she knew
her husband was a thoughtful, considerate man and would
take good care of his family. What's more, Li Lisan was now
working under Lin Biao, who used to be Yomei's suitor
and was the number one leader of the CCP in Manchuria,

in charge of both military and civilian affairs there. Even
though Lin Biao had married someone else, he would surely

Clockwise from top: Yomei, Lily, Inna, Lisa

treat her and Lily decently, despite the possibility that he
might not regard them as his close friends anymore.

The train chugged slowly and stopped at most of the
small stations. On the way, Lisa often talked to Yomei
and Lily about the brutal realities of the red revolution,
and her revelations were an eye-opener to them. Now
they understood why so many Chinese expats in Moscow
were leery or afraid of Li Lisan. According to Lisa, he had
been purged several times in the Soviet Union and once
had even been imprisoned, under the charge of spying for
the Japanese. Before leaving Moscow, Yomei and Lily had
agreed between themselves that they wouldn't mention
the shady aspects of Soviet life once they were back in
China, not only to preserve a heavenly image of the first

socialist country but also to protect themselves, because they knew that most of the time troubles came from a loose tongue. Now they were convinced that there'd been more prevalent abuses of power and even merciless suppressions of dissenters within the USSR. No wonder many Soviets turned reticent and dropped their eyes whenever the name Stalin was brought up.

Lisa also talked about her love for her husband. They had come to know each other when Lisa was seventeen. At the time she had just graduated from a vocational school, specializing in the craft of printing, and in response to the Party's call, she'd gone to Siberia, where she worked as a designer of page layout at a publishing house in Khabarovsk. There, Li Lisan was editing a small newspaper, *The Times of National Salvation*, and often went to the printshop, where they got to know each other. He encouraged her to continue her education, so she enrolled in a teachers college, majoring in foreign languages. Meanwhile, he was busy publishing the paper, in support of the war against the Japanese invasion of China. When they got married in Moscow in 1936, they were given a room in the Hotel Lux by the Comintern, for which Li Lisan was working. But their peaceful time didn't last long. One night in February 1938, the Department of Internal Affairs came and spirited him away. They threw him in jail. Lisa was promptly driven out of the Hotel Lux and had to return to her mother's. Most of her friends began shunning her. Much worse was that the Party branch of her school held a meeting attended by more than five hundred people and demanded that she sever her ties with Li Lisan, who had become "an enemy of the people." But she couldn't believe he was a reactionary and refused to leave him. She was expelled from the Communist Youth League (Komsomol) and had to surrender her membership certificate on the spot, in the presence of the entire school.

Afterward, irrespective of others' suspicion and scorn, she began to look for Li Lisan. Hard as she tried, she couldn't find out where he was. Not until a year and a half later did she come to know he was in Taganka Prison. Right away she started to deliver clean clothes and food to him. Toward the end of 1939, thanks to Yomei's father's intervention, he was finally released and was able to rejoin Lisa, but they no longer had a home of their own and had to live at her mother's place. Then for a whole year, he had to go to the Comintern regularly to do self-examination and confess his "crimes." His self-criticism writings were always typed by Lisa, and altogether the sheets were as thick as a hefty book manuscript. Then, the following year, he was told that the CCP had expelled him, and as a result he couldn't find regular work in Moscow anymore. Thanks to his skills in both Russian and Chinese, the Foreign Language Press employed him as a part-time translator, giving him piecework wages. For many years neither he nor she thought he would ever see his native land again.

Yomei had known some parts of Lisa's story and told Lily that indeed it was her adoptive father who had intervened with the CPSU and helped get Li Lisan out of prison. That further proved the truthfulness of the couple's story to Lily, who began to look up to Lisa, regarding her as an experienced revolutionary. Between themselves, Yomei and Lily talked about the Lis and believed that theirs was a picture of genuine love. Indeed the Lis were totally different from most Chinese Communist couples, particularly the top CCP leaders and their wives. Yomei said to Lily with feeling, "One must marry only for love, like Lisa." Lily agreed, "We'd better remain single if we can't find someone we love wholeheartedly." The two of them were so moved by their lofty sentiment and conviction that their eyes turned moist and their cheeks pink.

It took them seven days to reach Chita city, where they had to spend a night in the waiting hall of the station before they could board the train to Otpor. The station had domed roofs and a front portal with twin columns, and there was a special room for women with young children, so the three of them, together with little Inna, went in there and lounged in a corner while dozing. Before daybreak, they got on the train bound for Otpor. The trip to the frontier town was fairly smooth and lasted eight hours.

The customs at the border was a small port manned by soldiers. They looked through everything in Yomei's and Lily's suitcases, riffling through every book and sticking their hairy fingers into the pockets of their folded jackets and pants. Lisa had much more stuff, so they rummaged through her baggage more deliberately. They took out every article from her suitcases and bags and scattered them around like jettisoned goods. At the sight of their things in such a mess, Inna broke out bawling, stamping her little feet, but the soldiers just smirked, obviously accustomed to noisy tots. It took them more than an hour to get through the checkpoint, though in the meantime the drivers of a locomotive sounded its whistle again and again. But the soldiers just ignored the blasts.

The moment they stepped out of the customhouse, a young officer called to them. He ran up to Lisa and asked, "What's your name?"

"Lisa Kishkin."

"Thank goodness, you're here at last! They have been waiting for you since this morning."

Following his pointer, they saw a train with only two cars standing nearby. The officer waved and cried at the locomotive; two men hopped off and helped them get on the front car. They told the women that if they didn't show up today, they would have headed back to Manzhouli, a small city beyond the border. The train turned out to be at the disposal of the Soviet consulate in Manzhouli and was used for shipping mail, people, equipment, and provisions between Otpor and Manzhouli. The crew had been instructed to bring Lisa and her companions across the border. Now finally, they could head back with their mission accomplished.

As the train was running south, Yomei noticed that the borderland was largely deserted, with many fields lying fallow in the last rays of the sunset. Houses, mostly thatched and built of mud bricks, were uninhabited, some of them burned down and with trees and firewood scattered on the ground. She wondered why some crops were not gathered, having been apparently abandoned by their owners. There might have been fights in this area, where there must be bandits. After they had crossed the border, the landscape began to have more colors; hills were fully wooded, with dappled foliage. Wild waterfowl were swimming in ponds. Some fields had just been reaped, with sorghum and corn lying along the ridges waiting to be bound and then carted away. In front of some adobe farmhouses, cows, pigs, geese, and ducks waddled by rust-colored puddles. There were knots of children at play, chasing a ball or kicking a cloth shuttlecock. Some chimneys were belching out billows of cooking smoke. On the dirt roads, carts, mostly drawn by mixed packs of horses and mules, rolled leisurely. Once in a while a donkey appeared, saddled with a pair of filled panniers and treading along wearily, together with its master walking beside it and holding the reins. All the animals and people seemed headed for home.

Manzhouli was just six miles from Otpor, so in only twenty minutes they arrived at the small Chinese city. The platform was bustling with people, some of whom were foreigners. Yomei saw a stalwart Russian priest clad in black wearing a large beard and sauntering among the throng of passengers. As he was reaching the exit, some foreigners, mostly women, began to cross themselves, and a few tried to kiss his hands. Lisa explained to Yomei and Lily that they must be White Russians who had fled from the Bolsheviks and the red revolution. As they were wondering if they should get off and go to the small station house to wait for the next train, a squad of Chinese troops in quilted uniforms turned up, each shouldering a long rifle. The young officer of this group, wearing a "box cannon" (Mauser pistol) on his hip, caught sight of Lisa and came up, motioning her to get off the train. She became nervous, unsure if she should obey him.

Yomei jumped off and went up to speak with the man, who nodded and pointed at a long passenger train two tracks away. She came back and told Lisa, "They were sent here by your husband to take us to Harbin."

"You mean we must change trains?"

"Yes. The officer says the passenger train is more comfortable, with a sleeping compartment for us. They're responsible for our safety and will accompany us all the way to Harbin."

Four of the troops came up and carried their suitcases and bags off, following them to the passenger train. The young officer was leading the way, holding Inna in his arms, and asked her to call him Uncle, which she had no idea how to say in Chinese. Then he handed her to Lisa and said he had to go to the station to give his chief in Harbin a call to inform him of their safe arrival.

Yomei wondered aloud whether he had enough time before the train departed. "Don't worry," he assured her. "They won't leave without me."

· *Twenty-Nine* ·

The railroad trip from Manzhouli to Harbin was six hundred fifty miles, give or take, but it was unreliable, often disrupted by bandits and by floods from swollen rivers. That was why Li Lisan had sent a squad of guards to keep his family and Yomei and Lily safe on this leg of their journey. There were not many passengers on the train, and the four of them stayed in a private compartment, Yomei and Lily sleeping on the upper bunks while Lisa and Inna used the bottom beds. The next morning, the young officer came to deliver breakfast. Yomei and Lily were thrilled to see salted duck eggs and fried peanuts and fermented tofu cubes, together with rice porridge and twisted steamed buns. They hadn't eaten a warm Chinese breakfast for years and began to dig in with relish, while Lisa seemed bewildered by the food and just took a few bites. At lunch and dinner, there were braised chicken and smoked fish and assorted pickles, so they all indulged their appetite. To Yomei and Lily's amazement, Inna enjoyed the Chinese food that she hadn't tasted before. Her mother often urged her to be careful with the piping hot porridge or soup, so as not to burn herself.

The trip, which normally took less than fifteen hours, stretched to ten days. When they finally arrived at Harbin, it was already early October. Li Lisan stood alone on the platform to meet them. Yomei and Lily were surprised to see him in a U.S. military overcoat and green combat boots. He was quite eye-catching dressed like that. Why was he kitted out that way, even if the American outfit must be warmer and more comfortable? Yomei and Lily didn't expect to be hosted by him here. They were supposed to continue to Yan'an, and Harbin was a layover. But Li Lisan insisted they stay in the city a few days, saying he would let Yan'an know of their arrival here, so there was no hurry to continue west. He took them to his jeep parked in the small square before the train station, and together they headed toward his house downtown.

Most trees had lost leaves, and hoarfrost glazed the branches and the asphalt. His house with dormer windows was a Japanese bungalow that had five rooms and a glassed-in porch and a small flagstone patio in the back. Over dinner—noodles and sauerkraut stir-fried with sausage—he explained that Yomei and Lily should stay with his family while they were in Harbin, and that was why he'd taken them here directly. He told them that he knew the unusual relationship between Yomei and Lin Biao. Actually, more than a week prior, Lin Biao had heard about their coming this way and begun talking about his feelings for Yomei, whose imminent arrival seemed to be roiling him. He told his colleagues that he and Yomei had a long-term relationship and he had been expected to marry her. He was with his current wife, Yeh Qun, only because he had not resisted his colleagues' persuasion stoutly enough. But he had agreed to marry her and had even had two kids with her. Now he insisted that the marriage was a mistake and he wanted to marry Yomei instead.

Li Lisan's explanation disturbed Yomei, who hoped she and Lily could leave for Yan'an the following day, but their host said that would be rude and might make Lin Biao more agitated. Now the man commanded half a million troops, and the civil war with the Nationalists had just broken out—there was so much at stake that Yomei mustn't act impulsively and must discuss with him, Li Lisan, what she was going to do before she took any action. From Lisan, Yomei learned there was a theater group in town. At the moment they were preparing to stage some Russian plays in celebration of the October Revolution. He would definitely put Yomei in touch with them. That way, she could stay in the city a couple of days for professional reasons. Meanwhile, they could figure out how to meet with Lin Biao. In any event, she mustn't steal away without letting the man know and must act politely and reasonably. In other words, she mustn't do anything to upset Lin Biao, whose emotional state would impact the whole situation of the northeast. In short, their relationship was no longer purely personal, and was already entangled with the political and military situation here. In spite of their bafflement, Yomei and Lily agreed not to rush to Yan'an right away and to stay in Harbin for a few days.

The next morning Li Lisan gave Yomei the address of the local theater group, and after breakfast, she set out there. It was a four-story building off Gogol Avenue. They were rehearsing some plays, and Yomei was eager to see the rehearsal. She persuaded Lily to go with her. Together they took a long stroll downtown.

The city was known as the Far East Moscow. Indeed, it was inhabited by a lot of Russians, and there were also Koreans and Japanese, though the latter were usually

dressed like Chinese to avoid being recognized, now that
they were citizens of a defeated country who were stranded
in Manchuria. Yomei liked the atmosphere of the city,
which had Russian influence everywhere. Even some streets
were named after Russians, such as Nekrasov, Lomonosov,
Horvath, Vladimir, Yeager, Mikhaylov. Churches and
synagogues stood on some of Harbin's streets and plazas
here, unlike those in other Chinese cities, and downtown
there was even a Saint Sophia's Cathedral, imposing and
onion-domed like the grand churches in Moscow's Red
Square. Yomei and Lily saw flyers in Russian posted on
walls and utility poles. They also heard local Chinese toss
out Russian words on the streets. This was definitely an
interesting city, a metropolis enveloped in an international
atmosphere.

The theater group was actually a spoken drama troupe,
called the Aurora Borealis Theater Association. Today
they were doing a rehearsal of Chekhov's *A Marriage Proposal*,
a one-act play. They were going to stage a pair of short
plays in early November to celebrate the Soviet revolution.
One of the pair was *A Provincial Lady*, which Yomei had seen
in Moscow long ago but hadn't enjoyed that much, partly
because there was so much French used in it and she didn't
understand some of the foreign words. To her, Turgenev
as a playwright was a bit too elevated in style, operating
mainly in the aristocratic stratum. Yomei watched their
rehearsal of *A Provincial Lady* and was appalled, because
the Chinese translator hadn't accounted for the French
and Italian embedded in the Russian original at all.
Everything was put plainly in Chinese. As a result, the
play was not only drastically simplified but also amazingly
transparent. Nonetheless, Yomei didn't interfere with
such an adulterated effort and just told the acting group

that their rendition was very different from Turgenev's original play, some parts of which were hard to translate, though those snippets in other languages were essential for representing the culture of the gentry and the well educated. But she did help them with *A Marriage Proposal*, because she loved Chekhov. She had read the play long ago in the original Russian and had also seen it performed in Moscow. Both she and Lily noticed that the actors here spoke pure and refined Mandarin, which kept their diction clear and elegant, and which also meant they might go far in their acting careers. Yet to Yomei's surprise, the director of the two plays, a middle-aged man with thin eyes, was an amateur. He introduced himself as Niu Lang, a high-school history teacher. He loved Russian literature and had been asked to direct the pair of plays. Evidently Li Lisan's office had apprised them of Yomei's background, so Mr. Niu was delighted to have an expert who could evaluate their work and help them. He sounded warm and sincere, eager to get Yomei involved in their production.

Yet both Yomei and Lily could see that the performance of *A Marriage Proposal* was somewhat half-baked. The play was a comedy and should be entertaining and funny, but none of the spectators at the rehearsal laughed. Throughout the half hour, the play felt dreary, dragging on lifelessly to the end. Mr. Niu, the director, looked embarrassed, apparently knowing it flopped. "Please help us make it more engaging," he implored.

"Do you have an extra copy of the translation?" Yomei asked. "I read it only in the original. I need to take a look at the Chinese version."

"Of course, we have some extra copies," Mr. Niu said and turned to the actor who played the suitor Lomov. "Young Hong, go get a copy of the script for Yomei. She's an expert in spoken drama and studied theater arts for seven years in Moscow."

"I'll read the play tonight and will come to speak to the cast tomorrow morning," Yomei told the director.

They all thanked her, pleased to have her diagnose the problem. They seemed to appreciate her straightforward demeanor, which cut to the chase without any preamble. On their way back to Lisa's house, Lily said she was a tad disappointed with the theater group and that this city looked like a cultural backwoods. But Yomei was excited and said the actors were quite good. In fact, it wasn't easy to find a group who all spoke refined Mandarin. Also, Lily should keep in mind that Harbin at the moment was the only major city occupied by the CCP's army. Maybe this might be the place where they could start their careers in China. What she said lifted Lily's mood.

Yomei's hunch at the city's potential was indirectly verified by Lisa. At dinner, she told them that she had visited the Foreign Language School in Daoli district that afternoon and was impressed by its Chinese students, so she decided to live in Harbin with her husband while teaching Russian at that school. "To be candid," Li Lisan chimed in, "native Russian speakers are badly needed, so Lisa will be invaluable to the school." He dipped his pork bun into the vinegar saucer and then took a bite.

What they said got Yomei's mind spinning. She intuited that this place would be much better than Yan'an if she wanted to be an artist in spoken drama. A director had to have her own theater or she couldn't get anywhere.

That night she read the mimeograph of Chekhov's play carefully, paying more attention to the dialogue where the characters talk at cross-purposes, and found it so hilarious

that she even laughed out loud from time to time. The
translation was well done for the most part. She mulled over
the troupe's rehearsal and figured out the problem. To her,
the two male actors in the play were fine, but the heroine
Natalya was below par. So the next morning, she went to
the rehearsal venue alone, since Lily wanted to go with
Lisa to visit the Harbin Foreign Language School. Yomei
spent most of the morning with the actress, Jin Minju. The
slender woman was Yomei's age, and of Korean descent, but
she spoke Mandarin like a native speaker. She and Yomei
sat at a rectangular table, together with the director and the
other actors. She told Minju, "You acted like a squeamish
young lady. That contradicts the role of Natalya in the play,
who is neither a daughter of a rich renowned family nor a
pretty virtuous girl of humble birth. First, you shouldn't
wear a long white dress like you always stay indoors.
Natalya's mother died long ago and she has to manage the
family's estates, working both inside and outside the house.
She even works in the fields with hired hands. You should
put on some more peasantlike clothes, to make her appear
more experienced in hard work. Maybe she should wear
a bun instead of a long braid. Second, in the play she is
selfish and greedy and good at running the household, so
she must rule the roost. Even her dad must listen to her.
The tough life has already worn away all of her ladylike
qualities, so let her be loud, willful, truculent like a shrew.
She's so stingy that she wouldn't even hire a servant and
has to do everything by herself. That makes her a capable
and strong woman, an old maid few men are interested in.
That explains why she goes berserk when she gets to know
that Lomov actually came to propose to her, but that she just
outraged him and turned him away. So don't be afraid of
letting rip when you're acting her role. Some large gestures

can make her lively and more memorable. By the way, Minju, do you like dogs?"

"Yes, I do." The actress nodded.

"Have you thought why Natalya is so obsessed with her dog—why her mutt must be superior to any other dog?"

"I'm clueless," said Minju. "Maybe she just happens to like dogs."

"Think about Natalya's life. She lost her mother long ago and must have been lonely ever since her girlhood, so her argument with Lomov about the superiority of her dog, her longtime companion, must be absolutely sincere. Let her act in all earnestness in that part. That might make her funny, pathetic, also sympathetic to the audience."

"This makes sense," Minju said, her round eyes full of gratitude.

Mr. Niu put in, "I'm so glad you came to help us, Yomei. I can see you're a true professional. To be honest, you're the first Chinese person I have met who can read Chekhov in the Russian. Please help us through the dress rehearsal. You can save us from botching this play. We couldn't let ourselves go with abandon in the performance partly because we were acting with trepidation, fearful that we might spoil a classical piece."

Yomei smiled and said, "Actors have to depend on their own inner impulse to perform well. You have to let yourself go because you're also acting yourself onstage."

The actors at the table wrote down her remarks. Minju admitted that she was too careful about her own image, afraid that the audience might think of her as a shrew, a wayward harpy. From now on, she would act more freely.

Yomei explained that she wouldn't be able to see their premiere, having to leave for Yan'an to see her parents soon. But she would try her best to see another rehearsal of theirs and wished them a big success with *A Marriage Proposal*. They should keep her updated about their progress. She even mentioned that she might consider coming to Harbin to build a theater based on the Stanislavski method, which they'd heard of but didn't really understand.

That evening some friends appeared at Lisa's home. They were Liu Yalou, Yang Zhicheng (Grandpa), Zhong Chibing, and Li Tianyou. Like before, the one-legged Chibing was on crutches. They all said they had come to see their old buddies Yomei and Lily. Liu Yalou had changed some—he was stouter but still strapping and more eloquent, even exuding a faint scent of eucalyptus. Over Big Red Robe tea he had brought, they reminisced about their old days in the Soviet Union and had a lot of pleasant memories in spite of the hardship they'd gone through during the war years. Now, the four men were all key generals under Lin Biao, commanding field armies and in charge of major offices. Liu Yalou was more advanced in his career than the others, serving as the chief of the general staff of the CCP's army in the northeast, as Lin Biao's right-hand man. He was open about the intention of his visit now, saying Yomei should marry him without further delay, because he was still single, having waited for her all these years. (That was not exactly true. He had divorced his third wife in the Soviet Union before he returned to Manchuria, together with the Russian Red Army that came to fight the Japanese Kwantung Army the previous year. He had been single for just one year.) Yomei didn't enjoy being hemmed in like this, but she managed to treat them as her friends. To a large extent they were, as they had always been warm and friendly to her and Lily.

Yet their visit disturbed not only the two young women but also the Lis, who realized that Yomei's presence here made her the object of pursuit by both Lin Biao and Liu Yalou, even though she liked neither of them, so she'd better leave Harbin as soon as possible. Li Lisan was the CCP's chief liaison officer in the northeast and often rubbed shoulders with Americans. That was why he wore the U.S. military uniform, which made him stand out from his comrades. He told Yomei and Lily that he could arrange a flight for them to Yan'an within two or three days. Yomei was delighted to hear that. But how about that meeting with Lin Biao? asked Lisa. Indeed, her husband agreed, it would be rude to go away without seeing him. No matter what, Yomei mustn't just pass by Lin Biao's door without saying hello. Besides, Lin Biao was Li Lisan's boss and might bear him a grudge if Yomei just ignored him. Lily believed Li Lisan had a good point, and no matter how unpleasant it was, they ought to go see Lin Biao before their departure.

· *Thirty* ·

The next morning, together with Lisa, they went to pay a visit to the Lins, purposely doing this around ten o'clock so that Lin Biao might not be in. Yomei wanted to call on him without having to see him in person. In fact, Lin Biao usually left home early in the mornings for the headquarters in a western suburb. He had to oversee the training of all field armies under his command and prepare his troops for a major campaign that was about to take place. The sentry in front of the Lins' home, a light-blue Victorian, stopped the three women, who told him that they had been Commander Lin's old friends back in Moscow, and had come to see him. Lisa's Caucasian face and their ability to speak Russian to each other convinced the young man that they were people of some consequence, so he let them through.

Yomei knocked on the door, and a round-faced woman in an army uniform opened it partway and put her head out. "Who do you want to see?" She was pretty and in her late twenties, thin but apple-cheeked, and with caterpillar eyebrows matched by bright, fierce eyes that were a bit wide-set.

"Can we see Lin Biao?" Yomei said matter-of-factly.

The woman frowned and said proudly, "He's not in."
Few people used Lin Biao's personal name in front of his
wife. Everyone called him Chief Commander Lin.

Yomei went on, "Can you let him know Yomei and
Lily stopped by to say hello? We used to be his friends in
Moscow."

Hearing that and seeing Lisa standing behind the two
Chinese women, Mrs. Lin opened the door and let them
in. She took them into the living room, which was bright
and spacious, with tall bay windows. In spite of several
servants and orderlies at Mrs. Lin's beck and call, the
room felt untidy, as if the occupants didn't intend to live
here for long. The furniture, mostly mismatched, gave
an impression of serving only as stopgaps. At a massive
redwood desk, a pair of rickety ladder-back chairs stood,
the paint on them chipped in places. The missus's manner
seemed to show she knew who Yomei was. Though polite
in appearance, she must have been agitated; she said she
was Yeh Qun, Lin Biao's wife. Yomei turned to observe her
closely. Yeh Qun was not as pretty as his ex-wife, Zhang
Mei, and even a little sickly, but she must be better educated,
and was probably a college graduate. Yomei hoped she
wouldn't phone Lin Biao so that they didn't have to wait
to meet him in person. Much to Yomei's relief, Yeh Qun
seemed determined not to call her husband and just told
them that she would let "Chief Lin" know of their visit.

That moniker sounded odd to Yomei, then she realized
that Lin Biao was the commander in chief in the whole
northeast. In fact, he had become the CCP's number one
general, and was a really extraordinary man now. Still, she
didn't feel eager to meet him in person, being afraid of any
more entanglements with him.

The visitors stood up to take their leave, and Mrs. Lin saw them out. Again she thanked them for stopping by and said to Lisa that she was pleased to meet her in the flesh finally. Through Yomei's translation, Lisa assured Yeh Qun that she could come to the Lis' anytime, especially whenever Lin Biao wanted to have a cup of good coffee or a bowl of borscht.

On their way back, Lisa said Harbin was an interesting place and she wouldn't mind living here for some years. Both Lily and Yomei agreed. But Lily pointed out, "You need a fine theater for your directing work, don't you?" She spoke Russian for the benefit of Lisa, who couldn't speak Chinese yet.

"They have a small one here," Yomei said, "which is pretty good."

"Perhaps you should ask Lin Biao to build a big one for you," joked Lily.

"I might do that indeed if I lived and worked here," Yomei said. "For the art I love, I'd do anything."

Lisa smiled and remarked, "That's a true artist talking. The artist and the revolutionary are the same kind of person, willing to take risks and even live dangerously."

Though apparently flippant about her relationship with the CCP's chief here, Yomei felt a surge of unease. She wasn't sure how to deal with Lin Biao, the man who had promised to wait for her six years back. Now he'd already become a family man with three children, including the one left in the Soviet Union, so she must be very careful about him. Perhaps she'd best avoid him.

At the time, Harbin was the base of the CCP's army in the northeast of China, thanks to its proximity to the Soviet Union. Moreover, the previous year the USSR's

forces had crushed the Japanese Kwantung Army and
occupied Manchuria, so the CCP's troops could resort
to the Russian support—if they were in peril of being
annihilated by the Nationalist army, they could flee across
to the Soviet side and sometimes also into North Korea,
the same tactics used by Kim Il Sung's Liberation Army,
which used to operate freely in the triangular region of
Korea and Russia and China. With the Soviets' help, Lin
Biao had built the formidable Northeastern Army, more
than a half million strong. They had inherited all the
weapons and equipment the Soviets had seized from the
Kwantung Army, and had also recruited tens of thousands
of Japanese servicepeople, most of whom had special skills,
such as medical personnel, artillerymen, tank operators,
aircraft pilots, and engineers. Right before the Japanese
surrendered, Mao Zedong had dispatched his most
capable officers and cadres to the northeast to establish
this powerful base, from which the CCP's army could
eventually march inland to topple the Nationalist regime
and liberate the whole of China.

Although Yomei thought she and Lily could leave
Harbin without seeing Lin Biao in person, that very
evening he and his wife came to the Lis' home in a jeep.
Lin Biao was a little frail and even pallid, probably due
to all the work he did at the commanding headquarters,
where he had to spend more than twelve hours a day.
Sometimes when a battle was underway somewhere in
Manchuria, he even slept in his office so that he could
make assessments and give orders promptly. Yomei
was nonetheless pleased to see him and even felt a little
thrilled. The man was more handsome in a peculiar
way, more confident, with an assured manner, wearing
a broad, shiny belt and cutting a dashing figure. Both he

and his wife took off their fur hats and hung them on pegs in the anteroom and then rubbed the soles of their boots on the well-worn rug in there. At the sight of Yomei, Lin Biao rushed up and pumped her hand. "I'm so happy to see you here. Welcome!" he said in a husky voice.

She said, "Sorry we missed you this morning, but thanks for coming to see us." She deliberately included Lily in their exchange, so Lin Biao turned and shook hands with Lily as well.

Li Lisan was pleased to see his boss here at this hour— obviously Lin Biao was eager to spend more time with Yomei, so Li Lisan told his chef to prepare dinner so that they could eat together. Lisa went into the kitchen to oversee the cooking—she wanted to serve something Russian, specifically a rich Luosong soup, which was a Chinese-Russian borscht with cubes of wild boar, turnip, napa cabbage, cellophane noodles, and red pepper rings. She also told the cook to prepare a platter of cold cuts and liver terrine that she had bought that day at the Michurin Store on Gogol Avenue.

In the living room, coffee was served, together with a plate of chocolate truffles. Lin Biao enjoyed the rich coffee, but its taste seemed to puzzle his wife. After a sip, Yeh Qun arched her eyebrows, forming a pair of crescents on her squarish forehead, her funnel-shaped nose twitching. She placed the cup beside her elbow and wouldn't touch it again. Lily told her to take another cube of sugar if the coffee was too bitter for her. Mrs. Lin shook her head and said, "I'm good, just not thirsty."

Feasting his eyes on Yomei, Lin Biao said, "I hope you can live and work here. We need experts like both of you. Few of us can speak Russian. Even though the Soviet Red Army has withdrawn from Manchuria, there's still a lot of

Russian personnel in town and you still can be of great help to us."

Yomei couldn't stop smiling happily in spite of Yeh Qun's hawklike eyes, which were riveted on her all the while. "I'm a theater director by training, and that's also my profession, so I can only work with actors," said Yomei.

"That's a not a problem at all. We need artists too," Lin Biao went on.

But to his disappointment, Yomei explained that she and Lily planned to head for Yan'an soon because neither of them had seen their parents for many years. Lily's dad, already sixty years old, was in Yan'an now, living with his new wife, a twentysomething, though her birth mother, his first wife, was still back in their hometown in Linli County, Hunan. Evidently the Central Committee of the CCP in Yan'an had plans for the two young women, who were both well educated, fluent in Russian, and both from revolutionary families—therefore trustworthy to the Party. So Lin Biao didn't insist and only said their paths would definitely cross in the near future now that Yomei and Lily were back in the rank and file.

At dinner, Lin Biao was unusually talkative, saying his army was going to prevail in the northeast, and that the Communist revolution was likely to succeed in a few years. Li Lisan agreed with his assessment. All the CCP leaders used to think it might take two decades for them to seize the country, but now the goal was clearly attainable in the near future because the Japanese Imperial Army had exhausted Chiang Kai-shek's military power and resources, and because the CCP's army had grown many times stronger.

"There isn't another major city like Harbin. It's our number one urban base now," Lin Biao told Yomei.

"I've met with a local theater group. They're interesting and very capable," she told him.

"So please consider Harbin as a possible base for your career." He clinked glasses with her, then with the others.

Yomei enjoyed the red wine and took another swallow. She was pleased that the host served red wine instead of hard liquor, *baijiu*, which was too strong for her palate.

Lisa piped up, "I'm going to teach at the Foreign Language School here. It will be a great start for me."

After translating for Lisa, Lily added, "I'd love to live in such a Russified city too. I saw croissants and apple turnovers for sale in a patisserie and *chleb* the size of a car wheel in a store. There's also strawberry ice cream, smoked red sausage, pine-nut terrine, even foie gras. That's wonderful."

"True, you can get all kinds of Russian groceries here," Li Lisan chimed in.

Yeh Qun looked ill at ease and didn't seem to like the food. Halfway through dinner, she said she was getting a migraine and wanted to go home. Lin Biao's face fell, but he managed to appear cheerful. After the main courses, without having tea, he and his wife took their leave. They put on their hats and headed for the jeep that had been waiting for them more than two hours in the frosty night.

Lily smiled and said that Lin Biao hadn't been able to tear his eyes away from Yomei the whole time. Yomei slapped her on the shoulder and muttered, "He's a married man now, nothing will happen between him and me."

Lisa said to Yomei, "That couple might have some trouble tonight. I could see plainly that he'd been dancing attendance on you ever since he stepped in."

"I don't like that," Yomei said flatly.

Sharing the upstairs guest room at the Lis', Yomei and Lily had a heart-to-heart chat before going to sleep, just like they used to do back at the Hotel Lux in Moscow. "Tell me honestly," Lily said in the dark, "are you still not interested in Lin Biao? He's extraordinary, to say the least, isn't he?"

"He's married now," Yomei said. "I'd hate to become someone's mistress."

"What if he divorces his wife? You can see that they can't be living peacefully together."

"In any case, I don't want to be pilloried as a home-wrecker."

"So there's no possibility for you and him to be together?"

"He promised to wait for me six years ago, showing great patience. Then he married someone else in just one year. I cannot trust him anymore."

"Maybe it was Yeh Qun who pursued him. A man like him must've had lots of women around him."

"He broke his word nevertheless," Yomei said in an earnest whisper.

"What if he'd kept his promise?"

"That would've been a hard call. I might have been moved to agree to marry him since that would have proved he loved me wholeheartedly and that he was honest and kept his word. But still I couldn't say I love him. As a woman, I'm just not attracted to him. How about you? Say Lin Biao fell for you. Would you be willing to be his bride?"

"In total honesty, very few women could resist that. He's like a ruler of all of Manchuria, powerful and brilliant. In the Communist army he is regarded as a legend—a godlike figure of warfare. So I would say I'd be overwhelmed if that happened."

"What does that mean?" Yomei pressed.

"I'd be too muddled to think clearly." Lily giggled, then continued, "Perhaps in my heart of hearts, I wouldn't mind becoming Madame Lin. My family name is already Lin anyway."

"After he left his wife?"

"That would be the prerequisite."

"I wish I could have your frame of mind, Lily. I just can't say I love him. If I marry someone, I can do it only for love."

· *Thirty-One* ·

The next morning Yang Zhicheng's jeep pulled up in front of the Lis', and he jumped off and told his chauffeur to wait. He came personally to invite Yomei and Lily to dinner downtown. He said the hosts were just their three old friends: Zhong Chibing, Li Tianyou, and himself. "Please honor us with your presence," he said almost humbly.

"Why stand on ceremony like this, Grandpa," Yomei said, still treating him as a classmate of sorts.

Lily jumped in, "Where's Liu Yalou? He won't be at dinner?"

"He'll have a meeting at the headquarters, so there'll be just the five of us. Please come."

Yomei and Lily agreed to join them at the Garden of Apricot Blossom on Stalin Avenue. In the back of her mind, Yomei had some misgivings about the invitation, which somehow excluded Li Lisan and Lisa besides Liu Yalou. Maybe the three men just wanted to chat about their old days in Moscow where they had had a hard time with the two little sisters. In any event, Yomei and Lily were obligated to meet them for dinner. These men were the most senior officers under Lin Biao now, either commanding two or three field armies or running a major department of the Northeastern Army. Yang Zhicheng was in charge of its logistics. It was astonishing that they had all made such tremendous progress in their careers. They used to be merely ordinary expats in the USSR.

The Garden of Apricot Blossoms was an old Chinese restaurant, popular for its southern cuisine. When Yomei and Lily arrived around five o'clock, it was already dusky outside, the streets foggy and many pedestrians wrapped in winter gear and some older Jewish women walking their dogs, which were wearing little hoodies. The three men were already seated at a round table behind a screen embroidered with white cranes that were on the wing. Their woolen overcoats were draped over the backs of their chairs. Unlike their troops, who wore quilted jackets and pants, these three were top officers and often donned Soviet and even U.S. uniforms. Beyond the table spread a mirrored wall that brightened the room. Zhong Chibing was gesticulating excitedly with his thumbless hand as if beating time for a melody only he could hear. He told the guests that they'd chosen this place because they wanted to treat their two friends to a genuine Chinese dinner. Yomei could see that he was still a nervous man, traumatized by his many injuries and a lost leg. In contrast, Li Tianyou was composed as always, just saying he was delighted to see them in this northernmost Chinese metropolis. The moment Yomei and Lily sat down, a tall waitress came over, and with a pair of bamboo tongs handed them each a warm, fluffy hand towel. Grandpa told them, "We guessed you must have forgotten what a real Chinese meal tasted like, so we picked this place that specializes in southern food. Now, order whatever you like."

He handed Yomei and Lily each a large menu, bound in leather. Neither of them had any idea how to order in a fancy Chinese restaurant, so they deferred to the men. Zhong was a gourmand and familiar with the offerings here. He mentioned to the tall waitress eight dishes and also a seafood soup. Yomei was impressed and asked, "Do you often eat here?"

"Not this one particularly," Zhong said. "I've visited most of the restaurants in town, and this is a quality place."

Lily took a bite of a tiny soup bun, a type that she, though a southerner, hadn't tasted before but enjoyed very much. She asked the others, almost innocently, "Have you noticed that women in Harbin have fair, glossy skin? Lots of them are pretty and lovely."

The men laughed. Grandpa said, "How could we overlook that, considering we used to be bachelors, normal and healthy?"

They laughed again. Zhong said, "Women here also have fine figures."

That was true, but Yomei made no comment. Then Li Tianyou said, "Rumor has it that Chief Commander Lin decided to put our headquarters in the suburb because he feared our men might get too distracted by women in town."

"That can't be true," said Lily.

"Of course it's true," Grandpa countered. "With so many beauties around, it would be hard to keep discipline among our troops."

Their orders came, carried over by two waiters followed by the tall waitress, wearing a napkin over her arm. Along with the dishes were two miniature jugs of sorghum liquor, which neither of women would touch due to the strong alcohol it contained—it was sixty-five proof. Yomei could see that the dinner was a feast. She and Lily loved the dishes, especially the simple, rustic ones, such as garlic stems stir-fried with pork loin and the homestyle eggplant. In the middle of the table sat a platter holding a stout section of a sturgeon from the Songhua River. Neither Yomei nor Lily had ever eaten this fish before, though they'd heard and read so much about it. Grandpa used a spoon to scoop up a chunk of the sturgeon, placing it onto Yomei's plate.

Lily glanced at him and seemed to expect to receive a piece as well, but none of the men made such a move. Yomei asked Grandpa, "Why not give Lily a piece?"

"Sorry, my negligence," Grandpa said and served Lily a chunk of the fish as well, then added a spoonful of the gravy over the sturgeon. He turned to Yomei. "You saw Yalou two days ago. What do you think? Are you going to stay here and marry him?"

"I have no such plan," Yomei told him and shook her head.

Zhong butted in, "Look, Yomei, we've known each other for many years. You're such a nice girl that we would all feel good and comfortable if you and Yalou got together as a married couple. He's like a big brother to us, and you're a true friend too, like a sister."

"Besides," Li Tianyou picked up, "he's been single for a long time. Like he said, he's been waiting for you all these years."

"That's not true," Yomei said, looking him full in the face. "I met his previous wife, Su Liwa, in Moscow three summers ago. She told me he was her husband."

"See, you've been following Brother Yalou all along," Grandpa said excitedly. "They divorced two years ago, and Yalou has had no woman in his life since then."

"But please understand, I'm not the one supposed to help him out of his bachelorhood. There're a lot of women here. Why can't he ask for another woman's hand in marriage?"

"You're the only one who's good enough for him," Zhong jumped in again, his thumbless hand drumming the table. "He has declared he'll marry no one except for Sun Yomei. See, you alone can possess him heart and soul."

Yomei sighed and shook her head helplessly. Then Lily came to her rescue, saying, "Stop badgering Yomei, OK? No woman should be cornered like this. Please let Comrade Liu Yalou wait patiently. If he and Yomei are meant to be together, they will be. Nobody would be able to separate them. Stop acting as go-betweens. Just let us have a peaceful dinner, all right?"

That silenced the men. Grandpa apologized and said he couldn't help but worry about Liu Yalou because he was the only one among them who was still single, and he needed a woman to help stabilize his life.

"Does that mean you're all married, all saddled with a family?" Yomei asked in amazement.

"Yes," said Zhong, "we're all happily married and can fight Chiang Kai-shek devotedly now."

"How come you didn't bring your wives here to share dinner with us?" Lily sounded incredulous.

"I'd love to meet them," added Yomei.

"You will, of course," Li Tianyou said with a shrewd smile. "They'll come to Li Lisan's home to talk with you pretty soon."

Yomei finally realized that the dinner was just a prelude to a long battle they had designed—they were all determined to yoke her and Liu Yalou together. Unlike Lin Biao, Liu was a learned man, fluent in Russian and more knowledgeable of military theories, though Lin Biao was acknowledged as a brilliant commander. Nevertheless,

Yomei was not interested in either of them. For the rest of the dinner, she remained reticent, her mind in turmoil, and she could hardly taste her food.

That night she and Lily again chatted intimately. Lily was moody and hadn't liked the role she played at the dinner. She admitted that she felt like an appendage to Yomei. People invited her along only because they couldn't separate her from Yomei, as if she were her friend's bag. Look at what had happened at dinner. Although she loved the scrumptious food, she'd felt out of place. The dinner had nothing to do with her, so she shouldn't have gone to it. She was so upset that she broke down in tears.

"Please, Lily, don't feel this way." Yomei threw her arm around her waist. "I never thought it would turn out like this. I feel trapped too, and I should have thought of a trap like this before we left Moscow. We should have gone to Tihwa and taken the western route back to Yan'an."

"This is a fine city," Lily said, calming down some. "I don't regret having come here, but I just can't be dragged around for your sake."

"I see your point," Yomei said, turning tearful too. "We used to say we must treat each other like sisters. Now, to tell you the truth, I'm scared of those men. I'm at the end of my rope. What should I do?"

"We should leave for Yan'an right away," said Lily.

"That's true. Imagine those young wives coming over to persuade me. I can't stand that."

"That will make me miserable too. So let's leave as soon as possible."

At breakfast the next morning, they spoke about their intention to Li Lisan, who thought it was a sensible solution and agreed to arrange a flight for them with the Americans who were in town, who had a plane that flew to Yan'an from time to time. Li also said that Yomei's presence here had already caused some disturbance—people whispered about some friction between Commander Lin Biao and Chief of the General Staff Liu Yalou. The two men, it was said, couldn't stop bickering due to their obsession with a pretty woman from Moscow.

After breakfast, Yomei went to see the Aurora Borealis Theater Association on Zhongshan Road. Mr. Niu, the amateur director, had sent her a note to tell her they were going to do the stage rehearsal of Chekhov's *A Marriage Proposal*, so he had invited her to come and critique. She went alone, because she wasn't sure how long she'd be with the actors. She also meant to stay away from the Lis' home to avoid any young wives who might pop up to persuade her to marry Liu Yalou. So she left for the rehearsal venue right after breakfast. The theater was in a brick building with bow windows and grillwork balconies. When she arrived it was not open yet. She sat in a coffee shop nearby to read a copy of *The Far East Daily*. She noticed there were a lot of Jews in the city. She chatted in Russian with a middle-aged Jewish woman, who told her that many of her relatives and acquaintances were here. They were on their way to other countries, such as Australia, the United States, Canada, and Argentina. Usually such families would stay here only two or three years, waiting for their emigration papers to get through. If they could not make it to another continent, they might just go to Shanghai, where there was a large Jewish community and where there might be more opportunities for emigration.

Mr. Niu met Yomei in the vaulted-ceilinged lobby of the theater. He was raving about how the performance had improved—it was dynamic and moved swiftly now. They turned and went into the auditorium, which wasn't very

large but looked solemn, like the inside of a church, being
well furnished, with wood-paneled walls and carpeted steps
and red, plush seats. It was so cold in there that Yomei could
see her breath. She asked Mr. Niu, "Do you often stage plays
in here?"

"Almost every month," he said. "This has become our
troupe's venue, our playhouse."

His answer made her heart leap with delight—she
realized that she might have a real theater if she worked and
lived in this city. She asked again, "If you can use this venue
as you like to, why did you do rehearsals in the building off
Gogol Avenue?"

"It's easy to keep warm there. The heating costs a lot for
this theater, so we do most rehearsals in a smaller venue."

"That makes sense."

The trio of the acting cast was excited to see Yomei
again. Jin Minju said that her performance could make
spectators laugh out loud now. Some even couldn't stop
afterward when they spoke with her. Yomei watched their
run-through and could see the great improvement they'd
made. Minju was a totally different woman onstage now,
bold and expansive and self-indulgent. She wore sleazy
canvas overalls and a severe bun of hair like a peasant
woman, as if she had just returned from the fields. As she
was arguing with Lomov over the ownership of a small
meadow, she was outrageous and contentious, stopping
just short of calling him names. Yet when she came to
know he was here to propose to her, she lost it and went
blustery, yelling at her father for keeping her in the dark
about Lomov's true intentions. She even sat on the ground,
kicking her feet while bawling to demand that he go get that
man back at once. The spectators laughed so hard that some
of them bent over and clapped their hands.

Afterward, when Minju asked Yomei for more suggestions, she told the actress, "Try to make the scenes more connected and more fluid, like you are part of the drama even if you're absent from it."

"How would I achieve that?" asked Minju.

"Study the text thoroughly to get familiar with every part of the play, so even if you're not onstage, you can follow the drama mentally. Then once you step onstage, you can act as if you picked up from the previous moment."

"That makes good sense. I'll study the play again tonight."

"Yomei," Mr. Niu put in, "you said you might come work with us in the future. Can that be possible? We really need you. I'm just a schoolteacher and can't direct at all. This theater group needs a real director like you to grow and flourish."

The actor who played Natalya's father broke in, saying in a booming voice, "Please come to Harbin and join us. You can transform our theater completely and make us more professional. Then we'll become the best spoken drama troupe in the northeast."

Their earnestness moved Yomei. She said, "I'll think about this seriously, but I'll have to go inland to see my parents first. I'll keep you posted about my decision. I'm sorry I'll be away and miss your opening night."

They all thanked her and went out of the building to see her off. Deep down, in spite of all the frustrations and unhappiness with those generals, she felt she could work congenially with this troupe and build her own theater here. It might become a beacon of sorts in the sphere of China's theater, as Professor Gorchakov used to say: A director was not a candle flame but a torch.

That evening Li Lisan told her and Lily that they could join some American servicemen flying to Yan'an the following morning. Both of them were relieved, being finally able to head for home. Back in their room, they compared notes about their future plans. Lily said she liked Harbin and would like to live and work here eventually. Yomei shared her positive feelings about this city and made a deal with her friend: they'd try to persuade their parents in Yan'an to let them come back to Harbin in the near future. They promised each other that no matter what, they would never part ways.

Thirty-Two

At the time, the United States was working as a peace broker in China, mediating between Chiang Kai-shek's government and the CCP, so there was an executive bureau comprised of people from the three sides. In addition, the American military provided air travel between Nanjing and Yan'an. The planes often went to Harbin as well, where Li Lisan was in charge of communicating with the Americans. So he could put Yomei and Lily on a DC-3 to Yan'an as members of the CCP's negotiating group.

Except for the two of them, all the others on the plane were American servicemen. On either side, under a line of square windows stretched a long row of seats along the wall. In the back were some bulky rucksacks and a stack of folded parachutes. Before taking off, a young man stepped over and cried out numbers at Yomei and Lily while demonstrating how to buckle up and then how to put on a parachute, punctuating his sentences with "Roger?" Once they were airborne, the plane began to shake so turbulently that Lily threw up, though the vomiting made her feel a little better. Yomei felt ill too, retching continually. An American serviceman in a leather bomber jacket and a beret came over and said something in English that neither of them could understand. He must have been asking them if they needed help. Yomei just shook her head no and smiled. Both of them were amazed that the Americans weren't overbearing, as they'd been described by the Soviets. The young man just mopped Lily's vomit off the floor as though this were his routine work. He was polite and warm to them, smiling as if to amuse himself.

Yomei thought about her imminent meeting with her adoptive parents. The Zhous must be too busy to pay much attention to her now, but she should try her best to stay with them. Their home was more comfortable, and they had always treated her like their daughter. In fact, Yomei's birth mother, Ren Rui, was also in Yan'an at the moment, but she was just a low-level cadre and might not have her own separate housing, so Yomei could become a burden to her if she stayed with her. By all means she should present herself as the daughter of the Zhous in Yan'an. Zhou Enlai was a top leader of the CCP, second only to Mao, and she would need his endorsement for her career, but she also believed she must take care of her birth mother, who was living on her own after Yomei's younger brother had left for the Red Army in the northeast. If Yomei returned to Harbin, she wanted to bring Ren Rui along. Her mother might find that city more comfortable, and the two of them could set up their own home there. Better still, she'd heard that her younger brother, Mingshi, was in the Mudanjiang area and might eventually join them in Harbin. She was quite certain that as long as Father Zhou agreed to let her go to Harbin, her plan would work out.

About four hours later, the plane started descending toward Yan'an. Below them stretched endless yellow dunes and hills. Lily had never been here, so the sight of the legendary red base excited her. As soon as they landed, they

were led into a small shed, in which there was a phone.
A man in his late thirties with a smooth, kindly face said
in a heavy Sichuan accent that Lily should call her father.
Yomei recognized the man, who was Yang Shangkun, the
commander of the force that guarded the CCP's Central
Committee. In the same accent, she asked him if the Zhous
were home. He smiled, apparently appreciating her lapsing
back into the dialect of their home province. Yang said the
Zhous were not home and both were attending a conference
at the Regional Government, so Yomei had better go with
Lily first and might find her parents at the meeting.

Lily's call went through and Mr. Lin picked up. "Hello,"
she said in English, as many Russians did on the phone.

That seemed to have puzzled her father, who turned
silent. Immediately she corrected herself and began to speak
Chinese. "I just landed, Dad, and can't wait to see you."

"Just hang in there," the old man told her. "I'll send
someone over to fetch you."

People around them laughed, whispering about the
odd manner of this girl educated in Russia. Soon it was
said that she'd gotten her dad on the phone then begun to
speak Russian to him, which struck the old man dumb. The
gossip became a legend in Yan'an, where Lily was viewed
as a "foreign doll," unfamiliar with real life in China, so
much so that she didn't even know how to talk with her dad.

Within twenty minutes after the phone call, her father's
orderly arrived on a horse while dragging along another
horse for Lily, but she didn't know how to ride. Besides, how
could Yomei go with her if there was only one horse? Yomei
laughed and said she could ride, and maybe Lily could sit
behind her while they rode together. But Lily didn't know
how to do that either. She couldn't get on a horse at all.
This brought out more laughter among the men. Again

she called her father, who said he'd send a car instead. In
no time, a large Ford sedan turned up, and together she
and Yomei got into the vehicle and headed for the Regional
Government. It was said the sedan was one of the only two
in Yan'an. This must be true. Before going to Russia, Yomei
had seen only a minivan here. She hadn't come across any
sedans in Yan'an at all.

The cave house for guests at the Regional Government
was empty, so the two of them just sat on canvas chairs,
trying to relax. The orderly said the leaders were all at a
meeting and Lily's father would come momentarily. The
two of them closed the door and waited while nodding off.
Both were somewhat tired out by the long flight.

Suddenly the door of the cave house opened. In came
Zhou Enlai, who happened to be attending the conference
at the Regional Government and had just heard of Yomei's
arrival. He stood at the door scanning her up and down,
his eyes glowing intensely while his lean face broke into a
smile. Then he turned to look at Lily. Both women were too
flustered to say anything, just staring at him. He cried out,
"Why are you sitting there wordlessly? Why not get up to
welcome me and say something?"

They recovered their wits and cried out together, "So
happy to see you!"

Yomei rushed up and hugged him, saying, "I asked
Uncle Shangkun how to get home. He said you and Mother
were at a meeting here."

He smiled and told them that he and his wife were both
here today. The minute the meeting was adjourned, he had
come up to the cave house to see them. As he was speaking,
Mr. Lin turned up. The old man looked as if he had aged
a lot to his daughter, a patina of silver beard covering his
chin and slender jaw. At the sight of Lily, he smiled with

glistening, tearful eyes, saying he hadn't been so happy for a long time. "Please don't go, Enlai," he said to Mr. Zhou. "Yingchao is here too. Let's have dinner together."

"I'd love to share your table, of course," Mrs. Zhou said behind him and came in through the door. Instantly, Yomei stepped over and embraced Mother Deng tightly. She said, "I missed you so much, Mom! It's so nice to be with you again."

The Lins lived in an adjacent cave house, and the table was laid in there. Together with the Zhous was also Lin Bochü's new wife, Zhu Ming, a charming woman in her twenties with full shoulders who was merely two years older than Lily. Dinner was excellent by Yan'an standards—boiled millet mixed with rice, pole beans stir-fried with cured pork belly, fresh chili peppers sautéed with dried tofu, and also pumpkin soup. Lily and Yomei enjoyed the rustic food a lot and kept saying they were tired of bread and potatoes and this meal tasted so different and so delicious.

Halfway through dinner, Mrs. Zhou said to Lily, "I'm so glad to see you back. Finally your younger brother has his big sister to look after him."

As Lily was mulling over those words, her stepmother Zhu Ming put down her bowl and said, "My head is hurting." She stood and went into the inner room. She seemed nettled by Mrs. Zhou's remarks, but her husband ignored her and went on chatting with his daughter and the guests. Lily could see that it couldn't be easy for her father to live with such a young wife. It looked like she, Lily, might not be able to stay with her dad here peacefully and that she'd better leave with Yomei for Harbin soon.

After dinner, Zhou Enlai and Lin Bochü had to return to the meeting. Deng Yingchao was tired, so she lounged on a canvas chair for a catnap in the nearby guest room before leaving for Yang Jia Hill, where the Zhous' cave house was. Yomei and Lily also tried to take a nap, but they were too excited to nod off. When Mrs. Zhou woke up half an hour later, it was already dark. Yet she said she knew the way well, so they set out together. She led them along a dirt road while the three of them chatted animatedly.

Once they settled down in the Zhous' living room, they continued reminiscing about Moscow, of which Mother Deng had fond memories. The young orderly poured aster tea for them, then stepped away. Yomei continued to tell her about their evacuation to Ufa, describing the adventures along the way. The older woman was fascinated by the Party school in the Urals and remarked, "It was indeed like a large international family."

Lily mentioned Lucas, the young Frenchman, saying he'd had a crush on Yomei and had to leave with the Spaniards among the students. Yomei felt a clutch in her chest and told Mother Deng, "I never heard from him afterward. It's said he fell in battle in Southern Europe."

Mrs. Zhou sighed and said, "The revolutionary cause always incurs losses. We've lost so many friends and comrades."

After a moment of silence, Lily changed the topic and asked the older woman, "At dinner, you mentioned my younger brother. Why did my stepmother look so annoyed?"

Deng Yingchao sighed. "To be fair, I'd say she didn't take good care of your little brother. I shouldn't have let my tongue slip like that."

"I see. I'll speak with my dad about this," said Lily.

"Don't pressure your old father. He must already have a lot of stress."

"Sure, I'll be careful."

To their surprise, Zhou Enlai came back before nine o'clock; perhaps he was eager to see Yomei and spend more time with her. His wife seemed surprised by his earlier return and asked whether the meeting had already ended. He replied, "Not really. I just left before others. Our daughter is back. It's a special day for me, so I can take a break." He looked at Yomei again, his face alight with affection.

Yomei felt thrilled by his words, but managed to hold down her elation and let Lily chat with Father Zhou about the disbandment of the Comintern and the new occupants of the Hotel Lux. Lily insisted that by comparison, the Red International Aid, in spite of its resounding name, was rather parochial, not as effective as the Comintern. Zhou Enlai also asked about their impression of some Soviet leaders. Of that Yomei and Lily couldn't talk much since they hadn't met many of them in person. Lily mentioned Vladimirov, the head of the Party school outside Ufa, whose real name was Chervenkov, and whose brother-in-law was Georgi Dimitrov, the head of the Bulgarian Communist Party.

"Vladimirov was considerate and kind to us, and always ready to give us a hand," Yomei added.

Zhou Enlai tipped his head back and laughed. "His personal name is Valko. We met in Germany many years ago. He's an internationalist, a genuine Communist."

Yomei also mentioned Li Lisan and Lisa, saying they had been of great help to many Chinese expats in Moscow. Father Zhou nodded and agreed that Li Lisan was a warm, sincere comrade who was capable and trustworthy.

When Lily was ready to leave about an hour later, Mrs. Zhou asked their orderly to hold a lantern for her on the way home. Lily tried to refuse the company, then realized she was unfamiliar with the road. Zhou Enlai told her, "It's about a mile from here. You'd better let him show you the way or you might not find your dad's place on your own tonight."

After her friend had left, Yomei poured more tea for her adoptive parents and went on chatting with them. Father Zhou said, "What are your future plans, Yomei?"

"Lily and I like Harbin a lot. As a spoken drama director, I need a theater in a city to start my career. The Soviet dramatic circle actually planned to let me disseminate the Stanislavski method in China's theater."

"I see. What do you think of the Stanislavski method? Will it be useful for our theater?"

"Absolutely. It's already accepted and practiced internationally and will definitely enrich our theater. I met a local group of actors in Harbin who were staging some Russian plays to celebrate the twenty-ninth anniversary of the October Revolution. They're pretty good, speaking pure Mandarin."

"In that case, you might indeed need to go to a big city and have your own theater."

Mother Deng chimed in, "I'm happy to see that you're so clear about your future." She seemed pleased to hear that Yomei wouldn't settle down in Yan'an.

Before they called it a night, Father Zhou said Yomei should go see Chairman Mao the next day. That came as a surprise. She asked, "Why? Isn't Jiang Ching Madame Mao now?"

"Yes, that makes it more necessary for you to go and report your return to Chairman Mao. You see, it was he who approved your request for going to Russia to study seven years ago. Now you're back, so you ought to let him know you have finished your study abroad, mission accomplished."

"Thanks for reminding me. I'll go see him tomorrow," Yomei said. "My mother is in Yan'an now, so I must see her as well."

"Of course," Mrs. Zhou said. "You must see her as soon as you can. Give her our greetings. You should spend more time with her while you're here."

Mrs. Zhou said that the Zhous had rarely seen her birth mother. This made Yomei more eager to see Ren Rui. Before they turned in, Father Zhou said with a sober face, "Yomei, there's some bad news about your younger brother, Mingshi, that you should know."

Her heart lurched as he went on to explain that Mingshi had died in a battle in Jilin Province recently. She wept and wondered how her mother had taken this new loss. But the Zhous believed she was still ignorant of Mingshi's death, so Yomei had better keep mum about it for the time being.

· *Thirty-Three* ·

The next morning Yomei went to Mao's quarters. The outside of the courtyard looked unchanged, the same ancient camphor tree standing on top of the knoll above the cave house. But the sentries were different now and stopped her. She told them that she used to come quite often and knew both Chairman Mao and Jiang Ching personally, but they wouldn't let her in. None had met her before.

As they were speaking, Jiang Ching stepped out of a cave house and caught sight of Yomei. Ching came over and welcomed her, saying, "What a surprise! I'm delighted to see you back." She turned to the sentries. "This is Vice Chairman Zhou's daughter, Yomei, who just came back from the Soviet Union. Before she left to study abroad, she'd been our regular guest."

She took Yomei's hand and led her toward the cave house that was Mao's office. Passing the granite grinding stone in the courtyard, Yomei patted it as though it were a crouching animal, and said, "I know you."

Ching smiled and said, "You haven't changed, Yomei, still like a young girl."

"I'm twenty-five now."

"Do you already have a boyfriend?"

"Not really."

They stepped into the cave, in which Mao was holding a document and poring over it. Ching said, "Hey, my dear, see who's here."

Mao put down the document and his face lit up. "Sun Yomei, where did you come from?"

"Back directly from Moscow. I came to report that I've completed my studies abroad."

"You're taller now. How many years have you been away?"

"Seven."

"You've grown into a young lady, lovelier and more charming than before. Old Mr. Zhiming must be proud of you. Where is he now?"

"Still in Zhengzhou." Yomei was impressed that Mao remembered her maternal grandfather's name. The old man, a legendary educator, had come to visit Yan'an twelve years before, and Mao had treated him to lunch. Yomei went on, "I'll write to let him know you remember him."

"Give him my greetings too."

Mao looked exhausted, and slightly disheveled. Yomei knew he was busy and her presence at his office meant that she had fulfilled her obligations, so she took her leave and stepped out with Ching. They sat on little stools in the courtyard, leaning against an earthen wall and chatting while basking in the sun. Ching asked, "Did you act in plays in Moscow?"

"Not very often," Yomei told her. "In the beginning, I studied acting, so from time to time they gave me a role in a play. Later they wanted me to study directing. That suited me better, actually."

"That was a wise decision. Acting depends so much on looks and youth. A woman grows old quickly. Once you've lost your looks, your acting career is basically over. By the way, in what plays did you act there?"

"Nothing major except for *Three Sisters*—they let me play one of the Prozorov daughters."

"Which one of the three?" Ching pressed eagerly.

"Masha, the middle sister."

"You performed the role in Russian?"

"I had to. That was part of my coursework."

"I'm impressed." Ching said as if lost in thought. At this point, a little girl in cotton-padded trousers and a flowered bib came out of another cave house, waddling toward Ching with her arm raised. "Mama, mama," the child cried out while running over to Ching, who held her up and put her on her lap. The child's pants were open in back, revealing part of her naked butt. "This is my daughter Neh," Ching said to Yomei. Then to the girl, "She's my friend Yomei, call her Auntie."

The chubby-faced girl said, "Auntie."

"How old are you, Neh?" Yomei asked.

"Almost six," she said, spreading her right hand and raising her left thumb together to show her age.

"Neh was born the year after you had left for the USSR."

"How time flies!" said Yomei.

"Well, what do you think of me now?" Ching asked without looking at Yomei.

Yomei was perplexed. "What do you mean?" Ching gave a peal of laughter, then said, "Silly you, I mean what do you think of me now as a wife and a mother?"

"Pretty nice, I guess," Yomei said, a little embarrassed but still puzzled.

Ching's face dropped. "Actually I'm not doing that well. There're all sorts of difficulties for me. I've encountered so many enemies in recent years, having to deal with them one after another."

Astonished, Yomei didn't know what to say, having no idea whom Ching was referring to. For a while, she kept silent and wondered if she'd better take her leave. She stood up and said she had to go see her birth mother.

"Thank you so much for stopping by to see Chairman Mao and me, Yomei. Please come again so we can talk at length about arts and theater. It's so stuffy here." Holding Yomei's hand, Ching added rather mysteriously, "You're just back and are unfamiliar with the situation in this place, but you will know eventually. There're a lot of backward people in Yan'an, who have been mean to me and my child. Some want to do us in. You're the daughter of Vice Chairman Zhou, and are known as the Red Princess, and I'm Chairman Mao's wife, so we must unite against those miscreants."

Yomei got more baffled now, though she nodded. She could tell that Ching had become a cranky woman, even though she had a reputation for being suave and poised.

At the sight of Yomei, Ren Rui almost dropped her scissors to the dirt floor. She rose and hugged her daughter, saying, "Why didn't you let me know you were coming back?"

"I wanted to give you a surprise, Mama," Yomei said teasingly.

"You did. For a split second, I thought I saw an apparition or a doppelgänger." Her mother touched her heart as if to calm herself.

Yomei looked at her mother more closely. Ren Rui had aged a lot, her heavy-boned face slack now and her eyes a little puffy, as if she had just cried. Probably she had heard the bad news about her youngest son.

Indeed, when Yomei sat down next to her mother, Ren Rui said that Yomei's younger brother, Mingshi, had been killed in a recent battle in the northeast. Though Yomei already knew, she still couldn't hold back her tears and started sobbing. She hadn't spent a lot of time with Mingshi, but she remembered him dearly. He'd been a quiet child, a little shy but fond of wooden guns and slingshots. Before she left for the USSR, her little brother had been staying with a relative's family in Anhui Province so that he could go to school there. Just the previous year, he had come to join their mother in Yan'an, but the boy had been so enthusiastic about military life that he had kept begging Ren Rui to let him join the Red Army. He was merely fourteen, so she wouldn't allow him. Still he argued and begged, saying he had almost grown up and had begun sprouting facial hair. At last she gave him permission, and he went to an artillery regiment, which later transferred to Mudanjiang in eastern Manchuria. Despite Yomei's own grief, she had put on a cheerful façade when she had come to see her mother. She meant to keep her mother in the dark about the loss, but now Ren Rui already knew and seemed to have calmed down some. Rui was a noted old revolutionary, though she was only fifty-five. She was also an author, contributing to local newspapers and magazines regularly. Coincidentally she had just published a poem in *The Liberation Daily* titled "Seeing My Son Off to the Front."

Yomei saw a copy of the paper lying on her mother's dining table. She picked it up and read the poem and was touched. Some lines reminded her of the hard childhood that she and her siblings had gone through: "When you were five, your father was murdered, / And we had to live without enough clothes and food." Lines like those made Yomei tearful again. She regretted not having looked for her younger brother when she was in the northeast the previous month. If she'd gone to see him, their meeting might have altered his fate slightly and even prevented him going into the battle of his last days. But she hadn't known in what unit he was serving or his exact whereabouts.

Yomei went over to a corner of the room and washed her face with a towel soaking in a white enamel basin atop a wooden rack. Returning to join her mother, she calmed down some. Meanwhile, Ren Rui remained composed, her face stony. Evidently she had already cried out some of her grief.

Her mother said Yomei's elder brother Yang was also in the northeast now. He was married but didn't get along with his wife, who was still in Yan'an. The young woman wouldn't come and see her mother-in-law during his absence. Therefore, Yomei felt she must take care of her mother from now on. She told Ren Rui, "Can you move and live with me if I go to the northeast, say, Harbin?"

"I used to live in Beijing and Tianjin and won't mind living somewhere farther north," said her mother. "Truth be told, I prefer urban life."

"Then let's quit living as cave dwellers," Yomei said.

In fact, Ren Rui liked cities, where life was more convenient. She had lived in some major northern cities, and every one of them was better than Yan'an, which was like a big village. As she was growing older, she felt that life had become more difficult and even precarious here. Even though she was used to austere conditions, she now preferred to stay with at least one of her children, who had been scattered to different places, and she had lost touch with her youngest daughter, Yolan, and her second son,

Jishi. She loved Yomei more than her other children for her filial disposition and vivacious temperament. She'd better leave with her if they could find a safer place, where they could assemble the remainders of their family.

Yomei had picked up some groceries on her way here, so she cooked noodles for dinner. She poached two eggs just for her mother, saying she had eaten well at the Zhous'.

Over a bowl of noodle soup, she asked Ren Rui why Jiang Ching was so cantankerous, as if she'd been attacked right and left. Her mother said, "I can understand her anger. Some people at the Central Committee were against Chairman Mao's marrying her, but he was determined to be with Ching, even though he hadn't divorced Ho Zizhen yet. As a solution, the Central Committee decided that Jiang Ching must work only as a secretary in charge of Chairman Mao's life. She doesn't have an official position at all."

"What kind of job is that?" Yomei said. "To serve him only in bed?"

"You have an awful mouth, Yomei. Don't ever talk like that about Jiang Ching to others. I've known her for many years. She's crazy, with a mixed bag of ruses and schemes. Her rage is unpredictable and has no bounds. Remember in Shanghai how she was jockeying for major roles in movies and plays? It was ugly. She even slept with directors to get the roles she wanted."

"I remember that."

"Now that she's Madame Mao, those who once opposed her might have to eat humble pie."

What her mother said reminded Yomei of Xu Yi-xin, the man who had once been after her instead of Jiang Ching. She wondered if Ching still bore her a grudge for going with Yi-xin briefly. But that morning at the Maos', Ching had been warm and had even tried to befriend her. As for Yi-xin, he was also in the northeast now, under Lin Biao's leadership, so it was unlikely that Ching could touch him. Besides, the man had been very cautious—the moment he'd found out that Ching was becoming Mao's woman, he didn't do anything to ruffle her feathers again and married another woman within a year. He was smart and knew how to navigate perils.

After dinner, she brewed a pot of tea with loose leaves from a tea brick, and poured a mug for her mother. There was only one mug in this cave room, so she used the same noodle bowl for herself. Over tea, she asked her mother some other things, specifically about the conference here in December 1943. She wanted to know if Zhou Enlai had really gone to his knees in front of Chairman Mao.

Ren Rui sighed and said, "I wasn't in Yan'an at the time, but your aunt Ren Jun was here. She told me about the conference. Evidently Zhou Enlai had done that and even called Mao 'Emperor.' Of course, he might have lost self-control for a moment. Some people saw him on his knees, including your elder brother Yang, who was working for Uncle Zhu Deh at the time."

"Father Zhou is an extremely rational man. How could he do something like that?" Yomei mused aloud.

"Politics, it's like a war, in which the participants can easily lose themselves and act out of character. That's another reason we should stay away from a political center. Don't live a life of constant political strife. Don't marry anyone arranged by the Party. Many marriages of this kind have ended in divorce. It's awful to see that most men in powerful positions have abandoned their older wives and married younger women. So many of those ex-wives have remained single and consider themselves widows, although their husbands are still alive."

"Trust me, Mama, I'm not interested in power or wealth. I met Uncle Guo Moruo in Moscow, he also advised me to live a life centered around art."

"That's amazing, isn't it? He's an experienced man but has always been entwined with politics, so he knew what he was talking about. I used to think he was just a political animal and an incorrigible philanderer, but obviously he was no fool."

"He's a man of letters, at heart more like a literary scholar and an artist."

Then Ren Rui asked Yomei how well the Zhous had treated her as their adopted daughter. She told her mother, "They've been good to me, though I feel that Mother Deng is an extremely careful woman."

"You mean she's vigilant when you're around their family?"

"Somewhat like that. Why are you asking me this, Mom?"

"I've known the Zhous for more than two decades. They are good and powerful people, but they have their own problems too."

"What kind of problems do you know of?"

"Do you think they have as great a marriage as it appears?"

"I'm not sure."

"How often do they quarrel?"

"I have no clue, Mama. Only once did I see Mother Deng's face dark and twisted with anger. I overheard her snap at her husband, saying he was hopeless, but I don't know what that was about."

"You see, Zhou Enlai is a handsome man, while Deng Yingchao is plain and even hard on the eyes. There are always pretty women around Enlai, so it isn't easy for Yingchao to keep hold of him."

"You mean Father Zhou is a skirt chaser?"

"I wouldn't say that. He may be a decent man, but his wife could easily suspect he has other women in his life. I know he's been nice to you. Has Mother Deng ever been nasty to you?"

"Never. She's always been kind and warm."

"Be careful. Only a dumb woman would feel unthreatened by the presence of a pretty girl like you in her family."

"But it was Mother Deng who suggested that they adopt me. Why would she do that?"

"To establish the father-daughter relationship between you and her husband so as to keep him and you within bounds? Wasn't he excited when he spent time with you?"

"Kind of. He's happy and in high spirits when I'm around. Of course, Mother Deng can see that."

"So don't spend too much time with Father Zhou alone. Treat him only as a paternal figure, with respect and filial love. Tell me the truth, Yomei, are you attracted to him? If you are, you'd better stay away from the Zhous. It's not easy for a young woman to control her deep feelings."

"I lost my dad at age six, so I regard Mr. Zhou only as a father figure. Rest assured, I won't overstep the line I drew for myself long ago, on the very day they adopted me."

"You're a smart girl and know how to make good use of your special relationship with the Zhous. But remember, if you offend Deng Yingchao or even just arouse her suspicion, you might land in hot soup."

"I'll keep that in mind, Mama. That's why I should strike out on my own and we should go to Harbin to live our own life. We ought to reassemble our family there."

"It's a smart move. I'm glad you figured it out."

They chatted about Yomei's oldest brother Yang, whose marriage was floundering partly because the Party had arranged the couple's union—prior to which the two hadn't known each other well. It turned out that they couldn't share the same roof peacefully, since their likes and dislikes were too different. At the moment, the couple were living separately—Yang was in Tsitsihar city, two hundred miles northwest of Harbin, while his wife was still in Yan'an. Ren Rui feared that their separation might be precipitating the end of their marriage.

· *Thirty-Four* ·

Yomei and Lily met every day in Yan'an, even though they were staying with their own families. Neither of them was totally at home here. The Zhous were kind and considerate to Yomei, but she couldn't be completely at ease when she was with them. She remembered her mother Ren Rui's admonition and avoided spending too much time with Father Zhou alone. She also tried to be present when they had guests—intuitively she intended to affirm her unique relationship with the Zhous and her reputation as the Red Princess. By far, Lily's situation was more awkward. She loved her dad, but the old man had a twenty-seven-year-old wife who didn't care for the children from his previous marriages. Zhu Ming was polite to Lily, mainly because this stepdaughter of hers, educated in the Soviet Union, was fluent in Russian and would definitely become a significant figure in the CCP's cadre echelons. At least Lily was badly needed by the Party and could serve as a liaison of sorts with the Soviets. Old Mr. Lin was proud of his daughter and had often taken Lily to see some top CCP leaders, such as Chairman Mao, Commander Zhu Deh, General Peng Dehuai, and Chief Liu Shaoqi (of the CCP's Secretariat). Therefore, his young wife had been cordial to Lily. Yet Lily could tell that her little brother, only seven

years old, had been left on his own, and she resented her
stepmother's negligence. For that, Zhu Ming was often
talked about in Yan'an. To make matters worse, Lily could
see that the woman would sometimes throw a fit at her old
father randomly. That was too much.

Yomei and Lily met Jiang Ching in a small restaurant,
Victory House, across the street from the only local textile
plant in Yan'an, where Yomei and Ching had eaten together
a couple of times when they'd both been at the arts academy
here. At the table near the door sat a young soldier, Ching's
bodyguard. Ever since she became Madame Mao, she
couldn't go out alone, and was always escorted by someone.
Today she seemed in good spirits. Over mutton dumplings,
the three women chatted about life in the Soviet Union,
which Ching was eager to hear about. She even confessed
that when young, she had always dreamed of going abroad,
though her first pick would have been France. She'd also
have loved to go to California to see what Hollywood was
like, because she loved American movies, often saying in
private that she admired Betty Grable, particularly her
shapely backside, and that she wanted to see how films
were made in the United States. Yomei liked Ching's lively
personality today, which was congenial, less overwrought,
and even a little innocent. Such a positive impression put
her somewhat at ease. Unlike her, Lily hadn't met Ching
before and seemed to hit it off with this new Madame
Mao, though she had been close to Mao's ex-wife Zi-zhen.
Ching was quite honest with them, saying she needed
to meet people who knew things outside China, because
Yan'an was basically a village, which made her feel rather
claustrophobic. But once they toppled the Chiang Kai-shek
regime, they would establish the red capital in a metropolis.
And Yan'an would be at best like a hometown of the CCP.

"Do you know which city will become the new capital?"
Yomei asked.

"Beats me," Ching said with a grin. "It's too early to tell.
I guess even Chairman Mao hasn't figured that out yet. But
it won't be Nanjing, for sure."

"Nanjing is a pretty city, isn't it?" said Lily. Indeed, at
the moment it was where the national government was.

Ching answered, "But as a capital, it has been a tragic
place, captured time and again by rebels and foreign
forces."

"That's true. We should avoid a city like that," Yomei
said.

Ching also revealed to them that she was in poor health
after giving birth to her daughter. She said it was awful to
have a baby, that breastfeeding had cracked her nipples,
so she had quit doing it long ago. She had been ill and
exhausted all the time. Someday she might go to the Soviet
Union for medical treatment and recuperation. Eventually
she might live abroad for some years.

That came as a surprise to Lily and Yomei. Yomei told
her, "Don't go there alone."

Ching sensed something in that suggestion and asked
her to elaborate. Yomei and Lily described how some wives
of the top CCP leaders, like Ho Zi-zhen and Ah Jin and
Liu Ch'un-hsien, had fared in the Soviet Union. Some
Russians could be supercilious and even mean-spirited
to Chinese. At certain points, those three preeminent
CCP women had all been shut in mental hospitals despite
their protests and resistance. It would be better if Ching
could have a personal aide and an interpreter who could
help her facilitate things. What Yomei and Lily said made
Ching pensive, and she thanked them for sharing their
thoughts honestly.

Yomei offered to pay for the lunch. Though she didn't have enough of the Yan'an currency, bian notes, on her, she did have some rubles, which at least Ching might like to take. But Ching said, "No need, it's my treat. I've already taken care of it—I have an account with this place."

Yomei and Lily thanked her. Having said goodbye to Ching, the two of them began ambling along the Yan River, which was more like a serpentine creek, while discussing their intention to go to Harbin together again. Patches of chill hung in the air, and a large flock of sheep was descending a distant hillslope, heading back home. Yomei wanted to double-check with Lily so that she could present their plan to Father Zhou and get his support. Once he approved it, everything should proceed smoothly. Lily said, "Sure, I'll go with you and your mother. We're like sisters, so your mother is like my mother too." Lily had met Ren Rui and loved her.

In fact, she didn't know where her own mother was exactly, having lost touch with her after she'd left China eight years before. Whenever she asked her father about her, he'd say he'd also lost touch with his first wife, who was definitely still in their hometown in Hunan Province. He hadn't heard from her for a long time. Lily often resented her father's negligence of her mother, but the old man always said he had too many urgent matters to attend to at work. Indeed, it must be hard to live up to his reputation as one of the most honest and conscientious men in the CCP. Once in a while, Lily wanted to yell at him, but she always managed to hold back her temper. Now she was eager to leave Yan'an with Yomei, feeling she belonged to the bigger world. Besides, she'd still be able to work for the Party and be even more useful in a city controlled by Lin Biao's army now.

That night, Yomei talked to the Zhous about her future plans: she would love to go to Harbin and work with a spoken drama troupe there. At first, Zhou Enlai seemed flummoxed and asked, "You're just back. Why do you want to leave home again? And so soon?" He lifted a cup of rice wine and took a sip. Unlike most CCP leaders, he didn't smoke, but was fond of drink, even hard liquor.

Yomei said, "My profession is stage directing. People in Harbin speak excellent Mandarin, and with a fine group of actors, I can build a professional theater gradually. When I was there last month, I worked briefly with a spoken drama troupe. They are very good and have their own playhouse. They want me to join them so that we can produce some significant plays. What's more, there's a good deal of Russian culture in Harbin, which would make me feel more at home there."

"See, Yomei is already Russianized," joshed Mother Deng.

"There're so many cities in China. Why pick Harbin?" Father Zhou said as if still puzzled.

"But Harbin is our base," Yomei answered. "I can't stage revolutionary plays with impunity in another major city, can I? Besides, I'm your daughter and might become subject to attack."

"I see, but why not wait more patiently? After our revolution succeeds, you'll have more choices. Why not go to Shanghai, or Beijing, or Tianjin eventually? The theater scenes in those cities must be livelier than Harbin's, mustn't they?"

Mother Deng jumped in again, "Enlai, you should hear Yomei out. She does have her reasons. She must be eager to embark on some pioneering work, which we should encourage her to do." She turned to their adopted daughter. "How about your mother, Ren Rui? Will she let you go far away from Yan'an? She must be lonesome here, and I'm worried about her."

"She says she can go with me, and Lin Lily wants to go there too. She's fluent in Russian and can be useful to our government there. The other day, she and Lisa Kishkin visited the Harbin Foreign Language School, which invited them to teach for them. My mom also thinks it better to live in that city because my elder brother Yang is in Tsitsihar, in the same province."

"Will Lily's dad allow her to leave Yan'an?" Father Zhou asked and drained his wine cup. "I feel Lily can be more useful than just teaching Russian."

"Of course Old Lin will let her go," Mrs. Zhou put in. "You know Zhu Ming can get out of sorts without rhyme or reason. If Lily stays here, the Lins might have no peace. Old Lin needs a peaceful home more than anything else."

Zhou Enlai exhaled a feeble sigh and said to Yomei, "Then I guess I have to give you my approval."

Mother Deng added, "You also have our blessing, Yomei. Don't forget to write every month to share your good news and honest opinions with us."

"Sure, you two are my parents. I'll take care of you when you are retired."

Father Zhou laughed. "Then I'll join your theater. You know I used to act onstage at Nankai University."

"Really?" Yomei couldn't imagine what roles he could have performed.

"He played young women most of the time," said Mrs. Zhou. "So many girls were blown away by his performances. You can ask your mother, Ren Rui, about that."

Zhou Enlai said to Yomei, almost with regret, "If I had the time and leisure, I would learn the Stanislavski method too. Do keep me in mind as a potential actor."

He tossed his head back and laughed again, by accident knocking the wine cup off the tea table. Yomei picked it up from the brick floor at once. She saw his face shining with some feminine features that could indeed make him appear charming onstage. No wonder it was said that some men had admired and loved him too, that even some foreigners had called him an Adonis. She was delighted that her request had been accepted by her adoptive parents. Father Zhou would certainly help her birth mother, Lily, and her with the transfer orders and all the necessary paperwork. She couldn't wait to share the good news with Lily.

· *Thirty-Five* ·

When Lily told her father that Zhou Enlai supported her and Yomei's request to go to the northeast, Mr. Lin was pleased. He said he had been scraping together the money to have a set of winter clothes made for Lily but didn't have to do it anymore, now that she was going to Harbin and would be issued winter gear there. These days, everything was more expensive in Yan'an—inflation was so rampant that prices had quadrupled in recent years. Since arriving in Yan'an, Lily had been wearing a threadbare woolen coat, which looked exotic to the locals, who believed she must be a reporter from a big city or another country. Unlike Lily, Yomei had some old clothes she could put on and would be happy to share, but they were too small for Lily, whose frame was wider than hers.

Again they boarded a U.S. airplane, but this time with Yomei's mother, and one headed to Beijing. At the moment, in late November, the CCP and the Nationalist government were in the midst of negotiations mediated by the United States. The delegates from the three sides were all staying at the Beijing Hotel, the best one in the city. The CCP's participants occupied the second and third floors, while the Nationalist delegates used the fourth and fifth floors. As for the U.S. mediators, they stayed on the top floor. Yomei and Lily and Ren Rui were treated as members of the CCP delegation and given a corner room on the third floor, which was sunny, with windows facing both south and west, so they were pleased about their lodgings.

As soon as they settled down in the hotel, they went to see Yeh Jian-ying, the head of the CCP's delegation, who was staying in a small courtyard in Jingshan Alley, nearby. To their surprise, Mr. Yeh told them to stop heading for Harbin for now, but he didn't explain why, only saying there was a telegram from the northeast that urged him to halt them. He had forwarded the cable to Yan'an, so at the moment, he was waiting for a response from the Party's Central Committee.

They were baffled, but had to stay in Beijing for the time being. A couple of days later, Yeh Jian-ying heard from Zhou Enlai, so he called the three women over and showed them the reply. Vice Chairman Zhou responded with a touch of impatience that the decision of dispatching them to Harbin had been made long ago and the headquarters of the northeast had also agreed to receive them, so there was no reason to reject them now. How could the comrades in Harbin have changed the order from Yan'an? Yeh Jian-ying sighed, his eyebrows tilting toward his temples while his thick upper lip curled a little. He said, "Under such circumstances, the three of you can proceed to Harbin as planned."

They flew to Changchun, which was the next leg of their trip. From there they would take a train to Harbin, which was less than two hundred miles north. The CCP head in Changchun city was Wu Hsiu-chüan, a very capable officer who had graduated from a Soviet infantry academy and even joined the Soviet Communist Party in the early 1930s.

To their surprise, Mr. Wu also tried to dissuade them from going farther north, because he had just received a telegram from Harbin that urged him to stop them. The three women were outraged. Who was so persistent in stopping them on the way? Lily and Ren Rui wanted to return to Yan'an at once, but Yomei said they should wait a while and find out what was really going on.

As a compromise, Ren Rui and Lily went back to Beijing, where Rui had many friends, to wait for the final word there, while Yomei remained in Changchun, looking into their case. They boarded a U.S. plane again, but the flight was so bumpy that Ren Rui got sick and took to her bed in Beijing. Lily by now was quite attached to Ren Rui, who used to work under her father in Yan'an, where she'd been the keeper of the official seal of the Regional Government. Meanwhile, Yomei went to Wu Hsiu-chüan's office in downtown Changchun three mornings in a row and requested to see the contents of the cable. Finally Mr. Wu relented and asked his secretary to show her the telegram. It was from Li Lisan: "In the interests of our Party, please stop Comrade Sun Yomei from coming to Harbin. Lin Lily can come alone." Yomei was flabbergasted, having suspected that Li Lisan must have done this for Lin Biao. She couldn't understand why Lin Biao would backstab her like this. He was unlikely to be so treacherous. She dared to say he must still have some affection for her. Yet in any case Li Lisan, as a friend of hers, couldn't possibly have made such an effort to stop her on his own. Probably Yeh Qun had given her husband hell, forcing him to prevent Yomei from reaching Harbin.

When Yomei rejoined her mother and Lily in Beijing and told them the contents of the telegram she had seen in Changchun, Ren Rui felt outraged. Her daughter was just a common young cadre in the Party; how could Yomei's transfer to Harbin stand in someone else's way? But since this change served the Party's interests as the cable claimed, Yomei had no choice but to follow the orders. Still, she and Lily were reluctant to part ways, so together with Ren Rui, they stayed two more weeks in Beijing, working in the office of the CCP's delegation.

By mid-December 1946, the negotiations between the CCP and the Nationalist government had collapsed, so the Communist delegates and staff were supposed to go back to Yan'an and other red bases. But for days, their departure was delayed, which made them feel as if they were stranded in Beijing. Nowadays the city was rather chaotic. Every day thousands of college students took to the streets, demonstrating against a U.S. soldier's assault on a young Chinese woman and demanding the full withdrawal of the U.S. military forces from China. (Decades later the rape victim confessed publicly that the case had been fabricated by the CCP in order to start an anti-American movement.) Yomei, her mother, and Lily were uncertain where to go. The CCP's delegates lacked any means of transportation of their own, and they were not sure whether the United States would keep its promise to fly them out of Beijing. Their superiors primed Yomei and Lily for the worst, which might be imprisonment. Once in jail, the Nationalists would definitely interrogate them to extract information, so they'd better prepare to stymie the enemy's efforts. Under no circumstance must they admit they had come back from the Soviet Union, because such information might single them out as targets of interrogation and torture. They each packed into a bag toiletries, underclothes, and things needed for prison life. Fortunately, the United States kept

its word and began to fly the CCP's personnel out of the
city, except for those able to leave by train. All the people
were assigned to head for three red bases: Yan'an, Handan,
and Harbin. Already the delegation had sent a list of people
to Yan'an and let the Central Committee decide each
person's destination.

In its reply, the Party's Central Committee instructed
that Yomei and her mother return to Yan'an, whereas Lily
was to go to Harbin. Yomei didn't want to part company
with her friend, and together they went to see Yeh Jian-ying
in hopes that Lily could also return to Yan'an. Mr. Yeh took
out the list from the Central Committee, in which Lily's
name was among those bound for Harbin. In disbelief,
Yomei looked through the page and didn't find her own
name. "Uncle Yeh," she begged, "please let Lily and me stay
together. We have gone through cold and hunger together
for seven years in Russia and want to be together like
before."

Yeh shook his crew-cut head and grimaced in
frustration. His jugged ears seemed to be flapping a little.
"It's so difficult to please you girls. The Central Committee
has already decided the assignments, so we mustn't trouble
the leaders anymore. Bear in mind, Lily, you don't have to
fly if you go to Harbin. The train is quite convenient."

To Yomei's astonishment, Lily conceded, "Fine, I accept
the Party's assignment."

Coming out of Yeh's courtyard, Yomei strode away
without saying a word to her friend. She was beside herself
with disappointment. Back in the hotel, she took Lily to
task and said hotly, "This is a nail driven into my head
that I can't pull out: Why on earth did you change your
mind? Didn't we swear to be together no matter what?

Now you've gone back on your word all of a sudden. Why? I don't get it."

"I want to stay together," Lily stammered, then raised her voice. "But what could I do? I can't disobey the orders from the Central Committee. You and I are Party members, and we have to carry out orders from above."

"The Party is run by people. Why not contact your dad and ask him to intervene on our behalf?"

"How can I do that? My dad always says I must act the same way as a regular comrade. He never lets any of his children have extra privileges. I can't possibly ask a favor from him."

"Then we must figure out a way to keep you from going to Harbin." Yomei spoke as if to herself.

Her mother intervened, "You mustn't feel so sore about his, Yomei, and mustn't act so selfishly. Even though you and Lily part ways, you'll still be friends and sisters. So you two must treat each other as real comrades who just have to do different jobs in different places."

That stopped Yomei from fuming overtly, though when she saw Lily off at the railway station, the two of them sobbed for a good minute before Lily got on the train.

When the "all aboard" bell sounded, Yomei knocked on the window, which Lily lifted up. Yomei took out of her bag five hard-boiled eggs wrapped in a checked handkerchief, and handed them to her friend. "I forgot to give you this for the trip." She managed a grin despite the pressing sadness at the base of her throat.

"Thank you, Yomei! I'll keep you updated about everything."

"Yes, please send your letters to Vice Chairman Zhou's office in Yan'an. He can pass them on to me."

"Of course, I'll miss you, Yomei."

"Same here. Travel safely."

Yomei waved as the train shuddered into motion, sliding away while huffing out puffs of vapors. Her eyes were trailing Lily's window until they misted over. Then hot tears trickled down and stung her cheeks.

· *Thirty-Six* ·

After Lily's departure, Yomei gradually calmed down. Her mother's company helped her cope with the separation from her friend. Ren Rui said to her, "There's no banquet that doesn't end. Lily must have her own life. It's better to part as good friends before you tire of each other."

What her mother said made Yomei reflect on her friendship with Lily over the years. Indeed, Lily, even though a staunch friend and like a sister, had seemed like her companion in others' eyes. Except for Young Zeng, whenever a man appeared in their shared life, he had come for her, Yomei, without paying attention to Lily. During the past years, from time to time Lily had complained that Yomei's trouble with men had had nothing to do with her and that she'd been dragged into a quagmire merely for Yomei's sake. That was true. Somehow all the men attracted to Yomei had just ignored her friend, as if Lily were a little sister of hers, a mere teenager. That kind of neglect hadn't been fair to Lily, to say the least. It was time Lily stopped playing her sidekick.

That realization soothed Yomei, who was pleased that she and Lily had parted as good friends. Maybe with their respective pursuits, they both might thrive more; in other

words, such a separation might be necessary for their
growth. Yomei reminded herself that she ought to feel
grateful to have such a true friend in her life.

About a month after Yomei had been back in Yan'an,
Mother Deng handed her a letter one evening. She
recognized the tilted handwriting in ballpoint—it was from
Lily, whose penmanship was far better in Russian than
in their native script. Lily wrote that originally she was
eager to go to the countryside and participate in the land
reform there, but the Northeastern Party Bureau wouldn't
let her, saying she was much more needed as a translator,
so now she worked for Li Lisan's Liaison Department,
both translating documents and interpreting for foreign
experts and delegates. It was hectically busy in Harbin, but
she enjoyed the work and the environment, and for the first
time, she'd felt her life charged with a purpose—to serve the
revolutionary cause. Lily also revealed why Yomei had been
blocked from going back to Harbin:

"I broached the topic with Lisa and Li Lisan at their home
one evening and told them that we had been astonished and
outraged in Beijing and Changchun when we found out
the contents of the telegrams dispatched by Li Lisan. He
was perplexed, then asked, 'What telegrams? After you and
Yomei left Harbin, I never sent anything about either of you
to Yan'an.' I thought he was playing dumb. Then he recalled
an exchange with Yeh Qun in late November. Yeh asked
him to cable Yan'an to stop you from coming back, but he
wouldn't do it. He told her that you wouldn't interfere with
her marriage because you could marry Liu Yalou, but Yeh
Qun wouldn't listen and said there had already been run-
ins over you between Lin Biao and Liu Yalou. Yeh Qun told
him, 'Imagine that our commander in chief and the head of
the general staff fell out over a young woman. How could the

army operate properly in the battlefields? It would definitely undermine the troops' capability and even morale. So we have more than a half million men's lives at stake and must forestall such a disaster.' All the same, Li Lisan didn't send out any telegram, though he saw her point. He told me that it must have been Yeh Qun who dispatched the cables to Yan'an and Changchun surreptitiously, using his name. He felt betrayed and outraged, but couldn't confront her since her husband, Lin Biao, was his boss."

Lily also added that Yomei mustn't leak this secret to anyone, because its disclosure might compromise others, particularly Li Lisan.

Yomei was shaken by Lily's revelation but felt good that she hadn't gone to Harbin, where she might have gathered a great deal of lightning without being aware of the approaching rainstorm. Indeed, here in Yan'an, under Vice Chairman Zhou's aegis, she was quite safe and didn't need to keep her guard up all the time. When she had returned from Beijing, Father Zhou had asked her why such a telegram had appeared and whether someone in Harbin, such as Li Lisan or Lin Biao, disliked her. She explained as much as she could, even though she was also in the dark about the true situation. She told Father Zhou that she'd gotten on well with Li Lisan, who was avuncular to her all the time; she'd always felt at ease with him. Besides, his wife, Lisa, was a good friend. But Lin Biao was different—he had asked her for her hand in marriage, but she'd never agreed. When leaving Moscow six years before, he had said he would wait for her answer patiently, but then without any hint to her, he had married Yeh Qun and had two children with her in three years. Yomei emphasized to Father Zhou that she'd never been attracted to Lin Biao anyway, so she'd felt calm to see him and his wife in Harbin, but Yeh Qun

seemed agitated and unhappy, even rather hostile. Maybe the
telegrams reflected Lin Biao's domestic troubles—he wanted
to keep his wife undisturbed. Zhou Enlai's face fell after
hearing her explanation. He told her, "Don't ever interfere
with Lin Biao's marriage. He's the most brilliant officer our
Party has and is now commanding the entire Northeastern
Army. He mustn't be distracted in any fashion."

Now, with Lily's letter in front of her, she wondered
whether to share it with Father Zhou. Maybe she shouldn't
rush. Such a disclosure might get Li Lisan into trouble,
which was the last thing she wanted to do. So in the evening
she went to see her mother, Ren Rui, who was still ill and
hadn't resumed working yet.

Ren Rui believed Yomei must withhold the truth of the
telegrams from the Zhous because such a revelation would
stir up a hornet's nest in the Party: specifically, it might
jeopardize Li Lisan and Lisa. If the couple were Yomei's
friends, such a matter should stop here, buried in herself.
Now, Yomei might have more trouble down the road, since
Yeh Qun was evidently good at intrigue and scheming,
so Yomei must be careful. She'd better avoid the center of
politics and the domestic strife of the major leaders.

"What should I do to live in safety and peace, Mom?"

Ren Rui heaved a sigh. "You must always be the Zhous'
adopted daughter. That can protect you, so nobody within the
Party can hurt you without having to answer to the Zhous."

"I know that and will behave like a filial daughter to
them. Just now you said I should avoid the political center.
How can I do that?"

"Maybe you should request to go to another place where
you can direct plays for a theater?"

"But there isn't a city like Harbin under the Communists'
control yet. It won't be safe for me to go to Beijing or

Shanghai or Nanjing now. The Nationalist police will nab me just because I'm known as Zhou Enlai's adopted daughter."

"Maybe you should speak to the Zhous? I'm sure Mother Deng hopes to get you out of Yan'an, so they might find an appropriate place for you. Just be careful when dealing with all the problematic women, like Jiang Ching and Yeh Qun."

"Do you put Mother Deng in the same category?"

"No. She's basically a good and kindhearted woman, but she could feel threatened, especially when a pretty young thing like you appears in her household. So I won't say she's a bad person. I know Jiang Ching is difficult, with lots of vengeful fire in her vitals, so don't ever offend her overtly. I've never met Yeh Qun. Still, the telegram incident shows she is devious and can be vicious. You must be vigilant when mixing with those powerful women."

"I won't brush elbows with them."

"Then you should find your own niche where you can work and live safely."

Yomei spoke with her adoptive parents the following day. Father Zhou was pleased to see that she wasn't disappointed by her inability to join the theater group in Harbin. Both his wife and he felt that, although specialized in spoken drama, Yomei still needed to know China's reality to become a mature and useful artist, so she should join the comrades in the land-reform movement and also participate in fighting against the Nationalist regime. Right now, Mother Deng suggested, she shouldn't rush and perhaps should start by joining a small team of comrades in land reform and gradually figure out what would suit her better. The older woman assured her that someday she would definitely stand out, and that the Party would make proper use of her ability and talent. It was just a matter of time.

Thirty-Seven

Before the winter was over, Yomei went to the border region of Shanxi and Shaanxi Provinces, where she participated in land-reform work. Nobody among her colleagues knew she was from a revolutionary family or was the adopted daughter of Zhou Enlai, though by her exotic and refined manner they could tell she was from Russia and well educated. Nonetheless, people enjoyed her presence among them. She was vivacious and always humming a song or tune. In a way, she was like a young girl to them.

But clearly she was such a dramaturge that it would be a waste to keep her in a land-reform group for long, so soon she was transferred to the United University of Northern China, a school established by the CCP, where she became a professor in its Department of Dramatic Performance. Now she could teach drama theories and practice. Her classes were well attended, and she began to have a following. Besides teaching, she had to take part in propaganda work designed to promote the morale of the troops that had been fighting the forces of Chiang Kai-shek. Even though she was a professor, she was now also a cultural officer in the army, since the distinction between the military and the civilian services was often blurred at the time, and since

the school was part of the CCP's army. She didn't mind
that so long as she could teach theater arts, which was a
change from the propaganda work she could not avoid. The
latter had its own rules and methods, with which she was
unfamiliar and in which she did her best to participate.
Later she even went to the frontline at Taiyuan, where the
Communist troops surrounded the city and eventually took
it. Both civilian and military life enriched her, and now
she felt she had some basic grasp of what real life was like,
so that in the future when working on plays about China
and Chinese people, she wouldn't be lost in her artistic
pursuit. For her, art must be useful and reflect the spirit of
the times. She was determined to make her art "serve the
people and the land."

Meanwhile, her friend Lily had made a great deal of
progress too. Lily had become an expert badly needed by
the Party. Within a year after their separation, she began
to serve as the interpreter for one delegation after another,
helping the CCP's officials and cultural dignitaries on their
visits to Eastern Europe, where they attended international
conferences and gatherings. Yomei was happy for her friend
and could see that Lily was an important member in the
Party's liaison work. There weren't many young Chinese
fluent in Russian and familiar with the Soviet affairs, and
also trusted by the Party. In hindsight, Yomei could see that
it had been necessary for them to part ways the year before.
Now they each had their respective space for development,
though Lily at times would complain that she still wanted
to study; maybe she'd go back to Moscow someday to do a
graduate degree in philosophy or political theories. She felt
she wasn't good at organizing people or handling money,
both of which she had to do when she led a delegation
abroad. Sometimes she'd write a check for more than fifty

thousand rubles. She confessed in her letter to Yomei, "That is really nerve-racking, considering that in Moscow we used to live on the cheap, pitching kopecks and pooling our money together at the end of the month for half a kilo of salted herrings."

While the battle of Taiyuan was underway, the university's drama department stayed in Yuci, a suburban town south of Taiyuan. They took up a project—restaging a folk opera called *A False Alarm*, and Yomei was assigned to direct it, even though by profession she was an expert in spoken drama. This was her first theater project, so she accepted the assignment and went about the directing work conscientiously. The opera was small, with only two main characters, and even the production crew didn't take it seriously, feeling it was just a piece of propaganda, like a skit, which was intended to be performed in Taiyuan, after the PLA entered the city, to pacify the civilians. The opera shows how a fabric merchant in Tianjin city mistakes the Liberation Army for just another warlord's force that will kill and rob, damaging people's property and livelihood. It follows that the startled merchant fears that his shop will be nationalized, but after witnessing how the PLA soldiers help and care for civilians, the man changes his attitude, and at the end he becomes a supporter of this people's army, which turns out to be law-abiding and protective of the people's interests. So the initial fright, dispelled at last, turns out to be only a false alarm.

Yomei studied the text carefully and decided to add a prelude and a coda, both of which not only highlighted the central idea and extended the storyline but also gave the feeling of a complete opera. The fabric merchant now starts by chanting these lines added by Yomei:

On both sides of the Yongding River,
The wheat seedlings are green.
It's said that the PLA is going to attack Tianjin—
They have already leveled hundreds of strongholds,
And the barricades around the town
Cannot stop them, not at all . . .

Following those lines was the merchant's monologue about the possibility of his fabric shop getting nationalized. Thus, at the very beginning, enough dramatic momentum was generated and the story could move with a clear purpose. Yomei also revised a number of the original lines by adding some colloquial expressions to enliven the comic effect. She had the new script of the opera distributed among the production group and requested their comments. They all liked the revision and said they were amazed and eager to work with this young director, whose Russian training and education shone in the revised text.

On the first day of their working together, the poet Ai Ching, the vice president of the university, gathered the production crew in a classroom to meet with Yomei. The young men and women, in spite of their lovely looks, were all wearing the army's uniform, gray and drab. They were surprised to see the director step in wearing a cream-colored silk shirt and a polka-dotted skirt. She was not just pretty but also stylish and exotic. Her presence excited the group, who were already familiar with the folk opera but still eager to work with the young director. The band could play the music without rehearsal, though they'd have to create new melodies for the prelude and the coda.

During their rehearsal, Yomei found the lead actor, Chien Min, exaggerating the fabric merchant's doubts and fright so much that the small businessman seemed like a crook. She asked the actor, "Do you think the shop owner is a good man or bad man?"

Chien Min replied offhandedly, "A rogue of course. The lyrics already say what kind of man he is: 'People say the Communists kill, burn, take away everything you have.' He says he's afraid that his fabric store will be nationalized."

Yomei's face fell. "Why do you think of him like that?"

"Because nine out of ten businessmen are devious, taking advantage of people. We all know that no merchant is honest."

His words upset her, and she told him, "If you think that way, how could you act well? 'People say' means 'It's rumored,' reported by others, just hearsay. It doesn't come from the shop owner's own mind. He's just a common citizen, easily influenced by rumors. You must treat him as who he is, neither good nor bad, just a regular man with his own inner struggle and mental complexity."

Though the actor's performance improved considerably afterward, the others in the group hadn't changed their minds about the fabric-shop owner. At the dress rehearsal, the man's face was made like a greedy, ferocious landowner's. At the sight of Chien Min's crafty, ugly face, Yomei said, "No, no, it mustn't be like this. Let me help you change some." She redrew his eyebrows, making them thinner and curve a little, and also dulled the sharpness of his eyes' edges. Even his mustache fell at both ends. As a result, his face appeared softer and warmer, like that of the God of Wealth in folklore. The transformation amazed everyone. Chien Min looked at himself in a mirror and said, "This face gives me a clue how to play the role—he's worried and uncertain, but he appears friendly and even reliable."

"That's right." Yomei patted him on the shoulder. "If he doesn't look good-hearted and trustworthy, how can he keep customers?"

The play became an instant success, an exemplary piece of propaganda theater. The locals in Yuci town were bowled over by it, with some even following the troupe when it performed the opera inside Taiyuan city. Those who had seen it before all said the play felt like a brand-new work now.

Later, following the PLA's victories, the opera was staged in town after town and city after city in northern China. Finally, at the beginning of 1949, when Beijing had been peacefully taken over by the Communists, the troupe was summoned to perform *A False Alarm* in that metropolis, which hadn't become the new capital yet. It was well received everywhere in northern China and made Yomei known in the theater world.

· *Thirty-Eight* ·

I n the spring of 1949, many CCP officials and workers gathered in Beijing to make preparations for establishing the new central government. Plainly, the Nationalist regime was collapsing, and it was just matter of time before the Communists took over the whole country. After Yomei's drama group performed in Beijing, she was transferred to the preparatory staff of the new government and stayed outside Beijing from then on. She plunged into the frenetic work for the inauguration of the new government. Then the first women's conference organized by the CCP was convened in the city, which Yomei as well as Mother Deng attended. Hundreds of women gathered at the Beijing Hotel for the conference, including Yomei's aunt Ren Jun and her friend Lisa, who was invited as a Soviet expert.

Lisa hadn't changed much, though she had another daughter, who had just started to talk. Lisa's strong face brightened at the sight of Yomei, and they hugged and then went into a bar for coffee. Yomei placed the pink-faced baby girl, Alla, on her lap while conversing with her mother. The child was happy and grasped at a coffee spoon, which Yomei let her play with. Lisa said that she liked teaching Russian to the Chinese students in Harbin, but she was going to join the faculty of Beijing College of Foreign

Languages. That was why they had moved from Harbin. In fact, her husband was about to become a senior official in the new government, probably a minister of sorts. The new State Council would need his service in view of his deep connections with the Soviet Union and his Russian skills.

Yomei remembered the telegrams that had blocked her way to Harbin two years before and asked Lisa about the details. Her friend shook her head of thick chestnut hair, her amber eyes glazing over as though something hurt her. She told Yomei, "It was Yeh Qun who demanded that my husband cable to the Central Committee to stop you from going to Harbin. She's a flighty, unbalanced woman, saying that your presence in the city could have damaged the rapport among the senior officers at the headquarters of the Northeastern Army. I guess, she was jealous of you and felt threatened. Lin Biao often yelled at her."

"Do you mean their marriage is in trouble?" Yomei asked.

"I'm not sure. They often fight but seem to get on all right. Do you still want to go to Harbin to work with that theater group? They've been doing better and have put on some good plays, including Gorky's *Philistines*."

"I was just assigned another job, working as a Russian translator, at times also as an interpreter, for the Party's Central Committee, but you know that at heart I want to direct plays. I'm not interested in a political career."

"That might be a better choice, actually. Politics can be riddled with intrigues and frustrations. My husband often says that if he could start over, he'd become an architect or an engineer. It would be better if your profession is more or less independent of politics. I mean, you can earn your living without having to hold an official position."

"That's why you enjoy teaching?"

"Yes, I'm going to help the college here build their Russian department."

"Say, if I can't land a directing job eventually, can I come and teach in your department?"

"Teaching Russian?"

"Yes, I've never stopped reading books in Russian since I came back. Also, I've been doing translation for the central government these days, so I can say my Russian is better now."

"I can tell." They had been speaking Russian the whole time. She said to Yomei, "Personally, I'd love to have you as a colleague, but at this point, I don't know how much say I can have in the department. I'll do my best to help you, of course, if it comes to that. But I feel you'll have more important work to do, like Lily."

"In a letter she said she might eventually join the group of translators working on Chairman Mao's writings."

"You mean translating his works into Russian?" asked Lisa.

"Yes."

They went on talking about Lily, who was leading a CCP delegation on a trip through Poland at the moment, from where they would visit other Eastern European countries. In every way, Lily seemed to be thriving and might continue working abroad for the new Chinese government.

After kissing Alla once more, Yomei took leave of Lisa. Speak of the devil—in the vast vestibule of the hotel, Yeh Qun appeared, her face slightly pudgy now, and wearing two medals and a name tag on a blue lanyard around her neck. Yomei did a double take, a bit flustered, but tried to think of something to say to Lin Biao's wife, who, in her military uniform, was eye-catching in this crowd of civilians. Her husband had risen to be the number one

general in the PLA, and in recent years his army had won
two decisive battles that had wiped out most of Chiang
Kai-shek's major forces. It was said that Lin Biao would
definitely become a marshal once the new government
was established, and that if his health permitted, he'd take
charge of the Ministry of Defense. As Yomei was wondering
whether to ask Yeh Qun about Lin Biao's health—she had
heard he suffered from severe migraines and depression
and often got sick from the stress of battle operations—the
little woman looked daggers at Yomei, her eyes sharp with
malice and her mouth a flat line. Then Yeh Qun swung
away and muttered, as if to herself, "This is a large world.
Why always crowd together?"

At a loss what to say, Yomei merely watched the short
woman striding away, her shoulders stooping a little.
Her pants were so baggy that she seemed hipless despite
the broad spread of her bottom. Scandalized, Yomei was
agonizing over whether to catch up with Yeh Qun and ask
why she had sent the telegrams under Li Lisan's name,
feeding disinformation to the Central Committee, but she
thought better of it, realizing that such an act would have
stirred up more trouble. Yet the woman's barbed words and
menacing eyes convinced Yomei that Yeh Qun still viewed
her as an enemy, so she must be more careful in Beijing,
since Lin Biao had become a preeminent figure in the
CCP's leadership. At the moment, his army, more than one
million strong, was poised to cross the Yangtze to topple the
Nationalist government in Nanjing. Even though the man
might still have some affection for her, she preferred to have
nothing to do with him. It was groundless for Yeh Qun to
feel threatened, as though Yomei were determined to steal
her husband. This was insane. From whatever angle you
looked at it, this didn't bode well. Yomei reminded herself

to be very cautious from now on when dealing with the Lins. She'd better steer clear of them.

The encounter with Yeh Qun dampened Yomei's spirit, and for days she avoided the crowds in the hotel, tried to stay away from the women's conference, and worked as much as she could in the translation office of the central government. She had a lot to do, rendering official documents into Russian and vice versa.

Then she heard from her aunt Ren Jun that her mother was hospitalized in Tianjin city, so she requested a leave from her office. Knowing she was Zhou Enlai's daughter and Ren Rui was a revered revolutionary, her superiors told her to stay with her mother as long as she needed. Without delay she hopped on the local train to that city in the east. It was just a two-hour ride.

· Thirty-Nine ·

When Yomei arrived at Heavenly Tavern Hospital in downtown Tianjin, her mother, suffering protracted tuberculosis, was in bad shape, hardly able to breathe. At age fifty-eight, she looked older, pallid, and emaciated. It was believed that her new acute condition had been precipitated partly by her youngest son's death. In recent months, she'd gotten exhausted easily and couldn't function like herself as before. After her hospitalization, her eldest son, Sun Yang, came to Tianjin to care for her for more than half a month, but he had to return to the Tsitsihar region, so Yomei's arrival couldn't be timelier. She and her brother looked after their mother together for two more days, then he went back to the northeast, where a large backlog of work was awaiting him.

On the small bedside table was a new book, an anthology of revolutionary poetry that contained two poems by Ren Rui, including "Seeing My Son Off to the Front." Her son Yang had brought her the book, which she cherished so much that she often reached out for it. After Yang had left, her condition took a turn for the worse. At times, she murmured her daughters' names, even though Yomei was sitting by her side. She also whispered "Ren Jun"—the name of her youngest sister, who had been attending the women's conference in Beijing and would come see her soon.

Besides feeding her mother and helping her take pills, Yomei also changed her diapers and emptied her bedpan. In addition, she gave her a towel bath every morning. After the bath, at her mother's request, Yomei would also dab floral perfume on her to counter the faint sour smell exuding from her. At times when she was awake and alert, Ren Rui looked shamefaced, seeing, her daughter cleaning her up. She said she shouldn't have troubled Yomei like this, but her daughter shushed her, saying, "You must have done this thousands of times for me. Now it's my turn to do the same for you. Mama, just relax and let me do the work."

Ren Rui would breathe a sigh. She also asked Yomei about her adoptive parents, specifically whether Father Zhou was supportive of her future plan for a directing career. Yomei said, "He saw the play *A False Alarm* that we performed for the Central Committee at Shijiazhuang, and he liked it a lot. He urged me to direct more plays. But at the moment, things are hectic, and we are all busy working for the inauguration of the new republic. I guess that once things settle down some, there might be a new job for me. Everything will work out fine. Don't worry."

"You're a smart girl and know how to navigate in treacherous circumstances. You must always stay close to the Zhous and insist to others that you're their daughter. This is a way to protect yourself. Within the Party you must have powerful people's support. On top of that, you're almost twenty-eight. It's time you found a man and got married. That can put me at ease. Do you already have someone in mind?"

"No, Mama. Don't talk so much. You need more rest."

"I'm worried about you, Yomei. Tell me, what kind of man do you like?"

"I don't like officials or officers. I don't want to have a powerful man who's like a boss at home. That's clear to me."

"Why? You'll need a strong shoulder to lean on, won't you?"

"I'm more interested in art, not in power."

Her mother sighed and closed her eyes, one of her sunken cheeks, the right one, twitching a little. She said in a half whisper, "Keep in mind, an artist needs the endorsement of an organization, and it's hard to survive on your own."

"You mean without the auspices of the Party an artist can't accomplish anything?"

"Right. So don't let your artistic pursuit mislead you into a blind alley."

"I'll remember what you said, Mama." In spite of saying that, she didn't totally agree with her mother. What about Gogol or Chekhov or Ibsen or Goldoni? she wondered. Even Stanislavski didn't belong to any political organization and identified himself only as a director and actor—a theater artist. There must be artistic work undefined or confined by politics. It was common sense that arts could transcend political power and operate in a different orbit. If those great artists could exist in Russia and other countries, there must be some space in China where genuine artists could work and thrive. But she didn't want to counter her mother overtly. At the moment, Ren Rui needed to recuperate enough to leave the hospital soon. What was urgent was that Yomei must figure out a way to look after her mother once she was discharged from the hospital. If she herself wasn't always available, she'd have to find proper care for her mother.

Her aunt arrived the next morning, but Ren Rui's condition had just turned critical, as if she'd been doing her utmost to wait to see her youngest sister Ren Jun. When they finally met, Rui seized hold of Jun's hand while tears spilled out of her eyes. Then Jun buried her face in the quilt over Rui's abdomen and broke out sobbing, twitching her shoulders. She said Rui must get well soon now that they were finally about to establish their new country—it was time to rejoice and celebrate the victory. But with staggered breath and a faint whistle in her lungs, her elder sister said, "I might not be lucky enough to enjoy our new life. You and Yomei must take care of each other and also let our old dad know I won't be able to serve him anymore, but I will look after him in the next life."

Jun cried so hard that her arched back began convulsing. Among their siblings she was particularly close to Rui,

Left to right: Ren Rui, Yomei, and Ren Jun

having lived with her for so many years, and it was Rui who had taken her to Yan'an, where Jun had joined the revolution, attending the arts academy and performing in a drama troupe. What's more, Jun was only one year older

than Yomei, and they used to study and play together and
even sleep in the same bed. The two of them also entered
the same troupe in Shanghai together to learn how to act.
As a result, they were like sisters, even if Yomei always
called Jun "Sixth Aunt," so Rui had been like a mother to
her youngest sister Jun as well.

Ren Rui stopped breathing the next day. Numerous
officials from Tianjin municipality, including the newly
appointed mayor, came to bid farewell to her, since she
was well respected in the Party. Yomei cabled the Zhous
about her mother's passing, and right away it was arranged
that Ren Rui was to be interred in Beijing, the prospective
capital, even though the CCP had not yet designated its
own official burial site for its martyrs and distinguished
deceased comrades (such as the well-known revolutionary
cemetery at Babao Hill later on). Her body was put on a
train to Beijing, where a memorial service was to be held
in her honor. Then she'd be buried in Peace for Everyone,
a public cemetery. Yomei and Jun and some others
accompanied the casket on the train, all wearing a black
armband and a white paper flower on their chest.

At the funeral the next afternoon, Lily's father Lin
Bochü delivered a short speech, praising Ren Rui as
a dedicated fighter for the socialist cause and for the
establishment of the new China. He felt honored to have
been her longtime friend and to have worked with her for
many years in Yan'an. He said, "She was a model wife and
a great mother figure to many young people around her.
After her husband was murdered by the Nationalists twenty-
two years ago, she raised her four children alone, moving
around to escape persecutions from the reactionaries. She
taught the youngsters progressive ideas and compassionate
attitudes, and she never stopped writing for periodicals

in support of our struggle. She was a devoted educator whose passing is a great loss to us and to our Party. We all will miss her sorely and hold her dearly in our hearts as a beam of light and as an example of selfless dedication. Dear Comrade Ren Rui, may you rest in peace!"

Zhou Enlai, representing the CCP, inscribed the tombstone to acknowledge her as a revolutionary martyr. The following day, *The People's Daily* reported her passing and the solemn occasion of her memorial service and burial. It also stated that more than forty dignitaries had attended her funeral.

· *Forty* ·

Without her own housing yet, Yomei told her temporary work unit, the preparatory secretariat of the new government, her wish to stay close to her aunt Jun. Jun and her husband and two children were living in Bright Green Village near Beijing city's Donghua Gate. So Yomei was given a room next to Jun's home. After she had settled in, numerous family friends arrived to see her and Jun and give their condolences for the passing of Ren Rui. Father Zhou and Mother Deng also came to see them. At the sight of her adoptive parents, Yomei burst into tears, saying she felt so miserable about her mother's life, which hadn't seemed to have a single happy period. Mother Deng hugged Yomei and said, "Many women have lived a hard life like your mother's. That's why we must do our best to continue with the cause left by her—the liberation of womankind."

Those words calmed down Yomei. She rose and went into Jun's kitchen to brew a pot of fresh *pu'er* tea for her adoptive parents. In spite of her grief, she promised to go see them more often in the future, now that they were all living in Beijing. Hearing that, Father Zhou said, "Please take our home as your own from now on."

"I will of course, Dad," said Yomei.

Nowadays she felt more at ease just to call the Zhous Dad and Mom. Such a relationship felt more appropriate after her birth mother's passing.

Early in the summer, Yomei was invited to attend the first national conference on arts and literature, which was held in downtown Beijing. At the meeting she met many people in the field of theater arts and found that the small opera *A False Alarm* had earned her some reputation. She had become known as a stage director trained in Moscow, specializing in the Stanislavski method, which many of her Chinese colleagues were eager to learn. Except for Yomei, there was nobody in this country who had studied the method systematically. As a result, a few theaters in Tianjin and Shenyang and Jinan even tried to persuade her to join them. She was excited to see such opportunities, though at the moment she couldn't make up her mind about where to go yet. She just told those theaters that she would seriously consider their offers.

Against expectations, when the conference had ended, she was invited to join a delegation that was going to Hungary for the Second International Youth Festival (attended mainly by the socialist bloc countries), partly because she could perform and speak Russian—her presence among the Chinese delegates could make the group appear more international, capable of directly communicating with the participants from other nations. What's more, she could help the Chinese delegation with its logistical work and travel arrangements. She was savvy about life in the Soviet Union, which the group planned to visit after seeing a few other Eastern European countries. Yomei accepted the invitation readily and also wondered if this opportunity might be due to Father Zhou's help behind the scenes, but when she told Mother Deng about the invitation, the older woman was genuinely surprised. Her response convinced Yomei that she had been picked for the delegation mainly thanks to her professional qualification. She should feel more confident about herself.

She enjoyed the trip very much, in part because she was just a regular member in the delegation without any leadership role. At most, she occasionally served as an interpreter for some fellow delegates. That made her feel good and useful. In Budapest she could relax while mixing with young people from other countries; she also

Yomei in her late twenties

represented the Chinese delegation to sing a number of folk songs at a public gathering. She always enjoyed performing to an audience, which felt almost natural to her. (Her friend Lily used to joke that the stage-fright nerves in

Yomei may have snapped at birth.) On another occasion she even sang a few Russian songs, which were well received too. Among the twenty-some Chinese delegates, she stood out as a vivacious person, well informed about Eastern Europe and knowledgeable about arts and literature. She even made a handful of friends, who hoped to visit the new China in the near future.

After Budapest, the delegation went to Poland and Czechoslovakia, where they visited collective farms and vineyards and dairies. Yomei was excited to see how butter was churned, and how assorted cheeses were made. They also paid visits to factories that manufactured automobiles, tractors, combines, backhoes, and dump trucks. In Warsaw, they took a bus to the Lodz ghetto, where more than one hundred thousand Jews had been forced to work at the ordnance and munition factories and garment sweatshops for the Nazi military during the Second World War. There was a Jewish museum in the ruins of the ghetto, where the Chinese delegates presented a large wreath, leaning it against a segment of brick wall splotched with mold.

On top of everything else, they were impressed by the affluent and peaceful life of the Czech farmers. Many of the families in the countryside lived in villa-like houses and had their own vegetable gardens and farming machines. Most of the households had a large radio set, and many owned a sedan or truck. In spite of the national collectivization, the Czechs seemed to have managed to preserve parts of the traditional country life. Some of the Chinese delegates sighed, saying it would take decades for Chinese peasants to realize such a comfortable and prosperous life. Perhaps that was simply out of the question, considering China had so little arable land for such a large population—540 million people. Yomei could see that the quality of the Czech farmers' life must be superior to that of the Soviet farmers, but she didn't share this thought with the other delegates.

From Prague, they went to East Germany. Parts of Berlin were still in ruins, and there were lines at bakeries and grocery stores. The Chinese youth delegation made a trip to Hitler's Chancellery, which was in town. The place was largely demolished, and everywhere was rubble. They went inside the Führerbunker, which must have been a grand building, with a colonnaded entrance. A sign said this was the place where Hitler and his mistress Eva Braun had committed suicide as soon as they had held their wedding when the Red Army was approaching. Yomei followed the others, going deep into the bunker, wherein it was gloomy and dank now with the odor of mildew, but the air also felt charged, as though something was about to explode. On a large desk was spread a military map illuminated by a shaft of light pouring in from a small paneless window on the ceiling. A pair of white gloves was lying on the hardwood next to the edge of the map. There was also a thick magnifying glass on the desk. Yomei couldn't help but wonder how often Hitler had had to get out for fresh air and sunlight every day. Anyone who stayed in this damp, vaulted shelter for long could get sick easily. On the other hand, when it had still served as part of the Reich Chancellery, this place could have been bright and magnificent, with all its marble floors and massive windows and doors.

Stepping outside the damaged bunker, she saw a deserted flowerbed in which some geraniums were blooming, their pink blossoms flaky and scraggly, and there were a couple of red amaryllis flowers among them. She picked up a white pebble the size of a pigeon egg from the flowerbed and slipped it into her purse. She meant to take it back as a souvenir for Mother Deng, for whom she ought to get only something hard to come by in China, because Father Zhou was the premier now and the Zhous must have everything they needed. They lived and worked in the center of Beijing, in the Zhongnanhai compound, where only the few top leaders' families resided. Yomei felt good about this unique pebble, which could be a special present for Mother Deng.

From East Germany, their delegation took the train to the Soviet Union, where they planned to travel for a month. But in Minsk, they received a telegram from Beijing— Foreign Minister Zhang Wentian instructed that Comrade Sun Yomei go to Moscow immediately and report for duty at the Chinese embassy there. Yomei had to leave her fellow delegates and hopped on an express heading north alone. To her knowledge, Liu Shaoqi, now the number two leader in the CCP, had just come to the Soviet Union for an official visit. Together with Vice Chairman Liu was Wang Jia-hsiang, who was also an experienced leader and could speak Russian. Yomei knew both of them and called them Uncle. Moreover, Mr. Liu's children, Aichin and Yunbin, used to be her friends in Moscow, though later the Liu brother and sister both went to the international children's home in Ivanovo. The two had come to the Soviet Union right after Yomei. She'd heard that by now they had both married foreigners (having become "Musty Bread"), though their father disliked such international marriages and even demanded that they divorce their spouses. Perhaps this time Vice Chairman Liu might need her, Yomei, to help persuade his children to repatriate. In any event, it was odd that she had been summoned without any hint beforehand.

· Forty-One ·

Moscow hadn't changed much from three years before. The first snow had obliterated many of the distinct features of the cityscape, the trees fluffy and their branches slightly bent with icicles glittering in the cold wind. Now and again they dropped tiny clumps of snow. Along the street a few drainage grates were belching out whitish steam. Houses and buildings were all snowcapped. The order in the telegram stated that Yomei report to Ambassador Wang Jia-hsiang at 13 Kropotkin Alley. She knew the place, which used to be Nationalist China's embassy, but the diplomats of the old regime had all fled, so the premises were occupied by the staff from the PRC now. Yomei was familiar with the area, near Lenin Hill, and took the metro to get there.

Ambassador Wang Jia-hsiang was a slim, urbane man of medium height and in his early forties. He received Yomei on the same day she arrived. They'd met in Yan'an, where she'd taken a course taught by him. He had spent five years in the late 1920s in the Soviet Union, studying at Moscow Sun Yat-sen University while receiving medical treatment. Among the top leaders of the CCP, he was known for being levelheaded and good at tackling thorny problems. Yomei congratulated him on his brand-new position, which was the most important Chinese ambassadorship, equal to a foreign minister in rank. Ever since he was wounded in the abdomen on the Long March fourteen years before, he had been in frail health. Even now, he kept a hot-water bottle underneath his jacket when working at his desk. Yomei noticed the small bump above his lap and asked after his health.

"I'm doing all right," he said with a smile. "We've been hectic, working day and night to sort out things. We called you over to help us prepare for Chairman Mao's visit next month."

"Oh, finally he's coming. What's my job exactly?"

"Help us with interpretation and translation."

"But I'm not an experienced interpreter."

"Chairman Mao will have his official interpreter, so you won't need to translate for him on most of the formal occasions, but you can accompany him on his visits to local places, serving as a tour interpreter or a backup interpreter."

"You mean Mr. Shi Zhe will come too?"

"Right. He'll be the interpreter when Chairman Mao meets with the Soviet leaders. For the less formal occasions, you can step in to give him a break."

"All right, I can do that."

Shi Zhe used to be Uncle Ren Bishi's secretary in Moscow and also briefly in charge of the affairs of the Chinese children at the Interdorm. He had lived in the Soviet Union for fifteen years and served as a colonel for nine years in the Department of Internal Affairs, mostly working in Novosibirsk. In the CCP, he was known as a legendary police figure, partly due to the fact that he'd gone through special training by the Soviet intelligence agency. Soon after returning to Yan'an with his boss Ren Bishi and the Zhous in 1940, he was recruited by Mao as his personal interpreter. Thanks to his Russian skills and his deep connections in the USSR, he was revered by many Party leaders, especially by those who needed a Soviet backup and feared its disapproval, since most of the vital information to and from the USSR went through his hands. Every few years, the Soviets had even summoned Shi Zhe to Russia to brief his superiors, though he wouldn't always come to report for duty, fearful of the gossip about him in the CCP and of Chairman Mao's suspicion. In reality, his source of power was also his Achilles' heel, and later he was imprisoned partly for that, being accused of espionage for the Soviet Union.

Yomei was given a room in the embassy and began translating documents for them. She liked working with those diplomats, some of whom had fought battles back in China and were still injured. She came to know that Vice Chairman Liu Shaoqi had gone back to Beijing and taken his daughter Aichin along with him, even though she had just married a Spaniard. To Yomei, to break up the young couple's marriage was cruel, though it was done in the name of revolutionary needs. She wasn't very close to Aichin, who was five or six years younger than she was, but she felt awful for the young woman. It was said that even though Liu Shaoqi had tried hard, he hadn't succeeded in getting his son Yunbin repatriated. Yunbin had married a Russian brunette and was still studying at Moscow University, majoring in nuclear physics. To Yomei, Liu Shaoqi seemed crazy, though she didn't share her thoughts with anyone. If only Lily were here. Together they could have compared notes to figure out some secrets in the top circle and had a better sense of their own circumstances.

In fact, Lily had been in Moscow just three months before, keeping the company of Madame Mao, Jiang Ching, who had come for a medical checkup and treatment. Lily served as her interpreter on that visit and seemed to get along with that vain, crabby woman, who somehow appreciated Lily. According to what Lily and others had told Yomei, she had kept Jiang Ching company on most of her official visits to Eastern Europe. They even attended a state banquet that Stalin hosted in honor of Liu Shaoqi, on the second floor of his Kuntsevo Dacha, outside Moscow. On that occasion, Jiang Ching stood up and proposed a toast to wish Stalin everlasting good health. The supreme leader tipped his head back and laughed heartily. The toast pleased Stalin so much that his swallow-shaped mustache began flapping a little. In return, he proposed one too, saying "We feel honored to have Comrade Jiang Ching visiting our country." Soon, word reached Beijing that Stalin had drunk to Jiang Ching in Moscow, and it was said that Chairman Mao had been somewhat troubled by that, because by rule Ching was not allowed to get so actively involved in political events. Actually, Liu Shaoqi had spoken with Jiang Ching beforehand and advised her to keep a low profile at the banquet, but Lavrentiy Beria and Georgy Malenkov had happened to be sitting next to Ching at the table and both had urged her to propose a toast to make Stalin happy. That was why she stood up to drink to Stalin's health, regardless of the secret restrictions imposed on her. In Lily's letter, she told Yomei that on that occasion she, Lily, ran into Stalin in the parlor adjoining the dining room and that he chatted with her briefly, asking after Madame Sun Yat-sen. Yomei was happy for her friend, who had apparently begun to play a significant role in the CCP's top circle when they had dealings with the USSR.

That must be another reason Ching had insisted that
Lily stay with her during her medical treatment in the
Soviet Union. Lily even went with her on vacation at a beach
resort in Crimea, where they stayed in an ivy-wrapped brick
mansion on the Black Sea. Ching seemed to like and trust
Lily, but Lily didn't want to be too involved in politics and
was eager to continue with her translation work back in
Beijing, which she enjoyed more. Yomei couldn't see her
friend in Moscow this time—Lily had left the USSR with
Jiang Ching two months earlier. Yomei was a bit alarmed,
knowing her friend could be naive and too outspoken. She
hoped that Ching wouldn't hurt Lily.

Soon after the new China had been inaugurated
on October 1, 1949, the Central Committee, having
communicated with Stalin, decided that Chairman Mao
was to visit the Soviet Union right away. The trip was the
first time Mao would step foot in a foreign country. He was
anxious and wanted to use this visit to celebrate Stalin's
seventieth birthday as well. This meant he must present
some gifts to the Great Leader. But what should he bring to
Moscow? Mao asked people who were knowledgeable about
Russian life. Some suggested silk and brocade, and some,
brand-name teas, and some, liquors like Maotai and Five
Grain Sap. Having stayed in the Soviet Union for more
than three months for medical treatment and feeling more
qualified than others to opine on the birthday presents for
Stalin, Jiang Ching insisted that there must be vegetables
and fruits, tons of them, for the Great Leader and his
colleagues at the Kremlin.

As a result, Mao's list of gifts for Stalin's birthday was
long and extraordinary: big napa cabbages, thick scallions,
long turnips, winter bamboo shoots, large pears, sweet
tangerines—six thousand pounds of each of those—fresh

teas and Chunghwa cigarettes, all shipped by train, in separate wagons. More impressive, there were some presents that were somewhat artistic: a life-size embroidered silk portrait of Stalin, his front bust woven into two pieces of fine Hangzhou brocade, two porcelain placards bearing his portrait, ten porcelain plates with his images burned on them, a porcelain dinner set for twenty-four people, a pair of Peking longevity dishes with brass bases, two cloisonné tea sets, a pair of tall flower vases once owned by Emperor Kang-hsi (1654–1722), an ivory pagoda, two statues of Russian heroines carved on ivory, three ivory balls, an ivory set of eight gods, also an ivory dragon boat, a large reddish brass firepot, and a dozen pairs of ivory chopsticks.

In private, Ambassador Wang shook his head and said, "Why so many? How vulgar and ridiculous this whole collection of presents is!" Wang also grumbled that the gifts couldn't arrive all at once, and it would be hard for the embassy to deliver them batch by batch to the Kremlin. This might turn Stalin's birthday into an extended holiday season.

Yomei overheard his complaints but made no comment. Luckily there wasn't anyone else within earshot. Wang mentioned that at the beginning of that year (1949) Artem Mikoyan, the vice premier of the USSR, had gone to Shijiazhuang, the temporary site of CCP headquarters before it relocated to Beijing, and that on that occasion, the Soviet leader had brought only a piece of wool fabric as a gift for the CCP's Central Committee. Nobody had ever said that was cheap. Yomei was impressed and thought Mikoyan's present had been simple and even elegant, but she didn't join Ambassador Wang in grumbling about the absurd birthday presents shipped from China for Stalin. She wondered how the Great Leader could consume six

thousand pounds of Shandong scallions, delicious as they
were. Stalin was known for being fond of cultivating a
vegetable garden and a fruit grove at his Kuntsevo Dacha,
so it would have made more sense if they had presented him
with the seeds of some rare vegetables and a few saplings of
precious fruit trees in addition to a few samples of the fresh
produce. Evidently Jiang Ching's taste hadn't improved
much despite being Madame Mao. In a sense, she still
seemed uncouth.

Besides her role as an interpreter for Mao, Yomei
would also serve as his confidential secretary on his visit
to the Soviet Union. In fact, Jiang Ching had coveted
such a position and even asked Mao to bring her along on
this trip, but the Central Committee had turned down
her request because she didn't know Russian and might
not be able to work properly in the foreign environment.
Ambassador Wang revealed to Yomei that she was the best
candidate for this job, not only by virtue of her Russian
skills and her familiarity with Soviet life but also because
her parents had both been loyal revolutionaries and she
was Zhou Enlai's daughter. These days, the people at the
embassy were all somewhat overwrought, as Chairman
Mao and his retinue had already left Beijing by train on
December 6 and were approaching the Sino-Soviet border.
After entering the Soviet Union, the delegation would
stop at every major city along the way. Last weekend, a
vice foreign minister from the Soviet government had
left on Stalin's personal train with a group of servants
and two chefs of Chinese cuisine for the border town of
Otpor. He'd meet Mao there, then accompany him back to
Moscow. On Thursday, December 15, Ambassador Wang
set out for Yaroslavl city, more than one hundred and fifty
miles northeast of Moscow, to meet and welcome Mao and

his suite. Wang's Russian was serviceable, so he didn't need an interpreter for the trip. As arranged, Yomei and many staff members of the embassy were to welcome the delegates at Moscow's northern station (the Yaroslavsky Terminal) the following day.

Forty-Two

On December 16, around two o'clock in the afternoon, Mao's entourage on Stalin's personal train arrived at the Yaroslavsky station, and a group of senior Soviet leaders were at the platform to welcome him, including Foreign Minister Vyacheslav Molotov and Marshal Bulganin. They went into Mao's berth carriage to greet him and then accompanied him out of the train. The guests and the hosts walked together through a small military review. It was snowing lightly, and it was so cold that Mao, in spite of wearing a thick woolen overcoat and a black fur toque, seemed to wince in the biting wind. Originally the hosts had planned a much larger ceremony, but due to the foul weather, they had scaled down the welcome spectacle considerably. Mao delivered a short speech, saying he was delighted and honored to come and see with his own eyes what the Soviet Union, "the heart of the world proletarian revolution," was like. And he also thanked Stalin and the Soviet government for hosting him.

Yomei was standing at the front of the audience, among the members of the Chinese embassy, and she was amazed by the touch of feminine shrillness underlying Mao's voice, which she hadn't noticed before. He was obviously under the weather and sounded as if he was short of breath. As

soon as the speech was over, they all got into sedans heading
southwest toward a villa called Sisters River, which was
about twenty miles away from downtown. It was the place
where Mao was to lodge. He planned to stay in the Soviet
Union for three months, negotiating with the Russians,
visiting some factories and cultural sites, and also having
some rest and medical treatment. If possible, he'd go on to
visit Poland, Romania, and Czechoslovakia. Yet in spite of
the long visit to the Soviet Union that was planned, it was
still strange to put him up so far away from the Kremlin.
Mao and his colleagues all knew that state visitors usually
stayed at dachas on Lenin Hill, which was close to Red
Square. Yomei had noticed that Mao wasn't in a good
mood. He didn't smile, and his smooth face dropped the
whole time after they had left the train station.

Together with Mao was Mr. Shi Zhe, who had come
all the way from China on the same train. He was trusted
by the chairman, having served as his Russian secretary
for many years in Yan'an and then in Beijing. Yomei was
mainly an informal interpreter, which meant that whenever
Shi Zhe was tired and needed a break, she would step in,
especially when Mao met the Soviets casually, not on official
business. In addition, she was in charge of translating the
meeting notes, some of which, after being summarized,
would be telegraphed back to the CCP's Central Committee
in Beijing. So although she wasn't present at some formal
occasions, she was often around as an understudy of Shi
Zhe's. By and large she was informed well enough to follow
the general drift of Mao's business meetings with the hosts.
From the very beginning, she could tell that Mao might not
be happy about the location of his lodgings, even though the
Sisters River residence was also Stalin's personal dacha in
Moscow, the second one besides his chief one in Kuntsevo.

Though it was called a dacha, Sisters River was more like a villa, grand and white, three stories, with four massive columns at the front, and surrounded by birch woods. Yomei guessed that Mao's moodiness might be due to the fact that Stalin hadn't shown up in person to receive him at the train station. But then, Stalin was pushing seventy and in poor health, and it was understandable that he couldn't go there personally.

Yet a meeting between Stalin and Mao was already scheduled for that very evening at the Kremlin. The Chinese group arrived at the grand palace at six o'clock. When the gate to a hall opened, they found the whole of the USSR politburo standing in a line and led by Stalin to receive them. Stalin held Mao's hand and observed him carefully for a long moment. He said through his interpreter Nikolai Fedorenko's translation, "You look splendid, so young and in such good color! The Chinese people are fortunate to have a great leader like you. You have made tremendous contributions to the revolution and will lead your people to more victories."

Mao was moved and said, "It's a great honor to meet you in person at long last, like a dream come true!" Actually, in the past two years he had kept asking to come and visit Stalin, but the supreme leader had never given his assent, always making one excuse after another for his unavailability. That might explain why Mao had brought with him only a small staff of some twenty people—he feared Stalin might give him the cold shoulder and thus humiliate him as well as his colleagues. Rumor had it that in Stalin's eyes Mao was merely a hidebound peasant, a self-proclaimed Marxist who was shrewd and recalcitrant, though forceful. If Stalin didn't treat him warmly, Mao might shorten his stay in the USSR.

After everyone was seated, Stalin and Mao began conversing rather casually. Mao said that he used to have no voice within the CCP and had often been mistreated. Stalin told him, "Now you're victorious. The winner never goes on trial because nobody can condemn him. This is a universal principle."

Mao nodded and realized that was Stalin's way of acknowledging that they had over the decades backed the wrong factions in the CCP. Those supported by the USSR had lost one fight after another to Mao, who was indeed triumphant and had to be accepted by the Kremlin now.

Stalin asked Mao about the purpose of his visit, saying, "You've come a long way and can't go back empty-handed. Do we need to do something together?"

Mao replied, "We came to learn mainly, to see what you have accomplished. Your experience means the world to us. As for our needs, we would like to have something that looks nice and also tastes good, full of nourishment."

His last sentence was meant to strike a humorous note, but it was impossible for Shi Zhe to render the humor transparent, so Mao's words puzzled the Russians. Struggling as Mr. Shi did, he couldn't get the message across fully—China wanted something grand in appearance but also substantial. Mao's expression puzzled the hosts, and a lengthy pause set in. Then Beria, the Soviet police chief, broke out giggling—apparently he alone caught the joke. His small round glasses kept glinting.

Then Stalin said that Mao was welcome to go anywhere while he was here, and of course they'd do their best to play host, making his visit a happy and memorable experience. Stalin went on to talk about how the establishment of the People's Republic of China had tipped the scale of global power balance. Now the Soviet Union and the PRC must unite like true socialist countries so as to keep peace in the world while opposing the aggression of Western imperialism. Mao asked Stalin whether the global peace would last, saying "As a matter of fact, my colleagues all want me to ask you how to maintain peace in the world, because we need peace in order to rebuild our war-battered country."

Stalin said there was no threat to China's peaceful environment from now on, since Japan was still struggling to recover from its defeat and since the United States and Europe were still shaken by the Second World War. He bantered, "Who else? Do you think Kim Il Sung will invade China? In short, there'll be a decade or two of peace ahead of us if our two countries join hands in solidarity." (Neither of them could foresee the Korean War that would break out seven months later and plunge China into a three-year confrontation with the United States.)

Gradually Mao shifted to the topic of revising China's old treaty with the Soviet Union (signed by Chiang Kai-shek's government in 1945)—the PRC had declared they would abolish all the unfair treaties signed by the previous regime and was eager to take back Port Arthur and Port of Dalian and the Changchun Railroad (the Chinese section of the Trans-Siberian railroad). A few months prior, Liu Shaoqi had talked with Stalin about this matter, but Stalin hadn't given a clear answer. Now he explained to Mao that the old treaty, though unfair to China, had been made together with the U.S. and England as part of the Yalta Conference. If the Soviet Union changed the contents of the treaty unilaterally (relinquishing its holdings in China), the other powers might intervene and want to revise the agreement on the Kuril Islands and Sakhalin. What if Japan demanded the return of the Kuril Islands? This might complicate matters. So for now it would be better to keep the old treaty as it was, meaning the Soviet navy should continue staying at Port Arthur and China should not take over the railroad. Neither should the USSR relinquish its hold on Dalian too soon.

Mao was taken aback to hear that, but he agreed to consider the Soviet position on this issue. Stalin offered a possible solution, namely to keep the old treaty while revising its contents so as to avoid giving the Western Powers an excuse to demand any formal revision of the Yalta treaty. Mao even admitted that while considering revoking the current unfair treaty, the CCP leaders hadn't taken into account the Yalta treaty (though they had understood how important the Port of Dalian was to the Soviet Union, which had no ice-free seaport of its own), so more caution should be taken and there was no need to withdraw the Soviet navy from Port Arthur or revoke the old treaty right away.

Mao then mentioned the aid of three hundred million rubles that Artem Mikoyan had promised the CCP to seriously consider a year earlier. China was in shambles and needed to recover from the devastation of the civil war, so any help from the USSR would be greatly appreciated. Besides money, China would also like to have many experts of various fields from the USSR. Stalin was quite generous and agreed to grant all the aid the Chinese requested, as he had already given his word to Liu Shaoqi a few months before. Now he was willing to sign all the agreements on the aid. Mao was elated to hear Stalin's affirmation, saying, "This is the first time our two parties have signed a treaty on financial aid and it will definitely bring about a positive response in China."

They then talked about trade in Xinjiang and with Mongolia. Stalin agreed to help China open civil aviation in those regions that could facilitate trade, transportation, and travel. Following the issue of civil aviation, since China

didn't have its own air force yet, Mao hoped the Soviet
Union would provide air cover if China launched an attack
on Taiwan to reunify the country. That seemed to catch
his host unprepared. Stalin lowered his grizzled head to
give thought for a moment, then answered, "We would love
to, but that might invite interference from the U.S. If they
send over warships and aircraft to the Taiwan region, the
confrontation could get out of hand, so let us think more
about such a move and make our decision later. We'd better
be cautious about this."

Toward the end of the two-hour talk, Stalin expressed
his wish to read more of Mao's writings. Such a request
delighted Mao, because it was rumored that Stalin viewed
Mao as another Tito, not a real Marxist at all. Mao
informed him that the translation of his writings into
Russian was about to begin, and he had been looking
through the pieces to be translated. Stalin asked whether he
would need an expert to help with the translation. Again
Mao was taken aback, but recovered himself at once, saying
he welcomed any help of course. Stalin recommended Pavel
Yuqin, a philosopher who a few years later became the
Soviet ambassador to China. At the moment, however, Mao
slightly resented assigning such a theorist to help him, as if
to ensure everything must be politically correct. But Mao's
resentment eventually faded, because Yuqin did manage
to convince Stalin that Mao was a genuine Marxist, with a
great amount of practical experience. And for years, Lily
served as one of the translators of Mao's writings.

In spite of a good night's sleep, Mao was in a foul mood the
next morning that was caused by the stymied negotiation
over the revocation of the old treaty. That had been the

main purpose of his visit, but it had gotten laid aside at
the very first meeting. What an imbroglio he was in now.
He regretted having agreed to not revise the treaty right
away. He should have begged to differ at the meeting,
emphasizing that both sides should agree to disagree for
now. Now, without any development in this respect, he
might have to face criticism in China once he was back.
The more he mulled over this frustration, the angrier he
became. He told Li Jiaji, a staffer on his retinue, to remove
the spongy mattress, saying it tended to give him a crick in
the neck and make him insomniac as he was unused to this
kind of comfortable bed. He wanted real wood boards, like
the bed he had back home. Jiaji didn't know where to get
wood boards, so he asked Yomei to explain the matter to
Ivan Kovalev, the Russian official in charge of Mao's daily
life here, to see if they could replace the mattress with wood
boards. Yomei believed it would be inappropriate to make
a big fuss over such a trifle. Instead, she measured the bed
lengthways and crossways and then reported Mao's demand
to Ambassador Wang, who sent a junior diplomat to a
furniture store downtown with Yomei's measurements and
bought some boards. The mattress was replaced that very
evening, and Mao was satisfied with the new hard bed. The
Russian servants later told Yomei that Mao was a genuine
revolutionary, still living like a guerrilla in the wilderness.

Mao expected that Stalin would meet with him again
to discuss the unfinished business, but there was no word
from the Kremlin. Now he understood why he'd been
put up at such a faraway place—Stalin must have meant
to keep some distance from him and also to show that he
was not a major guest here. So Mao was galled, though
he knew that Stalin must be busy these days with so many
delegates from other Eastern Bloc countries coming to

celebrate his seventieth birthday. Nonetheless, Mao came up with a more bizarre demand—he wanted to have the toilet altered, claiming that sitting on the nice toilet would make his bowels seize. He needed the more primitive type he had back home—a small, rectangular porcelain bowl set in the floor of the bathroom so that he could squat over it. Yomei tittered on hearing such a demand and said, "My, this one is like a nail in my head that I don't know how to pull out." After considering Mao's new demand a moment, she reported it to Ambassador Wang, who sighed on the phone, apparently at a loss what to do. "My heavens, where could I find a mason who can change the toilet for him?" he wondered aloud. "Besides, that's Stalin's bathroom and we're not supposed to mess with it."

Yomei laughed, then said she was going to speak with Ivan Kovalev, who had lived in China for many years and must know what a toilet for squatting was like. So she went to see Ivan and explained Mao's demand. Kovalev cracked up and said no Russians but himself knew anything about such a toilet. Moreover, it was Stalin's bathroom and he'd have to get permission if he'd have anything done to it. Luckily he got approval from the Kremlin, and then sent over a mason to lay bricks around the toilet to construct a tiny terrace around it, and even built two steps for Mao to climb up to squat over the hole when he needed to defecate.

Yomei placed a roll of toilet tissue at the corner of the mini-platform, then turned to Mao and said, "Please be careful. Don't fall from this."

Mao laughed and said, "I'm not that frail and old. I just don't want to give them the impression that we Chinese are merely pushovers."

Yomei nodded and went on giggling. "Please let us know if you need something else, Chairman."

"Of course. What's our plan for tomorrow?"

"You told the Russians you wanted something nice to look at and also good to eat, so they made arrangements for you to visit a national museum of fine arts."

"All right, is the Russian winter always so cold?"

"Yes, it can be harsh and miserable."

"No wonder so many of Hitler's troops froze to death at Stalingrad."

Mao seemed pleased with the renovation of the toilet and even praised Ivan Kovalev, saying he was a clever fellow.

· Forty-Three ·

A few days later, on December 21, the Kremlin held a dinner party in celebration of Stalin's seventieth birthday. Mao was seated next to Stalin as the most honored guest. Nonetheless, Mao didn't look happy, being still mindful of the grim results of his first talk with Stalin. Mao gave a speech at the banquet, eulogizing the old man as the greatest leader of the proletariat of the world and as the elder brother of the Chinese people. He wished Stalin "an everlasting life, and always in good health." He even shouted, "Long live Comrade Stalin!" He also inscribed a couplet with a brush in his flowing calligraphy on two bands of glossy red paper for the supreme leader: "May happiness surround you like an ocean / May your life last as long as a mountain." The inscription delighted Stalin and impressed hundreds of delegates from the other countries. Some admired Mao's calligraphy, saying it was beautiful and vigorous.

The banquet was followed by a show, which Stalin and Mao watched in the same box on the balcony. Nevertheless, to Mao the birthday celebration was too long and tedious. It lasted nearly six hours. Not until one in the morning did the Chinese delegates head back to their lodgings in the suburb. On the way, Mao complained to Wang Dongxing, his chief of staff, a butler of sorts, saying, "I had no idea

Stalin's seventieth birthday,
Moscow, December 1949

that their birthday party would go on for so long. I didn't eat well or see anything interesting. For a whole evening I just clapped my hands, following others. When we're back, we won't hold our parties like that. If we give a banquet, we'll let people eat well. If a show is put on, let them get fully entertained."

The following day Mao phoned the Kremlin to express his wish to have another talk with Stalin, so a new meeting was scheduled for Saturday evening, just two days away. Again Shi Zhe and two others accompanied Mao to the talk, which dragged on for five and a half hours, but there was no substantial development. Stalin simply avoided the topic of the old, unfair treaty, which Mao was eager to get rescinded or revised, but the Soviets seemed determined to keep it off the table. As a result, Mao got more frustrated and often threw a tantrum in front of his staff. At lunch the next day, a dish of broiled salmon was served, but he jerked it aside and declared, "I don't want this, I eat only live fish." His spoon fell off the table, clattering on the parquet floor, and right away a Russian servant came with a replacement.

Yomei went to tell Ivan Kovalev what Mao wanted. The man shook his fleshy face and chestnut hair and said, "That's an odd demand, but we'll see what we can do."

Indeed this wasn't hard for the Soviets to manage. They could ship some live fish to the kitchen and let the Chinese comrades see the creatures before the chefs put a knife to them. It was whispered among Mao's staff that he had acted that way mainly because an unpleasant episode had cropped up in his mind. In January 1949, Mikoyan went to visit the CCP headquarters outside Shijiazhuang. He brought along a good amount of Russian food: sausages, ham, caviar, cheese, cakes, canned food—also vodka. At the welcome dinner, the Chinese side could provide only food produced in the countryside, fresh-killed pork and poultry, and there was also fish braised in soy sauce. Mikoyan and Fedorenko enjoyed the red wine and the Fenjiu liquor supplied by the host, but they wouldn't touch the fish, even though Mao urged them to try the product of the Hutu River. Mikoyan told Nikolai Fedorenko to ask if the fish had been alive when they had arrived at the kitchen. Mao told him that the fish had just been caught. Only after ascertaining that the fish were absolutely fresh did the Soviet visitors begin to eat the dish. This episode soon became a kind of scandal at the CCP headquarters. Now in Moscow, that memory suddenly nettled Mao, so he insisted on eating only live fish. This was just an act of histrionics, Yomei knew, but it later became a rule in the Soviets' treatment of Mao, who was said to eat only live fish. In 1957, on Mao's second visit to the USSR, Khrushchev instructed the catering department, "Mao Zedong doesn't eat dead fish." He also made sure that

Mao had a hard-board bed and a squatting toilet. Nikita Khrushchev seemed somewhat intimidated by Mao, who, as a revolutionary, was one generation older than he was and much more experienced. He once remarked, "Comrade Mao Zedong acts as if God must serve him."

A few days later Fedorenko came to see Mao and asked if he needed something. Mao could no longer hold back his temper and spluttered, "I came here not just to celebrate Stalin's birthday. If you want to keep the old treaty signed with the former Nationalist government, you can have it. And then I'll leave in a couple of days. See what I have been doing here. All I do is eat, sleep, and crap. How is this different from back home except that I gained several pounds of flesh?" He slapped the table, so irate that he couldn't continue.

Nikolai Fedorenko was stupefied. He was an accomplished orientalist in Russia and knew both Chinese and Japanese. He murmured, "I am sorry. There must be some misunderstanding. We'll see to this, of course."

After he'd left, Mao said to Shi Zhe and Yomei, "You're both experienced in dealing with the Russians. Can you guess how Stalin will respond to my outburst?"

Yomei shook her head, too stumped to reply, but Shi Zhe said, "Believe me, Chairman, I've known Fedorenko for more than a decade. He might not report your complaint to Stalin at all."

"That's true," Yomei chimed in. "Most officials here would do their best to avoid trouble. Nobody wants to make Stalin unhappy."

Mao sighed and said, "No matter what, we must do our utmost to protect China's interests. If they refuse to sign a new treaty favorable to us, I won't leave. I have time and can remain their guest here forever."

"So your outburst just now was only to show your discontent?" Yomei asked.

"You're a smart girl," Mao said with a shrewd smile.

It seemed that Stalin had been keeping Mao away on purpose to let him cool down some. Kovalev and Fedorenko suggested that Mao go out and visit some places, but Mao wouldn't do that, saying it was too cold and he was already somewhat sick. So he stayed indoors every day. To help him while away the time, Shi Zhe got hold of some documentary movies, which Yomei played for Mao in a small conference room. Mao liked watching biographical films, which for him was a good way to learn about a foreign country's history and culture. She showed him *Peter the Great*, *Alexander Nevsky*, *Napoleon*, *Leo Tolstoy*. He often asked her to stop to translate a snippet of dialogue or an episode for him. One afternoon, she showed a documentary on the Soviets' experiment and production of the atomic bomb. The blast was like a typhoon of fire that wiped out whatever was in the explosion zone, within a radius of several miles. More terrifying, after months there was still no sign of life in the area. Though Mao used to claim that the atomic bomb was merely "a paper tiger," this film shocked and shook him to the core. He asked his comrades with his eyes ablaze, "What do you think of the atomic bomb? Powerful, huh?"

Everybody nodded and admitted that they hadn't imagined the bomb could be so destructive and that it might be impossible to survive such a blast. Mao said, "By whatever means, we must make our own atomic bombs."

On New Year's Day, Nikolai Roshchin, the newly appointed Soviet ambassador to China, came to see Mao. There was a delegation of the Japanese Communist Party visiting Moscow and during their talk with their hosts, the subject of Sanzo Nosaka cropped up. He had been

spreading problematic views in Japan and even claimed
that the U.S. military occupation of Japan could help speed
up the democratization of their country. The Japanese
delegation would like to meet Mao and to have some issues
concerning Sanzo Nosaka clarified, now that their former
Party honcho had lived in Yan'an for some years. But Mao
refused to see them, saying he wasn't feeling well, his
head dizzy and heavy during the day. That was true, partly
because he couldn't continue with his regular schedule as he
did back in Beijing, where he used to work mainly at night.
Mao also informed Roshchin that he had decided to leave
by the end of January, thus cutting his three-month visit
down to one and a half. There was a huge backlog of work
awaiting him back home, he claimed.

Roshchin was surprised but obligated to report Mao's
words to the Soviet politburo. In truth, the top Soviet
leaders had been deliberating whether to sign a new treaty
with the People's Republic of China. A number of them—
Molotov, Shvernik, Mikoyan, Vyshinsky, Roshchin, and
others—felt that Mao's position in the CCP and in China
might be weakened if he couldn't bring back a new treaty, so
the USSR must assume some responsibility for preserving
the stability of its neighbor, the PRC. In the long run, the
new China's stability would help protect the USSR as well.
Stalin listened to their opinions attentively, though he
hadn't yet made up his mind.

Meanwhile, on January 1, 1950, a newspaper in England
claimed that Mao was under house arrest in Moscow,
saying that was why he hadn't shown his face publicly for
ten days on end. An English newspaper in Hong Kong
even reported that there had been a coup in Beijing,
engineered by Liu Shaoqi and Zhu Deh, so that Mao had
been forced into exile and could no longer go back. Such

fake news would tarnish the Soviet Union's reputation if
it were not corrected at once. Therefore, both the Russian
and the Chinese sides agreed to hold a news conference at
which Mao would answer questions raised by international
journalists so as to stop the malicious rumors. In a written
interview by a TASS reporter, Mao explained that the
length of his stay in the Soviet Union would depend on the
progress that the PRC and the USSR could make in solving
several issues: First, what to do about the old treaty signed
by the Nationalist government. Second, the ways in which
the USSR could provide a loan and various kinds of aid for
the PRC. Third, how to make a series of trade agreements
between the two countries. In brief, he was here working
hard with the Soviet comrades in the interests of China.
He was being treated as a state guest and enjoying his visit
tremendously.

Actually, the very fact that Stalin wanted Mao to speak
directly to reporters already indicated that he expected to
yield some ground, knowing Mao might bring up the issue
of the unfair treaty to the public. So Mao divined a positive
sign from this turn of events. Ambassador Wang was
also heartened by such a development. At the same time,
three countries—Burma, India, and Britain—announced
that they would recognize the People's Republic of China
in the near future and establish a formal relationship
with it. Apparently more Western countries might soon
acknowledge the new China. Now Stalin began to worry
that China might lean toward the West if more Western
countries recognized it and if the United States succeeded
in bringing about enmity between the PRC and the Soviet
Union, so he had to take measures to keep the USSR and its
neighbor as close as possible. Without China as its staunch
ally, a socialist bloc in Asia would be out of the question—

there would be no way to bring Korea, Vietnam, and Mongolia together if vast China didn't belong to the same Asian socialist bloc. In addition, recently the U.S. National Security Committee issued a statement that said the United States would adjust its Asian policy and forsake Formosa so as to disentangle itself from the civil war in China. In other words, the CCP should be entitled to liberate Taiwan and reunify the country if it chose to. In early January 1950, Harry Truman even made a public statement that Taiwan was part of China's territory and that the United States had no intention or responsibility to defend it. Clearly the United States was making an overture to the PRC in order to drive a wedge between China and the Soviet Union. Then, getting no response from the Chinese government, the White House went further—Secretary of State Dean Acheson gave a more elaborate speech at a press conference to express America's goodwill to China. He mentioned that the United States had never invaded China, and unlike other foreign powers, it had never held any concession in that country either. It was Russia that had robbed China of a large piece of land in Siberia (almost 1,500,000 square kilometers, a territory larger than Texas, California, and New Mexico combined) and it was Russia that had set up the puppet state of Mongolia, which the USSR had actually helped secede from China to create "a buffer zone" for itself. In short, the United States had always been a friend of the Chinese people over the centuries.

The United States' new approach gave Stalin the impression that America was making an effort to sabotage the alliance between Beijing and Moscow. So he must treat Mao differently from now on. Within three days, Stalin changed his original intention and agreed to sign a new treaty with the PRC and allowed Zhou Enlai to come to

Moscow to work out the details of the aid and trade with the Soviets. When Yomei had handed Mao the translation of the statement from the Kremlin, Mao glanced through it and sprang to his feet in rapture. He stretched up his arms and said, "Finally we have a breakthrough! Thank you for bringing this wonderful news, Yomei."

"Now you can go around and visit some places?"

"You bet. I just fumed at Stalin, but at last I can see that he isn't mean-spirited. He can be generous and farsighted, a great leader indeed."

Mao then called in Chen Boda, his political secretary, and dictated a long telegram to the Central Committee in Beijing to inform them of the new development and also to summon Premier Zhou to come to the USSR without delay.

Yomei could see both euphoria and pride in his dictation. Indeed, when he had reported to the Central Committee the stalemate after the first talk with Stalin, his colleagues in Beijing had responded that he should accept the Soviets' position and come back, but he wouldn't eat the dirt of humiliation and instead persisted willfully in his own manner and with his own agenda. Now this hard-earned victory delighted everyone. Once again, Mao had proved to his colleagues that he was a forceful and foresightful leader.

· Forty-Four ·

Zhou Enlai and his staff left Beijing on January 11, 1950, and it would take them about ten days by rail to reach Moscow. In the interim, Mao went to see the sights and to look at some areas of the USSR. Yomei accompanied him on most of these trips.

The next day they set out for Leningrad (the former Saint Petersburg), where Mao wanted to see the *Aurora*, the cruiser that had fired the first shot at the Winter Palace on October 25, 1917, and thus begun the October Revolution. In an essay Mao wrote: "A barrage of gunfire from the October Revolution sent Marxism to China." He meant that the Chinese Communist revolution had actually started from the barrel of the cruiser's forecastle gun. The large vessel was anchored on the Neva, at its estuary in the Gulf of Finland. Mao appeared moved while standing beside the *Aurora*, though she was rusted all over and obviously in mothballs, no longer seaworthy. A gangplank connected her with the bank, but it was iced over and looked slippery, so Mao didn't go on board to look at the interior. From there they strolled a little along the gulf. Everywhere was white, and the ice on the river and the gulf was four or five feet thick, they were told. From the Neva they went to see some defense works nearby, built

during wartime against the Nazi forces. They walked
past stone parapets and massive ramparts and concrete
batteries. Yomei could see that the scenery out below
must look splendid in the summer. Afterward they visited
Kirovsky Plant, which was one of the largest in the USSR
and manufactured a wide variety of machinery. Yomei was
impressed by the architecture of some workshops there,
which brought to mind stone castles with their vaulted
ceilings and wide, arched windows. Mao didn't seem so
keen about the machinery; perhaps he was more eager to
see the factories that produced warships and tanks and
artillery pieces, but their hosts didn't show them any of
those, probably because they were afraid the Chinese
might ask for some of the advanced weapons.

They also went to visit the National Museum of Fine
Arts near the Neva River. Mao was somewhat ignorant
of art, especially Western art, so he just strolled around
through the halls of paintings and sculptures. Seldom
did he stop to observe an artwork carefully. Yomei was
following him and Shi Zhe, but at a distance of ten feet. Mr.
Shi was interpreting for Mao on this occasion, since he, Shi
Zhe, was eager to see the museum too. Yomei always made
sure to be second fiddle in the role of Mao's interpreter,
though she was often asked to accompany him when he went
out sightseeing. Shi Zhe was quite touchy about his role as
the principal interpreter and wanted to do the work on all
formal occasions. That was fine with Yomei, who wasn't that
interested in official meetings anyway. As they were coming
out of the last hall and stepping into the chandeliered and
colonnaded atrium, a wiry, middle-aged blonde turned
up. She said she was the vice curator of the museum and
that they did have a section of Chinese arts but it was under

renovation at the moment and couldn't open to visitors. She apologized and then withdrew.

Mao grunted, "Of course they won't let us see the artwork robbed from China. They must have a plethora of those here."

Both Shi Zhe and Yomei were amazed by Mao's opinion. She didn't enjoy the visit to the magnificent museum because she couldn't look at the artwork at her own pace,

Yomei and Mao in Moscow

having to follow Mao around, who wasn't that interested and moved too fast.

Back from Leningrad, they went to visit the Moscow Metro. Mao was greatly impressed by the pristine state of the underground station, which was like a grand hall inside a museum. He said to Yomei, "The Russians must have a lot of marble quarries. They even built the subway station with marble." Indeed, inside the station marble was everywhere—stairs, columns, statues, even benches all made of marble.

"This is a rich country," Yomei said. "It has a great deal of resources."

"I guess it's always good to have a rich neighbor," said Mao.

The Soviet Ministry of Culture invited the Chinese delegates to attend the dress rehearsal of *The Red Poppy* at the Bolshoi Theater. It was a ballet set in Shanghai, produced specifically for the Chinese guests, since it presented a Chinese revolutionary story—a beautiful prostitute falls in love with a Russian sailor who teaches her proletarian ideas and its spirit, which she in turn disseminates to the dockhands. Yomei went to see the ballet with Ambassador Wang and his wife and two other Chinese diplomats. Except for Yomei, they all hated the ballet and believed it was based on a faulty premise, because China's Communist revolution hadn't started that way, not through prostitution. Worse yet, the Chinese women appeared to have bound feet in the dance. Yomei explained to her colleagues that all female characters in a ballet had to wear the small slippers called toe shoes, and that this had nothing to do with any bias against Chinese women. Yet Mrs. Wang couldn't be convinced and still felt disgusted. Likewise, her husband wrote a negative report to Chairman Mao and suggested shunning the opening night.

In private, Mao asked Yomei's opinion on *The Red Poppy*. She said, "I can see that its premise might be inaccurate, but as a piece of art, it's an earnest and high-quality work. World class, if I tell you the truth. It has integrated so many things and is kind of breakthrough in the art of ballet. The sailors' dance, the workers' dance, the Mongolian ghost dance, the girl's solo fan dance, the sailors' Cossack sword dance, all are small masterpieces. It's rare to see a ballet with so much masculine vigor and beauty in it. We Chinese can learn a lot from this performance, which shows how to blend high art with mass art and how to make the traditional aristocratic art express the gritty and dark reality of the common life. There is even a Chinese *yang-ge* in one scene that is lovely and gorgeous, although it doesn't look like a real Chinese folk dance anymore. But the ballet on the whole can be inspiring, the choreography, the music, the costumes, the setting, everything meticulously made. At least it's eye-opening, I would say. That ballet troupe must have spent more than a year working on it. It feels like a classic."

"You really love it, I can see," said Mao.

"Absolutely. I was thrilled about its artistry."

"Still, politically it's wrong, so we must be careful about our response to it. Here's Ambassador Wang's report on it. You can take a look."

Hearing that, she stopped raving about *The Red Poppy*, aware that her tongue had gone too loose. She took the report and promised to read it carefully. Of course, she wouldn't praise the ballet anymore after seeing how negative Wang's comments were. He even said it was "shameful and prejudiced," so he suggested not attending its premiere.

Zhou Enlai arrived at Moscow on January 20, and Yomei hurried to see him in his hotel. He looked a bit tired but spirited, excited about the progress Mao had made with the Soviets. He wanted to know whether Yomei enjoyed the kind of confidential work she'd been doing.

"Not really," she said. "You know I'm too naive to understand political maneuvers and strategies."

"There has been consideration about your future work. Are you willing to work for me in the State Council?"

"Doing what?"

"In the Foreign Ministry. They need Russian interpreters there. Also someone familiar with Soviet affairs."

"I see, but my specialty is spoken drama. Let me think about this, OK?"

"Take your time. It could be a good opportunity for you."

"My friend Lily speaks Russian fluently too. Why not also recruit her for the State Council?"

"She's been with Jiang Ching, who seems quite fond of Lily. It's strange that the two hit it off. Jiang Ching doesn't take a shine to someone easily."

"If you have Lily work in the Foreign Ministry, I can try to persuade her, and I can join her too."

"Good heavens, don't take the State Council to be our family's business. Don't breathe a word to Lily yet. She'll be fine, and there'll be important work for her to do. For now, just think about your own future."

"In actual fact, before I left for Poland with the youth delegation, Mr. Liao Chengzhi talked with me about directing a Soviet play, *Pavel Korchagin*, and I agreed, so I might work for him for a spell."

"But in what theater are you going to stage the play?"

"I have no idea. Mr. Liao said there might be some new theaters after the new China was established."

"Of course, we will set up some theaters to improve our people's cultural life, but is that what you want to do?"

"Yes, I prefer to work as a theater artist for the rest of my life."

"I admire that—a clear vision about your future and striking out on your own."

"Gorky said something like, 'When your work is voluntary, you will have a happy life.' I believe in that."

"That's wise. You have grown up indeed."

The next day Zhou's team plunged into negotiations right away. Unfamiliar with finance and trade, Yomei was not recruited for the talks. She could tell that perhaps due to Mao's satisfaction with her work, Father Zhou couldn't take her away from Mao's staff.

Zhou Enlai also received tickets for the premiere of *The Red Poppy*, but having heard about the ballet from Ambassador Wang, he hesitated to go see it. He asked Yomei about the performance. She told him it was a masterpiece, interpreted from an artistic point of view. "It's truly original, fantastic, and you'll enjoy it," she assured him.

"How did Chairman Mao respond to Ambassador Wang's report?"

"He said, 'Politically the ballet is wrong.'"

"That's his opinion?"

"Yes, his conclusion is based on Ambassador Wang's report, but the Wangs don't understand ballet. Mrs. Wang even grumbled that the Chinese women in the play all had bound feet. She didn't understand ballerinas have to wear small pointed shoes. Traditionally, ballet shows a good deal of the female body: long limbs and elegant backs, but in *The Red Poppy* there's no exposure of the female body. All the ballerinas wear traditional Chinese costumes, which are gorgeous and beautiful. It's quite moving to see what they have achieved. We can learn a lot from this production, which is a real eye-opener. You should go see it."

"I'll see what to do," he said thoughtfully, with a feeble smile.

To Yomei's surprise, Shi Zhe also hated the ballet and felt it was a kind of insult to the CCP, and he told Mao his negative opinion. So the chairman decided not to attend the premiere. Zhou Enlai followed Mao's decision and avoided the opening night too. Yet they couldn't simply boycott the ballet, so they sent Chen Boda over, representing the CCP. Still, this was a slight to the

Yomei and Zhou Enlai in Moscow

ballet troupe. Chen was merely Mao's political secretary, holding no prominent position within the Party or the government at all. He had studied in the Soviet Union in the late 1920s for three years and was a man of culture. Understandably, he enjoyed *The Red Poppy* so much that when the curtain was dropping, he stood and applauded vigorously. Later Mao heard of his warm response to the ballet and criticized him. Chen lost his temper and wouldn't see Mao the next day. But they had been together for more than a decade, so Mao didn't mind his petulance and just told the others to leave him alone.

In private Chen checked with Yomei to see if he hadn't overreacted to the ballet. Having heard her positive assessment, he sighed and said, "What a bunch of clodhoppers and locust-eaters, who have no idea what real arts are like." He put his stubby finger on his lips to indicate that she must keep his remarks confidential.

However, the Chinese leaders' refusal to see *The Red Poppy* made Yomei mindful. She grew more self-reflective and felt awful for the ballet crew. Evidently, however accomplished an artwork was, it had to suit the Party's political needs. Otherwise it would be hard for arts to get anywhere. This was a lesson she had to remember.

· Forty-Five ·

The new treaty was signed at last, and the Soviet side agreed to return Port Arthur and the Port of Dalian and the Changchun Railroad to China by the end of 1952. This meant the abolishment of the old treaty, showing the world that the two countries were united "like brothers." Premier Zhou's team had also managed to work out a series of treaties with the Soviets, and every one of these was signed formally.

On the morning of February 14, the Kremlin held a ceremony for the signing of the Sino-Soviet Treaty of Friendship, Alliance and Mutual Assistance, which both sides viewed as a monumental achievement. Zhou Enlai, the premier as well as the minister of foreign affairs, represented China in signing the treaty, while Andrei Vyshinsky, the new foreign minister, was the Soviet signatory. Zhou wielded a brush while Vyshinsky used a chunky pen. After the signing, the senior leaders of both countries took a group photo. Yomei stepped away but noticed from the side that right before the photographer clicked the shutter release, Stalin moved forward a bit, about half a step. Afterward she asked Father Zhou why Stalin had done that; Zhou smiled then said, "He wanted to appear taller." Indeed when the photo came out on the front page of *Pravda*, the two national heads looked similar in height. In reality, Mao was five foot eleven, at least two inches taller than Stalin.

That evening Ambassador Wang, together with his wife, gave a thank-you banquet at the Mittelberg Hotel, near the Kremlin. The embassy rented the whole first floor, and more than five hundred people attended the dinner party. Some guests were military officers, the chests of whose uniforms were decked with colored aiguillettes and glittering medals. The large hall was bustling with guests and servants. Wine flowed, while tobacco fumes misted the high ceiling a little. The main course of the dinner was hot pot, each large table spread with plates of shaved meats, seafood, and assorted vegetables. At the main table in the front were seated Mao and Stalin and six other dignitaries from both sides. Behind the two Great Leaders Yomei sat as their interpreter. Stalin wore his marshal uniform, with epaulets and red piping on the trousers, and he was smoking his stout pipe nonstop. The firepot in front of him was different from those on the same table. It looked more expensive; its brass gleamed under the four-tiered chandelier, and the pot outshone all the other ones, but the inside of Stalin's pot was coated with whitish tin. Yomei was puzzled, then realized what had happened. A couple of days prior she'd heard that the Soviet side had asked about this very firepot, just presented to Stalin personally as one of the presents for his birthday. They wanted to make sure that the brass was not poisonous. Evidently they'd taken measures to ensure food safety for their supreme leader by coating the inside of the pot with a layer of tin. The Russians always seemed to have misgivings about anything Chinese.

Before the banquet started, Stalin turned around and asked Yomei, "You speak Russian so well. How did you learn it?"

"I studied at the Russian Institute of Theater Arts for almost seven years."

"Ah, did you study with the late Konstantin Stanislavski?"

"No, he had passed away when I enrolled. Nikolai Gorchakov was my mentor."

"That fellow was Konstantin's student, an excellent director."

"I enjoyed his tutelage very much."

"Stage directing is a wonderful profession." Stalin leaned right toward Mao and said, "This beautiful young lady studied at our best theater art institute and she speaks excellent Russian. Why didn't she translate at our talks? It's rare to meet a foreigner who speaks Russian with such music and clarity." Fedorenko was seated at the same table and translated Stalin's compliments for Mao.

Mao said, "Her father was murdered by Chiang Kai-shek two decades ago, so in some ways, I saw her grow up. It was I who sent her over to study dramaturgy. Indeed, we should make better use of her talent and training."

Yomei was delighted to hear those words from Mao, translated to Stalin by Fedorenko. Before she could say something, two female servants came over, both giving off a faint scent of pineapple perfume, to help heat up the firepots on the table by making the bluish alcohol flames underneath taller.

Stalin picked up a fork and speared a thin lozenge of bamboo shoot and put it into his mouth. Yomei wondered why he was eating the piece raw, which wasn't right. Stalin said, "This is good, really tasty."

Mao smiled and with chopsticks picked up a piece from the same plate and dipped it into his boiling pot and let it cook for a moment, then took it out and ate it. He told

Stalin, "This way makes the vegetables and meats taste better."

Stalin chuckled and followed suit, placing shaved beef and vegetables into the steel strainer in the boiling broth. He kept nodding after tasting a shrimp, and said, "Delicious. You Chinese are real gourmands."

Despite the small tiffs between them in the past weeks, this celebratory banquet seemed to have finally brought the two leaders closer together. Afterward Mao thanked Ambassador Wang for organizing such a dinner of genuine Chinese cuisine. Yomei assured Mr. Wang that Stalin had enjoyed the food and liquor a lot.

Three days later the whole delegation was leaving Moscow. Before departing, Mao told Wang Dongxing to make sure to have the stopgap toilet in the bathroom removed. Everything in Stalin's dacha was restored to its original state, neat and immaculate. Some people led by Ambassador Wang, most with sleepy or bloodshot eyes, went to the train station to see the delegates off. Both Mao's suite and Zhou's team were taking the same train homeward. They were eager to go back, so the return trip was faster, in spite of the stops along the way they took to visit Nizhny Novgorod, Kirov, Omsk, Ulan-Ude, Chita, and other cities. Along the way, everything was white, and the train ride was rather tedious, though Zhou Enlai was always busy handling matters back in China. To while away the time, Mao wanted to learn some Russian, so Yomei was assigned to give him lessons in the evenings. He was bad at foreign languages. He said he'd been learning English for more than three decades, but he still couldn't speak it. At most he could read a newspaper article in English, but by and large he disliked anything Russian and even claimed that none of the banquet foods offered by the Soviets was better than a bowl of seafood noodles.

In the evenings, around eight o'clock, Yomei would go to his berth carriage and teach him some everyday expressions in Russian, such as "thank you," "very good," "excuse me," "goodbye," or "a wonderful book."

Mao's tongue was clumsy or lazy, never able to manage the retroflex r, so she tried to pick words and phrases that didn't require curling up the tongue. Mao seemed eager to have Yomei on his staff, perhaps thanks to Stalin's praise of her beauty and Russian skills. One evening, as the train was approaching Yekaterinburg, he asked whether she'd be willing to work for him at his side as his Russian secretary.

"How about Mr. Shi Zhe? He speaks Russian better than I do," she said and took a swallow of the red wine Mao had poured for her.

He was amused that she was so fond of wine and would offer her a full glass every time she came to teach him. He said, "Shi Zhe has been with me for ten years. It's time he got a promotion. Don't tell him I said this. He's a capable comrade and should play a more significant role in our Party."

"My field is theater arts, so it might be hard for me to change," she said honestly.

"Most women comrades would jump at such an opportunity, but I admire you for not being so eager."

"I would like to direct plays."

"All right, there should be plenty of opportunities for you on that front. Our country needs artists as well."

Usually Mao would chat with her rather casually after she taught him a couple of Russian words and phrases. Once, he even told her that Jiang Ching had asked him to take her along on this trip, but he had turned her down. "She's troublesome," he confessed. "She agitates and alienates others. Sometimes it's even hard for me to tolerate her."

Yomei was surprised that Mao was speaking about his wife this way. Probably he meant to insinuate that his marriage might have gone awry or that he might give up on Jiang Ching, who had indeed been barred from participating in any important political and official activities. Nonetheless, Yomei wanted to remain coolheaded and didn't even disclose Mao's revelation and invitation to Father Zhou—she simply wouldn't be involved in political ploys or maneuvers, which were beyond her most of the time. She'd best avoid them.

One evening, having left Kransnoyarsk, she went to teach him Russian again. Again, he had a full glass of red wine waiting for her. The lesson went well, and now he could manage "You're welcome" in Russian.

"*Pahzhaloostah*," she said.

"*Paronusha*," he repeated after her, his tongue sloshing a little. "This sounds like quarreling with someone."

She tittered. "That's a good analogy. Russian can be a harsh language." She downed the last swallow of the wine.

As they continued with the lesson, she felt dizzy. Things were turning misty around her, and even Mao's bulky face went out of shape and was somewhat equine now.

When she woke up before daybreak, her head was still woozy from the alcoholic fog. She was shocked to find herself lying next to Mao in his bed. She was half naked, without her underpants on. Mao was snoring lightly. She turned her head and wondered how this had happened.

She sat up and climbed out of the bed. He stirred and opened his eyes halfway at her. He smirked as if enjoying seeing her in such a state. Hurriedly, she struggled into her underthings and trousers while crying in shudders. She turned to face the wall, her back toward him, as her shoulders were heaving and her legs and hands shaking. A numbing pain shot through her, as if something had snapped in her chest and blocked her windpipe.

"Why ... why did you do this to me? You ruined me," she wailed in a quivering voice, still not daring to face him, her heart thudding in her ears.

"I could tell you were not a virgin. I don't like virgins anyway." He paused, then went on, "Please join my staff. I'll be nice to you." He lit a Chunghwa cigarette and took a drag, then blew two tusks of smoke out of the edges of his mouth.

"Let me alone!" she cried out between sobs. "I used to respect you like an uncle."

"But you're a woman now, like a ripe plum. You're sensuous and beautiful, much better than Jiang Ching. To be honest, I like you more. Ching and I haven't shared a bed in ages. Please join my staff. I need your help and will be considerate to you." He smiled with leering eyes but without opening his lips.

"I've known Ching for many years and can't do that to her. Please leave me alone!"

"Even though you don't want to work for me, keep in mind that I'll be happy to help you when you need me."

Wordlessly she swung away. Covering her cheeks with her right hand, she flounced out of his carriage. After wiping herself with her soaked handkerchief and a wad of toilet tissue in the bathroom, she went back to the staff's quarters and climbed up to her bunk in a compartment.

She lay down, her heart still galloping. She resumed weeping and wondered what Mao had done to her exactly. Evidently he had entered her or he wouldn't have talked about her loss of virginity. Why did he say she clearly wasn't a virgin? She hadn't had sex before; her torn hymen was probably due to the fact that she had often ridden horses in Yan'an in her midteens. That used to give her a sore behind. Mao was a monster, but also a god in many people's eyes. Now what could she do?

An hour later, the train pulled into Irkutsk. Most people got out to stretch their legs on the platform. Yomei got off too. At the sight of Father Zhou, she ran up toward him while glittering motes were flying over the snow ahead of her. She hugged him and burst out sobbing; her look of agony seemed to cut him to the heart. He realized something terrible must have happened, and said, "Did Mao do something to you, Yomei?"

"Yes, Dad. He raped me!"

"How did it transpire?" His eyes were smoldering.

"Last night, while teaching him Russian, I drank a glass of wine in his carriage and passed out. He dragged me into his bed and had his way with me. What should I do now, Dad?"

"Do you think the wine was drugged?"

"Yes, it was."

"Such a heartless animal!" Zhou's bushy eyebrows tilted to his temples while she was crying. He patted her shoulder and freed himself from her embrace, which might be too eye-catching. He whispered, "Calm down. Some people might be watching us. Don't act rashly. Don't tell anyone about this, or it might get out of hand. Do you remember Big Ox in Yan'an? This could become dangerous if you spread the word."

"I can't go and teach him again!"

"You don't have to. Just try to avoid him, but you mustn't tell anyone about this."

She nodded her agreement to swallow her shame and humiliation. Then a conductor jingled the bell to summon the passengers back onto the train. Yomei remembered Big Ox, the young guard who used to tell others that he and his comrades in arms had carried Chairman Mao in a stretcher on the Long March, because the Great Leader wanted to read on the way, but was unable do that on horseback. Besides, it was more comfortable to lie in a stretcher than to ride a horse, from which one could fall easily, whereas in a stretcher he could doze off whenever he wanted to. Big Ox was warned to bridle his tongue, but he prattled on about his unique task on the Long March again at a holiday dinner after he'd a few too many again. As a consequence, he was sent away, and Yomei had no idea where he was now—in any case, he was silenced for good. So now she must remain quiet about what Mao had done to her. Again she nodded at Father Zhou to assure him of her silence, and again she throttled the sobs surging up in her throat. The train sounded the departure whistle, and Father Zhou put his arm around her. Together they headed back toward the entrance of a passenger coach. She moved as though in a trance.

· *Forty-Six* ·

Back in Beijing, Yomei went to live at the Zhous' residence and office, West Flower Hall, in Zhongnanhai, the mysterious compound in which a dozen or so of the CCP leaders' families were living. It consisted of more than two hundred acres and had a lake inside that was more like a series of big ponds. Yomei had her own room in West Flower Hall. The building was a courtyard of sorts, composed of a dozen or so rooms plus a commodious living hall. In front of the main house, done in an ancient architectural style and with flying eaves, was spread a large flower bed planted with peonies and daffodils. Behind the house stood cypresses, white-barked pines, fruit trees—some branches were just sprouting yellowish leaves that were like tiny scissor blades. Yomei was known as the premier's daughter, so she could enter the most restricted residential areas within the compound without a pass.

These days she felt tired and looked gloomy and a little aged, having lost her usual vivaciousness. She no longer hummed songs or gave clear peals of laughter as she used to. Mother Deng clearly knew what had happened to her, though she had never brought up the topic or alluded to it.

Under the excuse of reviving her spirits, Yomei went to stay a couple of days with her aunt Jun. Jun was thrilled to

see the presents she'd brought back from Eastern Europe
for her children: chocolates, Polish dolls, layettes, onesie
pajamas, and velvet hoodie coats. Most of the clothes
were one or two sizes too big, so that the kids wouldn't
outgrow them too soon. When Jun asked her why she
looked so down, sapped of her glow, Yomei just said she
had been frazzled after the long trip, which after all had
lasted more than four months. She wondered if she should
disclose Mao's assault on her to Jun but decided against
it—she remembered that in Harbin Father Zhou had
again admonished her not to breathe a word to anybody.
One thing nagging her these days was whether she might
get pregnant. Though already fifty-six, Mao must still be
able to father children. From time to time, some woman
would turn up at Zhongnanhai with a baby, claiming that
the child's father was Mao. Although to date such a claim
had never stuck (the guards office of the Zhongnanhai
compound would tell the baby's mother that she mustn't
presume that the great clearheaded leader had lost count
of his own children), this might indicate that Mao was still
potent and fertile. Yomei had become alert to every little
stir in her lower abdomen. Not until mid-March, on her
third day at Jun's home, did she feel the throbbing cramps
and find her period coming at last. This was a huge relief,
which lifted her mood some. She heaved a sigh and said
to herself, "Finally I can pull this nail out of my head."
Together with the feeling of relief, a kind of dull calm
settled over her.

When Yomei went back to the Zhous' a week later,
Mother Deng smiled and said to her, "Look, who's here."

A young woman in her early twenties and with a strong
face and a head of raven hair stepped into the living hall.
Yomei was surprised to see her younger sister, Yolan, and

rushed up to her. The two hugged, their eyes glistening tearfully. Mother Deng said, "Now we have two daughters."

Yomei saw that another bed had been set in her room for Yolan. She realized that the Zhous may have brought her little sister over to elevate her spirits. Yolan had lived with their oldest aunt Ren Fukun's family back in their home province of Sichuan. After their father had been killed in the late 1920s, there was no way their mother Ren Rui could possibly raise all those children on her own. Fukun offered to help raise one of her sister's children, even though she already had three sons herself. So Ren Rui gave her youngest child to her elder sister. Yet at heart, Yomei never let go of her little sister. Even during the time when their family was all living at their aunt Fukun's home, Yomei would say to Yolan on the sly, "We have the same mother. Your mother is actually our aunt." The three-year-old could hardly grasp the full meaning of those words, though she was attached to Yomei and often followed her around and would get a piggyback ride from her. When their family was moving inland later on, Yolan didn't leave with them, since Fukun loved her, treating her as her own. Over the decades, Yomei had often thought of Yolan, wondering if they could ever be together again.

Yolan told Yomei that a half year earlier her adoptive parents had explained to her how their mother had left her with Aunt Fukun two decades before. Now that Yolan planned to attend college in Beijing, she should reconnect with her real family, including her siblings in the north. Aunt Fukun told her that Yomei, whom Yolan still remembered vaguely, was Premier Zhou Enlai's daughter now, so Yolan should try to rejoin her sister.

On arrival in Beijing, Yolan went to Zhongnanhai straightaway, but the guards stopped her, saying the Zhous had no relative like her. Then they phoned Mrs. Zhou, who, after figuring out who Yolan was, told them to send her directly to West Flower Hall. The Zhous believed her sudden presence in Beijing might help ease some of Yomei's anxiety and restore her lively spirit.

After dinner, the two sisters chatted away, deep into the night. Their elder brother Yang had just transferred back to Beijing, but was now at the state planning commission, which didn't have a permanent working site yet. Since he was single now, having divorced recently, he lived in a dorm, sharing a room with a colleague. So the two sisters had better stay together in the city. Yomei wondered if she and Yolan should look for a place of their own, and she even sounded the Zhous out on this, saying her sister's sudden presence here might inconvenience them. But both Father Zhou and Mother Deng insisted that Yolan stay with them for the time being, because they had already adopted her elder sister as a daughter. They said this was the minimum they should do for their late parents. Father Zhou suggested that they pay a visit to Zhu Deh, who had once gone to Europe with their dad to look for a way of saving China from the clutches of warlords and feudalism. Father Zhou had met the two Sichuanese men, Zhu and Sun, in downtown Berlin in the fall of 1922 and introduced them to the Communist Party. Yomei assured the Zhous that she and Yolan would go see Uncle Zhu, whose family was also living in the same compound, at Forever Happy Hall.

Yomei believed that for now Yolan should stay at West Flower Hall and get to know the Zhous better—eventually Father Zhou might help her get into a fine college in Beijing.

One afternoon the two sisters took a long stroll around the southern part of the lake in the Zhongnanhai

compound. As they were crossing the isthmus toward Ying
Terrace, the little island in the middle of the southern
pond, they ran into Jiang Ching, who was with Neh.
Mother and daughter were on the shore throwing cooked
millet to a school of koi, their fluffy whitish tails spread
like miniature gauze parasols. Yomei introduced Yolan to
Ching and told her that her sister and she had lost touch
for more than two decades and had finally been reunited.
Ching was wearing black-rimmed glasses. She looked well,
perhaps owing to her medical treatment and recuperation
in the Soviet Union the previous fall. She seemed glad
to see Yomei, though Yomei noticed a shadow flit across
her smooth face. Ching said to her, "I hope you had a
wonderful time in Russia. Please come see me so we can
compare notes and share our discoveries about the Soviet
Union. I also want to know how Chairman Mao spent his
time there."

For a moment Yomei was flustered, then collected
herself. She said, "Sure, I'll be happy to share what I know
with you."

Ching waved goodbye to both of them and left with her
daughter. Yolan was amazed to see that Madame Mao was so
young and said to Yomei, "She's pretty, isn't she? Do you see
Jiang Ching regularly?"

"Not really. I don't like her that much. Both our mother
and I got to know her long ago in Shanghai. But don't
tell Father Zhou and Mother Deng that we ran into Jiang
Ching. Ching can be troublesome. Most people avoid her."

"All right, I won't breathe a word."

Though Yomei had agreed to share her experiences
in the Soviet Union with Jiang Ching, she didn't go see
her at all. In fact, she was disturbed by Ching's eagerness,
wondering if Ching had heard something about the night

she had spent with Mao on the train. Ching must have
had "eyes and ears" on Mao's staff; they might have noticed
that Yomei had abruptly quit teaching Mao Russian in the
evenings, and must have guessed that something unusual
had transpired between Mao and her, and they might have
informed Ching of this on the sly. The more Yomei mulled
over this possibility, the more agitated she became and the
more resolved she was to avoid meeting Ching in private.
It might have turned ugly if Ching had demanded to know
whether Yomei had attempted to seduce her husband, the
Great Leader.

With those misgivings in mind, Yomei went to see Lily,
who was back in Beijing now and served on the translation
board of Mao's writings in the editorial and translation
bureau that was within the Party's Central Committee. Lily
was also involved in translating Stalin's collected works into
Chinese. Their mutual friend, Lisa, had moved to Beijing
on account of Li Lisan's new appointment as the head of
China's trade union. Lily didn't have her own housing yet,
so she stayed with Lisa. The two of them were quite close
now. Yomei and Lisa were friends too, but she didn't want
to be too involved with the Lis because of the telegram
scandal three years before and because she didn't want to
stir up trouble for Li Lisan—some people might accuse
them of having formed a Soviet clique. As a matter of fact,
Father Zhou had told her to be careful while mixing with
foreigners.

Yomei and Lily were having ice cream in a snack bar
on Wangfujing Street. The two had so much to catch up
on, but both seemed a little guarded due to their current
confidential work in the Party. Before the meeting, part of
Yomei had wanted to reveal to Lily that Mao had assaulted

her, but at the last moment she changed her mind, even though she still held Lily as her best friend. How could she convince Lily that she hadn't flirted with Mao at all? In most people's eyes, many women would want to have an affair with the great man and even to bear him a child. Therefore, she'd better not unburden herself of everything. Above all, the knowledge of such a secret might endanger Lily.

"So you seem to get on well with Jiang Ching," Yomei said to her friend, her tone of voice verging on a question.

"Yes and no. She said she needed my help when we were in Russia. But I could see she was a crank and can be bossy and demanding. It's hard for her staff members to work for her."

"When did you last see her?"

"Just three weeks ago. She wants to put on some Russian plays. You know, because she's not allowed to operate in the top political circle, she has become more interested in the arts, specifically drama and cinema."

"Really? What plays is she interested in?"

"I'm not sure. She mentioned Gorky and Bulgakov."

"That's impressive. She used to be an actress, so she's knowledgeable about theater."

"Keep in mind, she might enlist your help too. In fact, she mentioned you, and we talked about you at length."

"What did she say about me?"

"She said she had known you since you were a young girl. To her, you were talented, vivacious, and beautiful, but a little too naive and headstrong."

"What did she mean by that?"

"She said you were more like a boy than a girl. Isn't that true?"

"Probably. I used to be like a tomboy," Yomei said pensively.

"I remember when we first met, I was fascinated by your carefree manner. I think that by 'too naive,' Ching might have meant you didn't have political savvy and acumen. Come on, Yomei, you are like that, aren't you? You never like officials; neither do I."

"Goodness, they put too much egg yolk in this ice cream."

Lily nodded. "They might use it as a substitute for butter and milk, I guess. Many Chinese don't know what real ice cream tastes like anyway."

They both laughed. They also talked about their personal lives. Lily said there was a young man, a navy officer, courting her, but she was reluctant to go with him because he was quite obsessed with rank and power, always becoming awestruck when a senior official's name cropped up in conversation. Yomei smiled, saying her friend hadn't adapted back to China thoroughly yet, but on the other hand, they both ought to retain their innocence, which was their true color and part of themselves.

Yet what Lily had revealed about Jiang Ching's opinion of her brought Yomei both agitation and relief. She felt relieved because Ching seemed ignorant of what had transpired between her and Mao, while she was disturbed because she suspected that Ching might ask her to work on some Russian plays. If that came up, she had no idea how to respond. She knew that deep down, Ching was much more interested in power than in art and that it would be impossible to collaborate with that woman, who was vainglorious and capricious, always acting as Madame Mao and enjoying bringing others to heel.

So Yomei decided to continue avoiding Ching. With some bitterness, she remembered how Ching had intimidated others, including her first crush, Xu Yi-xin. Now, the woman definitely relished her status as First Lady. But she, Yomei, was Zhou Enlai's daughter, and as long as Father Zhou was the premier, Ching couldn't really hurt her. She could afford to ignore Jiang Ching.

· *Forty-Seven* ·

Meanwhile, Liao Chengzhi, the chairman of China's Youth Union, approached Yomei again. Liao also headed the National Youth Art Theater, recently formed but not fully staffed yet. He had been looking for talent for the company and invited Yomei to join them. She was delighted to accept the position of stage director in chief, which was the first appointment of this kind for a woman in the new China. She felt this job belonged to her, since she was known as the first red theater expert. "We produced the play *The Patriots* two months ago. It was a fiasco," Mr. Liao told Yomei, flexing his chubby fingers as if they had been burned. "The director was an amateur and had no clue how to tell a story. Many scenes felt disjointed as a result."

"I'll do my best," she promised, her eyes glittering with excitement.

"So like we agreed last year, our next project is *Pavel Korchagin.*"

Without delay, Yomei embarked on the task of directing the Soviet play. She also moved into the dorm of the theater so that she could get to know the production crew better. Besides, it was time for her to be on her own, though her sister, Yolan, would continue staying at the Zhous' until she went to college.

The choice of staging this play had been carefully made by the Youth Art Theater, because *Pavel Korchagin* was a eulogy of youth and a lesson about how to live one's life meaningfully for "the liberation of mankind." Politically and diplomatically, such a stage production in China's capital could also serve as an indicator of the two countries' cooperation, not just in economy and politics and the military but also in culture and arts. Yomei was aware of the international implications of the project, though eventually she also meant to introduce the Stanislavski method to China through the Youth Art Theater. In addition, *Pavel Korchagin* was her inaugural production, her first full-length play, of which she must make a success to salvage the new theater from the fiasco of its previous effort. Ultimately she wanted to build her own theater, though for now she had to focus on directing *Pavel Korchagin* to consolidate her standing in the circle of spoken drama. Once she was secure in her new position, she could build the theater according to her vision. One thing was clear to her: she didn't want a foreign theater and must make this one rooted in the Chinese soil. These days her busy work and high hopes buoyed her up, and she felt energetic again.

Besides studying the Russian play, by Bondarenko, and poring over the novel from which it was adapted, *How Steel Was Tempered*, by Nikolai Ostrovsky, Yomei was also doing a great amount of reading—the history of the USSR, narratives of the Russian civil war, Ostrovsky's letters and speeches, and numerous critical papers on the writer. She also looked at a good deal of paintings, photographs, slides, and movies. The reading helped her form images of the

characters and visions for the stage designs. She found
the Russian play somewhat disconnected, and its Chinese
translation clunky in spots, with some lines hard to speak
aloud, so she decided to revise the script thoroughly to make
it more coherent and more colloquial, so that it could be
transparent to the Chinese audience. Through extended
reading, she gradually grasped the heroic spirit of Pavel
Korchagin, a blind and paralyzed man who never gave up
and lived his life to its fullest. His spirit could be summed
up by the catchphrases he often used: "Long live life!" and
"Long live labor!"

To create a suitable poetic mood for the beginning of the
play, so as to immediately pull the audience into the scene,
Yomei added a song partly written by herself. She imagined
the melody based on a Ukrainian folk song she had heard
in Ufa long ago, and would ask a composer to create some
melodious music based on the folk song. For now she just
wrote out the lyrics:

> In the vast prairie of Ukraine
> A little river is flowing peacefully
> By a pair of tall poplars—
> This is our beloved homeland
> Where we have lived and died
> And will thrive for generations to come . . .

She wouldn't reveal the song to the cast yet, afraid that
doing so might set boundaries to the actors' imagination
and creativity. She would share it with them once all the
scenes had been revised to make the story more compact
and unified.

A major challenge was how to make best use of the
miscellaneous actors she had on her hands. Some of them

were from Yan'an, more experienced than she was as
revolutionaries, some from Shanghai, already established
in the field and even with a national reputation, and some
were from the northeast, quite young but full of promise.
The hardest choice was the role of the hero, the leading
man. At the very beginning of Yomei's directing work,
Liao Chengzhi, the president of the Youth Art Theater,
had recommended Jin Shan, the vice president of the
theater, for the role of Pavel Korchagin. Besides being
a spoken drama actor, Jin Shan was a movie star as well,
with the sobriquet "China's Clark Gable," so Liao believed
that his fame should help the play secure at least box office
success. Further, Jin Shan's wife, Zhang Ruifnag, was
also a huge movie star and well experienced in spoken
drama acting and would help bring a large audience if she
played Tonya, Pavel's lover. This also meant that Yomei
ought to accept the couple as the hero and the heroine in
the play. She couldn't pick one and leave out the other,
having to use them as a pair. She could see the advantage
in taking on both of them—since there was a passionate
kissing scene that might be easier to perform if the actors
were a married couple—this wouldn't violate the Chinese
audience's sense of propriety. She had no problem with
Zhang Ruifang, who was in her early thirties and still
pretty, with a youthful figure, but she had reservations
about Jin Shan. Shan was almost forty, getting fat in spite
of his lush widow's peak, and might not be able to represent
the youthful years of Pavel, who, according to the graphics
sent over from the Soviet Union, was thin and gaunt but
with a large bone-structure, which Shan didn't have. Yet
Shan was her superior, the vice president of the National
Youth Art Theater. He had been appointed to that position
because he had been a longtime Party member working in

the Nationalist regime in disguise. Initially it was hard for
the people at the theater to accept him as a colleague, let
alone a leader, and Mr. Liao had had to do some explaining
to them. He declared, wagging his pudgy index finger,
"Comrade Jin Shan was one of the biggest moles of our
Party, working in the reactionary ranks." Indeed, he had
done a great deal to promote the left theater and cinema
and for the war against the Japanese invasion, including
performing abroad to raise funds for the Chinese people
during the wartime. But unlike many Party members,
who were eager to grab powerful positions after the
establishment of the PRC, Jin Shan was thrilled to be able
to return to the art world when Liao Chengzhi offered him
a position in the theater. He wanted to remain an artist
performing onstage.

Besides those concerns nagging Yomei, in terms of both
artistic and political experience, Jin Shan was more senior
to her. More complicated was that fifteen years back, when
her mother had taken her to Shanghai so she could learn
how to act, she had been put under Jin Shan's protection
in a left-wing drama association, the Oriental Troupe. She
used to call him Uncle Jin, though he was merely ten years
older than her. Now, what to do? she wondered. Do you
believe he can carry the role of Pavel Korchagin? she asked
herself, but wasn't sure.

She decided to take a professional approach as the
director when dealing with Jin Shan. She showed him the
photographs of the play performed in Moscow. "See," she
said, "the span of Pavel Korchagin's life onstage is quite
wide, from sixteen to thirty-two. It might be a challenge to
you. Do you think you can fulfill the role?"

He chuckled. "Of course I'll be able to handle it. I
promise to lose some weight and make myself trim again."

"I hope it will work out well." Her tone of voice implied that she reserved the right to drop the leading man if she found him unsuitable.

Jin Shan himself had directed many plays, so he didn't really look up to Yomei in the beginning, but he was eager to prepare himself for the principal role. To play the teenage Pavel, he constantly practiced a young boy's movement and acts. When he walked, he jumped and skipped every few steps. He was also very careful about his diet and wouldn't eat his fill at meals. At the threshold of his apartment, he placed a board bench so that he'd have to leap over it whenever he passed the door. He began doing vigorous exercises too. Every morning he got up at the crack of dawn and jogged all the way to Tiananmen Square and around the neighborhood, running three miles. After that, he'd wake up his younger colleagues so that they could play basketball for more than an hour, all wearing jerseys and shorts and canvas sneakers. Every week, he dropped two or three pounds. Little by little, his gait became nimbler, and everyone could see that he looked younger now and began to have a gently curved-in waist, as if it were cinched. Partly due to his diligence, other actors got very serious about their physical shape too.

Yomei often emphasized that every one of them must live in the play emotionally even offstage, because one of Stanislavski's principles dictated that an actor shouldn't step onstage before he or she was already in the scene emotionally and psychologically. Jin Shan was gradually fascinated by Yomei's way of directing, which was an eye-opener for him. He had worked with several famous directors before, some of whom didn't speak much while directing. They'd hold a copy of the script while talking to actors. Jin Shan couldn't tell what other preparations

these directors had done, besides studying the script. But
the amount of work Yomei had been doing struck him as
stupendous and thoroughgoing—she knew every aspect
of the play, even some small historical details, such as the
décor of a regular Moscow apartment and the floral clothes
worn by Ukrainians (she told the acting crew that in the
Soviet Union younger people usually wore simple colors,
often monochrome, whereas older women donned bright
colors). More amazing, she didn't ask actors to memorize
their lines, nor did she allow them to read from the script.
She wanted them to *speak* their lines. If they couldn't
remember them precisely, they could take a look at the
text and then say their lines as if the words were their own
natural speech. Jin Shan could see that this was to harness
the inner creative impulses of the actors and also to make
them listen to others, which can be harder than speaking.
In the beginning they sat at a long table, each speaking their
lines. Then, when their verbal exchanges reached such an
intensity that they couldn't help but use gestures and body
language, they began to leave the table and chairs to get on
the rehearsal space, acting out the dialogue.

Jin Shan was also impressed by Yomei's revision of
Bondarenko's script. She had even cut an entire scene,
which tightened up the drama considerably. On the
whole, her revisions gave the play a natural flow. She also
resurrected a character, Sergei, and instead of letting him
get killed, the revised script kept him alive, still laughing,
confabulating, and dreaming with Pavel at the end. Such a
bold revision gave the story more hope and a brighter color,
which could help inspire the Chinese audience. Prior to
working with Yomei, Jin Shan had known the Stanislavski
method only in patches, and now he was appreciating this

comprehensive experience, which was so empowering and
liberating.

Many of the actors lived in the dorm, a two-story brick
building behind the theater, and their apartments were
all furnished with wood floors and central heating, which
were a kind of luxury at the time. The Jins' apartment was
upstairs, while Yomei's was on the ground floor. Living
in the same building made it easier for them to compare
notes on the play and discuss issues that occurred during
rehearsals. Sometimes Shan would go down and talk with
Yomei for hours on end. His wife, Ruifang, wasn't worried
about the time the two spent together, and believed that
their meeting was professionally necessary. Jin Shan often
got excited when a new idea came up, and Yomei gradually
relied on him as a kind of sounding board during her
revision of the script and in making stage adjustments, but
on the whole she was quite certain about her directing work
and seemed to have a plan for every facet of the project: she
was even meticulous about the lighting of every scene and
the variety of the wardrobe.

For Jin Shan, the role of Pavel was rather mysterious.
On one hand, he felt attracted to the hero; on the other, he
couldn't get close to him enough to grasp him. Every time
after rehearsing a scene, he'd feel exhausted, agonizing for
Pavel's sake. While rehearsing, he suffered and rejoiced
alternately. In addition, as the vice president of the theater,
he had to do some managerial work. Lately he had been
composing a long report on the theater's political studies.
So three nights in a row he hadn't slept, and during the
day, he still went to the rehearsal. One afternoon, while
doing the crucial second scene in which Pavel meets for the
first time with Sailor Zhukhrai, the revolutionary leader,

Jin Shan somehow lost self-control and began laughing unstoppably. Such hysterical laughter at times happens to actors under too much stress. But an experienced star like Jin Shan shouldn't have had such emotional incontinence. Everyone was shocked. When he had finally stopped, he said absentmindedly, "Why did I do that? Damn, I'm such a dope, laughing for no reason at all!"

Yomei knew that his random laugh must be due to exhaustion and pressure, but he was an experienced actor and should have been able to preempt such a mishap. Unable to respond properly, she dismissed the cast for the day. Jin Shan remained on the rehearsal stage alone and murmured, "Terrible, this is terrible!" Then he hugged a prop, a poplar trunk made of papier-mâché, and broke out sobbing.

Yomei stepped over and patted his shoulder. "You've been working too hard. Please don't blame yourself. You're such a dedicated artist that you'll do the role magnificently. For now, you must rest well so we can continue tomorrow."

He nodded wordlessly. Together they went back to the dorm building. She took him upstairs and explained the incident to his wife, who had come home earlier that day.

Yomei was fascinated by Jin Shan, who had been known as a playboy, having one affair after another for nearly two decades. She knew that a lot of women had been infatuated with him, and that one starlet had even committed suicide because he had not reciprocated her love. Yet for years, he wasn't able to stop behaving like a Casanova. It was said that he had once asked a poet friend to compose a florid love letter for him, of which he made several copies and sent them to different women, but later those women found out that they had received the same sugary words. Zhang

Ruifang was his second wife. She agreed to marry him
mainly because of his relentless pursuit of her—at one point
he had even threatened suicide. His ex-wife, Wang Ying,
was also a huge movie star and a spoken drama actress.
After leaving him, she went to Yale to study literature and
later became a writer and even performed the play *Put Down
Your Whip* in the White House for the Roosevelts.

Regardless of Jin Shan's problematic history with
women, Yomei was touched by his dedication. She could
tell that at heart he was a pure artist and ready to give
everything to a good play. He often told younger actors,
"You must act not only with your brain, but with your
feelings and blood. For an actor, there is no better ending
than to die onstage." Yomei also noticed the change
in herself of late—she was in a buoyant mood now and
laughed a lot, and was somewhat like her former self again,
especially when Jin Shan was around.

He came to rehearsal the next morning as if nothing
out of the ordinary had happened the day before. His wife
felt sorry for him, since her role was less exacting and she
enjoyed playing Tonya. So when he went downstairs to talk
with Yomei in the evenings, she didn't intervene, believing
he needed the director's stabilizing influence to sustain
him. Sometimes he stayed with Yomei for three or four
hours in a row. She always welcomed him, amazed that
time slipped by unnoticed when he was here. There were
always new things to talk about, and whenever they found a
new idea or figured out a solution together, his face would
brighten, his eyes flashing. Soon he came every evening and
stayed very late.

One night, when it was already past eleven o'clock, as he
and she were talking about a frolic scene in the wilderness

enacted by Pavel and Tonya, Shan got so excited that he hugged Yomei, then the back of his hand brushed her breast, as if inadvertently.

"Sorry, sorry," he said. "You're so charming, I've become too clumsy." His smile distorted his handsome face, his nose quivering a little, as if he were a gauche greenhorn.

"Don't worry. It's OK," Yomei said, blushing.

Her reply emboldened him. He embraced her again and kissed her on the mouth. From there, he proceeded to touch her, and she reciprocated passionately, stimulated by his male scent, which was pungent and intoxicating to her.

She enjoyed having sex with him and appreciated his experience in making love. Evidently he had slept with a lot of women. She liked that, liked to be taken by a man who could make her feel invigorated and youthful again. He told her that hers were the most beautiful breasts he'd ever seen, smooth and firm, thrilling to the touch.

"I can see you're a connoisseur of women. Tell me, how many breasts have you fondled?" she said.

"Gosh, how could I keep track?" He forced a small laugh, a bit embarrassed.

"I can see that you're a lustful goat, but I love you."

"I know. Please stay with me, always," he murmured and went on caressing her.

"I won't let you go. You're mine, body and soul." She kissed him on his nipple, on which there were two or three hairs.

But she had to let him go back to his wife around one in the morning. Ruifang was already deep in sleep when he slipped into their bed. She murmured something he couldn't understand. Probably she was having a pleasant dream, speaking playfully with somebody, her lips twisting a little.

Now his wife could tell that Shan and Yomei might be falling for each other. She confronted him one morning and asked bluntly, "Are you carrying on with Little Mei?" Ruifang used a former endearment for Yomei, whom she had seen grow up. It was kind of ridiculous to see this girl interfering with her marriage. But on the other hand, she had never loved Jin Shan and had agreed to marry him mainly out of respect and affection and friendship.

"To be honest, Ruifang," he confessed, "I'm so attached to Yomei. You know what a brilliant director she has become, and she's also a beautiful young lady."

"If you and she are serious about each other, you must be aboveboard with me. Otherwise I won't share the stage with you. I can't stand that people talk about me behind my back. Don't make a fool of me."

"I promise I'll be honest with you."

In spite of his promise, it was hard for Ruifang to remain composed when seeing him spending so much time with the younger woman, who Jin Shan claimed had become his psychological crutch. Yet Ruifang was the kind of person who couldn't tolerate anything that undermined her pride. She and Jin Shan had never quarreled, but after five years' marriage, she felt exhausted. So she simply moved out of the dorm building, though she still went to rehearsals as before. Even on the rehearsal stage, she couldn't always remain undisturbed, seeing how her husband was hung up on the young director, who seemed to enjoy playing the seductress. Clearly Yomei was in love, her eyes smiling all the time, and even her footsteps appeared suppler now.

As a matter of fact, thinking of herself as a home-wrecker was eating away at Yomei's heart. As soon as she heard that Ruifang had moved out of their apartment, she went to see

Jin Shan's wife, who received her rather politely. Yomei sat down in Ruifang's new room, which was still in disorder, and asked her bluntly, despite her pounding heart, "Can you tell me what kind of a man Jin Shan is? I want to stand on firm ground when dealing with him."

Taken aback, Ruifang managed to say "I'm not very clear about him. He seems a simple man at heart, but he likes to make things elaborate and complicated."

"You mean he's vain?"

"Not exactly. Perhaps he didn't have much real education and is basically self-taught, so he wants to impress others whenever he can."

Yomei still didn't grasp the full meaning of Ruifang's words, but this conversation convinced Ruifang that Yomei was serious about her feelings and intentions and that there might be no way to keep her and Jin Shan apart. So Ruifang proposed a divorce, which Jin Shan accepted. The collapse of their marriage became quite a scandal, but it didn't bother Yomei that much because Jin Shan had offered to marry her, saying he'd finally found a soulmate. Yet she wasn't sure whether to accept his proposal. She had to know more about him.

One night, as the two of them were strolling along Chang'an Avenue near Tiananmen Square, she said to him, "Shan, you must tell me everything about yourself or I won't know if I can marry you."

"What's there to talk about?" he said and paused under a streetlight, looking inquiringly into her eyes, in which tiny sparks were flitting. He said, "I'm just an actor and have made many movies. You know all of them. Also, I started to work for the Party secretly two decades ago, so you can call me an older comrade."

"Tell me about your major affairs." She looked into his handsome face, which turned a touch mysterious.

"Why do you need to know them?"

"You must have been intimate with some well-known actresses whose paths I might cross in the future. I don't want to be in the dark and ought to know whom I will be dealing with and where I stand."

"Fair enough. I'll tell you everything then."

He went on to recount the major relationships he'd had. He didn't include one-night stands and brief flings, which would have been too numerous for him to recall and explain. He just mentioned about a dozen women, focusing on his ex-wives: Wang Ying and Zhang Ruifang. He felt neither of them had really loved him, though he himself was to blame for the broken marriages. He promised Yomei that he'd treat her as part of himself and love her wholeheartedly. The two of them strolled around for five hours until the early morning traffic began to appear on the streets. They had to return to the dorm to catch a bit of sleep before going to work.

She believed him, convinced that he'd make her an excellent husband. Whatever others said about her role as a home-wrecker didn't bother her that much. To her, as long as the two of them loved each other deeply enough, their union should be justified. She was unafraid of accusatory fingers and barbed tongues. On the other hand, the fact that she had ruined Ruifang's marriage put her on the defensive, so she had to endure all sorts of gossip, rumors, and glaring eyes. She even went to see Zhang Ruifang again and talked about Jin Shan's intention to marry her. She apologized, saying that she and Shan really loved each other. Ruifang remarked that Jin Shan could marry a pretty young woman every other year and wouldn't hesitate to hop in bed with an attractive woman anytime. Yomei sensed the bitterness in her tone, yet the two women managed to reach an accord on the production of *Pavel Korchagin*. As a veteran actress, Ruifang behaved professionally and continued to play Tonya.

She also joined her ex-husband in the run-throughs and the dress rehearsal, which proceeded without incident.

Forty-Eight

The play premiered in early September and became a
spectacular success. The theater didn't sell tickets initially
and just invited some professionals and dignitaries
to attend the first two performances. Lisa and Li Lisan
were there for the opening night and congratulated Yomei
afterward for such a splendid inauguration of her directing
career. She introduced Jin Shan to the couple and also
translated for him when he chatted a bit with Lisa. Lisa told
him that she had seen the movie *The Midnight Song*, which he had
starred in. He laughed and said, "That was long ago, when I
was still a young boy." Li Lisan was also warm and friendly to
Jin Shan, saying he was glad to see that Jin Shan's handsome
face was smooth and scarless, because the protagonist Shan
had played in the movie, Sung Danping, had a hideous visage
burned by acid. That made them all laugh.

The audience of *Pavel Korchagin* were struck by the beauty
and originality of the production, and some had even
applauded at the very beginning, as soon as the curtain
went up, when no actor had uttered a word yet, just for the
vibrant scenery, which was so exotic and striking, the likes
of which they had never seen before. The only complaint
came from some conservative viewers who felt the deep,
wet kisses between Pavel and Tonya were over the top—they

said the two could have just hugged and smooched a tad
and didn't have to French-kiss openly for a full minute. But
young people loved to see this extravagant manifestation of
passion and love. Some even applauded at the scene.

Another reason for the play becoming an immediate
sensation was the actual love triangle in the production
crew. The leading man and lady, both big stars, and the
stage director had been entwined emotionally; nevertheless,
they had managed to put the play together and even made
it a hit. That was something unheard of, and therefore
many people were more eager to see whether this triangular
tension was manifested in the performance. In addition,
there was also another famous actor, Wu Xue, who played
the role of the revolutionary leader Zhukhrai. Such a cast
alone was extraordinary.

After the first two nights, the theater began to sell tickets
to the public. There was always a line at the box office. One
night as Yomei and Jin Shan were strolling around, hand
in hand and both wearing lightly tinted glasses, they saw
some people wrapped in blankets or thin quilts standing in
the line for the next day's tickets. The couple stepped away,
afraid of being recognized. Jin Shan was so touched that he
said "This has made me feel as if I'm having a second acting
life. Our play has revived me."

Yomei laughed and asked, "So you feel like the Emperor
of Spoken Drama again?" She was referring to the
nickname the public had given him back in Shanghai.

"Well, not an aristocrat, but a youthful man again. Even
when I'm with you in bed."

She whacked him on the shoulder. "You're a hopelessly
sensual goat."

He laughed. "You're not exactly a chaste maiden, are
you?"

"How could I remain chaste with a man like you?"

"To be honest, I admire your resolve and the kind of clarity you have about your own feelings."

"I respect Ruifang for her devotion to the play. She's a true professional. It must be hard for her to play the leading lady."

"Of course it's not easy, but she'll leave when the performance period is over."

Ruifang had just made arrangements with Shanghai Film Studio and would move to that city soon. She would also quit the stage and resume acting only on the screen. Her fame as a movie star would help her find work anywhere in China. Both Jin Shan and Yomei felt relieved to see her land an adequate position for herself.

Yomei invited Lily to the play's fourth night, on September 12. By then, Lily had left the Lis', since she had her own lodgings in the dormitory of her translation bureau. She was so struck by the beauty and grandeur of the play that afterward she hugged Yomei and murmured, "I'm so proud of you!" Her eyes welled with tears.

Yomei took her to a nearby dumpling house to have a snack. It was nearly ten o'clock at night, but there were still many customers in the restaurant. The two of them were seated face-to-face at a Formica table, at whose center a yellow laminated menu stood between the salt and pepper shakers. Still in the afterglow of the successful evening, they were each to have a bowl of wontons. Jin Shan was with the acting crew and couldn't join them. These days, after performances, he'd meet the members of the audience who were reluctant to leave right away, giving a brief talk about the production of the play and fielding their questions. Lily had congratulated him backstage, after the performance. She'd also met him a few times before and could see that he looked younger now, having dropped more than twenty pounds and fitting into the role of Pavel Korchagin well.

Spooning up a wonton from her steaming bowl, Yomei said, "You know, I'm going to get married soon."

"Who's the lucky groom?" Lily's eyes narrowed as she was smiling.

"You haven't heard?"

"No, tell me who your fiancé is."

"Jin Shan."

"Oh, doesn't he already have a wife?"

"They are divorced. I love him, so I want to get married."

"Why? You were never the marrying type."

"True, I used to be against matrimony, but lately I've realized that once you're married, you can concentrate more on work, and people leave you alone."

Lily put down her spoon and sighed. "Still, I'm surprised. Why did you pick Jin Shan? You used to have great suitors, some of whom have become pillars of our country." The inner edges of Lily's eyebrows rose, forming a caret below her full forehead.

"I can see you're underwhelmed. Tell me, is Jin Shan that mediocre to you?"

"Not because of that. As an actor, he's fine but somewhat washed-out. Compared to men like Lin Biao and Liu Yalou, Jin Shan is inconspicuous, to say the least. He's quite old for you, besides. Honestly, Yomei, I wish you had talked with me about your choice. I can't see what you love about him."

"As a matter of fact, I asked myself the same question, but I now have my answer: I love his artist's soul, and even his madness. When we're together, we have so much to talk about, whereas with men like Lin Biao and Liu Yalou I don't have a common language. How about you? Are you seeing anyone?"

"No, I'm not that interested in men, although a bunch of them had often popped up in my work unit."

"So the navy officer has stopped going after you?"

"He just disappeared."

"Why?"

"I have no clue. Perhaps because I couldn't help him with his career. It doesn't matter. I'm not interested in a sycophant like him anyway. I'm tired of men."

"That's only because you haven't met the right one for you yet. In due time, you'll meet someone who can make you feel like a different woman."

"Fat chance." Lily arched her eyebrows. "I want to go to Moscow to study again, to work toward a graduate degree, but it's out of the question for now."

"Why? Because of Jiang Ching?"

"She's part of it. She wants me to work for her, but I'm more suitable for desk work, so I've been trying my best to stay in the translation bureau under Shi Zhe's leadership. I like my colleagues there, who are all knowledgeable and can write well."

"It's a large work unit, isn't it?"

"Yes, almost like a ministry. When will your wedding be held?"

"We don't have a fixed date yet. Probably next month, after the performance period is over. I'll have to check with Father Zhou and Mother Deng to see when they can attend our wedding. I'll keep you posted."

"Do you need anything for your new home? I mean, what kind of gift can I get you?"

"Nothing at all. Please come to my wedding. That'll mean a lot to me."

A week later, Yomei went to see the Zhous. Her sister, Yolan, no longer lived with them, having moved to the

dormitory of the Beijing College of Foreign Languages,
where she matriculated as a Russian major. Yolan enjoyed her
school a lot, so she didn't go to the Zhous as often as before,
in spite of Yomei's urging her to keep stronger ties with the
Zhous. Such a close relationship would stand her in good
stead when dealing with the officials at her school. But Yolan
seemed to have settled down at the college and had a circle of
friends, though she still went to see the Zhous from time to
time. Yomei was happy for her. Nowadays when they met, she
sometimes spoke Russian with her and could tell the progress
Yolan had been making with her studies.

Before Yomei told the Zhous about her relationship
with Jin Shan, they'd heard of it. Word had gone around
that Zhou Enlai's daughter had become a home-wrecker
and had robbed Zhang Ruifang of her husband. After a
dinner of seafood soup and braised meatballs—"lion heads,"
a signature dish in Huaiyang cuisine, and Yomei's favorite
dish at the Zhous'—the premier, his forehead crimped,
asked her bluntly, "I'm told that you've been carrying on
with Jin Shan. How serious is this affair or whatever you
call it?"

Lowering her eyes, Yomei said, "Jin Shan and I love each
other. We plan to get married next month."

Father Zhou and Mother Deng looked at each other,
apparently astonished by her answer. Mother Deng said,
"Why such a rush? Do you really know him?"

"Yes, I'm known him since the age of fourteen."

Father Zhou smirked. "You were just a little girl at that
time and couldn't possibly get to know him well."

"But in recent months, I have seen how dedicated he is
to the theatrical arts. He's a real artist, a great one."

Father Zhou's face clouded over, giving a reproachful
smile. "Yomei, both Jin Shan and Zhang Ruifang used to

work for me, so I know them pretty well. They are both truly excellent actors, but you're going to marry a man with whom you will live for the rest of your life. There must be some sides to his personality that you might not be aware of. You mustn't rush."

"We only want you to be happy," added Mother Deng.

Yomei breathed a sigh. "Do you approve of my marriage?" She sounded frustrated, a flicker of impatience and shame in her tone.

Father Zhou said, "I know what kind of a man Jin Shan is. As a comrade and even a friend, he is a fine fellow, but as a husband, you ought to be careful before plunging into a marriage with him. He just divorced his wife for your sake and might do the same to you if he falls for another woman."

"Besides," Mother Deng joined in, "you should consider your reputation. It's hard for a woman to shake off a bad name. You should've been more prudent."

"If this is a scandal," Yomei went on, "it will blow over. For love, I'm willing to suffer and sacrifice."

The Zhous said no more and seemed aware of the futility of their remonstrations. Yomei realized that at heart they disapproved of her marriage, so she didn't persist. Instead, she asked them about their opinion of *Pavel Korchagin*. They both loved it and even said they could see a star rising in China's spoken drama, meaning Yomei had had a great beginning. They truly felt proud of her. At the same time, they advised her to be careful and learn how to manage success. Father Zhou told her that a Soviet newspaper had just reported on the performance in Beijing, and he would have a copy of the article sent to Yomei.

· Forty-Nine ·

The article on Beijing's staging of *Pavel Korchagin* appeared in *Izvestia*, a widely read newspaper in the Soviet Union. Zhou Enlai had a translated copy delivered to Yomei, so that she could share it with her colleagues. They were all thrilled to see that the news of their success had even reached Moscow. Evidently some people at the Soviet embassy in Beijing had seen their performance and reported back to their government. The article said that the director of the play had been educated in the USSR and adopted the Stanislavski method, to which the play owed its success. It also claimed that the Chinese audience had been so moved that after the performance, groups of young people had marched away from the theater while shouting in unison "Pavel! Pavel!" The name had become a synonym for hero in Beijing.

That was true. Yet the rave didn't lift Yomei's spirits that much. She was mindful of the Zhous' negative response to her imminent marriage. She talked with Jin Shan about this, but he wasn't fazed by the Zhous' reservations, saying that his life had been beset by gossip, rumors, and even slanders that said he was a pervert and madman and incorrigible philanderer, but as long as one produced genuine artwork, all those negative noises and reviling

words would fizzle out. "Talent and artistic accomplishment
will trump them all," he assured Yomei. So they decided to
go ahead with their plan for the wedding, on October 14.
She mailed out two hundred invitations. As for Father Zhou
and Mother Deng, she handed them the card when she
visited them the following weekend, and she hoped against
hope that they would attend her wedding.

Jin Shan and Yomei

On Saturday evening, October 14, Jin Shan and Yomei
were standing at the front entrance to the Youth Palace
on East Chang'an Avenue, he in a grayish-blue suit and a
scarlet tie, while she was wearing a burgundy swing dress,
which was quite becoming, setting off her exotic beauty.
Dozens of cars were parked in the side lot, as numerous
dignitaries came for the wedding. Among them were
Roshchin (the Soviet ambassador to China), General
Luo Ruiching (minister of public security), Feng Wenbin
(secretary of the Chinese Communist Youth League), Wu
Yuzhang (president of the People's University), and Jin
Shan's longtime friend Zhao Dan, the movie star, who
had come all the way from Shanghai. There were scores

of younger friends of the groom's and the bride's. Lily was
in Eastern Europe again with a delegation, so she couldn't
come. Neither could Yomei's elder brother Yang, who
was in Guangzhou on business, but Yolan came, wearing
a saffron skirt printed with butterflies and a beige vest
and serving as one of the two bridesmaids. The other one
was Oyang Fei, Feifei, whom Yomei had befriended in
Moscow. Feifei was wearing a houndstooth dress, black
stockings, and leather sandals, which made her look exotic
and younger than her age, twenty-eight. She and Lily
worked together in the same office, the translation bureau,
rendering Mao's writings and the CCP's documents into
Russian. She'd brought Yomei a tall tin of Russian chicory
powder, which she said tasted richer than coffee and which
was from both her and Lily. The two also gave Yomei a
gleaming Bialetti coffee pot, made in Greece.

The wedding wasn't very formal, being more like a big
reception. Tables and chairs stood along the walls of a large
hall on the second floor; its terrazzo floor was sprinkled
lightly with talcum powder for the dancing that some
attendees would be doing. The tabletops were spread with
candies, fruits, pastries, wines, sodas, peanuts, sunflower
seeds, and fancy cigarettes. At the sight of so many goodies,
the children there got excited and began attacking them,
with some even slipping a taffy or a maltose candy into
their pockets, while adults stood around chitchatting over
drinks. The kids, busy eating candies and fruits and walnut
cookies, ignored the bride and the groom at the front of the
room, who were being introduced to the guests formally by
Liao Chengzhi, the round-faced president of the Youth Art
Theater, who served as the emcee.

Yomei was agitated and couldn't stop looking around
in hopes of finding the Zhous. If they didn't show up, that

would be a blow to her, one she was afraid might signify that they might cut ties with her. Yet their presence here might also give rise to gossip—people might whisper that the Zhous endorsed their daughter's misbehavior. She told Yolan to stay near the front entrance and let her know if their adoptive parents turned up.

Meanwhile, Jin Shan looked happy and at ease, laughing and exchanging pleasantries with the guests, though Yomei, with her heart in her mouth, was trying to appear poised and rapturous. The groom was experienced with all sorts of occasions and had even mixed with ruffians and gangsters in Shanghai in his early twenties, so he was usually unflappable. He often said to his bride, "As long as we stay together as a loving couple, people will accept us eventually. Their current reservations shouldn't be a big deal to us."

Finally, a midnight-blue Volga sedan with a brass leaping deer at the head of the cowl pulled up at the front entrance. Out came Mrs. Zhou, holding a small red package that looked like a wrapped book. Instead of going up to her, Yolan turned around and called to her sister. Yomei hurried down the stairs and went up to Mother Deng. She said, "I'm so happy to see you here, Mom!"

"Of course I must come to my daughter's wedding."

"Where's my dad? He can't make it?"

"He has to receive a Hungarian delegation this evening, but he gives you his congratulations. I'm also representing him."

"Oh, I understand. We'll save some Mickey Mouse toffees for him." Yomei sounded slightly disappointed, wondering whether Father Zhou still disapproved of her marriage. He was displeased for sure.

Mrs. Zhou went up to the groom and said to him, while holding Yomei's hand, "I'm now giving you my daughter.

You must be considerate and kind to her, love and cherish her and grow old together with her."

"I shall of course, Mother," Jin Shan said with a little bow, then lifted a porcelain pot and poured her a cup of Dragon Well tea. He said again, "I know how lucky I am with Yomei. We will help each other and make progress together."

"Yes, you both must cherish such an opportunity in your life. Here's a present from Enlai." She handed him the red package.

Gingerly he unsealed it to find a copy of the newly issued *Marriage Law of the People's Republic of China*. Amazed, some people snickered and some laughed, saying never had they seen such a wedding gift. Yomei felt uneasy about this—she alone could fathom some of its implications. Father Zhou might still be uncertain about Jin Shan and in his eyes the groom might be an incorrigible playboy, so only in appearance had Father Zhou countenanced her marriage. This booklet might signify to the groom that in his new marriage, he must stop philandering as he used to and must do right by Zhou Enlai's daughter.

At this moment Jiang Ching arrived with two limousines, together with her child and stepchildren: Neh, Min, Anching, and Anying. The two sons, from Mao's second wife, were both in their late twenties. They came because they had known Yomei since her early days in Moscow a decade before. The troubled Anching was still slow in his manner and speech, though his elder brother Anying had become a strapping young man who people believed was a rising star in China's political scene, given that he'd fought in the Soviet army as a lieutenant during the Second World War and could speak both Russian and English. Yomei was delighted to see them and chatted with them in a casual and friendly manner.

"Here's my groom," she said, introducing Jin Shan to Anying and Anching. They shook hands as Anying said, "I've seen many movies you starred in."

"That was long ago," Jin Shan said, beaming. "I'm just a stage actor now, working for Yomei."

"You're a great artist," Anying said sincerely.

Yomei was about to ask him about his bride, knowing he'd just gotten married, but she checked herself, uncertain of his younger brother's situation. Maybe Anching didn't have a girlfriend yet.

Jiang Ching came over and presented to Yomei a gorgeous quilt cover, which displayed a pair of golden mandarin ducks with shiny blue feathers embroidered on the red silk. She shook hands with Jin Shan to congratulate him and wished the couple everlasting happiness. The groom gave a little bow and said he was very grateful to Ching for coming to his wedding. They had known each other since her Shanghai days. He had once been a tremendous movie star beyond her reach, even though they had performed together in Gogol's *The Government Inspector* and Ibsen's *A Doll's House*. She'd been his fan at the beginning of her acting career and had even had a brief crush on him. Now the old memories seemed uncomfortable to both of them, since she was the First Lady, one of the most powerful women in the country, even though she held no consequential office of her own.

Jiang Ching seemed unwilling to mix with the crowd, so she didn't stay long. When she took leave with her daughter Neh, she left behind one of her limos for her stepchildren. Yomei went down to see her off. Descending the wide stairs, Ching looked sideways at the bride, then said, "Honestly,

Yomei, I'm not that sure of your marriage." She glanced at Yomei, twitching her snub nose as if in disapproval.

"I love Jin Shan, you know."

Ching chuckled and said in a slightly grating voice, "Lots of young ladies have fallen for him. He used to be a dandy and surely has great taste in women. We ought to talk, Yomei. Please come see me in Zhongnanhai."

"OK, I will."

"Promise to come see me in a week or so."

"Sure, I will phone you from my parents' home before coming."

"See you soon then. Again, congratulations!" Ching held out her hand, her lips puckered a bit.

They shook goodbye. Yomei turned back into the reception hall. Some people were dancing in there now, and the music of "The Blue Danube" was floating in the room, where the air was faintly smoky. Yomei found Feifei and the Mao brothers seated in a corner trading small talk in Russian, which was easier for them to use. They were cracking sunflower seeds, drinking Cuban coffee, and laughing now and again. Anying, Anching, and Min hadn't left with their stepmother because they wanted to spend more time with the crowd and also to visit and "bust the nuptial chamber," making fun of the groom and the bride in the traditional way. Yomei felt uneasy about such a custom, but Jin Shan said they ought to indulge their friends and guests on this occasion.

Nobody could know that this was the last happy gathering that Anying would attend in China. Two days later, he would set out in secret for Korea as the official interpreter for Commander Peng Dehuai, and a month later he'd be killed there by a U.S. bomber while he was making coffee and frying rice with eggs for breakfast in a clapboard cottage. But tonight they all grew more youthful, full of hope and joy.

Luckily for Yomei, after nine, her young friends were all too tired to insist on busting her nuptial chamber. After seeing Mother Deng off in her blue sedan, she returned to the wedding hall and found her friends gone. Jin Shan said an officer had just turned up and summoned Anying away for some urgent business.

· Fifty ·

Yomei told the Zhous about Jiang Ching's eagerness to see her. Her adoptive parents were surprised, because this was unlike Ching, who was high and mighty, and reluctant to mix with others. Perhaps she had seen *Pavel Korchagin* and intended to recruit Yomei to work for her. If so, this might signify that she was going to interfere with the country's cultural work. So Yomei must be vigilant when dealing with her.

Due to her poor health, Jiang Ching no longer slept with Mao, but she was still the secretary in charge of his life and shared his residence in Zhongnanhai. The moment Yomei sat down in Ching's office, a servant came in and poured a cup of coffee for her, which amazed Yomei, since Mao drank only tea. Apparently Ching had her own lifestyle here.

Ching stepped in and sat down on the other armchair next to the tea table. She said, "Well, Yomei, I didn't expect you to be so fierce and so bold in the arena of love. I'm impressed."

"What do you mean?" Yomei asked, sipping the vanilla coffee.

"You took Zhang Ruifang's husband away. How many women could do that? She's one of the few movie stars I admire, and also a fine lady, a northern beauty. I wouldn't have dared to make such a gutsy move."

"Jin Shan and I really love each other."

"That's irrelevant. To have a fling with a man like him is different than marrying him. In other words, an affair is understandable—a lot of young women will go weak in the knees before him, but to form a lifelong union with him, that's a different matter."

"So you think I shouldn't have married Jin Shan?"

"That's right. I know he used to be a lady-killer, but things have changed and times are different now. Truth to tell, he isn't worthy of you."

"Why's that?"

"Look, there are statesmen and generals galore in the capital. Some of them are quite young and handsome and have become linchpins of our country. Most of them could easily outshine Jin Shan."

"But to my mind, he's a good match for me."

"You underestimate yourself, Yomei. You're known as the Red Princess, Premier Zhou's daughter, educated in Russia, beautiful, talented, smart. To be frank, the Zhous must have had high hopes for you and you may have let them down. People used to talk about who would be the lucky man you picked, and nobody would have thought of Jin Shan, who seemed already passé."

"Really?" Yomei smiled in amazement. "Well, beauty shines only in the beholder's eyes. Like to like: he is my best choice, so I don't think I married beneath myself."

"You're still green in life. Ideally speaking, a woman marries a man to find a shoulder 'strong like a mountain,' that you can rely on. Can Jin Shan become such a supporter in your life?"

"A mountain can be too heavy on your back, can't it?"

Ching giggled. "You're a sharp girl, but Jin Shan isn't that reliable, to say the least. I've known him for many years and even shared the stage with him a few times. Like numerous young women, when I was in Shanghai, I had a crush on him too, but that was silly. So many men who shone like stars early in your life turn out to be a mere red cherry at the tip of a cigarette."

"Well, at least Jin Shan is a fine artist, and we compare notes constantly in my directing."

"I can see that. In fact, I was deeply impressed by *Pavel Korchagin*, which is a gorgeous production. That's the main reason I want to talk with you. I hope we can collaborate in the future. You know I love theater and will be happy to make a contribution to China's theater arts."

Ching's words disconcerted Yomei, but she recovered her calm and said, "Of course, I'll let you know my future projects. Our next production is Gogol's *The Government Inspector*."

"Who is in the cast?"

"That's not decided yet. Jin Shan won't be involved, for sure. Mr. Liao Chengzhi has left our Youth Art Theater in Jin Shan's hands, so as the president, Shan has to do a lot of administrative work. We might collaborate with another theater and will form a joint production crew soon."

"When is the play going to open?"

"The spring after next."

"Please keep me updated about its development."

"Sure, I will." Yomei paused, uncertain if she could keep her word.

Ching went on, "I love that play, it's a masterpiece. I once played a minor role in it when it was performed in Shanghai. They wouldn't give me a major part, so I could only play the locksmith's wife. Jin Shan was in the cast too,

playing the royal inspector. He was adorable onstage, like
a real scapegrace, outrageous and shameless, and dropped
lies right and left. Yomei, my little sister, let us join hands to
create a new theater for China."

"Of course, I'll be happy to help if I can." Yomei
remembered that Jin Shan's first wife Wang Ying had played
the mayor's wife in the play in 1935, and that Ching had
served as Wang Ying's understudy—she was in Cast B and
would step in for Wang Ying if she was unavailable. At the
time, Ching had been resentful and even made a scene while
fighting to play the leading lady in Cast A. After so many
years, she seemed still bitter, galled by the memory of playing
the vociferous wife of a locksmith among townsfolk who go
to the fake inspector to voice their grievances.

Ching said, "We must join hands now, Yomei. I can
share everything with you, including my man."

Caught off guard, Yomei felt her cheeks heating up.
She wondered whether Ching knew about the night Mao
had spent with her on the trans-Siberian train, or whether
Ching suspected there'd been an affair between her and
Mao, or whether Ching's offer was even in earnest. Probably
the First Lady was just testing her to see if she might have
an eye on Chairman Mao. Finally Yomei found her words:
"Please, Ching, I have much more respect for you than for
Zhang Ruifang."

"I'm serious about what I just said. You know Chairman
Mao is a strong man and has never lacked women around
him. It will be better to have someone refined and pretty
than to let a floozy share his bed. Sleeping with loose
women can make a man coarse and vulgar. Besides, my
husband said he admired you."

"When did he say that? When I was seventeen? You
know I'm no longer a young girl." Yomei had heard that

Mao lived separately from Ching and often slept with other women.

"No, just last week, when he read the Russian article on your staging of *Pavel Korchagin*. He said you had won honor for China and for our Party."

That was a surprise. Yomei hadn't felt that way about the play's success and couldn't help frowning. She'd had no political motivation in staging *Pavel Korchagin* at all. A prolonged lull ensued while she was struggling in vain for words, her head held in her bony, long-fingered hands.

At last she raised her eyes and managed to say, "I'm a married woman now, a wife, so I'm obligated to be faithful to my better half. But I hope my position won't undermine our friendship or interfere with our dedication to the theater arts."

"Of course not. Jin Shan is a lucky man. I told him that at your wedding."

They both chuckled. Ching mentioned her experiences in the Soviet Union and said that many Russians had been quite supercilious to her, so hopefully the Chinese could best them in some kind of art, and theater was one of the areas where the Chinese might excel. Yomei agreed.

Later she told Father Zhou about Ching's artistic ambition without revealing her offer to share Chairman Mao with her. The premier, his forehead furrowed into a frown, said Ching's position as the chief of the cinema bureau in the CCP's Propaganda Department might not justify her interference with China's theater. He seemed to imply that her artistic endeavor could be just a pretext for political maneuvers whose purpose was still unclear, so Yomei must be careful when dealing with her in the future.

"Should I report to her on our theater's activities?" she asked.

"You don't have to if you feel reluctant," said Father Zhou. "Just don't offend her. She can be difficult and unreasonable."

"She's touch and go," Mother Deng chimed in. "She's a hornet's nest you mustn't poke."

"I will avoid her path then," Yomei said. She felt relieved and decided just to ignore Ching from now on.

· Fifty-One ·

The Chinese audience was familiar with *The Government Inspector*, which had been staged numerous times in China over the decades. Lately the Ministry of Culture planned to have it reproduced in the spring of 1952 to commemorate the centennial of Gogol's death. This was also an effort to strengthen the friendship between Red China and the USSR. Such an important project was given to both the National Youth Art Theater and Beijing People's Art Theater, which was an older establishment than Yomei's. So the directors and actors of both companies now joined hands in the production, which already had its own tradition in China. The crew saw the movie of the Soviet production of the play and aspired to do a better job than the Russians. Even though it was a masterpiece whose script was quite definitive, Yomei still did a good amount of desk work, reading critical papers on the play and writing out biographies of the main characters. In addition, she and her fellow directors from the People's Art Theater focused more on the small details, specifically the minor actors, whose performance ought to be more original, with fresh touches.

For the whole year of 1951, Yomei worked with the cast, most of whom were well experienced. Some were famous and had even acted in the same play before. Still, they enjoyed rehearsing with Yomei. She was full of passion and insights, and was so different from other directors they had worked with in the past. Besides, her laughter was infectious—whenever people heard her hearty laughter, they could tell that a rehearsal session was underway and going well. She made the rehearsal hall so lively and exciting that the production crew couldn't help but feel they were doing something significant and even sacred. What's more, she never imposed her own opinion on an actor. Instead, she'd try to elicit the actors' own responses and interpretations, emphasizing that an artistic performance must show an individual's characteristics, and that could only originate from within the actors' own creative impulses. Naturally she always stressed that actors must rely on their own creativity. No matter how small a role, it had to be played conscientiously. She told them, "There's no minor role, and there are only minor actors who're in the habit of performing sloppily."

At the same time, some actors were somewhat intimidated by such a young woman director, who was sharp, relentless, always outspoken, and totally different from a regular stage director. There was no way to hoodwink her if you slackened your effort. She treated the experienced actors the same as the others, irrespective of their seniority and fame. She demanded that every one of them write out a biography of the role they played, providing their analysis of the character's functions and significance in the play, including his or her relationship with the others and even what their character might do offstage. She kept reminding them that the Gogol play was not just a comedy but an artwork of high order, so they must make every effort to perform their roles creatively and with genuine feelings. All the humor must be rooted in total sincerity.

Lei Ping, the actress playing the mayor's daughter, Marya, was the same age as Yomei and had acted successfully in many plays before. In *The Government Inspector*, she just spoke a few lines, though she was quite active in several scenes, including some in which she didn't have a single line. To everyone's amazement, Yomei paid more attention to Marya's role in the wordless situations. She meant to have Lei Ping mentally occupied in every episode and kept asking her, "Marya, what are you thinking at this moment?" If Lei Ping couldn't answer clearly, Yomei would tell her how to make herself more involved in the unfolding drama. By no means should she just utter ahs and ohs. She must let herself be enthralled by the fake inspector's bragging about his exploits and adventures and must lap up everything he said. Sometimes, without any action onstage, it was hard for Lei Ping to get fully engaged, and Yomei urged her just to listen attentively. "In fact, it's harder to listen than to speak," she told Lei Ping. "Try to listen as the daughter of a provincial mayor. To Marya, whatever the dashing inspector from Saint Petersburg says must be true and fantastic. When he glances at her, how would she respond? That must be breathtaking, right?"

When coming to that moment again in the rehearsal, Lei Ping let out a shriek, which brought about peals of laughter among the spectators and felt entirely true. Yet Lei Ping didn't respond adequately later when the inspector begged for her hand. Yomei told Yu Chun, who was enacting the inspector, to give Marya a surprise. Yu was a seasoned actor, and he rushed over and jumped behind Lei Ping, who was startled with a jolt. "Great!" Yomei clapped her hands. "That's how Marya should respond, with a fright that looks real and comes from within. You must act physically, not just cerebrally."

She worked meticulously with everyone in the cast. She kept saying that for a role onstage, no matter how small, there mustn't be a single unoccupied moment. A good actor must participate in the drama from start to finish—even offstage, one must be emotionally involved. By and by, the experienced actors were no longer afraid of her finding problems with their acting; they were eager to improve their skills. They adored her as an expert dedicated to the art of spoken drama.

Scene from *The Government Inspector*, Beijing, 1952

Later, when the play was staged with rave reviews and embraced enthusiastically by the audience, the actors believed that they had bested the Soviet theater in staging this masterpiece. Lily saw it and had the same opinion, having seen it performed in Moscow before. Yomei's reputation as a major stage director in China had been further consolidated.

These months, Jin Shan wasn't directly involved in any stage production at all. As the president of the National Youth Art Theater now, he had endless meetings and had to find official support for the company's projects. As Yomei's direct boss, he tried to stay away from the plays she was working at, because it was whispered that the theater had become the couple's family business now. Such a remark disturbed Jin Shan and Yomei, but for now they had so much to do that they just ignored the wagging tongues. As long as the final product was superb, that could justify everything, so they had to focus on the productions.

While busy directing *The Government Inspector*, Yomei undertook another project, a children's play, which was the first endeavor of its kind in the new China. So it was groundbreaking work that she took very seriously, even though its full significance wasn't clear to her yet. Subsumed under the Youth Art Theater was a children's theater that was supposed to offer plays for a younger audience. It was Yomei's responsibility to provide artistic supervision for the children's theater, so she had to participate in its dramatic projects too. As early as the spring of 1951, she had started to work on a play called *Little White Rabbit*, which was based on the Soviet author Sergei Mikhalkov's children's story "A Lively Little White Rabbit." Yomei watched the movie of the short play made in the USSR and also read the original story, but for a full play she would need to expand the story and add new characters and episodes. She enjoyed the creative process, which was quite different from directing a play with a script already finished.

Now, after Yomei's re-creation, the children's play was full of drama and meanings: Little White Rabbit's home is occupied by a big red fox who also catches and eats rabbits, so all the rabbits in the forest flee at the sight of the fox. Then Little White Rabbit takes a double-barreled gun from a sleeping hunter and uses it to drive the red fox out of his home. He and Mother Rabbit tidy up the place. Many other rabbits come to congratulate them and want Little White Rabbit to share the gun with them so that they can keep the red fox and the gray wolf away. But Little White Rabbit has grown arrogant and won't share the gun with others, saying it's his, belonging to him alone, so all the fellow rabbits have no choice but to leave, except for Little Black Rabbit, whose parents are still far away in another forest. When Little White Rabbit falls asleep, Blackie takes a close look at the gun. To her horror, she finds both barrels empty, and she runs away and tells the secret to the other rabbits. A crow overhears the whisper and spreads the word in the forest that the gun has no bullets. In no time, the red fox and the gray wolf come back to attack Little White Rabbit and his mother's home. With the help of the other rabbits, the gun is returned to the hunter, who arrives in the nick of time and shoots the fox and the wolf dead. Little White Rabbit has learned a lesson and stops being selfish. Finally the forest returns to peace, in which all the rabbits live happily from now on.

Yomei's colleagues were all impressed by her script. The art committee approved it unanimously, so she embarked on the production without delay. But nobody in China had ever produced this kind of children's play before, and neither had Yomei studied any like it in Moscow. She had to come up with her own ideas and solutions during the production. She imagined the entire play set in a forest, in a fairy-tale world, so the mise-en-scène throughout must reflect such an environment. The rabbits' home would

be built of branches, wattles, and vines, and inside were
mushroom seats around a table made of a giant mushroom.
As for cushions and pillows, they were pumpkins and
squashes of various sizes and shapes. In every way, the
setting must exude a fairy-tale ambience.

But the cast, which consisted of kids and adolescents, was
the real challenge, because nobody had ever played a rabbit
before. Yomei told the children, "Don't be intimidated.
This is an opportunity to learn how to do it together."
She sent them to the zoo to observe how rabbits and foxes
and wolves live and behave. They went but found nothing,
because they didn't know what to look for. Yomei explained,
"We humans are also a kind of animal, so follow your own
instinct to see how they eat, sleep, interact with each other,
and especially how they treat the young." Following her
suggestion, the cast members went to the zoo again.

After several visits they found that in general, rabbits
were peaceful and friendly to each other and tended to eat
together without fighting for food. The grown-up rabbits
usually were good and helpful to the young. Conversely,
wolves and foxes were lone creatures and always ate their
own fill first, ignoring the young around them. As the
child actors were watching, one of the wolves growled and
charged at them from behind the bars, its mouth wide-
open. That scattered the youngsters, but the ferocious look
became stuck in their minds. Gradually they began to see
the difference between gentle rabbits and vicious wolves
and cunning foxes. To make them feel their roles more
intimately, Yomei told them each to raise a rabbit. The girl
who played Little Black Rabbit kept a small black one; the
boy in the role of Old Rabbit had a big adult one at home.
Every day they observed the rabbits more closely. They
discovered that when rabbits were frightened, their ears

would fold back. When happy, their ears would wag briskly. Bit by bit the actors began to feel able to act like a rabbit.

Nevertheless, on the first day of rehearsal, they felt so self-conscious that they didn't know how to walk anymore. Some would jump at every line of dialogue and some even skipped when they were supposed to just stand around. Yomei said they must relax and didn't need to imitate a rabbit at every move. Like a child, she too jumped and capered around to illustrate how to perform more naturally as their own character-rabbits, not like those in a cartoon. She explained they must act as themselves and imitate a rabbit only at a crucial moment to indicate they were a rabbit. In other words, for each of them seven or eight rabbit moves would be sufficient. That would enable them to move naturally onstage. Gradually the actors playing the rabbits, the fox, and the wolf all found their own ways of performing. From then on, the rehearsal proceeded smoothly.

But this wasn't good enough for Yomei. She took them to the West Mountain outside Beijing, where she picked an immense oak tree under which they rehearsed, while the band played on the grassy slope. The actors, some of them barely in their teens, felt they were in the natural world, with trees around them and grass under their feet. They walked, skipped, and ran in this animal world, full of fun and buoyance. In the mornings they set out for the mountain, where sunrays fell through branches and leaves and birds twittered and warbled nonstop. Everybody was refreshed by rehearsing in the actual forest. When they returned, they brought back with them the feeling of that world, which gave them more confidence while acting. To their surprise, Yomei wouldn't give them directions about any individual actor's gestures and moves onstage, and the only designed choreography was for groups, which was a kind of halfway ballet. They often danced together, all in altered leotards, although they wore normal shoes, and they didn't spin on their toes. Their dances were brisk and lovely.

Unlike spoken drama productions, Yomei emphasized the effect of music in *Little White Rabbit*, because it was a children's play and must be exiting and amazing to the young audience. She said such a play must be able to grab the viewers at the very beginning and carry them through the story to the end. Once under the spell, the audience would remain in the play, upset or tense or delighted as the drama continued. In brief, such a children's play had to flow effortlessly, like a long breath. The music and the choreography together enlivened the drama throughout. Thus, the band offstage and the performance onstage became unified, and at times even the musicians went wild, as if they were on a roller coaster surging up and plunging down. Everyone at the rehearsal could see that the crew was doing something fantastic and groundbreaking. This play would be a surefire success.

· Fifty-Two ·

Yomei told Father Zhou about the plays she had been directing. He was pleased to hear about them, saying they were excellent choices—politically safe, because both plays had already been accepted in the Soviet Union. He had always advised her to have more political awareness so that she didn't take up any problematic project. Yomei knew he had the recent movie *The Life of Wu Xun* on his mind. Perhaps he was still shaken by it. In late May of the previous year (1951), an article had appeared in *The People's Daily* denouncing that movie. It was said that the article had been approved and edited by Chairman Mao himself. It criticized the movie as a model of reconciliation with feudalistic and reactionary forces. Wu Xun, the hero in the movie, is illiterate and has witnessed how the poor are taken advantage of by the rich, who are educated and literate, so he starts saving in order to sponsor free education for the children whose families cannot afford to send them to school. Even when he is reduced to a beggar, he never changes his mind or course of action and even begs people to kick and punch him if they pay him. Finally, after three decades of panhandling, he has saved a small amount of money, which he uses to start a free school. When he dies,

Emperor Guangxu bestows on him the title the Begging Saint. The article sponsored by Mao condemned Wu Xun as someone who lacked fighting spirit and compromised too much. He is a picture of passive reconciliation.

Early in 1951, soon after the movie had been released, it was shown in the small auditorium inside Zhongnanhai, where Liu Shaoqi, Zhou Enlai, Zhu Deh, and other national leaders all saw it. They raved about it, particularly about the masterful performance of Zhao Dan and his wife, Huang Zhongying, both having been top stars for decades. Through "grapevines" in the Zhongnanhai compound, Mao heard about the enthusiastic responses of the other leaders and felt unhappy about this feudalistic story. Hence the negative article that appeared in *The People's Daily*.

Knowing Father Zhou was afraid of Mao, Yomei said, "I don't understand how come Chairman Mao has become so interested in arts in recent years. He was not like that back in Yan'an."

"True, the only arts that used to interest him were poetry and calligraphy," said Premier Zhou. "Someone else must be behind the campaign against *The Life of Wu Xun*." He looked rather exhausted, with new rings around his eyes.

Yomei said, "I see. It must be Jiang Ching taking vengeance on Zhao Dan and Huang Zhongying."

"Why did you say that?" he asked.

"The couple used to be huge stars in Shanghai, and Jiang Ching wasn't qualified to carry their shoes."

"Don't say this to others," interjected Mother Deng.

"Have you heard of James Yen, who's in the United States?" asked Father Zhou.

"No, I don't know who he is," said Yomei.

Mother Deng chimed in, "He started the Movement of the Mass Education and received funding from the U.N. and some U.S. foundations."

"So some people believe that *The Life of Wu Xun* is a eulogy of a man who has been viewed as a present-day Wu Xun," Father Zhou said.

"That feels like a malicious stretch," Yomei said. "He's far away, in America."

"You must be vigilant in your directing work," he went on. "Don't assume that the world of arts is pure and autonomous. In our country and our time, everything can become political. In fact, I shouldn't have said Chairman Mao was interested only in calligraphy and poetry. He has been obsessive about controlling the arts world. Remember the Yan'an Forum on Literature and Art?"

"Yes, we all studied his speech delivered at that conference."

"What he expressed are the tenets of our Party's policies on arts and literature. Be careful not to overstep the rules he specified in that speech: art must serve the people and must be part of the revolutionary apparatus."

"OK, I will keep that in mind. Thanks for reminding me, Dad. But Chairman Mao's view is basically derived from Lenin, who demanded that artists work as propagandists of sorts." At heart she had issues with such a view, because an artist ought to play more roles than that. For instance, Balzac declared he wanted to become a recorder or scribe of his time. In other words, he didn't have to be an active participant in history. Art ought to be its own autonomous office.

The premier said, "Yes, clearly Chairman Mao's view was borrowed from Lenin, but don't tell others that.

Evidently he's not satisfied with the status quo of our arts
and literature. He wants to make better use of them."

"So Jiang Ching actually represents her husband?"

"You're a smart girl. Do keep that in mind when you're
dealing with her."

"All right, I'm glad that the two plays I'm working on are
from the Soviet Union. At least they are politically safe."

Yomei had also noticed that more critical articles about
the Wu Xun movie had appeared in various newspapers.
Likewise, Zhao Dan and Huang Zhongying were
denounced and condemned for acting in it as leading man
and lady. They were treated as remnants of the old China
and would have to receive thorough ideological reform
so as to become useful artists in the new society. Yomei
had known them sixteen years before, in Shanghai, and
respected them. In their mistreatment she saw how vicious
Jiang Ching could become, so from now on she'd better give
that woman a wider berth.

Still, for months she wondered whether to invite Ching
to the dress rehearsals of both *The Government Inspector* and
Little White Rabbit. Jin Shan said she should. If Yomei felt
uncomfortable about that, he could have an invitation
sent to Jiang Ching in the name of the National Youth
Art Theater. But Yomei was not convinced. She told her
husband that if Ching disliked something in the plays, she
might demand that Yomei change it before the premiere.
That woman would definitely take offense if someone
disobeyed her. In any event, they mustn't invite trouble,
so Yomei simply wouldn't update Ching about the new
productions.

Since Beijing People's Art Theater also participated
in *The Government Inspector*, Yomei was able to premiere
the two plays almost at the same time in the spring of

1952. Both were well received. Because the Gogol play
was a collaboration of the two theaters and was another
adaptation, critics didn't give it the kind of attention a new
play deserves. Instead, they raved about *Little White Rabbit*,
saying it was masterful and a sui generis work in China's
theater and should secure Sun Yomei's reputation as a
founder of children's drama in the nation. Such high
praise unnerved her, though she got excited when a major
movie studio offered to make a film of the play. Lily saw
Yomei's *Little White Rabbit* and loved it, saying it was richer and
more meaningful than Mikhalkov's original. Her remarks
reminded Yomei that however effusive the praises were, the
play was an adaptation, not really an original work. She had
to be coolheaded about this.

Yomei with the film crew of *Little White Rabbit*

   Soon she received a letter from Jiang Ching, who had also
seen *Little White Rabbit* and liked it very much. Ching enjoyed
the beautiful choreography, which combined children's
dances with ballet and should serve as a model of how to
blend such foreign elements into China's own dramatic arts.
Ching also viewed the play as a landmark work that laid the
foundation of children's drama in China. She reminded

Yomei of their conversation a year and a half before, and hoped Yomei could collaborate with her. "Together we can revolutionize China's theater and ultimately usher in a new epoch in the history of our arts," Ching wrote. "I'm still looking forward to hearing from you."

In spite of the kudos, the letter disturbed Yomei. She intuited that Ching might not leave her alone and must be determined to take advantage of her directing skills. She wrote back to thank Ching for her generous words and also pointed out that *Little White Rabbit* was merely an adaptation from a short Soviet play, so she couldn't possibly be a founder of China's children's drama at all, even though she'd love to strive toward that goal. As for any collaboration with Ching, she eschewed the topic. She told herself that even if Jiang Ching forced her to work for her, she wouldn't give in. She had to develop her artistic projects independently, without anyone else's interference.

· Fifty-Three ·

In the early summer of 1952, Jin Shan led a delegation to North Korea. They intended to make a movie, titled *Brothers Bound Together*, to celebrate the solidarity between the Chinese and the Korean soldiers in the war against U.S. imperialism. As a film star, Jin Shan had fans in Korea as well. Kim Il Sung and Peng Dehuai, the commander of the Chinese forces there, were both supportive of the movie project and tried to facilitate the artists' work. Since the Chinese delegates had to collaborate with Korean actors, Kim Il Sung assigned a young woman, An Hsiang, as the interpreter and guide for the Chinese delegation. Miss An, pretty and in her twenties, with large eyes, silken skin, and an oval face, had seen the movies in which Jin Shan had starred, and now she followed him around whenever she could. She told him that her job was to make him happy. Indeed, she did everything to please him, peeling apples and pears for him, brewing tea, fetching warm bathwater, and even making his bed.

He was moved and also fascinated. Accustomed to rubbing shoulders with pretty women, he couldn't help dropping a double entendre now and then, so she started flirting with him too and even said he should stay in Korea for a year or two so she could take good care of him. By and by, they fell for each other and even moved into the same room, openly sleeping together. She made him feel like a young man again.

Miss An must have lost her head over Jin Shan, doing her best to captivate him, and paid no heed to the warnings from her comrades. Soon their affair was reported to the leaders of the Korean Labor Party. Chairman Kim Il Sung flew into a rage and ordered Miss An's arrest. After a brief trial, she was executed by firing squad. As for Jin Shan, the Koreans couldn't punish him directly, so they handed him over to the headquarters of the Chinese army. Commander Peng cursed him in front of other officers, saying it was shameful to revel in adultery while soldiers were fighting and dying in trenches on the front. He pulled out his pistol, about to shoot Jin Shan. But one of the generals on the staff stopped him, saying that Jin Shan was the president of the cultural delegation from Beijing, so they ought to let the State Council mete out the punishment. Commander Peng agreed to spare his life for the time being. He had Jin Shan thrown into the military prison at their headquarters.

Word came back to Beijing about Jin Shan's "crime" in Korea. It was rumored that he had been executed by Peng Dehuai for an affair with a top Korean leader's wife. Some said Jin Shan was simply an incorrigible womanizer and shouldn't have led the movie delegation abroad. What a shame! Due to his philandering, the international movie project was scrapped. More outrageous, on a personal level, was the question of how he could have betrayed Sun Yomei, his beautiful young bride, who surpassed him in both ability and looks.

In the National Youth Art Theater, different versions of Jin Shan's crime were circulating. Yomei heard some of them and was shocked and heartbroken. She went to the

Party's committee of her work unit and inquired about Jin Shan's situation, but nobody could give her a definite answer. So she went to the Ministry of Defense in the State Council. There the officers knew she was Premier Zhou's daughter, so they were polite and tried to respond to her inquiry as much as possible. First of all, she wanted to know if Jin Shan was still alive. A young colonel assured her that he was detained by Commander Peng but would be sent back soon. So for now she didn't need to be too worried about his safety.

Two weeks later, Jin Shan returned to Beijing under escort. But he was not allowed to go home and instead was put in a small dark room at Beijing Film Studio, in which he had to write out his confession and self-examination. The film company was furious at him, because his crime had ruined their movie project. Yomei was forbidden to see him, but she felt relieved knowing he was at least back in one piece. She remembered how upset Father Zhou had been about her marrying Jin Shan, and realized why he hadn't attended their wedding and had given them a copy of the new marriage law. He must have had an inkling that Jin Shan, fickle and sensual, was unreliable and couldn't be trusted as a husband. Now, his international scandal had become the talk of the town, of the country. Some people even said this was just retribution for Yomei's destroying Zhang Ruifang's marriage. She felt too ashamed to face the Zhous, so she didn't go see them for the time being, even though they must have been informed of the disaster in her marriage.

To Yomei's surprise, Lily popped up to see her without notice. Lily brought Yomei two croissants, saying she had just gotten them from Lisa. She and Lisa still saw each other quite often, though they lived in different districts now.

After pouring tea for her friend, Yomei began tearing into a croissant. "Mm, this is so delicious!" she said. "I haven't tasted a croissant in two years."

Lily looked stronger and healthier now, more like a refined young lady with a curvaceous figure, probably thanks to her frequent role as an official interpreter, which guaranteed a fine and rich diet, but she was still as naive as when she'd been a student back in Moscow. She had gone to the USSR the previous fall, serving as the interpreter for a CCP delegation headed by China's former ambassador to the Soviet Union, Wang Jia-hsiang, who was now in charge of the CCP's International Department. She told Yomei that she had met Stalin again while keeping Mr. Wang company. The Great Leader received them, just Mr. Wang and Lily, in his Kuntsevo Dacha again. Wang could speak some Russian, but he wanted Lily to be with him for such a private meeting lest he misunderstand Stalin or not be able to communicate his thoughts clearly. On the deck of the dacha, they had a long dinner and conversed late into the night. Stalin and Mr. Wang talked about the situation on different continents, specifically in Asia. Stalin's chevron mustache was completely gray now, but he seemed still energetic. He was relaxed and quite amiable. Toward the end of their conversation, he told Mr. Wang that Lin Biao had already recovered from his illness fully and could return to China. He said, "If he stayed here too long, he might get sick again as a result of idleness." Lily emphasized that what she said was strictly confidential, while Yomei nodded to promise to keep the secret. Apparently Stalin wanted Mr. Wang to pass his words on to Beijing. That was why Lin Biao and his wife, Yeh Qun, had come back soon afterward. Yomei had heard that when the Korean War broke out, Mao had asked Lin Biao to command China's forces on the Korean Peninsula, but Lin Biao wouldn't go, under the pretext of his poor health. Instead, Peng Dehuai was dispatched, while Lin Biao went to Moscow again for medical treatment.

Yomei could see that Lily had been quite active in the highest political circles, and she congratulated her friend for the progress she'd made in her career. But Lily wasn't happy about her involvement with those big shots at all and preferred working at a desk, translating and writing. She'd feel more at home in a study, she confessed. She couldn't understand why Jiang Ching would ask her to accompany her whenever she went to the Soviet Union for medical treatment. Ching already had a personal Russian interpreter, Zhang Guonan, a woman Yomei had met in Harbin long ago. In recent years, Guonan had gone to Russia several times with Ching. Lily was nervous whenever Ching introduced her, Lily, as her young friend to Russians. She wasn't sure why Madame Mao was so bent on keeping her around, though it was probably because Ching meant to show that she had an old revolutionary's daughter as a close friend. But that was just Lily's guess.

After another swallow of tea, she told Yomei the purpose of her visit: Mother Deng had asked her to come and speak with Yomei. The Zhous were angry at Jin Shan and worried about Yomei. Premier Zhou was so outraged that he declared that Jin Shan should be shot to match the death sentence the Korean woman had received. Fortunately, Luo Ruiching, China's police chief and minister of public security, dissuaded the premier, saying that the Taipei regime might utilize Jin Shan's death for propaganda purposes if the CCP had him executed. The Nationalists would say that Jin Shan was a good example of what happens when serving the Commies—even a top secret agent, a super movie star like Jin Shan, could come to grief on the mainland, being executed merely for an extramarital affair. So Father Zhou curbed his fury and didn't give the order for Jin Shan's imprisonment and execution. Mother Deng told Lily to pass their opinion on to Yomei that she must ally herself with the Party in such a case, because Jin Shan had become a criminal, politically dead. Yomei must protect her own career and political life, and avoid being dragged down by such a miscreant of a husband. In a word, she must cut her losses and divorce him.

Yomei wasn't surprised by the Zhous' admonishment, but she was unsure if that was the step she should take. She asked Lily, "Well, what do you think I should do?"

"If I were you, I'd leave him. He betrayed you and might do it again."

"You know I do love him, so I'll worry about him even if we are divorced."

Amazed, Lily persisted, "What will happen to Jin Shan if you leave him?"

"That will be the beginning of his end."

"Keep in mind that both your parents, the Zhous, believe it's time you left him. They're experienced revolutionaries and know what's best for you. Please listen to them."

"OK, let them know I cherish their opinion and will consider it carefully."

"But you haven't said if you'll divorce him. You must wash your hands of him, once and for all."

"Don't push me, Lily. I'll have to figure out how to get out of this bind alone."

"You've been acting like a petty bourgeois. The Party's position is already clear. Why do you still have misgivings?"

"Please don't pressure me!"

"All right, I've done my best."

"You've never loved a man and have no idea how hard this is."

"But I know right from wrong, and you must cut yourself loose now. What should I tell the Zhous? They're very concerned."

"Heavens, tell them that this is a nail in my head that I'll have to pull out by myself."

Yomei felt uneasy about her friend's attitude, but said no more. Before Lily left, they hugged. In spite of assuring the Zhous that she'd consider their opinion seriously, Yomei had no idea what to do. Her brother Yang and her aunt Jun had suggested the same—divorce Jin Shan without delay. They said that to get out of such a logjam, she had to use her head, not her heart. Just the day before, the Party committee of her theater had informed her that there'd be a meeting to denounce Jin Shan in three days and that she should attend it and express her position on his case, which had gotten more complicated by now. Lately the Party had started a political campaign in the arts world that was intended to correct the "decadent lifestyle and bourgeois attitudes" among some artists. And so Jin Shan, even though a veteran Party member, had automatically become a major target of the movement—a "big tiger." It was said that seven years earlier in Shanghai, he'd kept some gold bars for himself, even though those had been the funds given him by the Party for establishing a secret radio station, which had never materialized. "Where are the gold bars?" some asked. Even though Jin Shan insisted that he had returned them to the Party, nobody believed him. On top of that, when the Japanese army had surrendered in the northeast, he'd been sent there to take over the Manchurian Movie Studio. But so many pieces of its equipment and tons of films had vanished. Where did they go? Did Jin Shan sell them and pocket the proceeds? He couldn't give a clear, believable answer to any of those questions.

To prevent Shan from killing himself, the Party committee of the theater assigned two young men to accompany him all the time during his incarceration in the movie studio. At night they'd sleep with him in the same small room and would follow him when he went out to the bathroom. They even fetched meals for him from the dining hall, because he was not allowed to meet anyone, not even his wife.

Jin Shan's denunciation meeting was held in the Youth Art Theater's conference room. As required, Yomei attended. She sat back in a corner and kept herself inconspicuous—some people looked around but didn't even notice her, and many were eager to see how she would respond to Jin Shan's disgrace. Jin Shan shambled in, hanging his head, escorted by the two young men. He was seated in the front, facing the crowd, his shoulders hunched. Then people began to speak, exposing and condemning him. Some called him a leftover element of the old society, totally corrupted by a bourgeois lifestyle. Some claimed that he had been an inveterate womanizer and used to shamelessly brag about his exploits and his casual ways with women. Some insisted it was high time he'd gotten disciplined and expelled from the theater once and for all. Some argued that his punishment should be in proportion to the Korean woman's, because this was an international scandal for which he was equally accountable.

At last, Yomei was asked to speak. Slowly she went over to the front, looking Jin Shan straight in the face. He cringed, then bowed his head, his face perspiring as if steaming a little. She turned around and said to her comrades, "Jin Shan made an egregious mistake, a mistake he should never have made." She paused to hold down her emotions, then continued, "But I believe this is the last mistake he has made. I hope he will reform himself and return to our ranks in the near future."

To everyone's astonishment, Jin Shan broke down sobbing noisily, his nose blocked, both hands covering his face. People had expected Yomei to expose and condemn her husband like numerous wives had done in situations like this, to show their clear stand in accordance with the Party's position. To resolve on divorce would be the normal way of self-protection. Nobody had thought Yomei would take such a stand. Indeed, she perplexed everyone.

After the meeting, some people even blamed her, saying, "Why do you still try to save Jin Shan? He is not dependable and doesn't deserve your devotion."

An older woman told her, "I know you still love him. But he has already plunged himself deep into a shithole, so you'd better tear him out of your gut—a short, severe pain is better than long suffering."

Yomei never explained or defended her decision, though she knew that to many people, Jin Shan's career was over. She just said he would change, and she still viewed him as a comrade. That remained questionable—people could see plainly that there was more punishment in store for him, that he might be put into a different category of bad elements, such as that of a criminal.

Then, a week later, to Yomei's astonishment, Mother Deng came to the theater alone and showed up in the rehearsal hall. Apropos of nothing, she asked Yomei, "Is the nature of his misdeed determined already?"

Having known the Zhous for so many years, Yomei instantly grasped the full implications of the question and

answered calmly, "Yes, it's a lifestyle problem." That meant
Jin Shan was still a savable comrade.

Without further ado, Mother Deng spun around and
left. Yomei realized that the Zhous might not have been
fully convinced of the message delivered by Lily, so Mother
Deng had come to double-check with her to ascertain that
she, Yomei, did intend to keep her marriage. Through that
brief exchange, Mother Deng was reassured of Yomei's
position—she was still treating Jin Shan as a comrade and as
her husband. Had she said she would divorce him, Father
Zhou might have thrown him into jail and even had him
executed.

Yomei now could also see that the case was far from over.
There might be some more disciplinary action awaiting Jin
Shan. Sure enough, the decision about his case was handed
down within two weeks: he was expelled from the Party
and had to leave for the Shijingshan Power Plant, where he
would become a regular worker. This was a huge blow, since
he'd been a Party member for twenty years and had always
worked as an actor and a midlevel official. Not having any
industrial skill, he could work only as a menial hand. Still,
he was lucky, because Yomei was adamant about handling
his case as a misdeed committed by a comrade. That had
blocked the attempt to destroy him. So he went to work at
the power plant without a murmur. Fortunately he took the
punishment in stride and got along with his fellow workers.
In their eyes, he was still a movie star, one who had no airs
and loved shooting the breeze and wisecracking with them.
Unlike most celebrities, he wasn't afraid of hard and dirty
work. He labored like the others, and was often bathed
in sweat. So he managed fine among the workers, though
he couldn't go back home to live with Yomei anymore.
Nonetheless, his small dorm room at the factory never

lacked for visitors—a lot of men came to see him. They still adored him as an artist, and as a superstar. Yet he refused to take a photograph with anyone, saying he was nobody now and must avoid any photo opportunity that might get them and him into trouble.

Whenever Yomei went to the power plant to deliver clothes and cigarettes to him, she found him in cheerful spirits, and the people around him warm and friendly. She could see that he was no longer a dandy like before.

· Fifty-Four ·

Yomei had withdrawn into herself. Her heart was often wrung with pain, especially when she came to be aware of the gossip behind her back. But she kept up appearances, as if unaware of people's insinuations and attitudes. Deep down, she resented the way the Youth Art Theater had disciplined Jin Shan. He had served the Party for twenty-odd years, and they should not have stripped him of everything and then dumped him into a factory as a daily drudge. Talented as he was, he could have been more useful in other ways.

Because of his absence from the theater, she had to do additional work in his stead now. So she slowed down some in her directing work, as if she no longer had her former enthusiasm for producing plays. She had been trying hard to get Jin Shan out of the power plant, but to date couldn't find a way. She thought of asking Father Zhou to help but decided not to. She even suspected that deep down, Father Zhou must despise her husband, if not hate him outright. It had become clear that Jin Shan would have to find his own salvation. Nobody but Shan could save him.

In the summer of 1953, a Russian theater expert came to Beijing to work on a cultural exchange project—he was to direct Chekhov's play *Uncle Vanya*. At the sight of the director's

name, Reslie Mironov, Yomei's heart skipped a beat. It can't
be him, she told herself, as she remembered her classmate at
the theater institute in Moscow who played Masha's husband
Kulygin in *Three Sisters*. To her knowledge, that young man,
her close friend, had disappeared on the Demyansk front,
and even his parents had written to her about him being
listed as "missing in action." For a whole decade, she'd
thought he'd fallen in the war.

At the reception, held in the Soviet embassy, she saw
the Russian director, now middle-aged, limping some,
apparently crippled; his face was misshapen and marred
with two slanting scars, and even his nose was twisted to
one side. She wasn't even sure if he was the Reslie Mironov
she had known. She went up to him and introduced herself.
At the mention of her name, his gray eyes shone. Right off
she recognized the familiar, frosty sparkle. She said, "We
met in Moscow in the early 1940s. Do you remember?"

"Of course, I'm so happy to see you, Yomei!" His voice
was rather hoarse now, quivering a little.

The two of them moved away from the crowd and
sat down at a small round table in a corner of the room,
where they sipped fizzy kvass in etched amber glasses.
Over the drink and a small plate of crab canapés, they
talked about the years after he had gone to the front
of Demyansk. He mentioned that his mother had told
him about Yomei's letter when he returned home, many
years later. He had been injured in the army and treated
in a hospital for seventeen months, and then sent to a
sanatorium, where he stayed for three years. Later, after
being demobilized, he didn't go back to Moscow. Instead,
he enrolled in the Leningrad State Institute of Theatre to
finish his degree in stage directing there. After graduation
he started his directorial career. To date, he had produced

a half dozen plays. But now that he was disabled, he lived with his sister's family outside Leningrad. He had read articles about the success of *Pavel Korchagin* in Beijing and knew that the director had studied the Stanislavski method in the Soviet Union, but he didn't make the connection with Yomei.

She smiled and said, "They used my official name: Sun Weishi, but my friends and colleagues still call me Yomei, like people at our alma mater did." She noticed that he was rather reserved in spite of his happiness at meeting her again, perhaps because he was damaged physically and she was already married. But she was enthusiastic about the project he was doing. Officially she was supposed to help him in the production, so she told him that he could use any resources at her disposal. He wanted her to collaborate with him too, feeling that with her help he could do a better job in directing *Uncle Vanya* in Chinese, which he couldn't speak.

He saw *The Government Inspector*, which was still being performed at the People's Art Theater, and was impressed by the Chinese cast. But the Chekhov play was a different kind, not a comedy but more poetic and subtle and manifesting the undercurrent of life, so he would need some different kinds of acting talents. She saw his point and promised to help.

Soon Reslie began looking to cast *Uncle Vanya*, but the search wasn't going well. At their next coffee meeting, Reslie told Yomei about his frustration: He'd found two excellent actresses, but he couldn't find a suitable actor for Uncle Vanya, though he had auditioned four men already. He sighed and said, "It's amazing that China, such a big country, can't give me an actor talented enough for my leading man." He sounded disappointed, a wormlike vein throbbing at his temple. He let out a small sigh.

Yomei took his remark as an inadvertent slight, so she offered an impromptu suggestion: "Maybe you can give my husband a try. He played Pavel Korchagin three years ago and also starred in some movies."

"Of course I'll be happy to meet him and see if he can play Uncle Vanya. Can you accompany me when I go see him? I don't speak Chinese, you know."

"No, I can't. Right now he's working at a power plant under a kind of education or reform program. It's inconvenient for me to see him now. Actually, I'm not allowed to. But I can find a translator for you."

Reslie was amazed, but agreed to meet with Jin Shan on his own. He smiled quizzically, as if he surmised some trouble in her marriage. She didn't explain the true situation, which was that she couldn't help Jin Shan overtly in this case. The interpreter she recommended was Yolan, who was a junior in college and almost fluent in Russian.

But that very afternoon, Yomei hurried to Shijingshan Power Plant and found Jin Shan in a workshop, which was like a large barn with all the doors wide-open. She called him out. Taking his hand in both of hers, she pulled it to her waist. She fixed her eyes on his pale face and said, "A Soviet director wants to see you and discuss the possibility of working on a play."

"What play?" He looked baffled.

"*Uncle Vanya*. It's a culture exchange project. A friend of mine, Reslie Mironov, came two weeks ago and has started directing the play. He has tried several actors for the lead role but didn't want to take on any of them, so I suggested you. Hope you will seize this opportunity."

"But I'm a semicriminal now."

"It won't matter if the Soviet director believes you're suitable. He will insist on recruiting you. That might get you out of here."

"OK, I'll do my best. Yomei, I miss you. Without you, I'd be done for."

"Don't thank me. This might be an opportunity to save yourself, but don't tell anyone I'm involved in selecting the acting cast."

"Sure, I'm not that moronic."

She wanted to give him a peck before leaving, but at this point a group of young women workers appeared, laughing and humming "At the Nanni Bend," the Red Army's song celebrating its agricultural production outside Yan'an. Yomei and Jin Shan swung toward the front gate of the power plant, where she took her leave of him and headed for the bus stop.

Reslie's meeting with Yomei's husband turned out to be quite productive. He immediately took to Jin Shan and could see that the veteran actor was superb, so he decided to sign him up on the spot. As Yolan interpreted, Jin Shan told Reslie that he hadn't completed his period of reform through labor yet, but the Soviet director said Shan was the only actor who could play the role of Voynitsky, Uncle Vanya. If the Chinese cultural officials didn't give him Jin Shan, he'd have to head back to Leningrad. Hearing that, Jin Shan grasped hold of Reslie's hand, his eyes filling with tears.

Soon, Jin Shan joined the cast. To take part in the rehearsal, he was able to stay home again, and now he and Yomei were back together in their apartment in the dorm building behind the playhouse. Jin Shan was working with fury on the role of Uncle Vanya, doing a great amount of

desk work. He pored over Chekhov's play and also read
his selected stories. He jotted down notes every day after
rehearsal so that he could make improvements the next
time. He told Yomei that finally he grasped the essence
of the Chekhovian art, or the spirit of Russian literature,
which was centered on this question: What should a good
life be like? Yomei was delighted to hear that and agreed
with him. She said that even the revolutionary literature
in the Soviet period still carried on the same essential
exploration of the human condition. Some themes in
revolutionary literature were actually derived from the
Chekhovian tradition.

Reslie told Yomei that he'd never met an actor who
worked as hard as Jin Shan. Once again she saw Jin Shan
as he'd been when practicing the role of Pavel Korchagin
three years before, giving everything he had to his
character. She was convinced he would shine onstage
again.

Reslie was pleased about the progress they'd been
making and about the quality of the production. Yomei
had helped him make small changes here and there in the
translated script to render the drama more transparent
to a Chinese audience. In Uncle Vanya's office she even
put an abacus for bookkeeping, which wasn't in Chekhov's
original, but Reslie agreed to use it to bring the drama
closer to the audience. As the associate director of this play,
Yomei emphasized time and again that the actors must
display the psychological complexity of their characters
according to their own interpretations. The hard work paid
off and made the play flow with ease from start to finish.
Reslie often said he'd have been happy if he were listed as
the second director of this production, because Yomei had
done so much and rendered the play more poetic and more

subtle, infusing it with the idyllic beauty of the Russian countryside. Some of the stage designs were bright and refreshing too, giving off a lyrical feeling that matched the human drama. But Yomei insisted on being listed only as the associate director, Reslie's sidekick.

The play opened in the spring of 1954 and became an international sensation. Some diplomats and experts in Beijing had seen the play in Moscow and unanimously praised the Beijing production, saying it was as good as the Soviet production, if not better. The National Youth Art Theater was packed every night the play was performed. Critics believed that its success marked a new height of China's spoken drama. In fact, the production of *Uncle Vanya* was the pinnacle of the new China's theater arts, because after 1954 a great deal of political interference hampered the development of spoken drama in the country and adulterated it with too many current ideological demands.

In addition to being staged in the Youth Art Theater, the play was also performed in Huairen Hall in the Zhongnanhai compound for the top CCP leaders. Premier Zhou, Zhu Deh, and many of the other most senior officials went to see it. Fortunately, Lin Biao was not living in Zhongnanhai; if he and his wife, Yeh Qun, had attended the play, it might have been hard for Yomei to deal with that woman's jealousy. The moment Zhou Enlai sat down, Yomei took Reslie over to introduce him to the premier. Reslie was nervous and kept rubbing his hands, but Yomei told him that Premier Zhou was her father. Mr. Zhou could understand some Russian phrases, and at the mention of him as her father, he laughed and said loudly to Reslie, "I am glad you two met here again. This is an amazing collaboration."

That put Reslie at ease.

The play unfolded naturally, and the flow of the drama and the deep current of life pulled the audience into its simple country scenes. At moments, Yomei could feel the audience holding their breath, as if they'd been part of that drama too. Coming to the end, the professor and his beautiful young wife, Yelena, have left, the country life returns to normal and tranquility, and from a distance rises a gentle melody played on the guitar. Uncle Vanya, his hair and beard gray, is hunched over his desk, his left hand still flipping the shiny beads of his abacus while his right hand enters sums into his ledger. His niece, Sonya, leans against him and says soothingly, her eyes looking faraway, "Poor Uncle Vanya, you're crying. There's never been happiness in your life. But we shall rest, we shall hear angels singing and shall see the bright stars. We shall rest." As her sweet voice lingers, the curtain drops.

A thunder of applause broke out. Then the curtain rose again and all the actors came onto the stage to greet the audience, except for Uncle Vanya, who was still at the desk, working on his abacus. The curtain fell again. Again, applause swelled. Once more the curtain went up, but Uncle Vanya was still at his work, as if nothing around him had caught his attention. Not until the curtain was lifted for the third time did he wake up, back to reality. Jin Shan stood up, looking tired, slowly stepped to the curved apron of the stage, and took a bow. The premier rose from his seat, followed by others, and everyone was clapping.

"He's divine onstage, I must say," Father Zhou whispered excitedly to Yomei. She felt a swell of pride to hear the high praise. It must also mean her husband's artistic career was finally restored.

Zhou Enlai and the other top leaders went over to shake hands with the actors. Holding Jin Shan's hand, Father

Zhou told him, "Welcome back to the stage. You're an amazing actor, and this is a great production."

Jin Shan bowed a little and said, "It's Yomei who saved me and gave me such a stroke of luck."

"So you must cherish her all the more."

"I won't make any mistake again. I'll love her heart and soul," he promised with moist eyes.

Yomei had been looking around, assuming that Jiang Ching might be among the audience, but there was no trace of her. She was bewildered and assumed that Ching's absence must have been intended. Chairman Mao didn't show up either, even though the State Council had made sure to deliver tickets to the Maos. Yomei felt that Ching might be resentful because she hadn't responded to her invitation to collaborate with her in revolutionizing China's theater. Yomei knew that woman was bullheaded and vindictive and might take umbrage at the slightest neglect. But right now, China and the USSR were in their honeymoon period, and *Uncle Vanya* was a culture exchange project between the two countries, so Ching couldn't do much to sabotage it.

The success of *Uncle Vanya* earned Jin Shan the sobriquet "Emperor of Spoken Drama" again. At the public meeting the following week, reporters asked him how he'd been able to express the play's psychological nuances so convincingly. He said, "Only work is my salvation, so I try to insulate myself in hard work." To convince them of the effort he had made, he pulled out two thick journals filled with his acting notes. He flipped through the pages to show his writing.

An editor at China Theater Publishing House happened to be in the audience. Afterward he approached Jin Shan and asked whether he might be interested in publishing his notes as a book. Jin Shan was thrilled to have such an opportunity.

Jin Shan in *Uncle Vanya*

After some editing, the book came out three years later as *The Creation of a Character*. On its front cover was a photograph of Jin Shan playing Uncle Vanya, in a dark suit and a polka-dotted tie. For decades, this book was a must-read for young aspiring actors.

Reslie didn't leave China after the success of *Uncle Vanya*. He was invited to put on the classic Chinese play *A Fan of Peach Flowers* together with Oyang Yuchien, a master stage director at the time. Delightedly he accepted the invitation.

· *Fifty-Five* ·

Both Lily and Lisa saw *Uncle Vanya* and wrote to congratulate Yomei on such a splendid production. After Yomei and Jin Shan went back to living together, Lily stopped coming to visit, partly because she and Shan didn't like each other. Perhaps she resented the fact that Yomei had never consulted her when she had decided to marry him. Now, she had once again ignored Lily's admonitions and would not divorce him, as if to show that her love for this man had no bounds. As a result, Lily and Yomei could no longer remain as close as before, though they still saw each other a couple of times a year.

In her letter, Lisa said she and two other Soviet women, Yomei's peripheral friends—Eva and Grania—had attended the play together, and they all had loved it. Yomei had known Grania for years; her husband Chen Changhao, Professor Chen, had flown to the Soviet Union on the same plane with Yomei in 1939. He had gone there for medical treatment for his gastric ulcer but later got stranded in the USSR during the war, where he worked in coal mines and also served in the Red Army. He then married a young Russian girl, Grania, who was illiterate at the time, having completed only the first year of elementary school. Lily and Yomei used to joke about the Soviet propaganda that claimed that the USSR had eliminated illiteracy, but Grania could hardly read. After coming to China with her husband in 1951, she had begun to acquire some literacy. She was a stout blonde now, working as a typist at the translation bureau together with Lily. As for the other Soviet woman in Beijing, Eva Sanber, she was quite extraordinary. She was a German Jew who, while working at the Comintern in 1934, fell in love with a Chinese poet, Hsiao San, who was fifteen years her senior. Hiao had been Mao Zedong's classmate back in their hometown in Hunan Province. The poetry he wrote was mediocre because he believed that poems should serve like knives and bullets in fighting capitalist oppression. Having lived in Europe for decades, he knew several languages and became an accomplished translator. In order to marry him in Moscow, Eva had to become a Soviet citizen first, or she wouldn't be able to live in the USSR, so she renounced her German citizenship and was naturalized. She lived in Yan'an for some years in the early 1940s. At the time, Yomei was studying in Moscow, though she had heard of the woman who was teaching photography at the Lu Hsun Academy of Literature and Arts in Yan'an. Not until 1952 did she meet Eva in person for the first time, at Lisa's home. Now, she was pleased by the three Soviet women's compliments on *Uncle Vanya*. Lisa even said it was "a triumph."

Thanks to the success of the play, Yomei received a job offer from the Central Academy of Drama. They wanted her to head the program for training stage directors and to teach the Stanislavski method, which had been universally accepted in China after the production of *Uncle Vanya*. The students were mostly young dramaturges from all over the country. By virtue of her Russian skills, Yomei could also assist the Soviet theater experts teaching at the academy. She sensed this might be a great opportunity for her to develop and disseminate the art of directing, since the students were rising powers in provincial theater circles and would form the base of China's spoken drama.

What's more, Jin Shan no longer had a position at the Youth Art Theater, which had treated him harshly and stripped him of his official position and wouldn't assign him a new job. It was time for Yomei to leave the theater. Although officially she was still the director in chief there, she wouldn't give as much time and energy to the Youth Art Theater as before.

Soon Jin Shan and Yomei moved out of the theater's dorm building. They moved into a courtyard with a red front gate off Zhang Zizhong Road in which several theater artists' families resided. The enclosure was at 3 Iron Lion Alley, and at that address lived Oyang Yuchien, the master dramaturge, Cao Yu, the famous playwright, and Sha Kefu, a writer and translator who was head of the Central Academy of Drama. Yomei and Jin Shan had bought a portion of a house—four rooms—for themselves, but they were reluctant to mix with others—their neighbors were all either celebrities or officials. Shan and Yomei had a wall built to block their tiny front yard so that they could have their own entrance at the back. Life was peaceful for them now. During the day, Yomei went to work at the Central Academy of Drama, and Jin Shan, though still carrying the baggage of political problems and still without a work unit, would participate in play or movie productions on his own—usually he was given a role or asked to direct a project for a theater or a film studio. The embezzlement accusations against him were dismissed, since he hadn't pocketed any of the Party's funds and had returned the gold bars as soon as the acquisition of the equipment for the radio station had fallen through. But he was a non-Party person now, more like a freelance artist—such a state of life could be frightening in the new society, where everyone had to have a work unit to be a respectable citizen. Yet he took such insecurity in stride and even mocked himself as "a free soul."

Jin Shan and Yomei

Although Premier Zhou seemed to have forgiven Jin Shan after his successful performance in *Uncle Vanya*, Shan wouldn't go to the Zhous with Yomei anymore. Father Zhou once asked her, "Where's Jin Shan? I haven't seen him for almost half a year."

"He's too ashamed to come and face you," said Yomei.

The premier chuckled. "He ought to turn the page. What has he been doing these days?"

"He's been directing a movie called *The Chrysanthemum Mountain*."

"Which studio is making it?"

"The Central Documentary Studio. It's a good movie, and he's quite passionate about it."

"Tell him to come see us when he's free."

"I'll let him know, Dad."

Even though she passed Father Zhou's invitation
on to Jin Shan, he still felt uncomfortable going to the
Zhongnanhai compound. At the Zhous', by custom he'd
have to call the couple Father and Mother. It was awkward,
so only on holidays did he go with his wife to visit her
adoptive parents. Whenever possible, he stayed home. Even
when Yomei's friends and students came to visit, he avoided
them, shutting himself up in his study. He knew that his
misdeed had harmed his wife's career as well, because their
superiors didn't like her way of keeping their marriage
intact, which had contradicted the Party's principles. As a
consequence, they didn't trust her anymore, even though
they couldn't punish her overtly. Now that he held no
official position, what he cared about was their family—so
long as Yomei stayed with him, he didn't give a damn about
what others thought of him.

By now Yomei's aunt Jun had moved to Tianjin,
where her husband Yida had a new job in charge of the
propaganda work for the city's labor union. But the couple
often came to the capital. Whenever they were in Beijing,
they would come to see Yomei and Jin Shan, for whom
they'd bring a carton of Great Gate cigarettes. In the
beginning Jin Shan didn't stay with them for long when
they were there, but Yomei kept telling him to stay around.
By and by, Jun and Yida began to get along with Jin Shan,
treating him with the ease and warmth they had before.
They still respected him. Yida, who was eight years younger
than Shan, often joked, "By our family tree, you should call
me Sixth Uncle." That Jin Shan would never do, but they
had become good friends. Because Yomei called Jun "Sixth
Aunt," Jin Shan did the same, even though he was nine
years older than she was. Oddly, he didn't feel embarrassed

at all when calling her that. As for Yida, Jin Shan treated
him more like a younger brother.

Among his friends and acquaintances, Jin Shan was
known for his excellent cooking. When Jun and Yida
were there, he'd make his signature dishes for the couple.
Jun would tease as the meaty aroma wafted into her nose,
"Mmmm, I wish we could come more often. We sure miss
your cooking."

Yomei gave a hearty laugh and told her, "Then you
should come every other weekend."

One Sunday afternoon in the fall, to Yomei's ecstatic
surprise, Lily came. Like everybody else at the time,
she just popped by without giving a heads-up. Yomei put
away the Goldoni play she had been translating. The two
friends sat in the living room and drank Iron Goddess tea
while Jin Shan stayed in his study. Lily didn't look happy,
because she had often been pulled away from her work
at the translation bureau. She was one of the translators
rendering Mao's writings into Russian, which she viewed as
her most important work for now. There were two Russians
at the project too, but their Chinese was limited, so Lily's
help was essential and integrated with the Russian experts'
efforts. Yet in recent years Jiang Ching had often called
her away, saying Lily was indispensable to her. Whenever
Ching made such a request, the leaders of the translation
bureau had no option but to let her go. Lily couldn't help
but believe that Ching was a hypochondriac who relished
endless medical attention.

Just last year, Jiang Ching had stayed in a sanatorium
called Liu Village on West Lake in Hangzhou city. She
even had her private yacht there. Probably because she

was tired of being alone, since Mao couldn't stay with her the whole time in Hangzhou, she approached Lily's boss in Beijing, Shi Zhe, and asked him to send Lily down to Liu Village to keep her company. Lily was unhappy about such an interruption, but had to go. The good news was that at Liu Village she had run into their mutual friend Yang Zhicheng, Grandpa. He was the vice president of the University of Military Affairs and a three-star general now, but he was in such poor health that he could hardly do any real work at his office. Grandpa and his wife were rapturous to meet Lily at the sanatorium. Zhicheng told Lily that he was elated to see Yomei's directorial career soaring. He reminisced about their old days in the Soviet Union with a lot of feeling, telling his wife that it was Lily and Yomei who had saved his life, helping him with bed and board when he returned to Moscow from Central Asia. "I was skin and bones, so famished that I almost ate my own tongue when they bought me a bowl of fish soup and warm bread in the hotel's cafeteria," he said, his eyes teary, then laughing.

Lily told Yomei, "Evidently Grandpa and his wife are big fans of yours, but somehow Jiang Ching didn't like you anymore. She once said to me, 'Yomei, that young girl, gives herself such hoity-toity airs now.' She seemed irked by something."

"She still treats us like teenagers," Yomei said. "She has approached me a couple of times and wanted me to collaborate with her."

"On what?" Lily's face was a little haggard, her bold eyes glowing while their lids flickered.

"I'm not sure of the specifics. She said together she and I could revolutionize China's theater. But she and I are not in the same boat—she's in pursuit of power, while I'm in pursuit of art and beauty, so it's like we belong to different species. If we've taken different roads, our paths mustn't cross."

"Ching's crazy and should stick with photography. She's a fine photographer, you know."

"I saw her work at an exhibition. She has her touches, but she wants to branch out into theater now."

"She tried hard to make me stay with her and even allowed me to use her yacht to visit some little islands and waterside villages. By the way, your reunion with your husband also gave Yeh Qun some relief, I guess."

"Why? Why would she feel relieved?"

"Last winter Lin Biao and Yeh Qun went to see Jiang Ching in Liu Village. I was with her when they arrived. I sat with them for only two or three minutes and then went out

Lin Biao and his wife, Yeh Qun

of the room, because Lin Biao was a major leader and might
have important business to discuss with the First Lady. I
just didn't want to be in their way. But when I went back two
hours later, Ching blamed me for leaving her alone with
the Lins. Yeh Qun had sobbed and claimed that I was rude
to her because I was your close friend, and still bore her a
grudge. That was insane, wasn't it?"

"Hysterical. How did Ching take it?"

"I told Ching that I'd left purely out of politeness and
respect. Lin Biao was a top military leader and Yeh Qun
had been his wife for many years. How could she still feel
insecure, threatened by you? She's a psychopath and worked
herself into a fury for no reason."

"Did you say that to Ching?"

"Yes. Ching smirked and said, 'That means Lin Biao
hasn't forgotten Yomei and may often have brought her up
in front of his wife. Fortunately, Yomei and Jin Shan are
back together, or else more trouble would start in the upper
echelons.' I said to her, 'You know, Yomei is quite modest
about herself, not interested in politics or power. She just
loves the theater.' Ching snapped, 'The arts are always part
of politics. The notion of artistic purity is totally bourgeois.
In any case, if you see Yomei, tell her I'm pleased about her
decision to preserve her marriage.'"

"What did she mean?" Yomei asked in genuine
perplexity.

"To some men in the highest circles, your divorce would
mean you were finally available, which might mean that
more marriages might fall apart."

"Heavens, we're in such a manic world!"

"Just be careful about Yeh Qun and Jiang Ching. They
are unbalanced and can do lots of damage."

"You should be careful about Ching too. Don't get too close to her. So many people despise her."

"I'm aware of that."

They also talked about the young man Lily had been seeing. He was an officer in the Ministry of Defense, but Lily felt that their relationship might not go anywhere, because he kept asking her for presents, particularly for things from abroad—kidskin gloves, a gilded fountain pen, a Swiss army knife, a pair of oxfords, what have you. She confessed she was no longer interested in men, much like Oyang Fei had, who had quit dating altogether, using the excuse that she couldn't understand the accented Chinese some men spoke. Both Feifei and Lily must have been deformed by their Soviet education, making them unable to fit in the new society here. In the eyes of many Chinese, they resembled foreign girls, wearing shoulder-length permed hair and blouses and skorts in the summer and woolen overcoats and even stockings in the winter (as if to show off their legs), whereas their women colleagues just wore thick padded pants. Some called them "foreign dolls" behind their backs, insinuating that they were out of touch with life in China. They were hard to please and always opinionated, tactless and outspoken to the point of being ludicrous. Even regular Chinese sodas and street food would upset their stomachs. They couldn't help but adopt superior airs. On top of that, they sometimes offended or embarrassed others unawares. At meetings, they talked at length as if they'd been in charge, and worse, their views were mostly impractical, coming only from books. They were like delicate flowers cultivated in a greenhouse, unable to survive the elements. If you married a woman like these "foreign dolls," you might never have peace at home.

Yomei sensed her friends' plight and said that Lily and Feifei must do their best to readapt themselves and think and behave more Chinese. But she amended, "Still you mustn't lose your innocence, your purity of mind and spirit. You must live your own life, even if you can't find a real companion."

"Bah," Lily grunted, "I don't need a man. Men disgust me. To tell you the truth, I feel safer and more comfortable when mixing with women."

"Actually, some women can be vicious and dangerous too."

"Name one for me."

Yomei did a double take. Though she thought of mentioning Jiang Ching, she checked the impulse, since Lily and Ching seemed to get along. Yomei realized that her friend might still be traumatized from seeing a man throw a woman into the ocean when she was a little girl on a steamer. Or maybe Lily was just frustrated by the fact she'd never gone with a man she could love wholeheartedly. What was wrong with her? Feifei had the same problem, even though she did get on well with her male colleagues. Their Soviet years seemed to have shaped their personality and mentality. It stood to reason that people viewed them like a different species. But Yomei knew they actually preferred a certain kind of man, someone like Wang Jia-hsiang, the CCP's former ambassador to the USSR, who was a revolutionary as well as a scholar, erudite and perspicacious and capable of solving hard problems, and who knew both Russian and English. She remembered that Lily had once quipped, "If only there were a younger version of Ambassador Wang in China! I would chase such a man to the ends of the earth!" Yomei had responded, "There must be some unpolished young fellow unnoticed by you yet. So keep your eyes peeled, and find a young man full of potential and turn him into a piece of polished jade, even though he might still look crude at the moment. A good relationship should make the two persons better than their former selves."

"You speak like a great educator." Lily clapped her on the shoulder.

"Young women often complain there aren't enough good men around, but most good men are products made by good women. We must try to improve them."

"So I must find a diamond in the rough?" Lily smiled, batting her eyes.

"Yes, that should be a goal. Keep in mind, no one is polished naturally."

Deep down, Yomei was glad she was different from her friends who had been educated in the Soviet Union and that she was fond of men, particularly a man like Jin Shan, with an artistic bent, articulate and percipient. She realized she may have meant to make him a better man all along, as if she were also a director of the domestic life.

Yet she and Lily both agreed to avoid any entanglement with the Party's politics. Life was short, and there must be more meaningful and enjoyable things to do. Lily firmly believed that a woman's happiness mustn't depend on a man in her life. That Yomei couldn't refute. When the rain had eased off, the sky brightening up, she helped Lily into her khaki windbreaker and told her to notify her before she came next time, so that she and Jin Shan could prepare a good meal for her.

"I just want to see you," Lily said, tying her hair in a violet bandanna. She stepped out into the damp, chilly wind, cradling an oilskin umbrella in her arm.

· Fifty-Six ·

Again Yomei received a letter from Yolan, who was in the USSR now. Before graduating from the Beijing College of Foreign Languages, she had been sent to the University of Leningrad to study Russian literature for three years. Yomei could tell that Father Zhou must have given Yolan a hand in such a career launch. Very likely, Yolan would become a professor someday. She was more at ease with Russian now and even wrote her letters in Cyrillic to Yomei, who always enjoyed reading her sister's slightly sinicized Russian. Yolan said she missed Beijing and Chongqing a lot but also cherished her time in the Soviet Union, where she had great teachers and friendly classmates. Also, Leningrad still had vestiges of the cultural splendor and elegance it had when it was Saint Petersburg. This letter contained a photo of her and a young man named Li Zongchang. They were both wearing skates and woolen neck warmers, standing on a public rink, beaming with arms around each other. Zongchang was rather skinny and bespectacled and had an intelligent face. He was studying chemistry at the same university in Leningrad. Yolan confessed they were dating seriously. Yomei was happy for her little sister, whose future seemed bright, considering her expertise in Russian literature and the young man she had picked. Zongchang looked steady and earnest and agreeable. They both would come back as soon as they finished their graduate studies there.

Yomei showed the photo to Jin Shan. He praised Zongchang and was happy for Yolan, saying the young fellow was truly extraordinary in spite of his nondescript looks. He was from the countryside in Jiangxi Province and out of tens of thousands of competitors had won a national scholarship for studying abroad. That meant he had a great deal of vitality besides talent. Jin Shan said with self-amusement, "It's good that Yolan has a Chinese boyfriend, so she won't come back like a foreign doll, another Lin Lily."

"Yolan was already in her twenties, a Chinese when she left," Yomei said. "She'll have no difficulty adapting back to life here."

Jin Shan added, "It's unhealthy to send young kids abroad and let them grow up in a foreign country unless they're meant to become foreigners who won't come back."

"Rest assured, Yolan will be less Russianized than I am," said Yomei.

Ever since they had married, Yomei and Jin Shan had been talking about having a baby. He was already forty-three and felt that fatherhood might demand too much of him, while she was also nervous about the prospect of motherhood, as she was always busy directing plays. They did try, but she simply couldn't get pregnant. Deep within, she suspected that it was Jin Shan's problem—he had slept with so many women that he might have caught some disease that made him no longer able to father a child. But she dismissed the thought and believed it might be too enervating to have a baby by herself anyway. She was even willing to stay childless as long as she and her husband could devote themselves to theater work. But once in a while, she couldn't help longing to become a mother.

At a family dinner given the previous fall for seeing Yolan off to the Soviet Union, Yomei had spoken with her brother Yang and his second wife, Shi Chee. Yang and Chee had married several years before and now already had a girl and a boy. Yomei said to them that they should consider giving her their next baby, which was already on the way. She promised to love and raise the child as her own. Her request threw Yang and Chee, though they did promise Yomei to think about it seriously. Chee was in her second trimester and would have liked to have another boy, because she believed girls were harder to raise. She told Yomei that she'd give her their third baby if it was a girl. After dinner, while Yomei and Chee were chatting about bringing up children, Yang talked excitedly to Yolan about the USSR, where he had stayed four months two years earlier, having been sent there to enroll in a training program in economics. He loved Russia, both the culture and the people, and also the landscape, though he had always missed noodles and rice when studying in Moscow. It was too bad that nowadays, already a father of two, he couldn't travel abroad as often as before.

Yolan teased him, "So marriage is a burden to you?"

"I won't say that. It has stabilized my life too, and the kids give me a lot of joy. Look, even Yomei wants to be a mother now. So don't wait too long to get married."

"Will Chee and you give away your next baby to Yomei?"

"We might indeed."

However, when Shi Chee delivered the child five months later, the newborn turned out to be such a husky boy that she and Yang became reluctant to let him go. So Yomei would have to figure out another way of adopting. In the

spring of 1956, she and Jin Shan heard that Duanmu
Lanhsin, a Shanghai movie actress, who was sick and
penurious, could no longer keep her twins. They had been
fathered by a lover of hers, who had been a movie director
and recently died of illness. Duanmu wanted to give away
one of her twins, so both Yomei and Jin Shan went to
Shanghai to take a look at the baby. At the sight of the child,
they fell in love with the twenty-one-month-old girl, who
was healthy and beautiful, her plump little hand grabbing
hold of Yomei's thumb while she was being dandled, as if
the child meant to claim her. Both Jin Shan and Yomei
had known Duanmu, who was pleased to see the couple,
knowing they'd be fine parents for her baby. So after
leaving one thousand yuan with the mother, Yomei and
Jin Shan brought the child back to Beijing. They named
her Little Lan and managed to obtain a Beijing residential
certificate for her.

The presence of the child in their family provided a
domestic center, and therefore more stability, for Yomei
and Jin Shan. They loved to carry Little Lan in their arms,
even within the household. They talked about finding a
kindergarten for her, but thought better of it. Instead,
they hired a nanny, since someone ought to be home when
they were out at work and since their household needed to
be more like a complete family now. The toddler seemed
at home with her adoptive parents and took them as her
playmates. She enjoyed taking a horse ride on Jin Shan's
back and playing with Yomei. She called them Dad and
Mom since day one. In the evenings, she enjoyed listening
to her mother read stories to her. When Yomei had work
to do, the nanny, Mansu, would step in, reading "small
people's books" (picture books) with Little Lan. The child's
eagerness to learn amused her parents. Jin Shan said Little

Lan took after her birth father, who had written small plays
and contributed articles to periodicals regularly. Jin Shan
also confessed to Yomei that he'd never thought it would be
so gratifying to be a father.

Indeed, the child gave him an excuse whenever he was
reluctant to socialize with visitors. He would carry up Little
Lan and withdraw into his study, as if to claim he'd better
take the child away so that guests could have a peaceful
time with Yomei. Some of the visitors would smile and say
they had never imagined him becoming a devoted parent.
Yomei was also grateful for the child's arrival, which gave a
center to their family. As a result, their life felt more self-
sufficient. Nowadays, seldom did she go and visit the Zhous,
giving the excuse of having to babysit at home, though
Mother Deng often urged her to bring along the child.
She and Father Zhou both wanted to see Little Lan, in any
case. It came to Yomei that they would probably claim her
daughter as a grandchild if they liked her.

Besides running the directorial seminar at the Central
Academy of Drama, Yomei had been translating some
theoretical writings on the theater arts for use as teaching
materials. She was also in charge of translating four of
Carlo Goldoni's plays, which were under contract with
the People's Literature Publishing House. She didn't know
Italian, but Goldoni's works were available in Russian, so
she translated the plays from the Russian sources. She was
the editor of the volume, and also translated two of the four
plays by herself, *The Servant of Two Masters* and *The Mistress of the
Inn*, while the other two were done by others. Yomei had
seen some of Goldoni's plays staged in Moscow and had
been deeply impressed. Now she'd like to stage *The Servant
of Two Masters* here. Luckily, her proposal for performing
the play was approved by the Ministry of Culture without

incident, so she began to assemble the production crew and even thought of forming a new theater for this play and her future work.

Her aunt Jun's husband, Yida, also loved Goldoni. Though in recent years Yida had been doing propaganda work in the Tianjin municipality, he used to be an actor and had been noted for several small roles. He and Jun were still living in Tianjin city, but whenever they were in the capital, they would come to catch up with Yomei and Jin Shan. Yida admired Yomei for translating and reproducing Goldoni's plays, which he said were real masterpieces and would be more valuable as time went by. "You can say they're already immortal," Yida said about Goldoni's plays. It was too bad he had stopped acting or he'd have done everything to join Yomei's production. Out of his love for theater, he was also respectful of Jin Shan, whom both Yida and Jun viewed as a great theater artist.

When the couple were in town, Jin Shan cooked a fine meal to show his appreciation of their visit. On the last Sunday of July, Jun and Yida came again, and Jin Shan made their favorite dish: braised pork. The whole house was redolent with the aroma of the dish. Jin Shan explained to them that he used a special rice wine for the pork, and that the flame under the pot must be kept low to stew the meat thoroughly and to collect the juice. He also put in a piece of rock sugar besides assorted spices, including aniseed and dried chili. "Above all," he added, "you must put your heart into your cooking. If you cook for someone you love, the food usually tastes better." That made everyone chuckle. Jun and Yida kept sniffing the air, saying they couldn't wait for dinner to start.

But as Jin Shan carried the pot to the dining table, he accidentally dropped it, and it fell with a thwack, the floor now strewn with browned pork cubes that surrounded his feet, steaming. An orphan chopstick was lying among the meat, while the other one had disappeared. He froze, too staggered to do anything. He released a deep sigh, standing there motionless. Yomei rushed over and set about cleaning the mess with a broom and dustpan and then wiped the floor clean with a terry cloth.

She told him, "Don't feel too bad about this. Jun and Yida are not strangers. You can make the same dish for them when they come again."

The guests tried to console him, saying they must not have any luck given that they wouldn't be able to eat something so nice today. They then made him promise to cook the same dish next time. Yomei placed a pot of boiled rice on the table. Before spooning the plump and glossy rice into bowls, she gave Mansu, the nanny, two ten-yuan bills and sent her to a nearby restaurant for some chicken and vegetable dishes.

· Fifty-Seven ·

1956 was a busy and productive year for Yomei. She hadn't severed her ties with the National Youth Art Theater yet, and was even directing a five-act play for them, *Gazing West at Chang'an*. It was a social satire whose script she couldn't risk revising because it was written by Lao She, the famous novelist and playwright, who was notorious for refusing to make any changes. He often told editors, "If you change a word of mine without my permission, that would be tantamount to theft or prostitution." So Yomei treated this play almost as routine work, though Jin Shan played the protagonist, an impostor, in Cast B, whose members served as the understudies of Cast A. The play was premiered in the spring and became an instant hit, partly because it was based on a true story known to the public: a clever crook fakes an official seal, which enables him to travel all over China with counterfeit papers; he lies about himself to obtain honors and recognitions, free plane tickets, large sums of subsidies, even a pretty bride, and eventually he becomes a high-ranking official in the central government; but three years later he is exposed and apprehended by the police. For decades the play was regarded as China's *Government Inspector* and is still performed today.

The week after of the premiere, hundreds of letters
poured in to the Youth Art Theater to express views on
the virtues and defects of the play, especially the narrative
presented by the script. But about the quality of the
production there was a consensus that acknowledged the
director's supreme skills and sensibility and also tact. That
summer *Gazing West at Chang'an* joined other plays in the
Beijing Drama Festival held by the Ministry of Culture
and garnered three top prizes for its outstanding quality:
One was for its cast's performance, one for its directorial
finesse, and the other was for the performance of its lead
actor, Yu Chun.

In the meantime, Yomei and her neighbor Oyang
Yuchien, the venerated playwright, opera actor, and stage
director, had formed the Central Experimental Theater
to produce new and foreign plays. Mr. Oyang, who had
studied in Japan and graduated from Waseda University,
was already in his late sixties and may have reached the
limit of his own career, so he was eager to collaborate with
younger artists, in particular Yomei, the Red Princess. In
addition to her exuberant talent and vivacious personality,
she seemed to have ample resources, and Jin Shan was
also well connected in the circles of theater and cinema.
Most of all, Mr. Oyang had been deeply moved by Yomei's
recent productions of Russian plays, which he himself had
not dared to touch, because he was more familiar with
European drama, not with Russian. Now, together, he and
Yomei managed to recruit a number of young talented
actors for the Central Experimental Theater, which Oyang
Yuchien headed while Yomei became its vice president and
its stage director in chief. Above all else, such a theater,
which aimed to be unorthodox, was attractive to aspiring
artists and a younger audience.

The first play they were to stage was *The Servant of Two Masters*. Since Yomei had translated this play, naturally she directed. It was such a masterpiece that ever since its first appearance in the mid-eighteenth century many countries had staged it. There was even a film of the Russian production of the play, which was the model that Yomei desired to emulate, though she didn't share her secret ambition with anyone except for her husband. Jin Shan believed she could do a better job.

Yomei combined the production with her teaching at the Central Academy of Drama. The directing class would graduate soon, so this would be their last project. She confessed to her students that one of her ambitions was to direct a great comedy, so she chose *The Servant of Two Masters* this time. She went on to explain, "What is a comedy? It's a branch of spoken drama, but it doesn't just make people laugh. The kind of slapstick that makes actors stretch their necks, stick out their tongues, and bulge their eyes is not comedy at all. That sort of thing debases comedy." One of the students raised his hand and asked what real comedy was to her mind. Yomei said, "The superior kind, for instance, Gogol's *The Government Inspector*, which can stir your soul besides making you laugh. In Gogol's words, to laugh through tears. That's to say, humor is mixed with pathos— earnestness and comedy go hand in hand."

She asked her cast of actors to propose the roles in the play for themselves. Then, to everyone's surprise, she picked You Benchang, a recent college graduate, for the role of Truffaldino, the servant of the title who fools around between two masters. Even Mr. Oyang was uncertain about Yomei's choice, because Benchang might be too young to carry the weight of the leading man. But Yomei was sure of her decision, having seen how the young talent acted in other plays. She argued that the theater had to nurture the younger generation. Her gut told her that this play might be around for a long time, so they must begin building the repertoire for their new theater and had better use a younger cast at the outset.

While they were rehearsing, an Italian troupe came to Beijing. It performed *The Servant of Two Masters* in the People's Art Theater, so Yomei's production crew and her directing students all went to see the performance. They were impressed by the vibrant presentation, the bright colors of the stage design, and the acrobatic feats enacted by the cooks and servants, but the splendid production made Yomei's crew diffident. They were unsure if they could match the Italians, whose acting felt more authentic. But she told them, "Bah, that's your fallacy. Goldoni wrote the play two centuries ago, and the Italian troupe is as removed from the original play as we are. So don't get intimidated. Authenticity is just an illusion, a feeling. We must take heart."

As if to deepen the students' concerns and diffidence, after seeing their rehearsal, the head of the Italian troupe remarked that their Chinese colleagues seemed to be doing a different play, not like Goldoni's work at all. Yomei didn't buy that and said to her crew, "You have all seen the Russian production of the play, can you say the Russians did a job inferior to the Italians?" They all shook their heads. You Benchang put in, "Personally I prefer the Russian performance. It's more earnest and funnier in a deeper, unsettling way."

Yomei said, "See, it's like turnip and cabbage, for which people have their own preferences. We shouldn't be intimidated by the foreigners and must stage the play in our own way. I'm sure a unique Chinese production will do great honor to Carlo Goldoni, because it will demonstrate the vitality of his art, which, regardless of cultures and languages, no circumstances can frustrate."

Her words inspired the crew, who continued to work on the play devotedly. When it premiered in the fall, it caused a sensation. To Yomei's delight, both Father Zhou and Mother Deng came to see it. They loved the performance, particularly the lively, funny servant played by You Benchang. At once, the young man became a rising star in China's spoken drama circle. He acted so brilliantly that the Ministry of Culture awarded him a top acting prize that year. Decades later, You Benchang grew into a virtuoso and performed in numerous TV plays and movies until 2009, when at age seventy-six, he entered a remote temple and became a monk.

Lily also saw *The Servant of Two Masters* and was blown away by it. She had seen the Russian production of the play in Moscow, but now she told Yomei, "Your version is better than the Russians'. I'm so impressed." Indeed, a lot of people showered panegyrics on Yomei's production. As she had foreseen, for many years the play remained in the repertoire of the Experimental Theater.

Yomei was delighted to hear Lily's praise, and after the performance that evening, she took her friend to a high-end European restaurant for dinner. They were having pappardelle with a thick ragout made of enoki mushrooms and seafood—shrimp and clams and baby oysters. In recent years, whenever Lily came, Yomei would take her out, knowing her friend and Jin Shan didn't like each other, but usually the two of them ate at neighborhood diners or a noodle joint. Today, Yomei wanted to celebrate the success of her staging of the Italian play, so the two were having something special. She told Lily that she had just come

into some money, having gotten paid for her translation
of Goldoni's plays—the book was forthcoming. Yomei
also revealed to her friend that theaters in Beijing were
eager to produce classical plays, because financially such
productions could hardly ever go into the red. The two of
them were each having a glass of grapefruit-flavored rosé.
Yomei raised her glass and said, "*Bon appétit!*" Lily responded
in French too, then drank to Yomei's new success. As the
two went on chatting, people at neighboring tables turned
to look at them, amazed that the two Chinese women's
conversation was peppered with Russian expressions and
that they were using the cutlery so naturally.

Soon all the nearby tables became vacant. Yomei
ordered lemon meringue pie for both of them. The dessert
came topped with a wavelike meringue baked brown. Lily
mentioned Jiang Ching again, with whom she had spent
the previous summer in Moscow and Yalta. She had been
reluctant to keep Ching company in the Soviet Union
and spoken to Premier Zhou about it, saying she had
more meaningful work to do at the translation bureau,
but he had urged her to stay with Ching. "It's even more
meaningful for you to work for Comrade Jiang Ching," he
told Lily. "Whenever she needs you, please do your best to
make yourself available." So Lily flew to Moscow and later
to Yalta. To her amazement, she found Ching's personal
interpreter Zhang Guonan already at her side, together
with two other Chinese women, Ching's nurse and maid.
Lily felt she was just a fifth wheel and grew more eager to
return to Beijing. She talked with Ching every day, begging
her to let her leave. At long last, Ching allowed her to go
back and deliver a letter to Chairman Mao personally.

"It's amazing Ching really likes you," Yomei said and put
a forkful of the pie into her mouth.

"I don't know. She just wants to make some use of me. Actually she wanted to know what you were up to. I told her that you were busy directing a play, as always. She wanted me to give her more details, but I couldn't."

"She's still interested in theater?" Yomei asked.

"You bet. She's passionate about drama and is also quite knowledgeable. To be fair, I enjoyed listening to her talk about literature and arts. She often says China must have a revolution in arts, and she seems eager to initiate it."

"She knows a lot about Beijing opera, which was her specialty—she started her acting career by singing opera, in spite of her mediocre voice. It's said that she began carrying on with Chairman Mao in Yan'an by singing snatches of opera for him in private."

Lily took a healthy sip of the wine—almost a swig. "Oh, that puts her passion for Beijing opera in perspective. She's kind of obsessed with opera. Last summer, she invited Master Cheng Yanchiu, who happened to be in Moscow with a Beijing opera delegation, to her sanatorium for lunch. I was there with them. Over baked trout and spaghetti, she kept complimenting Master Cheng, and she said that since the beginning of her artistic career, she had loved his performances but that she had been able to admire him only from afar. After lunch, she told her maid to close both doors so that nobody could see us from outside. Then she asked Master Cheng if he could sing the aria 'Tears Shed on a Wild Hill' to us. The old man obliged and began to sing in a lower but clear voice. It sounded odd, since he couldn't sing with full abandon. The second he finished, Ching clapped her hands and said, 'I'm so fortunate today, to hear you sing so close by. I love your performances, because you can always adapt to the needs of dramatic situations. I admire your capacity to reform your singing style and make it in keeping with the times. In brief, I appreciate your creative spirit. We all know there are two main schools in Beijing opera: your Cheng school and the one embodied by Mei Lanfang. I differ from Premier Zhou on this and we two have argued. He prefers the Mei school, while I love your school. For me, Mei Lanfang is too conservative. I prize creativity above anything else, but somehow the premier prefers the Mei school.'"

"She said that? It was kind of low," Yomei said.

"It was indecent of Ching to gossip like that, considering this was her first meeting with Master Cheng. But don't breathe a word to your father about what Ching said to Master Cheng, OK?"

"Sure thing, I won't stir up trouble," Yomei said. "In fact, Ching learned to perform Beijing opera briefly, but her voice wasn't good enough, so she gave up."

"That I didn't know. No wonder she's so obsessed with it. To be fair, your father was very considerate to Ching. He always asked me about her health and how well she was getting by. She was quite happy at Yalta and learned how to swim, I told the premier."

"Do you think the two of them really get along?"

"I'm not sure. At least in appearance, your father was very kind and nice to Ching."

"He's a picture of a gentleman, indeed."

"That's why he was so charming and gracious. To tell you the truth, I didn't like the way Ching was talking about your dad, considering he'd never said a negative word about her to me."

"I can't trust that woman. You must be careful when mixing with her."

"Of course. I don't think I will continue to work for her. When I delivered her letter to Chairman Mao, he apologized on her behalf, saying he was sorry for having taken me away from more important work."

"You mean the translation of his writings?"

"Yes, we have to work hard to stay on schedule."

Yomei refrained from revealing to Lily that there'd been friction between Father Zhou and Jiang Ching. She knew they disliked each other but had to appear cordial, at least on Premier Zhou's part. He couldn't afford to alienate Ching, behind whom loomed Mao. Yet what Lily had said about Ching's passion about drama slightly unsettled Yomei, since she knew the woman was willful and wouldn't give up easily once she embarked on something.

Sure enough, a month later Yomei received a letter from Jiang Ching. In it, Ching mentioned a large novel, *Tracks in the Snowy Forest*, which had just come out. She said that the People's Art Theater had been working on a play, *Taking Tiger Mountain by Strategy*, which was based on some key episodes in the novel. The play would be staged in the near future as a spoken drama. "I have read the script," Ching wrote, "and am impressed. I am wondering if it can be adapted into a Beijing opera. You are an expert, Yomei, so I am eager to hear your opinion. Ideally, as I said before, I hope we can collaborate on a play or a few in the future."

Yomei had read the novel but not the play script, so she had no idea how to respond to Ching's letter, which disturbed her to some degree. Ching had for years held a middling position in the Propaganda Department as the head of its cinema bureau, but lately she had been promoted to Mao's personal secretary, with a rank of vice minister. As a result, she was becoming a powerful figure in the Party, because at times she could represent the chairman. Because Ching's uterine cancer had been cured after four long visits to the Soviet Union in the past few years, she was

physically capable of more work now. It looked like Mao
had encouraged her to branch out into other arts. Yomei
showed Ching's letter to her adoptive parents. After reading
it, Father Zhou told her to be careful about Ching. "If you
don't want to deal with her directly, you must be polite and
respectful in appearance. Just don't antagonize her."

"I'll be cautious, for sure," she said.

About a month later, Yomei wrote Ching back, saying
she liked *Tracks in the Snowy Forest* very much, but that she
hadn't seen the script of the play *Taking Tiger Mountain by
Strategy*, though she'd heard of the project being already in
progress. She'd surely keep an eye on the play's production
at the People's Art Theater. As for adapting it into a Beijing
opera, she had no idea how. She wished she could have
given Ching a hand. "But I know practically nothing
about Beijing opera. I am sorry, Ching. This is beyond my
ability."

With that, she thought she could stop Ching's overtures
for some time. Now she had to focus on her own directing
projects.

· Fifty-Eight ·

After *The Servant of Two Masters*, Yomei started to work on a new play, *Joys and Sorrows*, by a young playwright, Yue Yeh. Yomei and her colleagues loved the play for its new perspective, which reflected the social reality of the times. As she put it, "I can feel a gust of fresh breeze blowing over the stage." Since Yue Yeh was still a novice, there were still some small missteps in the script, but he was available and Yomei could make changes in consultation with him. Together they meant to produce a play about "the people living in our time."

The story was a new kind of love triangle. The key male character is a high-ranking official in the Party, his current wife is an educated woman who joined the revolution a decade ago in the war against the Japanese invasion, and the other woman, the man's former wife, is a small cadre in the countryside, also working for the Party. Sixteen years ago, the man left his home village to join the Red Army to fight the Japanese invaders, and then he and his wife lost touch. By the end of wartime, they assumed they were no longer a couple. The man later came to know another woman and fell in love with her, so they got married quickly and had a child. Now by chance the three of them meet. The man is embarrassed and also apologetic to his former wife, who turns out to be understanding and still solicitous of him. He is touched and even thinking of getting reunited with her. In the beginning the two women can't help but be at odds. Yet as time passes, they begin to see each other's virtues, and both offer to withdraw from the marriage, but the man disagrees. Finally they live together under the same roof, even managing to do so harmoniously.

Such a story had happened to numerous officials in the CCP, and this kind of domestic problem was ubiquitous in the country now, so the play resonated deeply with many people. All the same, some critics seemed eager to find fault with it, because the story was not about workers or peasants or soldiers, and politically it felt rather aberrant, no matter how well it was embraced by the public. And soon four provincial theaters in other cities began performing *Joys and Sorrows* in collaboration with the Central Experimental Theater. It became a national sensation. During the first half of 1957, it was performed forty-three times in Yomei's theater alone.

An ardent lover of drama, Zhou Enlai saw Yomei's new production and praised it. He congratulated the acting crew and even took a photograph with them after the performance. The photo appeared in some major newspapers.

Despite the rave reviews and the play's popularity, soon adverse criticism appeared. Some said that the spirit of *Joys and Sorrows* went against the new marriage law, which clearly banned polygamy. Some argued that the ending posited an ideal ménage à trois, which mustn't be tolerated by a socialist society, because this amounted to a put-down of women. If we had been in the old society, the argument went, such a play could have been justified, but we were in the new China now and this was simply an anachronism, unacceptable.

Then the Art Committee of China's Theater Association held a conference on the play. At the beginning every attendee was polite and seemed ready to praise the production crew's effort. But Zhang Ying, a woman with a lumpy face and the editor in chief of the magazine *Dramatic Writings*, pointed out the negative resonance the play might produce, because in spirit it contradicted the new marriage law. She had to say it was mistaken to advocate "such a discordant sentiment." In a sense the play was backward and even feudalistic.

Yomei and Zhang Ying had known each other since 1937 in Yan'an, and both had been in the field of theater ever since. Appalled by Zhang Ying's critique, Yomei shot back, "Why so mean to the production crew? Only because you have the media in your hands can you feel so entitled to trash our play and to plant a reactionary cap on our heads. You know how difficult it is to bring out something new onstage, and genuine art doesn't originate from a correct topic or a righteous statement—it must be an expression of life and reality. But instead of encouraging others, you just want to kill our effort with your stupid theoretical cudgel. For goodness' sake, it's a seven-act play, and we all worked our tails off on it."

At that Zhang Ying lost it. She pointed at Yomei and raised her voice, blasting, "You're a great expert, educated in Moscow, so nobody can say anything negative about your play, right? And if anyone voices criticism, it must be sugarcoated, mustn't it?"

Muted for a moment, Yomei collected herself and said, "I'm not arguing for myself. I have to defend the people on our production crew. Mr. Shu Qiang is a revered actor, and this is his last stage appearance before his retirement. Liu Yanjin, in order to play the role of the former wife

well, worked so desperately that she cried many times
while rehearsing. I just can't stomach the dirt you've been
throwing on them so randomly. You can rationalize
anything you want to, but the play reflects the reality of our
times. That is the essential task we strove to fulfill. It's true
we didn't present a heroic figure in our play, but we showed
a piece of real life. We held the Chekhovian spirit as our
guidance. Besides entertaining the audience, we tried to
teach them to be kind and generous to others, so I can see
nothing wrong with the play. Chairman Mao just declared,
'Let hundreds of flowers bloom together and let hundreds
of schools of thought express themselves aloud.' I dare say
that our play is a theatrical flower."

Yomei's assistant director weighed in: "Our director in
chief worked hard on the play too. There's some technical
development in our production. Yomei managed to have
opened the fourth wall, the strictly kept barrier between
the actors and the audience. Such an attempt is a taboo in
the Stanislavski system, but we challenged this Russian
rule and succeeded in making better use of the space in
front of the stage by making the scenery slant and extend.
As a result, the setting gives a feeling of vastness that
matches the countryside landscape. Why not take into
account the technical development we accomplished in the
production?"

Zhang Ying couldn't go on arguing with them, because
she was an amateur in the art of stage production and
mainly good at working with words on a page. The leader
presiding over the conference seized the moment of
confusion and dismissed the crowd, saying, "Let us call it a
day. We might resume our discussion at another time. You'll
be notified."

Somehow Premier Zhou heard of Yomei's altercation with Zhang Ying. On Yomei's next visit to the Zhous with Little Lan, he asked her about the dispute, which she didn't deny. He looked serious and said she should have behaved less impetuously and tried to create a warm, congenial work environment for herself. He went so far as to say he would invite Zhang Ying over for lunch so that the two of them could patch up their quarrel. The woman used to work for Father Zhou, who knew her pretty well and liked her. Yomei was surprised by his offering to bring her and Zhang Ying back together. Maybe he'd just said that and might be too busy to invite Zhang Ying over.

But the following Thursday, Mother Deng phoned and asked Yomei to come home for lunch that Sunday. Having sensed this could be a rather serious occasion, she left Little Lan at home this time and went to West Flower Hall alone. While she was chatting with Mother Deng in the living room, Zhang Ying arrived. In no time lunch was ready—an orderly brought in four bento boxes, two small ones for the Zhous and two larger ones for the guest and Yomei. The small boxes each contained steamed rice and stewed yellow croaker fish and stir-fried vegetables, while the large ones had the same food, along with a pair of pot stickers as appetizers. Zhang Ying had eaten meals with Mr. Zhou a couple of times before, so this didn't feel like anything out of the ordinary to her. After lunch, over tea, the premier asked them, "I have heard you two fought over the assessment of *Joys and Sorrows*."

"We didn't fight," said Zhang Ying. "We just expressed different opinions about the play."

But Yomei admitted, "We did fight, but only with words."

Zhou Enlai laughed, placing his left arm on the back of the chair he was sitting on. "That was already something unusual between you two, considering you have been familiar with each other for such a long time and both are seasoned art workers of our Party. You ought to have behaved more reasonably, not butting heads in the open. Now you must make peace and shake hands in front of me."

Yomei held out her hand, which Zhang Ying shook. They grinned at each other, then at the Zhous. Both looked a bit embarrassed. Father Zhou went on, "In fact, you might also consider the play in this light: the story takes place before the new marriage law is issued, so it doesn't really contradict the law."

"That's true," admitted Zhang Ying. "The new law hadn't taken effect yet in the time of the story."

"I want both of you to promise me to treat each other as friends from now on. If you have different views, try to communicate kindly and patiently between yourselves first. Don't ever make a scene in front of others again."

Both women promised to do that and left the Zhous with revived congeniality. However, Yomei couldn't help mulling over Father Zhou's treating them to lunch and speaking with them as if to make a concerted effort to minimize the impact of their blowout. Why? It was true that he was passionate about theater, but never had he been so involved personally.

At the time Yomei couldn't figure this out, but in the fall more sinister criticism surfaced. A slew of articles published in various newspapers and magazines criticized the playwright and the theater for their problematic attitudes. Yue Yeh, the young writer, had become the target of vicious attacks. Someone wrote: "Although the play presents the life of peasants and cadres, in reality it is saturated with petty bourgeois sentiments." Another said that *"Joys and Sorrows* advocates bourgeois liberalization. Worse still, it applies the decadent attitudes of love to Communists and revolutionary cadres, so we have to intervene and criticize it." In essence, many argued, the play disseminated feudalistic views and vilified Communist cadres. Such negative criticism continued and blew up into a minor storm in the end— several people in the play's production crew got classified as "backward elements" and were disciplined. As the premier's daughter, Yomei was safe for the moment, though she was stumped. Now even Zhang Ying deeply regretted her carping article, which had inadvertently served as a prelude to the barrage of condemnation. If only she could have foreseen the vicious attacks triggered by her writing. It was impossible to reverse the trend now.

Yomei couldn't see any direct connection between the witch hunt and Father Zhou's effort to preempt it by making Zhang Ying and her reconcile, but there must be more reason for him to have made such a hasty effort. Perhaps some powers in the Party's upper echelons had a hand in this, but Father Zhou couldn't reveal to Yomei who they were. At heart she suspected that Jiang Ching might be behind the scenes, orchestrating the attacks.

One thing was certain: Ching was determined to make waves in the theater world. Sure enough, in the winter of 1957, Yomei received another letter from Madame Mao. Ching wrote that she was even more passionate about Beijing opera now. She again mentioned the play *Taking Tiger Mountain by Strategy*, saying it was being performed at the People's Art Theater and she hoped Yomei had seen it and given thought to her previous proposal: adapting the play into a Beijing opera. She also said there was already a group of writers and composers helping her with the libretto and the music for the adaptation. She wanted to do something original. For instance, using a full orchestra of Western instruments in combination with some traditional Chinese instruments. This way the music could be "more expansive and more physical." She emphasized that such an experiment was an example of the kind of theater revolution she had mentioned to Yomei before.

Yomei showed the letter to the Zhous, who seemed to expect such information. Father Zhou furrowed his brow and said, "Jiang Ching is getting busier again. Yomei, you must take precautions when dealing with her. Even if you are reluctant to help her, you must always be courteous."

"I won't collaborate with that witch. She's an amateur."

Mother Deng piped in, "That's all right, but don't ever offend her."

"OK, I won't. I'll always keep in mind that Jiang Ching is the First Lady."

About two weeks later she wrote back to Ching, saying she had gone to the People's Art Theater to find out how she could see their production of *Taking Tiger Mountain by Strategy*, but they'd told her that the show's run was already over. She felt bad about having missed this play. She confessed to Ching that in recent months she had been somewhat overwhelmed because of the attacks on her play *Joys and Sorrows*, and she'd had to try hard to hold the acting crew together. Some of her actors had been devastated by the vicious attacks. That was why she had neglected what was going on at the other theaters in town. She wrote, "Thanks very much, Ching, for alerting me to *Taking Tiger Mountain by Strategy*, which I am sure must have been excellent, considering the magnificent novel I enjoyed reading." However, Yomei reiterated her former position: She was completely ignorant of Beijing opera and unable to help

Ching adapt the play. "My field is spoken drama," she concluded. "I am sorry for not being able to branch out into Beijing opera."

Having mailed the letter, she thought that for the time being it might parry Ching's pestering, which seemed to have become chronic. For the next year she was going to take on some major directing projects.

· *Fifty-Nine* ·

Reslie, after directing the classic play *A Fan of Peach Flowers*, had taught a directing course at the Central Academy of Drama. In the spring of 1958, his long stint in China was over and he was about to return to the Soviet Union. Yomei treated him to a farewell dinner at Assembled Delicacies (Quan-ju-de), a place well known for its Peking duck roast. Lily came to join them. The three enjoyed such a private occasion, and Reslie, in shirtsleeves with the cuffs rolled back, kept saying he loved the duck and it was a pity he couldn't find such a fine dish in Moscow or Leningrad. Unlike Yomei, who was a hearty social drinker, neither Reslie nor Lily could finish a single shot of the fragrant Luzhou liquor. Reslie didn't drink in general, due to his medical condition.

After dinner and having hugged Reslie goodbye, Yomei and Lily went to a teahouse so that they could catch up. Lily had actually matriculated at the Soviet Institute of Social Sciences as a PhD candidate in philosophy and started her student life again in Russia. She had just come back because her father was very ill and might pass away at any time. In two or three weeks she'd go back to Moscow to resume her graduate work. She told Yomei that the relationship between the two countries was good now, and that the Soviets

as well as the comrades of the other Eastern European
countries were friendlier to the Chinese. Chairman Mao
was generally held as a contemporary Marxist theorist in the
socialist bloc. For example, to prepare for their qualifying
exams, every philosophy graduate student in the Soviet
Union now had to thoroughly know Mao's philosophical
essays, particularly "On Contradictions" and "On Practice."
Evidently in Eastern Europe Mao was esteemed as a major
leader of the international socialist movement, much more
respected than Khrushchev. Lily hoped to complete her
doctorate in three or four years.

Yet she seemed agitated, saying she couldn't articulate
why she'd lost her peace of mind since coming back to
Beijing. Taking a sip of pomelo tea, she asked Yomei, "Have
you heard of Case Eighteen?"

Yomei shook her head no. And Lily went on, "It's an
investigation that has dragged on for more than four years,
but it's gotten intensified of late." Seeing Yomei flummoxed,
she explained that the case originated from a letter Jiang
Ching had received on March 18, 1954, when Ching was
in Liu Village in Hangzhou. At the time Lily's father and
stepmother Zhu Ming were also staying in the sanatorium.
That was why Lily agreed to join Jiang Ching there at that
time. But Ching didn't reveal anything about the letter to
Lily, which she later learned went into great detail about
Ching's scandals and affairs in Shanghai in the 1930s. It
was a handwritten letter, mailed from Shanghai, and it
warned Ching to behave and stop meddling with political
affairs in the high circles of the Party's leadership and
reveling in luxuries. (Ching had seven limousines, and
when traveling on the train, she often brought along a limo
and her big white horse.) If she didn't mend her ways, the
letter said, she'd be exposed publicly, which meant everyone

would know what "a slut" she had once been. Ching went
into a fury and required the head of the police department,
General Luo Ruiching, to investigate the case and ferret
out the malicious writer. A secret investigation was soon
mounted. Ching believed the letter had been composed
by one of three kinds of people: top officials in the CCP,
or their wives, or people in arts circles who knew her
past. Because she had received the letter on March 18, the
incident was coded as Case Eighteen. A task force of some
one hundred people was assembled for the investigation,
and they compared the handwriting in the letter to that of
more than eight hundred people, and still couldn't identify
the writer beyond a doubt. There were some suspects, but
they all refused to admit any connection with the letter.

Among the suspects was a woman named Zeng Fei in
Shanghai whose husband headed the municipal Bureau
of Culture. Zeng Fei was a neighbor of Mao's ex-wife, Ho
Zi-zhen. Zi-zhen had been living in Shanghai after she had
returned from the Soviet Union. Zeng Fei was sympathetic
toward Zi-zhen, who'd been practically abandoned by her
ex-husband after she'd given birth to six of his children. It
was said that when she was released from a mental asylum
in Ivanovo, Zi-zhen could no longer speak, because she
had been shut in solitary confinement for more than two
years. When Chairman Mao went to Shanghai in February
1954, he didn't even pay a visit to Zi-zhen. That galled Zeng
Fei. Then, at a meeting of the city's leadership, Zeng Fei's
husband made a proposal that more aid be given to Ho Zi-
zhen. In light of Zeng Fei's discontent, the municipality's
investigators suspected she might have a motive. They
interrogated her and compared her handwriting to that in
the letter. The two indeed looked similar, but not identical.
Zeng Fei adamantly refused any involvement, saying that

the fact that she was unhappy about Comrade Ho Zi-zhen's situation didn't mean she hated Jiang Ching, whom she'd never met. Unable to prove any charge against her, they let her go.

The investigators also focused on people who had known Ching in the 1930s, before she went to Yan'an. Whoever had gossiped about her became a target now. They even seized a maid working for the household from whom Ching had rented a room at the time, but the old woman with a hunchback hardly remembered Jiang Ching at all, never mind her love affairs.

So the case was stymied. Lily had thought the investigation was over, but it had resumed lately. The investigators again started interrogating suspects and studying their handwriting. The resumption was due to Ching's vociferous complaint that someone had sabotaged the initial investigation. Luo Ruiching had no choice but to reopen the case. Ching even issued a deadline to the Department of Public Security for "ferreting out the criminal."

"That's crazy," Yomei said. "What if they simply can't find the wrongdoer?"

"Somehow this gives me the creeps," Lily confessed.

Yomei giggled and said, "Come on, Ching gets on well with you and can't possibly suspect you."

"That's true. She also knows my handwriting and yours too. Still I can't rid myself of the willies."

"Luckily there's the letter that shows the handwriting, or Ching might pin the blame on anyone who disobeys her. She tends to imagine enemies, and never hesitates to kindle enmity. Every a bush or tree looks like a snare to her."

"So you haven't heard of Case Eighteen?" asked Lily.

"Uh-uh."

"Your dad never mentioned it?"

"Father Zhou rarely talks about official business in my presence. I didn't hear of this case until now, from you. But take it easy. No ghost will knock at your door for a misdeed you didn't commit."

"You must be careful too. Ching heard you were about to put on Ostrovsky's *The Storm* and said, 'Yomei is getting too ambitious and might overshoot herself.' I said you were already well experienced as a director and should be able to do a fine job. Ching grunted, saying the play had been overproduced, almost staged to death, and it was hard to imagine that you could do anything new with it."

"Our theater wants to stage *The Storm* to honor the centennial of the play's premiere. Also to celebrate the tenth anniversary of the new China. The decision was made by our art committee, and it has little to do with my personal preference. On the other hand, I love *The Storm*, which can be a challenge."

"Don't be bothered by Ching's nonsensical opinions. I'm sure you'll do a great job. But beware of her jealousy."

"Thanks for warning me. Sometimes one doesn't have a choice—either to be envied or to be looked down upon. I prefer jealousy to contempt from others."

After Lily had left, Yomei mulled over Jiang Ching's snide remarks on her next project, which hadn't gotten afoot yet. She wondered why Jiang Ching hadn't disclosed to Lily the fact that she, Ching, had played the heroine Katherina in *The Storm* two decades before. That had been a major production in 1937 in Shanghai and must have been the second peak in Ching's acting career. The first one had been three years prior, when she had played Nora in *A Doll's House*, sharing the stage with Zhao Dan and Jin Shan and other famous actors. Probably she was reluctant

to mention her own participation in *The Storm* because
during the rehearsal period Ching, already married, had
been carrying on with Zhang Min, the director of the
play, and later had lived with him as his mistress. People
all knew she had become the leading lady because of her
intimate relationship with the play's director. It was a kind
of scandal that Ching must still dread to be unearthed, so
Yomei didn't mention to her friend Ching's involvement
with *The Storm* either. Such information might have put
Lily in danger. But Ching was right about the challenge
of staging the play, one of the founding works in Russian
drama and also one of the most successful productions
of spoken drama in China. On the other hand, its
magnificence made Yomei all the more eager to stage it.
The play had been produced several times in this country
over the decades, and there'd been also a movie adaptation
done in Hong Kong ten years before, though it was in
Cantonese. Yomei intuited that Ching might dislike
her effort to reproduce the play, which could awake the
memories of her erstwhile promiscuity among those who
had known her long enough.

Luckily the Soviet embassy assigned a theater expert
teaching in Beijing to assist Yomei in the production,
even though she could have done the job on her own.
It turned out that the Russian man seldom turned up
at the rehearsals; nonetheless, Yomei preferred to list
him as an associate director. His Russian name and
Soviet background could forestall sinister interference
from people like Jiang Ching. The project had become
international now, and as a result few dared to mess with it.

As usual, Yomei formed two acting teams and mixed the
young actors with the older, more experienced ones so that
the younger generation could learn and grow. Also, this way

Cast A and Cast B could alternate during the performance season. At times her crew was invited to another city to perform a new play, so it was more feasible to have an extra team that could be sent out. To everyone's surprise, Yomei chose Zhen-yao Zheng for Katherina in Cast A, because she had been impressed by Zhen-yao's portrayal of Mother Rabbit in *Little White Rabbit*. Now only twenty-two and a brand-new graduate from the Central Academy of Drama, Zhen-yao was flabbergasted by the assignment, feeling inadequate to be cast as the leading lady. In the play, Katherina is a young peasant's wife in a remote Russian town who has to live under the thumb of her cruel mother-in-law. Her husband, though kind and gentle, is a milksop and loves his mother more than his wife, so he listens only to the older woman and drowns his miseries in drink. Then Katherina encounters Boris, an educated young man, and the two fall in love and spend time together. Yet fearful of God's punishment and tormented by the pangs of conscience, Katherina confesses her affair with Boris to her mother-in-law and is beaten savagely. More outrageous, her lover Boris refuses to help her, so she eventually kills herself.

Zhen-yao felt that the wide range of Katherina's emotional turmoil was beyond her. Worse, she was unfamiliar with life in a primitive town on the banks of the Volga, even though she'd grown up in the countryside, in a county seat of Anhui Province. Yomei told her, "You're not supposed to copy actual life. Acting must originate from within yourself, and the seed of the stage reality must be rooted in your own being. I saw a Katherina in you, but of course she'll be a Chinese version in our play. Don't be intimidated. I'll help you and we can create a unique Katherina together."

At times, Zhen-yao was so moved by Katherina that she would laugh or weep unstoppably, and Yomei would do the same with her. Then she'd tell the actors at rehearsal, "It's always good to be stirred by the role you are playing. If you yourself are not moved, how can you move the audience? When I was preparing the script, I often had to pause to sob or laugh. Don't you think the pilgrim in the second act is ridiculous and funny?" Then again she started laughing heartily. She was directing as if she were acting too. Now and then she would toss out lines and even recite a snatch of the script in the Russian as if to show the sensation and the melodious resonance of the original words, as if to check whether she had missed something in her directing. She often quoted Auguste Rodin: "Art is feeling."

To make the script more animated and more communicable to the Chinese audience, Yomei shortened some long pieces of dialogue, specifically the preachy passages delivered by the pilgrim woman Feklusha and by the autodidactic artisan Kuligin. With this tightening, the drama moved faster and the acting became livelier.

To her surprise, You Benchang, the superb young actor who had performed the lead role in *The Servant of Two Masters*, volunteered to play a footman who didn't have a single line in *The Storm*. Yomei accepted his offer, believing he must have his own idea about how to perform the role. Indeed, by now the whole crew had adopted her principle: there's no small role, and there're only small actors. So no matter how minor a role was, every one of them prepared for it thoroughly. To play the silent footman well, Benchang studied all nineteen translations of the play and read some nineteenth-century Russian fiction and critical papers on the play. Yomei also shared some pictures with

Katherina, played by Zhen-yao

him, including volumes of Russian paintings. His fellow actors were all equally dedicated. As a result, when the play was performed, the audience found that even minor characters, such as pedestrians, servants, and the townsfolk, appeared like little stars, scintillating onstage, every gesture and every line of theirs charged with feeling and meaning. In addition, Zhen-yao, as Katherina, was lively and passionate and elegant in the performance, at times wearing an angelic smile that radiated an inner light. On the other hand, Yomei emphasized that for Katherina, to love Boris meant intense suffering mixed with happiness, so Zhen-yao must act out this harrowing contradiction, this inner struggle, that she was going through—even though Katherina knew she couldn't survive her affair with Boris, she couldn't hold herself back. In this production, her appearance among the vulgar and snobbish people in the town must manifest a conventional Russian critical verdict that stated that "Katherina is a ray of light in the kingdom of darkness."

Toward the end of 1959, a Soviet cultural delegation came to see the play. They were so impressed that the leader of the group said that watching the play, he felt as if he were seated in a Moscow theater. Though that was intended as high praise, Yomei wasn't pleased about it. To her, there were many new things in her production. Besides the brilliant acting, the stage design was also revolutionary, having challenged the fourth-wall principle established by Aleksandr Ostrovsky himself. The landscape in some scenes was slanted, with a ravine and tufts of grass and bushes, giving the impression that it sloped away from the audience's feet to the back of the stage, where the Volga was flowing. Such a design opened the forbidden fourth wall fortified by many Soviet directors. Yomei's stage design manifested an original approach that should be valued as a contribution to the development of theater arts. Yet the Soviet delegates paid no heed to such advances and seemed to believe they themselves were superior in everything.

Jiang Ching also saw the Central Experimental Theater's production of *The Storm*. She wrote Yomei a note, saying that she was greatly impressed by the fresh and vibrant performance and that Yomei was already a superb stage director, with a distinct style and touches. Ching had been working with some writers and composers for the Beijing opera *Taking Tiger Mountain by Strategy*. Though fully occupied with the opera, Ching added that she still hoped Yomei would collaborate with her in the near future. She reminded Yomei not to indulge herself in art for art's sake. "Arts must help make revolution," Ching wrote. "In other words, arts must be useful and serve a purpose. That is the source of artistic vitality."

Yomei couldn't see eye to eye with Ching on this matter. She believed some artwork could transcend time, and she hoped to achieve that kind of work. On the other hand, she knew that purity could also vitiate the arts. Still, too much emphasis on artistic utility might reduce art to the level of vulgarity. She aspired to create work rooted in history but also able to rise above it. She shared Ching's letter with Jin Shan, who smiled and said, "It's not easy to get positive feedback from that woman, who's unpredictable like the weather in June. You'd better be more careful when dealing with her."

"She and I don't travel the same road—all she wants is power and vanity, so there's no need for me to mix with her."

Jin Shan smiled. With Little Lan sitting on his knee, he had been showing the five-year-old how to tie her shoelace into a knot of bunny ears. He said to Yomei, "You're so arrogant. Keep in mind that Jiang Ching is the First Lady now and might not always take your rejection with poise and nonchalance. I know her, she's vengeful. You'd better appear friendly to her and somewhat cooperative."

"Whenever I spent time with her, I'd feel like I'd eaten shit. Sorry." She clamped her hand over her mouth, aware that their child was listening. She went on, "I am allergic to Jiang Ching. No, I'll never mix with her."

"I know you won't change. I just mean to remind you that the way you've been treating Jiang Ching might backfire. There must be another way of dealing with her."

"I just don't want to deal with her."

Jin Shan sighed and said to the child seated on his lap, "You have a pigheaded mom, Little Lan."

"I want to grow up pigheaded like Mom," the girl said in an earnest cry.

That cracked up both her parents. Yomei laughed so hard that tears came to her eyes.

· *Sixty* ·

Soon after Yolan and Zongchang returned from the Soviet Union, they got married. She became a lecturer of Russian at Beijing University, while he worked at the Institute of Chemistry, Chinese Academy of Sciences. They had their own apartment in the city, provided by Zongchang's work unit. Their home wasn't too far from Yolan's school, but she still had to take the bus to work. Right before Yolan came back, Yang and his family had moved to Sichuan, where he was working as the Party secretary of the Southwest Normal College. For years, Yang had wanted to enter the field of higher education, and he enjoyed his new position, which he felt was rejuvenating him. Because he was far away in Chongqing, Yomei and Jin Shan had become Yolan's only family in Beijing, and they intended to help the newlyweds set up their home.

Though Yolan and Zongchang both drew a standard salary for a college graduate—fifty-six yuan a month— they still had money problems, because he, as the oldest son of his family, was obligated to help his parents in the countryside. Two of his younger siblings were still going to middle school, so he had to send remittances home every month. Aware of their financial difficulties, Jin Shan gave the couple a generous wedding gift—a set of fine furniture bought from a downtown store. It consisted of a bed; a double-door armoire; a rectangular dining table, shiny and made of hardwood, which could seat eight, and a pair of date-wood corner shelves. The dining set was too big for their poky apartment, but the couple accepted it with gratitude. Jin Shan told them that he had just struck gold, having been paid for a movie he had directed, and that money was always like water flowing through his hand, coming and going unpredictably. He meant he was a spendthrift, so they should take the gift like a windfall.

Indeed, Jin Shan couldn't save, so Yomei handled their family's finances, even though she wasn't that good at balancing the books either, often going over budget. Fortunately, as artists and authors, they always had some extra money coming in.

For years, Jin Shan, with the cap of "rightist" on his head, hadn't been able to participate in most of Yomei's productions. So he had struck out on his own and found work mainly by virtue of his reputation and talent as an actor and director. Unable to find a theater in Beijing willing to take him on, he went to provincial cities, where his name and ability still could secure him employment, although it was mostly temporary, paid on a piece rate basis. In the past few years, he'd been affiliated with a theater in Zhengzhou, the capital of Henan Province, and had produced a number of plays, all of which were didactic, because the projects were usually assigned to the theater by the Propaganda Department of the provincial administration. Yet among them, his play *The Red Storm* stood out as a work with serious artistic distinction. He wrote the play and directed it. He also played Attorney Shi Yang, one of the lead roles. His insuppressible talent was shown fully in the production of this play—he had written the

script in two weeks and started working on its direction
only seventy-two hours before its premiere. Such a speedy
production was in keeping with the spirit of the Great Leap
Forward movement at the time, when the whole country
was racing ahead helter-skelter, naively believing that in
fifteen years China could become such an affluent country
that its industrial power would surpass that of England,
and that soon afterward, Communism would be realized in
the country—thus China would have made a "leap forward"
into a blissful utopia.

The Red Storm, about the labor union's struggle with a
warlord, did strike a chord with the audience and was so
well received that Beijing Film Studio offered to have it
adapted into a movie. This delighted Jin Shan, so in the
following year, 1959, he was busily working on the movie.
He wrote the screenplay and directed the picture. To some
extent, he was still thriving career-wise and had never
stopped producing plays and movies. Yomei was happy
to see him continue with his artistic pursuit and that his
adversity had not diminished him. The movie came out
later that year and was greeted with wide acclaim. For two
months, Jin Shan basked in the rays of its success.

Then, to Yomei's surprise, Lily dropped out of graduate
school and came back from Moscow. She called Yomei and
they talked briefly on the phone. She told Yomei that it was
impossible to continue to stay in the Soviet Union anymore.
Just two months before, Young Zeng, the vain man they
both used to despise, had been arrested by the KGB and
sent to a labor camp on Sakhalin. Then many Chinese
expats in Russia began to repatriate.

"What's the charge against Yong Zeng?" Yomei asked in
surprise.

"Espionage, selling intelligence to China."

"Gosh, he used to be so proud of kissing up to the Soviets that he acted like he was above all of us. Obviously the Russians never treated him as one of their own."

"What's more ironic is that he was naturalized in the USSR long ago, so the Soviets can handle him any way they like now—China can't possibly intervene on his behalf. Even though he's like a buffoon to me, I feel bad for him. His mother is still alive in the countryside of Jiangsu Province, near Zhenjiang."

Yomei and Lily didn't speak intimately at length on the line, afraid that the operator was listening in on them. In fact, part of some operators' jobs was to eavesdrop on telephone users to collect useful information for the police. The day after Lily's call, Yomei went to see her in the dorm of the translation bureau. She and Oyang Fei shared a sizable room, so the three of them sat at a square table under a pair of fluorescent lights. They drank coffee and cracked spiced pumpkin seeds while chatting in Russian, since Oyang Fei's spoken Chinese was still shaky—at times she couldn't come up with the right words or expressions. Lily said it was out of the question to continue with her graduate studies in the Soviet Union anymore because of the quarrel between the two Communist Parties. In recent years, the USSR had made stupendous achievements in science and technology and surpassed the United States in many areas, such as launching a new type of nuclear submarine and planning to send the first man and woman into space soon. The Eastern Bloc countries were all thriving, and socialism would likely prevail in the world. So Khrushchev believed that from now on, the socialist countries should concentrate on peaceful development so that they could eventually trump the capitalist countries economically and culturally.

Chairman Mao, on the contrary, argued for the use of force to defeat the capitalist powers. Mao claimed that "the east wind has already overwhelmed the west wind," and that no reactionaries would ever make themselves scarce unless you forced them to: "No dirt will leave the floor without being swept away." In the beginning, the leaders of the two Parties, the CPSU and the CCP, began to argue among themselves. Then, in November 1957, Mao announced at an international congress held in Moscow that the socialist countries must unite to wipe out capitalist societies in the world by force. He went to so far as to claim, "Why should we be scared of a global war? The world has two billion people. If half the population is destroyed, there will still be one billion survivors. China has more than six hundred million people now. If we lose half the population, we will still have three hundred million with us. So we are not afraid of any war, not even nuclear attacks."

What he said shocked the audience, particularly the leaders of some Eastern European countries. Antonin Novotny, the head of the Czechoslovakian Communist Party, too frightened to hold his coffee steadily, whined to others, "My country has only twenty million people. It's unthinkable to take that kind of loss: three hundred million lives! Comrade Mao Zedong must have gone out of his mind." After that conference, the objections to Mao's stance increased among the Eastern European comrades. By and by, the Soviet leaders began to view Mao as a dangerous, hotheaded maniac, so the two countries could no longer maintain a congenial relationship.

Yomei remembered that Mao had actually been shaken by the documentary film on the atomic bomb that she had showed him in Stalin's dacha at the end of 1949. Why did

he now declare he wasn't afraid of nuclear blasts at all?
The man must be either hypocritical or insane. But Yomei
didn't share her view on this matter with her two friends.

Lily went on to explain that the tension between the
USSR and the PRC made her graduate studies difficult, and
that there were too many official lines she had to toe, even
in Moscow. She was often required to express her views on
Chairman Mao. It would be suicidal if she said anything
against the Great Leader back home, because her words
would be relayed to the CCP eventually. So she decided
to keep mum and often got criticized by her Soviet peers.
Finally, she couldn't stand it anymore and had to decamp.

"When will you go back to continue with your graduate
work?" asked Yomei.

"I have no clue," Lily sighed. "Maybe I won't be able to go
there anymore."

Oyang Fei mentioned that she had met a senior
economist from the USSR recently. The man was quite
critical of the Great Leap Forward, though the movement
was currently going full steam in China. To him, the whole
thing seemed harebrained. He said, "Why such a rush? Why
must you Chinese dash into Communism? Isn't a socialist
country already good enough for you? I wouldn't mind
living in a socialist society for a few generations. It would
be better to keep the realization of a Communist society as
a long-term goal, a supreme vision. Why waste resources
on one Potemkin project after another? It's dangerous to
realize your ideals too soon, like having your prayer fully
answered. It would be better to have a perpetual goal you
can strive for."

Lily had even heard some foreigners call Mao a rash,
heartless peasant. But she reminded Yomei and Feifei,
"Don't tell anyone this. I just repeated what I'd heard."

"Sure thing, we must keep our conversation confidential," said Yomei.

Lily went on, "I met Lisa and Grania last Saturday. Believe it or not, they're both supportive of the Great Leap Forward, saying China must ramp up the realization of Communism. Again I argued with them. They don't understand the reality here, since they are living in bubbles. Even more ridiculous, they both thought China should treat them as Soviet experts, with a bigger salary, better housing, junkets and yearly leave to go home, top medical care, et cetera. I told them that they were making a lot more than a regular Chinese does, their families were far better off than others, and by any means they mustn't think China was a wealthy country. As a matter of fact, I suspect they've been misled by their Chinese husbands. So many people around us are blinded by their enthusiasm and reveries, and they have no idea what the world outside China is like. They all believe China is a rich, strong country."

"Do you think the Korean War might have something to do with it?" Yomei asked.

"Definitely. The war boosted the confidence of the Chinese people, who were misled by propaganda. Many believe that in every way China can match the number one superpower in the world, the United States. That's why the Central Committee has always referred to the war as a great victory."

"But China suffered horrendous casualties," Feifei piped in.

Lily said, "Generally speaking, the loss of soldiers' lives doesn't count to the top leaders."

"That's true. That's why I try to stay in the world of art," Yomei said. "Politics can drive you out of your mind and drain away your humanity."

She was truly uninterested in politics, but she could see
that the country might be heading toward disaster. People
seemed too zealous about the vista of a Communist society,
having no idea China was still poor and shabby, and far
behind most industrialized countries. As an artist, she
didn't trust any mass movement and instead just preferred
to stay within her own field, in pursuit of artistic beauty.
Gradually their topic shifted to Yomei's directing work.
Her next project was *Black Slaves' Hate*, a play based on the
American novel *Uncle Tom's Cabin*. She was uncertain of this
project, because she had never been to the United States and
had no concrete sense of the place and the people. But her
friends assured her that she'd do a superb job. Both Lily
and Feifei could see that Yomei had become top in her field.
Feifei said, "The other day I heard that you were regarded
as one of the three best directors around."

Surprised, Yomei asked, "Who are the other two?
There're many ahead of me, for sure."

"Jiao Juyin and Huang Zuolin."

"I'll be damned! They're both masters, older than me by
a generation."

Lily joined in, "I've heard the same opinion. Yomei, now
you're reaching the top. I'm proud of you. Those two best
directors are men. You're the first woman stage director in
the new China, the best of our generation. I wish I could
be artistic like you, but I don't have a creative bone in my
body."

"Come on, there're still a lot of challenges ahead, but
I'm just happy about my job at the theater," Yomei said.
She respected those two master directors—Jiao Juyin had
studied in England, and had even spent some time with
Bernard Shaw, while Huang Zuolin, based in Shanghai
now, had been educated in France. In other words, the two

master directors were unique and magnificent in their
own ways, shaped by the European traditions. Yet Yomei
was much younger and might be more promising, if not as
accomplished as those two yet. All the same, it was amazing
that the top three stage directors currently in China had all
been educated abroad. She seemed to represent the Russian
tradition. Though she was not entirely comfortable about
this affiliation with the Soviet Union, such a revolutionary
background should be some kind of protection for her.
Also, she had joined the Party twenty years before and
was a red expert with Yan'an provenance. As long as she
didn't make major political mistakes, she should be safe
and able to continue staging the plays she loved. She was
aware that many people used to believe that she had made
such headway in her career mainly thanks to her unique
relationship with Premier Zhou, but by now people in the
theater world all reckoned her as a significant force. She
had earned that recognition with genuine work.

· Sixty-One ·

The Chinese translation of *Uncle Tom's Cabin* was published in 1901. The two translators, Lin Shu and Wei Yi, described the process of their translating Harriet Beecher Stowe's novel as follows: "We two wept then translated, and translated then wept, lamenting not only black people's bitter life, but also our four hundred million yellow people who will become miserable successors to blacks. Furthermore, yellow people's calamity will not be long before it strikes. There is already a ban on Chinese workers in North America, and our compatriots are mistreated in many countries—these facts indicate that we are not that different from black people, and actually we might be in a worse situation. From their erstwhile suffering as slaves we can imagine our future. We are becoming *yellow niggers*."

Lin Shu was a famous translator and translated more than two hundred novels and plays, from Tolstoy to Shakespeare. But in point of fact, he didn't know any foreign words. He collaborated with others who could read English, French, Russian, and Spanish, and those who could explain the stories to him. They team-translated, paragraph by paragraph. Lin Shu was such a lively, rapid writer that he declared that the moment his partner finished explaining a paragraph, he had already put it

on paper. In spite of numerous imprecisions, every title
he rendered was embraced by the public enthusiastically.
Some became classics.

His translation of Stowe's novel came out with an altered
title: *A Chronicle of Black Slaves' Lamentation*. It became an instant
sensation, and several major newspapers serialized the
story in China. A group of Chinese students in Tokyo were
mesmerized by the novel. They had a drama club, Spring
Willow Troupe, that decided to adapt it into a play. Yomei's
current neighbor Oyang Yuchien was a key member of
Spring Willow Troupe, and he took part in the adaptation,
playing a white man in the play. It was staged in 1907 and
was so well received that soon afterward, several cities in
China also put on versions of the play. Later, in the early
1930s, it was performed widely in Ruijin, the CCP's Soviet
base, to deepen people's understanding of racial oppression
in the United States. Now, decades later, when the United
States had become the citadel of world capitalism, the
Central Experimental Theater, headed by Mr. Oyang
Yuchien, decided to stage the play again so as to reveal
these dark pages of American history and also to honor the
semicentennial of spoken drama, a new genre, in Chinese
theater. But the early script of the play had been lost, so
Mr. Oyang decided to write a new play based on *Uncle Tom's
Cabin*. With Yomei's help, he produced the lengthy script,
making it closer to the spirit of the current time, when
people on different continents were all engaged in fighting
against racism and the so-called final stage of capitalism—
imperialism. Already seventy-one and with his memory
failing, Mr. Oyang had to depend on Yomei to produce
the play, but he served as a consultant, giving her ideas and
suggestions occasionally. His reputation also helped protect
the project from too much official interference.

The new script was titled *Black Slaves' Hate*. It was a massive play, with nine acts and more than forty characters. Besides the animus highlighted onstage, the slaves were more active and determined in their struggle against the slave owners, fighting for their survival in the land they'd been shipped to. In the novel Stowe advocated for the humane treatment of the slaves snatched from Africa; she held that the educated Africans should eventually be returned to their homeland, where they could start a normal life and build their own democratic countries. Such a notion was already obsolete, and the new play ought to show that the black Americans' future lay in fighting for their own decent livelihood in America and for equality and justice. So even the protagonist, Tom, was altered. He is no longer a passive Christian who followed the Bible's teachings to the letter. When refusing to flog his two female slaves as he was ordered to by his master, he exchanges words with his cruel owner, Legree, with dignity and deep passion. Tom tells him: "True, my body was sold to you, but my soul belongs to myself. Although you can make me do the heaviest work, what's in my mind is different from yours. I'm afraid we'll never be the same . . . You can flog people like cattle, but I'll never raise my hand against an innocent person." Tom's condemnation bruises his master's pride, so Legree begins punching him, then orders his underlings to throw Tom into a deserted barn infested with vermin. He means to starve him into submission. Yet unlike in the novel, in which Legree beats Tom to death, in the new play the unyielding Tom is tied to a tree and set on fire. He is burned to death, which is more striking and more powerful onstage.

Swallowed in flames, Tom makes his last speech: "I used to think everybody could be moved by kindness, but today

I have realized that American bosses like you cannot be brought around by kindness. You will have to pay the debt you owe. Even though you don't pay now, the account will be settled sooner or later. Do you think you can clear the debt by burning me to death? No, the debt you have carved on the hearts of the sufferers will never be wiped out." So Tom is a totally new character in Yomei's production and is meant to be a fighter.

In preparing the new script, Yomei abided by the words that John Brown had bequeathed his children: You must hate, hate with an intense passion the source of evil—slavery. She was trying to instill some of John Brown's spirit into Uncle Tom and the other characters, especially George and his sister Cassy.

At every opportunity, Yomei emphasized the slaves' enmity, which in turn must also inspire rebellious actions. The undercurrent of the drama is clearly class struggle, which reflects the global élan of the 1960s.

Mr. Oyang Yuchien loved the new script, which bore his name as its author, and which was approved by the theater's art committee within a week after Yomei had submitted it. Then she began to assemble the various actors and to rehearse the initial scenes.

None of the actors had been to America. All the impressions and understanding they had were mainly from writings. Even though Yomei had seen

Uncle Tom, played by
Tian Cheng-ren

the old movie of *Uncle Tom's Cabin*, the black-and-white film
wasn't that helpful either, because the new play was much
more intense and fiercer in its theme of class struggle
and had to have more colors. Still, the movie gave her a
picture of what a slave owner's mansion on a plantation was
like, white and grand and wrapped with a veranda. It also
showed the interior of the slaves' quarters. But the stage
design mustn't copy the American movie and had to be
brand-new and reflect a distinct Chinese sensibility. It had
to manifest a new spirit. Recently Chairman Mao had made
a public statement condemning American imperialism and
racism, and supporting the civil rights movement in the
United States. So *Black Slaves' Hate* had to reflect the struggle
of the present time as well.

During their rehearsal, Patrice Lumumba, the
Congolese popular leader, was arrested and murdered by
the authorities of his country. A short documentary film
that showed him being apprehended and executed was
shown to the Chinese public. With his hands bound from
behind, Lumumba was forced onto the back of a truck; he
turned around, his eyes blazing with hatred. Yomei told
the actors that the flames in Lumumba's eyes must be a key
mental reference in their performance—the oppressed had
to fight to survive and must never have any illusions about
the oppressors. The acting crew nodded in assent and felt
more excited about such a powerful dramatic project.

Nevertheless, there were additional small, specific
problems that had to be solved case by case. Hsiao Chih,
the lithe young woman playing Cassy, couldn't imagine
what the female slave, who was skilled in witchcraft, was
like. Yomei couldn't explain to her in concrete terms and
images either. Then one day she chanced upon a statue of
a black woman at the home of Liao Chengzhi, the former

president of the National Youth Art Theater. The statue had been presented to him by a friend of his in Guyana. With excitement, Yomei took Hsiao Chih to Mr. Liao's home, where they looked at the statue. The actress was struck by the vivacious beauty of the female figure and kept tutting with praise. Yomei asked her, "Don't you think Cassy's stage image should be like this, lovely, evocative, and kinetic, also memorable?" Hsiao Chih nodded in agreement. Thus she became able to proceed with her enactment of Cassy.

In act seven, Tom is viciously flogged by Legree, his new owner. Conventionally the director would ask the actor to show the pain, asking him to moan loudly and even howl. There was little else one could do. But Yomei wouldn't take the well-trod path. She put twenty-five slaves onstage—when the whip falls on Tom with loud cracks, all the slaves groan and swing their heads from side to side as if being flogged at the same time. As a result, the whole stage trembled with their agony. Every spectator on the rehearsal ground was struck by this drastic manifestation of pain.

Toward the end of the play, Cassy and Emmeline want to flee north together with Tom, but he won't go and instead urges them to set off without him, because if Legree finds out about their escape, he might dispatch men to track them down. Also, Tom is injured, unable to walk normally. While the two women are leaving, he smiles at them as his way of seeing them off. "That smile must reveal the kindness and depth of his soul," Yomei told Tian Cheng-ren, the tall scraggy actor playing Tom. "This smile is also meant to assure Cassy and Emmeline not to worry about him."

Cheng-ren worked so hard on that smile that for a time he seemed unable to smile naturally anymore. Then one afternoon, Lei Ke-sheng, who was playing George, teased him. Young Lei said, "Brother Tian, you're not Mona Lisa, no need to make your smile too mysterious. Just imagine your wife gave birth to a husky baby boy this morning." People around laughed. Cheng-ren smiled. Yomei caught

Cassy and Tom in *Black Slaves' Hate*

that flitting smile on his face and cried out, "That is the smile you should give to Cassy and Emmeline, with a touch of bliss!" So from the next day on Cheng-ren grabbed Lei and wanted him to see if he was reproducing that smile. Eventually he managed to do it with ease onstage. When the play was performed, some people commended that heartbreaking but beatific smile, shaded by a veil of moonlight, saying it displayed so much of Tom's generous character.

The play turned out to be a huge success. Several rave reviews appeared in newspapers, including a long laudatory article in *The People's Daily* by Tian Han, a top playwright serving as the head of the theater bureau in the Ministry of Culture. A visiting African writer saw the play and enthused, "This is so different from the novel and so nuanced. The director is a genius!" One evening a few

Congolese among the audience wouldn't leave after the curtain dropped. They begged the crew to perform the play in Africa and even said that at least it should be recorded on film so that more people could see it. Premier Zhou came to see it too and was greatly impressed. He told Yomei, "I saw several productions of this play, and yours is by far the best." He also invited the crew to perform it in the Huairen auditorium in Zhongnanhai, where many top leaders saw it, including Liu Shaoqi, Zhu Deh, Chen Yun, and Deng Xiaoping.

Jiang Ching also saw it. She sent along a note of congratulations, saying Yomei must be the number one female spoken drama director in China now. Ching also mentioned two "amazing plays" she'd been working on: *Taking Tiger Mountain by Strategy* and *The Legend of the Red Lantern*. She was converting them into Beijing operas. Yomei wrote back to thank Ching and said she couldn't wait to see Ching's operas. She realized it would be impossible to separate theater from politics and that she might not be able to shun Ching altogether. She'd better learn how to deal with her without making an enemy of her or being exploited.

· *Sixty-Two* ·

n the fall of 1961 Lily's stepmother Zhu Ming committed suicide as a consequence of her involvement with Case Eighteen. Though Lily had never been close to Zhu Ming, the death of her stepmother plunged her into a crisis—she feared that Jiang Ching might turn on her. Her father had passed away the year before at the age of seventy-four, so some of the privileges Zhu Ming had enjoyed were no longer available. The young widow, only forty-one, became depressed, and recently she had tried to sift through her late husband's papers (planning to write a memoir one of these days), some of which seemed to fall into the category of classified information. Unsure how to handle them, she wrote a letter to Yang Shangkun, the chief of the General Office of the CCP's Central Committee, to request guidelines and also to express her wish to retain some of her former privileges, such as special medical care, an annual winter jaunt to the south, and a summer vacation at Beidaihe, the northern seaside resort for senior officials. Over the years, Yang Shangkun had participated in the investigation of Case Eighteen, and was familiar with the letter that had threatened Jiang Ching to expose her sordid past in Shanghai if the First Lady didn't mend her ways. For seven years, the case had remained uncracked because they couldn't find anyone's handwriting that matched the one in the letter.

As Yang Shangkun was reading Zhu Ming's letter, he found the handwriting familiar but couldn't place it. Then it flashed across him that Zhu Ming's script might resemble the one in Case Eighteen. So he called the Department of Public Safety, which at once sent over two graphologists. They compared Zhu Ming's letter with the one addressed to Jiang Ching seven years earlier. Without difficulty, they concluded that the two letters were by the same hand.

They called in Zhu Ming. Without any equivocation, she admitted she was the perpetrator. Her composure and prompt admission amazed the investigators. She confessed that long ago, back in Yan'an, she had heard people whisper about Jiang Ching's sordid past in Shanghai. After she and Lin Bochü had gotten married, she came to know more about Jiang Ching's abuse of privileges in Yan'an, such as eating fried meatballs twice a week, wearing a fox-fur robe, even washing her hair with eggs. Zhu Ming resented Ching's lavish lifestyle, which became more extravagant after the establishment of the new China. Ching ate eggs every day, but she'd have only the white and there mustn't be a single drop of yolk in her food. She liked crabs, but would eat only male crabs. When she had chicken, the bird must be young and weigh around half a pound. Zhu Ming was convinced that such a corrupt woman might undermine Chairman Mao's integrity and revolutionary spirit. Her opinion was shared by some of the investigators in secret, so they didn't treat her harshly and even let her go that very day.

Then, to everyone's astonishment, she poisoned herself as soon as she was back in her home, convinced that Jiang Ching would never let her get away with impunity. Her

suicide shocked many people. Despite the breakthrough
in Case Eighteen, the investigators couldn't figure out her
motivation for threatening the First Lady. Someone said
perhaps Zhu Ming had resented Jiang Ching's demand that
her stepdaughter Lin Lily keep her company constantly
in Liu Village, although the Lins were staying nearby in
Hangzhou at the same time and couldn't spend time with
their daughter Lily. Or Zhu Ming might have envied the
privileges Ching enjoyed: the big villa house, the new yacht,
the flock of servants. Yet nobody could make the woman's
motivation more concrete and precise, let alone explain it
clearly to Jiang Ching. The investigation group summoned
Lily and questioned her. They demanded to know how often
she and her stepmother had talked about Comrade Jiang
Ching. "Never," Lily replied. "Zhu Ming never mentioned
Comrade Jiang Ching, who she knew was friendly to me."
In fact, Lily was also truly bewildered, unable to come up
with any explanation of her stepmother's animosity toward
Ching. Neither did she have a clear idea how Zhu Ming had
come to know so much about Jiang Ching's past, though
it was probably from her late father. Lily claimed she was
totally ignorant of Ching's personal history. Though she
had heard snippets about her from Yomei, she didn't want
to drag her friend into such a case.

"My stepmother and I hardly spoke to each other," she
told the investigators.

"What do you think might be her motivation to write
that nasty letter to Comrade Jiang Ching?" a rotund official
asked.

"I've no clue," Lily said. "She never shared her thoughts
with me. How could I tell? Actually she and I were like
strangers, and I never liked the way she treated my younger
brother and my dad."

So they let Lily go. Nonetheless she was disconcerted, uncertain if Ching might treat her as an offender as well because Zhu Ming had been her stepmother. She knew her late father had never liked Jiang Ching and had been among those opposed to Mao's marrying her. Her stepmother Zhu Ming may therefore have been influenced by her father, but she wouldn't bring up anything about her dad to the investigators. Still, Ching must have known her father's attitude and might treat her differently from now on. Yomei heard about the Lin family's morass from Mother Deng. She phoned Lily, and they agreed to meet the following weekend at her dorm.

Lily looked shaken and kept sighing, her face haggard. As Yomei sat in an armchair in her friend's room, Lily told her, "The Internal Security Office interrogated me and wanted to find out what I knew about Jiang Ching. The truth is my stepmother never mentioned Ching's past to me. Zhu Ming was a difficult woman and would often throw a fit in front of my dad, so I didn't like her and always stayed out of her way. That was why I didn't often go home to see my dad, not wanting to seek unhappiness."

"But you did know something about Ching's scandalous past," Yomei reminded her.

"It was true my dad never liked Ching, but he wouldn't talk about her to me. All I know about Ching's past was from you."

"So next they might bring me in?"

Lily tittered. "Rest assured, I didn't mention you at all. I just played ignorant with them."

"We must be more careful from now on. Even if Ching has lost the traces of the case after your stepmother's death, she might not give up easily and might take out her rage on someone else."

"That's why we must give her a wide berth."

"It's not that simple. She has written to me every year and wants me to work for her."

"On some plays?" Lily wondered.

"Yes, she said she wanted to make a brand-new theater for China, but I don't know anything about Beijing opera and cannot help her at all. Besides, you know I dislike her."

"To my knowledge, she has a lot of enemies in the Party, so you'd better not collaborate with her. Otherwise you might alienate others."

"Still, every time I must give her a solid excuse or she might think I despise her."

"Then get some good excuse ready for her. Gosh, I wish I could return to Moscow to finish my graduate degree, but the two countries keep getting more hostile to each other, and there's no way I can go back. The philosophy institute in Moscow won't even bother to answer my letters anymore, as if I'm no longer their student."

"Remember how simple and hard but happy our life was in the Soviet Union long ago?"

"Those carefree days in our youth are gone like smoke and will never come back again."

"Life continues and we cannot afford to be too upset, Lily. We have to plug away at the work at hand."

"That's true. 'Only work can save you,' my dad used to say. Tell me, Yomei, are you happy about your married life?"

"To be honest, not totally, but my daughter gives me a lot of happiness. I've had more joy from being a mother than a wife. Why did you ask?"

"Someone, an older man, is after me, but I'm not sure if I should accept him. He's a high-ranking official and his wife just died, but he is also old-fashioned. I feel I'm already

past the age for a happy marriage. It's my convoluted path
of life that has made me so different from the comrades
around me here. Deep inside, I feel I don't need a man for
my happiness."

"That's true. Like I told you, I love Jin Shan mainly
for his artistic soul. We do have a common language, but
I wouldn't say my happiness depends wholly on him. He
needs me more than I need him."

"Still, you two are a fine couple now, I must admit. An
older colleague told me that marriage was like an aviary,
it's easy to get in but hard to get out. That has made me
hesitate."

Yomei laughed, then said, "She must have serious
trouble at home."

"It was a man who said that."

"My, I guess many women must feel the same. But don't
be so affected by negative opinions like that. You must
follow your own heart and head."

"I have no compunction about remaining single for the
rest of my life, and neither does Feifei. We are both inclined
to believe in celibacy. Now we're a pair of old maids in
others' eyes—they call us half Russians. Some even whisper
that we're more likely to be lesbians or hermaphrodites."

"Don't pay mind to what others think. So many people
subsist on disparaging others. It's just a way to make up for
their own inferiority, to soothe their egos. You have your
own life to live and must spend your life the way you prefer."

"Oh my, I thought I was more rational than you, Yomei.
Now I can see that you're coolheaded too."

"Living with Jin Shan has made me more patient, I guess."

"I'm sure you've also made him a better man."

Indeed, these years Jin Shan had begun depending on
Yomei all the more, though he often undertook his own

projects, continually directing plays or movies. He was a
force in the world of theater and cinema and often said with
a touch of bitterness that he didn't need any work unit, and
that he himself was a work unit. The truth was that he was
still in disgrace as a person expelled from the Party and
couldn't have a home institution.

As if to prove his worth, he worked very hard, sometimes
even around the clock. Yomei urged him to slow down
some, but he always said he was the heart of the projects he
worked on, and others relied on him. Then, while directing
Li Xiucheng, a historical play about a key leader of the Taiping
Rebellion, he collapsed in the rehearsal hall in a downtown
school building. Some young actors carried him by turns on
their backs to the Friendship Hospital. All the way he was
unconscious, saliva dripping out of the corner of his mouth.

The diagnosis was a heart attack. Fortunately, the doctors
managed to bring him around and stabilized his condition.
When Yomei arrived at the hospital, he was out of the woods,
and was transferred to a ward shared with two other patients,
though he was still on an IV drip. He opened his eyes a slit
and moved his hand, which she took hold of right away. He
said, "I am dying, sweetheart. Don't miss me when I'm gone.
I'm sorry. All I've done is drag you down."

"Stop, Shan!" she said. "You will recover and get well
soon."

"You're still so young, Yomei. I wish I could accompany
you for many years to come. But it's a tragedy in a woman's
life to marry an unworthy man. I know our marriage has
diminished you a lot. So after I'm gone, find another man
who can give you more help and a better life."

"Please stop this nonsense, Shan! You must think of our
life together in the future. Think about the long haul ahead
of us. I need you to be with me, so does our daughter."

"Bring Little Lan with you when you come again. I miss her."

"We shouldn't let her miss school, but I'll try to bring her along in the evenings and on Sundays. For now, rest well and sleep as much as you can. If you need something, write it down in case you forget to tell me."

Due to his hospitalization, Jin Shan had to let the associate director of their historical play take charge for the rest of the production. He had already done most of the work, so the play would be staged according to his vision and plan. For two months, he stayed in the hospital and Yomei came every Sunday and sometimes also in the evenings on weekdays. Whenever she brought Little Lan with her, the girl nestled against her father, and once in a while she even fed his meals to him with a spoon. That made him happy and talkative. The child would blow on the hot food on the spoon as if he were her charge. Both Yomei and Jin Shan often commented that Little Lan would make a great nurse. Indeed, the girl enjoyed nurturing people and animals.

One evening, as Yomei, seated next to his bed, was peeling a mandarin orange for him while he was asleep, he woke up and moved his hand a little and shook his head. "How are you doing today?" asked Yomei.

"Not well. Oftentimes I feel suffocated." Indeed, his breathing was laborious and ragged. Obviously he was struggling to speak. "Yomei, maybe this is the end."

Her heart tightened and she said, "Don't think like this, Shan. You will recover."

He shook his head. "My heart condition is chronic. I can tell it gets worse each time when . . . an attack comes."

"Think positive thoughts, please. When you get out of the hospital, let's produce a play together. Again, you'll

play the leading man and I'll direct the play." She said
this despite the fact she might not be able to make such a
decision to resurrect him officially on her own.

"I'm sorry, Yomei." His hand squeezed her wrist hard.
"All these years I've been nothing but a burden to you. After
I'm gone, you—"

"Stop that! We're husband and wife. We came together of
our own free will. I love you, Shan. For my sake, you must
get well soon. Our family needs you."

But his condition began taking a turn for the worse,
and from the next morning on, an oxygen mask was put
on him. Beside his bed a steel oxygen tube was slanted
on a dolly like a small torpedo. He was gradually losing
his speech. Word about his condition spread, and many
friends and leaders came to see him, assuming this might
be their last meeting. One afternoon a senior official from
the Ministry of Culture arrived and found Jin Shan's face
clouded, while his lips kept twisting, as if he was in pain
and unable to get his words out. The man bent over and
said, "Jin Shan, come again. What do you want to tell me?"

Shan opened his mouth but closed it again, his face
contorted. Yomei scooted over with a fountain pen and a
notepad. She told him, "Shan, write it out if you can." She
put the pen in his hand and placed the notepad next to it.

With limp fingers he scrawled: "Without a Party card, I
can't go meet Marx down there."

Yomei almost gasped at those words, realizing that
Jin Shan was still bent on salvaging his reputation and
regaining his lost past. But she said nothing.

The senior official returned to the ministry and
reported Jin Shan's last request to its Party committee.
Everybody realized this was a dying man's wish, so they held
a meeting that very night, at which it was decided to restore

his Party membership, and that Jin Shan must be informed of this rehabilitation without delay.

It was snowing the next morning. Yu Lin, the young Party secretary of the National Youth Art Theater, came to the hospital with a large bouquet of red roses wrapped in cellophane. He had phoned Yomei beforehand, so she was waiting for him in the ward. Jin Shan no longer belonged to the theater, but it was their Party committee that had stripped him of his membership, so they were responsible for taking him back now. Yu Lin announced to the patient solemnly: "Comrade Jin Shan, I hereby inform you that our Party committee had restored your membership. From now on, you can take part in all the activities within the Party. Congratulations!" He gave Shan the bouquet, then a copy of a new pamphlet from the CCP Central Committee on fighting against revisionism that was intended to reach every Party member. From now on, Jin Shan would receive this kind of document regularly. He wept like a child while burying his face in the flowers. It began snowing beyond the window, the feathery flakes sticking to the panes.

Yomei was moved, seeing her husband so happy. Before Yu Lin left, Shan told Yomei to get him a banana, which at that time was a rarity in northern China in the winter. Also, it was in the midst of the famine, when many people were starving. Yu Lin was ecstatic to have the large banana, saying he'd give it to his twins, who had never tasted this tropical fruit.

Afterward Yomei went to the hospital every other evening. On account of Shan's illness, she reduced her workload. Instead of staging a full play, she tried to do something lighter so that she could spend more time with her husband.

Much to her surprise, in December 1962, she received a large envelope from Jiang Ching, which contained a libretto that was more than eighty pages long. A letter was attached to the script. Ching said that this was the opera that she and a crew had been working on. It was tentatively titled *The Legend of the Red Lantern* and was adapted from the movie *Always There Are Revolutionary Successors*. The music for the opera wasn't done yet, but two composers were busy working on it, so Ching had sent along only the lyrics to seek Yomei's opinion and also to see how the two of them could collaborate on this project.

Having paced up and down at home for two hours, Yomei wrote back to Ching and apologized for her inability to join her for now because Jin Shan was seriously ill. He had already been hospitalized for nearly two months, and she had to carry out her "wifely duties." Nor could she comment on the libretto in much depth. First, she knew nothing about the movie, which hadn't been released yet, and neither could she tell how well the adaptation had been done, though it looked impressive. Second, she assumed that in a Beijing opera, music and words must match, working together in harmony, but she had no musical sheets as a reference now, so she couldn't make a judgment. Yet she added that she had read the libretto quickly and liked the story, which was engaging and powerful, and at times humorous. She concluded by saying, "I'm sorry, Ching. I have to do my best to save Jin Shan's life now. I wish I could participate in your project, but this is out of the question for me now."

Now it was imperative for her to take up a less ambitious project for the next season lest Jiang Ching believe that Yomei had just put her off by giving unjustified pretexts. To avoid producing a major play, she suggested staging a series of Chekhov's small comedies for an evening. This was approved. Without delay, she picked four one-act plays by Chekhov for the next season: *An Anniversary, A Marriage Proposal, The Boor,* and *An Unwilling Martyr.* She was familiar with them, especially the first two. She had played a small character in *An Anniversary* while studying at the theater institute in Moscow and had briefly directed *The Marriage Proposal* in Harbin. As for the other two plays, *An Unwilling Martyr* needed minimum directing because it was mainly a long conversation between two characters with almost no action at all. In contrast, *The Boor* is shot through with action—a lady accepts a male creditor's challenge to a duel, but the two of them, in spite of their noisy wrangling, wind up in each other's arms. The comedy was a boisterous farce and wasn't difficult to direct, given that her actors were now more seasoned, creative, and versatile. Yomei felt comfortable about her choices, which would likely entail less work. And the short plays could definitely entertain and move audiences.

· Sixty-Three ·

Soon after Jin Shan had left the hospital, Yomei's brother's family moved back to Beijing from Sichuan, where Yang had headed the Southwest Normal College for several years. Yang's former boss Zhu Deh, the nominal commander in chief of the People's Liberation Army and a vice chairman of the PRC, wanted him to write his biography. Yang had worked as his secretary for many years in Yan'an and then in Beijing, so he felt obligated to undertake such a project, regarding Zhu Deh as a father of sorts. The old man, already in his midseventies, used to be a sworn brother to his father and had treated Yang like a son, even though Zhu Deh had a son of his own, who was a locomotive driver in Beijing. It was whispered that the old man was extremely shrewd, believing that to be a common laborer would be a good way for his son to survive the endless political upheavals. His belief turned out to be right—his son, though relegated to a small train station where he took charge of a warehouse for three years during the Cultural Revolution, eventually died of a natural cause, of a heart condition, but left five children for the Zhu family.

Now Yang was back in the center of the CCP again, where he knew life could be troublesome and even

treacherous, but he was willing to work for Zhu Deh for a
third time. As a matter of fact, he was the best candidate
for writing Marshal Zhu's biography. Few who knew the old
man well could write better than Yang, who had studied
in Japan for some years in the early 1930s and had been
acknowledged as one of the most capable official writers in
Yan'an. Since the office of the CCP's Central Committee
didn't have housing for Yang at the moment, his family—
his wife and three children—was staying at the PLA's
guesthouse at the edge of Beihai Park. Yang had once owned
a courtyard in downtown Beijing that had been presented
to him by a friend of his father's, but after the Communists
had come to power, he had donated the property—three
small houses surrounding a tiny yard—to the country.
At that time, in 1949, while divorced and still single, he
had been living in the Zhongnanhai compound, next to
Zhu Deh's residence, for the sake of work, and he'd never
thought he might need his own housing someday. Now he
regretted a bit having given his property away. But he didn't
worry much about his family's inadequate housing yet,
certain that this problem would be solved pretty soon once
he started his work here. As long as he had a room where
he could work on Marshal Zhu's biography, he wouldn't
complain. The PLA's guesthouse did provide him with a
small office on the top floor in addition to a suite for his
family.

Yomei and Jin Shan invited Yang's family over
for a gathering. Yolan and Zongchang also came and
brought with them a large watermelon and a magnum of
champagne.

Little Lan got excited to see her three cousins, Yang and
Shi Chee's children, two of them younger than she was. Yang
and Chee's oldest child was Bing, a lovely girl the same age as

Little Lan who was a bit frail. Bing's younger siblings were boys, Ning and Ming. The two girls, Lan and Bing, were both second graders, but the boys were still too young for elementary school. It was drizzling outside, the sky gray and low, so the kids couldn't go out to play in the tiny yard. Little Lan had some bric-a-brac under her bed, among which were a couple of dolls. She pulled out a box of children's picture books, and the four of them gathered in her room, the girls reading while the boys built things with toy bricks.

Meanwhile Jin Shan was making his signature dish, braised pork cubes. Yang's wife, Shi Chee, a slender woman with an angular, heart-shaped face, had brought a large cured white fish, a special product of Sichuan. Jin Shan had eaten this kind of fish before and was excited to cook it. He cut the fish and steamed it in a pot. He didn't have many relatives himself, so Yomei's siblings were like his own. He enjoyed having family gatherings, and even the noise made by the kids filled the house with life. Now and then, Jin Shan let out a wisecrack. He told Yang and Shi Chee that Yomei had saved his life again, having helped him recuperate from the heart attack, so from now on he preferred to stay home and just help his wife with her work. Yang smiled and said he was so delighted to see that Jin Shan had finally become "a model husband."

After dinner, Yomei and Yolan chatted about their respective work. Yolan liked working at Beijing University, and this semester she was teaching a selected-reading course, which included Pushkin and Turgenev and a few authors of the Soviet period, like Gorky and Isaac Babel. She mentioned a novel she had just read—*The Brothers Yershov*, which a Russian colleague had loaned to her. She was told that the book might be problematic but was immensely popular in the USSR at the moment. In fact, ever since its publication four years earlier, the novel had been in the center of controversy. The author, Vsevolod Kochetov, was already known in China. His previous novel, The Zhurbin Family, had been a bestseller here, and he'd been held as an exemplary practitioner of socialist realism. His new book, Yolan said, felt nostalgic. It questioned the current political trends in Soviet society. Evidently the author preferred Stalin to Khrushchev, similar to the Party secretary, a main character in the story, who laments at the end of his life, "If only Lenin were alive!" Indeed, it was extraordinary for such a novel to have seen print, considering that Khrushchev was still the boss of the CPSU. Yomei was fascinated and said she'd get hold of a copy of the book and read it. There was a foreign language bookstore downtown, so she'd go there and buy a copy.

Yang had heard of the controversy, and he said some top CCP leaders actually appreciated the views and sentiment expressed in the hefty novel, whose Chinese translation had come out the previous summer. There had been some discussion within the CCP's top circle about this book, which seemed quite timely and evoked some sympathy among the CCP leaders. They believed that like in the Soviet Union, there was also deep-seated corruption among their comrades in China, many having gone astray in their pursuit of self-interest and forgotten the original vision of the revolution. Some had betrayed the proletariat and even themselves, becoming obstacles to progress. Yang had overheard a senior cadre in his office saying, "This is a timely book, a poignant reminder for all of us." It was also true there had been grumbles in the CCP about Khrushchev's denouncing and demonizing Stalin. Mao believed that some of the Soviet leaders had strayed from the original course of the revolution started by Lenin.

Thus they had committed the misdeed of revisionism, which Mao was determined to fight. So it was high time for a correction—this novel could serve such a purpose. The inside information provided by Yang made Yomei want to explore the possibility of adapting the novel into a play, given that she had liked Kochetov's previous books. Over the years she had learned that it would be safer to produce a Soviet or traditional Russian play, because those cultural officials and hacks above her tended to leave such a production alone, not daring to mess with it. Aside from politics, if a work could cross linguistic and cultural barriers and find an audience in another country and language, it meant the work had great vitality, and was almost without exception artistically superior.

After dinner, having eaten ice cream that Jin Shan made, the guests were ready to leave. Yolan helped Yomei wash the dishes, then both families left. The children were in jubilant spirits, each taking with them a gift from Aunt Yomei—Bing got a baby doll, Ning a toy plane, and Ming a wind-up gunboat. But Little Lan hadn't joined them in devouring the ice cream that she loved. She said she had a headache. Jin Shan saved a small bowl of it for her.

After the guests were gone, Yomei went into her daughter's room and found her lying in bed, her face buried in her flowered pillow. Yomei touched her head and neck and decided the girl's temperature was normal. "All right," she said, "come eat your ice cream or it will melt in a jiffy."

The girl stepped into the kitchen and sat down at the table, eating the ice cream while gulping down her tears. Alarmed, Jin Shan asked, "What gives? What makes you cry like this?"

"Ming said you two are not my real parents. Is that true?"

Yomei and Jin Shan glanced at each other, for a brief moment too stunned to say anything. "Why did he say that?" Jin Shan asked Little Lan.

The girl went on in a moist, snotty voice, "Dunno, maybe because I wouldn't let him take away my set of Monkey King books. He said, 'I'm gonna ask Aunt Yomei for them. She's my real aunt but not your real mother.' I called him a liar, but he told me, 'Go ask Aunt Yomei when she adopted you.'"

"That little squirt is an asshole," Yomei said.

"You are my real parents, aren't you?"

"No, Ming is right," Yomei said. "We adopted you when you were a baby, and you have brought so much joy to us."

"Yes, Little Lan," Jin Shan added, "we're one family. We've taken you as our flesh and blood. You're our daughter, our only child in every sense. You're our pride and joy."

"Who're my birth parents?"

Yomei managed to reply, "Your father passed away long ago. Your mother was too ill to raise you on her own, so she let us have you."

"Where is she?"

"She's in Shanghai, but we haven't been in touch since you came."

Jin Shan said, "I knew your father, who was a smart, elegant man. Your mother was beautiful too."

Yomei explained, "We didn't mean to keep you in the dark for good, Lan. Your dad and I talked about this, and we both believed we should let you know the truth when you grew up. So we will share any information on your birth mother in case you want to know and even look for her."

At those words, Little Lan got up and fell into Yomei's arms, crying hard. "You're my mother! Dad is my real father. This is my home."

"We're so happy to hear this, Lan," said Jin Shan. "We couldn't imagine this family without you. You're heaven-sent to us. You know that Mother Yomei loves you as much as if she's afraid you might melt like a chocolate in her hand. In the beginning, you wouldn't sleep at night, so she just held you in her arms pacing about the room for hours at night."

"Sometimes your dad did that too—the second he put you down, you cried again, so he had to keep holding you, walking around and humming a nursery rhyme."

At those words, Little Lan beamed with a smile. "I can see I'm so lucky. I could've become an abandoned baby."

"You joined us and made this family complete," Yomei said. "It must be fate that threw us together, so we must love each other and live happily."

Jin Shan added, "I'm so glad we can talk about this openly now, Little Lan."

"I'm happy to know the truth, Dad and Mom. I love you." She smiled in spite of her tearstained cheeks.

Yomei and her daughter, Little Lan

· Sixty-Four ·

Yomei didn't find the Russian original of *The Brothers Yershov* in the foreign language bookstore, but she bought a copy of its Chinese translation and read it over a weekend. She was impressed by its plainspokenness— it confronted the degenerate trends and official corruption in the Soviet Union, which were believed to have deviated from orthodox Marxism and Leninism. The latter holds that class struggle is a fundamental feature in a socialist society, so the proletariat must be firm and aggressive in suppressing the remnants of capitalism and the bourgeoisie. The novelist seemed truthful to the point of bluntness. Still, with Dostoyevsky's masterpiece *The Brothers Karamazov* looming in the background because of its title, Kochetov's novel felt like a piece of reportage, lacking in psychological acuity despite its vast canvas and large cast of characters. On the other hand, it did have magnitude, which Yomei always prized in a literary work. According to what she had witnessed in the USSR, she believed its descriptions of the bureaucracy and the corruption in the Communist Party there. She intuited that a dramatic adaptation of this novel in China might have international repercussions. In recent years, the CCP had been accusing the USSR of straying from its original vision—a move driven by revisionism and opportunism—and purposely slowing down in its advance toward a Communist society. Yet Yomei's gut told her that this novel, as a literary work, might be too deeply entrenched in history, feeling more like a thriller that mainly served current politics, so she shelved the idea of adapting the novel into a play.

Then, to her surprise, Zhou Yang, the deputy head of the CCP's Propaganda Department, called and invited her to a small meeting. On the phone, he didn't elaborate and only revealed that they would like to see if she could stage a play adapted from *The Brothers Yershov*. Luckily she had just read the book and wouldn't appear uninformed, and, knowing the novel now, she could form a professional opinion on the adaptation. She had known Mr. Zhou Yang long ago in Yan'an, where he had been a major literary theorist. He had published numerous theoretical essays, translated some critical writings by Chernyshevsky, a handful of Gogol's stories, and *Anna Karenina* in its entirety. Since 1949, he'd been a tsar-like figure in the world of arts and literature in the new China, though Mao had never completely trusted him on account of his landowner family background. Mao and Jiang Ching believed Zhou Yang was too soft in his dealings with artists and intellectuals, in particular not aggressive enough in curbing the bourgeois trends among them. Yomei could tell that if Zhou Yang was now interested in adapting *The Brothers Yershov*, powerful people in the CCP's high echelons must be behind it.

In Zhou Yang's office, Yomei met two other men, one of them she had also known in Yan'an—Lin Mohan, who was in his early fifties, thin like a rail and wearing round wire glasses. Like Zhou Yang, Mr. Lin was also a theorist, having written a good number of critical essays and a handful of small plays. The other man was quite young, probably not thirty yet. Zhou Yang, his pudgy face smiling good-naturedly, introduced the slender young man, Shao Yan-hsiang, to Yomei, saying, "He's an excellent poet, and he's been adapting *The Brothers Yershov* into a play."

Shao had seen Yomei's drama productions and looked happy to meet her. He said, "Finally we've met in person. I used to watch you only from a distance." He placed a hand above his mothy eyebrows as if it was a visor.

That made Yomei laugh. "Come on, you're talking as if I were a celebrity, not approachable."

"Of course you are a star—I mean in the field of spoken drama," Shao said.

Both Zhou Yang and Lin Mohan threw back their heads and laughed. They said they had known Yomei when she was still in her midteens. Indeed, who could have known that their Little Mei would morph into such an accomplished artist, an iconic figure to young people in the field of spoken drama? The two men said they couldn't help but feel in awe.

Seated around a table with a checkered top and gunmetal legs, they began to talk about the business at hand. Zhou Yang explained that the CCP's Propaganda Department had been planning to turn *The Brothers Yershov* into "a political alarm bell" so as to admonish Party members against slipping into a capitalist track and becoming obstacles to social progress. Zhou Yang had assigned Shao Yan-hsiang to work on the play script two months before, so the young poet was already deep in the middle of writing. Both Zhou Yang and Lin Mohan believed that Yomei would be the ideal director for this adaptation. Hearing their suggestion, Shao was thrilled, saying Yomei would also be able to help him with the script, given that he was a novitiate in playwriting and needed some guidance.

Yomei realized this project was as serious as a political task, so she just accepted it, saying that the play would have to be entertaining in its own fashion, even though there were many exciting scenes and rich lines of drama in the novel that were impossible to present onstage, such as the accident at the smelting furnace and the machines that could handle a huge block of red-hot steel nimbly, "like playing on the piano," and that were "celebrating the sublime rhythm of labor," as the novel claimed. Above and beyond that, the love relationships among some men and women in the novel had to be made more engaging. She added, "The theater has limited space and time for such an immense story, so we must figure out how to compress it without losing its power. Our stage designs must be fresh and striking too, since the setting of the story is a coastal city. Maybe we can put a part of an open hearth onstage, with a backdrop of ships in a large busy harbor. We will have to figure out how to present the workshop scene, where molten iron sprays with flying sparks. There'll be a lot of difficulties, but every challenge can be an artistic opportunity."

All three men were artists and intuitively understood the particular needs of the stage adaptation. Yomei also suggested cutting the parts of the novel that were about staging a new play, called *The Okunves*, which eulogized heroic labor and the patriotic spirit of the workers in fighting the Nazis. Toward the end of the novel, the success of the play coincides with a victory over corruption and fraud in the steel plant. To Yomei, the most efficient way to vitiate theater was to have the drama business proper as a subject—a play must never become a piece of metadrama. She even believed that this part of the plot, strife and success in the city's theater, might be a weak one in the novel, even though it might have been necessary, adding a dimension to the canvas of society that the story presented. Still there wasn't enough space for such a presentation onstage, and to dramatize a play within a play would be too self-conscious. At least it might feel too artsy, a tad contrived, and she wanted to avoid that.

Zhou Yang nodded. "Yomei, you're an expert. I trust your judgment. Why don't you take part in preparing the script as well?"

"Yes, please give me a hand!" the young poet begged. His thin eyes lit up as he smiled good-naturedly.

Yomei agreed, feeling pleased about the arrangement. Before leaving the Propaganda Department's office building, she chatted briefly with Lin Mohan in the foyer, where an old man with a spray bottle was watering potted plants lined up beneath lofty windows, and now and again digging his fingers into the wet soil. Mr. Lin, holding a vellum briefcase, was waiting for his car. He confessed to Yomei that he couldn't fully participate in the adaptation of *The Brothers Yershov* because he'd been working on some projects for Jiang Ching. Yomei was amazed, but also a bit relieved. This meant Ching might be too occupied to bother her anymore. Mr. Lin said he'd been revising the lyrics of the Beijing opera *The Legend of the Red Lantern*. He added, with a smile bordering on self-amusement, "Believe it or not, I'm also working on a ballet for Comrade Jiang Ching."

"You mean *The Red Detachment of Women*?"

"Right, that's the project."

"But do you know how a ballet is made?" Yomei asked innocently, her translucent eyes fixed on his thin face. "I mean the music, the choreography, the story, everything must be unified and harmonized in a ballet. It's an art of high order, very hard to do."

"I know." Lin laughed, showing nostrils full of tufty gray hair. "Truth to tell, I'm a total layman. My job is mainly to make sure every part of the ballet is acceptable to our Party."

"How can you predict whether it's acceptable?"

"We can abide by the Party's policy on literature and arts—from the people, about the people, and for the people."

Yomei sighed. "It must be difficult for you to work like a censor, isn't it?"

"I'm just trying to do my best. Comrade Jiang Ching encourages us to master the art through making it, so at worst this can be a unique experience."

"Then I hope you enjoy it," Yomei said.

"I do. We all feel like doing something original and significant. Comrade Jiang Ching always emphasizes that art must affect life and shape society, so in a way we feel we're creating a new culture for the multitudes."

"Like engineers of the human soul?" She quoted from Stalin's instruction for artists and cultural workers.

"Somewhat like that."

Yomei realized that theater may have become Jiang Ching's gateway to power, the power to shape the country's cultural life and its people's minds. Yomei said no more, unwilling to throw a wet blanket on Mr. Lin. She knew that Ching was unlikely to produce original art. Most times Ching borrowed from different sources and even appropriated the work of others without acknowledgment— her productions usually gave no credit to the original authors and instead listed only Jiang Ching as the producer. Yomei was glad she had been able to stay away from that vainglorious woman.

Sixty-Five

S hao, the young poet, had written most of the script
already, and Yomei liked what he had done. She could
see that the young man had a refined, poetic sensibility
that tended to keep the actors' diction too elevated, so here
and there she toned it down a little, explaining to Shao that
the actors had to speak naturally. As a rule, the language
ought to be common speech, relying on the words people
used every day. Overall, the script had captured the main
points of the novel's dramatic conflicts, but Yomei wanted
to add something original, since this would be a foreign
play made for a Chinese audience. She would like to have
a more memorable woman character that was based on
the role of Lyoliya, who was portrayed in the novel as
damaged, scarred, scrawny, and hard on the eyes. Yomei
wanted Lyoliya to be somewhat beautiful, inside as well as
outside, with a shapely figure in spite of her face, which had
been mutilated by the Nazis. She wanted Lyoliya to carry
more weight, so as to give the story more historical depth
and gravity. In addition, Lyoliya's love for Jima should
be rewarded with a semi-union in the end. Yomei talked
to young Shao about her ideas for the revision, which he
thought made good sense. He agreed, "We shouldn't stick
too close to the novel. We are doing a play for the Chinese

audience. The play ought to be more poetic and more intense than the novel, since it's much shorter. We must make it more expressive and more resonant."

So in the play, Yomei let Lyoliya, a second-tier character in the novel, carry a great deal more weight. She had an actress chosen for Lyoliya already: she gave the role to the svelte Hsiao Chih, who had played Cassy in *Black Slaves' Hate*. Due to the drastic differences between Cassy and Lyoliya, Chih was intimidated and said she might not be able to do it. "We're all tyros in this," Yomei told her. "That makes our work more exciting." She assured Chih that she would help her find a new way to play such a damaged woman, but Chih must follow her guidance. The young actress agreed.

The task Yomei assigned Chih was simple: learn to play the guitar. She even hired a teacher for Chih and told her to practice diligently and learn how to strum it while singing. So every day Chih just took a guitar lesson and practiced a couple of simple chords. This wasn't easy for her, never having touched such an instrument before, but she practiced it devotedly, at least four hours a day.

Yet once the rehearsal started, Yomei left Chih alone, just telling her to continue with her guitar lesson and learn how to sing while plucking the instrument. Yomei even had a Russian folk song composed for Lyoliya. Chih often splayed her hands to show others her fingertips, callused from all her playing. Indeed, she'd been practicing continuously, even though she often got bored. As the weeks passed, she felt somewhat agitated when watching others rehearse actively. Everybody seemed to be having a great time on the rehearsal stage, laughing and wisecracking, but why was she left alone? Why did they often skip her part to practice other scenes?

Then one morning Yomei said to Hsiao Chih, "All
right, now you perform a song on the guitar for us."

Confidently, Chih wrapped her face with a white scarf
and sat down, then plucked the strings as she began to sing
in a slightly husky voice. The acting crew gathered around
to listen and was impressed. Nodding her approval, Yomei
said, "Good, let us rehearse your part now. Lean the guitar
against the bench. Keep in mind, it's not yours, it belongs
to Jima Yershov. You should carry only a backpack when
you come here to see him for the last time." In the play,
Lyoliya appears to say goodbye to her friend Jima—she
won't be able to come to see him on weekends anymore.
Prior to the war, she had been a lovely girl with a natural,
innocent manner and charming looks, but after the Nazi
troops assaulted her and mutilated her body and face,
she felt humiliated and ruined, unable to live among the
people who knew her. Chih, as Lyoliya, stopped outside
Jima's house and put her hand on a picket fence, while
her other hand held the strap of her backpack. She looked
hesitant, as if changing her mind. Yomei interrupted Chih
and said, "Now tell me how you see the character Lyoliya at
such a moment."

Chih, who had read the novel twice, told her director,
"She is in pain now, almost unable to tear herself away from
the fishing village familiar to her, because she's afraid to
meet strangers and also to lose her only friend, Jima, who
she believes loves Kazakova, the pretty young engineer in
his workshop. To Lyoliya's mind, her life is about to change
forever. She'll be more lonesome and maybe more isolated
from now on." Chih used to think that this character wasn't
essential since she wasn't a worker at the steel plant, the
center of the struggle against corruption, but Chih didn't let

out that thought. Yomei nodded and said, "Lyoliya appears only a few times in the play, but she's a vital character. The war started by Hitler inflicted endless destruction on common people, and Lyoliya, as a victim, damaged in both body and mind, represents an accusation against fascism and a justification for the serious efforts to remember the past." Indeed, with her ruined life standing in sharp relief, most fashions in arts and literature appear superficial and frivolous.

Chih nodded and felt a bit enlightened and began to see the significance of the role she was playing. Yomei turned more specific, saying, "A wedding just ended beyond this fence, but you've almost lost the ability to love like a normal woman—to become a bride and a mother, because the Nazis mutilated your body and looks, and you cannot give birth anymore. When you hear the jubilant chatter from the wedding and see the cheerful crowd, how do you feel?"

Stirred and touched, Chih stepped over to the stone bench, sat down, and picked up the guitar, playing it while singing in a sorrowful contralto voice:

Along the bank of the Volga River
There's a craggy cliff
Covered by thick green moss.
For so many years no one has come here . . .

She was too emotional to continue, so she lowered her head, her cheeks bathed in tears.

"Jima, why are you still standing there?" Yomei cried at the actor who played the chief foreman at the steel plant. At this point of the drama, he was supposed to rush over and embrace Lyoliya, but he was so spellbound by Chih's performance that he forgot what to do. Everyone could see that this episode would be a shining point in the play—a resounding climax. Both Yomei and Shao were pleased about this revised episode. This bright conclusion might lift the drama from grisly history to the realm of the human heart. It was how the play got charged with more feeling.

When the rehearsal was nearly completed in the fall of 1963, how to present *The Brothers Yershov* to the public became an urgent issue, because it was a play full of political implications that might have international repercussions. On the weekend prior to the dress rehearsal, Yomei went to the Zhous, bringing along Little Lan, whom Father Zhou and Mother Deng both loved to see. The girl was nine years old now, and already wearing a red pioneer neck scarf at school. She used to be naughty when her mother took her to the Zhous' residence and had even dropped and broken some tableware. Grandpa Zhou had once pointed his chopsticks at the girl's round face while saying to Yomei, "You've spoiled her rotten—she's like a wild thing now. If you continued to indulge her like this, she'd soon climb up to our roof and tear off the tiles. You must rope her in." But now the girl, already a third grader, was demure and respectful, knowing Grandpa Zhou was one of the most powerful men in the country and that she must behave at the Zhous'.

Over lunch—moo shu vegetables and seafood soup— Yomei told Father Zhou and Mother Deng about the problem of knowing how to present the play to the public. The premier was aware of the adaptation Yomei had been doing. In fact, the project had support from the top circle of the CCP. "You mean Chairman Mao approved this production too?" Yomei asked in amazement.

"Not exactly. Chairman Mao must have read about the anti-Khrushchev slant presented in the novel, but he doesn't pay much attention to these kinds of matters nowadays. He doesn't read contemporary fiction. Still, anything against Soviet revisionism and opportunism ought to be favored by our Party."

Yomei didn't ask more questions, aware that in recent years Mao had been forced to "stay away from the frontline of the central government," having given up most of his power as a result of the famine (in which tens of millions of people were starved to death) and the debacle of the Great Leap Forward. It was believed that the real powers in the government were Liu Shaoqi, Zhou Enlai, and Deng Xiaoping, and that Mao might have lapsed into being a mere figurehead. In a sense, Mao had become a toothless tiger.

Father Zhou said he should see the play first, and then would think about what kind of venue might be suitable for it. His instinct told him not to show it to the general public like a regular production. "We'll have to consider how the Soviets might take it," he said.

In spite of his hectic schedule, Premier Zhou managed to attend the dress rehearsal the following Thursday. He was bowled over by the intensity and the striking vigor and beauty of the play. Afterward he kept saying to Yomei, "You did a great job with the adaptation. The play must have become a different work from the novel, maybe equally good if not better. I can see that it can serve as a textbook for the comrades of our Party, to remind us of the danger of corruption and of forgetting our original ideals." But he believed it might be unsuitable to open the play to the general public because it disclosed some of the underbelly of that socialist society: bureaucracy, greed, the petty maneuvers of power struggles, wicked manipulations of others, selfishness, hedonism. It was disheartening to see such a prevalent obsession with ranks and positions and rubles in the USSR, where corruption and avarice had undermined the foundations of socialism. More worrisome, such an exposure might boomerang, making the public more aware of the seedy aspects of the current Chinese society and reminding the audience of venal elements among their own officials. In a word, the play could backfire on the CCP if it was seen by the masses.

After exchanging views with the Party's Propaganda Department, the State Council decided to stage *The Brothers Yershov* in a smaller auditorium inside the Great Hall of the People instead of in a large public theater. All Party members in Beijing were required to go see it as part of their political education. Thanks to the required attendance as a political study, which meant most Party branches in the capital had to purchase tickets collectively, Yomei's theater production enjoyed a financial success her company had never had before.

· Sixty-Six ·

n spite of the smaller venue and the limited public access, the play became quite popular. It was performed in the Great Hall of the People for three months. Many top leaders of the CCP went to see it. President Liu Shaoqi and his wife Wang Guangmei liked the play so much so that they met the acting crew and Yomei and took a photo with them, which was published in major newspapers. Zhou Enlai, a lifelong theater lover, saw the play again and praised its unique sensibility and its colloquial language. Zhu Deh also loved it, but he was so frail that Sun Yang had to go with him twice to let the old man finish seeing the entire play. Zhu Deh told Yang, "Your sister is extraordinary, already a master of stage directing. She's still so young and has a brilliant career ahead of her. Your father in the netherworld must feel proud of her now."

That year, 1963, Yomei was forty-two. Compared to the other top drama directors in China, she belonged to the rising generation, among whom she stood at the forefront as the most accomplished. Yet such a distinction gave her more unease than peace.

Late that summer, she received a phone call from Jiang Ching's office inviting her to a private meeting with Ching. What's up now? she wondered. On the phone she asked

Ching's secretary about the purpose of the meeting, but the young man sounded unclear and just said Comrade Jiang Ching would like to discuss some cultural issues with her. Yomei felt that this invitation was ominous— Ching might have a new knife to grind. Yomei had just undergone appendicitis surgery, which had for a week made her feel as if her right leg was shorter than her left leg, and she wondered whether to tell Ching that her medical condition prohibited her from coming. But she decided not to mention the surgery, which was minor in any case. She was loath to appear as a malingerer, even in Ching's eyes. Thank heaven she'd always been in good health.

The following week, she went to Ching's office in Copious Garden, which was Mao's residence in Zhongnanhai. The moment Yomei was ushered into the living room, Ching stepped in with splayed feet and waved at a servant to pour tea for the guest. Ching sat down and crossed her legs at the knees. She was wearing green beaded slippers. Yomei observed Ching's feet, both in dark-blue socks, and wondered if Ching had six toes on one foot, as legend said. Ching began, "Congratulations, Yomei, on *The Brothers Yershov*. It's a remarkable achievement, and the awards it has received are all well deserved." The Ministry of Culture had just given the production team prizes for best dramatic creation and the best performance of the year.

"Thanks. I'm glad you like the play," said Yomei. "That means a lot to me."

"I guess the Soviets won't be pleased by our dramatic adaptation. Your play is sharper and more poignant than the novel. Also it's beautiful in a stark way, gutsy and austere, which I greatly admire."

Uncertain what Ching was really driving at, Yomei tried to tone down the talk about her success a bit, saying,

"Truth be told, I can't feel complacent about this. Our work was adapted from Kochetov's novel. Whatever our accomplishment, it is derivative by nature."

"Still I was very impressed. What's your next project?"

Yomei was startled, yet managed to reply, "We've been doing a new play, *The Fen River Flows Forever.*" In fact, she wasn't sure of this new project, which had run into resistance from some official censors who were set against it, saying it was vulgar in its presentation of the current countryside—mainly a reference to the loud folk music and the frolicsome folk dances Yomei had put onstage. She couldn't help but wonder whether Ching might have a hand in posing the obstacles to their new production. It was so hard to do genuine theater nowadays, especially in the capital. The positive acceptance of *The Brothers Yershov* was largely due to political circumstances, also because few people dared to speak against a project sponsored by the CCP's Propaganda Department.

Jiang Ching asked again, "Have you seen the play *Cuckoo Mountain* staged by the Shanghai Youth Theater?"

"No, I've heard that the Central Youth Theater is going to mount it in Beijing. I'll go see it when it's staged here."

"It was a good play but still has some problems. I would like to convert it into a Beijing opera. You're an expert and a renovator in theater arts, and your input will be invaluable to me. Can we collaborate to turn *Cuckoo Mountain* into a Beijing opera?"

Unsettled, Yomei said, "What do you expect me to do, Ching?" She knew the play was about how a peasant armed force in the Hunan region fought the local bandits three decades before and eventually joined the Red Army on Jinggang Mountain, so she suspected that Chairman Mao might be behind this play: Jinggang Mountain used to be his base. Within the Party he had often bragged that he was

always primed to go there and wage guerrilla warfare again
if he failed in any power struggle with his political rivals.

"The play obviously has some serious problems," Ching
said in an edgy voice about *Cuckoo Mountain*. "We'll have to fix
those problems first so as to tell a good and correct story,
then we can figure out how to make it into a Beijing opera."

"Ching, I'm afraid I can't participate in such a project.
First, if the play has problems, we should point them out
and let the production crew make the changes. It's their
play, so we can't just take it away from them and turn it into
a different thing. In other words, they have the copyright
and we ought to handle this professionally."

"Nonsense. The notion of copyright is obsolete, it's a
capitalist idea. Nobody should make money from the rights
anymore. We must produce some revolutionary model
plays to set high and correct standards for China's theater.
Chairman Mao says there's too much foreign and feudalistic
stuff on our stage and screen nowadays. You've produced
many foreign plays. Do you think you have committed
no political mistakes in your productions?" Ching's lens
flashed at Yomei while her lips were pursed.

A silence ensued. Yomei was somewhat petrified by
Ching's insinuations. The woman could always find fault
with her work, one way or another. Such a person could
even pick a bone in an egg. What should Yomei say now?

"Sister Ching," she finally managed to respond, "we've
known each other for more than two decades. You know I
can't hurt our colleagues' feelings like that. Honestly, your
request is hard for me, like a nail in my head I don't know
how to pull it out."

"If working together with me will hurt you that much,
then forget it. I'm sure our paths will cross more often in
the future. Let us leave the door open for now. I will need

your help, so consider my offer of collaboration seriously
and give me your final answer soon. OK?"

"I'll think about it for sure."

Yomei talked to Jin Shan about Jiang Ching's request.
He was alarmed, knowing the woman could be retaliatory
and vicious and wouldn't leave Yomei alone, so he suggested
she speak to Father Zhou and see if the premier could come
up with a solution. Jin Shan believed there must be some
political motivation in Jiang Ching's effort to break into the
field of theater again, so Yomei must be cautious and avoid
becoming a target of Ching's attack.

That Saturday evening, Yomei went to West Flower Hall,
the Zhous' residence. She told Father Zhou the series of
operas that Jiang Ching had been doing: *The Legend of the Red
Lantern*, *Taking Tiger Mountain by Strategy*, and now *Cuckoo Mountain*.
And there was also the ballet *The Red Detachment of Women*.
Probably some other theater projects were also underway,
since Ching, as the First Lady in the CCP, had infinite
resources and could make use of many people, organizing
them into teams and utilizing their talent and creativity
for her plays. Father Zhou looked amazed. He said Jiang
Ching couldn't be acting on her own. He seemed to imply
that Mao was the mastermind behind Ching's efforts, but
Father Zhou wasn't explicit about this. Yomei sensed he
meant that Mao had been using his wife to regain control
over the field of arts. Probably Mao wanted to return to
the center of political power through the avenue of arts
and propaganda. By occupying the stage and the screen, he
could place himself as the supreme leader in the minds of
the multitudes again.

Father Zhou sighed, then said, "Jiang Ching might
intend to take over the fields of culture and arts. That's her
way to impact people's mental life. So don't contradict her."

"All right, I'll be extra-cautious, but I can't humor her either," Yomei said. "The way she treats others' work is unprofessional and amounts to robbery, like plucking fruits from others' orchards without paying the owners. I can't lower myself to her level."

"Don't ever tell her what you think. She might take it out on you if she feels insulted and frustrated. She's unpredictable, like a nasty child's face."

"What should I do then?"

"Let me think about this. There must be a way to do your own work without getting in her way."

"But I've never interfered with her work at all. She has come to me again and again in spite of my refusal to collaborate with her. Each time she makes me feel as if I've just eaten a bug. She's unscrupulous and at times even threatens me, saying I may have made some political mistakes in producing so many foreign plays. Gosh, she politicizes everything. For her, art must be part of the revolutionary machine and must serve politics unconditionally—artwork must function as a banner or a weapon."

"That's Chairman Mao's stand too. So don't argue with Jiang Ching about this principle, which has already been adopted as our Party's policy on literature and arts. It's already sacrosanct. If you're not sure how to respond to Jiang Ching, just keep mum or change the topic. Give me a little time so I can figure out a solution, OK?"

"Sure, I'll listen to you."

Yomei felt agitated afterward, knowing she'd have to take up a new project soon or Jiang Ching, seeing her unoccupied, would return to her again. She and Jin Shan talked about Ching's efforts—the operas and the ballet. He saw more implications in her projects. Apparently, by weaponizing theater, she intended to play a more powerful role in politics and society. It looked like Mao was behind her, using arts as a breakthrough point to regaining the controlling power he had lost to Liu Shaoqi and Zhou Enlai after the great famine, so at all costs Yomei must stay away from the vortex of the political struggle. Having known Ching for decades, Jin Shan believed that she would settle old scores with those artists who had once slighted her or just surpassed her, and she would show them who was boss in China's theater and cinema now. It looked like Yomei might have no choice but to cope with Ching.

A week and a half later, Mother Deng called and asked Yomei to come for dinner the following Saturday. Yomei went over alone. This time Premier Zhou made a bold suggestion: She should leave Beijing for a remote place where she could continue with her theater work. He had in mind Daqing, the oil field in Heilongjiang Province, since there must be rich material from which she could draw inspiration for her art. She was taken aback by such a suggestion and didn't see the full implications yet. The oil field was far away, in the wilderness between Harbin and Tsitsihar. She said, "Little Lan is just ten years old and still needs me. What should I do about her?"

"You can take her with you," piped in Mother Deng, dipping a porcelain ladle back into the fish casserole sitting in the middle of the table, which was covered with a mauve cloth. Evidently, the Zhous had talked about this between themselves.

"Yes, why not?" Father Zhou said. "That will give her a different kind of education—to live among the masses at the bottom of society would toughen up Little Lan mentally and physically. There's nothing to lose for her."

"That's true," Yomei agreed. "It can be a salutary experience for her. I'm going to talk with Jin Shan and will let you know my decision soon."

"Take this as a temporary assignment. It will be safer for you to stay away from Beijing for a couple of years. You can come back once you finish your work at the oil field. Let's hope by then Jiang Ching will have something else to occupy herself with and will leave you alone."

"Do you think I should invalidate my Beijing residence?"

"Of course not. Treat your move to Daqing as taking a long stint far away."

"I see. I'll talk with Jin Shan about this."

Mother Deng joined in with a smile, "I can see you are so nice to Jin Shan. He ought to cherish you as a devoted wife, a great wife, I'd say."

"I do love him, Mom."

Father Zhou interjected, "I hope he will live up to your love, though." He sounded a touch piqued.

Maybe he still viewed Jin Shan as a rival for her love. No wonder Jin Shan hadn't come to see the Zhous in recent years, giving the excuse that he'd feel awkward. Probably besides feeling ashamed, as he claimed, he sensed some negative vibes at the Zhous'.

When she explained Father Zhou's suggestion to Jin Shan, he was astonished and kept silent for a good minute. Then he said, "That's not a bad idea actually. I have a gut feeling that there must be real drama in the life of the oil workers and that we can create genuine art in the northeast."

"You said 'we.' Does this mean you will join me there?" Yomei asked.

"Of course I'll go with you. I'd be restless if you went alone. Our family will move to Daqing and stay there a few years. The world is so vast, we shouldn't cocoon ourselves in a single place like Beijing. What's more, the oil field belongs to the Ministry of Petroleum Industry, which is within the domain of the State Council."

"What do you mean?"

"Father Zhou can protect you that way, since you will work under his jurisdiction."

"I see. That's why he suggested I go to the northeast—to stay beyond Jiang Ching's reach."

"That's right. Everyone knows Ching is vendetta personified. The farther you stay away from her, the better."

"True, we can keep out of her way, if we can't join her in hurting others. She views anyone who refuses to collude with her as her enemy."

"What's more," Jin Shan continued, "Chairman Mao said recently that Chinese theater and cinema must devote more attention to the workers and peasants and soldiers. So it will be safer for us to go join the oil workers and create fine plays about them."

"That's a good reason for us to head for the northeast. If we make plays about the oil field, no one can find fault with our work. We may even blaze new ground in spoken drama if we are lucky."

Yomei was pleased that her husband would be able to move with her to Daqing, and Jin Shan's decision cemented her resolve to leave Beijing.

Ever since he had recovered from the heart attack, Jin Shan had been semiretired and didn't go to the provinces alone for movie or drama projects anymore. He preferred to stay home, just to keep Yomei and Little Lan company. Every morning he'd go to a nearby park to practice tai chi, and he also enjoyed picking up groceries at the marketplace and cooking for his family. Now, even though his health had stabilized, he still didn't want to strike out on his own again, so he wanted to go to Daqing with Yomei if she was headed that way.

Once they decided to accept Premier Zhou's suggestion, Yomei wrote a letter to Jiang Ching to inform her of her job change—from now on, she would live and work at Daqing Oil Field as a kind of "education" so as to find dramatic inspiration "from the actual struggle of the workers in the northeast." In short, thanks to this new job assignment, she'd be away for some years at least. This implied she wouldn't be available for the dramatic projects under Ching's auspices from now on.

Sixty-Seven

Yomei didn't move to the northeast right away, since she had to pick up the slack in the production of *The Fen River Flows Forever* after the official critics and hacks had attacked it. Some actors were so unnerved by the abrasive criticism that they began considering how to wiggle themselves out of the cast, yet Yomei wouldn't let their labor go to waste and wanted to make sure the play ran for at least two or three weeks.

After the performance period was over in March 1964, she joined a group of artists to go and visit Daqing Oil Field. This large delegation, organized by the Ministry of Culture, comprised more than forty dignitaries—writers, musicians, composers, actors, and directors like Yomei. Yet unlike the other delegates, she had her own plan, wanting to see what life and work were like in that place. When they arrived, the land was still frozen everywhere, cloaked with snow. In spite of the howling wind and the iced-over roads, she enjoyed the visit and was moved to see the workers and their families so dedicated to the struggle of opening this oil field, the first large one in China, a country generally believed poor in petroleum deposits. Partly thanks to this oil field's production, Premier Zhou had declared the

previous fall that by the end of 1963 China had become
basically self-sufficient in petroleum products.

To entertain the workers and leaders of the oil field,
the delegates performed their works in a makeshift
auditorium—a large felt tent. Yomei got on the platform and
read a poem, "I Want to Sing," which she had written the
night before:

> *I want to sing of these heroes,*
> *Sing of their zestful life and brave struggle.*
> *From all corners of our country*
> *They've gathered in this wilderness,*
> *Making the land yield all the riches*
> *That will sustain generations to come.*
> *I want to sing of the callused hands*
> *That sink drills and swing mattocks*
> *To open a new path for our old nation . . .*

People were amazed by her resonant voice, charged with
youthful passion, even though she was already in her
forties. The poem showed her genuine feelings about this
place and the tens of thousands of people here, and it also
reflected her vision for her future work. She intended to put
down roots here and create plays celebrating the life and
dedication of the workers and their families.

The cultural delegation stayed at the oil field for ten
days, and then all its members left except for Yomei. She
believed she must know more about this place and the life
of these people, particularly their daily work and struggles.
In all likelihood, the oil field would be richer than any big
city in artistic material, and she intuited that she should stay
here as long as possible. By familiarizing herself with the

oil field and its employees she might eventually be able to produce plays that could represent the workers' indomitable spirit and manifest a different kind of dramatic beauty, raw and fresh and energetic. In short, she'd have to mix with the inhabitants to understand them well enough for her artistic creation. Above all, both she and Jin Shan had to make their art useful, as their contribution to the construction of this socialist country. To some extent, they too believed in the pragmatic function of the arts, a part of which was to serve the revolutionary cause. In spite of their dedication to the art of the theater, neither of them, given their circumstances and backgrounds, considered it possible to exist entirely outside of politics. They both saw that to serve the revolution was also their artistic mission, and therefore their art must take root at the bottom of society and must reflect the spirit of the times. Although they were artists at heart, they were also revolutionaries and Party members. This dichotomy within them made it unthinkable to separate their artistic pursuit completely from the ruling power, the Communist Party.

So Yomei went to the leaders of the oil field and expressed her wish to move here. They were amazed and also delighted to see that a highly accomplished theater expert, let alone one known as the country's number one woman spoken drama director, was willing to leave the capital for their frontier town of Sartu. "Sartu" is a Mongolian word that refers to a remote, isolated area, meaning "the place from which the Moon rises." Usually such a backwoods town didn't attract artists from big cities at all, so the leaders all welcomed Yomei. They even assigned her a suite in the guesthouse, because she'd told them that her husband would come and join her, since they both wanted to work to promote the cultural life at the oil field. But Yomei didn't accept the suite: instead, she wanted the same type of housing as a regular employee. Her wish was approved, and she moved into a three-room unit in a row house, with mud walls and a roof covered with red clay tiles, the regular kind of housing used by the workers' families. Her neighbors, warm and friendly, had no idea that she was Premier Zhou's daughter from Beijing.

To mix with the workers more easily, she asked the leaders to let her join a work unit. They issued her a set of canvas overalls and a hard hat and a pair of rubber boots and sent her to an oil well, where she met a famous model worker, a driller nicknamed Iron Man Wang, who was a national hero at the time. Wang looked rustic and was of medium height, with coppery skin and a rugged face that was often lined with dust. He was such an unflagging derrick man that he even bragged, "When the oil workers give a howl, even the Earth will tremble thrice." He always urged his fellow workers to "make the impossible possible." It was his drilling team that had first struck oil in Daqing and thus marked the beginning of the new era of petroleum production in China.

Soon Yomei and Iron Man Wang became close friends. He tried to dissuade her from staying on the drilling site, saying it could be dangerous, but she wouldn't listen, determined to experience what the workers were going through. She even moved into a tiny room in one of the derrick hands' makeshift dorms, which were made from derelict train cars placed at the site. She also ate in their canteen, where the food was decent and plenty—these oil workers were at the frontline of China's industrial development and better supplied than other workers. Moreover, Heilongjiang Province, known as China's granary, never lacked basic foodstuffs. Soon Yomei learned that Iron Man Wang's mother, wife, and youngest daughter all had a medical condition that was partly due to malnutrition and an iodine deficiency, but he didn't make enough money to buy medicine and nutritious food for them. So she asked Jin Shan to send over some drugs and canned meat and fish, which she passed on to the Wangs. She also gave the Iron Man a Japanese-made transistor radio, a rarity at the time, so that he could keep up with news. By and by, Iron Man Wang began to call her Sister Yomei, their friendship further cemented. Whenever she was unsure of something, she'd turn to him for advice.

As time went by, she noticed that many women here, especially the workers' wives, were also actively participating in the oil production, though indirectly and in their own ways. They didn't appear at the drilling rigs, but they did all the logistic work that ensured an adequate life for their husbands. They took part in road constructions, in opening farmland to grow fresh produce, in raising cattle and milk cows; and from the spring to the fall, many of them worked in the black-soil fields, planting, thinning out seedlings, weeding, and harvesting. Every team of housewives grew a lot of soybeans so that they could make bean sprouts and tofu in the wintertime. They even mixed mud with bits of straw and used the mixture to ram-build the walls of the dorm houses. Others even repaired and drove trucks and the "iron oxen" (tractors). They also staffed stores, the post offices, dining centers, kindergartens, the clinics and the hospital, and the tailoring and mending shops, where they worked foot-powered Butterfly sewing machines. Intuitively Yomei felt it was on these women she must focus her attention. Dramatically speaking, it might be difficult to produce a play about the actual struggle at a drilling rig, whereas the domestic sphere could be rich and fascinating and more resonant. So she often joined the women in their homes and at their work sites.

Her intuition turned out to be right. She found the women's activities exciting and meaningful, and she began to mingle with them more often, joining their work and chatting with them at length. At night she would scribble down notes to keep records of the day's activities and her discoveries. Little by little her journal with a green plastic cover was filled up, and then she bought another one. In the early summer, she befriended Lu Ju, a cowgirl who tended cattle for the oil field's life section and took the animals to the grassland every day. Though she was small-framed, Lu Ju was hardy, holding a long whip with a sharp sickle stuck in her belt. People pegged her as a tomboy who wasn't afraid of the wild animals she encountered when pasturing the cattle on the hillsides and in the wilds. Time and again, she had run into wolves, which followed the herd, and she had fought them with her sickle. Once she had even killed a wolf. People advised her to stay close to the oil field with her large herd, since there were bears roaming in the forests and bushlands. Or they told her she should arm herself with a hunting rifle. But she always set out with just a sickle.

Yomei and Iron Man Wang

Yomei approached Lu Ju and asked to go out with her to pasture the cattle in the wilderness. Seeing such a beautiful lady with such a refined bearing, Lu Ju said, "Are you sure you can do it?"

"I'm as strong as you," said Yomei. "Don't look down on me."

"There are lots of mosquitoes and horseflies."

"If they haven't eaten you up, I'll be OK too. I'm sure my flesh doesn't taste better than yours to them—you're so young, your blood must be fresher."

Early the next morning, they set out together with the herd, more than a hundred head of cattle, taking them to graze on the dew-soaked grass on a hillside. It was cool and pleasant before sunrise. In the distance, the oil derricks stood, one after another, some shaded in billowing haze. Yomei observed them—the patches of fog around the wells made the metal frames resemble small Ferris wheels in slow motion. Those drilling sites were so far away that one had to take a bus to get there. Yomei reminded herself to have some photographs of those derricks taken from the distance, so that they might serve as a reference for her stage design in the future.

When the sun was high above the treetops, beating down in full force, it got hot. With the morning dew gone, the air flecked with insects, some of which were circling over their heads, Yomei took off her boonie hat, waving it to shoo them away. She said, "My goodness, the mosquitoes here are like small dragonflies and droning like bombers." She used her hat to keep a swirl of them at bay.

The two of them were sitting on a large rock, watching the herd below them. The sun was blazing relentlessly, and soon the scorching heat dispelled most of the mosquitoes, while some glossy bluebottles flickered around, humming fitfully. Lu Ju was local, born here, though her parents had emigrated to the northeast from Shandong Province thirty years before. She was familiar with this area and could tell Yomei the names of the birds that called and tooted. She also said that life at the oil field was better than in the villages because there was a regular income and enough food in the canteen, so she liked her work here. "My only regret is I didn't go to middle school," she confessed to Yomei. Yomei suggested that she attend the night classes, but Lu Ju shook her bird's nest of hair, saying, "My head is too dense to hold anything in it. I guess I was born to herd cattle, to lollygag in the wilds."

"But there's a literacy class in the evenings. You can sit in on it for free."

"I tried it once, but it didn't work for me."

Yomei enjoyed the cowgirl's company and chatted with her casually. Lu Ju had brought lunch in an army satchel—water and buns stuffed with green cabbage and ground roe venison. Around noon, when the sun was flaming just above their heads, they began to have lunch. They ate slowly. Yomei couldn't help but wonder what she might have felt like if she had been a cowgirl here like Lu Ju, who was so content and carefree.

On the third day of their cattle-tending, Yomei began to have sunburns on her face and neck. Lu Ju teased, "See, I told you this work wasn't for a city lady like you."

Yomei countered, "You know, I once worked in the fields when I was in my teens."

"Where was that?" Lu Ju narrowed her eyes, looking incredulous.

"In Yan'an."

"My, you mean you're a Red Army woman? But you look so young."

Pleased by the compliment, Yomei simpered. "I was a soldier there and also a student."

"Still if you were in Yan'an before the new China, that means you're an official."

"I've been working at a theater, just a stage director." In spite of saying that, she was actually a midlevel cadre. She earned one hundred twenty yuan a month, twice the amount that a skilled worker made here. But she didn't explain to Lu Ju in detail because she wanted to stay as close as possible to the cowgirl.

That afternoon a pair of yellow wolves appeared at the edge of the pine woods. The beasts looked sickly and famished, their fur in clumps. They were roaming around and watching the cattle with ravenous eyes, as if they were about to attack a calf. Lu Ju was startled and sprang to her feet. She handed the sickle to Yomei and said, "Use this if they come near the herd." She then strode to the wolves while brandishing her long whip with loud cracks. She yelled at them, "Go away, beasts. If you come close to my herd, I'm gonna flay you to death!"

She rushed to the wolves, swinging the whip forcefully. It had a leather tip and could cut like a knife. Fearful that the beasts might turn on Lu Ju and that there might be more wolves lurking in the woods, Yomei followed her, wielding the sickle. The wolves shied away, then turned around and headed for the woods, their hindquarters so scraggy that the bones stuck up the skins as they were trotting away. Yomei breathed a sigh of relief and noticed the soft down on her own arms standing on end. She also got goosebumps, while her heart was still pitter-pattering. Slightly out of breath, she asked Lu Ju what she would do if a large pack of wolves appeared.

"Then I'll be on the defensive. With only a pair of them, I can afford to play tough," Lu Ju said.

"You mean to bluff?"

"That's right. The second you hightail it, they'll pounce on you and your herd."

"How many wolves are living in this area?"

"All told, two or three score, I guess."

"How about bears? If a bear appears, can you chase it away with a whip?"

"Not really. There're a couple of black bears on that mountain, but usually they don't attack cattle. As long as there are crops in the fields, they don't bother to prey on a large animal like a cow or bull. It's tigers that are more dangerous."

In spite of her apparent calm, Yomei was a bit disturbed by the encounter. She was concerned about Lu Ju's safety. The cowgirl urged her to stay home the next day, but Yomei insisted on coming along. She didn't want to give Lu Ju the impression that she was scared of wolves, so she continued to tend cattle in the wilderness for another two days. But she spoke about the wolves to Iron Man Wang, who was a leader in the oil field's labor union. Indeed, what if a sizable pack of the wild animals appeared and attacked the herd? Brave as Lu Ju was, she couldn't possibly keep them away and might even put her own life at risk. So they ought to assign another hand to go with her. This way the two could work as a pair, helping each other in the wilds. Iron Man Wang agreed to consider Yomei's suggestion seriously, but he gave Lu Ju a Mosin-Nagant rifle and twenty bullets instead of a human companion, since she was in the militia and knew how to shoot. She was pleased about the weapon and always kept its bayonet raised when she set out in the mornings.

Yomei had a portrait of herself taken by a young photographer in front of some oil derricks. She was pleased to see her features now, slightly weather-beaten and with a few sunburned patches on her face. She mailed the headshot to her husband, Lily, her sister Yolan, their brother Yang, and Aunt Jun. She meant to show them how well she had acclimated to Sartu and that she was living like a regular worker now.

In his reply, Yang wrote that his biography of Marshal Zhu Deh was already at the printer. Now that he was done with the book, he wanted to transfer to a new work unit, ideally to a college in Beijing. In principle, Uncle Zhu Deh had agreed to help him transfer, but it wasn't clear yet where he'd go. He praised Yomei for having given up the comforts and privileges of the capital for the sake of making genuine art. He said he was proud of her.

Yomei also wrote a long essay titled "Daqing Correspondence," which described the life and struggle of the workers and their families, particularly how the wives coped with the difficulties inside and outside their households. She copied the long piece in triplicate and sent them to her husband and Lily, asking them to comment. They both thought it was rich and significant material out of which she must make a new play. They urged her to get the essay published. Later Yomei also mailed a copy of the essay to her brother Yang, who had just become vice president of the People's University in Beijing. Yang enjoyed the piece very much too and told her to get it published somewhere. But she didn't send it to a magazine until a year later. At the end of 1965, it came out in the biweekly *Red Flag*, the Party's number one magazine. By then she and Jin Shan were already coming to the end of rehearsing their play *The Rising Sun*, which was in spirit based on the long essay and which praised and celebrated the dedication of the workers' wives to the opening of China's largest oil field.

· Sixty-Eight ·

On January 6, 1965, Jin Shan and Little Lan arrived at Sartu to join Yomei. It was good timing. The spring festival was three weeks away and school was in winter recess here—Little Lan would have some time to adapt to the new environment. It was cold outside, but the mud-walled house, heated by coal stoves, was warm and cozy. The window panes were frosted over, displaying wavelike patterns that blazed against the sunlight, and every family's front entrance was covered by a thick cotton curtain over a solid wooden door. Outside there was snow everywhere, but Little Lan still went out to join the neighbors' children, riding a sleigh on slopes, fighting merrily with snowballs, whipping tops on the flat iced ground, skating on a pond close by. They also caught sparrows and wrens and orioles with a wicker basket propped up on the rim by a short stick attached to a long string—when the birds got under the basket to eat grains spread on the ground, the string would be pulled to trap them. Soon Little Lan got frostbite on her ears, so Yomei made sure the child wore earmuffs and a fur hat and mittens whenever she went out. If it was too cold, she'd make her daughter put on a thick face mask to keep her nose from freezing.

Back in Beijing, Little Lan had been an average student,
but the elementary school here was weaker in pedagogy and
she skipped the third grade. She joined the fourth graders
directly when she started.

Ever since the first snow, the wives in the workers'
village, the residential compound at the oil field, had
stopped going out to work. The land was frozen, so most
of their activities had to be indoors now. Lately some
young women, together with a few literate men, formed
a dramatic group, intending to create skits regularly to
entertain the oil workers and inspire others. Prior to Jin
Shan's arrival, Yomei had seen *The Broad Road*, a one-act
play made by the amateur actors in the General Machinery
Plant. It was about controversy and conflicts in the
workers' families, mainly between husbands and wives,
who were divided in their attitudes toward the women's
participation in the logistical work of the oil field. Some
believed they must take part in some production activities,
such as opening crop fields and growing produce to
improve the diet of the workers' families, whereas some,
especially those from big cities, felt too embarrassed to
do such heavy farmwork. Toward the end of the play, the
group that supported participation in the production
activities prevailed, and they even rallied to the slogan
"Make revolution with five shovels," which meant to
start women's supporting activities with primitive tools.
The play was still rough in spots, but it was lively and
full of promise, so Yomei gave the amateur drama
group some tips that helped improve their performance
quite a bit. Once it was staged, the audience responded
enthusiastically, so it was performed more than ten times
in various plants in the oil field. Many people from local
communities came to see it too.

The week after Jin Shan's arrival, Yomei took him to the Third Plant to see *The Broad Road*, whose liveliness and intensity threw him into ecstasy. Afterward, back in their mud-walled house, he continued to rave about the short play, saying it was an eye-opener and full of potential. It might embody a different kind of drama, one that unfolded on a small domestic scale and spread beyond to the large terrain of the new society. Yomei agreed and could also see the play's potential in exploring women's roles in the socialist revolution and in the new China. She and Jin Shan talked about the skit until two in the morning, convinced that they could create a full-length play based on *The Broad Road*. Since Yomei was a better writer than Jin Shan, she set to work on the script.

The next day she went to the headquarters of the General Machinery Plant and spoke with its leaders, describing her intention to create a full play based on that skit. They were excited and assigned an assistant to help her with the script and also to facilitate the rehearsal down the road. On top of that, they gave her an office in which her crew members could gather and discuss their work. But for now, besides the assistant the only other member on her crew was her husband. Jin Shan and Yomei often joked that they were running "a real mom-and-pop shop" here. Whenever she encountered a problem in writing the script, she would talk with her husband, who was well experienced in stage production and could always offer some useful advice.

Winter was long here and there weren't many activities in Sartu, so it was easy for Yomei to stay indoors and concentrate on writing. Every evening she and Jin Shan compared notes, which was also the time when she could brief him on her progress. They envisioned that the

play, not having a title yet, would be made up of six acts
and populated with a large cast of characters, mostly
women, given that the play was about the experience of the
housewives at the oil field. Jin Shan was elated whenever
they talked about its progress, and he kept saying this new
kind of play might be a breakthrough in China's spoken
drama. Yomei thought it could be a milestone in her career
too, if it was well made. Motivated by that grand vision, they
worked hard, with a peculiar kind of intensity they had not
experienced before.

A month later, a draft of the script was ready, and Yomei
showed it first to her friend Iron Man Wang. At the sight
of the title, *The Rising Sun*, Wang beamed, saying, "What a
great title. It reflects our wives' indomitable spirit." He
read the play that very night and spoke with Yomei the next
morning. He told her that the script had blown his mind,
though he had a couple of small suggestions, mainly about
the accuracy of some details. For instance, some of the
women were actually illiterate, and the work-team leader in
the play shouldn't have asked every one of them to read out
a long article by turns. While Wang was speaking, Yomei
jotted down his comments.

"Please don't take what I'm saying too seriously," Wang
said with genuine embarrassment. "I'm just blathering."

"These are important details and can help us make the
play more authentic." She went on scribbling her notes.

She accepted practically every suggestion Iron Man Wang
offered. Jin Shan was confident about the script now, saying
the oil field leaders should be pleased about this project and
support it wholeheartedly.

Indeed when the script had been presented to them,
they went into raptures, saying this play looked "cunningly
slight" but was actually "thick and heavy," meaning "full of

tremendous import." So they were totally supportive of the project. They told Yomei and Jin Shan that they could have as many people and resources as they wanted. However, in spite of their full support, the leaders still had doubts about its production—where on earth could they find the actors good enough to perform this forceful play? They hoped Yomei and Jin Shan could use their connections in Beijing and get a bunch of star actors over to participate in the stage production. To their surprise, Yomei said the play mustn't use any professional actors at all. She and Jin Shan preferred to have regular housewives and workers for the cast. Though not fully convinced, the leaders agreed to let them pick those who Yomei and Jin Shan believed could act onstage.

Yet the process of picking the right amateur actors was arduous, partly because the workers and their wives were from different regions of the country and spoke their own dialects. The play needed those who could speak good Mandarin at least. Besides, the actors should have a decent physical appearance and be able to understand their parts and act them out. Very often after auditioning for a whole day, Yomei and Jin Shan couldn't decide on a single person. It was particularly difficult to find suitable male actors, who ought to be articulate and have a bearing that fit the drama onstage. So Yomei and Jin Shan kept their eyes peeled for suitable candidates. For two days they interviewed men for the role of Chief Wang, who in the play had his doubts about the housewives' ability to open crop fields and grow produce and build mud-walled dorm houses. Then, as Yomei and Jin Shan went to watch "the good news team" of the General Machinery Plant rehearsing their new skit, they saw a young man step on the stage to deliver a prop for the actors—a chalkboard that was still naked with the natural color of the wood. The round-faced man set up the board, then ran away while the actors looked unsatisfied about the unfinished prop, saying, "This is only a brown board." In a flash, the deliverer came back with a black coat and hung it over the board. He said, "See, it's a blackboard now." People all laughed. Jin Shan and Yomei asked Yang Dasheng, the assistant assigned to them by the oil field, "Who is that fellow?" They were told that the young man was Mu Rongchang from the supply center. Both Yomei and Jin Shan declared, "He should be Chief Wang in our play."

For two weeks, they couldn't find a suitable actor for Master Li, a backward character in the play who grumbles about his wife's going out to toil in the fields with a hoe or shovel, saying her workplace should be their home, around the kitchen range. Then Yomei remembered a cameo actor in *The Broad Road* who had appeared only on that evening when Jin Shan had seen the skit. One of the actors was sick, so the plant's propaganda chief grabbed hold of a substitute from somewhere. The man hadn't acted onstage before and couldn't remember all the lines on such short notice. Yomei was amused by the impromptu arrangement and told him that he didn't have to say the exact lines, that he could speak in his own way insofar as the meaning was the same and clear. So the man agreed to join the cast, and he acted naturally onstage. Later the propaganda chief told Yomei and Jin Shan that his name was Sun Zaoli, and he was their projectionist. In the beginning, Zaoli had refused to step in for the sick actor, saying he couldn't perform onstage at all. He screwed up his broad eyes. "Never done it, not interested," he told the propaganda chief, who was trying to persuade him to fill in. But the chief promised to treat Zaoli to roast beef and fried potatoes and a bottle of wheat liquor, so the man agreed to try. Yomei was impressed by his performance, so now she remembered Zaoli and invited him to join their crew. But the projectionist refused to act anymore and didn't even respond to the summons from General Machinery Plant's headquarters. Then the plant's supervisor went to Zaoli's dorm at night and ordered him to come with him. Still Zaoli begged off, saying he was no material for the stage. The supervisor told him, "Cut out all this mischief! Director Sun Yomei went to General Manager Song to ask for you because you didn't show up at the rehearsal today. If you don't join the crew, I might get fired. Come along now." Manager Song Zhenming was the head of the entire oil field and had become Yomei's friend and totally supported the production of *The Rising Sun*, believing it might make the oil field better known to the whole country. That was why she'd gone to him directly for help.

Thus Yomei coerced Sun Zaoli into joining the acting crew. Zaoli was very talented and learned the art of acting fast. Some years later he became a stage director too, one pretty active in the local drama circle.

The workers' wives in the play were less difficult to find, since the women all were to act out their own lives and work. Most of them were naturals for their roles. Both Yomei and Jin Shan were satisfied with the female actors, even feeling they would be scintillating onstage. After all the other roles had been filled, there was still a key role, Party Secretary Luo, that remained vacant. Such a character must appear upright, strapping, with a deep resonant voice, but thus far, they hadn't found a man fitting the role.

Wang Yuanpu was a culture clerk at the oil field. Ever since Yomei and Jin Shan had started working on the play, he had been helping them select actors, because he was familiar with the workers and their families and also with the arts circles in Sartu. He knew that these days both Yomei and Jin Shan had been worried about the role of Secretary Luo, but he couldn't think of anyone suitable either. Then one night, on leaving their office, Jin Shan said, "Yuanpu, why don't you try the role of Secretary Luo?"

"Me? That won't do. I've never acted before," Yuanpu blurted out.

"At least give it a try," Yomei urged.

Wang Yuanpu stood five ten, had a rich clear voice, and had also graduated from high school. Such a twelve-year education was rare among the people here. It wouldn't be easy to find someone with his kind of qualifications. So Jin Shan thought he could be a possibility.

For some reason, in spite of turning down the offer, Yuanpu began to memorize Secretary Luo's lines once he was back home. He paced up and down his small family room and at moments paused to watch himself in a mirror on a wardrobe. Even at meals he couldn't stop rehearsing the lines in his head.

A few days later he plucked up his nerves and told Jin Shan that he'd like to join the cast. Once at rehearsal, he was exceptional, showing an intuitive understanding of the drama and what was expected of him. Both Yomei and Jin Shan were delighted to settle on him. Now, finally, in the early fall the cast was formed. By then, the script had been revised several times and was more polished and ready.

The rehearsal proceeded well, in part because the amateurs were acting out themselves and their own lives. They didn't need a lot of training and they followed the director's instructions faithfully because they hadn't formed their own ways of acting yet. Yomei tried to preserve the original rawness in their performance. Whenever someone strove to be like a professional, she would stop him or her, saying, "No, no, that doesn't sound right, it's too much like stage dialogue. It must be Little Yang [her assistant] who taught you to speak like that, right? Don't try to be refined and artsy. Speak in your own manner and in the way in which you feel comfortable."

When they had corrected themself, Yomei would say, "This feels comfortable, doesn't it? Now you can stand up and speak while you move around. Try to be yourself."

One woman complained that she didn't know how to walk onstage, as if her feet no longer belonged to her. Yomei was surprised, then said, "No idea how to walk? How did you come into this room? Now, start from the beginning—push the door open, step in, take off your headscarf and your overcoat, then sit down. Repeat the whole process once more."

Seeing the woman moving at ease now, Yomei enthused, "This is wonderful. How naturally you can do this!"

She mixed intimately with the women in the cast and often laughed and wept with them when the drama reached a hilarious or heart-wrenching point. At times touched and overcome with emotion, she collapsed with them on the rehearsal ground, their arms wrapped around each other while they were laughing or sobbing together with abandon. Jin Shan said he had never before worked with a group of actors who could get so deep into the drama.

In late fall, the play premiered in the oil field. People were struck by its liveliness and authenticity. The most common response was "It's so real!" After the first night the crew performed more than ten times in Sartu, and every time the auditorium was packed, elbow to elbow. Some people sat on the steps along the walls and some stood on their feet in the back. The leaders of the oil field were moved, and declared, "*The Rising Sun* is a brand-new kind of

drama that shows the brave spirit of our oil workers and
their heroic wives." They also reported their conclusions
to Beijing. Soon orders came from above that the amateur
troupe go to the capital to perform for the general public
and for some senior leaders.

At first the actors thought this was just a regular
invitation asking them to perform a couple of times in
Beijing at most, but the play took the capital by storm
and was staged again and again. People hadn't seen such
a dramatic work before, one whose actors were actually
workers and their family members, enacting their own
life and struggle onstage. The play became a cultural
phenomenon—a breakthrough in theater arts. It didn't even
have an author, since Yomei was listed only as an "adapter"
at that time. Such an approach was absolutely original. The
production crew even went to perform on college campuses
and at army barracks in the Beijing area. One day Yomei
told the crew to get ready for an important performance.
Toward the evening they realized they were going to
Zhongnanhai to perform for the national leaders in the
small auditorium there. They were beside themselves with
joy, never having thought they'd reach such a destination.

Many leaders and their families went to see the play,
including Liu Shaoqi, Zhu Deh, and of course the Zhous.
They were all struck by the fresh presentation of the vast
landscape dotted with oil derricks in the backdrop and also
fascinated by the workers' struggle, their wives' labor in the
crop fields, and the construction of the mud-walled houses.
The women's collective activities served to define their
new roles in the new society. When their production team
displayed their produce in barrows—colossal pumpkins,
long turnips, large napa cabbages, mammoth sunflowers
the size of car wheels, giant potatoes that each weighed over

four pounds—the audience was amused and applauded.
Rarely did a play show so much of the rawness of life. At
the end, when the song "The Workers' Families Make
Revolution at Daqing" started and a team of housewives
strode across the stage raising a broad red banner, Premier
Zhou, evidently moved and proud, rose and applauded. The
entire audience followed suit.

The moment the curtain fell, Yomei ran up to the
crew and told them all to gather onstage. She said,
"Look who's coming!" Following her forefinger, they saw
Premier Zhou, accompanied by the top officials of the
Ministry of Petroleum Industry, ascending the side stairs.
Overwhelmed with joy, the acting crew rushed over to
shake hands with the premier. Many of them were still in
their denim overalls or cotton-padded jackets, a few women
in roomy slacks and washed-out jackets, and some were
wearing huge red flowers on their chests. Jin Shan called
to his assistant Yang Dasheng to go over and keep people in
order, but that was impossible. Premier Zhou kept shaking
hands with them patiently, now and again pausing to chat
a little. Oddly, some women broke out sobbing, and none
of the other actors could control their emotions anymore.
Tears were flowing among the whole crew. Yomei was
dazzled and also touched. These people from the bottom
of society had never had such an opportunity to meet a
top leader like Father Zhou. So she stepped aside and just
looked at them, feeling proud and rapturous as well.

Premier Zhou went to the front of them and said loudly,
"Let us sing a song together to celebrate your success."
Without hesitation, he started the first line of the song "We
Are Marching on a Broad Road." The whole crowd began
following him in one voice, while he raised his left arm to
beat time. Within seconds the entire auditorium joined in.

Later Yomei revealed to the acting crew that Premier Zhou had actually had a snack prepared for them, but seeing the tears gushing out of their eyes and given that it was already so late, he didn't order that the sweet fruit dumplings be served. Everyone on the production crew felt regretful, blaming themselves for having tear ducts soft like sponge; otherwise, they could have shared a night snack with Premier Zhou. That would have been something they could brag about to their children and grandchildren. Sun Zaolin, as if still playing the role of the backward husband, told them, "You've never gotten so overjoyed as to forget what to do next, huh?" That was also his way of lamenting the missed snack prepared for them by the premier.

· Sixty-Nine ·

Premier Zhou loved the play and saw it three times. He told Yomei that she should produce more plays like *The Rising Sun*. "This is pioneering work," he said. "There should be a second and then a third play of this kind." He also urged her and Jin Shan to form another team of actors, so that *The Rising Sun* could be performed in various provinces as a model play that combined professionalism with the masses in the artistic production. Indeed, in this respect, the play was a trailblazer. Following Father Zhou's instructions, Yomei and Jin Shan assembled a Cast B of actors, which soon began to perform in the provinces of central China together with Cast A. Wherever the two acting groups went, they were enthusiastically received. During the first six months of 1966, the play was performed 210 times and more than a quarter million people saw it. It made history in Chinese theater—no play had ever reached such a vast audience so quickly. The Ministry of Culture decided to make a movie of *The Rising Sun*, so without delay Yomei and Jin Shan returned to the oil field to plunge into filmmaking. More experienced in cinema than Yomei, Jin Shan wanted to follow the same format of the spoken drama production and avoid using professional actors in the film. Soon the two of them began auditioning people to find actors for the movie while working on the screenplay too.

Meanwhile, a lot had been going on in Beijing. In the early spring of 1966, the Central Experimental Theater and the National Youth Art Theater merged. Even though they were absent from the capital, Yomei and Jin Shan were both appointed as stage directors at the new theater. Now, after fourteen years, they were working in the same company again. They heard that a political campaign had begun in the newly established theater that had been partly triggered by Jin Shan's proposal to put on the representative plays by Tian Han and Yang Hansheng. The plays had somehow become labeled as "poisonous weeds," though in truth they were already modern classics of Chinese drama. It was said that Kang Sheng, the man responsible for political purges two decades earlier in Yan'an who operated behind the scenes most of the time, had masterminded this struggle in arts circles. He was in charge of the Party's ideological work, and political intrigues were his forte and field of action. Yomei had known Kang Sheng for many years, and in the early 1950s Kang had written her long, obsequious letters that praised her productions and commented on traditional Chinese theater and arts in general. Apparently the sickly, conniving man had intended to curry favor with her because she had served as Mao's interpreter in the Soviet Union, where Kang had assumed she had deep and extensive connections. He might also have believed that an intimate relationship between Mao and Yomei might develop, since many pretty women, given such an opportunity of being around the top leader, would make what they considered the best use of it, exercising their charm over Mao. Kang Sheng couldn't imagine that Yomei would pay no mind to the Great Leader, not even treating him as an interesting man. Yomei always had misgivings about Kang's warmth and friendliness toward her. She knew he and Jiang Ching were very close, and were both from Shandong Province, and that it was Kang Sheng who had in Yan'an introduced Jiang Ching to Mao, so Yomei had always been on guard when dealing with the wily Kang. Now, he seemed to have come to the foreground, helping Jiang Ching claw her way into the world of arts. Knowing the deep connection between Ching and Kang Sheng, Yomei and Jin Shan shared a strong foreboding, both afraid that something ominous might be in the offing.

They were further convinced when Father Zhou visited Daqing Oil Field in early May. The premier met them privately, and together they took a walk after dinner. He revealed to them that the situation in the CCP's top circle was irksome, even precarious at the moment. A large political movement seemed on the way, so both of them must be very careful from now on. He urged them not to appear too close to the Zhous, because if his political opponents couldn't hurt him directly, they might turn on some of those who worked for him or were related to him.

"Can I write to you like before?" Yomei asked, quite disturbed.

Zhou Enlai's face dropped a bit. "Just be careful about what you say in your letters. Always assume that some other eyes will read your letters before they reach me."

"Then I'll try not to write if I can't speak my mind," said Yomei.

Father Zhou breathed a sigh, looking around to make sure no others were within earshot and sight, other than his guard behind them. He said under his breath to both Yomei and Jin Shan, "Just be alert and try to grow another pair of eyes on the back of your head."

What he meant was that they must exercise their vigilance against political intrigues, which might come from every direction and which seemed to grow more rampant and more malevolent day by day. They had to learn how to protect themselves and avoid doing anything beyond the pale. The premier couldn't tell them explicitly that the Cultural Revolution was about to break out. It was initiated by Mao as a way to incite the masses to smash governments at all levels and to take power back from Liu Shaoqi and Deng Xiaoping and their followers—the so-called capitalist roaders, those who pulled the revolution in a capitalist direction. Mao was willing to turn the whole country upside down as long as he could regain the supreme power in China.

As Father Zhou hinted, in late May the Cultural Revolution broke out, and on some level this began to reshape everyone's life and throw the entire country into a lawless state. All remaining performances of *The Rising Sun* were called off, and all the actors were sent back to their work units. Changchun Film Studio wrote to Jin Shan and Yomei and revoked the movie contract. All these setbacks, in fact, might have just been repercussions of more ruinous happenings in the top circle: apparently someone had intended to deliver a blow to Premier Zhou by striking down his pet theater project, embodied by *The Rising Sun*. Again, Yomei could see the traces of Jiang Ching's hands behind this.

Then they heard from their work unit, the new theater, which summoned both of them back to Beijing to "join the Cultural Revolution." They had no choice but to return. Having heard that schools and colleges in the capital were in chaos, they decided to let Little Lan stay in Sartu for some time, where education continued and life was still normal and safe and where the girl was treated as Yomei's daughter. She already had many friends and would be helped and protected by the people of the oil field. Above all else, she could stay with the Nius, who had become close friends of her parents. So Yomei and Jin Shan went back to the capital in early summer without Little Lan.

They found Beijing in chaos and could feel tension in the air. Everywhere there were Red Guards from the provinces, and their presence made the city appear younger, teeming with youthful faces. Many groups of the Red Guards raised flags emblazoned with slogans like "Right to Rebel!" "Wipe out Evil Elements!" "Carry on Class Struggle!" "Defend the Party's Central Committee!" Those young people swarmed into the capital to get reviewed by Chairman Mao in Tiananmen Square, where waves of flags surged like a red sea. Hundreds of thousands of them had come, traveling free and getting free board and beds along the way as well as in the capital. The whole country seemed to be on the move, the youngsters wearing army jackets and caps and scarlet armbands, their waists cinched with leather or canvas belts. They trekked on foot or rode buses and trains to Beijing. Even the Red Guards leaving the capital after being reviewed by Mao didn't go home directly, and instead they'd headed for other places to mobilize the masses to join the revolution, which was like a firestorm swallowing the whole land.

Soon after Yomei returned to the capital, she received a note from Jiang Ching inviting her over the next weekend, saying they'd have some important matters to discuss. Both Yomei and Jin Shan were agitated by the invitation, which was like a summons. They couldn't fathom what the woman had up her sleeve, yet Yomei had no option but to go and meet her.

She had heard of the success of Jiang Ching's opera *The Legend of the Red Lantern*, which had premiered in Beijing the summer before. It had garnered numerous rave reviews and also been hyped as a revolutionary model play. Even Chairman Mao saw it and praised the performance, so the opera became a feather in Ching's cap. Ever since being back in Beijing, Yomei had avoided seeing the opera, unwilling to have anything to do with it. Now in her meeting with Ching, she'd better not touch this topic. If it came up, she must provide a reasonable excuse for not having seen the play. Perhaps she could say she'd been far away in the northeast and missed out on the performance.

She went to the Zhongnanhai compound to see Jiang Ching. The moment she sat down in her office on Mao's premises, Ching came in and shook hands with Yomei, smiling without opening her mouth. She told a servant to bring some fruit. In an instant, a wisp of a woman, in her early twenties and with a bony face and two short pigtails, stepped in, carrying a single huge pear and two porcelain plates stacked together. She put the fruit on a table and unwrapped a napkin to produce a stainless-steel knife that was about a foot long, with a curved blade. She was ready to peel the giant pear in front of Ching and the guest. Yomei was astonished by the size of the knife, which looked more suitable for slaughtering hogs.

She was also amazed to see such a golden pear with a smattering of russet specks on its skin. It weighed more than three pounds, she guessed. Never had she seen such a humongous fruit. "What kind of pear is this?" she asked.

"Dangshan pear from Anhui Province," Ching said. "We received a couple yesterday."

Ching motioned for the servant to go ahead. Wordlessly the woman began peeling—under the blade a ribbon of the peel unfolded while the white flesh was being revealed. On the other plate the peel piled up without a break. It extended many feet long, and was coiled up in whorls. Within a minute, the peeling was done. Then the woman cut half of the pear into cubes the size of tiny match boxes and put toothpicks on them and placed the plate on the tea table between Ching and the guest.

"Now try this, Yomei," Ching said.

Yomei picked up a piece and took a bite. It was juicy, sweet, and fragrant. "This is yummy. Thank you so much, Ching. This is the first time I've tasted Dangshan pear. What a treat!" She also thanked the servant, who left noiselessly with the peel and the core and the wrapped knife. The uncut half of the pear was still sitting in the plate on the table.

"Take as much as you want, Yomei," Ching said and gave a tight-lipped smile.

"Thanks. I must have a second." She picked up another piece.

"Yomei, I saw your play *The Rising Sun*," Ching said with her chin lowered to her neck. "It's really impressive, and I love it. What a cunning play. It seems simple and small, but it has tremendous resonance and extensive ramifications."

"Thanks very much for your generous words."

"Now I'm wondering if we can collaborate to turn it into a Beijing opera."

Flabbergasted, Yomei stopped chewing and didn't know what to say. Ching pressed on: "Like I told you, together we can make a revolution in China's theater. Your new play could serve as a harbinger of China's new revolutionary drama."

At last Yomei found her words, saying, "I cannot decide on my own, Ching. You see, I'm not the author of the play, which was a collective effort. I was listed merely as an adapter. If I treated it as my own work, people at the oil field would be outraged and say I have appropriated the fruit of their collaborative labor. It will be unethical for me to do that. I'm sorry, Ching, I'm not at liberty to use this play freely. My hands are tied."

Jiang Ching's face fell, pinkish patches appeared on it, and her upper lip curled. She said, "For so many years I've been eager to work with you, Yomei, but you've never honored my wish. You know that patience has never been my strong suit. I'm tired of repeating my requests and can't cozy up to you forever. So for heaven's sake, take this as my last invitation."

That struck Yomei dumb. She stared at Ching's face, on which a malevolent smirk emerged. Ching rose and said, "I used to think we could work together as a pair—you were in charge of spoken drama while I ran Beijing opera. Now it looks like I'll have to fight alone and within the field of Beijing opera. This is a warrior's fate, to go on fighting alone."

"I'm sorry, Ching. I wish I could join you."

"Because of your refusal, we won't be able to do much in spoken drama, which is the last stronghold of reactionary artists. What a pity—that a red and trustworthy expert like you cannot be of much use to us. You know, Chairman Mao always appreciates you."

"I'll do my best to make myself useful for the revolutionary cause and also to live up to his appreciation."

In spite of turning Jiang Ching down firmly, Yomei felt quite rattled. Jin Shan was also startled, believing that *The Rising Sun* was dead unless they let Jiang Ching harvest the fruit of so many people's collaboration. No matter what, he and Yomei would not allow that to happen. Yet he knew

Ching's personality. She used to pursue some male directors doggedly, willing to do anything for them, including sleeping with them, so as to secure a major role in the plays they were directing. He told Yomei that Ching would surely wreak vengeance on her, though he couldn't tell in what fashion. So they'd better be more vigilant at work and keep a low profile.

At last the revenge came, like a bolt from the blue. In mid-June the Red Guards at the People's University ransacked the school leaders' offices and detained Sun Yang. They even denounced him publicly in the Culture Square, forcing him to stand on a stool and wear a papier-mâché dunce cap and a heavy wooden placard on which were inscribed "Capitalist Roader" and "Traitor." Those words, together with his name, were crossed out in red ink, as if he were about to be executed. The placard was so heavy that the steel wire cut into the flesh of his neck. The Red Guards also paraded him through the campus, where big-character posters were everywhere, condemning Yang and the other school leaders as "a black gang." Yomei had never seen so many political writings handwritten in big characters and posted on walls in public spaces. What a bizarre way for the masses to express themselves and expose others. Among the denounced, Yang had been singled out as a special target because he was labeled a foreign spy. What was even more outlandish, the Red Guards fabricated their own charges against him, which said he had been developed by the Japanese Chrysanthemum Bureau, one of the four major Japanese intelligence agencies, when Yang was studying in Japan, and later the Chrysanthemum Bureau had planted him in Yan'an, at the side of Zhu Deh, to collect intelligence for the Japanese Imperial Army. No wonder he still had some nipponized mannerisms, such as often bowing to others, which actually gave him an air of sophisticated humility.

The Red Guards incarcerated Yang in the basement of the school's main building and beat him every day to extract information needed by the leaders at the Central Committee of the Cultural Revolution. They told him that he must expose his former boss Zhu Deh, who was nothing but an old bandit, not a hero that Yang had eulogized in the biography he'd written. It was whispered that Chairman Mao had blown a fuse when he saw the hefty book describing Marshal Zhu Deh as the founder of the Red Army. To Mao's mind, Zhu Deh had been closer to a warlord who had contradicted him time and again in the CCP, ever since the mid-1920s. To present Zhu Deh as the founder of the Red Army was to undermine Mao's leadership of the armed forces. As Mao had declared repeatedly: "Political power comes out of the barrel of a gun." For decades Zhu Deh had been a thorn in Mao's flesh, but there'd been no way to get rid of him, thanks to Zhu's seniority and reputation in the Party and the army. That accounted for the detainment of Sun Yang, which was a way to strike Zhu Deh from the side. In Mao's eyes, Yang had been Zhu's lackey and loud eulogist, and as such he must be reined in and silenced.

Yomei was devastated by her brother's arrest. At this point she was still unsure whether his punishment was part of Ching's revenge. She could tell that Kang Sheng and Jiang Ching both resented the biography Yang had written of Zhu Deh. But the old man was so revered, few people in the Party could touch him. Yomei and Jin Shan talked about such a turn of events, and both believed that there must be some bigger power behind Jiang Ching and Kang Sheng who intended to bring down Zhu Deh. Evidently it was

Mao behind them, because Zhu Deh was ranked well above Jiang Ching and Kang Sheng and used to be together with Mao. Now that a major biography had been published as if to erect a verbal monument to the old man, Mao couldn't tolerate such a personality cult—nobody in the Party should surpass him in reputation. He alone should occupy the limelight and get all the acclaim. But Yomei and Jin Shan could talk about the labyrinth of this power struggle only between themselves, not daring to voice their opinions and conjectures to others.

Yomei tried hard to get Yang out of the Red Guards' clutches, but to no avail. She went to see Uncle Zhu Deh and found him very upset by Yang's arrest, but the old man couldn't figure out a way to save him either. Zhu Deh had even asked Premier Zhou, who headed the Central Committee of the Cultural Revolution, though he seemed like a figurehead who was unable to manage the mass movement at all. The premier was only drifting with the bloody torrent of the revolution. It was Jiang Ching and her clique who ran the committee. Zhu Deh asked Zhou Enlai to intervene on Yang's behalf, but Zhou had just grimaced and said his intervention might only backfire. He told Zhu Deh, "Many people could have remained safe, but because of my intervention, they got hurt and even destroyed." Though somewhat puzzled by Father Zhou's equivocation, Yomei felt he might have his reasons.

Then more trouble flared up for Jin Shan and Yomei. Big-character posters appeared on the bulletin boards at the theater, then everywhere, even inside the lobby and the corridors of their office building, even on the street, where mats were fixed on trees and utility poles so that more posters could be pasted to them. The accusers called the Youth Art Theater and the Central Experimental Theater "a pair of citadels of the bourgeois artists," mentioned many plays produced by them as "poisonous weeds," and also listed many leaders of the theaters as reactionaries and capitalist roaders. Among the condemned, Jin Shan was naturally ranked at the top, since he already had some historical baggage on his back. He was named as a diligent disseminator of feudalistic and bourgeois sentiments. His wife, Sun Yomei, was his helper and a sympathizer of the Soviet revisionism. The two were a really a corrupt pair and even strolled around arm in arm publicly without shame and often spritzed themselves with reeky, exotic perfumes. Someone also pointed out that Yomei preferred coffee to tea—"she is a Russian slave and a worshipper of foreign stuff."

Those condemnations upended their world—Yomei felt as if heaven and earth had traded places. She couldn't help but wonder what sort of revolution this was. It was more like an act of mass destruction; so many people, suddenly possessed by vengeance and schadenfreude, had degenerated into fearless and bloodthirsty fiends who were relentless in exposing each other to save themselves. Yomei tried to hold her tongue, convinced that she hadn't done anything wrong and should be safe. Over the years the two theaters had produced so many revolutionary plays and earned the public's respect and support. So how could the Red Guards overnight turn them into sources of "poison and spiritual corruption"?

Jin Shan remained calm in appearance, having gone through numerous denunciations and condemnations before, but Yomei couldn't stomach this kind of far-fetched smearing. She often felt her gorge rising at the thought of those groundless accusations and at how people confused rhetoric with facts. It was hard for her to remain taciturn—

she'd always been outspoken and aboveboard, like someone transparent. Furthermore, she had always been red, born and bred, and known as the Red Princess since the Yan'an days. How could she have become "a black-hearted reactionary" all of a sudden? This made no sense.

When she finally expressed her objection and complaints, the revolutionary task force at the theater believed she had the wrong attitude, and, regardless of the specific issues she brought up, they just attacked her more viciously to subdue her. She didn't know that many of her colleagues had already gone through this kind of maltreatment and had been made tame and obedient. On account of her stubbornness, she had become a special target, and both she and Jin Shan were ordered to join "the black gang," who would be denounced publicly. The revolutionary task force ordered them to admit their wrong deeds and crimes and reform themselves through menial labor, including mopping floors and stairs, cleaning toilets, wiping windows with rags, and sweeping the front and back yards and the parking lot.

One afternoon in late August, a band of Red Guards led by a teenage girl came to the theater. Together they wanted to discipline "some reactionaries and evildoers." Most of the actors and staffers held back at the sight of them and remained quiet and bowed their heads and kept busy working to make themselves unnoticeable. Somehow the girl commander caught sight of Jin Shan and demanded, "What kind of family are you from?"

He answered, "My father was a small businessman, but he died when I was one year old."

"Businessman, huh?" the girl went on, scowling. "That means he was a capitalist, so you're a son of a capitalist. No wonder you've become a reactionary."

Yomei glared at the moon-faced girl, wondering at how ridiculous this was. Then the teenage leader, the girl, caught her resentful eyes, stepped up to her, and demanded, "How about you? What's your role at this theater?"

"I'm a director," said Yomei.

"Doing what?"

"Staging plays."

"So you have produced plenty of poisonous weeds, one patch after another?"

Yomei didn't bother to respond, just looking her in the face.

"What's your family background?" the girl persisted.

"Revolutionary martyr."

"Revolutionary martyr, is it?" Her slitted eyes raked Yomei up and down. "Then you have betrayed your red origins and become a black element in our society."

"Ludicrous," Yomei grunted contemptuously.

That incensed the girl, who waved at the Red Guards behind her and ordered them, "Teach her a lesson to set her straight!"

Two teenage boys rushed up and grabbed hold of Yomei's arms. Then, with a large scissors, they began cutting her hair. She struggled to resist, but more Red Guards joined in and restrained her. They dropped clumps of her hair to the floor, and in a wink of an eye they opened a naked cross on her crown, which they called "the yin-yang hairdo" due to the contrast between her black hair and her whitish scalp now.

In fact, the violent act was gratuitous. The Red Guards were just passing by and had no idea whom they manhandled. They cut Yomei's hair for fun and to punish her stubborn attitude. But such a random act cut her to the quick. After they'd left, she looked at herself in a mirror, then began sobbing. With ravaged hair, how could she go home?

Jin Shan found a flabby wig from a pile of stage costumes in a back room and told her to put it on. Quietly the two left for home. That night, Jin Shan clipped off the rest of Yomei's hair so that her head became bald, but it was still in fine shape, round and smooth. He was amazed that even without her luxuriant hair, she still looked as elegant as a model nun. He said, "My, you may have been a princess in your previous life. Nobody can destroy your beauty. Even without your hair, you still look so beautiful."

"Well, beauty is truth and truth is beauty," she said with slight irony. "Damn, I'm still so arrogant." She tittered.

"Besides an arrogant heart, what else do we have as an artist? We're all megalomaniacs in a way."

"That's right. I can see you are similar to me. At heart, you look down on those in power. Many of them are mere clowns in gorgeous caps and gowns."

He laughed without a word and went on clipping the soft hair on her nape.

Every day they went to the theater to work, but all they did was mop floors and clean bathrooms. They were also expected to read the big-character posters hanging all over the place. They used to enjoy strolling along Chang'an Avenue between the theater and their home and often go out for a walk after dinner, but nowadays they didn't go anywhere after work and only stayed home.

Even so, they were not left alone. There were all sorts of people who came to their house on the pretext of special investigations.

· *Seventy* ·

One afternoon in midfall, three men came to ask Yomei and Jin Shan about Iron Man Wang in the oil field, the model worker known throughout the country. The stocky one of the three investigators declared, "The so-called Iron Man is a fake. He joined the Nationalist ranks in his early twenties and has just pretended to be loyal to the Communist Party. Now you must help us expose him."

At those words, Yomei couldn't keep mum anymore, her blood in flames and her eyes smoldering. She asked them, "If you say Iron Man Wang was a Nationalist, then you must show some evidence. You can't malign someone this way. Show me your proof if you have any; otherwise you're committing a vicious calumny."

The same short, hatchet-faced man, apparently the leader of the trio, responded, "Of course we have evidence, we have ironclad evidence, solid like a mountain."

Jin Shan stepped in, "If so, why bother to ask us? We didn't get to know him until recently, and we're totally ignorant of his past."

That seemed to have gagged the investigators. Yomei seized the moment of their confusion and added, "Yes, I met him in 1964 for the first time. You all know that the

Nationalist Party disappeared from the mainland fifteen years prior to that."

The tallest one of the three persisted, "But he isn't a model worker as he has been portrayed. At least you can help us prove he's a fraud."

Yomei said, "Bah! We have no idea how he became a model worker in the oil field, but we spent some time with him and saw with our own eyes how dedicated he was to his work and how kind and considerate he was to his fellow derrick men. I respect him. In every way I must admit he's a good Iron Man, one who absolutely deserves the moniker."

The three investigators were incensed and insisted that neither Yomei nor Jin Shan nor the big shots behind Iron Man Wang could protect him anymore. He was nothing but an iron statue with feet of clay who could be toppled easily. In fact, they claimed that Iron Man Wang was already in jail, so it would be futile for Yomei to defend such a black-hearted traitor. She and Jin Shan were astounded by the news and asked where Iron Man Wang was imprisoned, but the investigators refused to tell them, just smirking as if relishing the pain and shock that transfixed the couple. They reminded Yomei not to be in collusion with that wicked man.

There was another group from the Ministry of Culture who wanted to know how Yomei and Jin Shan had started working on *The Rising Sun*. These investigators were experienced officials, not regular Red Guards. Yomei insisted that she herself had volunteered to go to the oil field after reading the heroic deeds of the workers there, particularly the long reports in *The People's Daily* on Iron Man Wang. She surmised the implications of their questioning, so by any means she didn't want to implicate Father Zhou.

The leader of this group, a bespectacled man with a flat face, seemed dubious about her reply. He pressed on, "Who were the officials behind your dramatic project?"

Yomei realized they meant to link her project to the State Council, so she said, "No leaders were involved at all. The whole thing started from the entertainment group in the General Machinery Plant of the oil field. They made a skit by themselves, titled *The Broad Road*, which took both Jin Shan and me by surprise. We were so moved by it that we decided to expand it into a full-length play. Of course we went to talk to the leaders of the oil field, who were all supportive."

Jin Shan reiterated the same story, emphasizing that the short play had blown him away and praising the leaders of the oil field for their support and enthusiasm. In brief, everything had come from the grass roots and there was no power from above that had intervened. Nonetheless, the investigators were skeptical. One of them, a middle-aged woman, asked Yomei, "So nobody in the State Council gave you any instructions?"

"Absolutely not."

"Then how come the troupe went to perform inside of Zhongnanhai?"

"That was not planned at all. When we brought the play to Beijing, invited by the Ministry of Petroleum Industry, we thought we were going to stage it here just two or three times. The actors told their families that they'd go back for the spring festival. But once we started to perform in Beijing, the play ran wild and we got more and more invitations. Finally the Office of General Affairs in Zhongnanhai heard of us and invited us over."

In their answers, Yomei and Jin Shan tried to distance Premier Zhou from the play as much as they could. Obviously the investigators suspected that Zhou Enlai

had masterminded the dramatic project, probably as a
countermove to the revolutionary model plays that Jiang
Ching had been producing. That must be why both the
stage play and movie of *The Rising Sun* had been called off.
Yomei and Jin Shan were amazed to see that without any
premonition they had gotten entangled in politics of the
highest circle, as if fighting at the artistic front for a faction
and engaging the First Lady head-on. As a consequence,
they were unwittingly confronting Chairman Mao. How
naively they used to believe that art could stay totally
detached from power. Deep down, Yomei could see that
from Father Zhou's point of view, after he had seen the play,
she and Jin Shan could serve as a counterforce against Jiang
Ching's effort to break into the political arena through
the avenue of theater arts. That may have been why Father
Zhou had suggested forming another acting crew so as
to disseminate *The Rising Sun* in the central provinces and
creating a second and even a third of such a play. The
premier may have meant to let their play outshine Jiang
Ching's dramatic efforts. Luckily, Yomei and Jin Shan
hadn't taken up another project right away, which might
have plunged them deeper into the politics of the top
circles.

Then one evening two men came and said they were
from the Committee of the Cultural Revolution, which
was the highest office in charge of the mass movement. The
instant they sat down they began to question Yomei about
Zhu Deh's reactionary deeds and words. She turned aghast.
How could they dare to doubt that revered old man, who
used to be ranked together with Chairman Mao as one of
the two supreme leaders of the Red Army? She gave them a
hard look and then said, "Why do you have the temerity to
come investigate Marshal Zhu Deh, who is my uncle? He

and my father were sworn brothers. How could you expect me to say anything against him?"

"Don't be so smug! Get a grip of yourself," one of the men spluttered. "Comrade Jiang Ching said Zhu Deh was just a warlord plus an opportunist."

"If Jiang Ching believes so, then you should ask some leaders more senior than her. They've known Uncle Zhu Deh much longer than Jiang Ching has."

"Who are those?" asked the older one of the two, who had a doughy face and gave a gappy grin.

"Go ask Chairman Mao how Zhu Deh led more than ten thousand troops to join him on Jinggang Mountain. If Zhu Deh were a warlord, he wouldn't have bothered to join the Communist Party, would he? He and my dad both wanted to liberate the common Chinese people from the oppression of feudalism and bureaucratic capitalism. They were revolutionaries through and through."

The younger investigator, in his thirties, jumped in: "You're talking as if your father and Zhu Deh were born revolutionaries. Don't feel so complacent. Maybe your father was merely a flunky serving a warlord. He would become a target of our investigation too, if he were alive."

"My dad was murdered by Chiang Kai-shek. He was a revolutionary martyr. How dare you pass that sort of judgment on him!"

"How can you prove that—I mean your father's martyrdom?" the older investigator said, hefting himself up and turning his chair. He sat on it again, sideways now, as if this was more comfortable for his ass.

"Go ask Premier Zhou," Yomei told him. "It was he who introduced Zhu Deh and my father to the Communist Party together."

"When was that?"

"1922 in Berlin," she answered, blazing up. "You'd better bone up on your knowledge of the Party's history before coming to see me again."

They both looked frustrated, their faces heated with colored blotches. The younger one said through his teeth, "Stop bragging about those old farts. They've only appeared red, but at bottom they have all become capitalist roaders."

"Shut your stinking mouth!" Yomei growled, shaking with a flare of anger. "I came to know Uncle Zhu Deh and Premier Zhou even before I could walk. They're my heroes. If you want to get any negative information on them, don't ever come here—you won't get anything from me. Also, tell those who are behind you, stop heckling those top leaders who have more important work to do. No one has time for this kind of claptrap and idiocy."

They looked astonished. The older one said, "Don't blow your top like this. We just asked you to help us to figure out some problems and facts unclear to us."

"But those are wicked questions, and I won't bother to answer them."

"OK, we understand."

Nevertheless, before leaving, they warned Yomei that she must bear in mind that her brother Sun Yang could help them clarify Zhu Deh's case. At the mention of Yang, she went ballistic. She pointed at the door and shouted, "Get out, both of you! You're not welcome here!"

They stood up, dropped their cigarette butts on the floor, then turned to the door. She picked up the butts and felt her blood throbbing with rage. She and her husband looked at each other speechlessly.

Time and again, Yang became the center of investigators' questions. They wanted to know whether some foreign powers had been involved in producing Zhu Deh's

biography, particularly the Soviets. One man even asked
Yomei, "Doesn't your brother Sun Yang have lots of Russian
friends?"

"I don't think so," she replied. "Yang went to the Soviet
Union for only a few months in 1953 to attend a cadre-
training program. Afterward he had no contact with
anyone there. He doesn't know Russian, and is unable to
mix with the Soviets. To my knowledge, the Russians never
liked Marshal Zhu Deh and viewed him as a hick of a leader.
Why would they sponsor the writing of his biography? They
haven't supported Chairman Mao or Premier Zhou that
way, and they were more international in their eyes. Your
question makes no sense and bothers me terribly. It's like a
gnat that flew into my mouth."

That shut the man up, but then he managed to continue,
"You must cooperate with us, because Sun Yang's problems
are extremely serious. Comrade Jiang Ching already says
he's not just a capitalist roader but also a running dog of
Zhu Deh's."

"Sun Yang used to be Zhu Deh's secretary. The job was
assigned to him by the Central Committee. It was his duty
to serve Marshal Zhu conscientiously. I can assure you that
Sun Yang is an honest and upright man."

"Then why did he work against Chairman Mao?"

"He never did!"

"We have a letter he wrote to the Central Committee,
complaining about the Great Leap Forward."

"He did mention the awful steel product he had seen.
Keep in mind that he studied in Japan and knew that
industrialization couldn't be realized overnight. How
could you justify that type of mass production of steel,
surrendering metal containers and beds, kitchenware,
even watch belts, to the backyard smelting furnaces? You

all have seen what sort of trash those furnaces produced—
they couldn't even produce pig iron, let alone high-quality
steel. It's common sense that no country could modernize
its industry that way. On top of that, you all know that
during the famine years a lot of people starved to death in
the provinces. That resulted also from overcollectivization,
didn't it?"

Jin Shan was perturbed by Yomei's outspokenness
and jumped in, "You ought to look at Sun Yang's entire
history and see how much work he has done for the Party.
In many ways he was a picture of selfless dedication. All his
colleagues loved and respected him. Where can you find a
better president for a university? There aren't many such
good and capable men around."

Again the investigators were nonplussed. Still, before
leaving, they told Yomei that her brother's case was far from
over and he might be incarcerated for a long time, maybe
for some years. She'd better be more cooperative so that they
could solve his case sooner. Their remarks unsettled her.

Since the fall, she had been trying desperately to find a
way to get Yang out of the incarceration. She had heard that
he was confined in the basement of the university's main
building and was often beaten at night. Out of despair, she
wrote a letter to Father Zhou to report Yang's persecution.
She begged him to intervene on his behalf, considering
Yang had a young wife and three small children at home. At
least they should let him return to join his family at night.
Given that Yang had worked for the Party for more than
three decades, they should treat him with basic decency.

The letter was mailed out, though Yomei was uncertain
if the premier could receive it. For more than a month, she
didn't hear a word from him. Probably the Zhous were also
in a tight spot, unable to protect others. That must be why

Father Zhou had told her in the oil field last year that she shouldn't visit his home too often lest his opponents pounce on her.

Though loving him like a father, she began to have misgivings about his integrity and smoothness. Recently one incident had disturbed her considerably. Two months before, Jiang Ching had gone to the Great Hall of the People to join a meeting presided over by Premier Zhou. Before she arrived, her assistant had phoned Cheng Yuan-gong, the premier's chief of guards, to tell him that Jiang Ching would need to eat lunch before she attended the meeting. So at the sight of Ching, Yuan-gong said to her, "Your lunch is ready in the Jiangsu Hall. Premier Zhou and the other leaders are in the meeting. You can join them after lunch."

Jiang Ching had forgotten about the lunch arranged beforehand by her assistant, so she blew her stack, convinced that Yuan-gong was blocking her way to the meeting. She blasted, "You're just a dog of Zhou Enlai's, but you treat me like a wolf. Come," she motioned to others around, "have him arrested!" But people were too stunned to act, a few turning aside and speaking in nervous whispers.

Later Jiang Ching told Wang Dongxing, the chief of general affairs at Zhongnanhai, to apprehend Yuan-gong, but Wang refused to carry out the order and told others, "With just a wild conjecture Jiang Ching worked herself up into a fury. She can't use me like a loaded gun." He had known Yuan-gong since the early 1940s in Yan'an and trusted him, so he couldn't see any reason for arresting the man. Yet his disobedience riled Jiang Ching up, and she spoke to Zhou Enlai directly, demanding that he get rid of Yuan-gong.

Yomei had known Yuan-gong for more than two decades and treated him like a younger brother. So when she heard him describing this manic incident, she got worried, but he said the premier wouldn't listen to Jiang Ching, an irascible woman who'd see red on all sides, so he, Yuan-gong, would be all right. But just three weeks later, he disappeared from Zhongnanhai, and Yomei had no idea where he was now. Rumor was that he'd gone to a labor camp in Jiangxi Province. Evidently Father Zhou had caved in to Jiang Ching and dismissed his chief of guards, who had served him loyally for twenty-five years. Such an outcome agitated Yomei, making her see that Father Zhou wouldn't be that reliable in helping her brother Yang, since he too could be coerced by Jiang Ching. What's worse, it was the premier's habit to sacrifice people close to him so as to save his own skin. He was always afraid that Mao might get rid of him. He was like a lizard that, if seized from behind, would sever its tail to survive.

Yomei's anxiety grew more acute when she went to see Zhu Deh. The old man and his wife both sighed and were genuinely concerned. The old man said, "Yang was with me for so many years. I know what kind of man he is. His only fault was that he worked for me conscientiously and wrote my biography. It was I who ruined him." He turned tearful and kept blinking his bleary eyes, his rustic face turning stony.

Yomei said, "Don't feel so bad, Uncle Zhu. I'm more worried about Yang's wife, Shih Chee, and their three children. Their family is shattered, and how can they survive? Maybe I should go beg Father Zhou and Mother Deng to help, since Father Zhou heads the Committee of the Cultural Revolution." From a bowl she picked a Roma tomato, which the Zhus had grown in their tiny garden. She took a bite. The fruit was sharp and pungent.

"There's no use," Zhu Deh said. "I spoke with Premier Zhou about Yang last week. He knew Yang well and could see plainly that the false accusation was malicious, purely a fabrication. But your father Zhou told me, 'Many people could have remained safe, but because of my intervention, they got hurt more and even destroyed.' So the premier can't do anything for Yang either."

Yomei wasn't sure of that, knowing Father Zhou was a shrewd and resourceful man. Apparently these days he had been busy protecting himself. There was no doubt that he loved power so much that he was willing to sacrifice anything and anyone for it, including some of his close comrades. Yomei thought of sharing her doubts with Jin Shan, but she refrained. Despite the letdown, she'd still take Premier Zhou as a father figure, whose defects she was eager to conceal from others. But she did speak with Yolan about the difficulties in getting their brother rescued. Lately Yolan had visited Shih Chee, who was terribly worried about her husband. In his most recent letter Yang told Chee, "Maybe I am already behind the times—the revolutionary movement is moving so fast that I can no longer keep up with it." Yolan had also run into some trouble with the Red Guards at Beijing University, but so far she was safe, in spite of her Soviet education. She too believed that Father Zhou might not be willing to help their family anymore, having to protect himself from Jiang Ching, behind whom loomed the ultimate power—Mao himself. In the eyes of Mao and Ching, Yang must have been Uncle Zhu Deh's frontline soldier, and had to be shot down.

· Seventy-One ·

Unexpectedly, Lily came to see Yomei one morning in late February 1967. It was a dry, cold day, not having snowed since December. She was wearing a navy woolen coat and an orange headscarf, which made her stand out among pedestrians wrapped in drab wintry gear of coarse fabrics and dull colors. She was a research fellow at the Philosophy Institute of the Chinese Academy of Social Sciences. In spite of the low-key title, her job was actually a distinguished one, because the academy served as a kind of think tank for the central government. She congratulated Yomei on *The Rising Sun*, which she believed was a genre bender, never having seen any play like it before. But Yomei told her that the play had run into a dead end, with its movie project scuttled too, apparently due to Jiang Ching's interference.

Shocked, Lily heaved a sigh. She said she too was in hot water of late, mainly because she had taken the step of defending their friends Lisa and Li Lisan, both having been under investigation for months. Lisa was accused of being a revisionist plus a Soviet agent, but she refused to admit any wrongdoing. More outrageous to their interrogators, Li Lisan openly swore that Lisa was innocent. Their accusers pointed out that he was her husband, so his testimony mustn't count. But Lily argued against them in front of her comrades and the leaders of the academy, saying nobody could have known Lisa better than Li Lisan, the two having lived and worked together for more than three decades, abroad and domestically, so of course Li Lisan must be qualified to offer his proof of Lisa's past. Lily also told Yomei that some investigators had questioned the Lis, as well as herself, about Yomei's involvement with their "Soviet clique." Fortunately, over the years Yomei had been too busy to see them regularly. At most she'd gone to the Lis to give Lisa some free tickets, especially when she staged a Russian play. Evidently some people were eager to nab the "Soviet cabal," which also included Oyang Fei, who was interrogated as well.

To Yomei's astonishment, Grania, too, was labeled a revisionist. The woman, hardly literate, couldn't possibly have any idea what "revisionist" meant. Lily said, "It boggles my mind that all sorts of people are utilizing this Cultural Revolution as an opportunity for reprisal and for self-advancement. It was Grania's husband, Chen Changhao, who had accused her of gathering intelligence for the Soviet embassy in Beijing. He wrote a long report to the Party committee of the translation bureau, saying Grania was 'a revisionist and a Soviet spy.' The truth was that he wanted to dump her so that he could live with another woman. Those two got married recently, while Grania is jailed somewhere in spite of her severe diabetes. I also spoke in defense of Grania, who is as innocent as a duck to me. There're so many men who just make me sick. They lie as easily as breathing, even to themselves!"

"Heavens, how come the Cultural Revolution is bringing out the worst in so many people and has reduced them to the level of ferocious beasts?" Yomei hadn't met Grania's

husband for two decades, but he was the professor who had
flown to the Soviet Union on the same DC-3 with his son
and Yomei twenty-eight years before. It seemed as if all
the misery and suffering over the decades had made the
man more trivial and more perfidious. Who is to say that
suffering ennobles human beings by purifying their souls!
The opposite is also true—suffering can also make one
wretched and wicked.

Lily went on, "You know what surprised me most?
Kang Sheng used to write me long, sugary letters, especially
when I was working for Jiang Ching. But two weeks ago,
at a meeting in our academy, he said in front of everyone,
'Don't bother about Lin Lily. She's already a revisionist as a
result of her Soviet education.' That man is sneaky and evil.
He enjoys tormenting others, as if he could thrive only by
hurting people."

Yomei said, "He used to write me long letters too, acting
like an uncle of sorts, but later, after I had fallen out with
Jiang Ching, he stopped writing and joined her in attacking
our plays. I'm wondering why he used to pay so much
attention to us, even though we were nobody in the echelons
of power."

"Well, you're so naive, Yomei. You're the same innocent
girl like back in Moscow. I can tell you why. Because we used
to be close to Chairman Mao, you were his interpreter in
Moscow, and I often accompanied his wife abroad. Kang
Sheng may have assumed that you would collaborate with
that woman and run China's art world sooner or later.
Now that we have turned out to be different from what he
expected, he has crawled out of his hole and helps Jiang
Ching make a revolution in the cultural world. Just be
vigilant about their motivations and schemes."

"You must be careful about what you say, Lily. Nowadays people seem to have lost their minds. There's no logic in this life anymore."

"You know, Yomei, you should let your hair grow back. You used to have beautiful hair."

"I don't mind having lost my hair. We don't rehearse or do any real work. I don't go to formal events anymore. Every day we mop floors and clean bathrooms and wipe windows, so there's no need to keep myself presentable at all. Besides, some Red Guards are vicious—they'll cut my fine clothes, so I wear canvas overalls to save some work for them." She grimaced.

Lily snuffled, her eyes glistening while tears trickled out. "How did the beautiful life we dreamed of come to this?" She let out a deep sigh.

"I used to believe that I could pursue my art with a pure heart and total dedication, but now I can see that even the art I love so much is not pure at all. Everything has been tainted by power and politics."

"You're right, Yomei, but don't say that to others."

"Sure, I can share my thoughts only with you."

Lily peered into her face. "Not even with Jin Shan?"

"Come on, he's my husband, still a soulmate."

"You don't regret having married him?"

"Not at all. At heart he's a fine man and I can trust him."

Lily made no more comment and seemed amazed by what Yomei had told her. She exhaled, then said, "It must be you who have made him a better man. It's hard for me to love a man wholeheartedly now, having seen so much ugliness and sordidness around me. I prefer to live alone. To be honest, I miss our Moscow days, when we were so innocent and pure, a happy pair of budding revolutionaries, even though life was hard then."

"Yes, so much is lost, gone like a mirage."

Jin Shan cooked a fine meal for Lily—a large bowl of noodles with poached eggs and cured pork and turnip and carrot slivers in it. He hadn't joined their conversation but was grateful to her for coming to see Yomei. He told Lily that these days few friends called on them. "Only investigators turn up, one group after another."

After lunch, Lily took her leave after giving Jin Shan a side hug, and Yomei went out to see her off. It clouded over. On the way to the stop for the 13 bus, Yomei mentioned that she must try to get Sun Yang out of the Red Guards' clutches. Lily was still unsettled by Yang's arrest; to her mind, he was a model revolutionary. She had read his book *The Ethics and Virtues of Communism* and regarded him as a true red scholar, and Yang had also served in the Red Army and fought as a solider. How could it be possible to pin a wicked label on a man of such strong moral fiber? "Times are mad," Lily said. "So many people have become nothing but fighting animals."

At this point a bus pulled up, so she hugged Yomei tightly and then got on board. Yomei waved as the bus rolled away. Like in the old days, she blew her friend a kiss. That was the last time they saw each other.

Yomei was not allowed to attend the meetings in which Yang was denounced, since she herself was also under attack and the Red Guards at her theater had limited her movement. During the day, she and Jin Shan had to stay on the premises of the theater, and at night they weren't free to leave home either. From Yang's wife, Yomei learned that he was unyielding as before, refusing to admit any wrongdoing or give evidence for Zhu Deh's "crimes." Instead, he praised the old man's honesty and integrity and his plain lifestyle, despite his high rank and the privileges attached to his position as the nominal commander in chief of the People's Liberation Army. Although he had been beaten up repeatedly, Yang seemed to remain a naive man. He even wrote to the two hostile revolutionary factions of his school: "You can all turn on me, but please stop hurting each other!" He was afraid their fierce fights might destroy each other as well as the university.

His wife, Shih Chee, also revealed that their three children were getting beaten on the street. Some small bullies kept calling them names—"Sun Yang's bastards" or "Little Jap lovers" or "wolf puppies." As a result, Ning, the older boy, was reluctant to go to school. Every morning his mother had to drag him there. Such a situation must not continue, and Yomei realized it would not change unless Sun Yang's status was reinstated. With him classified as an enemy of the people, everyone felt entitled to abuse his children. So she had to find a way to get him out of the Red Guards' hands.

For months Yomei had been trying desperately to rescue Yang, but couldn't make any progress. Late in the spring, she decided to write to Jiang Ching directly and beg her for mercy. For her brother and his family, she was willing to swallow her pride. She wrote:

> Dear Comrade Jiang Ching,
>
> I am writing to report my brother Sun Yang's case. Last summer some Red Guards of the People's University detained him and publicly denounced him on a platform. They have not only imprisoned him but also physically abused him, calling him a capitalist roader and a traitor and a foreign spy. To date, he has not been allowed to go home to see his family, and as a result his three little children are living a fatherless life

and in fear. They are often attacked on the streets, partly because their father is in disgrace, being classified as an enemy of the people.

Ching, you have known Yang since the Yan'an days. He worked for the General Affairs Office as a secretary for Commander Zhu Deh, and later he went to the northeast to fight Chiang Kai-shek's army. After 1949, he transferred to the field of high education, serving as a college leader in both Sichuan and Beijing. His whole life has been subordinated to work and duty. You might also know the articles and books he has penned over the decades, in which he has expressed his profound love for our Party and his deep belief in the revolutionary cause. I dare say that Sun Yang is a model Party member, honest, clean, considerate, and generous to his colleagues. There is simply no evidence to justify the accusations against him.

My dear Ching, I know we might have different views on theater arts and I might not be able to catch up with your grand vision, but I do respect you and admire your energy and sensibility. I have always told others, "Comrade Jiang Ching is aesthetic and well versed in several arts." I didn't mention your calligraphy, but I had that in mind as well, being deeply impressed by your flowing, forceful brushwork. Even though we don't always see eye to eye, I respect you from the bottom of my heart. Ching, I know a lot of people used to be mean to you, but please let bygones be bygones so that you can feel more at peace. Life is short, given to us only once, so we should do our best to live cheerfully, beautifully, meaningfully (I am quoting Chekhov). I beg you to intervene on Yang's behalf and help us save his family.

Many thanks in advance and always yours,
Sun Yomei

The letter, though making Yomei feel as if she had eaten a fly, was mailed to Mao's residence directly. In the following weeks, she grew more anxious and expected to hear from Ching. She and Jin Shan talked about the possibility of Ching's leniency. He knew Ching was vindictive and selfish, but Yomei had once been friends with her, and in her letter she'd done her best to flatter the woman, who always enjoyed flattery and welcomed praise. So Yomei was hopeful, feeling that Ching might lift a finger to have Yang released.

· *Seventy-Two* ·

But throughout the summer, the persecution of Yang continued. Some people from the Central Committee of the Cultural Revolution went down to the university and kept talking about Sun Yang as a traitor and a foreign agent. Yomei finally saw that Jiang Ching had ignored her appeal and might even enjoy seeing her suffer on Yang's account.

On September 6, both Jiang Ching and Kang Sheng spoke about Yang at a public meeting attended by the revolutionary masses from various colleges in Beijing, including many from the People's University. Kang Sheng announced, "Sun Yang is a major secret agent, no doubt about that. The People's University is a hotbed for evil elements like him." Jiang Ching told the Red Guards, "You must teach Sun Yang a lesson. Don't treat him with any leniency. He's an agent serving the Japanese, the Soviets, the Nationalists—he used to be in cahoots with the Blue Shirt Society, which was a fascist organization in the old China." Most of the college students had never heard of that name and couldn't tell how bad that secret society had been, so back on campus they got more violent in abusing Yang. Jiang Ching's words stoked the fury of those blind, ruthless young people.

Yomei became more agitated. If she didn't get Yang out of incarceration soon, he might perish in the Red Guards' hands. As a last resort, she decided to go see Mao in person and beg the Great Leader to help rescue her brother. She knew that Ching, even as Madame Mao, couldn't see him freely, because they already lived separately, and that to see him, Ching would have to schedule an appointment beforehand. So this would be a challenge to Yomei too. Worse, if Ching came to know she had seen Mao personally, Ching might go berserk and became more vengeful. But at all costs, Yomei had to save her brother and his family. Since she didn't care what might happen to herself, she began to think about how to make an appointment with Mao.

Long ago she had happened to befriend a nurse on Mao's medical staff, calling her Sister Wu. Yomei phoned Wu and asked her to put in a word for her. "Just tell Chairman Mao that Sun Yomei would like to see him in person," she told Nurse Wu. "If he doesn't respond, don't mention it again. If he agrees to see me, ask him what time I should come. It's kind of urgent, Sister Wu. I beg you to help my family and me."

"You have to be more specific about why you want to see him. That's required."

"OK, tell him that Sun Yomei wants to report her work to him."

"I'll do that, but I can't promise any results."

"Understood. Whatever the outcome, I appreciate your help."

"Don't forget to send me some play tickets."

"Goodness, Sister Wu, I wish I could offer you some again. But nowadays we can't stage any new plays except the revolutionary model plays produced by Comrade Jiang Ching. I assume you've seen them, haven't you?"

"Yes. I don't need tickets for them."

Nurse Wu knew Yomei was the Red Princess and hers was a revolutionary family that had given the Party a number of martyrs, so she agreed to help her. Above all, Yomei knew Mao personally, so the nurse was willing to help. At her mention of Yomei to Mao, his eyes flickered and his lips curled a bit. He said, "Certainly I'd like to meet her. I'm glad she hasn't forgotten me."

Nurse Wu was amazed by the reply; obviously the Great Leader seemed interested in receiving Yomei. Few people could get close to him these days. He was already celebrated as a red sun, casting warm rays on everybody and everything in the country.

The time was settled on the following Monday, at midafternoon. Yomei wondered if she should let the Zhous know her move, but decided against it. For more than a year she hadn't gone to see them, and Father Zhou seemed to be having difficulty in keeping his own skin intact. Yomei had seen big-character posters exposing the premier, saying he had opposed Chairman Mao over the past four decades. She'd also heard that at a small meeting Jiang Ching had even slapped the premier's face, but Zhou Enlai had just smiled without losing his composure and even urged the First Lady to keep her temper. Later Ching apologized to him and admitted she'd been mistaken to act that impulsively. Zhou forgave her in front of many people, and those who witnessed the reconciliation between the two all praised the premier for his magnanimity. "What a gentleman," they said. But Jiang Ching also griped to some people in private, "Zhou Enlai can start a rebellion even when he's on his knees."

When Yomei arrived at Copious Garden in Zhongnanhai, after entering Mao's room, where most of the books lining the walls were thread-bound editions, with yellowed spines, she was surprised to see him so aged, his bulky face a little bloated and his eyes barely open. Nurse Wu has said he was just up from a siesta. Indeed, he still looked sleepy. Since their return trip from Moscow seventeen years earlier, Yomei had seen him a few times, only at public gatherings, where he had appeared rather spirited and healthy, and was sometimes seated under his own oversize portrait. But now she could see clearly that he was ill and exhausted, wearing cotton shoes, whose low black uppers were squeezing his ankles, which must be swollen. One of the shoes had a hole at the toes, revealing the white sock he was wearing. His hands looked waxy and marked with age spots. Both of them rested on his lap, with their fingers interlaced. Yomei could tell that he was a senile wreck, and then she realized he was pushing seventy-four. Mao's dotage reminded her of a line in one of his early poems: "I believe a human can live two hundred years." What irony! Then again, with his kind of pressure and strife, even a man with an iron constitution might go to pieces quickly. Beyond question, Mao was already in the twilight of his life. This realization cast a shadow on her mind.

He smiled, revealing tea-stained teeth, and his face looked a little doughy. He said, "I'm glad to see you, Yomei. I've heard you are very active in theater circles and produced some fine plays." Behind him on the wall hung a scroll of wild, flowing calligraphy by Huai Su, an eighth-century monk from Mao's home region. The words in the piece had been inscribed so freely and erratically that Yomei couldn't recognize their meanings at first glance.

She suppressed the urge to observe the calligraphy more carefully and said to Mao, "I'm a stage director at the

Central Experimental Theater and enjoyed my work there. But lately because of the Cultural Revolution, things have gone topsy-turvy, and we can't stage plays anymore."

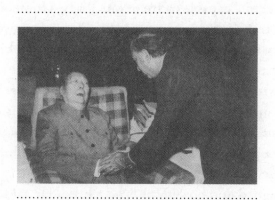

Mao in his later years

"I've heard of disruptions here and there, but they are unavoidable. We're in the midst of a revolution, which has to break the old stuff to create something new."

"You mean we are going to have a new kind of theater?"

"Correct. There was too much foreign and feudalistic stuff on the stage and the screen in our country. It's high time we started over. That's why Jiang Ching has been active in producing the model plays."

"I see. I wish I had understood the purpose of her efforts earlier. She's been very active indeed."

"You're an expert in spoken drama, and you should help her. We need new arts that serve the masses instead of just the elite."

"I see. Thank you for the instructions."

He tried to laugh, but the laugh seemed to have stifled itself. His upper lip curled a bit. They went on talking about life in general. Yomei mentioned the disappearance of order and rules, to which he listened attentively. She then brought up her brother's case as an example of the absence of law now. She said, "Chairman Mao, you know Yang. In a way, you saw him grow into a revolutionary soldier and then into a capable cadre of our Party. How could he become a traitor and a secret agent for foreign powers? The Red Guards at the People's University have jailed him in a basement and beat him every night. If this continues, he might die in there. Worse, he has three small kids. With such a criminal name labeled on him and with his absence from home, his family will be destroyed by the masses. Please take pity on him and help him get released. He's red at the bone, you know that."

Mao sighed and bowed his head a little. He said, "Throughout our Party's history, there has been constant abuse of power and mistreatment of our own comrades. We should look into Sun Yang's case. Thank you for telling me about him."

Mao's assistant, a curvaceous woman in her midthirties, stepped in to remind the visitor that it was time to wind things up. Indeed, Mao looked tired. Yomei stood to take her leave. Before turning away, she stretched out her hand, which he held for half a minute before letting it go.

Riding the bus home, she mulled over her meeting with Mao. She was unsure if Mao would help rescue Yang and could tell that Mao had been behind Jiang Ching's interference with the world of arts and theater. So evidently, by refusing to collaborate with Ching, she might by chance have been pitting herself against the highest power in China. Such a thought gave her a chill, though the air was balmy and sultry and even the chocolate-brown vinyl seat on the bus was hot under her thighs. By instinct she could tell that Mao was no longer attracted to her—there was no longer the kind of subtle sparks from his features as there had been seventeen years before. Maybe he was just an old man now, too feeble to be sexual anymore, or perhaps she'd lost her beauty and vivaciousness. But she wouldn't worry about the loss of her charm, believing it was a natural part of aging. She was more concerned about Yang's safety and sanity. She was told that people had heard him screaming at

Jiang Ching, Zhou Enlai, and Kang Sheng

night. Apparently they applied electric rods to him, besides whipping him with leather belts.

That night she talked with her husband about her meeting with Mao. Jin Shan was alarmed by Mao's urging her to help Jiang Ching with the theater revolution. This indicated that all the attacks on their colleagues and on the plays they'd produced in recent years had been orchestrated remotely, by Mao himself. It also signified that nobody, not even Premier Zhou, could protect them if Jiang Ching took them as her enemy. So at least for now they had to appear more conciliatory, and not confront or provoke her. Jin Shan was also unsure if Mao would help get Yang out of jail. Clearly Mao disliked the idea that Zhu Deh's biographer remained at large. In his book, Yang described Marshal Zhu as the founding father of the Chinese Red Army. That was the high crime that Jiang Ching's collaborator Zhang Chunqiao in the politburo had accused Yang of. Evidently, Mao must be behind the scheme for getting rid of all the forces assisting Zhou Enlai and Zhu Deh. Very likely, Yomei was regarded as a disciple of the premier's. She was already in a dangerous plight and had to figure out how to save herself.

Jin Shan's analysis of the situation made sense to Yomei, but it was already too late for her to reconcile with Jiang Ching. Besides, she simply couldn't do anything to please that power maniac, never mind produce model plays for her. She had to find another way to deal with her.

As Jin Shan predicted, Yang was more severely abused in the following weeks. Yolan, a mere Russian teacher at Beijing University, was allowed to see Yang once a week. She reported to Yomei that their brother's face was bruised and swollen and that he could hardly speak now. "If this continues, he might die in their hands soon," she told Yomei. "He seemed delirious, and kept saying he felt too antiquated to keep abreast of the revolution anymore. I think he must be depressed."

"Anybody can get depressed if abused like he has been. Yang should've never come back to Beijing." Yomei heaved a long sigh.

"That's true. Our folks in Sichuan have been safe. This place is dangerous, too close to the emperor." Yolan stuck out her tongue to show that was a slip. An elongated dimple appeared above her chin.

To preempt further attack from Jiang Ching, Yomei sneaked to her aunt Jun's home to inform her of their family's woes. After stepping in, Yomei took off her cap, and at the sight of Yomei's bald head, Jun burst into tears. She'd heard that Yomei was under investigation and interrogation by the Red Guards but hadn't expected to see her maltreated like this. Yomei used to have abundant, wavy hair, but now it was all gone. Evidently those so-called revolutionaries intended to humiliate her so as to break her spirit. But Yomei smiled and said, "I'm already accustomed to those crazy bullies. Sixth Aunt, I came to remind you to get rid of everything associated with the top leaders of our Party, particularly with Jiang Ching."

Puzzled, Jun said, "I have nothing to do with her. After the new China was established, I've never run into her. She and I revolve in different orbits—our paths have never crossed."

"How about the photo she signed with her former name, Lan Ping? Remember she gave each of us a picture of herself before she was leaving for Yan'an thirty years ago?"

"You mean the ones she presented to us when we were at the Shanghai Eastern Spoken Drama Theater?"

"Yes, she gave each of us a headshot of herself and signed it."

"I might still have it in my album."

"Get rid of it right away, because it can be evidence against you. Jiang Ching has gone out of her mind with vengeance and wants to eliminate any trace of her past. So whoever knows about her past may be in jeopardy now. If she sees that photo, she might label you as a counterrevolutionary and wipe you out."

Jun seemed incredulous. "I know Ching is flighty, but Chairman Mao should be able to restrain her, shouldn't he?"

"It's not that simple, Sixth Aunt. I went to see Mao last week and begged him to help get my brother Yang released, but Mao was noncommittal. I had the impression that he was no longer his former self. He might be behind Jiang Ching, instigating all the violence and disorder in society."

Jun frowned, her bangs half-gray now. She mentioned Yeh Qun, Lin Biao's wife, who had been quite active of late. Jun said that that was another vengeful woman who hated Yomei. Now that Yeh Qun had also come to the foreground of the political arena, she could be destructive too. Yomei promised to be careful and to play the fool if the investigators questioned her about Jun and her husband Yida. Jun said she'd do the same and refuse to admit to any recent communication with Yomei. In brief, the more separated they appeared from each other, the safer it would be for both of them.

· *Seventy-Three* ·

Yang's wife, Shih Chee, was arrested in early September by the Red Guards of the People's University, where she was a lecturer in Chinese. Such a turn of events devastated Yomei. Now with both parents absent from home, how could their three children survive? Yomei couldn't go to the school to find out what had happened to Shih Chee, since she herself was also under investigation, forbidden to appear there. She went to Yolan instead and asked her to care for Yang's kids. Yolan already had two children, a boy and a girl, both toddlers, but she was willing to take in Bing, Ning, and Ming. But she was often hard up herself for money—her husband's family in the countryside was poor, their livelihood depending on his monthly remittance.

Yomei knew Yolan's plight and said she would help her financially as long as their brother's children had a place to stay. With that promise, Yomei began to give Yolan forty-five yuan a month, more than a third of her salary, enough to feed the three kids. She felt somewhat comforted by the temporary arrangement, though they still had to find a way to help Yang and his wife out of the Red Guards' clutches. Or at least get Shih Chee back so that the children could return to their home.

Yomei wrote to Jiang Ching again, mainly about Shih Chee's arrest. She begged Ching to take pity on a young mother who had three small children. The kids were innocent and mustn't be made orphans like this. She concluded: "Please show some mercy, Ching! You are a mother and must know how harmful this disruption is to the children's upbringing."

On the morning of October 6, the loudspeaker on the campus of the People's University was broadcasting "The Cavalry March," and some people were humming along to the melody as they walked. Then the music stopped. After a crackle, a female voice announced, "Sun Yang, the former vice president of our school, took his own life last night as his way to escape the charges of distorting our Party's history and espionage for foreign countries. As Chairman Mao teaches us, 'Everyone dies, but some deaths are lighter than a goose feather and some weigh more than a mountain.' Sun Yang's shameful death is clearly lighter than a goose feather and won't stop us from struggling against him and his wicked deeds."

People started to spread the word of Yang's death. Yomei collapsed when she heard of it and began sobbing convulsively, as though she were crying her insides out. For a good while she could hardly breathe and felt her heart in a knot. Then, having recovered some from the shock, she rushed to campus to see Yang's body. She simply didn't believe he had killed himself. People all knew that nowadays the majority of so-called suicides were actually murders. Even those who had taken their own lives in most cases had done so because the torture had been too much for them to bear. At the front entrance to the main building of the university, she ran into Yolan, who too had hurried over the moment she'd heard the sad news. A group of Red Guards blocked their way, saying they were not allowed to see the corpse of Yang, who had become a counterrevolutionary now, as the act of suicide was a betrayal of the country and the people. Therefore, even though Yomei and Yolan were his sisters, they were not allowed to see his body.

Yomei lost her calm and yelled at a man who must have been a Red Guard leader, "Sun Yang is our brother. Even if he were a criminal, as his family members, we are entitled to say goodbye to his body." Again tears were streaming down her cheeks.

Still, they wouldn't let them go down into the basement. As the wrangling grew louder, an officer, a leader of the revolutionary task force, came into the lobby and asked what this was about. Yomei said, "Our brother died in your hands, so we must see him for the last time."

The middle-aged officer, who had a pencil mustache and fleshy ears, waved them through but said they could stay no more than fifteen minutes. In such sultry weather, the body might begin to smell anytime and would have to be shipped away without delay. A girl led them down into a small room, where Yang was lying face up on the concrete floor. He was already reduced to skin and bones. His face was emaciated, marked with dark bruises and speckles of viscous blood. A long gash slanted on his balding crown, while his thin arms lay along his sides as if about to move, but his hands were crushed at the knuckles, some of his fingers swollen with broken nails. In every way, he appeared to have already been beaten to a pulp before he breathed his last. Yomei pulled up the left cuff of his pants and saw that his kneecap had been smashed, the whitish bone visible. Yolan couldn't stop crying, while in a rush of hatred, Yomei spat out at the Red Guards, "This isn't over—we'll settle accounts with you!"

From there the two sisters went to Zhongnanhai
directly. They told the sentries there that they wanted to
see Zhu Deh's family. Zhu's office responded to let them
in. Yomei didn't go to the Zhous straightaway for fear that
someone might report their appearance there to Jiang
Ching. The two sisters told Mrs. Zhu, Kang Keching,
about Yang's death. The three of them sobbed, their arms
wrapped around each other. Zhu Deh was ill, bedridden, so
they mustn't disturb him with the sad news, but Aunt Kang
promised that his office would look into the case. Yomei
had no doubt about that, because the old couple had treated
Yang like a son of theirs. From the Zhus', she phoned the
premier's home and told Mother Deng about Yang's death
and asked the Zhous to help find out the true cause. Mother
Deng sounded shocked and promised to pass the word on
to Father Zhou, saying that indeed they mustn't let Yang die
with a criminal name.

On their way home, Yomei and Yolan talked about the
promises given by the two top leaders' wives. They were
unsure of the outcome, but right now they had to make sure
Shih Chee was all right. On her arrival home, Yomei found
Jin Shan arguing with some Red Guards, who had come
to warn his wife not to step out of their house. Yomei told
them that she would have observed their rule, but what had
happened was an emergency—she'd had to respond to her
brother's death. That pacified the Red Guards somewhat,
who left after having warned her not to leave home again.

After a simple, early dinner, Yolan left for the People's
University again, to see Shih Chee, who must have found
out about the tragedy by now. Indeed, after hearing of
Yang's death, his wife had blacked out in her cell. When she
came to, she demanded a full explanation of her husband's
demise. She didn't believe he had killed himself. She yelled

at the Red Guards nonstop, so they struck her to shut her up. They pushed her face against the concrete floor so forcefully that two of her front teeth broke. She later told Yolan that they had openly said she'd better follow in Yang's footsteps—they even left a sharp scissors on the windowsill and tied a nylon rope to a hook on the door lintel. "Those murderers are just man-eating beasts in human skin," she said to Yolan.

Although Yomei couldn't go see Shih Chee herself, she asked Yolan to let their sister-in-law know that they would look after her three children and that whatever it took, Chee must survive, because their enemies wanted them to perish so that there wouldn't be any witness left to hold the criminals accountable someday. Shih Chee, through Yolan, promised Yomei that she would live on for the sake of the children. So from then on, she became somewhat docile and didn't challenge her persecutors overtly.

Seventy-Four

Yomei couldn't figure out whether her visit to Mao and her letters to Jiang Ching had precipitated her brother's death. It was very likely that Jiang Ching had come to know about her meeting with Mao and become more vicious, though Yomei hadn't mentioned to the chairman anything against her. In a way, she regretted having gone to see him, since evidently her visit hadn't helped protect Yang and might have brought him more torture. Even her entreaties for Ching's compassion might have only provoked her or shown Yomei's own vulnerability.

In mid-December she wrote to her daughter in Daqing Oil Field and asked her to come back for the spring festival in late January. In the letter, she wrote that she was going to invite her cousins over so that Little Lan could celebrate the holiday together with Bing, Ning, and Ming. Yomei didn't mention Uncle Yang's death and just said, "Something happened in their family. I will explain when you are back." She also enclosed thirty yuan for Little Lan's train fare and a five-pound national grain coupon so that she could get food on the way. Mother and daughter wrote each other quite often, at least twice a month, but Yomei had not revealed to the girl her and Jin Shan's troubles yet. She wanted their daughter to be undisturbed and to concentrate on her schoolwork in Sartu.

One early morning, about a week after the letter was sent out, Yomei and Jin Shan were still in bed when someone banged on their door. Jin Shan got up to answer it. Yomei sat up and looked out of the window. It was still pale gray outside, and the streets quiet, without traffic yet. Who would be here before daybreak? she wondered.

In came a group of policemen, all wearing felt hats with the earflaps let down. "Are you Jin Shan?" a gruff voice asked.

Yomei stepped out of the bedroom, buttoning up her jacket, as Jin Shan answered, "Yes, I am. What's the matter?"

"You must come with us," a thickset cop said.

"Where to?"

Without another word, two men rushed up and grasped Jin Shan's arms and clapped handcuffs on his wrists. Yomei stepped in between them and shouted, "Wait a second. He's not a criminal. Why did you cuff him?"

Their leader, a scrawny man with a lined face and a bulbous forehead, took out a piece of paper with a big round seal at its bottom, accompanied by the signature and the square signet of the official who had authorized the arrest. "Here's the warrant," he told Yomei. "Are you his wife?"

"Yes, what's the charge against him?"

"Can't say for sure. We were just ordered to haul him in. I need you to sign this." He put the paper on the table.

"You must first tell me what crime he committed."

"He's a counterrevolutionary. Never mind then, even if you don't sign, he's still a criminal we can pick up." He took back the warrant and waved at the other three men, who stepped forward, and together they dragged Jin Shan away.

Yomei followed them into the yard, while her husband shook his head, indicating she should stop and that he'd be all right. They put him into a white minivan and pulled away. The vehicle let out a raucous blast.

That afternoon a team of Red Guards came. They announced that they wanted to rifle through Jin Shan's house for evidence of the crimes committed by both Yomei and him. She had no choice but to let them conduct the search, though she was certain that neither of them was guilty of anything. The Red Guards rummaged through their chests, drawers, bookcases, and wardrobes, combing through their letters, books, and albums. For some reason, they took away all Yomei's letters from Chairman Mao, Jiang Ching, Zhou Enlai, Zhu Deh, Kang Sheng, and other dignitaries. Some of the letters were in Russian, and the Red Guards bagged them all in a gunnysack. They also confiscated her albums of photos, some of which were historically valuable, such as those she and Mao had taken together in Moscow. She intervened, saying they couldn't just make off with her personal memorabilia. A girl with a square, mannish face, who must have been a leader, told her, "Comrade Jiang Ching instructed us to seize whatever looks suspicious from you, especially pictures, so we're just carrying out the orders from the Cultural Revolution Committee."

Yomei realized this was also part of Ching's revenge, so she made no more objection and just stood against a wall, arms crossed, and let them search every nook and cranny of her home. They collected a lot of Jin Shan's letters and papers too. They seemed to be after something specific, but none of them was explicit about their goal and they all just kept going through their possessions. One young man found a bank deposit book of Yomei's and was wondering whether to include it as part of their booty, but he put it back in the sideboard drawer. Yomei breathed a sigh of relief. Just two days prior, she had sent a woolen coat and her main bankbook to Jun's and asked her aunt to keep them for her for the time being. Now she was amazed that the Red Guards seemed uninterested in anything monetarily valuable. They had filled four burlap sacks with her and Jin Shan's belongings, mostly papers, letters, photos, posters, slides, and some books.

Before leaving, they locked the glass-front bookcases and pocketed the keys. They also sealed with bands of red paper all their cupboards, desks, chests, and the sideboard. They inscribed big crosses in black ink on the sealing paper, then told Yomei that nobody was allowed to tamper with the seals.

After putting things back in order, Yomei wondered what to do. She knew that she shouldn't go to a relative or friend in such a state. That would have depressed others, if not compromised them. So she forced herself to cook dinner, just boiling a bowl of leftover rice and stir-frying some cabbage and cured pork. No matter what, she had to eat to keep up her strength. While at the wok, she noticed the end of a volume of Chekhov's plays sticking out from behind the cupboard. Someone must have dropped it there inadvertently. It was a hefty book with a morocco binding and in Russian; fortunately the Red Guards hadn't taken it. So after dinner, she sat down, an afghan wrapped around her shoulders, copying passages from *Three Sisters*, a play for which she always had had a soft spot, because it was the first Russian play in which she had acted a significant role. That had been two and a half decades before. How time had flitted, like a shadow that passed swiftly—so many things had appeared, then disappeared. She went on hand-copying the play, mainly to take her mind off things around her and from the thoughts frightening her. She feared that Father Zhou was reluctant to help her family anymore, unwilling to confront Jiang Ching and Mao. That was entirely possible. Yet in a time like this, she had to continue by any means. Later, lying in bed, she recited some final lines from *Uncle Vanya*: "We will say we have sobbed and suffered, that we had a hard and bitter struggle, and God will have pity on us, and we will see a new life, a bright and glorious life." She kept murmuring those words in the Russian until she fell asleep.

The next morning she again went to the theater to join the political studies and a denunciation meeting. In the afternoon she was also ordered to join a public rally, though thus far she hadn't been put on the platform yet. For a whole day she was thinking about what to do. She'd have to find a way to get Jin Shan out of those bullies' hands.

At her wit's end, she decided to turn to Lin Biao for help, believing that he, as the Party's vice chairman, should be in a position to look into her husband's case. Just the year before, at the Eleventh Plenum of the CCP's Eighth Congress, Lin Biao had been announced as Mao's successor, the second most powerful man in China now, and above all, he was in charge of the entire PLA, having military power in his hands. So he might be able to overrule Jiang Ching in some cases. That night Yomei wrote:

My Respected Vice President Lin,
  How time is flying. Although we haven't seen each other for eighteen years, I have often seen you in newspapers and documentary films. Since 1950, I have been a stage director in Beijing and have produced some fine plays. I enjoyed my profession and found it

rewarding and enriching. But since last fall, things have changed drastically. My brother Sun Yang was seized by the masses at the People's University and jailed in a basement there. He was accused of spying for Japan, the Soviet Union, and Chiang Kai-shek's regime. The Red Guards paraded him through the streets and put him up on platforms for denunciation. In the freezing weather, they forced him to bow as low as possible, with his hands bound behind his back. As a result, his dripping snot formed icicles below his nose.

Needless to say, the accusation against Yang was groundless and ridiculous. You met him three decades ago in Yan'an and saw how he grew into a capable cadre and soldier. I dare say he was one of those most dedicated workers for our Party and country. Two months ago it was announced that Yang had killed himself, but this was obviously a lie. I went to see his body, which was battered, his skull broken and his knee smashed. As a devoted Party member, even after his death, Yang mustn't be treated as a traitor, nor as someone who committed suicide.

More outrageous, his wife, Shih Chee, was also arrested before his death and accused of being a traitor. She went to school in the new China and has never been abroad or worked with foreigners. How could she possibly become a traitor? Whom would she betray? And for whom? The charge was nothing but rubbish.

Yang and Chee have three small children. Because of their parents' arrest, the kids have become homeless. At the moment, my younger sister, Yolan, tries to look after them, because I am also under attack— my home was ransacked and my husband Jin Shan has been arrested (the charge is quite vague: "counterrevolutionary"). Both Jin Shan and I have been accused of spreading foreign and bourgeois culture. Of course, we are innocent. He has worked for our Party since the early 1930s, and you know what I was like when I was a young girl. I would say Jin Shan and I are both red from head to toe. I would even venture to claim that at some point you and I were comrades fighting in the same trench. How could I be a traitor to our revolutionary cause?

*Now, dear Vice President Lin, I am writing to ask for your help,
not to rescue me but to save my brother Yang's family by getting his
wife, Shih Chee, out of incarceration. Of course, I hope you can also
look into Jin Shan's case so that he will be treated properly or released.
I always have fond memories of you and believe you are a generous and
kindhearted man. That is why I have made bold to write you directly to
beg for your help. Many thanks in advance.*

Always yours,
Yomei

She didn't ask for a lot from Lin Biao, because she believed
what she needed from him was an attitude or a gesture. As
long as he expressed his interest (perhaps in secret, with a
certain amount of pity) in protecting the Sun family, Jiang
Ching might hold back from attacking them.

Yomei sealed the letter and wondered where to send
it. Usually Lin Biao resided in Maojiawan, an alley in the
western part of downtown Beijing, but during hot summer
days he often lived in the Zhejiang Section in the Great Hall
of the People because there was air-conditioning in there.
It was winter now, so Yomei mailed the letter to Maojiawan.
She hoped against hope that Lin Biao still had enough
affection for her that he would lift his hand to protect her
family. This should be easy for him.

She didn't know that all letters addressed to Lin Biao had
to go through his office, which was headed by his wife, Yeh
Qun. Yomei's letter was intercepted by the small woman,
who flew into a wild rage after reading it. She said to her
secretary, "That slut will never change, still attempting
to seduce my husband." Without explaining, she just set
the letter ablaze, so Lin Biao knew nothing about Yomei's
request for help.

· *Seventy-Five* ·

Yomei had also thought of Liu Yalou, the bright-eyed man who used to court her persistently. Yet after their meeting in Harbin in February 1950 (he got on the train to meet with Mao), she had lost touch with him, even though he too had moved to Beijing later on. For many years Yalou had commanded China's air force and also served as vice minister of defense. Although not as powerful as Lin Biao or Father Zhou, Yalou would have been able to help her readily. Also in his favor was the fact that he didn't have a personal office headed by his wife like Mao and Lin Biao did, making him easier for Yomei to contact. But the passionate, energetic man had died two years earlier of liver cancer. It was true that Yomei had always given him a wide berth, yet when the news of his death was announced on the radio, she felt sad and wandered in a poplar grove outside the town of Sartu for two hours alone until the twilight thickened. The news broadcast had said Liu Yalou's passing was a national loss, considering he was only fifty-five, but Yomei felt it was like her own loss as well, even though she couldn't talk about it to anyone. From the radio she learned that in Beijing all the national leaders, except for Mao, attended his funeral, at which Lin Biao delivered a moving speech. More than one hundred thousand mourners

gathered on the streets to bid farewell to him for the last
time. Along the streets, his hearse rolled through, and some
national flags flew at half-mast. In spite of Yalou's notoriety
for womanizing and for being relentless in factional
fighting as Lin Biao's right-hand man, his passing made
Yomei feel aged all of a sudden, as though a page of her life
had been turned. Despite herself, her eyes were swimming
in tears.

She also thought of Xu Yi-xin, the first man who had
touched her. Still handsome, he was also in Beijing now.
For decades he had been in the foreign service, working
as an ambassador to several countries: Albania, Norway,
and Syria. Just the year before, he had returned to China
to take the position of vice foreign minister. The other
day she had seen him receiving a Vietnamese delegation
in a documentary movie that showed the current news.
Somehow Yi-xin looked smaller than before on the screen,
a bit shriveled. Since leaving Yan'an for Moscow, she had
not met him in person, but with the benefit of hindsight,
she seemed to understand him better and even felt grateful
that he had protected her. He was smart enough to cut ties
with her as soon as Jiang Ching began living with Mao.
Yomei wondered whether to write to him and ask for help,
but she thought better of it, knowing that his efforts on her
behalf might bring trouble to him and his family, and even
to Yomei herself, because Jiang Ching might get riled up if
she assumed that the two of them had been secretly intimate
over the decades. Better to let sleeping dogs lie.

It was already the holiday season. This year the spring
festival was on January 30, which was less than a week away.
No matter how mad life had become, she ought to make her
home a little comfortable and festive for her daughter, who
would be back soon. Without breaking any of the sealing

paper, she wiped all the furniture and tidied up the house. She also made some meat jelly in a dutch oven, a dish Little Lan loved. Yomei wondered if she was already on her way home.

Little Lan boarded the train in Daqing five days before the holiday. In Harbin she would switch to the train bound for Beijing. The ride was long and crowded and exhausting. She tried not to drink liquid for fear of having to fight her way to the toilet. Fortunately she'd bought some biscuits and apples before getting on board. It took her three days to arrive at the capital.

It was still dark outside, so the girl stayed in the train station for two hours in order to let her mother sleep until it got light. Around six o'clock she started out for home on foot. The streets looked different from two years before, with some areas littered with trash—leaflets, candy wrappers, ice cream cartons, soda bottles, cabbage roots, coal cinders. On the power lines perched flocks of crows, dozing despite the waxing daylight. The birds looked frozen numb in their sleep. This was so different from the mornings in Sartu, where at this hour the air would palpitate with showers of birdcalls. As Little Lan walked along, big-character posters appeared on walls and bulletin boards. Near the former National Youth Art Theater, she saw some of the posters denouncing her parents, calling Jin Shan a foreign stooge and an incorrigible womanizer and Yomei a counterrevolutionary and an advocate of abominable bourgeois sentiments and lifestyles. One poster quoted Jiang Ching's most recent verdict: "Sun Yomei was a wolf sleeping beside Zhou Enlai." One even mentioned Little Lan, saying she wasn't Yomei's real daughter but an illegitimate child by a promiscuous actress in Shanghai. The adoption of such "a foundling, born out of wedlock," indicated that Sun Yomei had always allied herself with the corrupt and the decadent. Indeed, she was rotten to the core and must be reformed thoroughly in this mass movement. Though Little Lan had known Yomei wasn't her birth mother, the poster still wounded her to the quick and brought tears to her eyes. Hurriedly she turned away and headed for home.

When she arrived, she found Yomei wide-awake. Her mother hadn't slept a wink the whole night, waiting for her.

"Thank goodness you're back!" Yomei said to her daughter.

"What's going on in town? Why are there so many big-character posters everywhere?"

"The Cultural Revolution is in full swing, and we've become targets. That's why I didn't want you to come back to school here."

"Where's my dad?"

On hearing that Jin Shan had been taken away and jailed somewhere, Little Lan burst into tears and cried wretchedly, her hand wet with tears. To her, he was a kind, indulgent father, a good man in every way. Why did they treat him as a class enemy? This was beyond her.

Yomei took out the breakfast she'd made two hours earlier—noodles with cabbage and tofu and baby shrimp in soup. She said, "You must be hungry. Let's dig in." She also placed a ramekin of meat jelly on the table.

Mother and daughter began eating. Yomei explained that a few days before, some Red Guards had come to ransack their home for criminal evidence and took away four gunnysacks of their things. Before leaving, they sealed their chests and desks and cupboards, so it would be inconvenient and too depressing to have Little Lan's cousins here to celebrate the spring festival, and they'd better have the family gathering at Aunt Yolan's home. Little Lan nodded while eating. She was groggy and could hardly keep her eyes open. So the moment she was done with breakfast, she went to brush her teeth and then got into bed. She slept for a whole day. Yomei felt happy to hear the girl snoring lightly in the bedroom.

That night Yomei told her daughter what had happened to Uncle Yang and Aunt Chee. Little Lan sobbed again. She couldn't believe that her cousins, who used to bask in so much parental love, had suddenly become orphans of a sort. Her mother was right that they shouldn't have the family gathering in this house, where everything would remind her cousins of their loss, and she and her mother should go to Aunt Yolan's instead. "If we go there, we ought to bring some holiday presents for my cousins," Little Lan said. "I wish I had brought back something we could use for that."

"No worries," Yomei said with a smile. "I've bought some new things for them."

"I got a little gift for Bing from Sartu."

"That's good. I hope it will please her. She's a big girl now, I mean mentally. She's a precocious child."

They went to Yolan's home two days later, on the eve of the spring festival. In the meantime, Little Lan had bought three packs of small firecrackers for Ning, Ming, and Lai (Yolan's six-year-old son), even though she'd never felt close to the boys. Mother and daughter went to the dorm of the science academy, which was Uncle Zongchang's work unit. It was cold and cloudy, the sky starless, yet the city was vibrating with holiday festivities—now and then explosions of fireworks burst as if a battle was underway. The aroma of holiday cooking wafted in the air, mixed with a touch of gunpowder. Yolan's three-room apartment was on the fourth floor of a slapdash dorm building, which had no elevator. When mother and daughter reached Yolan's door, Yomei was huffing and puffing a bit, but she noticed that Little Lan still moved with ease in spite of carrying the big parcel of presents. She was pleased to see that the girl was stronger now—her life in the oil field must have been wholesome.

Yolan hugged Little Lan and then took the parcel they'd brought. Yomei told everyone that these presents were from Jin Shan as well. Ning and Ming each got a pair of suede boots, while Bing had a pea-green corduroy jacket. As for Yolan's children, they each received a canvas book bag and a pair of lambskin mittens. There was also a butterfly barrette for the four-year-old girl. Then, from her tote bag, Yomei took out a roast duck wrapped in wax paper and tied with kraft string. She said to Yolan, "I picked this up on the way."

Zongchang opened the package and chuckled while nodding his head of salt-and-pepper hair. He told Yomei, "We talked about whether to get a braised chicken or a roast duck. Luckily I bought a big chicken. Now this duck will make our dinner a feast."

Yomei handed her sister a wad of cash—her subsidy for their brother's three children. (For the holiday she had added an extra twenty yuan.) She said, "Let me give you this now in case I forget." Yolan took the money without a word and put it into her side pocket, as if she were afraid the others might see it.

Little Lan presented to the three boys each a pack of firecrackers, which delighted them. She also gave Ying, Yolan's daughter, a cloth doll, which the girl embraced with rapture. Then Little Lan handed to Bing a patch of white birch bark in a large envelope. She said, "People in

the forest use this as paper. Some write letters on it." Bing
showed the smooth and glossy bark to her brothers. They
were all fascinated. Even Aunt Yolan was amazed, saying
she had read about birch bark in Russian novels but never
seen it. Now this was really precious. She wished she could
have borrowed it from Bing and shown it to her Russian
literature class. This would have been an eye-opener to
the students. What a pity that she didn't teach that course
anymore. The students and teachers were busy making
revolution nowadays, acting as if they could subsist solely on
fanatical slogans and destructive activities.

Yolan's confession surprised Yomei, who asked, "Didn't
you go to the countryside in Leningrad? There must be
birch woods in the city too."

"I saw birch trees there of course," Yolan said, "but I
didn't see a large piece of the bark prepared like this—like a
piece of paper."

"Too bad I didn't bring back an extra piece," said Little
Lan.

Soon they sat down to dinner, which had six dishes,
including rice porridge with dates and peanuts and
assorted beans mixed in, steamed buns stuffed with red-
bean paste, and boiled taro potatoes. The latter was a
rarity that Zongchang had bought on the black market for
triple the usual price. The boys were eating the chicken
and duck ravenously. They all enjoyed the double-sautéed
pork, a Sichuan specialty of Yolan's. Apparently they
hadn't tasted much meat of late. Yolan told them not to pig
out on everything for now. There'd be beef dumplings at
midnight, so they ought to save some of their appetite for
the first meal of the New Year. The boys said they wanted
to finish dinner quickly so that they could go out and
set off firecrackers. But their uncle and aunts wouldn't

let them out for fear that they might run into bullies on
the streets who might rob them of their firecrackers.
So the boys were allowed to join the seething and
festive explosions in the neighborhood only from their
balcony. They had no choice but to light their strands of
firecrackers from up there, while they kept giving battle
woops and delighted shrieks. Uncle Zongchang had
prepared a variety of fireworks for them too, so they had
plenty to play with.

Meanwhile Little Lan and Bing retired to a bedroom
and chatted between themselves. Lan told her cousin
that she enjoyed life in the oil field, where people were
straightforward and friendly and easy to get along with.
But it was very cold in the winter in Heilongjiang, and the
landscape was white from late October to April. They also
talked about their future plans. Bing somehow longed to
become a soldier, though she was just thirteen, whereas
Little Lan wanted to study medicine to become a doctor.
Knowing that most colleges were already suspended in
Beijing, she only hoped that schools would reopen soon.
But unlike the classless furlough enjoyed by youngsters in
the capital, education in Sartu continued, and students
there still had schoolwork up to their chins during
midterms and finals. Little Lan would have to go back
soon for the spring semester. Bing said she'd probably go
visit Lan in Sartu when her mother was back home again.
Little Lan promised to accommodate her if she came in
the summertime. Summer was more comfortable in the
northeast, she told her cousin, whereas winter was no fun.

In the living room, the adults began making dumplings.
As they worked around the kneading board, Yomei, with
little Ying seated on her lap, told them that she had just
written to Lin Biao in hopes that he might get Shih Chee

out of the Red Guards' clutches. Yolan and Zongchang were
both surprised. She asked Yomei, "Do you think Lin Biao
will get your letter?"

"I have no clue. I was so desperate—I just sent the letter
to his Maojiawan residence."

"His staff might intercept the letter, don't you think?"
asked Yolan.

"I had to run the risk to save Yang's family."

Zongchang chimed in, "I wonder why Jiang Ching had
Jin Shan apprehended. Shan has never talked about her and
can't pose any threat to her at all."

"Did he offend Jiang Ching in the old days in
Shanghai?" asked Yolan.

"I don't think so. She doesn't seem to hold a grudge
against Shan personally. He used to work under the
leadership of Premier Zhou, so Jiang Ching might want to
get some information about Father Zhou from Jin Shan."

"Maybe more than that," Yolan said. "Obviously Jiang
Ching hates you to the very marrow of your bones, so she
might want to get something against you from him too. In
other words, she means to hurt you in every way she can.
She's such a vicious harridan."

"Believe me, Jin Shan won't give them any information
of that kind. But what you said makes sense. That must be
another reason for them to seize him. This also means I
must be their real target. Well, I'm ready. Come what may."

Zongchang shook his delicate chin. "You're talking like
you're going to become a revolutionary martyr."

"You must be more careful," said Yolan. "Try to deal
with Jiang Ching reasonably and perfunctorily."

Yomei realized that she should take preemptive measures
and avoid compromising Yolan and Zongchang. If they ran
into trouble, Yang's three children would have nowhere to

go. So she told them, "I mustn't come too often, mustn't get you implicated."

The two sisters agreed that from now on they'd meet at the Monument to the People's Heroes in Tiananmen Square every Saturday at eight in the evening to compare notes and catch up. Zongchang also thought it was good to exercise more caution from now on.

Yomei had noticed that her daughter, already pubescent, was one and a half inches taller than before. Most of her clothes were too small now, and Little Lan needed new jackets and pants, but Yomei was short on cash at the moment, having spent the remainder of her salary for the holiday, besides giving sixty-five yuan to Yolan. Then she remembered she had a small amount in a deposit book, but it was in a sealed sideboard drawer. Together mother and daughter steamed the band of paper with a mug of hot water and then peeled it away. Yomei was thrilled to see there was still about two hundred yuan in the booklet. She went to the bank and took out the cash, and then mother and daughter set out shopping. Yomei bought Little Lan a woolen sweater, a pair of suede boots, two corduroy jackets, and two pairs of denim pants. The girl was excited to have these new clothes and the ankle boots.

Yomei told her that she had left a duffel bag at Jun's home. In the pocket of the woolen coat was another deposit book, which had more cash in it, more than two thousand yuan. If she, Yomei, was imprisoned and Little Lan came back to Beijing, she could collect that bag from Jun, to whom Yomei had already made clear that she should surrender it only to someone of their family. So if her parents were not around, Little Lan would inherit the fine coat and the savings.

Yomei's words made her daughter down in the mouth. The girl turned tearful and said, "Why are you talking like you're going to prison or somewhere dangerous? Please wait for me at home. Remember I'll come back for medical school."

"That's my dream for you too. Of course I'll stay well and take good care of your dad when he's back."

"Do you think he can endure all the abuse in jail?"

"He's tough inside and will survive. He knows I love him and am waiting for him at home, so he'll always have hope."

"I feel awful about Uncle Yang, though."

"Keep in mind that neither your father nor I will ever commit suicide. If we don't survive, that means people have laid their hands on us."

Little Lan left for Sartu the following weekend, bringing with her two tins of White Rabbit toffees and a sack of assorted preserved fruits for the Nius, the family that had taken her in at the oil field. The girl had promised to write Yomei more often, at least every other week. She already looked willowy, pretty like her birth mother. She would definitely grow into a beauty. Yomei was glad that Little Lan wasn't interested in theater or cinema at all. In this country, it was always safer to remain common and average. That must be why Uncle Zhu Deh had made his only son drive a locomotive. People all knew the bird that stuck its head above others would get shot first, but still few were content to stay ordinary and inconspicuous. Life shouldn't be tiresome and fearsome like this, obscured by shadows and secrecy. It should be more expansive and more liberating, imbued with light.

Seventy-Six

Jiang Ching looked through the things seized from Yomei's home. She was struck by the photos that showed her with Yomei in her midteens. How lovely the girl was in the pictures, and her as well—she had been a young woman in full bloom. She was also surprised by a spate of photographs of Yomei and Mao, taken in the Soviet Union. Carefully she went through the letters between her and Yomei. As for the pile of correspondence between that woman and Premier Zhou and Kang Sheng and Zhu Deh, Jiang Ching's assistants had already looked through them without finding any evidence that could be used to incriminate Yomei. Ergo, Jiang Ching ordered them to burn all the letters and pictures. She kept only one photograph, one that featured the premier shaking hands with Yomei and the acting crew of *The Rising Sun* after their performance.

Equipped with this photo, Jiang Ching went to see Premier Zhou at West Flower Hall. Zhou looked startled at the sight of her dark face, but he smiled with ease after she had sat down on a crimson velvet davenport. Without preamble, she handed him the envelope containing the photo. She said, "I found this: so you tried to sabotage our effort and make your own cultural revolution in an underhanded maneuver, didn't you?"

He took a look at the photograph and said, "You misunderstood me, Comrade Jiang Ching. Sun Yomei produced that play to celebrate the oil workers who were so dedicated to our country's petroleum industry. They're heroes and ought to be presented in our arts."

"But you intended to make some model plays with Sun Yomei's help, didn't you?"

"I'm not that interested in theater at all. I'm just an amateur, a dilettante at most, but now I can see that it's your turf. Don't be angry, and forgive me for overstepping. Have some tea. This is fresh Dragon Well from Hangzhou."

She took a sip and put down the cup. "Tell me the truth—you have been behind Sun Yomei's efforts, haven't you? You've been working against Chairman Mao and me all along. Now you've gone too far, carrying out your own plans. Even if you don't like our food, you mustn't set up your own kitchen."

"Easy, Comrade Jiang Ching. Please don't assume I'm at odds with you. I didn't know what you had in mind, and you've never revealed your intentions to me. Besides, Sun Yomei is just a stage director and has done nothing wrong on purpose, and she just followed the spirit of Chairman Mao's 'Speech at the Yan'an Forum on Literature and Art.' As a theater expert, she's supposed to celebrate heroic workers and their families."

"But the outcome of this play undermines the revolutionary model plays we have been making. I can see clearly that you've been attempting a countermove."

"It's just a piece of spoken drama that has nothing to do with Beijing opera."

"Still, it was becoming a movement, performed everywhere. There was even a movie to be adapted from it. So with this pet project of yours, you intended to sidetrack our effort to regain the world of theater, particularly in the sphere of spoken drama. It's the last citadel of reactionaries, which we must storm."

"Well, I had no idea a common play could be construed like this."

"Now we have decided to arrest Sun Yomei. I will have the warrant sent over for you to sign. Please sign it soon. It's time Sun Yomei reaped what she sowed."

Zhou looked stunned, his face dark and a bit haggard. He said, "I will consider it of course."

Jiang Ching went on, "Well, you must prove your innocence if you want to continue to head the Central Committee of the Cultural Revolution." He understood he was merely a figurehead in that office. Even his position in the CCP was precarious—he was totally at Mao's mercy now. Although Jiang Ching did not elaborate on her threat, he knew that if he couldn't prove his innocence, he might be removed from the standing committee of the politburo. If she was dead set against him, with Mao's backing she could bring about his downfall. Such a dire prospect unnerved him, so he might have to ally himself with Jiang Ching, which would be equivalent to standing with Mao.

Jiang Ching's visit roiled the premier, who discussed the matter with his wife that night. They both saw that this might turn into a falling-out with Jiang Ching, so they had to do everything to patch up the rift. If it wasn't repaired in time, such a schism might also antagonize Mao, so they had to make amends quickly.

The warrant arrived the next morning. It gave counterrevolution and espionage for the Soviet Union as

Sun Yomei's crimes, so she was to be apprehended without delay. The premier showed the warrant to his wife, and they both sank into thought for a long while. Then they talked about what to do. Mrs. Zhou believed he had no option but to sign it if he wanted to keep his post. Beyond question, Mao was behind Jiang Ching's revolutionary activities now, and to oppose her was to confront Mao, who could be ruthless in crushing his opponents. So Zhou Enlai had to beat a retreat. He uncapped his fountain pen and signed the warrant for Yomei's arrest. That sealed her fate.

Throughout the premier's political career, he had betrayed people close to him numerous times, even when he was aware that the betrayals might destroy them. He once had even signed a warrant for the arrest of his younger brother Tong-yu—he also provided detailed information on Tong-yu's whereabouts and on his family members. His brother was seized and imprisoned for seven years. Premier Zhou was a masterful politician and knew how to protect himself, and he didn't hesitate to sell anyone or anything, including his soul.

Jiang Ching was pleased with having Zhou's signature on the warrant. The next day, she began to make plans for hauling in the entire Soviet gang—Lisa Kishkin (who was already a widow but who didn't yet know that her jailed husband Li Lisan had killed himself with sleeping pills a few months before), Oyang Fei, Grania Chen, and Sun Yomei and Lin Lily. For months Jiang Ching had been making plans for their apprehension. Her instructions for arresting them stated that they were all revisionists, traitors, and foreign agents, so they were enemies of the people's dictatorship and must be brought to justice right away.

But in Yomei's case, Jiang Ching wanted to keep her hands clean, at least in appearance. Recently she had

learned that Yomei's letter to Lin Biao had been intercepted
by Yeh Qun. Obviously Vice Chairman Lin hadn't seen the
letter. Given his enduring affection for Yomei, he might
have intervened on her behalf if he'd heard about her
distress. She also knew that Yeh Qun hated Yomei's guts
and had over the two decades claimed she would kill Yomei
if she could lay her hands on "that slut," so Yeh Qun had
better step up and do the dirty work so as to protect her
own marriage. Jiang Ching went to Maojiawan to see Lin
Biao's wife. Her visit flustered and overwhelmed the small
woman. Ching pushed up her cat-eye glasses and told Yeh
Qun, "We have common enemies, and now finally we are in
a position to get hold of them and make them pay for their
wrongdoings. Can we help each other in this matter—I will
apprehend your enemies, and can you nab mine so that we
can get even with them?"

"Certainly I'll do whatever you want me to do, Comrade
Jiang Ching," Yeh Qun said in an obsequious tone of
voice, handing Ching a peeled tangerine. "Try this, it just
arrived."

Jiang Ching popped a section into her mouth,
chewing it with her lips slightly bunched. She continued,
"I know you hate Sun Yomei, who has been my enemy for
a long time, ever since our days in Yan'an. Now, I have
her detention warrant here, and you can handle her as
you like."

Eager to please the First Lady, Yeh Qun promised to
follow Ching's directives and bring in Yomei and "subdue
that fox spirit," who, to her mind, had been looming over
her marriage for decades, eager to take her husband away
from her. She would cut Yomei down once and for all.

"Do this secretly, with reliable hands," Jiang Ching said.
"Of course, nobody will know."

"Also, you'd better break that woman's arrogant spirit and destroy her beauty."

"Sure thing, once I have her in my hands, she'll be a goner before the end of this year."

Jiang Ching said no more, though she was surprised by Yeh Qun's hatred. If this small woman wanted to get rid of Sun Yomei, let her. This would at least keep her own hands clean.

Thus, a nefarious net began to be cast over Yomei, who was still busy trying to get her husband out of his confinement, even though she hadn't found out his whereabouts yet.

As agreed, Yomei and her sister met at the monument in Tiananmen Square that Saturday evening. They sat at its foot and compared notes about the current situation. Three days before, Yolan had gone to see Shih Chee, who was jailed in the same basement where her husband Yang had been murdered. Chee told Yolan to thank Yomei for helping with the three children's keep and for trying to get her out. Still the Red Guards wouldn't leave Chee alone, forcing her to confess her husband's "crimes." Apparently they intuited that some of them might one day have to answer for Sun Yang's torture and death, but they couldn't figure out how to absolve themselves, assuming that the more of his crimes they could prove, the more justification they might have when they were held accountable for his demise. So they pressed his wife hard for criminal evidence against Yang, but Chee always insisted on his innocence.

"The two boys are not doing well," Yolan told Yomei. "I can see they're traumatized. On the streets, kids often call them little bastards fathered by a foreign agent."

"Tell Ning and Ming that their dad wasn't an agent or traitor," Yomei said. "As soon as the Sino-Japanese war broke out in 1937, their father quit school in Tokyo and returned to China to fight the invaders. He was a hero in every sense. Also, if Yang were a stooge hiding beside Commander Zhu Deh, how could the Red Army have won one victory after another for so many years?"

"I'll talk to them. The boys are terrified to go to school."

"If necessary, do you think they should stay home for the time being?"

"Probably, we'll see. By the way, Yomei, you must be careful. The other day, Jiang Ching said to some college Red Guards that you were 'a beauty snake' and 'a time bomb sleeping next to Chairman Mao.' People have been whispering about that, as if you were having an unusual relationship with Mao."

"Jiang Ching is a fractious woman and has extraordinary powers for vengeance. I've known her since I was fifteen, and we used to be friendly to each other. In recent years she asked me to work on some plays for her, but I refused because I knew nothing about Beijing opera. That was the source of her fury. As for Chairman Mao, I once worked for him as an interpreter in the Soviet Union. Other than that, I'm not close to him at all. You know I'm not interested in politics. Jiang Ching can't wait to topple Father Zhou so that she can control the central government entirely. That's why she wants to get some negative information on him. We must do what we can to protect Father Zhou, who's our safety net."

"I see. I was wondering how come she'd flown off the handle like that publicly. She's really nuts and malicious."

"If they approach you, just deny any deep connection with me and the Zhous. You can say you got reconnected with me only when you came to college in Beijing and then we lost touch for several years when you were in Leningrad. Tell them that you've never been close to me because we didn't grow up together. In short, the less you are related to me, the safer it will be for you and Zongchang. Remember, just play dumb with them."

"OK, but I'm still worried about you, sister."

"I'll be fine. Jiang Ching doesn't have any evidence against me. I'm clean inside and out."

Jiang Ching's public remarks provided Yomei with another perspective on her relationship with the woman—Ching seemed to suspect there had been an affair between her husband and Yomei. That might explain why Ching had once wanted to talk with her about Mao's official visit to Moscow. She may have heard that Mao kept Yomei in his personal carriage for a whole night on the trans-Siberian train, so that Ching couldn't help but treat her as a mistress of Mao's. This put Yomei in a predicament—she couldn't clarify the truth to Ching. Worse, there was no way to know what Mao had told his wife about her. In other words, Ching's vengeance wasn't purely political or artistic. She might be driven by the instinct of a wife, doing her damnedest to save her marriage and face. If so, Yomei might be in serious danger.

She'd heard that a beautiful movie star in Shanghai had been recently imprisoned, having been accused of having an affair with Chairman Mao. The woman, from a capitalist family, was interrogated and tortured, evidently by Ching's lackeys. As a result, she jumped out of a building, but she didn't stop breathing at once. When the rescuers were carrying her on the back of a rickshaw to the hospital, words, like half-masticated food, kept seeping out of her blood-foamed lips—"I didn't . . . didn't seduce Chairman

Mao . . ." The woman's face was swollen, having been
slapped by the soles of shoes the night before, and she killed
herself because she couldn't satisfy the investigators sent
over from Beijing, was unable to write out what had really
transpired between her and Mao. Yomei had known the
movie star personally and remembered her lovely dreamy
eyes and svelte figure, though she was nearly forty back
then. Yomei also knew from hearsay that the woman had
been enmeshed with Mao, having met him on the sly several
times, which had made Jiang Ching green with jealousy and
malice. It was said that even during the final days of her life,
the woman was still dreaming that Mao would intervene
on her behalf, but the Great Leader had totally forgotten
her, probably due to the chemotherapy she'd gone through
for her breast and brain cancer in recent years, which had
ruined her looks and health. The image of the movie star's
last gasp of life upset Yomei and enabled her to see how
fatal such an accusation could be. So she had to defend
her innocence at all costs and had to speak up for herself
whenever she could, even though it would be impossible to
reason with Jiang Ching.

To date, Yomei hadn't told anyone about what Mao
had done to her. Only the Zhous knew, although she was
sure that Jiang Ching may have had eyes and ears around
Mao, keeping her apprised of any unusual happenings that
occurred when Mao traveled. Probably Yomei should just
insist that nothing had happened between her and Mao.
Still, it would be hard to prove her innocence. Clearly
Chairman Mao would never admit any wrongdoing, and
only others would be to blame for his malfeasance or crimes
and pay for them. Who dared to point a finger at him! Now,
how could she get out of this logjam? Impossible. She kept
saying to herself, This is a nail I can't pull out of my head.

The following night she sneaked to her Sixth Aunt's and asked to hear Jun's opinion. She trusted her, having grown up together with her and always taken her as a confidante. Jun's children and husband had all turned in, so she and Yomei were alone, sitting at the dining table and sipping the rice wine Jun brewed herself. Yomei explained why Jiang Ching had been so ruthless to her and her family. She described the incident with Mao on the train in February 1950 and also emphasized she had never been interested in Mao as a man, even though fifteen or sixteen years earlier Jiang Ching had told her that she was willing to share her husband as long as Yomei agreed to collaborate with her.

Jun pulled a face, then said, "Good heavens, I never thought this could get so messy. You were smart not to agree to have a special relationship with Mao. Jiang Ching couldn't have been serious. She may have just been testing you. It was good you didn't take the bait."

"How could she want to trap me?" Yomei was baffled.

"First, no woman would want to share her husband that way, especially considering hers is such a powerful man. Second, she might just have wanted to see how you'd respond—if you had showed some interest, she would have been convinced that there had been an affair between you and Mao."

"That makes sense. Do you think I should spill everything to Jiang Ching now, just to tell her what her husband did to me?"

"No, don't do that. How can you say Mao was a rapist? Such an accusation would never stick. It might backfire. The Central Committee would get rid of you if you embarrassed the Party's number one leader."

"Premier Zhou said the same thing—not to breathe a word, so it looks like I'll have to remain a loose woman in

Jiang Ching's eyes. If I had known Ching viewed me this way, I wouldn't have gone to see Chairman Mao last fall. What should I do now?"

"Just say you respect and worship Mao as our great savior. Present yourself as a pious woman."

"Do you think Jiang Ching will buy that?"

"I'm not sure. But you can't afford to be too confrontational."

"Sixth Aunt, if Ching's flunkies come to question you, say you know nothing and that I've never shared my secrets with you."

"OK, I can feign ignorance."

"Also, try your best to protect Premier Zhou. I know he's under vicious attack, so we must make sure he's safe."

Jun poured more wine into Yomei's cup. "Of course I'll do my best to protect Zhou Enlai as well. He's a big tree that can shelter all of us, so we mustn't let him fall. Have some more of this wine."

"I've had enough. You're so smart, Sixth Aunt. Jin Shan is not around, so you're the only person I can turn to for advice."

"Does this mean you told Jin Shan about your incident with Mao on the train?"

"No, you're the only person I've told, except for the Zhous."

"Don't tell your husband. The truth might be more destructive than we can imagine."

"I'll keep this to myself, of course. This stays only between us, OK?"

"Sure, it will rot in me."

Yomei returned home to find a letter from her daughter in the mailbox on the front gate. Little Lan informed her that school had resumed in Sartu and she was doing well, though math class was getting more difficult—they were going to start pre-algebra this semester. Her pals and some aunties often praised her new outfits, particularly her suede ankle boots. She wanted her mother to rest assured that all was well with her.

Yomei planned to write her daughter back in two or three days. After washing up and brushing her teeth, she poured some hot water from a thermos flask into a rubber bottle and placed it inside her quilt so that it would keep her feet warm while she was asleep. The house was rather cold, but she was reluctant to stoke the stove to heat the entire room, so she used a hot-water bottle instead.

· Seventy-Seven ·

The next day was Friday, March 1, and Yomei went through another session of self-criticism at the theater. This already felt like a routine to her. By the end of the day she was exhausted, but wasn't allowed to go home before dark. She had taken to wearing a fur hat nowadays. Her hair had grown back some, though she was still uncomfortable to show her short hair.

After a lonesome dinner, she went to bed early, hoping she could get up before daybreak to write a letter to Little Lan. She planned to enclose fifty yuan for the Nius' two children, who would need spring clothes soon. Hardly had she fallen asleep when someone rapped at her door and a voice yelled, "Open it, open up now!"

Yomei woke with a start, her heart drumming. She climbed out of bed but didn't dare to answer the door at night. She asked, "Who is it?"

"Investigators. We came to ask you a couple questions," a gruff voice said.

"It's already so late. Why not question me tomorrow morning? I will come to work as early as I can."

"Open the door. If you don't, we'll break in," the same voice cried.

She had no choice but to obey them. The second she opened the door a crack, they pushed in. Two men grabbed hold of her and dragged her away. She struggled to get free, but in vain.

They pushed her into a jeep and drove north. The car made so many turns that she soon lost her bearings. About a half hour later they stopped at a prison, which seemed to be near Deshengmen, still downtown. She was led into a room on the second floor, in which four men were waiting for her. None of them looked like the police. Three were actually in an air-force uniform—green jackets with four pockets and dark-blue pants. She couldn't see why military personnel were involved in her case. Then it dawned on her that Yeh Qun might be behind them. This meant that Lin Biao might not have received her letter. That woman could be more vicious than Jiang Ching. Or maybe the two were in league in persecuting her now. Even so, she wouldn't cooperate with them.

The moment she sat down on a wooden folding chair in front of the interrogators, the leader of the four, a middle-aged man with a large, mobile Adam's apple, asked her, "Sun Yomei, now you're a criminal and must fess up if you want to receive leniency."

"I'm clean and innocent," she said.

"Clean? Give me a break. Tell us, how often do you go to bed with Zhou Enlai?" guffawed the same man, named Hou Min. He must have been pushing forty, and already had rounded shoulders and a beer paunch hanging over his belt.

Thrown by the question, she couldn't say a word for a good while. Then she collected herself and said, "Stop springing such questions on me! I am Zhou Enlai's

daughter, so I love him as a father. You have no right to talk
like that."

Hou was tongue-tied for a moment. He shot a Great
Production cigarette out of a pack on the desk and lit it with
a match. He then resumed, "Sure, he's your sugar daddy.
Remember where you are and who you are. Stop inflating
your sense of self-importance. You must behave yourself in
this jailhouse, or you will get more than you can carry."

"You think you can frighten me into obedience?"

"We just need some truthful information from you."

A weasel-faced man in civvies, fluttering his crafty eyes,
added, "We've seen so many people fall to pieces in here.
Don't presume you're superior to others." He scratched
his bald scalp as if he were combing hair. His pointy ears
twitched a little.

"Still, I'm a stickler for facts and can't lie," said Yomei.

While they were speaking, a young man sitting in the
corner by the small window was busy jotting down notes.
Yomei glared at the leader contemptuously and said, "You
won't find me useful to you."

"But you could be useful to some of the male inmates,
who haven't seen a woman for years." Hou gave a lewd,
gummy grin, showing his long teeth.

She clammed up in disbelief and felt the sudden
strumming of her heart, while her mouth went dry, her
throat burning. She felt the blood draining from her face.
He smirked again and went on, "We know you and Zhou
Enlai were often engaged in hanky-panky. Did you lose
your virginity to him? Does he still feel you up from time to
time? Tell me what color his underwear is."

Though still numb with terror, she managed to reply:
"Your shameless nonsense makes my ears wilt. You're
talking like a hoodlum. Why not ask me about Chairman

Mao's underwear?" A glint of pride flickered in her eyes. As she was speaking, she regained her composure. She told them in a supercilious tone of voice, "I'll tell you what, in Moscow I served as Chairman Mao's personal interpreter, so I would check his clothes, which were laundered by the Russian servants. But I can't tell you what kind of underwear he used, because there're rules that forbid me to leak classified information. Let me just say Chairman Mao wore navy socks. Remember, you're not supposed to gather this kind of information. Make a notch on your nose—don't forget it."

All the interrogators looked dumbfounded, apparently unfamiliar with some of the Russian idioms mixed in her retort. Then another man, in his thirties and thin like a pole, with a crew cut, said, "You think we don't know you often tried to seduce Chairman Mao? Why did you do that?"

"You're talking farts! Stop insulting the Great Leader. You're committing a crime now by speaking about him like that."

"All right," their head, Hou, joined in again, "let's skip that. We know you're a whore, born and bred, regardless of the innocent airs you have put on. Tell me how you exercised your charms on Vice Chairman Lin Biao."

"You can go ask him. He was my friend in Moscow and was warm and kind to me, partly because I was his ex-wife Zhang Mei's close friend. He's a gentleman through and through. You mustn't speak out of turn like this or I will report you to his wife, Yeh Qun."

The fourth man with a pimply face jumped in, hissing through his teeth, "Do you think you're still the Red Princess, living in Zhongnanhai? Ridiculous. Now you're a counterrevolutionary, an enemy of the people. And you must behave and cooperate and tell us what really happened between you and Zhou Enlai."

"Here's the nail I can't pull out of my head: Why are you so interested in what happened inside the top leaders' pants? Can't you be more respectful and speak like a decent man?" She shook her face with a look of revulsion.

A lull followed. Hou said again, "All right, it's getting late and you need time to clear your head to become more reasonable. We'll continue tomorrow."

With a wave of his thick hand, he told the guards to take her to room 302. Two men stepped over and pulled her up and dragged her away.

The solitary cell was damp and dingy, reeking of sweat and urine. The whitewashed walls were grayish under a twenty-five-watt bulb. The blanket on a narrow pallet may have been used by numerous inmates before, but Yomei covered herself with it fully, afraid she might get ill otherwise. However dire her situation was, she had to survive and join Jin Shan to resume their life together. By now she was more convinced that her apprehension had as much to do with the theater arts and political struggle as with the wifely jealousy of the two most powerful women in China, Jiang Ching and Yeh Qun. Whatever their scheme, she must do everything to preserve the last remnants of her dignity. When she got out of prison, she might try to persuade Jin Shan to move somewhere far away from Beijing. They could live in a provincial city and devote themselves to an obscure local theater, like her second brother, Jishi, who had been living an undisturbed life back in Sichuan. Yes, start fresh, anew. She wouldn't mind cutting ties and living in total isolation. If possible, she'd adopt a different name. To survive, one had better remain a cipher on the periphery and manage to become

self-sustainable. It was too perilous and maddening to
stay near the center of political power. Maybe they should
move to Sartu, where Little Lan was now. It was simply
too precarious to be a significant artist in this country,
where no genuine art could exist outside of politics.
Any extraordinary talent that emerged in arts would get
noticed by the powers that be and would be harnessed to
serve a cause or a political purpose. There couldn't be
any artistic independence to speak of. That was viewed
as separated from the multitude, therefore by nature
bourgeois and reactionary. So she and Jin Shan had better
reassess their condition and figure out a proper modus
vivendi.

Yomei didn't know that the other members of the so-
called Soviet cabal had been arrested as well. Lily had also
been apprehended the night before and brought to the
same prison, though they couldn't possibly have been aware
of each other's circumstances and whereabouts. Yomei
was in the hands of the air-force men, whereas the other
members of the gang were held in another building and
handled by the police, who interrogated them to gather
information on the other "Soviet agents," including Yomei.
Fortunately, none of them said anything negative about her
and all insisted on her innocence and her dedication to
the theater arts. Those women were not physically abused.
In contrast, Li Lisan, because of his denying that Yomei
and the other women were working for the Soviets, had
often been punched and kicked by his interrogators before
he had committed suicide the previous summer. Once he
was battered unconscious, with two teeth knocked out of
his head. Due to the repeated torture, he took an overdose
of sleeping pills. In his last letter, he vowed to the Central
Committee that he had never betrayed the Party or the

country. But at this point, none of the Soviet gang was aware that he was already dead.

The next day the interrogators asked Yomei many questions about Li Lisan and obviously were trying to frame him as a spy for the USSR and as a traitor to the CCP, even though he had died ten months before. Apparently they were trying to gather evidence that might be used to absolve themselves—once Li Lisan was proved to be a class enemy, his destruction could be justified and his case closed.

Yomei insisted that Li Lisan was selfless, a paragon of a good man. "I don't think you can find a more dedicated comrade than him," she said.

"We know you two are working hand in glove for the Soviets," Hou said and grinned, one of his cheeks bigger than the other.

"The truth was that for a long time," Yomei explained, "Li Lisan was believed expelled from the Party, so we all shunned him in Moscow. Still, he was busy editing a newspaper in support of China's fighting against the Japanese invasion. No one but his wife Lisa stood by him. Theirs is a great example of a couple's mutual devotion and love. She refused to condemn Li Lisan and believed he was a good, pure man, a genuine revolutionary. For that she was expelled from the Komsomol, and became a scapegoat. In the early 1940s, Li Lisan lived in total obscurity, from hand to mouth. When the composer Sinn Sing Hoi appeared in Moscow, sick and destitute, and nobody helped him, it was Li Lisan who fed and sheltered him. We thought Lisan had a house of his own and went over to take a look. It turned out that he and Lisa were sharing a room with her mother and her sister's family, but the Lis let Sinn Sing Hoi use their only bed while the couple slept on the floor with their baby. What else

could you expect an expelled Party member to do but help
a dying comrade like that? The Chinese expats talked
a great deal about Li Lisan, and all were touched by his
generosity and devotion to the revolutionary cause. No,
you can't get a single negative word about him from my
mouth. Neither can you force me to say any fabricated
nonsense about him."

"But even his wife admitted he kept delivering secret
intelligence to the Soviet embassy here," Hou said.

"That's preposterous. I've known Lisa Kishkin well
enough to tell you she isn't that kind of a person and would
never inform on her husband. She's a stalwart wife to him,
steadfast like a rock."

"Didn't she herself often go to the Soviet embassy too?"

"Again, why are you kicking up such a fuss? Why make
an elephant out of a fly? Why not use a bit of your common
sense? She's from the Soviet Union and of course she had
to go to the Soviet offices in town for paperwork and for
business reasons. Even a hedgehog can understand that."

A bespectacled man jumped in, "Talk to us in Chinese.
We don't understand the foreign expressions you're so fond
of tossing out. There's no need to show off. Also, drop your
Russianized manner. You're no longer in Moscow. You're
an inmate here, the same as everybody else."

"I spoke to you like this only because I assumed you were
reasonable human beings."

At that, another interrogator, with cross-eyes and a
pockmarked face, rushed over and struck her on the cheek.
Instantly her chin was streaked with blood. He hissed,
"We're also responsible for getting rid of your arrogance, so
don't put on airs in front of us."

The strike almost knocked her out. She sucked in her
breath, her head ringing. Their leader waved a squarish

hand, and the guards stepped over and dragged her back to her cell again.

Lunch was turnip soup with a corn bun, which tasted mildewed and even had weevils in it. The previous day, Yomei had thrown the inedible food out of the small opening on the door, saying it would upset her stomach and make her sick. But today she closed her eyes and just ate the food without tasting it. No matter what, she had to eat and live to fight another day.

· *Seventy-Eight* ·

A t night she often heard inmates in other cells
screaming and yelping as they were being hit.
Most of them were men, though once in a while a
female voice, sharper and more heart-wrenching, pierced
the walls. There were also paroxysms of wailing and noisy
protests. Once she heard a male voice calling his attackers
"Daddy" and "Uncle" and "Grandpapa," begging them
not to beat him. Yet someone gave a shrill bark of laugh,
sputtering, "We can stamp you out like an ant." Then they
resumed savaging him. "Ow, ow! Please don't hurt me,
Papa! Spare my life!" the inmate kept howling. Shrieks of
laughter followed.

This was hell. Yomei felt a pang of fear, as though
her blood was on the cusp of curdling. No matter what,
she'd have to keep her wits together so as to deal with
the interrogators. She felt a nerve on the right side of
her head throbbing with darts of pain. Although her
proximity to the violence made her nerves overwrought
and frayed, sometimes she'd sing a song, a Russian song, to
cheer herself up—"The Evening in a Suburb of Moscow,"
"Katyusha," "The Hawthorn Tree," "Troika," or "Heroes of
the Fatherland"—but most times no sooner had she started
singing than a guard would bark at her to shut up.

By now it had grown clear to her that the powers behind her interrogators were Yeh Qun and Jiang Ching, whose names she'd once overheard the men whisper among themselves. Every day they took her to the interrogation room and spent several hours questioning her. Sometimes one or two of them turned violent, punching and slapping her. Once a man hit her in the chest and grasped her breast, saying they must squash her pride. She swatted his hand away and asked him whether he had a sister or a mother.

As the interrogations continued, the team of men became worn out. They had spent so many days already, but didn't make any progress. She had simply yielded no useful information. She had become a hopeless case. The more frustrated they were, the more violent they got, so physical abuse and harassment became part of the daily process. But she always appeared superior to them in spirit and couldn't help but look down on them. They all could feel their inadequacy in subduing her. As a result, some new interrogators stepped in, and the two groups rotated. Still, they couldn't make her cooperate.

Without fail, their interrogations would lead to Zhou Enlai. Their job must be to dig up enough dirt on the premier so as to topple him. They even tried to surprise Yomei by asking her unexpected questions so that she might divulge something valuable to them unwittingly. Once Chief Hou asked her, "Isn't there a scar on Zhou Enlai's chest?"

Nonplussed for a moment, Yomei managed to reply, "He has many scars on him. I saw the one left by the operations on his right arm at the Kremlin Hospital. I know what's behind your question. Why not ask me what his genitalia are like?"

The other three men laughed through their noses, while Hou's pudgy face turned the color of pork liver, which made the freckles on his cheeks nearly invisible. Expressionlessly, Yomei said, "Premier Zhou is my father, so stop trying to make me throw dirt on him. I do love him, but only as a father of mine."

Two of the interrogators shook their heads and breathed out a sigh. She didn't know why. Were they sympathetic to her? She hoped so.

Alone in the cell, she often mulled over her life and work over the past two decades. She felt she had been too innocent and ignorant. She had used to believe art could hold its own autonomous dominion in society and that she could live a fulfilled life by dedicating herself to the art of spoken drama. Now she could see that she had been mistaken. In this country, arts and politics were always entwined, and most of the time arts were subdued to become handmaids of politics. If she could start over, she might have tried to live a different life that would have little to do with politics or even art. But for now, she had to endure all the torture and humiliation. She was sure that Father Zhou must be looking for her and would come to her rescue soon.

The interrogation continued every day, save Sundays. One morning they brought up the name Reslie Mironov and asked if she had a promiscuous relationship with the Russian man. She answered, "I did like Reslie, partly because we were classmates at the Russian Institute of Theater Arts and we played as a couple in Chekhov's play *Three Sisters*."

"Not as a couple in real life?" asked Chief Hou, smirking suggestively.

"He went to join the Red Arm to fight the German invaders. For many years he was listed as having fallen in the line of duty. I thought he had sacrificed his young life for his fatherland."

"Didn't you invite him to come to Beijing and collaborate with Jin Shan in *Uncle Vanya*?"

"No, first of all, I've never had that kind of clout. Second, I didn't know he was still alive. His appearance here was a shock to me. You can go ask my old colleagues in the Youth Art Theater how Jin Shan was picked for the role. Reslie interviewed many actors for Uncle Vanya and didn't find any of them suitable. Then he heard of Jin Shan and they met. He signed up Jin Shan on the spot."

"How did he come to know of Jin Shan?"

"I recommended my husband to him. Look, the play was a collaborative project between the USSR and China, and I was assigned to be its associate director. I recommended Jin Shan also out of my national pride—Reslie complained he couldn't find a suitable actor in the whole of China, so I didn't want him to think there was no Chinese man capable of taking such a role."

That silenced them. Then Hou asked, "So there's no extramarital affair between you and that Russian expert?"

"Why can't you think of a normal relationship between a woman and a man, like friendship, respect, affection, camaraderie? Reslie might have had a crush on me before he joined the Red Army, but he was injured and crippled and seemed content to live a single life with his sister's family in Leningrad. The man had a lot of dignity and a strong will, and I respect him for that."

That again dampened their eagerness to probe her romantic experiences with foreign men. That night she thought about the questions about Reslie. Evidently they must have come from someone privy to the theater business. Those air-force men, knowing nothing about Russian drama, couldn't even have come up with the title *Uncle Vanya*, to say nothing of Reslie Mironov. Again, Jiang Ching may have been supervising them in prying open her mouth.

Then another round of interrogation puzzled and also amused her, making her wonder if Ching was supervising them closely enough. They asked her about her staging of Ostrovsky's *The Storm*. They viewed the production of such a classic Russian play as evidence for Yomei's spreading foreign culture and bourgeois sentiments in China. In particular, she had done her damnedest to disseminate the Stanislavski method.

Hou sucked in his breath and said, "How the hell could your poster describe Katherina, the heroine of the play, as 'a ray of light in the kingdom of darkness'? Clearly Katherina is just an adulteress, unable to hold her legs together. Why did you publicize such a crazy woman, who betrays her husband? Did you intend to advocate adultery? And to undermine our society's moral order?"

"I'm appalled to see you're so ignorant of arts and literature," Yomei said. "You can't tell how much Katherina suffers in the household and in a far-off backwater town."

"Suffering from what?" He snorted a laugh. "Give her a shovel or a hoe and make her work in the fields. That would consume her lust and cure her mental problems. You call that play a work of art? If it's art, it's bourgeois art and shouldn't be shown in China, not in our proletarian society. By nature, you're just a reactionary."

"You're such an ignoramus. You should check with Comrade Jiang Ching whether she played the role of Katherina in Shanghai in 1937. The play was directed by Mr. Zhang Min, who chose Jiang Ching as the heroine, the adulteress. She was gorgeous onstage. It was a major development in her career. Please go ask Comrade Jiang Ching, whose name was Lan Ping at the time. She'll be happy to enlighten you on this."

That silenced them all. They looked at each other in perplexity, and then the two younger ones grinned, as if amused. Back in her cell, Yomei couldn't stop chuckling. She wondered how Ching would take it when she read the interrogation notes about The Storm. But then the interrogators might suppress those notes about Jiang Ching's past. In the old theater circles it was known that Zhang Min, a director of some repute, had decided on Ching for Katherina only because she was sleeping with him, acting as an adulteress in real life since she was married—her husband, Tang Na, attempted to kill himself time and again because of her frequent affairs.

The interrogators had gotten paper and pens delivered to Yomei's cell and demanded she write out her confessions, but to date she hadn't put down a single sentence. She always emphasized that she was red inside and out and had done nothing wrong. None of them was qualified to criticize her, let alone chastise and abuse her. They seemed to respond to her position by beginning to question her about some other people she knew.

One day they asked her about Lin Lily. Chief Hou said, "Didn't she always have the hots for white men? Didn't she have a big-nosed boyfriend like her younger sister did, who married a Russian?"

"No." Yomei was alarmed and wanted to defend her friend by any means. "Lily didn't feel safe around men because she was traumatized when she was four years old—she saw a man throw a woman into the ocean from a passenger boat. Also, she met some obnoxious men in Moscow, like Young Zeng."

"What's his full name?" Hou persisted.

"Zeng Yongfu. We just called him Young Zeng. He worked at the Comintern and always bad-mouthed others and gave us orders. Vice Chairman Lin Biao knew him. Young Zeng worked for him briefly, but I don't think Lin Biao has a good opinion of him."

"I don't believe that Lin Lily is not interested in men. How about Wang Jia-hsiang?"

"That's ludicrous, beyond all bounds. Lily used to work for Ambassador Wang in the Soviet Union. They had to go to places together for work."

"How can you explain this?" The bespectacled man handed her a photograph.

Yomei took a look. In the picture, Lily leaned against Mr. Wang and smiled blissfully. To some extent they did look like a couple, though she was a generation younger than he was. Yomei knew Lily liked Mr. Wang and might even have developed a crush on him, but that didn't mean there was an affair between them. To her knowledge, Mr. Wang was very rational and careful and wouldn't take advantage of Lily. Besides, Mrs. Wang was a charming lady and always accompanied him—the couple loved each other dearly. Yomei told the interrogators, "Look, Lily was his interpreter and respected him like an uncle. In fact, they often went to official events together, only the two of them. For instance, in 1953, they went to Stalin's Kuntsevo Dacha for dinner and spent many hours alone with Stalin. There couldn't possibly have been another Chinese present on that occasion. This photo was nothing but a memento of an official occasion."

"But they are intimate like lovers in this photo."

"Lily is innocent like a young child. She has a pure heart. Don't you dare smear her like this."

"We'll find out. Wang Jia-hsiang will have to give his explanation about this."

Yomei was shocked that Mr. Wang had also been detained. Why were so many decent and capable people under investigation now? To her knowledge, there was no feud between Mr. Wang and Jiang Ching. What was this country coming to? So many people had become targets of the revolution, as if the revolution had to consume some lives in order to sustain its turbulent momentum. She hoped Lily, who was often too outspoken, was careful with her tongue this time. Above everything else, she hoped Lily was safe.

ily was also interrogated frequently, but neither she nor Oyang Fei were physically abused. Still, Feifei had lost her mind, she was at times catatonic and delirious, and had to be sent to a mental asylum. As for Lily, she wasn't cooperative at all, believing she was mistreated by some people in the Party. She and Yomei were in the same jail at the time, but they were unaware of each other's imprisonment. Like a regular inmate, Lily was allowed to stay outdoors in the back of the premises for fifteen minutes a day, while Yomei was kept inside around the clock.

Compared to Yomei, the other women of the Soviet cabal were merely small fry, and none of them was a significant target of investigation. On top of that, there was no personal hatred involved in their cases. Yomei's situation was far more perilous. To her surprise, she was questioned also about her relationship with Xu Yi-xin, who was still serving as a vice foreign minister at the moment. Evidently Jiang Ching hadn't forgotten the cold shoulder that man had given her three decades before. One afternoon Hou said brazenly to Yomei, "Tell me, how many times did Xu Yi-xin sleep with you?"

Yomei insisted that they had never been real lovers. Yi-xin had been after her, but as soon as Jiang Ching started living with Chairman Mao, Yi-xin stopped meeting her, Yomei.

"Why was that?" Hou asked.

"Because Jiang Ching had a crush on him, and he wouldn't want to complicate his relationship with women, I guess. But actually there was no real relationship developing between him and me. To put this bluntly, he was afraid of antagonizing Jiang Ching, who had begun keeping Chairman Mao company."

"We are supposed to look into him as well. Didn't he often run after female students at Lu Hsun Academy of Literature and Arts?"

"Like I said, he was just one of the school leaders, and he also taught an introductory course in social sciences. He was intelligent and spoke Russian. Plus with his good looks, he was attractive to many young women. It was some female students who chased him, not the other way around."

"So you fell for him and opened your pants to him too? Didn't he have a birthmark on his butt cheek?"

"I won't answer such shameless questions. You'd better find another way to gratify the voyeur in you, or else you might infuriate Comrade Jiang Ching. She was fond of him too, though Yi-xin may not have reciprocated her affection. Why bring back those unpleasant memories to Comrade Jiang Ching? You ought to respect her privacy and let what transpired remain undisturbed."

That stopped them from asking anything further about Xu Yi-xin, whose future seemed precarious to Yomei now. Evidently Jiang Ching would never forget even the smallest grievance and might take revenge on him as well. He shouldn't have returned to Beijing before he was retired—it would have been safer for him to remain an ambassador abroad, wandering from country to country before his retirement.

In midsummer of 1968, Yomei collapsed, physically unable to go through the interrogation sessions anymore. She was in delirium and often talked incoherently. She would yell at someone, "Don't drive this nail into my head!"

The interrogations could no longer continue, so they left her alone. But to make her more obedient, once in a while they put her into a male cell and let the inmates use her. No matter how she protested and resisted, the bestial men had their way with her, even when she had blacked out. The order from above was secretive but clear: "Crush her spirit, destroy her body. Do not let her survive this year." So the prison personnel meant to have her finished off as soon as possible so as to end this nightmare.

Except for the interrogators, very few people knew Yomei's true identity. Because of her isolation and the pseudonym they'd given her, it was safe for them to do whatever they could to her. Therefore, they just let some male inmates torture her as a kind of reward for their "good behavior." They'd say to the prisoners, "Here's a woman back from Moscow. You can use her as you like." By then, Yomei had lost her voice and was deranged and at times unconscious.

Meanwhile, Yolan tried desperately to find out where Yomei was, but without success. She went to West Flower Hall in Zhongnanhai and begged Father Zhou to help rescue her sister, but the premier said he had assigned people to look into the case and couldn't find Yomei's whereabouts. That must have been true—as soon as they

arrested her, her persecutors had changed her name to
"Sun Fraud."

Then, one day in the summer of 1970, Yolan was told
to go to the prison at Deshengmen to get her sister's death
certificate. She hurried over, and they handed her a piece
of paper that stated Sun Yomei had died of a cerebral
hemorrhage two years before. Yolan asked for her sister's
ashes, but they told her, "Her body was disposed of like
those of all counterrevolutionaries. We haven't kept any of
their ashes, so we have nothing to give you."

She left in stupefaction and with bitter tears. Swelling
with anger, she went to Uncle Zhu Deh's home the next day
and told the Zhus about Yomei's death. Both Mr. Zhu and
his wife broke down, sobbing bitterly. Mrs. Zhu said with
a crumbled face, "You Suns are a family of loyal martyrs.
Our Communist Party owes you Suns a deep apology, but
there's no way to make up for your losses!"

Yolan also went to inform the Zhous of the tragedy. To
her amazement, they had known of it long ago. Mother Deng
said, "Your sister was too fiery and too unyielding to survive
in prison. Originally your father and I thought it would be
safer to keep her in jail as a kind of protection, since even
if they detained her, they'd have to proceed by the rules.
But who could've imagined they'd kill her like that? When
Father Zhou heard of her death, he insisted on an autopsy
and a thorough investigation. But they had already cremated
her." While saying those words, Mother Deng kept a blank
face, so Yolan couldn't tell whether she was sad or angry or
really concerned. But the old woman's words threw her deep
in thought. Why did Father Zhou sign Yomei's detention
warrant in the first place if he meant to protect her? Yolan
kept wondering and couldn't help but feel that the Zhous had
played a part in her sister's destruction as well.

More unforgivable, if the Zhous had known of Yomei's demise long ago, why didn't they notify her? It seemed that in this case their hands were not clean either. Later she told Sixth Aunt Jun about Father Zhou's signing Yomei's arrest warrant. Jun was outraged and couldn't help but curse that smooth, crafty man, saying he was "a smiling snake" and had thrown her niece into the claws of those tigresses—Jiang Ching and Yeh Qun. He was their accomplice.

Indeed, Yomei may have been troublesome to the premier, but his signature sealed her fate. No decent father would have sacrificed his daughter that way. No wonder it was said that Zhou Enlai was hypocrisy personified, even though he was viewed as the number one "warm man" in the CCP. Yolan went to Yomei's home every two or three weeks to keep everything in order and to water the pots of camellias and orchids that Jin Shan and Yomei had been fond of. Every time she was there, she'd make sure to feed Jin Shan's goldfish in the aquarium with dried water fleas. With a little coal shovel, she scraped the moss away from the slate path in their tiny yard. Before the wintertime, she took the flowers and the fish to her own home and brought them back in the spring.

Back in June 1969, Shih Chee had been released, so Bing, Ming, and Ning had returned home and joined their mother. Then Chee was sent to Jiangxi Province for labor reform, and her three children went with her. The following summer Zongchang was diagnosed with stomach cancer and became an invalid for almost two years before he died. Yolan was left alone with their two children, though she managed to raise them on her own. Fortunately she still had her teaching position at Beijing University, where she devoted herself to helping her students, although most of them weren't eager to learn Russian anymore. It was English and Japanese that had were now the popular foreign languages. Even the radio broadcast English lessons in the mornings and evenings. In her department many lecturers of Russian had switched to English, struggling to learn the foreign tongue that was more useful in the world. But Yolan remained a Russian teacher and didn't change anything in her profession or in her life. In the following years she never did contact the Zhous. She wanted to have nothing to do with them.

Rumor had it that when Lin Biao heard of Yomei's death toward the end of 1969, he had taken his wife to task. He said to Yeh Qun, "I knew you and Jiang Ching killed Sun Yomei. You and she simply can't let anyone be and will destroy whoever is brighter and prettier than you are. If you two rotten cunts go on like this, you will ruin everything, including yourselves!"

· *Eighty* ·

After more than seven years' imprisonment, Lily and Jin Shan got out of jail in the early summer of 1975, within days of each other. The incarceration had ruined their health, so neither of them were able to work like before. Lily went to stay with her elder sister's family, while Jin Shan returned to his home. Finally they came to know that Yomei had been killed long ago. Crushed and wrecked, Jin Shan was resolved to keep his home as it had been when Yomei had lived there. He was frail, having in seven years' imprisonment aged at least two decades, and couldn't manage on his own, so Yolan came every weekend. She cooked for Jin Shan and helped him tidy up the house. He was often off his head, taking Yolan as her sister, calling her Yomei and even patting her. She didn't blame him, though he would apologize when his senses returned.

She was touched by his attachment to the memory of her sister. Sometimes she stayed in Yomei's room on weekends. Gradually Jin Shan depended more and more on her help. As they got to know each other better, he proposed to her, with the provision that they keep everything in the house as it had been as when Yomei had been there. Without a second thought Yolan accepted the offer—she too wanted to remain faithful to her sister's memory. The two of them went to the local office and got a marriage certificate, but they didn't hold a wedding, feeling there was nothing to celebrate. It was fate that had thrown them together, assembling them as one family again. Jin Shan loved Yolan's children and accepted them as his own, though somehow he fell out with Little Lan, grumbling about her friends, who had borrowed his precious books but never returned them and also about her having a boyfriend, who was nothing but a dandy in his eyes. As a result, the girl no longer acknowledged him as her father, though she always thought of Yomei as her mother.

Jin Shan and Yolan lived peacefully in spite of so many historical events taking place. In 1976 alone, Zhou Enlai died in January, Zhu Deh passed away in June, Mao Zedong breathed his last breath in September, and in the following month Jiang Ching and three of her close accomplices—the Gang of Four—were overthrown by a coup mounted by Marshal Yeh Jian-ying and Deng Xiaoping. The gang was arrested and thrown into prison. Their overnight downfall was celebrated throughout China by common citizens. At her trial, Jiang Ching insisted on her total innocence, crying out, "I'm Chairman Mao's dog and would bite whoever he set me upon." To her mind, there was simply no one entitled to try her. Later she hanged herself in her prison cell, with handkerchiefs tied together and fixed to a small iron shelf that supported her washbasin. She claimed she was to join Chairman Mao in the netherworld. Years before, in the fall of 1971, Yeh Qun and her husband, Lin Biao, perished in a plane crash in Mongolia as a result of their failure in the struggle against Mao. Scared of Mao's retaliation, the couple had fled China, but their plane hadn't been able to reach the Soviet Union and crashed. Their bodies were buried together with those of their followers in a stopgap grave dug at the site, in the wild prairie outside Öndörkhaan, except for Lin Biao's head, which was collected by the KGB and later pickled in formalin. All those powerful figures disappeared as if a gust of wind had swept them away and scattered them like puffs of smoke. In spite of everything, Jin Shan and Yolan continued to live uneventfully.

Then Yomei's reputation was restored. All her "crimes" were dismissed. The only accusation remotely true was that she had personally gone to Lisa's home a few times to give her some free theater tickets (which had been treated by her persecutors as Yomei's way of passing intelligence on to Soviet agents). On June 9, 1977, the Ministry of Culture held a memorial service in honor of Yomei, which was attended by more than two hundred people, mostly her friends and colleagues. Many couldn't hold back their tears and spoke about their love and affection for her and about what the loss of such a brilliant stage director meant to contemporary Chinese theater, and also to themselves. Memory after memory, all were stained with tears and blood, mixed with grief and joy—

"Sun Yomei was a transparent person and an endearing artist. It was the Cultural Revolution that prevented her career from reaching its peak. She is a people's martyr among our artists and a people's hero among our artists. In this aspect, no artist can be compared to her. She is a nonpareil, in a class of her own." —You Benchang, actor

"Sun Yomei is by all accounts a founder of the new China's new theater. She was a torch blazing like a beacon for all the latecomers in our field. Her work still can teach us how to navigate the sea of theater arts." —Zhou Zhi-qiang, president of the National Theater of China

"Every play she directed gave you a new sensation. She always experimented with new methods and new forms. People who saw her plays all had such an impression: some of her plays were like a series of pictures of life, full of the aura and the feeling of reality; some were like sets of oil paintings, abundant, raw, bold, thick with colors; some flowed like lyrical poetry; some were like a symphony, lively and fresh, lingering with meaning and emotion afterward." —Jin Zhenwu, actor

"One of the most salient features of Comrade Sun Yomei's directing was that she emphasized what was behind your lines. She demanded that actors substantiate their characters' inner lives and must imagine every specific monologue to find the precise unspoken lines. Once the inside of a character was filled and specified, the character's language and movement onstage would become active and powerful, and then the thoughts and feelings could become more realistic." —Jin Shuzhi, actress

"I can forgive Jiang Ching many bad things she did, but one thing I will never forgive her: the murder of my dear friend Yomei. Why destroy such a brilliant, beautiful woman, who was harmless to everyone?" —Lisa Kishkin

"Sun Yomei was straightforward, so her words were sharp, even piercing. Everyone, however experienced or famous, was equal on her rehearsal stage, no more than an actor. When taking part in her rehearsal, you were excited but also antsy. With her

help, you always could find something new and get
enlightened. But once she caught any defect you had,
you'd have to pay for it. She was good at imitating
you, so through her imitation, your defect would be
enlarged and even stretched. The observers around
you would laugh out loud while you didn't know how
to take it, beyond being embarrassed, of course. It
was like placing germs under a microscope, so you
wouldn't dare to touch them again. Therefore, those
imitated and embarrassed by her learned the most
from her. Her acumen and fearlessness daunted
you, while her generosity and open-mindedness
encouraged you to make bold and get better. This
individual's personality had so many solid facets,
unforgettable." —Yang Zongjing, stage director

"My mother was always kind and considerate to others,
and she was never guarded to anyone. In the early 1960s,
there was the famine, and whenever her acting crew came
to our home to discuss a play, she would ask our nanny
to stir-fry some flour, then let everyone have a bowl of
it mixed with sugar. A down-and-out actress named Jin
Minju from the northeast once came to our home because
her husband was branded as a 'rightist.' When the woman
was leaving, my mother gave her a fine fur overcoat, the
only one she had, because the woman was wearing thin
clothes... Mother enjoyed playing with me like a little
girl. Together we jumped rope, skipped and danced over
a chain of rubber bands, played hide-and-seek, kicked the
shuttlecock, played hopscotch, made origami creatures
and colored pinwheels, flew kites and paper planes, built
temples and vehicles with toy bricks, and tossed marbles,
though she was already close to forty... She was always
fun. She was almost never made-up but always glowed

with beauty and ease. Her beauty was true, coming out from within." —Little Lan

"She was a big director but had no airs. Once, rehearsing a play, she let You Benchang chase some refugees. I was playing a refugee, and while escaping from Benchang, I couldn't stop in my tracks and hurt my back and broke a rib. I was hospitalized. It was in the middle of the famine, and without enough food, I was bloated and couldn't sleep at night, suffering from a psychological disorder and being emaciated. Sun Yomei often went to the hospital to see me and gave me some sleeping pills, saying they were from Russia, so I should take one tablet only when I really couldn't sleep. Later she also gave me a bottle of vitamin B_{12}. The capsules were in a pink bottle, and were very precious at the time. I still have the bottle at home. During the Cultural Revolution, when I heard she was gone, I gripped that bottle and cried for hours... In real life she was a scatterbrain. She bought a monthly bus pass but used it only three times and later had no idea when it expired. Once she purchased a floor lamp in Guangzhou and consigned it for shipment to Beijing. After a long time, when we were rehearsing *Joys and Sorrows*, as the senior official was sitting in the living room and reading a newspaper, Yomei said, 'Well, if only there were a floor lamp while he's reading the paper'—she stopped and went spacey. We were all at a loss and asked what happened to her. She said, 'I have a chrome floor lamp somewhere at home. But I don't know where it is nowadays. I remember paying for it.' By then, half a year had passed. She had actually forgotten to collect the lamp from the railroad cargo office. On the other hand, we were often amazed by her photographic memory when she worked on a play." —Song Geh, actor

"When we were performing *The Brothers Yershov* in
the Great Hall of the People, my baby was sick and I
was overwhelmed at home, so I couldn't concentrate
onstage, and many things went wrong: I missed one of
my scenes, my beard fell off, even the fly of my pants was
not buttoned. One night, Vice Premiere Chen Yi came
to see our play, and Yomei accompanied him. But they
couldn't find me, so they had to drop the curtain and
look for me again. Afterward Yomei's chauffeur told me,
'Director Sun wants to replace you.' I said I was prepared
for that, knowing I had embarrassed her and my fellow
actors... The next day Yomei told me to come to her home
in the evening. I thought she'd dress me down. When I
arrived in the evening, she was writing at a desk. I said,
'Comrade Yomei, I'm here.' She just uh-huhed. She kept
scribbling directing notes in Russian, so after waiting a
while I said again, 'Comrade Yomei, I'm here.' Without
raising her head, she said, 'I know. There are two baked
pies on the dining table. You should eat them.' I said,
'Comrade Yomei, you can criticize me and even curse me
if you want to.' She said, 'I've heard you're a good father
and a loving husband, but you must also be a fine actor.
You can go now.' I was stupefied and wondered, Is this
all? She didn't blame me but fed me and even gave me a
pack of expensive Phoenix cigarettes, telling me not to let
Jin Shan know. That was in the famine time! From her
home in Iron Lion Alley to our theater's dorm, I wept all
the way, murmuring in my heart, Rest assured, Comrade
Yomei, I'll become a good actor!" —Lei Keh, actor

"Sun Yomei was carefree, open, very transparent.
She was fond of laughing, and her laughter was loud and
clear, endearing and infectious... She had charming
eyes that showed love and hate plainly. For her, right

and wrong could not stand together; good and bad must
not mix. At rehearsals, if she found you showing talent,
her eyes would smile, narrowing a little. But if you
did a sloppy job, she wouldn't give you a second look at
rehearsal. Her personal history, her artistic talent, her
charismatic personality, her love for life and theater, her
ambitious artistic pursuits, and her beauty, combined
with her natural and unbending disposition, all made
her stand out and appear unique. You can sing the
praises of her personality endlessly." —Shen Ling, actress

"I've heard that Yomei was beaten so severely that her
body was covered with cuts and bruises. The medical
verdict is that she died of 'subarachnoid hemorrhage.'
But her family didn't see her body, and even her
ashes were gotten rid of because she was branded as
a counterrevolutionary. The other day I took part
in a meeting that was supposed to condemn Yomei's
persecutors. But nobody mentioned Yeh Qun, Lin Biao,
and those involved in torturing her to death. I simply
can't resign myself to this cover-up!

"I can't help but despair at the loss of such a theater
artist at the peak of her creative powers and brilliance.
Who killed her? How? Why has no one stepped up and
explained it to us clearly? This is to do her a double
wrong. Whenever I think of her radiant smile and
ringing laughter and her graceful figure and her quick
and supple movements, and how all have disappeared
forever, my heart can't help bleeding and seething with
hatred... When we were young students in the Soviet
Union, Yomei and I both saw a marvelous, lofty vista
ahead of us after our revolution succeeded and after the
new China was established. Neither of us could have
imagined awaiting us was such a brutal future." —Lin Lily,

who always believed that Lin Biao may have had played a hand in destroying her friend

"Sun Yomei's case is hard for me to mention. It always gives me nightmares. Even after so many years, I still can't think of it. Sun Yomei was tortured to death in just half a year in prison, because there had been orders from above, which wouldn't let her survive the year [1968]. On the other hand, she had a personality like a mountain tit. A tit cannot be caged, because the moment you put the little bird into a cage it starts bumping into the walls of bars and won't stop until it kills itself. Sun Yomei was like that, too unbending to survive imprisonment. At the beginning of her interrogation, I joined them once, but after that, I stopped going. I was allowed to join them, but I was too scared to go. That was not an interrogation at all, that was abuse. To be specific, it was to humiliate her. In a formal term, it was a violation. They pulled her hair, whacked her across the mouth, punched her in the sides, and shouted obscenities. Once I asked my team leader why they tortured the woman like that. He showed me her file. After reading it, I realized this case was enormous, handed down from the very top. Those interrogators soon got exhausted, and during a smoke break, they would chat, saying the woman had a devil of a temper and would rather break than bend. She was uppity and delusional, acting like she were still living in Zhongnanhai. They whispered that her life was such a mess that it had been mixed up with three of the most powerful men and two of the most powerful women in China—nobody could survive that kind of entanglement, to say nothing that she was merely a stage director . . . I was not on duty the day she died. I went home to fetch

something, then I got a call that said she had died and I
must go back right away. So I hurried over. On arrival at
the jail, I saw them carrying her out on a stretcher. What
a horrible sight! She was naked and partly covered with
a white sheet, her hands and feet still shackled, her face
bathed in blood—a nail was hammered into the top of
her head." —Investigator Feng

"Among our entire Second Red Generation, Sun
Yomei was the most talented and the most accomplished
one. Many top national leaders viewed her as such too.
The four-star general Luo Ruiching raved about her,
'She is the first theater expert our Party has produced,
a real red expert!' . . . She might be entitled to say to
others, 'The world is ours and the country is ours,
so we must say and do what we can' . . . On the other
hand, Sun Yomei spent so many years studying abroad
that she became muddleheaded. She simply didn't
understand China's millennia-long bureaucratic system,
which dominated everything. Her eyes saw only one
man among all the extraordinary figures—the actor Jin
Shan." —Zhang Langlang, writer and painter

· Eighty-One ·

Jin Shan had been feeble ever since he was released from prison. He limped a little and had to use a cane when he went out of his house, so he stayed home as much as he could. But soon after marrying Yolan, he resumed the movie project *The Rising Sun*, which he and Yomei had started briefly ten years before and which was still suspended. He had no funds or power for such an effort, but he wanted to resurrect it lest he have no time to complete the movie. These days, he was working on the script, which still bore Yomei's craggy handwriting in blue felt-tip pen.

Under Yolan's care, he got much better in 1978 and more active again. Soon he was appointed the president of the National College of Theater Arts, the highest learning institution of its kind in the country. His appointment was mainly due to his reputation and artistic accomplishments, but he wasn't well enough to carry out all the duties of the office. He also began to serve as a stage director and intended to restage some older plays, including *Under Shanghai Eaves* (1937), *Heavenly Spring and Autumn* (1941), *Return on a Snowy Night* (1942), and *Qu Yuan the Poet* (1942). The authors of those plays were still alive, and they all wanted Jin Shan to resurrect their representative plays. That kept him busy, though he didn't rush to reproduce them, wanting to do one fine job at a time. Meanwhile, he never stopped working on the movie *The Rising Sun*, but it was impossible to assemble the original acting crew, and most of the workers and their wives were no longer available. It was unlikely he could find a new cast of mass actors from the oil field, which supported his resumed effort all the same.

Ever since holding the office as the president of the theater college, he had developed an interest in TV drama, which he believed was the future of public entertainment. He did some research to figure out the direction of this popular genre— there were more than seven million TV sets in the country at the time, and if China Central Television broadcast a play, it could instantaneously reach millions, which it would take more than fifteen years for a play performed in the conventional way to reach. He talked about TV drama whenever he could, to the public and to cultural officials. Later he became the head of China's TV drama association, and also the editor in chief of *The Arts of TV Drama*. He dreamed that someday the movie *The Rising Sun* would be such a success that a TV play would follow on its heels.

He worked very hard at his theater college and often skipped lunch to save time. He sometimes brought with him a sizable piece of bread. At noon, when his younger colleagues came to report on their work, he'd break the bread in two and give a piece to the person, saying, "Let's share this, half and half." He'd begin eating while listening to the report.

His colleagues urged him not to work so hard, saying he didn't have to come to the president's office every day, since they could go to his home to report to him. He'd sway his head from side to side and say, "No, no, you'd have to struggle to board a jam-packed bus, whereas I have a chauffeur." His colleagues were amazed that he was still a debonair man after so many losses and so much suffering.

In the summer of 1979, he went to Sartu to select actors for the movie. He was received without any fanfare, since he wanted to keep the project as low-key as possible. When his car pulled up at the entrance to the oil field's administrative building, dozens of people were standing in line to welcome him. Some of them were new faces, but he shook hands with everyone. Nobody said a word, but all were tearful. Many in their fifties, some sexagenarians, a few septuagenarians, all the older people wept in silence while smiling too. Jin Shan's appearance, in a navy short-sleeve shirt and brown loafers, seemed to bring back to them the glorious memory of their erstwhile hardship and struggle in producing *The Rising Sun*, the play that had made them briefly famous.

Nevertheless, it was not easy for him to find suitable actors anymore. Most young people were no longer interested in such a movie, which was alien to their lives. What's worse, he didn't have a budget and couldn't tell the potential actors how much they could make from acting in the film. Never had he expected that funding would be the major obstacle to such a project. Formerly, insofar as the offices above had granted approval, the movie would be made, because the cost would be covered automatically and because few people expected to make money from acting in a movie. Now, the most he could tell them was that the film would be made once they formed a fine acting crew. Nonetheless, many of the interviewees asked about the pay without hesitation and also considered it a decisive factor. As a result, his trip to the oil field wasn't fruitful—he didn't find many suitable actors at all.

In spite of the constant setbacks, he never gave up on the movie project, which he sometimes felt was like a quixotic task. Yolan supported his effort and gave him a hand whenever she could. As long as something contributed to the memory of her sister Yomei, she'd do anything to help him.

On the evening of July 6, 1982, Jin Shan again had a heart attack. He dropped his chopsticks and a slice of cucumber on the table and couldn't continue with dinner. He broke into a sweat and had trouble breathing. His body felt numb below the waist. Yolan could tell it must be angina again, and as soon as she helped him move to a fabric settee, he passed out.

He was taken to the hospital nearby, but it was only for senior officials with a rank higher than a minister. Jin Shan didn't have that kind of status, so he was left comatose in the hallway for three hours. Not until midnight, after direct interventions by the head of the CCP's Propaganda Department and by the minister of health, was Jin Shan rushed to an ICU. By then he was already breathing his last.

He passed away around four the next morning. His last words were murmured to Yolan, "Yomei, Yomei, that's so beautiful..."

· *Author's Note* ·

This novel is largely based on the stage director Sun Weishi's life. Because "Weishi" is hard to pronounce in English and might upset the cadence of sentences, I instead used "Yomei," a name which sounds warm and lovely in English and which Sun Weishi adopted in her personal correspondence. Likewise, her friend "Lin Li" is named "Lily" in this novel. "Lily" is the name that Lin Li actually used in the Soviet Union.

Most of the events and details in this novel were factual, but there were still many holes in Sun Weishi's life story, which I had to rely on imagination to fill so as to create a full narrative. The arch of the plot here closely follows the journey of her life, which was widely known in China, incredible though it seems at times. Reality is often more fantastic than fiction, so I did my best to remain faithful to Sun Weishi's life story. For the information on her life I am mainly indebted to the following authors and their books:

Lin Li, *Miscellaneous Memories* (*Wangshi Suo Ji*). Beijing: Central Document Press, 2006.

China's National Spoken Drama Theater, Ed., *An Innocent Heart: For the 91st Anniversary of the Birth of Sun Weishi (Wei You Chi Zi Xin)*. Beijing: Xinhua Publishing House, 2012.

Shen Guofan, *Zhou Enlai's Adopted Daughter: Sun Weishi*. Beijing: Contemporary China's Press, 2014.

Xian Jihua and Zhao Yunsheng, *The Emperor of Spoken Drama: a Biography of Jin Shan (Huaju Huangdi: Jin Shan Chuan)*. Beijing: China's Cultural Association Press, 1987.

Nikolai M. Gorchkov. *Stanislavsky Directs*. Translated by Miriam Goldina. New York: Funk & Wagnalls Company, 1954.

· *Acknowledgments* ·

My heartfelt thanks to people at Other Press: Judith
Gurewich, Yvonne Cárdenas, Alex Poreda, Janice
Goldklang, Elizabeth Kennedy, and John Rambow. Their
careful and hard work refined this novel.